The
Visitors

The
Visitors

A Novel

SALLY
BEAUMAN

HARPER

NEW YORK ▪ LONDON ▪ TORONTO ▪ SYDNEY

HARPER

A hardcover edition of this book was published in 2014 by HarperCollins Publishers.

THE VISITORS. Copyright © 2015 by Sally Beauman. All rights reserved. Printed in the United States of America. No part of this book may be used or reproduced in any manner whatsoever without written permission except in the case of brief quotations embodied in critical articles and reviews. For information address HarperCollins Publishers, 195 Broadway, New York, NY 10007.

HarperCollins books may be purchased for educational, business, or sales promotional use. For information please e-mail the Special Markets Department at SPsales@harpercollins.com.

FIRST HARPER PAPERBACK EDITION PUBLISHED 2015.

Map by Viv Mullett, The Flying Fish Studios Ltd.

Library of Congress Cataloging-in-Publication Data has been applied for.

ISBN 978-0-06-230270-0 (pbk.)

15   16   17   18   19   OFF/RRD   10 9 8 7 6 5 4 3 2 1

For Ellie and her parents, James and Lucy

CONTENTS

A PLAN OF TUTANKHAMUN'S TOMB

BURIAL CHAMBER

21'

13'

TREASURY

12'6"

15'8"

Sealed doorway

ANNEXE

14'

ANTECHAMBER

26'

8'6"

12'

Sealed doorway

Sealed doorway

PASSAGEWAY

30'

Stairway down

Entrance

6'

All measurements are approximate

E

G

THE VALLEY OF THE KINGS

VALLEY OF THE KINGS

Tutankhamun
Merneptah
Ramesses VI

Ramesses I
Seti I

Qurna

'CASTLE CARTER'

'THE AMERICAN HOUSE'

KARNA

NILE RIVER

LUXOR

Winter Palace Hotel

CAST OF CHARACTERS

(the names of fictional characters are italicised)

CAIRO, 1922 and later

Lucy Payne, aged eleven, visiting from England
Miss Myrtle Mackenzie, from Princeton, New Jersey; *in loco parentis* and escorting Lucy
Hassan, their driver and dragoman
Herbert Winlock, an American archaeologist, field director of the New York Metropolitan Museum of Art's excavations near Luxor
Helen Chandler Winlock, his wife
Frances Winlock, his young daughter

Howard Carter, an English archaeologist, in charge of the Earl of Carnarvon's excavations in the Valley of the Kings
George Edward Stanhope Molyneaux Herbert, 5th Earl of Carnarvon, of Highclere Castle, Hampshire; amateur archaeologist and collector of antiquities
Lady Evelyn Herbert, his daughter, aged twenty
Poppy d'Erlanger (formerly Countess of Strathaven), a beauty, bolter and divorcée
Lady Rose, her young daughter, and *Peter* (Viscount Hurst), her infant son
Wheeler, her maid
Marcelle, Lady Evelyn Herbert's maid

Albert Lythgoe, curator of the Metropolitan Museum's Department of Egyptian Art: the museum's *éminence grise*

Arthur Mace, an English, Oxford-educated archaeologist, working with Lythgoe in Egypt. Associate Curator at the Metropolitan Museum, in charge of its Egyptian conservation work

Harry Burton, English archaeologist, also part of the Metropolitan Museum's team in Egypt, and its acclaimed photographer

Minnie Burton, his rebarbative English wife

Madame Masha, the familiar name for Countess Mariya Aleksandrovna Sheremeteva, formerly a prima ballerina in Moscow; directrice of an exclusive Cairene ballet school

Fräulein von Essen, one of Madame Masha's long-suffering pupils, and *Frau von Essen*, her mother, both visiting from Berlin

Lieutenant Urquhart and *Captain Carew*, young officers in the British army, attached to the British Residency, serving in Egypt at a period when Cairo is under martial law

LUXOR, 1922–3

El-Deeb Effendi, a senior officer in the Egyptian police force, seasoned detective and admirer of the works of Arthur Conan Doyle

Mrs Lythgoe, Albert Lythgoe's wife; in charge of the domestic arrangements at the American House, the Metropolitan Museum's sumptuous dig headquarters near the Valley of the Kings

Michael-Peter Sa'ad, head cook at the American House

Abd-el-Aal Ahmad Sayed, the senior servant at 'Castle Carter' (Howard Carter's home near the Valley of the Kings), and **Hosein**, his much younger brother and fellow servant

Ahmed Girigar, Howard Carter's senior *reis* or foreman, in charge of his excavating team in the Valley of the Kings

Ahmed Girigar, his namesake and grandson; aged six, one of the excavation team's water boys

Pierre Lacau, Director of the Antiquities Service, in charge of all excavation in Egypt, and keen to reform its practices – a radicalism that does not endear him to his archaeological peers

Rex Engelbach, Chief Inspector for Antiquities, Upper Egypt, and thus directly responsible for supervising all finds made in the Valley of the Kings

Ibrahim Effendi, his deputy inspector

Mohammed, Ibrahim's relative and sometime rival, an energetic informant; head cook on the *Hatshepsut,* a houseboat at Luxor hired by Miss Mackenzie and Lucy Payne

Arthur 'Pecky' Callender, an Englishman, formerly an engineer on the Egyptian railways; an old friend of Howard Carter, brought in to assist with the work on Tutankhamun's tomb

Alfred Lucas, a distinguished English chemist working for the Antiquities Service in Cairo; enlisted to work with Arthur Mace on the conservation of objects found in the tomb

Dr Alan Gardiner, of Oxford, the greatest philologist of his era, and an internationally renowned Egyptologist; friend to Lord Carnarvon; advising on inscriptions in the tomb

Dr James H. Breasted, of Chicago, an equally renowned Egyptologist, advising on clay seals in the tomb

A. S. Merton, special correspondent in Egypt for *The Times*; Howard Carter's long-time friend

Arthur Weigall, special correspondent for the *Daily Mail*; Howard Carter's long-time enemy

Valentine Williams, special correspondent for Reuters

H. V. Morton, special correspondent for the *Daily Express*

A. H. Bradstreet, special correspondent for the *Morning Post* and *The New York Times*

CAMBRIDGE, 1922 and later

Dr Robert Foxe-Payne, classicist and Fellow of Trinity College; Lucy's father

Marianne Emerson Payne, his late wife, Lucy's mother; an American heiress

Nicola Dunsire, a young blue-stocking, putative descendant of Sir Walter Scott; recently studying at Girton College, now Lucy's governess

Clair Lennox, Nicola's alarming friend, once her fellow Girtonian, now an artist

Eddie Vyne-Chance, a handsome, iconoclastic Cambridge poet with a thirst for alcohol

Dorothy ('Dotty') Lascelles, now training to be a doctor, and *Meta*, a scornful classicist, both Girtonian friends of Nicola Dunsire

Mrs Grimshaw, wife of a Trinity College porter, cleaner at Dr Foxe-Payne's house in Newnham for many years

Dr Gerhardt, a Cambridge don once enlisted to tutor Lucy in German and French, and his sister *Helga Gerhardt*, a Fellow of Girton; both friends of Dr Foxe-Payne

Mr Szabó, a Hungarian dealer in antiques and curios

HIGHCLERE CASTLE, HAMPSHIRE, 1922

Fletcher, a former ditch-digger on the Earl of Carnarvon's estate, said to be a rogue

Streatfield, Lord Carnarvon's butler

Almina, Lord Carnarvon's wife, 5th Countess of Carnarvon. The heir (and allegedly the illegitimate daughter) of the millionaire banker, Alfred de Rothschild

Dorothy Dennistoun, a woman with a reputation; one of Lady Carnarvon's closest friends

Helen, Lady Cunliffe-Owen, another friend; sometimes a reluctant medium at Lord Carnarvon's seances at Highclere

Brograve Beauchamp, candidate for the National Liberals in the forthcoming election; an admirer of Lord Carnarvon's daughter, Lady Evelyn

Stephen Donoghue, a great flat-racing jockey, winner of the English Triple Crown and (several times) of the Derby

HIGHGATE, 2002

Dr Benjamin Fong, an alert American Egyptologist; formerly of Berkeley, University of California, now a Fellow of University College London; conducting research for a high-budget jointly funded BBC/HBO television documentary

ONE

Sphinx Girl

Here we are in Egypt, *land of the Pharaohs, land
of the Ptolemies, country of Cleopatra* (as one says in high style) . . .
What to say? What would you like me to write? I have hardly got
over the first bedazzlement. It is like being thrown, fast asleep,
into the middle of a Beethoven symphony . . .

Gustave Flaubert, letter from Cairo to Dr Jules Cloquet, 15 January 1850

I

When I'd been in Cairo a week, I was taken to the pyramids; it was there that I saw Frances for the first time. It was January 1922, and Miss Mackenzie, *in loco parentis*, my guardian for our travels in Egypt, planned our visit with great care. She believed that if I could see the pyramids, 'One of the greatest wonders of the ancient world, remember, Lucy, dear,' and see them in the most powerful way possible – at sunrise – they would effect a change. They would stimulate; they would enthral; they would *snap* me back to life, and persuade me to re-engage with the world. For six days she had postponed this visit: I wasn't yet strong enough. On the seventh day, the great moment finally arrived.

Miss Mack, who had been a nurse in the war, believed in timetables as well as pyramids. She was convinced regimes were therapeutic. So the day of our expedition was planned with zeal. The list she drew up in her neat looped handwriting went like this:

5 a.m.: The Pyramids at Giza. Departure prompt.

Noon: Picnic luncheon at the Sphinx, in the shade of her paw.

2.30 p.m.: Return Shepheard's Hotel. Obligatory REST period.

4 p.m.: Tea on the celebrated hotel terrace. An opportunity for *conversazione*.

5 p.m.: Attendance, by invitation from the great lady herself, at Madame Masha's legendary dancing class. Duration, one hour. Benefits, inestimable.

'You see, Lucy,' Miss Mack said, 'if truth be told, and although I am an old Egypt hand, my contacts in Cairo are just a little bit rusty.

What we need is an *entrée*. Friends, dear.' She regarded the list sadly. 'Fun.'

I had forgotten what 'fun' was. It had disappeared into the fume and smoke that afflicted my mind then. But I was an obedient child, grateful to Miss Mack for her vigour – her 'pep', as she called it. I knew that my listlessness alarmed her; I knew that behind all her exhaustive planning lay anxiety, even fear. So I tried to reassure her: I rose early, in the Cairo dark. I endured the dousing with eau de cologne that kept flies at bay, and the sand shoes and the long socks; I accepted the cotton gloves: 'Never insert your fingers into crevices, Lucy. The pyramid stones are notorious – beware of scorpions *at all times*.' I submitted to the panama hat: that was to protect me from the fierce Egyptian sun – at least, that was the ostensible reason, the one Miss Mack always gave. Costuming complete, she turned me to the cheval glass, and we both inspected me. Should I snatch the hat off, expose the tragic state of my hair? The small girl in the glass met my gaze. Eleven years old, and she looked seven: thin as a reed, pinched around the nostrils, wary about the eyes. *What a little nothingness*: she was no one I recognised.

I turned my back on the girl and followed Miss Mack downstairs to the palace of hubbub that was the lobby of Shepheard's Hotel. Escorted by a flurry of flunkies in ballooning white trousers and red boleros, I crept out in her wake to the flaring torches, the hotel steps and the eddying darkness beyond. A fracas ensued. Miss Mack, American, fiercely republican and principled, believed in frugality but was a woman of generosity. She scattered *baksheesh* like manna from the heavens: she bestowed her bounty on everyone, the beggars who swarmed throughout Cairo, the fake and the genuinely afflicted alike, the ragged half-starved children, the street vendors, jasmine-sellers and snake-charmers, the touts who, crying, '*Antika, sweet lady, first class, very ancient*,' produced from their sleeves scarabs manufactured the previous day. Her soft heart had been spotted within days of our arrival, and the instant she appeared on the hotel step she was surrounded by an importunate horde.

I waited in the entrance as the inevitable turmoil commenced, then, feeling the familiar faintness, sank down on the stone steps between the sphinxes either side. Below me, the hotel's *safragis* were reminding Miss Mack that there was unrest in Cairo, that she must not contemplate setting off without a dragoman. When this appeal failed – as an old Egypt hand Miss Mack scorned guides – the hotel servants, clustering around her and shouldering the beggars aside, began insisting she hire a motorcar: a line of gleaming tourist cars now waited outside the hotel where, in her youth, a multitude of donkey boys had plied their trade. I saw Miss Mack hesitate: the night before she had been loud in her condemnation of automobiles – *dust, gasoline fumes, speed, convenience*, where was the romance, the poetry there? Now she glanced towards my seated figure, and I saw her reconsider. There was a risk in overtiring me . . . The hired cars were expensive, and all her thrifty instincts argued against them. But on the other hand my maternal grandparents, American grandees, formerly estranged and unknown to me beyond their handwriting, were now languidly assisting, wiring top-up funds, paying Miss Mack a 'retainer' and insisting money was no object – as indeed, in their case, it was not. They had insisted that on this voyage no expense should be spared.

'Perhaps an automobile might be advisable after all, Lucy,' Miss Mack said, fighting her way past the encircling *safragis,* and returning to the steps. 'We must not exhaust you. Maybe this wasn't wise – such an early start . . . '

I rose to my feet, and held on firmly to the hotel balustrade. If I concentrated hard, I could banish that smoky confusion from my mind for brief periods. I knew Miss Mack's plans and it seemed cruel to disappoint her. I said, 'Oh, please – not a car. I was looking forward to the carriage – and look, Hassan is there as usual, across the road.'

Miss Mack wheeled about. Beyond the shrieking crowd of hawkers and professional beggars forever on duty on the hotel steps, she glimpsed her paragon. There he sat, on the far side of Ibrahim Pasha Street, bent over the reins of his carriage, waiting for custom that was, these days, infrequent and poorly paid. His attitude was one of stoic resolve; on glimpsing Miss Mack, he lifted his hand in salute. In an instant she was resolute again. Out came her purse; munificent tips were conferred. Hassan was whistled across; bags, baskets, rugs, stools were transferred in seconds; the carriage hood was drawn up; and I was installed, Miss Mack beside me, confident once more and ready for anything in hand-made tweeds. Hassan's horse pricked its ears and neighed; the sound startled a pair of red kites, tireless scavengers that roosted in the palm trees of the Ezbekieh Gardens opposite.

They rose up with a clatter of wings, circled overhead, and gave us a fly-past. 'Now, Lucy,' said Miss Mack in a hopeful tone, 'now your great adventure begins.'

Hassan was Miss Mack's paragon for many reasons: he was a kind, knowledgeable man and he cared for his elderly horse in an exemplary way; his carriage was resplendent with shining trinkets, powerful amulets and charms. He spoke English, French, Turkish and Arabic, and in his youth had served in the British army under Lord Kitchener . . . Miss Mack sang his praises for the expedition's first half-hour. I was tired from all the dressing and packing and loading and *talk*. I examined the dark sky and the fantastic glitter of the low-slung Egyptian stars. I breathed in the sweet talcum scent of the lebbek trees. Cairo, which I thought of as a city of consternation, was strangely quiet at this hour.

'How well I remember the first time I made this journey to the pyramids, Lucy,' Miss Mack was saying. She wiped a tear from her eye. 'We took a carriage just like this one. I was only a child, a little older than you are now. Just twelve, and it was the first time I'd ever left Princeton. Why, it must have been 1878 – can it really be that long ago? The excitement! "Now, Myrtle, prepare yourself," my dear father, God rest him, said to me. But I was screwed up to such a pitch of excitement that I could *not* stop fidgeting. I was hopping about like a bug on a blanket – and then, on the horizon, as the sun rose, I saw . . .'

I made no comment. We had now crossed the Nile; the towers and minarets, the jasmine and sewage scents of the city were behind us. Far in the distance I heard the rumble of a tram, the cough of a car engine. The dark of the desert enveloped us; I breathed in its antiseptic air. With a low muttered imprecation, Hassan turned the horse's head, and we entered the narrow road that Miss Mack referred to as the Allée des Pyramides. Abandoning reminiscence, she was now attempting another approach. A history lesson, I realised, had been continuing for some while. I felt a passing sympathy for her: in the face of my silences, she was indefatigably well-meaning; she did *try* . . .

'What I want you to remember, Lucy,' she was saying, 'is that for the ancient Egyptians, sunrise was a resurrection. They believed that – that after the heartache of death, there would be a rebirth. It was as predictable as the rising of the sun each day . . . ' Clasping my hand, she added: 'Try to think of that, Lucy. It might strengthen you. I trust it will, dear.'

I did not reply. After a polite interval, I extricated my hand from hers. Miss Mack, perhaps discouraged, fell silent. How cold the air was! How regular the clip-clop of the horse's hooves. Hassan's charms and trinkets jingled. I could dimly see the avenue of acacia trees either side of the road; they had been planted, the guidebooks said, in honour of the beautiful Empress Eugénie of France – but when? In some other century, some other world . . . Smoke coiled in my brain: I watched the lovely Eugénie dance a graceful if unlikely gavotte on the desert sands with Napoleon Bonaparte; they both turned to bow obeisance to a pharaoh who'd died three thousand years before. This pharaoh was wrapped in a swaddling of death bandages. As I watched, his *ka* detached itself from his body, turned to beckon us sternly towards the perils of the underworld, then stalked off down the *allée* ahead. We followed. A bird cried out forlornly from the branches of the acacias. Somewhere in the darkness a jackal howled.

I crept closer to Miss Mack's reassuring warmth and bulk. She hesitated, then put a comforting arm around my shoulders. If I fell asleep, I knew what dreams would come. I resisted for as long as I could, but after a brief fight the tiredness and darkness claimed me. Fast as anaesthetic, equally irresistible: I went under within a quarter of a mile.

2

'Lucy, dear – you're looking exhausted,' said Miss Mack, later that morning. 'Perhaps all three pyramids were too ambitious? After all, one pyramid is much like another, and we've done Cheops most thoroughly. Maybe we should have our luncheon a little earlier? You're so pale and washed out. I think I'll park you by the Sphinx, dear – just for a second while I tell Hassan our change of plan. If you stay in the shade, here behind her left paw . . . There's no better place for a picnic than the Sphinx's paws. Some people favour the tail area, but I cannot agree.'

I sat down obediently on the camp-stool provided. The pyramids, a dark sapphire when I'd first glimpsed them against the citron of the desert sky at dawn, were now glittering painfully. Groups of camel touts were arguing at a distance; an intrepid male tourist, assisted by Arab guides, was clambering up the Great Pyramid to laughter and cries of encouragement from a group of smartly dressed young Englishwomen standing below. 'Keep going, Bertie,' one of them called, her voice carrying clearly across the sand. 'Nearly there, darling one. Only another eighty thousand feet to go . . .'

'The water flask, Lucy,' Miss Mack said, inspecting me intently. 'I'll leave it with you – are you feeling thirsty? You're very *white*. Are you sure you're all right, dear?'

'Truly, I'm fine. I'll just sit here and read the guidebook.'

'Very well. I'll be two ticks, and I'll stay in sight all the time.'

Miss Mack scurried off across the sand towards the palm trees in whose shade Hassan had laid out a mat and was praying; it was two hundred yards away. Such guardianship! I considered the flask, which I knew contained water that was absolutely *safe*: Miss Mack had supervised its purification, its boiling, cooling, filtering and bottling – ever-vigilant, she left nothing to chance. I unscrewed and uncorked it, took a swallow of water, felt nauseous at once and spat it out on the ground.

Nine months previously, walking across fields in Norfolk on a hot perfect May day, my mother and I had stopped to ask for directions and glasses of water at a remote farm. We had been visiting my father's sister, Aunt Foxe, and exploring the area on the coast still famous as 'Poppyland'; wandering inland, we'd become lost. The farmer's wife had brought the glasses of water to us on a tray, and we drank thankfully, sitting in the shade of her apple orchard. The trees were in blossom, hens pecked at the grass: my mother Marianne, revived by our holiday, had lost the careworn look she so often had at home in Cambridge; she looked pretty and young again. 'This is idyllic, Lucy,' she said. 'Isn't this the most marvellous place to have happened upon? How clever of you to spot it, darling. And isn't this the *best* water? How pure it tastes. So cold and refreshing – it must be straight from their well.'

And so it was – that was established later, when enquiries were made. By then, my mother was dead of typhoid and I was expected to share her fate; but Miss Mack had been there to nurse me and, by some quirk that my father described as merciful, I survived. Now here I was, teleported to a desert, sitting in the shade of the Sphinx's massive paw. I inspected its weathered crumbling stones. No scorpions that I could see.

'The word "typhoid" is taken from the Greek *typhos*, Lucy,' my classicist father had explained. 'It means "stupor", but the term was also used to describe a hazy state of mind. This disorientation, or "smokiness" as you insist on calling it, is a well-documented symptom of the disease. It's known to linger on, after the illness has apparently run its course. It will pass, I promise you. But you must learn to be patient, and give it time.'

Eight months since my alleged 'recovery', and the fogginess had not cleared. My father really should not make promises he could not keep, I felt. Yet that seemed disloyal: those remarks had been made when we'd just spent our first Christmas without my mother, a period that had been painful for both of us. All I could remember of those weeks were walks around a cold, foggy, deserted Cambridge, and one terrible expedition along the banks of the Cam towards Grantchester, in the course of which my silent father broke down. Turning away from me, hiding his face, he'd left me there by the riverside. Walking at a brisk pace towards the town, he disappeared. After an interval, I too set off and reached home without incident: *no harm done* . . . I decided I'd write my father a letter that very night: I would describe the pyramids and the Sphinx and Hassan. I'd describe the further delights of the day, as laid out in Miss Mack's master plan. I'd say nothing of Empress Eugénie; nothing of a hallucinatory pharaoh. I'd make everything *lucid,* including my improving health and gratitude. Yes: a lucid letter from daughter Lucy. I began to word it, stopped at *Dear Father,* and scanned the sands.

The heat of the morning was pleasant, still bearable, and just sufficient to make the light bend, waver and deceive. In the distance, Miss Mack was supervising the unloading of baskets, a small folding table and snow-white napery. I took another swallow of water and forced it down. I turned my gaze towards the Great Pyramid, where the man called Bertie had finally reached the summit. He removed his tweed cap and shouted, 'Huzzah!' Loud cheers came from the spectators below. Bertie, it seemed, had come prepared: from inside his Norfolk jacket he produced a small flag and waved it victoriously. I raised the field glasses and focused them. The flag was a Union Jack. Bertie fixed it between the stones at the pyramid's summit where it fluttered briefly. There were more cheers, then groans as the flag blew away.

Behind this group, I saw, a large car was approaching, bumping its way across the sand. It described a circle, made for the Sphinx, reconsidered, and finally came to a halt in the shade of some palm trees about fifty yards away. I watched as its occupants climbed from the car: first, a young but portly man, balding and with a markedly high, prominent forehead, wearing a flamboyant bow tie; then a woman, festooned with scarves; and finally a girl of around my own age, who jumped from the car, ran a few yards, and then performed a cartwheel. I watched as she followed it up with a somersault, and then reached into the car and fetched out desert gear. A fly-switch, a pair of dark glasses. I stared in astonishment as she put them on. Such sophistication, dark glasses for a child, how I envied her this protection from the punitive light; how free she looked, how her dark hair, almost black, shone.

'Hot, hot, *hot*,' she called to her mother – was it her mother? They were the first words I heard her say. 'Daddy, it's *baking*. I told you it would be.'

Her voice was light, discernibly American. Her father shrugged. 'Sure it's hot if you insist on gymnastics. Try sitting down.'

'May I climb a pyramid before lunch?'

'Don't be fresh, Frances. That's not funny and no, you may not. Neither before lunch, nor after it. It's vandalism, as you very well know. Now sit down and eat your sandwiches. I'll test you on your hieroglyphs when you've finished. Did you learn the six I set you?'

'Kind of.'

'Kind of won't do. Accuracy is all. Helen, is that confounded picnic ready or not? This was a damn-fool idea – I'm due back in Cairo in an hour . . .'

Their voices faded; they withdrew out of sight behind the palm trees. I was wondering dreamily if they too were apparitions, when Miss Mack, followed by Hassan, rejoined me. The table was unfolded, a cloth spread upon it; baskets were opened, and the bounty of a Shepheard's packed lunch was revealed. Cold roast quails and a pilaff; sweet quince pastries, dates and greengages. Miss Mack and I ate in state at the folding table, with plates and knives and forks and linen napkins; Hassan, who, at Miss Mack's insistence, shared this plenty, squatted on the ground. He had brought with him some flat Egyptian bread, which he unwrapped from a cloth bundle. He then shinned up the Sphinx's foot, placed the bread carefully in full sun on the paw-knuckles, allowed it to warm through, and shinned down again. Explaining that his wife had made it for him, he offered it to us to share. Miss Mack froze: seeing I was about to accept some, she shook her head at me.

'Excellent bread,' Hassan said, somewhat mournfully: I felt he was used to such offerings being refused. '*Shamsi*, you see? Sun bread. You will like it – that is sure.'

'Indeed we would, Hassan,' Miss Mack said firmly. 'But my friend Lucy has been ill, you see, so we have to be very careful what we eat.

That is tremendously kind, but we have so much already, and we wouldn't dream of depriving you.'

Hassan gave up with melancholy grace. He seemed saddened – I hoped not affronted. I scraped at my plate, pushing the food back and forth into little piles. I could eat very little. The meal took an age. We were still scarcely halfway through when I heard voices, then a car engine. The acrobat girl was departing. I watched her disappear in a shimmer of light and a cloud of dust – and she couldn't have been an apparition since Miss Mack also registered the exodus.

'Automobiles,' she remarked, with a frown. 'At the pyramids! Some people have no sense of respect. They might remember – this is a holy place. It's a *burial* ground.'

We inspected the burial ground again when lunch was finally finished. Miss Mack was reinvigorated, determined to evoke *some* spark. All three pyramids and no escaping them: kingdoms, dynasties, reigns; probable building methods; alignment with compass points and stars; number of pharaonic wives and daughters buried in adjoining necropolis . . . The sun was now directly overhead. I squinted at the wives' section of the necropolis. It was only partly excavated, and the sands were encroaching on its rough jumble of stones. Any decoration or inscriptions they might once have had, had been long scoured and obliterated by millennia of desert storms.

Wandering away, I leaned over one of the burial pits. Miss Mack, reading from her guidebook, had informed me it was an unknown princess's tomb, stocked with wine, fruit, and grain to sustain her in the afterlife. Now it was about ten feet deep – a dazzle of debris. An emerald-green lizard darted for a wall crevice. A faint breeze brushed my skin. I watched the sands shiver beneath my feet – and realised that this burial place was not deserted after all: moving in the shadows below me was a girl. She was about my own age, thin, wiry and alert. I could see she was trying to escape the pit. She made a series of nervous runs at its encircling walls, as if meaning to climb or jump them. She advanced on its boundaries, then backed off again. After a while, she seemed to sense my presence: she raised a hand to shield her eyes from the sun's glint, lifted her transparent face and turned to look at me. We stared at each other, hard and long. I raised my small box camera to capture her on film, and at once, as swiftly as she had manifested, she disappeared.

Should I inform Miss Mack of this interesting mirage? I knew if I did I'd be dosed up with aspirin and confined to base again. I said nothing. Miss Mack was gathering up our belongings: time to return to the hotel. She looked dispirited; I think she felt the pyramids had been woefully ineffective, and was now pinning her hopes on the afternoon's dancing class.

3

The young man paid his first visit to me today. He had come to interrogate me on the subject of a tomb – a very famous tomb. His name is Dr Ben Fong. He is an American scholar, formerly of Berkeley, California, now a Fellow of University College London. He is writing a book (*another* book!) about the most famous discovery ever made in the Valley of the Kings. A television documentary, a co-production jointly funded by the BBC and some American channel, perhaps HBO, is also being planned. Its working title is *Tutankhamun's Tomb: The Truth*. Laid-back, photogenic Dr Fong will be fronting this alliterative, high-budget, four-part marvel. The book and the TV series, he informed me, are 'linked in' and interest in them is 'awesome'. He dropped this information early on in our interview, when still under the illusion that I'd find this prospect impressive, even flattering. He's quick on the uptake, however, and unlikely to make that mistake again.

This first visit was preceded by a polite letter, citing Dr Fong's impressive academic qualifications, his previous books, and his Egyptologist contacts and friends, including the one who recommended approaching me, who had provided my address. That man, an expert on the transcription of papyri, is an acquaintance I've not seen in twenty years. The letter was followed by several emails. Dr Fong expressed gallant surprise that a woman of my great age should be 'computer-savvy'. In view of that unpromising start, I have no idea why I agreed to see him: was my curiosity aroused? I doubt it. I think it's simply that in winter my arthritis can be vicious, I don't get out as much as I'd like and can experience cabin fever even here in London. Loneliness, of course, had nothing to do with it — no, I agreed to see the man because he pressed me, and I was bored.

These days I tend to spend winters in England, and summers either in America or elsewhere. Where I go and when I go now depends on no one but myself: this, as I'm always telling people, is a pleasant state of affairs. My journeyings depend on the current state of my arthritis — also on mood. Since it was January when we met, and the arthritis was in its winter ascendancy, Dr Fong came to my house in Highgate. It is an old and beautiful house, if overburdened with stairs, and it is set at the top of the highest hill above London. It has a fine view across the famous Highgate Cemetery, where people as diverse as Karl Marx and George Eliot are buried; I find this stupendous view, over burial crosses and guardian angels towards the towers of the new London, very useful. I can usually divert my guests' attention with its wonders for at least ten minutes, which gives me ample time to assess them. Dr Fong proved impatient, however. I hadn't got beyond early thirties, keen-eyed, modish hair, wearing a wedding ring, pity about his shoes, when, four minutes in, I found myself installed in my chair by the fire, Fong opposite me, notebook in hand and pencil poised. Between us, on a small table, lay a tape recorder. Without preamble, Dr Fong switched it on.

'Just say something, Miss Payne, so I can check sound levels . . . Great, that's fine. What an incredible room you have here! So many books, quite a library of them. And amazing paintings, I mean like *seriously* amazing. Is that a . . . could it be . . . ? Wow, yes it is. Professor Yates did warn me, but even so. I see you keep a *shabti* figure on your desk. A very beautiful one too. Would it be—'

'A fake?'

'Genuine, surely?'

'The bazaar in Cairo. Bought in 1922, the year I first went to Egypt. One of the more unscrupulous dealers. I was a child. Eleven years old. Green in judgement. So, alas, no.'

I was not warming to this interviewer. *Game on*, I thought. I suspect Dr Fong came to the same conclusion — but then the *shabti* in question, one of the small faience figures made to serve an Egyptian king in the afterlife and placed in his tomb for an eternity of servitude, was genuine. I knew that, and Dr Fong knew I knew.

We fenced around for forty-five minutes. I may have divorced two husbands, buried a third, and generally led what has been described as a rackety life, but for the past two decades I've lived alone. I've reverted to the solitude of my childhood, and reacquired old habits, one of which is caution. I'm nervous with strangers and suspicious of them. I dislike taking others into my confidence and avoid doing so. As I've outlived most of the friends who *had* gained my trust, there are precious few confidantes these days. Dr Fong did not fail to point this out: he ran through a roll-call of eminent men, including all those involved in the astonishing discovery and excavation of Tutankhamun's tomb, all those that I first met in Cairo, as a child; those I knew at Luxor and the Valley of the Kings. Every last one of them was dead as a dodo. Drawing breath, he then described me as a unique living witness to the greatest archaeological discovery ever made, and to the extraordinary and historic events that galvanised Egyptology in the decade from 1922 to 1932 . . .

'No, 1935.' My mind had strayed elsewhere. The words were out before I could stop myself.

'Nineteen-thirty-five?' He gave me a puzzled look. 'Sorry – I don't follow. Howard Carter discovered Tutankhamun's tomb in November 1922. It was opened in the presence of his patron, Lord Carnarvon, later that same month. It took ten years to document, conserve and remove all the artefacts. The last of them left for the Egyptian Museum in Cairo in February 1932, Miss Payne. All done and dusted well before 1935.'

'Of course. Memory failure. I apologise.'

'Your memory seems fantastically good to me. If mine's in such good shape when I get to your age – *if* I do, of course – well, I reckon I'll be pleased.'

'You're too kind.'

'Am I missing something here? Nineteen-thirty-five? I'm not aware that . . . Could you be thinking of 1939, when Howard Carter died? I guess that must have been a significant date for you: the end of an era? You went to his funeral, I hear. Not too many people did. *Not* a well-attended departure. I was going to ask whether—'

'Another time, Dr Fong.'

'Hey, no need to be so formal. Call me Ben. Everyone calls me Ben.'

It took me a further half-hour to curtail the interview. As far as Dr Fong was concerned, I was merely a source of what journalists call 'colour', I'm sure; an old woman who might provide the odd anecdote or *aperçu* he could use. I could tell he was on the lookout for evidence of Alzheimer's, or some other depressing variant of mental decay. He cannot have expected any revelations of significance, not from someone who'd been a mere child at the time. And if he had been expecting revelations, I intended to disappoint him: I'm still bound by ancient loyalties – he'd learn nothing of significance from me.

But I should have remembered how remorseless scholars can be: the questions were interminable. I tried everything – hauteur, old-lady vagueness, silence, even incipient tears; none of it washed. When he inserted a new tape in his machine, inspiration came at last. I produced my photograph albums. They are numerous and large. I felt sure that page upon page of faded sepia snaps would ensure a quick exit. They were taken with the Kodak box camera Miss Mack bought me in Cairo, first used on our pyramids expedition, then taken on to Luxor and the Valley of the Kings. It's many years since I last looked at these photographs, and they tug at my heart.

I turned the pages of the first album. There were all the distinguished men whom I had known in another country, another era, another life, acquaintance with whom explained Dr Fong's presence now. There were their wives and children. There were the places so central to my existence then: the Winter Palace Hotel on the banks of the Nile where Miss Mack and I stayed when we travelled on from Cairo to Luxor; Howard Carter's house in the desert; and, just a mile or so away, the house where I stayed with Frances. It had been built by the Metropolitan Museum of Art shortly before the Great War. Its purpose was to house the team of archaeologists excavating in Egypt for the Met, several of whom were co-opted to work for the Earl of Carnarvon and Howard Carter, once the astonishing discovery of Tutankhamun's tomb had been made.

The Metropolitan House – or the 'American House', as it was usually known – was at the centre of social life in the Valley area at that time; it was a hive of gossip and intrigue. But the photographs I'd taken conveyed nothing of the house's immense size, or the magnificent desolation of its position, facing out across the desert, with the crags of the Theban hills directly behind it, and behind them, hidden from view, the Valley of the Kings. My pictures had been taken from too close a perspective: all you could see were meaningless angles of walls, a fragment of window, a little segment of dome. The photographs were small, often poorly lit or slightly out of focus – yet they brought a lost world back to me. They unleashed a clamour so loud I was surprised Dr Fong could not hear it. Silently, I passed the album across. How the dead pester and beseech the living! How importunate they are.

'Fascinating,' said Dr Fong, turning the pages rapidly. 'You know, I can never get over the clothes the archaeologists wore. Ninety degrees Fahrenheit at least, more in the Valley, and much more inside Tut's tomb – and they're kitted out in tweed suits, vests, neckties – how did they stand it? Is that Lord Carnarvon?'

'It is.'

'Thought I recognised the hat – you can't exactly miss it.'

'It's a wide-awake hat.'

'You're kidding – I must make a note of that. Gives him the look of a Mississippi river-boat gambler I've always thought – was Carnarvon a bit of a dandy? Kind of vain, maybe? Autocratic, would you say?'

'He could play the English milord when it suited him. Much of the time his manner was diffident. Are you asking me to describe him?'

'I guess I am.'

'He was – debonair.'

There was a silence. The tape faintly whirred. Dr Fong betrayed signs of impatience.

'That's *it*? Debonair?' He peered at the tiny picture. 'And the young girl next to him? It's kind of hard to make people out – the pretty one, arm in arm with Howard Carter?'

'Lady Evelyn Herbert. Lord Carnarvon's daughter. She always accompanied her father to Egypt then, as you'll know.'

'Oh, right. Okay.' Dr Fong glanced at his watch, and turned the page. He was now looking at a larger group portrait, a bevy of archaeologists lounging against the stone walls erected around the entrance to Tutankhamun's tomb. He perked up at once. 'Ah, now I recognise most of *these*. The Metropolitan Museum men. That's Herbert Winlock – the one at the back, very high forehead, flamboyant bow tie? No mistaking *him*. I really admire his work: a great archaeologist and a great writer too . . . That's Mace, and Lythgoe . . . and the man wearing breeches is Harry Burton? What a photographer! Magnificent. How he contrived those pictures in such appalling conditions, inside Tut's tomb, cramped conditions, inadequate light – it's astonishing.' He paused. When I didn't respond, I saw puzzlement again. 'You have *seen* Burton's photographs, right?'

'I was there when he took them. So, yes.'

'And these?' He flipped a page, scanned the images, and shook his head. 'No. This is new to me. I don't recognise anyone here . . .'

I leaned across to examine the picture. It had been taken on the steps outside the American House. Mrs Lythgoe, the senior wife, was speaking to one of the servants. Harry Burton's wife, Minnie, was wearing a long woolly garment designed to flatter her hips. Helen Winlock, who was dear to me, had been caught in a hand gesture I remembered her making a score of times a day: it indicated she had lost something and was in search of it: sometimes her spectacles, or her watercolours, sometimes a missing child.

'Wives,' I said. 'Living at the Metropolitan House those first seasons. Several of the archaeologists brought their families with them to Egypt.'

Dr Fong glanced down at the photograph. Mrs Winlock and her fellow Metropolitan wives merited twenty seconds. He turned a page. 'And these two children. Who are they?'

'The dark-haired girl on the right is Frances, the Winlocks' daughter . . .'

'And the one on the left?'

'That is me.'

There was a silence. Dr Fong muttered an expletive. 'You look – I guess I wasn't expecting . . . what's with the hair?'

'I was recovering from an illness. Long story. Not of any interest to you.'

'Sorry if I sounded rude – it caught me by surprise, that's all. You look—'

'I know how I looked, Dr Fong.'

Reaching across, I took the album from him and handed him a different one. 'Let me show you the pictures I took of the pyramids,' I said warmly. 'They'll be of interest, I know. Most people find them absolutely fascinating. A lost world, Dr Fong.'

If faded out-of-focus pictures of the pyramids in the 1920s did not dislodge him, nothing would. They are, in my experience, a soporific that's guaranteed. Add in a few animated old lady anecdotes inducing terminal ennui, and most visitors discover a pressing appointment. In less than five minutes Dr Fong again checked his watch; in another five, he produced his BlackBerry, consulted its screen and announced he must be going – forgotten a meeting, so interesting to hear my reminiscences, would make use of the invaluable insights I'd provided, privilege to meet me, would try to be in touch again, felt sure there was more I could contribute, but unfortunately had to leave . . .

Result. Within minutes he was hastening down my front steps and I was able to close the door on him. I stood in the shivery hall; it was still only mid-afternoon, but in London in January on an overcast day, with snow threatening, my house exists in a permanent and sepulchral twilight. I could feel the ghosts gathering. They're now as familiar with my house as I am. They like to cluster, especially by the stairs. Today their mood seemed amicable; it is not always so.

I returned to my sitting room. There, too, I could sense movement, excitement: something, perhaps Dr Fong's questions, perhaps the photographs, had caused disturbance. Sharp as the crack of a whip: electricity in the air.

4

'Farewell to the Pyramids . . . ' Miss Mack said, as we climbed back into Hassan's carriage; one flick of his whip in the air – and we were back in our rooms at Shepheard's, bang on schedule. The louvres were closed, the ceiling fans switched on, the linen sheets folded back and the mosquito net arranged protectively around me. Miss Mack announced she'd retire to her room to write up her journal: she had literary ambitions and planned to write some form of Egyptian memoirs one day – a day I secretly thought would never come. 'You have a good rest, Lucy, then you'll be ready for tea and the great ballet class,' she said, closing the door.

Most afternoons, however tired I was, I fretted wakefully through these periods of enforced rest. I would try to read – *Treasure Island*; my mother's beloved Tennyson – or I'd write in my diary, or I'd simply lie there and stare at the ceiling, watching the ceiling fans inexorably revolve. That day I fell at once into a deep and dreamless sleep. So soundly did I sleep that the 4 o'clock tea-on-Shepheard's-terrace deadline was well past when I woke. If Miss Mack regretted this lost opportunity for *conversazione* and celebrity spotting, she concealed it well.

'Why, Lucy, you *do* look refreshed,' she exclaimed in delight. 'There's some colour in your cheeks at last. Exercise and rest – and lots of new *interests*, I knew they would do you good! And since I have what I feel I may call *extensive* nursing experience, I know whereof I speak, dear . . . Now, we've just time to get you ready – Madame's class begins in fifteen minutes. A quick wash and brush-up . . . Can you manage a little mint tea?'

Closely supervised, I washed my face and hands and changed my petticoat. Miss Mack felt my forehead and took my temperature. *Normal*. I was back to *Normal*, and had been all day. I sipped the cool mint tea, hoping Miss Mack wouldn't expatiate on her nursing experience. On the outbreak of war in 1914, with an impetuosity that was characteristic, she had taken the first available ship to England and enrolled as a VAD. After training in London, and a period in France at a military field station, she had been posted to Egypt, to the hospital at Alexandria where those men fortunate enough to survive the Gallipoli campaign had been transferred.

Most were hideously wounded: over the past few weeks I'd heard long descriptions of amputations, septicaemia, gangrene – and the indomitable courage of dying British and Colonial servicemen. Miss Mack had a fascination with the gory, and a brisk manner when describing it. I wanted to hear no more. I'd had enough of death. Death had been stalking me for months and it was time he gave me up, took himself off and found some other prey. I'd imagine him hiding in my room, in its huge and sinister catafalque of a wardrobe; sometimes, at night, I'd smell his bandages, his mouldy mummifying bandages . . . I edged away as Miss Mack began to select fresh clothes for me, eased back the wardrobe door and peered inside. Empty apart from clothes. Nothing lurking. Death *definitely* not there today.

Laid out for me on my bed was a clean outfit and yet another hat. I scowled at it, and Miss Mack sighed: 'Now, don't be difficult, dear. We can't have sulks, not now. I want you to make a good impression. I thought, the Liberty print dress? It suits you charmingly. And the hat with the matching riband – now, don't be silly, Lucy, look, I'm wearing a hat too, best bib and tucker, I hear Madame is a stickler for such things . . .

'I wonder,' she went on, somewhat nervously, 'should I address her by her title? No, I guess I'll stick to "Madame"; after all, we are meeting her in her *professional* capacity. People say she can be very *grande dame*, but the thing to remember, Lucy, is that before that terrible accident, she was a great artist, a prima ballerina, so a certain temperament is only to be expected. And then she's Russian, and in my experience *all* Russians are excitable. So we can't be sure how she'll react, Lucy, when we actually meet her. She is very choosy as to whom she admits to her classes, I hear – I believe she's turned down several little girls of the most – well – *irreproachable* background, and for no good reason that anyone could see. But if she takes a shine to you, as I'm *sure* she will, dear, it should open doors. It will give you a chance to meet some girls your own age, to make some nice friends in Cairo . . . '

This lengthy speech took us out of our rooms, down the great central staircase, and past the famous ebony statues of nubile, bare-breasted Egyptian maidens at its foot; Miss Mack ignored them stonily and averted her gaze. It carried us on through the lobby and into the hotel's famous Moorish hall. This large space, surmounted by a vast glass dome, had a clubby atmosphere: it was an unofficial male preserve. Groups of English officers lounged in leather armchairs; *safragis* carrying trays and soda siphons moved soft-footed between tables; government officials conferred with colleagues from the British Residency, rustled the pages of *The Times*. Englishmen to the right of us, Frenchmen to our left . . . According to Miss Mack, this huge room was subject to an invisible divide: this gulf she called the Channel, or la Manche, according to mood.

The British, who, as Miss Mack put it, ruled Egypt while pretending it was a Protectorate, were on our right: they drank Scotch whisky. The French, who ruled over all matters cultural, including the great domain of archaeology, were on our left, drinking champagne. Both sides of the Channel united at once in the face of female trespassers. The Englishmen stared with cold indignation; the Frenchmen looked upon us more mildly, then, defeated by a charmless child and a spinster who was stout, and neither pretty nor young, sighed in a philosophical way. Miss Mack, sensing this inspection, her colour heightening, marched on. I suspect she overheard the remarks about her hat, which sported a rusty bow and was worn at a peculiar angle, over her left eye. '*Affreux*,' murmured a Frenchman. 'Bloody *hell*,' muttered an English subaltern.

We passed into a series of dimly lit, Persian-carpeted corridors, Miss Mack talking all the while. *Ballets Russes*, *Revolution*, *Count*-this and *Prince*-that: bombarded with associations that related to Madame but meant little to me, negotiating a maze of bewildering ante-rooms, I could feel my mind fogging up again. I tried to concentrate on the few hard certainties that Miss Mack had drilled into me.

One: I must sit still, not fidget, and watch the ballet class carefully. *Two*: I must not remove my cardigan, as that would reveal to all and sundry the shocking emaciation of my arms. *Three*: I must not remove the hat under any circumstances, because we both knew what happened when I did. *Four*: while I must answer if addressed directly, I should not proffer information unasked or blurt things out, as I tended to do ... Yes, yes, it was *true* that I had contracted typhoid and that my dear mother had died of the same disease; the fact that my father was immersed in his academic work and holed up in his Cambridge college was also true, if an inelegant way of expressing it ... But to add that I was here in Egypt with Miss Mack because he couldn't decide what to do with me, though in due course I'd no doubt be parcelled up and sent elsewhere ... well, that was *not* true. It was just plain hurtful. That kind of remark embarrassed people. It was ... *too much information*, as we'd say now.

Must, must not, I muttered to myself as, at the end of a long corridor, we finally came to a tall pair of mahogany doors. From beyond them came the sound of piano music, abruptly halted by a loud banging sound. It was followed by a tirade so fierce that we both froze.

'*Non, non, non!* Fräulein von Essen, Lady Rose, this is excruciating. Never in my life have I seen such *lumps*. Back to the barre, *mesdemoiselles! Alors, nous recommençons* ... Now, *adage, s'il vous plaît. Stretch, stretch* ... No, not like some vile ostrich, like a *swan* ...The arms, *so.* The feet, *so.* Young ladies, have you set out to make me suffer? Continue like this and I'll throw you out of my class, every last one of you. Music! One, two, three, four – *allongez, allongez* ... Ah, mon Dieu! *Allongez, mademoiselle* ...'

Under cover of the music, Miss Mack finally risked opening the door. She crept around it and I followed her. I saw a huge room, its size doubled and redoubled and distorted by the looking glasses lining its walls. At first glance, it seemed filled with scores of small girls wearing white leotards, white hairbands, and gauzy white skirts that grazed their knees. On the count, this ghostly *corps de ballet* moved in unison. Then, as my panic subsided and the room calmed, I found I could begin to differentiate between the reflected and the real. To my left, beyond the gilt chairs reserved for the ranks of mothers and nursemaids, and next to the piano and accompanist, stood a woman who could only be the legendary Madame Masha: it was by this name that she was familiarly known throughout Cairo, her real name, Countess Mariya Aleksandrovna Sheremeteva, being a mouthful no one could pronounce. She was tiny and terrifying, wearing a flowing dress, her raven hair parted in the centre, slicked back against her skull and fastened in a bun, ballerina-style; she was armed with a long tapering stick, which she banged on the floor to emphasise her demands.

Beyond her, lined up with their right hands clasping the barre, was a group of just seven, no, eight little girls, all of about my own age or younger. Their flushed faces were fixed in concentration, they had beads of sweat on their brows. The child at the front was, I gradually understood, the Lady Rose who had incurred Madame's wrath before we entered. She was the smallest child present, plump, clumsy, erratic in her footwork and on the verge of tears. Next to her was the unfortunate Fräulein von Essen, scarlet with exertion, out of breath and visibly wilting. Fifth from the front, performing the exercises of the *adage* with cool precision, was a pupil whose grace marked her out from her companions. Even with her dark hair sleeked back inside a bandeau, I recognised her at once as the pyramids' girl.

As I watched, Madame advanced upon her, stick raised. She touched her lightly on the shoulder with the tip of her stick and, motioning the other girls to stop and to watch, said: 'Enough. Mademoiselle Winlock shall demonstrate. Frances, *ma petite*, come forward. *Attention, je vous en prie.* We shall move on to the allegro. Mademoiselle, *if* you please, you will show them how it's done.'

The pyramids' girl began to dance – and it *was* like a dance, not a series of exercises. Each move flowed into the next, to Madame's barked commands. *Entrechat, demi-plié, grand jeté, fouetté*: I was watching grace, balance and an astonishing accuracy of footwork performed at speed. I was transfixed with admiration: I had never attended a ballet, knew nothing of the art, and had never suspected what dance might be. '*Ballon*,' said Madame. 'Mademoiselle Frances, *on essaie le ballon, s'il vous plaît …*'

There was a stir in the room, a craning of necks, a new concentration on the faces of the watching girls – just enough for me to understand that, whatever a *ballon* was, it was difficult. There were a few preparatory graceful steps, then the child's feet flickered in a series of lightning scissor moves and without appearing to jump or to leap she simply rose in the air, as weightless as a bird. I gasped at this magic and, before I could stop myself, clapped my hands. The girl returned earthwards, landed, missed her step, twisted her foot, and fell in a heap on the ground.

'*Pas mal*,' Madame pronounced, ignoring the fact that Frances Winlock's face had whitened with shock and pain. She shrugged, adding, as she turned away, '*Vous voyez — c'est difficile.*'

Beside me, Miss Mack shook her head: I think she was reconsidering the wisdom of my joining this ballet class. 'Oh, the poor child! I hope she hasn't broken anything,' she murmured. 'It'll be a miracle if that ankle isn't sprained. And she danced so charmingly too. A little praise might not go amiss. Or sympathy ...'

Madame overheard this comment. She turned to look at Miss Mack and me, fixing us in the glare of her huge tiger eyes. I shrank away, fearing some burning reprimand. She gave us a look of scorching contempt, then turned her back on us. Clapping her hands once with a sound like a pistol shot, she dismissed the class.

5

In the mêlée that ensued as the girls ran off to change out of their ballet clothes, and a crowd of mothers and companions clustered around Madame, Miss Mack and I held back. We hovered nervously on the fringe of the group, and I found we were next to a woman I now recognised as Frances Winlock's mother. She had changed her dress since I'd glimpsed her that morning at the pyramids, but still looked dishevelled, as if the garments she'd chosen to wear to Madame's class had been an attempt at smartness undermined by last-minute changes of heart. Numerous drifting scarves were thrown about her neck; perhaps, undecided as to which best suited her, she'd simply given up and elected to wear them all. Her manner was agitated; her eyes, which resembled her daughter's, were both intelligent and kind.

'Oh, isn't this *awful?*' she said to Miss Mack. 'It's such a battle-ground, everyone fighting for attention . . . And Madame is a Gorgon – I always mean to protest, then she glares at me, and I freeze. She will *push* Frances, and make her do things she's not ready for – she's only eight, you know, but people forget that because she's tall, and advanced for her age.' She paused, and smiled. 'I'm sorry, I'm running on, and we haven't been introduced. I'm Helen Winlock. It's my daughter that had the fall . . . I haven't seen you here before. Are you thinking of enrolling your daughter in Madame's class?' She turned to me, with a wry expression. 'Are you sure you're ready for that? It's nothing short of tyranny. Frances has been reduced to tears many times – you must be about the same age, I think? How old are you, my dear?'

'I'm eleven,' I replied firmly. I was used to these misconceptions and found it prudent to correct them fast.

Mrs Winlock, embarrassed at her mistake, began on an apology. Miss Mack, always ready in my defence, came to my rescue. As she later told me, she had at once recognised that Mrs Winlock was not only a fellow American, but also a woman of sympathy; she had noted that her accent was Boston Brahmin and 'pure Harvard yard'. Drawing Mrs Winlock aside, she embarked on a now-familiar tale. I could hear only some of the phrases, uttered with emphasis and heartfelt pauses, but it was easy enough to join up the narrative: this was my history, my identity. I might not believe it, but I knew it by heart.

No, neither the child's mother *nor* her aunt, merely Lucy's unofficial guardian . . . known her dear mother Marianne from way back, had attended her New York christening, her coming-of-age party . . . Happened to be in England and thus on hand when the great tragedy occurred . . . Typhoid, horribly sudden; poor Marianne succumbed to complications, Lucy desperately ill, everyone fearing the worst. Luckily had *extensive* nursing experience, and, in the end, child pulled through . . . Hair had to be shaved, taking an *age* to grow back, made her painfully self-conscious, other difficulties too, acute loss of weight, loss of appetite, grief and listlessness . . . Everyone in state of despair, father at his wits' end, immersed in his work of course, not very good with children anyway, well, what scholar ever was? Yes, a don at *Cambridge, England* . . . Oh, Mrs Winlock was familiar with the world of academe? Well, then, she'd know the situation was *hopeless*, father simply hadn't the remotest idea how to care for a child, also . . . Here Miss Mack lowered her voice, so I caught only two words, '*Bad war.*'

Those two words were familiar: my mother had used them once a day: they were a diagnosis that explained everything, the aloofness, the outbursts of temper, the nightmares and the night screams. My father had volunteered in 1914: he left home for the army when I was four and returned when I was eight. I knew this silent stranger had fought in France, though he never spoke of it. Once, when I asked him to show me where the Somme was and handed him an atlas, he threw it across the room, and it struck me on the forehead, drawing blood. *Bad war, bad war.* I'd met several other men in Cambridge

afflicted by that disease; I'd glimpsed several victims among the officers here in Cairo — their twitchy unpredictability gave them away,
as did a certain deadness in the eyes. Had anyone experienced a good
war? I knew better than to ask.

I stared at the floor, which had begun to undulate. Miss Mack's saga
had resumed . . . So, crisis situation, but she herself, old Egypt hand,
had had a suggestion to make . . . Prolonged period of convalescence.
Voyage to warmer climes — much better than the prospect of an
English winter. Only difficulty, *insufficient funds* . . . at which point,
Took Charge, wrote the maternal grandparents, who, thus far, hadn't
lifted a finger to help . . .

Here, Miss Mack drew breath. I knew what was coming next: the
bid for sympathy was made: the bid for status would follow as
inevitably as night followed day. Mrs Winlock was listening to this
story with close attention, and with what seemed genuine interest.
Unlike many of the women Miss Mack had buttonholed on my
behalf, both on the voyage out and this past week in Cairo, she
betrayed no signs of impatience. Lowering her voice again, Miss Mack
moved on to the next twist in the tale.

Child's father brilliant classicist, distinguished Norfolk family, but
could be his own worst enemy, always had advanced, even Socialist
views . . . a trait that had *not* gone down well with Marianne's
family . . . They'd met in London on Marianne's first visit to Europe.
Married inside three months, cut off without a dime, all contact with
her family severed . . . No, didn't make one *ounce* of difference when
the child was born, though you'd have thought that might have softened their stubborn attitudes and overcome their stiff-necked pride.
But perhaps Mrs Winlock, as a fellow American . . . oh, and a
Bostonian? Well, then, she'd understand just how plain bone-headed
such families could be, especially when it came to a clan composed
of *Emersons, Stocktons* and *Wigginses* . . .

Miss Mack paused. Mrs Winlock's eyes widened as the information sank in. 'Stockton — as in railroads?' she said faintly.

'*And* Emerson steel.'

There was a silence. Upon Helen Winlock's face came an expression familiar to me. It was compounded of surprise, awe, pity and
deepening distaste. I began to edge away.

'I wrote them,' Miss Mack said, with an air of finality. 'I wrote the

Emersons — and I did *not* mince my words. And they relented — well, to the extent of funding this little expedition of ours. What the future holds, I cannot say. But I will tell you, Mrs Winlock, that I'm just about *burned* up with all this snobbery and injustice and when I look at that poor child there, it breaks my heart. She's lost a mother she adored. She's been desperately ill. What she needs isn't some stuffy old woman like me. She needs *fun*. And some friends her own age who can take her out of herself, don't you agree?'

The pitch seemed over-blatant to me. I was retreating, shame-faced, when I saw Helen Winlock do something unexpected: instead of uttering the platitudes and evasions that this appeal of Miss Mack's usually evoked, she gave every sign of being moved. Her interpretation of the appeal seemed to differ from mine: colour rose in her cheeks; with a low exclamation of sympathy, she rested her hand on Miss Mack's arm, and then awkwardly embraced her. Miss Mack sighed and grasped Helen Winlock's hands. In the midst of the mêlée of returning children being reclaimed, the two women stood there clasping one another, exchanging what seemed to be consolation or endearments as if they were the oldest of friends.

I was not used to such demonstrations. 'Let us *try* to avoid hysteria, Marianne,' my father used to say on those occasions, increasingly rare, when my mother had betrayed strong emotion. I backed away, inching a path through the chattering influx of little dancers, now transformed into ordinary girls wearing skirts and blouses or dresses such as mine. One by one they were collected: Fräulein von Essen was marched off by a uniformed nanny. The hapless Lady Rose was greeted by a sweet-faced young woman so exquisitely dressed, so astonishingly fashionable, that I stopped to stare.

'Rosie, darling,' she cried, swooping across the room and bending to embrace her. 'What a perfect duck you are — you looked just like a little rosebud when you were dancing. I'm *fiercely* proud of you, and I intend to show you off to the whole of Cairo. Will you let me take you to tea on the terrace tomorrow? Your mamma says I may . . . Now, shall we toddle off? You must be utterly exhausted, darling — that wicked witch shows you poor girls *no* mercy. She really is an old battleaxe . . . Oh, Madame! Here you are! I'm so glad I came. It was an absolute education, I never realised art involved such *hard* work.'

'And why would you?' Madame replied, with a flash of her eyes.

'Do I see any evidence of hard work in your face? In your hands? Pah, lady's hands, idle hands.'

'Now don't be cruel, you monster,' the young woman answered with a smile. 'You know I try. And you shan't intimidate me – I know your ways too well. *Mille mercis pour tous ces compliments.* Now, listen: Pups telegraphed this morning. He'll be here next week, and he says you're joining us for dinner before we leave for Luxor? Oh, *good.* Yes, here at Shepheard's, we thought – a whole *heap* of people, some friends from London and Poppy d'Erlanger – she and I travelled out here together – oh, and Howard Carter, of course—'

'And your mother?' Madame interjected. 'Will dear Lady Carnarvon not be joining us?'

'Darling, unlikely. She may change her plans, but she's in Paris.'

'Again?' said Madame, with a small lift of her eyebrows. The two women exchanged a look I could not interpret, and the younger made a wry face.

'Yes, *again* – but what can one do?'

'Very little, I imagine,' Madame replied. 'I shall be sorry not to see her, but delighted as always to see your father. I look forward to the dinner. Send him my *félicitations* . . .'

'Oh, I *shall.* It's *so* lovely to be back – Poppy and I are having a whale of a time. I'm thinking of buying a canary – did Howard tell you? If I do, I shall take it with us to the Valley to bring us luck. Now, I must fly . . . Pups sends *masses* of love, by the way.'

Leaning forward, she embraced Madame, who chuckled, bestowed a kiss on Madame's sallow rouged cheek and, clasping Lady Rose's hand, turned to go. She drifted past me, still chattering away. I caught a drift of her scent – jonquils, iris – and then the vision was gone. I watched Madame scythe her way through the last clustering of children and guardians, and saw that Miss Mack, flanked by Helen Winlock, was nerving herself to pounce.

'Madame, if I may just introduce myself,' I heard. 'I am Myrtle C. Mackenzie. Of Princeton, New Jersey. I wrote you a note, you may recall? Concerning my little friend over there, Lucy Payne? Lucy . . . Lucy? Where has the child hidden herself . . .'

I had hidden myself behind the piano, crouched down by the stool, where short-sighted Miss Mack was unlikely to spot me. I could sense the saga was about to start up again; I'd reappear when it was over,

I told myself, and not before. Madame was receiving the abbreviated version: Miss Mack was no fool, and no doubt sensed that with a woman like Madame it was futile to play the sympathy card. The status card, however, given the intake of her classes, might prove a trump. If plain Lucy Payne were denied admittance, perhaps a grandchild of steel and railroads might make it through the door? *Emerson*, I heard, *Stockton*, *Wiggins*. My cheeks flamed. I imagined Madame's scorn, poor Miss Mack's chagrin. As I peeped out from behind the shiny ebony of the piano, I saw my guardian was agitated, and Helen Winlock had now entered the debate. Madame stood listening to both women with an expression of stone.

'*Impossible*,' I heard. '*Je regrette, ma chère Madame, mais votre fille*—'

'*Miss*. I told you, I am *Miss* Mackenzie. And Lucy is *not* my daughter. Heavens! This is so darn difficult. May we stick to good plain English, please?'

'English? But I thought you were American?' Madame said silkily.

'And so I am. A Yankee and proud of it!' Miss Mack, who knew sarcasm when she heard it, was becoming heated. She raised her voice; her hat was now tilting dangerously over her left eye. As I shrank back again behind the piano, I felt a small hand brush my arm. Turning, I found myself face to face with Frances Winlock.

'Hello,' she said, without ceremony. 'I've been watching you for a while. I was watching you this morning too, through my field glasses. I recognised you as soon as you walked in. You're the Sphinx girl, aren't you?'

'And you're the pyramids' girl. You're an acrobat. You did a cartwheel. You wore sunglasses. I was watching you too.'

We gazed at one another warily. After a long appraising pause, Frances Winlock held out her hand, I solemnly shook it and we introduced ourselves. Close to, I could see that she was indeed younger than I'd realised at first, though she was tall for her age, almost on a level with me. Unlike her untidy mother, she was immaculately turned out in a navy blue pleated skirt and a neat, white blouse with a Peter Pan collar. She wore socks and sandals identical to mine. Her shining dark hair was cut in a bob to her shoulders, parted on the side and pinned back from her high forehead with a slide or, as Miss Mack would call it, a bobby-pin. She had a clear complexion and an air of radiant health. Her eyes and the brilliance of their gaze were the first thing you noticed about her – until she smiled, that was. Her smile lit her face in a way and to a degree I'd never seen before. She smiled now, and I risked the question to which I'd longed for an answer all day: 'I've been wondering – did you pass your hieroglyph test?'

'Oh, you heard that?' The smile disappeared. 'No, I failed. One out of six. Daddy was mad at me. But they are hard – really hard.'

'Never mind. You're sure to get them right next time,' I said. She seemed so crestfallen that I felt anxious to console her. 'And you danced beautifully.'

'No, I didn't. Half the steps were wrong, and then I messed up that jump.'

I glanced down at her ankle, which was visibly swollen. 'Have you sprained it?'

'I don't think so. I can walk on it. Just twisted it – it hardly hurts at all.'

That was untrue, I thought. Frances shuffled her weight from foot to foot experimentally, and winced. Changing the subject, she quickly asked me why I was in Cairo, how long I was staying there. She also asked why was I so thin and – peeping under the brim of my hat – what had happened to my hair? She was the first person I'd encountered who had been this outspoken and her directness undid all my resolutions: before I could stop myself, out the story came. I was just reaching the end of this blurt and had got to the 'parcelled-up' phase when Miss Mack, accompanied by Madame and Helen Winlock, discovered my hiding place.

As I looked from face to face, Miss Mack's flushed and anxious, Helen Winlock's sympathetic, Madame's a mask of arrogance and impatience, it became obvious that Miss Mack was fighting a lost cause. 'Ah, Lucy,' she said. 'I'm afraid this is not promising. Madame's classes are full and it really doesn't look as if—'

'This is the child?' Cutting her short, Madame leaned forward to examine me. I felt the full glare of those predator eyes of hers. 'I will question her myself. *Vous permettez, mademoiselle?*'

Miss Mack and I, unsure whom she addressed, both nodded. The inquisition was brief and to the point. In rapid-fire time it elicited the information that, despite having reached the advanced age of eleven, I had never attended a ballet performance, a ballet class or indeed any other kind of dancing class in my entire life. Furthermore, I neither rode, nor played tennis, and my swimming was unreliable. I was not, Madame deduced, *sportive.*

'*Enfin* – what *can* you do, child?'

'Well, I read. I read a lot,' I said desperately, casting around for an answer and giving her a Cambridge one.

Madame raised her eyes to the heavens. 'Do you *wish* to dance, Mademoiselle?'

'No. Yes. That is, I didn't, but—'

'*Incroyable* ... Still, I must not be hasty. You have been ill, I must make allowances. I shall be fair. Fair play, as the English never cease reminding us. We shall see with our own eyes. Child – remove your hat, please.'

I did so. Miss Mack gave a small mew of distress and protest; no one else said a word.

Madame recovered first. 'Let us continue,' she said. 'Child – bend over and touch your toes ... Now, stand straight, raise your arms above your head, and lower them slowly – *slowly*, Mademoiselle. *Enfin*, remove your shoes, hold on to the barre and raise yourself on your toes – *comme ça, vous voyez*?' She demonstrated. I copied. She sighed. 'Extend your left leg, point the toe and raise it as high as you can ... *Mon Dieu,* but you're stiff, I've seen a chair, a table, with more animation. *Ça suffit.*' She began to turn away. 'We will not waste each other's time any longer.'

'That's not fair, Madame.' To my astonishment, Frances Winlock pushed past me and spoke. 'There are umpteen girls in our class who can't dance very well and never will – and you didn't turn them away. Lucy wants to learn, she told me so. And besides, you're not giving her a chance. She's – she's – she's very – *acrobatic*. She can do these amazing handsprings and cartwheels. Somersaults too ... '

This lie was brazen: I blushed to the roots of my tragic hair. It was stated with wide-eyed innocence and in a tone of such heartfelt conviction that Miss Mack was completely taken in. 'Why, Lucy, dear, I never realised—' she began.

Mrs Winlock gave her a sharp nudge, and said quickly, 'Frances, that's quite enough. But perhaps my daughter has a point, Madame? After all, Lucy will be moving on from Cairo to Luxor in a few weeks, just as we shall, so it's only a short-term arrangement. Surely you could fit her in? Imagine how much she'd learn from a teacher such as you! And I know Frances would love it if you could . . . She and Lucy are *such* friends.'

I said nothing. I could see Madame was not deceived for an instant. She knew that Frances was lying, and I could no more perform a cart-wheel than I could read hieroglyphs. I was an impostor, a fake – and about to be exposed as one. All she had to do was ask me to demonstrate. I saw her eyes gleam with that malicious possibility, but then she seemed to change her mind. Possibly Frances and her mother weighed more with her than all the Stockton and Wiggins and Emerson tribes put together: maybe she felt like playing up to her own reputation for unpredictability; perhaps it was simply that the blatancy of the lie amused her.

She looked intently at Frances and at me. A long fraught silence ensued, and then she laughed. 'Well, well, well – you have talents I should never have suspected, Mademoiselle,' she said in a dry tone. '*Eh bien*, you will be on trial, but since your friend vouches for you, you may attend my class next Tuesday. By then I shall expect you to have learned the first five ballet positions; if you haven't – out on your ear. Mrs Winlock, Miss Mackenzie – you have exhausted me. I wish you good day.'

She swept out of the room. When I was sure she was gone I thanked Frances for her generous lie, and her mother for intervening, and Miss Mack for pressing my case; but I was incoherent. I was experiencing fierce emotion, of a kind I'd almost forgotten, and had assumed long gone.

'There, there,' said Helen Winlock, 'let's say no more about it. I reckon we should celebrate, don't you? Miss Mackenzie—'

'Myrtle, my dear, please.'

'Won't you and Lucy join us for dinner tonight? I'm letting Frances stay up. If we dine quite early? My husband Herbert will be so pleased to meet you – he's an archaeologist, out here working for the Metropolitan Museum of Art. I'll introduce you to a whole bunch of our archaeologist friends if you think you can bear that—'

Miss Mack's face lit up: as she was a devotee of tombs and temples, nothing could have delighted her more. She demurred, but was soon won round.

Later that evening, wearing my best dress and with my patchy tufts of hair artistically concealed by a scarf, I found myself at a huge table in the very centre of the glittering Shepheard's dining room, Frances seated next to me and explaining in a whisper who everyone was. That was the first time I met her father, Herbert Winlock, and the colleagues whose photographs now rest in my albums, forever frozen at that supreme moment of triumph that was almost a year away.

'And who is that?' I asked, indicating a man seated near her father, who seemed somewhat isolated and withdrawn, neither participating in the repartee nor sharing the easy manners and good humour of the other guests. So far, the only remark he'd made, was a curt, 'Tommyrot'. It had come at the end of a long discussion between Frances's father and the man she had pointed out as the senior curator of Egyptology at the Met, a small, quietly spoken Bostonian named Albert Lythgoe. Neither seemed to mind the brusque comment: Lythgoe raised an eyebrow, Winlock grinned, and they continued their discussion serenely.

'That's Howard Carter,' Frances replied. 'He's an archaeologist too. He works for the Earl of Carnarvon, who has the concession to dig in the Valley of the Kings. Mr Carter is an especial friend of mine. I'll introduce you one day, but be warned, Lucy: he has one devil of a temper. Daddy says he's the rudest man he's ever known.'

Howard Carter seemed to resent the lack of reaction to his 'Tommyrot' remark. He slopped some wine in his glass and slumped back in his chair, staring off into space. He was in his late forties, I judged, hawk-nosed, dark-haired, ill at ease, broodingly assertive even when silent. After a brief interval, he rose to his feet and, without a word to his companions, walked out.

I watched him leave with interest. To me, Mr Carter looked like an outsider – it takes one to know one, of course.

TWO

The Opening of the Mouth

The 'Opening of the Mouth' was an important Egyptian
ritual in which an inanimate object, such as a statue or one who was
no longer alive, like a mummy, was symbolically brought to life . . .
different adzes were used for the symbolic cutting open . . . and
several mummies have been found on which there are small
cuts in the bandages in the region of the mouth.

www.britishmuseum.org

6

Cairo was a relatively small city then, not the spreading metropolis it has become since. The haunts favoured by visiting Americans and Europeans were limited in number, so I saw Howard Carter often over the following days, though it was some time before I'd actually be introduced to him. He was not staying at Shepheard's, I learned, but at the Continental Hotel across the Ezbekieh Gardens, where the Winlocks also had their base. Like them, he visited Shepheard's daily, using it as an informal club.

Frances gave me nuggets of information: she said his father had been an artist, who specialised in portraits of animals, that he was the youngest of eleven children and his family had been poor. He'd been farmed out as an infant to two spinster aunts and brought up by them in Norfolk – there his grandfather had been a gamekeeper on a large estate, and there both his parents had been born. That interested me: with my dual nationality, I had a good ear for accents, and the expert Miss Mack had sharpened it. I was familiar with the unmistakable pronunciations of rural Norfolk from my visits there. Carter's voice, with its clipped consonants and drawling upper-class vowels, sounded fake. Practised yet unnatural, it had an actorish ring, retaining no trace of his native county that I could hear.

'Whereabouts in Norfolk?' I asked.

'Swaf-something? Swath-something? I forget.'

'Swaffham? It's a little town. Some cousins of my father's live near there.'

'Then you should tell Mr Carter – he'll like that. But I don't think he goes back there very often. He came to work in Egypt when he was seventeen. He didn't have a degree or anything – not like Mr Lythgoe who lectured at Harvard or Mr Mace, our conservationist, who studied at Oxford – or Daddy, who is so brainy and has degrees from Harvard *and* Leipzig.' She frowned. 'He never talks about it, but I reckon Mr Carter scarcely went to school. He could paint well, though – his father taught him. So someone pulled strings and he was given a job in Egypt, copying tomb paintings . . . He'd never left home, and he'd had very little training, but within a few months he was digging at el-Amarna with the great Flinders Petrie, imagine that! He worked for a while as an inspector for the Department of Antiquities – they control archaeology in Egypt – and he's been here ever since. Well, he leaves in the summer, we all do – you can't stay in Egypt then, not when it's one hundred and forty degrees, and you certainly can't dig. But he has a house in the desert that's known as "Castle Carter", so his *home* is here. At least, that's what he says.'

My interest grew: a man who'd escaped schooling? A castle in the desert? Frances was so much better informed than I: I didn't know where el-Amarna was or what it signified; I'd never heard of Flinders Petrie. Something about Howard Carter fascinated me – perhaps the fact that I could not decide which aspects of him were genuine, and which fakery or pretence. He had a piratical air, though he disguised it beneath a Homburg hat and gentlemanly, well-cut suits. He had a natty, substantial moustache, large white teeth that flashed in a threatening way when he smiled, a long chin, and sleek hair; he seemed given to mischievous satiric flourishes, raising his hat with great zeal to female guests, for instance, as they crossed paths in the lobby.

'Good morning, my *dear* lady,' I once heard him say to a bewildered English visitor who had recently arrived, and who – to judge from her perplexed expression – had not the least idea who he was. And then, on another occasion: 'Frau von Essen! *Guten Morgen, gnädige Frau* . . . and still in occupation, I see. Is Berlin not calling to you?'

This remark – made at a time when the Great War was fresh in everyone's memories and when Germans experienced prejudice in British-ruled Egypt – might have been a barb, or mere politesse. Haughty Frau von Essen bridled and gave him a cold stare, to which he responded by baring his teeth in that alarming grin, clicking his heels, and sauntering out of the lobby whistling.

Over the next few days, I became something of a Howard Carter sleuth; I found myself looking out for him and, more often than not, I'd be rewarded. I'd see him strolling across the Ezbekieh Gardens, carrying a silver-topped cane, the professional beggars giving him, I noticed, a wide berth. Or he'd be taking tea on the terrace at Shepheard's, sometimes in the company of Lord Carnarvon's daughter, Lady Evelyn – the elegant young woman I'd glimpsed at Madame's dancing class; more often in the company of the rich older women who were its habitués, and with whom he seemed a great favourite: they were always gushing compliments, hanging on his every word.

'So I shinned down the rope to the cave,' I overheard him say one afternoon, 'a two-hundred-foot drop below. It was the middle of the night and pitch dark, but I caught the thieves red-handed . . . Yes, a tomb built for Queen Hatshepsut, so my hopes were high . . . A sixty-foot passageway into the rock, two hundred tons of rubble to clear, and all we found was an empty unused sarcophagus. The tomb was so well hidden Hatshepsut could have lain there unmolested for millennia. But she ruled as a king, and was determined to be buried as one. So she constructed a new tomb for herself in the Valley, where it was plundered in antiquity like all the others. A king's status she aped, and a king's fate she shared.'

'Oh, Mr Carter, *too* exciting, how marvellously *brave*,' one of the admirers sighed – and I silently agreed.

What I thought of as my best Carter sighting came at the celebrated Mena House Hotel in the desert outside Cairo. It was a place where the rich – British, American, Egyptian and European – went to swim, play tennis or golf, to admire the antiques, to sample the delicious food – or simply to see and be seen. It had originally been built by the Khedive, the then-monarch of Egypt, as a sporting lodge for desert shooting parties; and such shoots, organised by British officers, were still popular. They'd massacre ducks at dawn on the Nile marshes, then assemble at the Mena House for hearty breakfasts of porridge, bacon and eggs.

The interior was that peculiar marriage I'd begun to recognise as Anglo-Oriental: you'd be served Earl Grey tea while lounging on divans; your scones or Victoria sponge cake would be served by a man in Bedouin robes. You could stroll outside to admire the famous herbaceous borders, where Egyptian gardeners in djellabas kept up a constant watering regime. You'd discover that, thanks to determination, an inexhaustible supply of money and dirt-cheap labour, the lavender, delphiniums and roses of an English manor house garden could be made to thrive in the desert, within yards of the pyramids.

Carter was alone that evening at Mena House – and he showed no wish to greet or even acknowledge the numerous friends and acquaintances of his who were present. In misfit-mode, scowling and abstracted, he made his way across the terrace, ignoring those who called his name or rose to waylay him. From the windows of the crowded hotel dining room, I watched him stroll outside, and then make his way across the lush lawns, from which the view of the nearby pyramids was justly famous.

Carter lingered there, in the lurid after-glow that follows an Egyptian sunset, framed by palms, oleanders, roses and dahlias; he was staring in the direction of the desert and the darkening blood-red sky. After a while, he took out a silver cigarette box and a gold holder, lit a cigarette and stood smoking it contemplatively. Outlined against the violent mauve of the oleanders, with the vast black shape of a pyramid looming over him, he remained there for some time. I watched the pyramid creep up on him – a celebrated and eerie effect, caused by some trickery of the light. This uncanny advance continued; then, when the pyramid had crept so close it seemed about to crush the garden and Carter with it, he extracted the cigarette from its glittering holder, threw a precautionary glance over his shoulder, tossed the stub into the flower borders and turned to go.

I expected him to return to the hotel and was sure he would come across to our table: we were with the Winlocks; Lord Carnarvon's daughter, Lady Evelyn, had just joined us, and she had known Carter from her childhood, as Frances had explained. Surely they would catch his eye and, seeing such old friends, he'd gladly join us? I nerved myself for a meeting, but Mr Carter never materialised; when I next looked out to the gardens, darkness had fallen and he had vanished into thin air.

By then, and just as Miss Mack had hoped, I was discovering what *fun* was. The days of dutiful perambulations from one must-see tourist site to another, and of religious readings from the guidebooks, were over. We'd dispensed with the regulation afternoon rest period, and abandoned the practice of early, melancholy suppers in our rooms. Now, as Miss Mack liked to say, there simply weren't enough hours in the day to fit in the delights Cairo offered: every morning, Frances and I practised ballet steps; in the afternoons, we explored the city, with her mother as our guide. As each day passed, I learned more about Frances herself – that she had been born in Cairo, which made her an honorary Egyptian, she said; that she had a younger sister, just a shrimp of two-and-a-bit, who was too young to come to Egypt; that she loved the desert and the Valley of the Kings – but also the wild places of America, in particular Maine, where her family spent summers by the sea, in a house on a remote island.

With Frances at my side, Cairo opened up to me. I explored the Mousky bazaar with her, wandering the labyrinth of dark lanes and getting lost in the section where they sold antiquities. There, Frances and her mother showed me how to bargain, and tried to train my eye: could I not see? This *antika* was an obvious fake, but that one, ah, *that* was the real thing. We made a visit to the famous Gezira Sporting Club to watch a polo match, and there, after a long and incomprehensible series of chukkas, the two teams of sweating British officers lined up, and Lady Evelyn presented the captain of the winning team with a silver cup. It was on that occasion that I met for the first time, and was fleetingly introduced to, Lady Evelyn's friend, Mrs d'Erlanger, the woman I'd heard her mention that first day at Madame's dancing class.

I'd glimpsed the astonishing Mrs d'Erlanger before, speeding through the lobby at Shepheard's, circling its dance floor in a dress that seemed to be made of liquid silver. I'd watched her run down the steps of the hotel and jump into a car driven by a dashing English lieutenant. I'd seen her in the Sudan courtyard at the bazaar, rifling through a heap of ivory tusks, bargaining for a leopard skin and tossing aside ostrich plumes. I'd watched her decide to buy all of the furs, and then, a second later, none of them . . . I knew she had travelled out from England with Lady Evelyn and would be continuing on to Luxor with her once Lord Carnarvon arrived, but I couldn't believe she could be pinned down in such a way. She fascinated Frances, and she fascinated me: I thought of her as an exotic and beautiful bird of passage – an impression Helen Winlock confirmed that day at the polo match. Following my gaze across the gardens to the clubhouse terrace, where the vivid figure of Poppy d'Erlanger could be seen, first at Evelyn's side, then separated off by an eager phalanx of polo players, she sighed.

'She's exquisite, isn't she, Lucy?' Helen said. 'Those eyes! But she isn't a woman you can rely on, you know – not like Evelyn . . . dear Eve's only twenty, and Poppy d'Erlanger must be, oh, twenty-eight, at least, and she has children too – but Eve is so sensible, whereas Poppy is – well, thoughtless. Lord only knows what goes on in that beautiful head of hers . . . She's always agreeing to do this or that, she was supposed to lunch with us last week – but then she simply doesn't turn up, and forgets to send word, or she stays five minutes and then disappears without explanation. She's famous for bolting . . . ' She laughed. 'And famous for her charm too, so she's always forgiven.'

Poppy d'Erlanger bolted on the occasion of that polo match: one minute she was there, and I was being introduced and shaking her thin, cool hand, and we were making our way into the clubhouse for the post-match tea; the next, there was a vacant chair, and emissaries were being dispatched in quest of her. After a long delay, we learned Mrs d'Erlanger had left the club a few minutes before.

'She drove off with Jarvis, I think,' said the young captain who'd gone in search of her. He had returned out of breath, hot, disgruntled and possibly envious. 'At least, I *think* it was Jarvis. But someone said it might have been that swine Carew.'

Evelyn seemed disconcerted by this news, but, covering up for her friend, she said lightly: 'Of course – I remember now. She mentioned that to me. And please be kind about that swine, Carew. He's the sweetest man, a *very* old friend of Poppy's – and he's a second cousin of mine, you know. Now, there's Indian tea and China – and, oh how divine, they've made us one of those Gezira ginger cakes . . . '

Frances and I were pressed into service, handing plates around. The moment passed, but I noted how gracefully Evelyn had handled it, and how effective her gentle reproof had been. I returned to my chair at the edge of the group and listened distantly to the ex-pat gossip with which I was becoming familiar: the horse races, the duck shooting, the latest doings at the Residency . . . The young officers moved on to discuss the rise of the nationalist Wafd Party, the current political unrest and the need to 'nip it in the bud fast' before 'things got out of hand'.

'The thing is, Lady E, one can't trust Egyptians an inch – they're devious,' said the most voluble of them, an earnest, fresh-faced young lieutenant by the name of Ronnie Urquhart. He fixed Evelyn with his frank blue gaze: 'The sooner we abandon all this defeatist talk of "independence" the better. Give up the Suez Canal – when it's our passage to India? The very idea! No: what works in Delhi will work in Cairo – we need to crack down hard. Did you hear about the demonstration last week? Right outside the Residency, a bunch of nationalist ruffians, waving flags and shouting slogans. On Lord Allenby's doorstep! Infernal cheek. We put a stop to *that* little game pretty fast. What we need to do now is pull in the agitators, get them off the streets and . . .'

I think Helen Winlock was bored and disagreed with the views being expressed, though she said little. Miss Mack took on these young men once or twice, and challenged them in a sprightly way: she was listened to with grave courtesy, and then ignored. I was imagining the vitriol the officer's remarks would have provoked in my father – not a man who tolerated fools. I was glad when Miss Mack cut short this tirade, which had now moved on to 'Gyppo trouble-makers', and rose to her feet.

'When Egypt gains independence, Lieutenant Urquhart,' she said, fixing him with her keen republican eye, 'which it will very soon, that much is obvious, then many of your so-called agitators will be elected members of a democratic Egyptian parliament. Are they to be deprived of freedom of speech then as they are now? No, don't answer me, Lieutenant, I must go.'

We left the clubhouse, with its leather armchairs, its faint cooking smells of roast beef and over-boiled cabbage, its atmosphere that was part gentlemen's club, part English prep school. We passed through the gardens and came out into the street; two armed sentries smartly saluted at the gates, and beyond them the clamour of Cairo reclaimed us. Frances seemed used to such contrasts, but my head was aching, my hat itched and I felt that familiar smoky dislocation as we set off along the dusty road. We threaded our way past Arabs riding side-saddle, past a pungent camel train; we negotiated a route through the crush of hawkers and beggars. It was time for evening prayers: the cries of the muezzin came from the minarets of the mosques, rising like discordant music above the din of the streets. At last we reached the corner where the loyal Hassan was waiting for us; climbing into the carriage, I touched his Eye of Horus amulet.

'What a collection of young hotheads,' Helen said, glancing back at the club. 'Aren't they insufferable, Myrtle?'

'Well, my dear, I do try to make allowances. Most of them are so very young, and they've been taught those opinions from the cradle. But the days of their precious Protectorate are numbered. So one has to ask – are they blind? Do they *think*?'

'Are they even capable of thought? I often doubt it. My, but King and Empire can get mighty tedious . . .'

'Helen, it *can*. I get this irresistible urge to mention the Boston tea-party . . .'

Helen laughed, and linked her arm in Miss Mack's. 'Save your breath, Myrtle,' she replied. 'They just might not have heard of it. History isn't their strong point.'

Those episodes of confusion and smoky uncertainty continued, and would still afflict me at unpredictable moments. But they became more infrequent – the influence of Frances seemed to drive them away. How different it was to tour the Coptic churches or Saladin's citadel in her unpredictable company. How much more rewarding to explore the hot vast Egyptian Museum with her and with her father, who'd sometimes take time off to give us expert guidance. With a genial Herbert Winlock at my side, I could patch up some of the gaps in my understanding. I learned that el-Amarna, where Mr Carter had first dug as a young man, had been a magnificent city, built by the heretic king Akhenaten, who had abandoned the royal city of Thebes and cast aside the old gods, imposing a single deity, the Aten, or sun god. Peering into the museum's dusty display cases, I could examine the broken statues of this king, and admire the reliefs that showed him with his six daughters and his wife, Nefertiti: the queen whose name meant '*The beautiful one is come*'.

'Did one of Akhenaten's daughters inherit his throne?' I asked Herbert Winlock. I was drawn to these long-dead daughters, who were depicted very small.

'Not so far as we know,' he replied; he was always tender with my ignorance. 'It wasn't impossible for a woman to rule, Lucy: Hatshepsut, for instance. She seized the throne after her husband the king died, and ruled her empire for thirty years with great success and great ruthlessness – and when you come to Luxor, I'll take you and Miss Mack around her mortuary temple. But in that era, she was an exception.'

He leaned forward and we both examined the carved relief that held pride of place in this cabinet: Akhenaten with Nefertiti, *en famille*. The tiny daughters were at play: the stone was cracked and chipped, and sections were missing, but if you examined it closely, you could see that the rays of the sun touched each member of the family, and that the rays ended in hands, which appeared to caress, or to bless them.

'So, to answer your question, Lucy, we're not sure who ruled after Akhenaten,' Herbert Winlock continued. 'It's an era that's virtually undocumented. But it wasn't one of his daughters. We believe there were two short reigns after his death: a king called Smenkhkare of whom we know nothing beyond a name, and then another, Tutankhaten, later known as Tutankhamun – but we know next to nothing of him either.' He sighed. 'That's the fascination of Egyptology, Lucy: how much we know – and how little. It's like flashes of intense light – and then a great impenetrable darkness.'

He broke off and glanced around. We could now hear the sound of footsteps and quiet voices. Two men had just entered the far end of that gallery: one, a familiar bulky figure in a Homburg hat, was Howard Carter; the other a distinguished-looking man who was unknown to me.

'Isn't that Howard?' Helen said. 'Who is he taking on the grand tour this time, Herbert? Someone important – someone useful?'

'Lord Northcliffe – owner of *The Times*. He's over here for the latest conference. Howard said he'd wangled a meeting with him,' Winlock replied. They exchanged a wry glance.

'I daren't look. Is Howard being *very* charming?' Helen smiled.

'Sure is. And won't thank us for interrupting him,' Winlock answered, and led us quickly into a side gallery.

It was filled with mummies – I remember that, for they haunted my dreams for months afterwards: case after case of them, in a silent space a hundred yards long. There they lay, bandaged, shrouded, white, peaceable and threatening. At the very end of the gallery, in a special case of their own, were the smaller mummies: children, infants and tiny babies. Frances, whose face had set in an obstinate mask of indifference, reached for my hand, and I clasped it. When we reached the case containing the babies, Helen came to a halt. She had paled, and was fighting back tears.

'Get me out of here, darling,' she said quietly to her husband. 'Please – surely you know a way out.'

Winlock did. All the corridors in that labyrinth of a museum were familiar ground to him; within minutes we had left the stifling hush of the galleries and were outside in the shocking heat of the sun. Across the street, an altercation was taking place, of a kind we often glimpsed: two Arabs were being lazily beaten by Egyptian policemen; a British officer stood watching, aloof and indifferent, his revolver drawn. After a while, in a bored way, he raised the gun skywards and loosed off a shot. The shouts and cries instantly stopped, and everyone scattered. One of the policemen shouted an insult in Arabic as the offenders fled; the officer holstered his gun and strolled off. The museum-pitch beggars who had held back to watch this sideshow then spotted Miss Mack, by now a well-known mark throughout Cairo; without hesitation, they and the *antika* hawkers moved in.

Miss Mack scattered *baksheesh* with her usual abandon, but recoiled when she saw the souvenirs on sale. A mummified hand? A collection of crumbling, evil-smelling mummified toes? No, she would *not* buy such horrors . . . I could see this refusal pained her, for the toe-hawker was a small boy of great beauty, perhaps five years old, barefoot, wearing clothes that were in rags. His eager face clouded – but disaster was avoided: he just happened to have two scarabs in his pocket and they also were for sale. Miss Mack bought both with alacrity.

'Miss Mackenzie, those are both very bad fakes,' Frances said, in her direct way. 'And you paid twenty times too much for them.'

'I know, dear,' Miss Mack replied humbly. 'Now I look at them, I can see – they're even worse than the last lot I bought. They really are hideous. Still,' her face brightened, 'the money will buy that sweet child a meal or a pair of shoes, so it won't be wasted.'

She set off with a new spring in her step. The little boy was already being roughly robbed of his spoils by the man who controlled that particular band of infants – but this exchange took place behind her back, and she walked on, oblivious.

When we'd returned to the hotel, I asked Miss Mack why Helen Winlock should have been so distressed by the museum's mummified babies. The question had been puzzling me: surely she must have seen them many times before?

Miss Mack knew the answer, I suspected: she and Helen had become very close by then. With a stern glance, she informed me that Mrs Winlock was a grown woman, who, like all grown women, had experienced sadnesses. 'What a child you are for questions! Curiosity killed the cat, Lucy,' she said tartly, turning away.

7

We had then been in Cairo almost two weeks, and my entry test for Madame's dancing class was coming closer by the day. Miss Mack had decreed that we'd need two further weeks to exhaust the delights of the city; for the final stage of our journey, we'd then travel up the Nile to the Valley of the Kings and the temples of Luxor – though Miss Mack, disdaining the modern name, would insist that our destination was Homer's 'hundred-gated Thebes'. Once there, our itinerary was formidable; when drawing up her lists, Miss Mack's eyes would gleam at the wealth of mind-improving, life-changing spectacles that lay in wait for me. That smoke would begin to drift behind my eyes again as she quoted guidebooks and flourished photographs. I was trying not to see the prospect that lay in wait beyond those marvels – my return to England, and the uncertainties that awaited me there. I clung to one sure comforting fact: we had an open invitation to visit the Winlocks and their fellow archaeologists at the American House. They promised that, when we went to the Valley of the Kings, they would accompany us and Frances would be my personal guide. If Mr Carter was in the right receptive frame of mind – and who could tell if he would be? – we might also visit him at Lord Carnarvon's dig.

'Carter has a *plan*,' Herbert Winlock explained to us one day, when he joined us in the cool marble halls of Groppi's café for ices and mint tea. 'For decades now, everyone's been saying the Valley's exhausted and there are no more royal tombs to be found. Carter won't accept that. He hasn't just *dug* in the Valley, he's spent years analysing the known tomb locations, the water courses, the rock formations – and he believes there is at least one last tomb to be found. He's narrowed his search down to a triangular area – Carter's golden triangle, we call it. The plan is to work through that, section by section, removing all the old spoil from previous digs, and going right back to the bedrock.'

'Heavens!' Miss Mack cried. 'How arduous, Mr Winlock.'

'Arduous, expensive – and so far unrewarding,' Winlock said. 'He and Carnarvon have been working their way through that darn triangle of his ever since the end of the war. This will be their fifth year in the Valley, and they've virtually exhausted it. So far, they've found a cache of thirteen calcite jars – interesting but not very . . . They were dug out of the ground by Lady Carnarvon herself two years ago. An act that was more surprising than the find. Almina Carnarvon is a remarkable woman, but—'

'She certainly is,' Helen put in. 'Whether she's staying somewhere two days or a month, she never travels with fewer than seventy-two pairs of shoes. If that isn't remarkable, I don't know what is.'

'But her interest in archaeology is less warm than her interest in footwear, certainly these days. It's lost its charm for her, I hear – though people say that it's her money that funds the Carnarvon digs. And it's Rothschild money, of course, so I guess it's pretty inexhaustible.'

Winlock exchanged a narrow glance with his wife, who then gave Miss Mack a similar glance, equally veiled. '*Alfred de Rothschild's natural daughter,*' she said, leaning towards Miss Mack and lowering her voice to a whisper, though both Frances and I caught the words. Miss Mack blushed and dropped her spoon. A peculiar reaction, as Frances and I later agreed: surely all daughters were natural? Was there such a thing as an unnatural daughter? Such episodes – and they were frequent – made understanding *anything* very difficult, as Frances often complained.

'They're hiding something,' she'd say to me, 'and I intend to find out what it is. I shall dig and dig until I get to the bottom of it.' I was recruited to assist with this task, which by its very nature seemed to me archaeological. Frances disagreed: no, she said – it was *espionage*.

On that occasion, Miss Mack jumped in fast. Consigning Lady Carnarvon to the region of the unmentionable, she reverted to the safer subject of the Valley of the Kings. 'How fascinating, Mr

Winlock!' she cried. 'Poor Mr Carter, poor Lord Carnarvon – all that hard work. Those piles of spoil are mountainous. Five years of toil! Down to the bedrock! And have they found *nothing* beyond those vases?'

'Virtually nothing,' Winlock replied. 'And don't forget *partage*, Miss Mackenzie. By rule of the Antiquities Service, administered, as we all know, by our *great* friends, the French, any finds are divided fifty-fifty between the permit holder and Egypt. So seven of those calcite vases went straight to the Egyptian Museum here, and the remaining six winged their way home to Lord Carnarvon's country seat . . . I guess they're now part of his collection at Highclere Castle. That's a poor reward for the kind of money he's been spending. Carnarvon wants a royal tomb, even dreams of an intact one, I suspect – and so does Carter. So, as you can see, they're both optimists and romantics – because *if* they should find such a thing, it would be a first. Every single tomb ever discovered in the Valley has been robbed – very thoroughly robbed – in antiquity.'

'Well, that is true, of course,' said Miss Mack, nodding sagely. 'But perhaps they'll make a breakthrough even so,' she added: she too was an optimist and a romantic. 'After all, the Valley is a mysterious place. It may yet have more secrets to reveal!'

'Let us hope so,' Winlock replied in a dry tone. It was difficult to tell whether he thought Carter deluded, or a man who was on to something. 'Anyway, last year Carter was clearing the ground by the tomb of Ramesses VI, but that area's infested with tourists and it's now the height of the season. So he's switched locations, and when we make our trip, we'll find him slaving away in a different part of the Valley altogether. Eve will be there – she never leaves her father's side, so, if Carter's in one of his foul moods, we can always talk to her . . . Or to Lordy.'

'Lordy?' Miss Mack's eyebrows rose.

'Lord Carnarvon has a surfeit of names, Miss Mackenzie.' Winlock smiled. 'No less than five birth names, plus his title, plus "Pups", as Eve calls him; plus "Porchy", which is what his family calls him – his courtesy title was Viscount Porchester before he inherited the earldom, you know. That makes a grand total of eight names. That's more than the pharaohs: even they stuck at a modest five. So we Met renegades call him "Lordy".' Winlock's smile widened. 'Not to his face,

naturally. He's an interesting guy, and I have a lot of time for him —
but, put it this way, I wouldn't want to risk *lèse-majesté*.'

When Miss Mack and I travelled on to Luxor, we were to stay at the
Winter Palace Hotel on the banks of the Nile, looking west across the
river towards the Theban hills — that much had now been decided.
Once there, our time was limited, for the date of our return to
England was fixed. Even so, we would go *everywhere* and see *everything*.
Only one aspect of the master plan remained undecided: how should
we travel upriver? The Winlocks, Mrs d'Erlanger and Lady Evelyn,
together with her father, who was due to arrive from England very
soon, would all be travelling by the overnight Wagons Lits train,
which would cover the journey in some twelve hours. Howard
Carter would also be journeying to Luxor by train, going ahead of the
Carnarvons to get the dig under way.

This uniformity of choice alarmed Miss Mack: the alternative to
the White Train was to travel upriver by boat, always her preference.
But should we journey in a swift, economic way via a Thomas Cook
steamboat, or by the more expensive, picturesque means of a houseboat or *dahabiyeh*? After days of indecision, Miss Mack finally made
up her mind: both the train (dull and commonplace) and the
dahabiyeh (slow and extravagant) were ruled out: QED, the Cook's
steamboat it had to be. I reported this plan to Frances immediately.

'A hard decision,' Miss Mack cried, over dinner at Shepheard's, on
the first occasion this decision was publicly discussed. 'I was tempted,
Lady Evelyn — I first sailed up the Nile with my father on a *dahabiyeh*
called *Kleopatra*. I shall never forget it! We flew the Stars and Stripes,
and we had a piano, and our own library . . . Ah, the dawns I saw! The
pelicans diving for fish! In fact, it was such a wonderful experience,
I mean to write it up as a memoir one of these days. But times
change, and I must be realistic. The young man at Cook's was *most*
helpful. So I've made up my mind. A *dahabiyeh* could take weeks. The
steamboat will get us there in four days. The fares are so reasonable.'

'And the company so intolerable,' said Herbert Winlock, stealth-
ily refilling her champagne glass. He glanced across at his wife, and
at Evelyn, who had joined us for dinner that evening; both were suppressing smiles. 'Miss Mackenzie, I can't allow it. Do you really want
Lucy to experience the Nile for the first time from the deck of a

steamboat, with all that noise and nasty cramped little cabins, and a crowd of ignorant tourists hell-bent on buying hideous souvenirs, complaining about the heat and the food and the flies? An old Egypt hand such as you are? Surely not?'

Miss Mack's egalitarian views fought a battle with pride in her status: she hesitated. 'Well, I guess you have a point, Mr Winlock, but—'

'Herbert, please. And as Helen addresses you as "Myrtle", may I not do so too?'

Miss Mack blushed scarlet as she acquiesced. Herbert Winlock could be charming, and I think he genuinely liked Miss Mack, as well as being amused by her. For her part, she had been predisposed in his favour by the immediate devotion she'd felt for his wife, and archaeologists could do no wrong in her eyes. Winlock was head of the Metropolitan's Egyptian excavation team; Rudyard Kipling, her supreme hero and favourite poet, had visited one of his digs years before – a meeting that in her view sealed Winlock's own heroic status. Within two days of making his acquaintance, she'd pronounced him courtly, witty, highly intelligent and an erudite tease with a dramatic taste in bow ties. By now there were distinct signs that he was the latest paragon – for example, a tendency to quote him ten times a day.

With his customary skill her paragon now sensed his moment and pressed home his advantage. 'Besides,' he added wickedly, 'what was that phrase – "No expense spared"? I think the Emerson and Stockton coffers could stand it, don't you, Myrtle? Would the cost of a *dahabiyeh* bring the railroads to a halt and close down the steel mills?'

'Well, that is true, of course,' she replied, visibly wavering. 'I want Lucy to experience the Nile the best possible way. But those *dahabiyehs* are so darn slow—'

'They *are*,' Frances put in. 'If the wind drops, or you get stuck on a sandbank, you can sit there for ever – that happened to you once, didn't it, Eve?'

'Well, perhaps not for ever, Frances,' Evelyn said, 'but you can get becalmed for days and even the most beautiful river can get boring. Anyway, I'm my father's daughter – I like *speed*, just as Pups does. So I adore the train – I love whizzing through the dark – and then waking up with the desert on one side and all the hubbub of Luxor on the other.'

'And there's a dining car on the train,' Helen put in, 'and mighty civilised it is. French food, lovely wine, the desert flashing past—'

'And efficient plumbing, Helen.' Evelyn laughed. 'Which definitely *cannot* be said of *dahabiyehs* or the steamboats.'

'That is true,' Miss Mack conceded, beginning to look anxious. 'The plumbing in all boats leaves much to be desired.'

'Daddy always says the steamboats can be very *unhealthy*, don't you, Daddy?' Frances said, on a note of innocent appeal – and it was then I began to understand that there was an agenda here, that Frances had initiated it, and that the Winlocks, aided and abetted by Evelyn, intended to push it through.

'Unhealthy? Heavens above – I hadn't considered that, which is very remiss of me. I have to be mindful of Lucy's welfare, she . . . Do you really think that, Herbert?'

'Well, I wouldn't wish to alarm you,' Winlock replied, straight-faced. 'But there can be a rat problem – Nile rats are gigantic, you know. And those boats vary greatly in their standards of hygiene . . .'

He left the sentence hanging, leaving it to his wife to execute the *coup de grâce*.

'You must decide, Myrtle,' Helen said. 'But of course, if you and Lucy *were* to take the train, we could travel up together. Why, Frances and Lucy could even share a sleeper.'

Poor Miss Mack! She was now in a state of consternation. I could see which way she was leaning; the mention of giant rats had made the train journey a near-certainty. I had no doubt that it was Frances who had engineered this outcome, and I was touched by her wily determination. But I was beginning to feel tender towards Miss Mack and knew the best solution would be to let her down gently. I suggested we go and inspect the steamboats minutely, and then decide.

'Oh, Lucy!' Miss Mack burst out, when we'd returned to our rooms. 'I was in such a fret – but I feel much better now. How sensible you are! We'll inspect those darn boats first thing tomorrow. I shall pay close attention to the plumbing systems. Then I'll know what to do.'

'Of course you will,' I replied cautiously: that ganging-up had made me anxious. I was experiencing a seeping sense of disloyalty.

'What a dear, good child you are, Lucy,' she said, and, for the first time since I'd known her, she dropped a kiss on my forehead and gathered me in her arms. I returned the hug awkwardly. No one had embraced me since my mother died. I was unsure how to respond. Out of practice, I suppose.

'The train?' Frances asked, on my return from the steamboat inspection the next morning.

'The train,' I replied.

'That *is* what you wanted?'

'I wouldn't have minded any of the alternatives.'

'Liar! You were angling for the train as much as I was, Lucy Payne.'

'No I wasn't. I stayed neutral.'

'Not true! And don't look so goody-goody. You don't fool *me*.'

I wondered who was right about my character, Frances or I. Linking her arm in mine, she marched me up the great staircase at Shepheard's: it was time for my daily dancing practice. Thanks to Frances, I'd now learned the five basic ballet positions. I hadn't *mastered* them, and couldn't claim to perform them well, but I had learned the rudiments. We were now ready for the final push: the day of Madame Masha's test was fast approaching.

We'd been unable to use Madame's studio at Shepheard's to practise – that was out of bounds, but we'd needed a barre, so had improvised. We'd ended up in the huge mausoleum of a bathroom next to my bedroom; there, the daylight was dimmed and filtered through windows of pearly glass, which gave our exercises a ghostly air. But there was a long towel rail of about the right height, and a door we could lock, so there was no danger of any outsider glimpsing my ugly, patchy hair or witnessing my clumsiness and ineptitude. At first, I had practised with Frances alone. Then, on the third day, we'd been joined by Lady Rose, the little girl whom I'd seen at

Madame's class – she claimed she needed extra practice too. That morning, I discovered, we were to be joined by Rose again, and also by her infant brother Peter, otherwise known as Viscount Hurst, aged three. This did not please me – and neither did the fact that Frances had kept this development a secret.

'Why do we have to have *them*?' I complained, drawing Frances aside and into my bedroom, leaving Rose and Peter at play in the bathroom beyond. 'It's bad enough having that stupid, stuck-up Rose. Now we're landed with a three-year-old cry-baby with a ridiculous title as well.'

'Oh, come on. Peter can't help the title. He's not a cry-baby, he's cute. And Rose isn't stupid or stuck-up – when you know her better, you'll like her. Besides, it's not their fault, it's their mother's: she insisted on bringing them out to Egypt, and now they're in Cairo she's always dumping them on someone – usually Eve.'

'Rubbish. They must have a nanny or something.'

'They did. But she was a snoop, so she got fired two days in. Meanwhile, their mother's always gadding about somewhere. Eve says she's got a new man – I overheard her.'

'A *what*?'

'A new man – you know. One of those flirty-flirty sort of things.' Frances batted her eyelashes hideously. We stared at each other and then giggled.

'But I don't understand,' I said, when we'd finally stopped laughing. 'How can their mother flirt? She's a *mother*. She's *married*. What about her husband?'

'Ah,' said Frances, giving me a measuring glance. 'Well, that's kind of tricky. You see, she divorced her first husband, and now she's finished with her second husband too – people say *he* got his marching orders before she sailed for Cairo with Eve. So I guess she's on the hunt for a *third* husband, and that takes time. Which is why we have to look after Peter and Rose, and why you have to be nice to them.'

I considered this. I was wavering.

'Also,' Frances continued, 'Rose and Peter's father, who was the first husband of course, is a man called Lord Strathaven. He's an earl too, like Eve's father, and he's horrible. Peter and Rose hate him. But Peter lives with him because he's the heir, so he can only escape for holidays, and Rose lives with her mother because her father can't be bothered with a stupid girl.'

'Oh, poor Rose – does she hate her mother too?' I asked.

'Of course not,' Frances replied airily. 'She adores her – everyone does. She's really sweet-natured and good fun. It's just that she isn't like most mothers and she isn't around much. But you must know that – you've met her.'

'Met Rose and Peter's mother?' I met many people at Shepheard's in the course of the day, and was finding it hard to navigate their bewilderment of names and titles. 'I haven't met anyone called Lady Strathaven.'

'Don't be silly. I *told* you: she's divorced. She *used* to be Lady Strathaven. Three years ago she was *still* Lady Strathaven. But she couldn't bear living with the horrible earl a second longer, so she bolted. She escaped two months after Peter was born. Now she's Poppy d'Erlanger.'

'Mrs *d'Erlanger* is their mother? But I've never seen her with Peter or Rose.'

'Of course you haven't – I *told* you, Poppy is too busy finding husband number three, so she leaves them with Eve, or her maid Wheeler, or whoever else she can persuade to look after them. Anyway,' she made an impatient gesture, 'if her plans work out, she won't be Poppy d'Erlanger much longer, she'll be Poppy-someone-else. And just think, she and Rose and Peter are all coming to Luxor too, so we'll have ringside seats when Poppy finally decides who to marry next. My money's on that Carew man we saw playing polo at the Gezira . . . Now, can we get on with this dancing class?'

It was shaming how little I knew, I thought, as we returned to the echoing bathroom. This world of multiple divorces was as foreign to me as the world of the pharaohs. Frances was light years ahead of me. None of this appeared to shock or confuse her; she simply took it in her stride with a sophistication she'd acquired in Cairo. In the fustian Cambridge circles in which I'd grown up, divorce equalled disgrace. Yet here was Rose with a mother who'd already dispatched one husband, possibly two; a divorcée who was welcomed on all sides at Shepheard's . . . I was never sure whether to believe all the things Frances told me: I had much to learn, I realised.

Before we began our ballet practice we played a game; Rose and

Peter had already begun it before we rejoined them. The huge, marble-floored and -walled bathroom contained the largest bath I'd ever seen, mounted on a marble plinth with four couchant lions as feet. By the time Frances and I returned, both Rose and her little brother were lying down in this sarcophagus.

'We're playing mummies,' Rose announced. She crossed both her brother's arms on his chest, and then settled herself beside him, her right arm next to her body and her left arm across her heart. 'Look, Peter's a king and I'm a queen,' she added.

So, she too must have visited the Egyptian Museum, and learned these funereal differences, I thought: she was observant, I had to give her that.

'Oh, *excellent*,' Frances said. 'Shall I perform the Opening of the Mouth ceremony?'

'Does it hurt?' Peter asked, on a piping note of apprehension.

'Of course it doesn't, silly,' his sister replied. 'How can it hurt? You're *dead*.'

Frances found my toothbrush and advanced on the bath. In a priestly way, reciting some incomprehensible and eerie hocus-pocus that she claimed was a spell from the Egyptian *Book of the Dead*, she made an ugly levering gesture with the toothbrush handle, first at Rose's mouth, then Peter's.

'There,' she said. 'This is the most solemn moment in your entire funeral. Now you're alive again and your *ka* is freed. He guides you on the sacred journey, down to the underworld. When you get there you will be presented to Osiris, the god of the dead, and you will get *judged*. Peter, Rose, are you ready for that?'

Rose and Peter, still lying in their bath sarcophagus with their eyes shut, had a brief conference. Peter, not surprisingly given his age, had no opinion on the matter. Rose did: 'Yea, we are ready and pre-pared . . .' she intoned in a sepulchral voice.

'Right,' Frances continued, 'this is the moment of truth. In fact, Ma'at, who's the goddess of truth, is watching, and so is Anubis, the great black jackal god, so there's no faking. Now your heart will be solemnly weighed, on a *huge* set of scales, like the scales of justice, but much bigger. On one side there's your heart and on the other side there's a feather—'

'A *feather*?' Rose sat up. 'They weigh my heart against a *feather*?'

'Yes, they do,' said Frances firmly. 'And if they don't balance out, boy, you're in trouble.'

Peter opened his eyes. The word 'trouble' affected him at once; his lips wobbled, and he made a grab for his sister's hand. 'What kind of trouble?' Rose asked recklessly.

'*Big* trouble,' Frances replied. 'If the scale that side goes down it means your heart is heavy with *evil*. It means you have a bad heart because you've done bad things in your life. So this huge horrible hairy monster comes along and gobbles you up. And that's it: no afterlife for you.'

'That can't be right,' Rose said, in a Sunday-school voice. 'What about forgiveness? What if you *repent*?'

'You can't repent. Egyptian gods don't forgive. It doesn't *work* like that. You are what you've done. And if you're bad, bad, *bad* . . . that's it, you're finished.'

At the repeated word 'bad', Peter made a small whimpering sound, covered his eyes with his hands and clung to his sister. Rose lay down again and hugged him.

'On the other hand,' Frances added, kindly, quickly and diplomatically, 'if you have a *good* heart, like you, Peter, and you, Rose, then everything is hunky-dory. Your heart and the feather balance perfectly – and off you go to paradise, which is just like this life, only much better and even more beautiful, and you – you live by the Nile and the sun shines and . . . and there are no more tears, only joy and rejoicings, and you have nice things to eat and lots of servants to do things for you. For ever and ever . . . That's if you're a king, of course.'

She paused, then continued in a helpful, pedantic way: 'Meanwhile, it's pretty neat being a mummy, because of course you don't rot, not if the priests have done their job properly, anyway . . . They've left your heart in, because you'll need it for the weighing ceremony, but they've taken out your liver and lungs and all the gut-stuff and pickled them. And they've pulled your brains out through your nose with a special hook—'

At the mention of brains, noses and hooks, Peter could stand it no longer. He uttered one long agonised wail, then sat up. Large tears plopped silently down his flushed face.

'Now look what you've done,' Rose said, also sitting up and

putting her arms around him. 'Honestly, Frances, you are the absolute *end*. He's only three . . . now he'll have nightmares.'

'He has nightmares already, you told me so.'

'That's because of Papa and his tempers. You don't have to make it *worse*. Why do you have to be so gruesome? Now you've really upset him . . . Oh, hellishness! There, there, Petey – don't cry, it's all right. Frances didn't mean it.'

'Yes I did. It's the *truth*. You asked—'

'Oh, put a sock in it.'

'Give him to me,' I said. 'I have some barley sugar in my room. You'd like that, wouldn't you, Peter?'

I held out my arms and the small trembling boy was bundled into them. He looked at me apprehensively, and wriggled at first, and I wasn't sure how best to hold him, but I made the kind of soothing noises I could remember my mother making to me, and they seemed to have the right effect. I took him to my room, and found the barley sugar stick, and broke off a piece for him. He seemed to like its amber colour and twisted shape; he certainly liked its taste. The tears ceased.

It took a long while to suck the sweet down to nothing, and by the time he'd done that he'd forgotten Frances's scare stories – although I had not. I cuddled him tight and kissed his forehead, and told him that of course he was a good boy and not a bad one – he seemed very anxious on this point. When his eyelids began to droop, I tried to settle him for a nap on my bed. But the second he realised I was leaving him alone, he clung to me and began to cry piteously, so in the end I took him back to the bathroom, where we could keep an eye on him while we practised our dance steps. Its marble floor was cold and hard, but I made a deep, warm nest for him out of the enormous, soft towels that Shepheard's provided; he snuggled down into them, put his thumb into his mouth, and in an instant was asleep.

Later, when we'd finished our exercises, he woke up, toddled over and took my hand. He couldn't pronounce my name, so he called me Lulu; he told me I had funny hair, but he liked it. I bent to kiss him again – he looked vulnerable, his skin still flushed from his sleep, and so sweet and trusting, that my heart gave a strange lurch. At his earnest request, I called him 'Petey' and he continued to call me Lulu. It was under this new name, and in this new guise, that, later that day, I was finally introduced to Howard Carter.

9

We were taking tea on the terrace at Shepheard's when the meeting with Carter took place – and at our very own table. This scheme, initiated by Frances and endorsed by Rose, had been effected with the combined assistance of Helen Winlock, Miss Mack and an indulgent Evelyn. She had charge of Rose and Peter again that afternoon – Poppy d'Erlanger was, as usual, not in evidence. The waiters had entered into the game, installing us at one of the best tables, and bringing us double portions of cucumber sandwiches, biscuits with icing and cakes. There was a brief battle between Frances and Rose as to who should have the honour of pouring the tea. Rose had just won this tussle, and I was busy settling a cushion on Peter's chair next to me, so he could reach the table, when I caught a waft of tobacco and lime cologne, and, looking up, saw Howard Carter.

Removing his hat with a flourish, he bowed to us with great ceremony – or mockery.

'Lord Hurst . . . Lady Rose – Frances, my dear child – what a splendid tea, and the most fashionable table on the terrace too. Am I permitted to join you?'

He made a curt gesture that brought the waiters hastening to his side, a chair was produced, and he had seated himself before Frances and Rose, both pink with delight, had graciously informed him he could do so. He smiled that disconcerting smile of his, and I saw his penetrating brown-eyed gaze rest upon me.

Frances, alert to the social niceties, was beginning to introduce us, when Peter interrupted. 'Lulu,' he said, banging the table with a teaspoon that Rose quickly confiscated. He liked the sound, and repeated it in an ululating way: 'Lulu, Lulu, Lulu.'

I had a feeling Carter already knew who I was, having perhaps discovered my connection to Miss Mack, and to steel and railroads. Something in the measured assessing stare he gave me suggested this, but if it were so he disguised it, merely nodding his head at me, and drawling, 'Delighted,' in a way that made me fear I should dislike him. I sat there on tenterhooks, nibbling a cucumber sandwich, hoping he'd redeem himself.

'So do tell us, Mr Carter,' said Rose, a good mimic, playing the hostess, 'how much longer shall we have the pleasure of your company in Cairo?'

'Just a few more days, Lady Rose,' he replied. 'I'll wait until Lord Carnarvon arrives – then I'm off to the Valley.'

'Well, I should think *so*,' Frances put in. 'I can't understand why you're still here. It's late in the season for you. Why aren't you in the Valley working?'

'Because, Frances, I was ill last November – I had to have an operation in London, and then I was convalescent for six long weeks.'

'Not a *serious* operation, I trust,' said Rose, pouring tea.

'No, no – a mere bagatelle, involving gallstones. Lord Carnarvon's surgeon wielded the knife, so I was in very safe hands. And then I stayed to recuperate at Seamore Place – that's Carnarvon's Mayfair town house, you know, so I was well looked after.'

I swallowed the sandwich and stared at the tablecloth. I despised all name-dropping, and this was clumsily done; my disappointment deepened.

'I couldn't get out to Cairo until last week. So it will be a short season for us in the Valley this winter. It will be February before we start and we'll finish off in early March. But we'll be back up to strength for a full season this coming October. Meanwhile, I've been employing my time in Cairo very usefully.'

'Have you been *dealing*?' Frances asked, her clear voice carrying to the adjacent tables.

Several heads turned, and Carter flashed that dangerous smile. Leaning forward, he said quietly: 'Frances, I've used my eyes and my expertise. And I think certain collectors – and certain museums – will be pleased with the result. But let that be our secret, and don't use that word, especially here in this nest of gossip mongers.'

'Have you found some marvels?' Frances asked, lowering her voice to a whisper.

'One or two . . . yes, one or two. And my good friend Tano was generous enough to throw in a few small trifles. I'd been racking my brains as to who might like them – then I saw you all here, and I found I had my answer.'

Reaching into his pocket, he withdrew some tiny parcels, wrapped in shiny white paper and sealed with red wax. I had been expecting three: to my surprise, there were four. Carter handed them to each of us in turn.

'For me?' I said. 'But you don't know me, Mr Carter.'

'On the contrary. We've just been introduced. So don't argue.'

We all unwrapped our parcels eagerly. We three girls had each been given a single and exquisitely worked bead: Frances's was obsidian, Rose's carnelian, and mine lapis lazuli. Peter also had a bead, made of silver, and in the shape of a hippopotamus.

'Ippo!' he cried, delighted. He had difficulty with aitches.

'Oh, they're beautiful,' said Frances, flushing with pleasure. 'That is kind of you.'

'Beautiful, and three thousand years old. Give or take a century.'

'Did they belong to a queen, Mr Carter?' Rose asked, in a hopeful way.

'Maybe. Or to a king. Once part of a bracelet or collar, perhaps. They're stolen goods, of course.'

'Stolen?' Frances was gazing intently at her bead.

Carter shrugged. 'Oh, stolen by some tomb robber, almost certainly. But nothing to worry about – we can forgive a theft that took place two thousand years ago, can't we?'

'They couldn't be – they weren't part of the Three Princesses' treasure hoard, were they?'

'Never heard of it.'

'But you must have done, surely? I thought—' She broke off as Carter gave her a sharp glance, and then continued quickly: 'Well, wherever they came from, they're lovely. Look, Lucy – yours is carved to look like a nasturtium seed.'

We all thanked him. Carter fell silent. He perhaps found our childish enthusiasm irritating, or was becoming bored – as I'd learn, his mood changes were sudden and often inexplicable. Having given the presents, he seemed to lose interest in them and in us. He asked our permission to smoke and lit a cigarette, using that silver box and gold holder I'd glimpsed before. He drummed his fingers on the table, his eyes on the other guests thronging the terrace; I think he was noting who was there and with whom. He gave the impression of distancing himself, and dwelling on some private grievance, while half listening to our prattle. Rose was telling him at length about the game we'd played that morning in my sarcophagus bath, and Frances's enactment of funeral rituals.

'She performed the Opening of the Mouth ceremony,' Rose was saying, 'and it was horrible. It made Petey *howl*—'

'Frances, you should know better than that,' Carter interrupted sharply. He swung around in his chair to face her. 'These were profound beliefs. Not a joking matter.'

'I wasn't joking, I was *explaining*,' Frances protested.

'To a three-year-old? What were you thinking of? Don't do it again.' He paused. Frances had coloured, and I could see she was hurt by this sudden reprimand from her hero. 'You've been in the Valley,' he continued. 'You've been in those tombs. Did they teach you nothing? Tell me, were you never afraid?'

'Well, no, not often. Maybe once, when the candles blew out and it was dark. But Daddy said I was being superstitious and foolish.'

'Your father was wrong. Take it from me.'

Frances flinched and subsided into silence. We all stared at Carter, who had raised his voice and now appeared angry. Peter put his hands over his eyes and began to tremble.

'But I thought you *liked* the Valley and the tombs, Mr Carter,' Rose said. 'You live so close to it. You've worked there for years and years and years. You've made so many discoveries. Everyone says you—'

'Oh, they do, do they? Then everyone is wrong. As usual. The Valley can be the most hateful place on earth. Or its opposite. Remember that. Frances, don't meddle with matters you can't understand. Learn respect. And watch your tongue in future.'

With that, he rose to his feet, gave us all a curt nod, then turned and walked out. I stared after him, trying to understand what could

66

have provoked this sudden harsh change. Both Peter and Frances were now in tears, and even Rose was disconcerted.

'Gosh, he really is frightfully rude,' she said. '*And* that cigarette holder is made of gold, which is such a *boast*.'

I comforted Peter and thought over this encounter, trying to decode it. It was not the mention of the 'Opening of the Mouth' game that had caused the problem, I decided; it might have seemed that it was, but I felt the true cause was something that had been said earlier. That evening, when I had Frances alone, I asked her in a casual way who were the three princesses she had mentioned, and what was the story of their treasure. Frances was too quick for me; she clammed up at once.

Defeated, I tried out the term on Miss Mack, who had never heard of such a hoard; she then asked Herbert Winlock if *he* had heard of it. She did so that night, across the dinner table at Shepheard's. Several archaeologists from the Met were present that evening, including Albert Lythgoe, the conservationist Arthur Mace, and the photographer Harry Burton; they were deep in some abstruse argument. Miss Mack's question instantly silenced them.

'Three princesses? No, that's not ringing any bells,' Winlock replied, after a considering pause and in an easy tone. 'But there are rumours of treasure hoards being discovered every other month, you know, Myrtle. These stories float around Cairo and Luxor, and very occasionally they're true. But most of the time it's the dealers who've invented them – it's just their way of driving up prices. You'll confirm that, won't you, Lythgoe?'

Albert Lythgoe nodded. He was somewhat prim, with faultless manners, though his gentleness concealed a steeliness of will, as I'd begun to notice. 'I surely will,' he said in his urbane way. 'Egyptian antiquities dealers are the best storytellers in the world, bar none. Ripping yarns . . . no one can touch them for inventiveness, Miss Mackenzie – not even your hero, Rudyard Kipling.'

'Exactly.' Winlock smiled. 'If half their tales were true, then the infamous tomb-robber families of Qurna would all be millionaires, Myrtle – and they were still living in mud huts the last time I passed that way.'

'But the Treasure of the Three Princesses – a stolen *hoard* of treasure — it does sound so very intriguing! It was Lucy who heard about it. You picked up on it at once, didn't you, dear?'

'Really?' Winlock turned his lazy, amiable gaze towards my end of the table, and fixed me with his eyes. Frances, who was seated next to me, bent over her plate and began to crumble a bread roll with great concentration. 'What very sharp ears you must have, Lucy,' Winlock went on. 'Now I'm intrigued. Who mentioned this fabled hoard to you?'

'No one mentioned it to me, exactly,' I replied. 'I overheard someone talking about it in the Mousky bazaar the other day.'

'Ah, of course. The bazaar. Well, that figures,' he replied, in an imperturbable way, and changed the subject.

I judged him successfully deceived, but I was wrong. A short while later, when Winlock thought himself unobserved, I saw him catch his daughter's eye. Frances, flushed, her manner repentant, met his questioning gaze. Her father frowned, tapped his finger against his lips in an admonitory way – and then winked at her.

Under the tablecloth, Frances's hand reached for mine and clasped it. I knew what it meant, that clasp and the mischievous grateful glance that accompanied it: it meant I was thanked, that there were secrets here. I could accept that. I too had secrets – who doesn't?

The next morning, with time running out and Madame's test imminent, Frances redoubled her efforts to improve my ballet. First position, second, third, fourth, fifth: when I'd finally contrived to make one foot point east while the other pointed west, she seemed pleased.

Turning away, and frowning into the glass at our mirrored reflections, she said in a casual way: 'By the way, did I ever tell you the story of the Treasure of the Three Princesses? It was the most fantastic *hoard*, Lucy. It was found during the war, in 1916, I think. There had been heavy rains, the sands shifted – and there it was. It was found by some men from Qurna, who did what they always do with finds like that: they fenced them – to a dealer in Luxor. His name is Mohammed Mohassib. When we go to Luxor, I'll show you his shop. It's – munificent.'

Examining her reflected feet, she began to perform the first five ballet positions. 'Mohassib then did what *he* always does when a hoard like that comes his way. He parcelled it up into small lots, and put out feelers for buyers. He tried playing them off against one another, as the dealers always do. The jewels were fabulous, Lucy, and their price was sky high – and if someone hadn't intervened the collection would have been broken up and scattered around the globe . . . Someone *did* intervene, though. Several people intervened, in fact: Lord Carnarvon, Mr Carter, Mr Lythgoe – and my father.'

She performed a pirouette. 'They decided it was time Mr Mohassib was taught a lesson, so when he approached the Met, he was told it wasn't interested . . . which rattled him badly. When other buyers heard the Met wasn't buying, they lost interest too, so the price started to drop. And then, abracadabra! Mr Carter stepped in and bought them, on behalf of Lord Carnarvon . . . But Lordy was just a front for the Met, and – imagine this, Lucy! – he sold them on to us at cost price: that was the secret deal all along! Mr Carter got a percentage, I think – and everyone gained. We got the collection intact for the Museum, and at a *very* good price. Lordy had the pleasure of outwitting one of the wiliest dealers in Egypt, and Mr Carter's become financially secure for the first time in his life – at least that's what Daddy's saying . . . It's taken all these years to acquire the jewels, and Mr Carter snaffled the very last batch of them the other week – isn't that splendid? I expect he'll pass on the good news to Lord Carnarvon when he arrives. Any day now, Lucy!

'I hope I've got the details right,' she continued, giving me a small reflected glance. 'That's the story I've *heard*. Some people were talking about it in the bazaar.'

'Of course they were. And in Arabic too.'

'My Arabic improves by the day. As yours does, Lucy.' She laughed and pressed one finger against her lips. 'Now, where were we? Ah yes, the first five positions.'

I performed them, and better than I'd ever done before. Frances clapped approvingly.

'Well, well, well! Who'd have thought it?' She planted a kiss on my cheek. 'At last you're learning, Lucy.'

I O

The next day – it was the momentous day when I performed my test for Madame, and passed it – I was whisked down to a celebratory tea on Shepheard's terrace with Frances and her mother. There we were joined by Evelyn, and – astonishingly – by her elusive friend, Mrs d'Erlanger. Some while after that, by a mysterious process, caught up in the currents of rush and confusion that seemed always to attend her, I was transported to the bedroom of Poppy d'Erlanger's suite at Shepheard's: I can still smell the lilies, the smoke of Turkish cigarettes, and the musky scent she was wearing.

'Hellishness! Rose, Peter – please help me,' Poppy was saying, on a note of nervy desperation. 'Whatever shall I wear for dinner tonight? Look at these horrid things! What possessed me to buy them? Eve, Frances, Lulu – advise me. I simply must make the right choice.'

We'd been in the room less than ten minutes, and Mrs d'Erlanger was standing amidst an ocean of clothes. A spring tide of chiffons and silks was lapping around her; a torrent of lace, organdie, fur and tweeds was cascading from her wardrobe onto the floor, and this flood was now several dresses deep. A flotsam and jetsam of frothy underwear, scarves, hats, gloves and shoes had been cast up on every surface in sight. One exquisite green snakeskin shoe with a diamanté buckle had drifted towards my feet, and Frances, seated next to me on the carpet, was awash in the foam of a lace nightdress. Peter, half asleep on my lap, was stroking some polar silvery fur, while Rose – a practical girl, as I was discovering – was extracting a tangle of silk stockings from the debris.

Evelyn, who, like Rose, seemed used to this spectacle, was sitting on a chair near by, waiting for the weather to calm and the tide to ebb: her attitude was patient and resigned, as was that of Poppy's maid, the statuesque Wheeler, who was standing to attention next to the wardrobe. This was a huge catafalque, very like the fearsome one in my own room; ten minutes before, the contents of that wardrobe, and of several chests of drawers, had been in impeccable order: now, chaos had come, but Wheeler's broad features remained impassive; she surveyed the detritus lapping around her ankles with studied detachment.

Audience and advisors, our sacred mission to help Poppy decide what to wear at the dinner the newly arrived Lord Carnarvon was giving at Shepheard's that night, we three girls were in a trance of dresses. I dearly wanted Poppy to choose a dress of black velvet; Rose preferred the emerald-green silk; and Frances favoured the slick of shocking pink satin that had been made for Poppy, I'd just learned, by an artist called Elsa Schiaparelli, a friend of hers in Paris.

How intoxicating that room smelled – never had I seen so many flowers in one space. Great bouquets of roses and deep-throated lilies and orchids spilled from vases on every available table. Poppy herself, as vivid as any of these flowers, stood in the sea of clothes, snatching up one dress, discarding it carelessly, then pouncing upon another with little cries. She had changed into a silk kimono embroidered with scarlet dragons, and tiny slippers with silver heels, decorated on their toes with thistledown pompoms. Her black shingled hair shone in the lamplight: falling forward in rippling waves across her face, yet cut as short as a man's at the back, it was shockingly modern, exposing her white neck and giving her a misleading air of porcelain fragility. Her dark blue eyes, restless in their gaze, were tragic in their expression. She was tall and astonishingly thin, she was all angles and surprises: she was the most beautiful thing I had ever seen in my life. *The beautiful one is come,* I thought. I wondered how I could have considered Eve's looks remarkable: next to her friend, her quiet grace and prettiness were eclipsed; she was a crescent moon in comparison to Poppy's meridian sun.

'Oh, do get a move on, Poppy,' Eve said now, in a good-humoured way, but stifling a yawn. 'This is taking such an age, darling. You know you look divine in all of them. Just remember, Pups thinks you're

71

frightfully *fast*, which amuses him no end. So don't disappoint him, and choose accordingly.'

This remark seemed to increase Poppy's uncertainty; she moaned and began pouncing, pulling, tossing and ferreting around again. Frances and I exchanged a look: we had witnessed the arrival of Lord Carnarvon the previous day, so we could understand why Mrs d'Erlanger might consider him a stern judge of appearances.

We had stationed ourselves in the lobby of the Continental Hotel where, like Howard Carter and the Winlocks, the earl was staying; we took up our position early, determined to get a good view. Even by the standards of the Continental, which were as high as Shepheard's in this respect, it had been a magnificent arrival. The manager and a line of under-managers were there to greet him: Lord Carnarvon made his entrance wearing that wide-awake hat, as made famous in an earlier era by Alfred, Lord Tennyson. Thin, elegant and superbly nonchalant, he wore a long dark woollen overcoat with a rich fur collar; he leaned on a cane with a handle carved from some improbable pink stone – made to his design by Cartier, we learned, when we quizzed Eve afterwards. True, he had a slight limp, but he moved at a rapid pace, taking immediate possession of the hotel as if it were his home and its staff his servants; in his train came his valet and his doctor – he usually travelled with his own physician. Four lordly trunks and thirty-seven pieces of leather luggage, each stamped with his coronet and monogram, brought up their wake: we counted.

'Fast, *fast* …' Poppy d'Erlanger sighed. 'I wish you hadn't said that, Eve – you've just made it worse. Wheeler, which of these dresses would you say was the *fastest*?'

'I really could not venture an opinion on that, madam,' replied the impassive Wheeler, speaking for the first time since this onslaught began. 'But I'd say they were all fairly speedy.'

'The blue? The imperial yellow? I adore that. Have I worn that yet, Wheeler?'

'Not in Cairo, madam. You thought of wearing it to the Residency, but settled on the blue chiffon with the sapphires. The last occasion on which you wore the yellow, the *only* occasion, was at Lord Carnarvon's birthday dinner at Highclere Castle.'

'Oh, well, that's no good then. Your father will have seen it, Eve. So that's out, *and* the blue …'

Poppy turned her tragic eyes to the dresses again – and I saw that the need for a decision really did pain her: this was no affectation, but an anxiety close to fear. She knew that she was judged by her looks. Had it never occurred to her, I wondered, exquisite as she was, that she might be judged on any other score, her sweetness of temper, for example, or her innate kindness and generosity? Presumably not – yet these qualities of hers were very evident. They became obvious after ten minutes in her company.

'Oh, please wear the emerald green, Mamma,' Rose said. 'You look so splendid in that. It's my favourite – and Petey loves it too.'

Peter woke up briefly, said, 'Geen, please, Mamma,' and went to sleep again.

'No,' said Frances, standing up, and fishing from the rainbow pile that slick of architectural pink satin. 'You should wear this. It's the fastest thing I ever saw in my life. And you must wear lipstick.' She looked covetously at the line of lipsticks drawn up for battle on Poppy's dressing table. 'A scarlet one, I think – one that *clashes*.'

'Heavens!' Poppy cried, snatching at the dress. 'Are you *sure*? What a little genius you are, Frances. Yes, yes, I see it now. Wheeler – be an angel and get it ironed, will you? It seems to have got crumpled somehow. Oh, and my bath needs to be drawn and I shall need my fur – no, not that one, the *dark* one . . .'

'Poppy, are you mad?' Eve stood up and stretched. 'Fur? It's insufferably hot – and it will be worse in the dining room.'

'I know, I know, but I might need it *later*. I might be trotting on somewhere.'

'Oh, Poppy – what are you up to? Trot on *where*? I do wish you wouldn't.'

'So do I. But even so, I *might*. Of course, I'm resolved *not* to, but I'm so bad when it comes to temptation. I solemnly intend to resist to the last – and then I just sort of cave in. Why does that happen? It's a complete mystery.'

'Well, I hope you're not planning something stupid, darling,' Eve said. She gave Poppy a searching look, then turned and motioned to us that it was time to leave.

'I'm not planning *anything*, Eve. Truly I'm not. I never do plan.' Poppy shook her head sadly. 'I think that's the problem. I just sort of ricochet around from moment to moment. But what can you do? I am what I am ... Now, children, best beloveds, before you go – you've all been such *bricks*, and I'm so grateful ... you must take something lovely with you. Is there anything here?' She looked around in bewilderment at the sea of clothes, from which we were carefully extricating ourselves. 'Hellishness! What a muddle – how did that happen? No, nothing here, they're all *very* unsuitable ... I know! Something from my dressing table – anything – some little bauble, something pretty – you choose.'

We hung back at first, but Poppy insisted. Politely ignoring the litter of diamond rings and ivory bracelets and exotic black Sobranie cigarettes with gold tips, and the amber cigarette holders and choco-late boxes and books and letters that were scattered on the table, we each made a decision. Rose selected a pink swansdown powder puff; Peter chose a nail file that he stuck in his waistband and claimed was a dagger. I very much wanted a book, entitled *The Mysterious Affair at Styles*, which was hiding beneath a pot of Parisian cold cream, but a book seemed greedy, so I chose a tiny phial of scent, which smelled of sophistication. Frances chose one of the armoury of lipsticks.

'You are such a colossal *clot*, Frances,' Rose said loftily as we left the room. 'Why did you choose that? Your mother will have forty fits – you can't possibly wear it.'

'Well, you can't wear a powder puff either,' Frances retorted. 'And I don't care. It's the colour of rubies. It's blood red, and it's gorgeous. When I'm grown up, I'm going to wear red lipstick all the time – not just in the evening like Poppy. I shall wear it at breakfast.'

'*Breakfast?* Bet you don't dare.'

'Meanwhile, I shall take it everywhere and get it out from time to time, and look at it.'

And that was exactly what Frances did that very evening. Before we went downstairs for dinner, we visited Rose and Peter to say good-night, and left them in their room, Rose with the powder puff on her nightstand, and Peter with his nail-file dagger under his pillow. They were being watched over by Wheeler, and by Eve's maid, Marcelle. The two women, who could scarcely have looked more different, one being twice the size and twice the age of the other, seemed good friends. Wheeler heaved herself into a capacious armchair and settled down with her knitting; Marcelle stretched out on a chaise longue, crossed her elegant legs, and offered us chocolates from a box that Poppy, who never touched them, had given her.

'Save me the soft-centres, mind,' she said in a voice that was firmly London – not a hint of France, despite her name.

We both selected more chewy specimens; Marcelle inserted a violet cream in her mouth, sighed, and opened a book; it was called *The Sheik*, and had a promising cover.

'Did you see the film of it, Wheelie?' Marcelle asked, waving the book. 'Ooh, how I wept. I love a good romance, I do.'

'I can't be doing with that flim-flam,' Wheeler replied stolidly. 'Give me a good murder, that's what I like. Something you can get your teeth into.'

'You've got no imagination, Wheelie, that's your trouble.'

'Better none than too much,' Wheeler pronounced, with finality.

Frances and I wished them goodnight. She had smuggled the lipstick, in its gilded case, and hidden it in her pocket – she showed it to me as we went down the stairs; during dinner she continually took it out under cover of the starched white damask tablecloth. She would examine it, gloat over it and then hide it again.

As we always went down to dinner early, it was an hour at least before the Carnarvon party of twelve arrived and was ushered to a table near us. Greetings were exchanged, and Poppy, who was seated on Carnarvon's left, wearing her short shocking-pink dress, blew us a scarlet kiss. Madame Masha took in our presence with her tiger's eyes, grandly inclined her head and took her seat to the immediate right of Carnarvon. Howard Carter, who was seated next to Poppy, greeted then ignored her; he immediately turned to Eve, on his left, and engaged her in a low, emphatic conversation.

The archaeologists at our own table watched this arrival covertly, but minutely. When they could be sure of remaining unheard, a buzz of speculation passed from side to side. 'How do you think Carnarvon is looking?' Lythgoe said, in a low voice to the Winlocks.

'Not well,' Helen replied. 'Even frailer than last year, poor man. I know Eve is terribly worried about him.'

'There was talk of yet another operation, I gather,' said Winlock. 'But he decided against. Couldn't face it – and who can blame him?'

'Egypt will do him good,' Helen said gently, turning away to Miss

Mack. 'It always does. His verve will soon return if they make some finds this winter.'

'And if they *don't?*' Lythgoe's eyes met those of Winlock across the table. 'How long do you reckon Carnarvon will go on?'

'Difficult to say. But if Lordy does decide to pack it in, the concession to dig in the Valley would be up for grabs. Not that that interesting possibility has ever crossed our minds—'

'Never. Hadn't given it a second's thought. Scout's honour.' Lythgoe smiled thinly.

'They've virtually exhausted the areas inside Carter's triangle,' Winlock continued in a pensive way.

He glanced around the table, and having satisfied himself that the general buzz of conversation ensured he and Lythgoe could not be overheard by Carnarvon's party, he leaned forward and lowered his voice. I was seated next to him, spooning up an ice. I concentrated, made myself invisible and listened.

'In fact, Carter's moving the current dig well *outside* his golden triangle,' Winlock went on. 'I find that pretty strange – it could mean he's got some new lead.'

'Maybe he's simply biding his time,' Lythgoe said. 'He had that operation back in November, he's still not back to full health. This season is a very short one for him. February to March? That's nothing by Carter's standards. My guess is he's pinning his hopes on their next season. When is he coming back out here? Has he told you?'

'Hasn't said a word to me – but he told Frances: next October. That's the schedule, but looking at Carnarvon I have my doubts. Lordy's spent a fortune, his health is poor. Suppose they draw a blank in the next month? He might well feel it's time to call it a day. Of course if he *does* jack it in, this will be Carter's last dig in the Valley.'

'Indeed.' Lythgoe waited a beat. 'Unless someone else hired Carter, of course. Any friendly millionaires sniffing around?'

'A friendly millionaire who was prepared to work alongside Carter, indulge his hunches, suffer his moods?' Winlock laughed. 'That breed of millionaire is damn near extinct. You're looking at the last of the species, right over there.'

'True. Besides, the day of the amateur excavator is over. Lordy is the last of his kind in that respect too.' Lythgoe, who never touched alcohol, took a sip of water. 'Welcome to the brave new world of the trained professional. Welcome to the universities and the museums, to scientific excavation, performed by men bristling with doctorates.'

'And the millionaires who top up their funding, who ask nothing more than a gallery be named after them – I'll drink to that.' Winlock raised his wineglass. 'On the other hand . . . ' He hesitated. 'What about *instinct*, Albert? The nose for a tomb. The natives have that. Carter has it. In spades. And you won't find that on the curriculum at Harvard.'

'Instinct can always be hired. Carnarvon hired it, and if he *were* to pull out—'

'Someone else could hire it. The Met, for example.'

'Feelers? Soundings? I rely on you there.'

'Of course. But I've had to tread warily. Carter's loyal. I've stressed it's hypothetical for the moment, depends on Carnarvon, what he decides, not sure if the Valley would ever be for us et cetera.' Winlock threw up his hands. 'Christ – *I* don't know. Do we even want to consider this? Maybe the Valley *is* exhausted and we'd be mad to waste time and money on it. Maybe Carter's right, and there's a tomb right there in that damn triangle of his. Maybe, one fine morning Carter will say to his workmen, "Try digging there today," and ten seconds later it'll be, "*Allahu Akbar*, Mr Carter-sir, look what we've found!" I haven't a clue any more. I believe one thing today and another tomorrow. Maybe Carter's a genius with an ace up his sleeve. Maybe he's a misguided dreamer – and a fool.'

Lythgoe smiled. I think Winlock's volatile nature amused him. There was a brief interruption then, while the waiters cleared plates, and the two men lowered their voices. Next to me, Frances had made a small scarlet lipsticked cross on her palm and was inspecting it critically. Across the room, at the curtained entrance to the restaurant, some difficulty seemed to have arisen: I could see waiters bunching and gesticulating; they had been joined by the tall and august figure of the manager. From the Carnarvon table next to us, came the drift of animated voices and laughter. Poppy had just said something to Madame Masha, who laughed. '*Méchante*,' I heard her reply, with a flash of her tiger eyes, and in a tone of throaty amusement. Then the waiter leaned across in front of me, arranging tiny dishes of silver and crystal. Frances took a date, I took an almond. The waiter departed. The two men's conversation had continued.

'In which respect – I'm going over to the Antiquities Service's bunker tomorrow. I'll be lunching with our dear friend the Director,' Winlock was saying. He made a sour face. 'He who decides who will dig where. God the Father in person for two long hours – now won't *that* be a treat? If he tells me yet again that it's time to reform the rules of *partage*, I won't answer for my actions: "Ah, but *mon cher* Monsieur Winlock, surely you can see, everything you find belongs by right to the Egyptian nation. Yes, yes, it's your museum's money that's funded the dig, and your expertise that led to the discovery in the first place, but that is neither here nor there, *mon ami*. The days of the fifty-fifty division are over." What humbug! The man's in his element at the moment, playing both sides against the middle, endorsing the Protectorate when he's drinking cocktails at the British Residency and all the while sucking up to his new Nationalist friends.'

'Pierre Lacau can see which way the wind's blowing,' Lythgoe replied. 'He's always had that gift. Frankly, he's capable of anything. But, rest assured, it's always been a fifty-fifty split, and that's the way it will stay, whether Egypt gets independence or not. I can bring considerable pressure to bear on Lacau and his Nationalist buddies and I've already set the wheels in motion. He's not going to push *us* around, or the British – not if he wants any excavating done in this country. Not if he wants any more pretty toys for his Egyptian Museum.'

'Stop talking shop, you two,' Helen interrupted, turning back to the two men. 'It's bad form *and* it's indiscreet – Howard has very sharp ears. Shall we have our coffee on the terrace? It's so noisy in here, and it's stiflingly hot. I'll join you there. Myrtle and I will just get the girls up to bed. They're exhausted – look, poor Lucy is half asleep.'

Frances and I rose obediently. She pocketed her lipstick and I began to plan the diary entry I'd write as soon as I was alone in my room. I'd report the conversation between Mr Winlock and Mr Lythgoe. I must remember also to report on such important matters as Mrs d'Erlanger and her fast dress. Frances and I said our goodnights, and as we turned to leave, I glanced across at the Carnarvon table. I could see at once that something had happened, something significant had happened, in a few short minutes: I'd missed the event's cause, but its after-effects were evident.

All laughter and conversation at Carnarvon's table had ceased; several of his guests were exchanging startled uneasy glances. Poppy d'Erlanger had become rigid in her chair, staring across the dining room towards its curtained entrance. I saw colour come and go in her face. Madame Masha, turning to follow her gaze, frowned and said something in a low voice to Lord Carnarvon. Poppy seemed to hesitate, and then, as Eve put out a hand to restrain her, she abruptly rose to her feet.

At once, all the men at the table also stood. This movement, and the scraping-back of chairs, caused heads to turn across the dining room. Miss Mack and Helen, who had been negotiating their way through the crush, found their way blocked; we all came to a halt. Frances and I were now immediately next to the Carnarvon table.

'No, no – please, don't let me interrupt things,' Poppy was saying, motioning the men back to their seats.

'Poppy, *don't* . . . Let my father deal with this,' Eve interjected, and Madame seconded this, saying, with a grimace: '*Quel spectacle, ces hommes là! Restez ici, ma chère.*'

Poppy seemed not to hear these pleas. She began to move away from the table, and as she did so Carnarvon attempted to stop her. I saw him lay his hand gently on her arm, and he said something inaudible.

'Porchy, no – truly,' she replied. 'That's fearfully kind and gallant of you – but I caused it so I must deal with it. No, really, I insist.'

And with that she sped across the room, threading between the crowded tables, her chin tilted, her expression fixed and her attitude defiant. Every head in the room turned; the din of conversation faltered and diminished. She came to a halt at the entrance. Two men in evening dress were there, I saw – and some altercation between them must have occurred, for one had his fists clenched and blood had spattered on his starched white dress shirt, while the other, restrained by waiters, was struggling to free himself and was white with rage. A boy had been sent running for assistance and the cluster of anxious *safragis* was having difficulty in keeping the two men apart.

'I have never seen anything so silly and uncivilised in my life,' Poppy said, addressing both men in a clear voice that carried to all corners of the dining room. 'What on earth are you thinking of? This is breaking my heart. Come away and stop upsetting people. I can sort this out in five minutes.'

She was carrying that dark fur. Tossing it over her shoulder and tucking her tiny bauble of a handbag under her arm, she stalked out of the room. There was a last flash of shocking pink from her dress, and then she was gone. After an uncertain pause, when it looked as if hostilities might break out again, the two men were forced apart and finally disappeared after her, surrounded by a flurry of *safragis*. At once the dining room came alive: an electric excitement crackled and flickered from table to table; laughter broke out among one or two groups and then was drowned by the buzz of revelation, the rising din of scandalous delight, the roar of claim and counter-claim.

'Gracious!' Miss Mack said, in a low voice to Helen Winlock. 'My dear, who were those two men – whatever was that about?'

'I'm not sure,' Helen replied, her face troubled. She spoke so quietly that I had to strain to hear. 'But the man with dark hair and blood on his shirt front . . . I'm pretty sure that was Mr d'Erlanger.'

'Oh, Helen!' Miss Mack gave a gasp. 'Quickly – let's get the children safely to bed.'

The following morning, it was discovered that Poppy d'Erlanger had left the hotel. When it was reported that her bed had not been slept in – and whether that was true or not, everyone seemed to believe it – the smouldering gossip took fire. Poppy did not reappear that day, was absent from the hotel the next, and was still absent the day after. By then, Shepheard's was an overheated hive of furious buzzing rumours.

'She's disappeared,' said Frances, who was electrified by these developments. 'What can have happened, Lucy? It's a mystery – we must solve it.'

We tried. Lord Carnarvon and Evelyn were the people in the best position to confirm or deny the rumours – as was Poppy's devoted maid Wheeler; all three of them remained tight-lipped, refusing to say anything. This silence did nothing to quell the talk – it created a vacuum that new rumours rushed to fill, as Frances and I quickly learned. The word was – though no one could say from whence it came, or on what authority – that one of the two pugilists had indeed been her estranged husband, d'Erlanger, and the other a young British officer well known at the Gezira Sporting Club. Poppy had bolted again, that was generally agreed, though whether with d'Erlanger, or the officer, was disputed. She was now in the South of France, or Italy, or – some claimed – Kenya. She'd left by train, said some; no, by private plane, said others, asserting she'd been seen boarding one at Cairo aerodrome. She'd planned it and gone for good, said her detractors, of whom there were many, their numbers growing by the hour. No, it had been a spur of the moment decision, said those who championed Poppy. The fact that she'd left her children behind *proved* this was yet another of her maverick exploits; Poppy would remember them, return repentant and bundle them up again as she always did; why, she adored Rose and Peter, and although she could be neglectful of them, no man would ever persuade her to part from them.

Eventually, on the fourth day, both Lord Carnarvon and Eve attempted, in a discreet but ineffective way, to quell the talk. Reluctant to dignify this tittle-tattle by comment of any kind, yet seeing that their silence had been counter-productive, they took to saying that Poppy would return any day now. They had to say that, I suppose; as was widely known, the following week was fixed for their departure to Luxor, and Poppy and her children were supposed to be travelling with the Carnarvon party.

It was during this incendiary period that I first became truly aware of Minnie, wife to Harry Burton, the photographer on the Met's team of archaeologists. Both he and his wife were English; they lived in Florence when not in Egypt. I'd encountered them before – it was difficult to miss blonde-haired Minnie Burton, who liked to queen it in the hotel dining room. Harry Burton was amiable and universally liked, but his wife was another matter. Helen Winlock detested her, I think, and Winlock himself, who referred to her as Queen Min, avoided her. In the wake of Poppy's disappearance, Mrs Burton and the haughty Frau von Essen, still at Shepheard's, had formed an alliance; presented with a first-class scandal, they were now in their element.

Frances and I were partisan and determined to discover the truth, but this proved exceptionally hard, for Miss Mack and Helen were as tight-lipped as Eve and her father. We tried to pump Wheeler and got nowhere; we tried Marcelle, with higher hopes, but even Marcelle, a fount of information on many diverting subjects, refused to be drawn. Time for another tactic.

'*Espionage*,' Frances said. Accordingly, we eavesdropped, we spied, we took to prowling around the terrace at Shepheard's; there we quickly discovered that the most fertile time was four-fifteen, and the most fertile area was Mrs Burton's table. A large pillar adjoined that table; lingering in its vicinity several days in succession, we gathered a few scraps of information, but nothing concrete. On the fourth day, when Frances was out with her mother, I escaped Miss Mack's clutches and returned to the terrace alone; there I found the Burton coterie in full flood, and, sitting alone at a nearby table, concealed by a potted palm and apparently immersed in *The Times*, the spruce figure of Howard Carter.

'Frances not with you?' he said, as I backed away, about to turn tail; before I could answer, he gestured to the waiters, who arrived in a rush. In an instant, I found I'd been seated in a chair opposite him, and tea was being poured. 'So,' Carter went on, 'you're spying unassisted today, are you? My task too. I'm here for Eve. We may as well join forces. Now . . .' He pushed a book across the table. 'You pretend to read this and I shall pretend to read my newspaper, don't speak and we'll get along fine. I have excellent hearing and I'm sure you do too.'

It did not occur to me to disobey him. I bent my head over the book, an account of the tombs in the Valley of the Kings, written in 1820 by the great showman of Egyptology, Belzoni. The conversation at Mrs Burton's table had paused while I sat down amidst the flourish of waiters, but there are advantages to being an unremarkable and charmless little bookworm, and the chief advantage is invisibility.

Within five minutes, the animated discussion took fire again, and I learned the following. *One*: the appalling scene witnessed by everyone in the dining room on the night of Poppy d'Erlanger's disappearance was *as nothing, my dears*, to the scene that followed it, which had been of considerable duration, continuing into the lobby, erupting into the Moorish Hall, and finally breaking out anew on the steps outside Shepheard's, where (as Mrs Burton now had it on *unimpeachable* authority) the men concerned had vowed to kill each other. *Two*: both men, dragged apart by various friends, had eventually gone their separate ways, after which, and not five minutes later, the *sheer nerve* of it, Mrs d'Erlanger was seen leaving Shepheard's in her disgraceful pink dress and her ostentatious sables, at night, *alone and unescorted*, as Minnie Burton could testify, having at just that second, and entirely by chance, passed through the lobby and thus *personally* witnessed this scandalous departure.

This revelation drew gasps from the coterie, but Frau von Essen felt she could improve on it. She'd been informed today that Mrs d'Erlanger had wired for her luggage to be sent on; this proved that *die Schlampe* had no intention of returning. Furthermore, that very morning her dearest friend, Grafin Mariza von Hollenstahl, had sent her a telegram from the South of France, informing her that the 'missing' woman had been seen in Nice, two days previously, strolling along the Promenade des Anglais, without a care for her children or her reputation, on the arm of the man she had shamelessly cuckolded in Cairo, namely her estranged husband, *der Jude,* Jacob d'Erlanger.

'Well, well. What a nest of vipers,' Carter remarked when, running out of revelations, the coterie at the next table departed. He put down his newspaper and met my gaze. My face was a hot scarlet and observing this, he added: 'Speak German, do you?'

'A little. I've had lessons.'

I lowered my eyes. Those Cambridge lessons had made it easy to translate *der Jude.* I didn't know what *die Schlampe* meant. But then I didn't know what 'cuckolded' meant either.

'Malice and prejudice need little translation.' Carter frowned. 'I've endured plenty of gossip, rumour and lies in my time – have you?'

'Not really, no. I'm too young, I suppose. And I'm – dull. Not promising material.'

'Now there we differ. I do not find you dull. Quiet, very. Reserved, certainly; but dull, no. You're an observer. I am also an observer. I've observed you observing, Miss Payne, and I made a mental note of it.' He folded up his newspaper and retrieved his book. 'So, what do you think – shall we let this kind of talk continue, or put a stop to it?'

'Put a stop to it – except one can't. People like Mrs Burton enjoy it too much. It's meat and drink to them.'

Carter bared his teeth in a smile. 'That is true, in the long term. But in the short term, something can be done. So, let's see … Refutation? Retaliation? I always enjoy retaliation. What do you say to that idea?'

'I say – yes. But have you a plan, Mr Carter?'

'I always have a plan. I'm methodical to my fingertips.' He rose. 'Thank you for joining me. My salutations to your friend Frances. Make sure that both of you are here on the terrace tomorrow at four-fifteen prompt, will you do that?'

*

The next afternoon, at four-twenty precisely, the thin and elegant figure of Lord Carnarvon was to be seen strolling across the crowded terrace at Shepheard's. The cynosure of all eyes, he seemed to make for the table at which, among a large party, Frances and I were seated: a strong number of witnesses had been assembled. Eve was presiding, the Winlocks, Lythgoes and Miss Mack were there; Madame had joined us, as had several prominent members of the English and American community in Cairo. Howard Carter was also present, stationed alone at a table near by.

Mrs Burton, unsuspecting, became alert, preening and gracious when Carnarvon, pausing in his amble across the terrace, came to a halt at her table. He greeted her and Frau von Essen, and their party, and then asked in his diffident, courteous manner if he might join them. The two women assented with one voice, and I saw Mrs Burton give several quick covert glances around the terrace, making sure that this tribute to their status was being widely appreciated. Flustered but triumphant, she sent waiters scurrying for more tea, while the more controlled Frau von Essen made a great show of introducing the earl to the other women at her table. Both then embarked on general vapidities, knowing better than to raise the subject of Poppy d'Erlanger in front of Carnarvon; he raised it himself, after a few charming pleasantries.

'I hear that the gossips have been positively inspired by the subject of my friend Mrs d'Erlanger,' he drawled, his manner mild and possibly amused. His quiet voice was slightly raised. 'The malice and inventiveness on exhibit really are remarkable . . . even for Cairo, which as we all know puts the drawing rooms of London to shame.'

Minnie Burton, who was in the act of raising her teacup to her lips, replaced it in its saucer with a tinkling sound. 'I abhor gossip, Lord Carnarvon,' she began, as Frau von Essen nodded regal agreement.

Across the terrace, there was a rustle of speculation, then a perceptible hush. His manner imperturbable, Carnarvon continued: 'I share that abhorrence, Mrs Burton, and yet I hear that the most fanciful stories – well, I suppose one must call them outright lies – are being bandied about in this very hotel, where one might have thought people would be better informed, or at the very least have higher standards. So unmannerly! So vulgar.'

'Indeed,' said Minnie Burton, looking rattled. 'But then all gossip is vulgar, Lord Carnarvon, as I've always maintained. I make a point of—'

'I am sure you do,' Carnarvon said, giving her his diffident charming smile — a smile that did not reach his eyes. 'I certainly hope so, for where you lead, others will follow. Such ill-informed talk is, of course, beneath contempt.'

'Beneath contempt! So very true,' echoed Mrs Burton, with enthusiasm.

'Yet it seems to be believed. It really is distressing for Mrs d'Erlanger's friends — and I have been her close friend for most of her life, since she is, as you may know, my god-daughter . . . As I say, it really is most distressing to learn that these vicious lies are being uttered, even accepted as gospel . . .'

'Absolutely, Lord Carnarvon. Wicked nonsense. I have never—'

' . . . when the truth of the matter is that Mrs d'Erlanger's father, a very old and dear friend, fell seriously ill a few days ago. And, being the loving daughter she is, Mrs d'Erlanger left her children in our care and rushed to his bedside the instant she received the wire. Friends of mine stepped in, and they flew her to France that same night.'

'*Mein Gott*, but this is terrible news,' Frau von Essen said firmly.

'Terrible,' echoed Mrs Burton. 'I pray she reached him in time. May I enquire . . . ?'

'How kind. Yes, he has pulled through. Fortunately, it was not as serious as feared; the doctors diagnosed pneumonia, but it seems they were wrong. You know how alarmist doctors can be.'

'Yes, yes,' Minnie Burton broke in, her eyes alight with the wild hope that Carnarvon might be diverted. 'Doctors *are* alarmist. I've often observed that. In my view—'

'And luckily her father is at his villa in Nice,' Carnarvon continued unstoppably. 'The climate there is kind . . . so the good news is that Mrs d'Erlanger will be returning very soon. Providing her father's health does not deteriorate, she'll travel back from France and join my daughter and me at the Winter Palace in Luxor, just as we planned. She hopes to book her passage in the next few days. Isn't that splendid news? I'm so glad to bring it to you. Should you hear any more of these tales being bandied back and forth, you'll now be in a position to correct them. I rely on you, my dear ladies.'

Both Mrs Burton and Frau von Essen had registered the silence on the terrace; they had perhaps begun to understand the nature of the reprimand and of their own humiliation. Without waiting for a reply, Carnarvon rose to his feet, made a polite bow and then ambled across to our table. There he ate a shortbread biscuit and drank a cup of Earl Grey tea; he left shortly afterwards with Howard Carter.

'Verdict?' Carnarvon said to him, with a chortle, as they left our table.

'Game, set and match. Painful to watch.' Carter gave his patron an appraising glance. 'Remind me never to cross you.'

'Or me you, my dear fellow,' Carnarvon replied in an affable way. Both men laughed, and strolled off together towards the lobby.

After that, there could be no going back: any deviation from the plans Carnarvon had announced, and the rumours would have sparked again. His departure for Luxor was, accordingly, a leisurely, conspicuous one, the gossip mongers and their spies being given good opportunity to confirm the presence of Mrs d'Erlanger's children in the Carnarvon party. On the same evening, Miss Mack and I left Shepheard's for the station, driven, as always, by the loyal and gentle Hassan. Miss Mack bestowed a final munificent tip, and it was a sad parting. As I climbed down from his carriage, he pressed a small gift into my hand: it proved to be an *ankh*, the looped Egyptian symbol of life, made of shiny tin. I wrapped it in my handkerchief with Howard Carter's lapis lazuli bead, my other most prized possession.

The light was fading, and the muezzins had begun the call to prayer as we made our way onto the crowded platform for the White Train to Luxor. Miss Mack, in a crisis of nerves, found, lost and regained our tickets. I was instructed to stand still in one particular spot, and not *move an inch* in case she lost me. I obeyed, and out of the swirl and confusion on the platform, an aching loneliness and melancholy settled upon me.

I could not shake it off; it would not depart – even when our friends arrived, and we were caught up in the bustle of finding our compartments. Evelyn, her father and their entourage were further down the train, but we were in the same carriage as the Winlocks; Frances and I, as promised, were sharing a sleeping cabin. Peter and Rose, supervised by Wheeler, had the cabin next to us. The excitement of exploring these tiny rooms and testing out the bunks was intense. Yet the undertow of apprehension and sadness remained; it strengthened as, with a banshee scream, the train jerked, jolted and, gathering speed, pulled out of the station. Frances, who had made the journey before, was sanguine; she quickly prepared for bed and went quickly to sleep; I stayed wakeful, nervous and alert in the dark, listening to the pulse of the wheels as we powered south, hour after hour, through the desert.

I lay there thinking of Peter, who had been frightened and fretful in the confusion of the station. He had clung first to Wheeler, then Rose, then me: he kept asking for his mother, something he rarely did, for he'd always seemed inured to her absences. So insistent were his cries, and his efforts to pick her out among the crush of passengers, that I too became seized with the conviction that, at any moment, the crowds would part, and there Poppy would be, hastening towards us. I envisaged her in that same pink dress and dark fur – which was absurd, I knew. I also knew, perfectly well, that such a manifestation was impossible: it took days to sail from France to Egypt, and Poppy d'Erlanger had not yet left France. Still the obstinate vision persisted, and from thinking of Rose and Peter's mother, I fell to thinking of my own – something I'd learned never to permit.

On we rushed through the dark. I thought of the twelve gates of night through which the ancient Egyptians believed the sun passed during the twelve hours of darkness. One by one the perilous gates opened and closed, and I began counting them, hoping that the arithmetic might make me sleep – still I stayed wakeful.

It was a fast train, but it made some stops en route – and at one of those stops, I crept out into the corridor in my dressing gown and slippers. It was cooler there, and through the window I could just make out a tiny station building, lit by one guttering oil lamp, palm trees fringing it, and beyond a vast blackness sprayed with stars. Further down the platform, Arab porters were loading baskets into the luggage van, but long after doors had slammed, long after the men had departed and their voices had grown faint, then inaudible, the train remained stationary in this nowhere place, while an invisible clock ticked, another underworld gate shut behind us and the gate ahead opened wide. It might have been midnight, or much later – I'd lost count. I was thinking how far away England was, how far away, how unreachably far, my mother was, when the door of the compartment next to mine quietly opened, and Wheeler stepped out into the corridor.

She was as taken by surprise as I was, I think, for she started, pressed her hand on her chest, and then, recovering, shook her head in reprimand. 'What are you doing out here?' she said in a sharp way, and then more gently: 'It's three in the morning.'

'I couldn't sleep, Wheeler.'

'Me neither.' She sighed. 'Peter couldn't settle, poor little chap. But I've got him off at last, so I nipped out for a quick breather. It's that hot and stuffy in those cabins. And those bunks weren't made for a woman my size.'

'I expect – maybe Peter is missing his mother?'

'Could be.' There was a silence. Wheeler hesitated, then turned me to face her. In the dim bluish light of the corridor, she gave me a long inspecting look. She said: 'And you, Miss Lucy? Are you missing yours?'

I wasn't sure how much Wheeler knew of my story; most of it, probably, as she was the kind of woman who absorbed information the way a bank absorbs money – and who guarded it like a bank, too. I said nothing, and Wheeler seemed satisfied with that answer. A few moments passed, while we both stared out at the stars in silence, then Wheeler rummaged in the pocket of her dressing gown. She brought out a flask, poured a thimbleful of liquid into the flask's cup, and handed it to me.

'Cherry brandy,' she said. 'Swallow it down in one. It'll ease your mind. You'll be off to sleep in no time.'

'I've never drunk alcohol. I'm not allowed.'

'You're allowed now. I shan't tell. It's the middle of the night. We're in the middle of nowhere. Get it down you. And wipe your eyes, pet – you must have got a smut in them.'

She passed me a clean handkerchief. I wiped my wet eyes, and drank the cherry brandy in one gulp. It was sweet and viscous; it made me cough, then it smoothed warmth down my throat and into my stomach.

Wheeler patted my head. 'That hair of yours is starting to grow back,' she remarked, in a kind way, turning me to face her again, and inspecting it closely. 'It's still a bit on the tufty side, but it'll even out soon, you'll see. I'm good with hair, you know – I have a knack for it. Mrs d'Erlanger swears there's no one to touch me with hair. When we're in Luxor, you come and see me one day, and I'll get my scissors out, and my lotions and potions, and by the time I've finished you won't know yourself.'

'I don't know myself now,' I burst out. 'Can't you see that?'

That reply was wrenched out of me before I could think. At that exact moment, the train gave a jolt, and above the rumble of the wheels as it began to move came the sudden piercing cry of a child in distress.

It frightened me badly. I clutched at Wheeler for protection. The cry seemed to have come from inside my own body; it seemed to judder up from the floor of the carriage, lodge itself in my lungs and then escape from my mouth – but I felt that couldn't be the case and so, as its echo died away, I asked Wheeler if it could be Peter who had cried out. She put her head on one side and listened impassively. When the cry did not repeat itself, she said that perhaps it was, but if so, he'd just been dreaming.

She said: 'You're an odd one, you are. And close. But that's all right: I'm the same way myself.'

Then she ushered me back to my cabin, telling me that Peter's bunk was the other side of the partition wall from mine; if the crying started up again, she advised, I must tap on that thin, that paper-thin, dividing wall: my tapped signals would be comforting.

I returned to my bunk, and lay back into the tilt and rush of the train. Occasionally, as I tossed and turned, a cry or a sob would be audible; but whenever the sounds grew louder, and threatened to wake Frances, I did as Wheeler advised. I'd tap a soft Morse-style message on the panels, and the crying was soothed, and died down.

We rattled on through the dark, on through the dark. Not wanting to think of what might happen after Luxor, or of my inexorable return then to England, I lulled myself by thinking of the places that still awaited me here in Egypt. I listed them again and again in my tired mind: a Winter Palace of an hotel, Carter's castle in the desert, the American House – and beyond them, the Valley of dead kings. The wheels took up this refrain: into the Valley, into the Valley, said their iron voice. *I must remember to warn Peter about scorpions*, I thought. I fell into a sudden pit of sleep, just as the last gate of night swung open and the edge of the window blind began to colour with the promise of sunrise.

THREE

Three-Thousand-Year Effect

I, Philastrios the Alexandrian, who have come
to Thebes and seen with my own eyes these tombs of
astounding horror, have spent a delightful day.

Ancient Greek graffito in a Valley of the Kings' tomb

I 2

Today, at nine in the morning, I received a phone call. Thanks to the arthritis, now in full winter ascendancy, it is taking me an hour to get myself out of bed, to wash and dress, and creep down the stairs. I'd just completed this whimpering descent, and was staring out at the gloom that was Highgate, when the phone on my desk rang. I snatched at the receiver, expecting to hear a welcome, familiar English voice, only to be greeted by an American one: 'Hi, it's Ben Fong here,' it said, in very warm tones.

An unpleasant surprise: it was a month since Dr Fong had visited me; I'd been sure I'd never see him again, and, unless my mind was giving out (always possible at my age) he was now a safe two thousand miles away, filming his Tutankhamun docu-spectacular. 'You must be in Egypt, Dr Fong,' I said. 'Are you phoning from Cairo – or Luxor?'

'No, Highgate tube,' he replied, in the tone of someone imparting very good news. 'I'm on my cellphone. Five minutes away. I was wondering if I could zip up and see you.'

'*Highgate?*' I couldn't hide my dismay. 'No, you can't,' I added, thinking fast. 'I'm on my way out. The cab is at the door now.'

'I couldn't catch you later? Like this afternoon, maybe?'

'No, you couldn't. I'm tied up all week. I'm very busy *indeed*. Why aren't you in Egypt?'

'Long story.' He gave a gusty sigh. 'Script problems, budget problems, crew problems – you name it. We've had to delay the start. I'm getting seriously pissed off. Sorry.'

'So when are you *leaving*?'

'Ten days – two weeks maybe.' There was a pause, during which I digested this bad news, then he added, in a gloomy, embittered tone, 'And that's if the schedule doesn't change again . . . Let's not go there.'

'The taxi man is getting impatient. I have to leave.'

'Sure, okay – sorry to have sprung this on you. I'll email – I really need to see you, Miss Payne. I—'

'I'm losing you,' I said quickly. 'You're breaking up. Goodbye, Dr Fong.'

I switched the phone to answer mode and crept across to the windows. The taxi was imaginary, of course, but paranoia took hold: with cellphones, a person may *say* they're in one place, while being somewhere quite different – for instance, ten feet from one's front door.

I peered out into the impenetrable murk that is Highgate, north London, on a wet day in February: no sign of Dr Fong. Did I trust him to get back on the tube train and go and pester someone else? No, I did not. I thought it entirely possible he'd jog up the hill in his regrettable white trainers, and hang out in one of Highgate's super-fluity of coffee shops: I envisaged him in Starbucks, lurking over a skinny latte.

The last time I'd seen him, there had been several lines of enquiry Dr Fong seemed keen to pursue. I'd dodged them once, successfully, I felt, and didn't intend to do so a second time. I closed the window shutters, bolted the front door, and lit the fire – I do have central heating, but it's ineffective; the boiler, plumbers tell me, is dying. I made myself some strong coffee, and, several millennia later, still agitated, I sat down at last. My armchair of choice, chintzy, faded, with sagging springs, has reached that stage of age and neglect at which such chairs become, for a brief period, truly comfortable. It forms an island, surrounded by albums, diaries, journals and bundles of letters: the markers, milestones or tombstones of that hideous route that fools fondly call 'memory lane'. These – all of them – related to Egypt. Picking up a worn guidebook to Hatshepsut's temple, I turned the pages, and an old picture postcard fell out.

It showed the baroque wedding-cake frontage of the Winter Palace Hotel. Directly below its terrace and gardens lay the wide expanse of the Nile. The disposition of palm trees, feluccas and *dahabiyehs* was arty: a Cook's steamboat, dominating the river scene, was disgorging passengers the size of ants. The sepia image was faded and some chemical deterioration had made the image unpleasantly sticky, but I could still make out a large inky arrow marking one particular window on the hotel façade.

Turning it over, I saw it was dated February 1922, and addressed to Dr Robert Payne, Trinity College, Cambridge. In a small pinched hand, the girl I then was had written:

The arrow marks my room, Daddy! Yesterday, Miss Mack and I explored Karnak, and today the temple of Hatshepsut. Our visit to the Valley of the Kings keeps getting postponed. We sail for England at the end of next week. I hope your new course of lectures is going well and that it is not too miserably cold in Cambridge. It is hot, hot, hot here. I have learned to read a hieroglyph! Miss M exhorts me to send good wishes.

    Your loving daughter, Lucy

There was a postscript that had been heavily crossed out: with the aid of my magnifying glass I could decipher two horribly cramped words: *I hope*. The rest of the afterthought was illegible – so what I had hoped, or why I'd decided to communicate this hope to my father, was irrecoverable. I examined the card; melancholy clenched around my heart. There was a stamp, but no postmark. This uninformative missive was never sent – perhaps, knowing my father would dislike the exclamation marks, I'd sent a different one.

I could remember the hieroglyph I'd learned, however: it was Frances who taught it to me.

'Okay, what can you see?' she would ask, as we stood on the terrace at the Winter Palace. We'd be watching the sun begin to sink behind the hills on the horizon opposite; this was a dangerous moment – to the ancient Egyptians, it meant the sun was about to make its nightly journey through the perils of the underworld, from which, if one of the gates of night failed to open, it might never emerge; to me it meant Frances's brief visit was drawing to a close; shortly she'd return to those hills and to the American House with her mother. From our vantage point, I could see the wide grey-green expanse of the Nile, the brown sails of feluccas, a man driving goats towards the ferry below and, on the far bank, a plume of white dust that marked the progress of Lord Carnarvon's hired motorcar: he was returning from his day's expedition to the Valley, Eve at the wheel, one of the boys from Castle Carter clinging to the running-board. You could set your watch by this punctual daily return. *What can you see, Lucy?*

'I see the sunset,' I replied.

'Very observant. And where do you see it?'

'I give in: on the horizon.'

'And the word for horizon is?'

'*Akhet.*'

'Which, when you write the hieroglyph, looks like?'

'A little squashed hill, with a dip in its centre, and a small round ball resting in the dip.'

'Progress. We'll learn another next time. Oh, hellishness, it's time for the ferry.'

She glanced over her shoulder: in the distance, but coming closer by the second, were the monitory figures of Helen and Miss Mack, shaded by parasols and deep in conversation; at the landing stage below, the ferry-whistle blew.

Nerving myself, I said: 'Miss Mack and I will be leaving soon. It's coming closer and closer. The days go so fast – oh, I wish I could come with you, Frances.'

'So do I. Daddy's been very tied up at his dig, and the Lythgoes have been entertaining endless Museum donors; too many millionaires to woo – that's what's held things up. But don't worry, the guest rooms will be free soon. I'm working on it.'

'Promise?'

'Cross my heart and hope to die,' she replied, kissing my cheek, and then running off to join her mother.

When Frances made a promise, it was always kept; when she said she was working on something, she meant it was semi-achieved. A few days later came the invitation to Miss Mack and me: would we like to join the Winlocks for two nights, staying at the American House, and, under their guidance, explore the Valley? Miss Mack sent a note of acceptance; I danced for pure joy. Then I applied myself: wanting to look my best for this visit, I pleaded with Wheeler until, with an affectation of grumpiness but actually with zeal, she agreed to get out her scissors, lotions and potions and transform me.

*

'Snip, snip, snip,' said Wheeler. 'And stop fidgeting about – I'd prefer not to slice your ears off.'

I stopped fidgeting and steeled myself to look in the mirror: I was seated in splendour in the d'Erlanger suite, at what would be Poppy's dressing table when she finally made it to Luxor. Its surface was prepared for her return with scent sprays, powder pots and elaborate jars containing the secrets of eternal youth; the sense of Poppy's presence was so strong that I kept expecting to see her face in the glass. It was a triptych of a looking glass too: instead of beauteous Poppy, it reflected in triplicate my sad hair, and the expectant faces of Rose and Peter, perched on stools either side of me.

'Pretty Lulu,' Peter loyally pronounced, patting my hand.

'No, not pretty,' said Rose – an honest girl. 'In fact, you still look a bit *strange*. But Wheeler will improve things, and it is growing back . . . sort of. Besides, short hair is very *it* – Mamma says so.'

'Enough!' Wheeler said, flourishing scissors. 'I need silence, not you two chattering on and putting me off my stroke.'

And she began combing and flicking and snipping and smoothing, working so fast that her fingers became a blur, and my damp tufty hair – freshly washed, soothed with a scented cream, and smelling flowery and exotic like Mrs d'Erlanger's – lay flat against my scalp one moment, and the next stood up as if electrified. It was parted in the centre – Wheeler shook her head in disapproval; then on the left, then on the right; at last Wheeler cried, 'Got it!' and parted it on the left again, but lower. 'It's putting up a fight – but I'll get the better of it. Oh, you would, would you?' she said, addressing a lock more rebellious than the others. 'I know how to deal with the likes of *you* . . .'

The offending lock was thinned, sheared, then twisted into obedience around a curling iron; eventually, with a sizzling sound, it gave up the battle. Peering into the mirror, I began to see that, as promised, something *was* happening: the thin face in the glass belonged to someone I distantly remembered, a ghost girl I recognised.

Rummaging in a drawer, Wheeler brought out what she called 'a fixative'. She rubbed this secret substance between her palms, applied it lightly as if anointing me, and then stepped back to admire her handiwork. 'You'll do,' she pronounced.

'Not half bad,' Rose concurred.

'Is it Lulu?' Peter asked, looking anxiously at my reflection, and then at my face – and, possessed with sudden happiness, I told him it was, and danced a jig with him. Shortly after that, it was time to leave to catch the ferry. I danced my way to the door, and, pausing on the landing outside, heard Peter's voice, raised in sudden alarm; as I'd come to understand, all partings, even brief ones, distressed him.

'Go *too*, want to go *too* . . .' I heard him cry, and Rose hushed him.

'Darling, you can't – you're too little. It's too far and too hot and too tiring. Petey, please don't cry. I'm staying here with you, and Lucy will be coming back, don't worry.'

'Soon?'

'Very soon, Petey – I promise. Word of honour.'

'With Mamma?'

'No, not with Mamma, Petey. But Mamma will be here soon too. It's just that she has further to travel than Lucy, doesn't she, Wheeler? So it might take a while. Mamma has to catch a boat and then a train, and—'

I heard a quavering uncertainty enter Rose's voice: Wheeler at once took charge. 'All things come to those as wait,' she said. 'And from what I hear, we shan't have to wait much longer. Why, I wouldn't be surprised if your mamma wasn't on the boat right now . . . And as for Miss Lucy, it's two days and two sleeps and you'll be seeing her again. Now, let's go out on the balcony, and we'll watch out and wave goodbye, shall we?'

I looked back as I reached the hubbub of the ferry. Miss Mack climbed aboard, but I paused to scan the hotel façade, until my gaze arrowed in on the right balcony. There I could see them – and can see them still: a tall woman, in her maid's black uniform; a small fair-haired girl, whose head just reaches above the parapet, who is semaphoring with both hands, and a little boy, lifted aloft and per-suaded to wave; his indistinct shape catches at my heart. I call out, but of course he cannot hear me.

On the opposite shore, I was handed out onto the jetty and there were Helen and Frances, and the donkeys that would carry us to the American House. 'Present,' Frances said, giving me a welcoming hug, 'you'll need these.'

To my delight and surprise, she handed me a pair of dark glasses. I put them on. At once, the world changed. *New hair and new eyes*, I thought, as I climbed onto my donkey, and we set off towards the hills.

We made our way through the green fertile zone that spread out along the bank of the Nile and, after half an hour or so, reached the crossroads where we turned inland. There, the lush fields of papyrus, rushes and palm trees abruptly ended and desert began. The rough track climbed, gently at first, then more steeply. Ahead of me I saw the cliffs and crags that concealed the Valley of the Kings, and could make out the chief landmark: the high bare pyramidal hill called el-Qurn. There, the cobra goddess Meretseger had her abode; her name meant 'She who loves silence'. She was the deity protecting these hills and their tombs, spitting a deadly venom into the eyes of anyone who defiled them.

Her domain was desolate but fiercely beautiful. My sunglasses made the hills appear uniformly black and forbidding, but when I removed them, their rocks transformed into fantastic corrugations and crevices of pink limestone, with clefts the dark purple of plums. It was burningly hot. I wondered how the donkey boys could tolerate the heat of the sand on their bare feet; but they seemed impervious, scampering ahead of us, singing and chattering, or returning to urge their animals on. The path grew steeper and the crags crept closer, until at last, crouching in close under the shoulder of el-Qurn, I saw the American House. Surmounted by a central dome, fronted by an immense arched veranda, long, white, low and assertive, it was twice as large – no, three or four times as large as I'd expected.

'Oh, how splendid it is! Why, it's vast,' cried Miss Mack, reining her donkey in. 'Helen, it's magnificent.'

'You must tell Herbert – he helped design it. Pierpont Morgan put up the money for it, you know – he was a trustee of the Museum then. It was to be called "Morgan House" in his honour, only it turned out his money wasn't a gift after all, and he insisted it be repaid. So we forgot Mr Morgan and his mean ways, and rechristened it "Metropolitan".'

'Quite right,' said Miss Mack, dismounting. 'There is nothing meaner than a mean millionaire. And I've known a few mean millionaires in my time,' she added.

We ushered her inside, before she could launch herself on the familiar saga of Emersons or Wigginses. Helen then took us on a guided tour: we were shown the bedrooms – a bewildering number of them, enough to accommodate all the Met's team and numerous guests; we admired the airy dining room under the dome, with its long oak refectory table; the well-stocked library; the common room, with its fireplace surmounted by blue De Morgan tiles; and the working areas of the house, including the map room, the dark room where Harry Burton developed his photographs, and the storeroom for finds. The atmosphere of the house was calming: the white plaster walls, brick arches and tiled floors were traditionally Egyptian in style, but the furnishings, chaste and rectilinear, were by modern American designers. There was a monastic, scholarly hush to the building. Frances and I were to share a room at the back, well away from the adult residents, whom we were not to disturb – out of range of Minnie Burton, who was not fond of children.

Frances led me there and we stood at our bedroom window: situated at the far end of the house, close to the servants' quarters, it looked directly across the sands and scree towards the honeycomb of Theban tombs in the hills. Nets to exclude scorpions were stretched tightly across the glass; one of the panes had been opened a crack, to admit a faint exhalation of hot sterile desert air.

I turned to examine the room: twin beds with white counterpanes; ceiling fans; photographs of her family, set up like a small shrine. 'Let me introduce you,' Frances said, picking them up in turn.

This was her great-grandfather, who had been the first director of the famous Harvard Observatory, and this was her grandfather, a curator of the Smithsonian in Washington DC. The photograph central to the shrine showed Herbert Winlock as a boy standing on the steps of that august institution, holding a toy telescope. In the faded picture next to it, Helen's father, a Harvard architect, was standing on the stoop of a magnificent brownstone in Beacon Hill, Boston, holding hands with two children – an infant Helen in Alice-in-Wonderland garb, and her brother, mutinous in a sailor suit. I gazed at them curiously. Another era: it seemed unimaginably remote, and I said so.

'Well, it isn't,' Frances said. 'That picture was taken in 1892. My mother was five. Thirty years ago – it's the blink of an eye.'

She turned to a collection of small objects arranged next to the shrine of photographs: most had been brought back from her father's digs, or discovered by Frances herself. They had been laid out like offerings, I saw, beside the last of the photographs, a small faded picture whose details were hard to decipher, but which showed a house by the sea and two figures, who might have been a girl and a boy. Next to it were a bleached bone from a jackal's paw, many stones, selected for colour or symmetry, and numerous flakes of limestone, with faded lines just visible on their flat surfaces.

She picked up one of these. 'Look, Lucy,' she said. 'This is my great prize. These are ostraca – they turn up by the hundred on every dig. The workmen used them like little notebooks when they were working on the temples and tombs. Sometimes they'd draw a caricature, and sometimes they'd write words, nothing important, just like a shopping list, or they'd draw a plan of the tomb they were working on. This is my favourite: it's a dog, and I found it at Deir el-Bahri. Daddy let me keep it. It's someone's pet dog, don't you think? Both it and its owner have been dead for three thousand years.'

I inspected the small lively dog: it was panting and possessed a joyous feathery tail. With great care, Frances replaced it, and picked up the photograph.

'And this is my little brother,' she said, fixing me with shining eyes. 'It's his favourite ostraca too – he loves dogs. So I put it where he can see it, for company. His name is William Crawford Winlock: he's named after Daddy's father, but we call him Billy. He was two years, eleven months and two days old when he died. That's our holiday house, at North Haven, which is the island I told you about, off the coast of Maine.'

I leaned closer and peered at the picture. The clapboard house Frances was indicating was built at the summit of a sheer bank; below it was a boathouse, with a large jetty and landing stage raised on piles, at the shoreline, just feet from the waves. This dead brother had never been mentioned before.

'We go to Maine to stay at that house every summer – and in this picture, it's the summer of 1918. Daddy was in the army then, still fighting in France. But we were there. And that's where my brother Billy died: he fell off that jetty, and drowned in the cold blue waters of Penobscot Bay.'

I can't remember what I said, but I must have said something, for Frances patted my arm in a consoling way. 'Yes, it was very terrible,' she went on. 'We were all there – my grandparents, and my mother and me. I was five – well, almost. It was the day my mother took me for my first race in a sailboat. There was just one tiny moment when everyone was looking the other way, fussing with picnic baskets and waterproofs, and that was the moment when he fell. But that's the way of things. They're fast. You know that too.'

'I do,' I replied. I closed my eyes, Egypt vanished and I was back in my Cambridge bedroom: my mother bent over my bed and stroked my forehead. I drifted into sleep, and when I woke from that long hot feverish sleep, she was gone. I opened my eyes again, and looked at the photograph. From its shadows, two figures emerged: I saw a small girl, who I realised was Frances, and a little boy, with bright hair, clutching her hand. Now I understood that reaction of Helen Winlock's in the museum in Cairo.

'He has very fair hair. He's a dear little boy. He looks like Peter,' I said, after a pause.

'Perhaps. But Peter cries – and Billy never did. And he talked more than Peter does. He likes coming to Egypt with me, and when I've been somewhere, like Daddy's dig, or the Valley maybe, I come home and describe it to him. I've told him all about you, of course, and he gave me permission to tell you his story. Normally, we keep it a secret – it doesn't do to broadcast important things around, and besides, it makes my mother cry, to be reminded, you know. But Billy considers it's right to tell you. You don't blab. And besides, he knows you're my closest and most particular friend.'

'Am I truly, Frances?' I asked anxiously; this honour was unexpected and powerful.

'Of course,' she replied, in a tone of careless reproof, as if I were being exceptionally obtuse. Turning away, and with a matter-of-fact air, she lifted my suitcase onto one of the beds and, moving to the washstand, poured some water into a bowl.

'Right, time to wash and brush up,' she continued, in a businesslike way. 'No need to unpack, the servants will do that. Then coffee on the veranda with the Lythgoes and my parents. That's the routine . . . You'd better know what you're in for,' she continued, as I washed my dusty face and hands. 'The *past* – and then, just when you think at long last it must be over, *more* past. Albert Lythgoe will tell you how Daddy was the most brilliant student he ever tutored at Harvard – and also the most rebellious one. Then Mrs Lythgoe will start in on her famous father Rufus, who ruled the American School of Archaeology in Athens with a rod of iron, and didn't permit women to excavate . . . She'll tell you how Albert proposed to her at dawn on the Parthenon – imagine Mr Lythgoe, proposing! You'll have to inspect the silver coffee service the King of Greece gave her as a wedding present . . . it goes on for ever! Meanwhile, Minnie Burton will carp from the sidelines, and boast about how her father ran the British army single-handed. You have to listen to all this, and not yawn or fidget once. I do it this way.'

Frances turned full face and assumed an expression of lively attention, eyes satirically wide. 'After that,' she went on, 'there's the ceremonial signing of the Visitors' Book, and then my mother loses her spectacles and her watercolours, and finds she's packed them, and Daddy cusses a bit, and then – at long last – we mount the donkeys again . . .'

'And we go to the Valley?'

'We go to the Valley. Eve is thrilled that you're coming, and so are her father and Mr Carter, she says. We're in their good books for some reason, all our espionage at Shepheard's, I think – anyway, they're laying on a picnic lunch for us.'

'In the Valley itself?'

'Better than that. In the Valley *and* in a tomb,' Frances said, performing a cartwheel.

The tomb selected for our picnic was sited at the far end of the Valley, in a remote ravine well beyond the most visited burial sites. It was a place of uncertainties, devoid of paintings or inscriptions, Herbert Winlock explained: scholars disagreed as to which king had commissioned it. It had been quarried a short distance into the rock, then abandoned, but this was not unusual, he added: Egyptian kings could be capricious when deciding their final resting place. All the tombs in the Valley were numbered and identified according to a system first evolved in the nineteenth century; they were referred to as KV 15, KV 24 and so on. Frances and I had by then adopted the acronym 'KV', which, when spoken, and particularly when hissed, sounded like the Latin warning *cave*, or the schoolboys' *cavey*. It was now our watchword of choice, used when adults circled near by. 'KV, Lucy,' Frances had said several times that morning when Minnie Burton had come threateningly close to our whispered conferences. *Beware, beware*: I examined the entrance to the luncheon tomb – no painted number; unidentified.

The tomb had a low, dark entrance, set under a rocky overhang. Facing north and protected from the rays of the sun, it looked like some natural fissure. Pausing and looking back the way we had come, I thought the unknown king had rejected a magnificent site to wait out eternity. Here, the wide central section of the Valley was invisible and the hills closed in, their rocks scoured into soaring columns. It was a wilderness place, and the heat was intense, yet the atmosphere was peaceful, the only sounds the murmuring of rock doves and the mew of kites circling the blue updraughts high above. My mind was still lingering on Frances's little brother, and how he had died. Now that I knew his story, the way in which I saw his parents had irrevocably changed. How often did they think of him? I wondered, as Herbert Winlock led the way cheerfully into the tomb, and Helen, lingering behind, peered about the rocks in search of Frances and me, giving that now-familiar gesture of the hand, the gesture that betrayed her nervousness, her instinct to locate missing children and gather them in. 'Ah, there you are,' she said. 'Come along, my dears.'

Turning to follow her, I ventured into the dark tomb, and found myself in a dining room. I looked around in astonishment: in the centre of the shadowy space, a long table had been erected and eight chairs arranged. The table was draped in a starched white damask cloth; each place setting had a large array of glasses, silver cutlery, crisp linen napkins, and gilded plates decorated with the initial 'C'. Lined up with military precision was an array of chutneys and pickled fruits bearing the labels 'Fortnum and Mason'.

'Prospero's feast,' Helen murmured. I was wondering if the initial 'C' signified Carter or Carnarvon, and marvelling at this display, when I realised that our hosts were waiting for us. Eve, together with Howard Carter and Lord Carnarvon, stood together in the recesses of the tomb, flanked by four Arab servants wearing white turbans, white gloves and white galabiyas, all four drawn up to attention like footmen. Eve came forward to greet us, but our two hosts hung back inspecting the new arrivals. Once we had all crushed in to the narrow space, they embarked on introductions – Carnarvon diffident to the point of languidness, Carter ill at ease and voluble.

'Lord Carnarvon, if I may introduce Miss Mackenzie, in charge of my little friend here, Miss Payne, making her first visit to Egypt, and to the Valley.' He dropped his voice, and I caught the words 'Emerson', 'Norfolk' and then 'Trinity'.

Once I'd been stamped and labelled, Carnarvon shook my hand, smiled, and murmured: 'Cambridge . . . my own alma mater, Miss Payne – and Trinity was my college too. Only lasted a couple of years, though, found it all a bit boring, trekking off to lectures at dawn, couldn't wait to go travelling, bought a yacht and took off for the Cape Verde islands instead . . . Miss Mackenzie, delighted . . . Frances, my dear, and Helen . . . now, isn't this amusing? I thought, after that long hot ride you've had, maybe something refreshing?'

Several bottles of champagne appeared, and while the four servants busied themselves with glasses, Carter began bustling back and forth, barking commands in Arabic. Turning to us, with much nervous jocular rubbing of the hands, he said, in his odd staccato way: 'Cold cuts. Of necessity. "The funeral baked meats" as the bard put it, at least I think he did . . . Delicious too, chosen by Eve from the stores at my house. Now let's see . . . we have tongue, potted fowl, pâté de foie gras . . . '

'And the most delicious *shamsi* bread, made in Howard's kitchens this morning,' Eve put in, coming to his rescue. 'Now, where shall we all park ourselves?'

The informality of 'parking', I noted, was followed by strictly observed placements: Lord Carnarvon ambled to his place at the head of the table, with Miss Mack, as the oldest woman present, seated on his right hand; Helen was seated on Carter's right at its foot, with Frances on his other side. On the strength of being a newcomer, I think, I was placed on Carnarvon's left. Herbert Winlock, who never cared where he sat, ended up in the middle, with Eve opposite him.

'Well now – this looks delicious,' Winlock said. 'A great improvement on the old days when we archaeologists all roughed it. What was it the great Flinders Petrie survived on, Carter?'

'Sardines,' Carter boomed. 'His famous sardines! First, he made a hole in the can – drank the oil, claimed it was very nutritious. Then he opened it and scoffed the sardines. Followed it up with a dozen oranges. That was breakfast. And luncheon. And dinner.'

'Heavens!' said Miss Mack. 'And was this diet inflicted on you too, Mr Carter?'

'It was. All Petrie's assistants had to endure it – most of them fled for the hills within a couple of weeks. He also despised tents, insisted you manufactured your own mud bricks and then built your own shelter with them – the fellahin could have done it in half the time. No plaster on the walls either – didn't approve of such luxuries – I've never slept anywhere so infested with spiders and scorpions . . . So, I can rough it if I have to, but I'm in favour of luxury whenever possible. Some foie gras, Helen? I can recommend it. Abd-el-Aal, wake up! Do you expect people to reach for things?'

He muttered a few commands in Arabic; Abd-el-Aal, the oldest of the men serving us, who was also the most senior of them, I thought, nodded serenely. He waited until he judged himself unobserved, then sidled up to the youngest of our waiters, a boy of about fifteen; he gave his ear a sharp yank and his ribs a sharp nudge. The boy, who looked terrified, scurried around the table to Eve. Lifting one of the salvers, he tipped a generous, pinkish mess of potted chicken onto Eve's plate. Its coating of gelatine quivered, then at once began to melt.

'How delicious, Hosein, thank you,' Eve said, with a sweet and reassuring smile in Carter's direction.

'And you, Mr Carter – did you flee for the hills, like Petrie's other assistants, or did you stick it out?' Miss Mack enquired. I could see that she, like Eve and the Winlocks, was attempting to ease Carter's nerves.

'Stuck it out. This was at el-Amarna, Miss Mackenzie. I was seventeen, been in Egypt less than six months – knew nothing, green to the gills. Everything important I learned from Petrie. Walked me off my feet for hours every day in the boiling sun, worked me like a dog, half starved me – but that man showed me how to use my eyes and he taught me how to excavate. Taught me to discard nothing, examine everything, record everything.' He broke off, then gave a wolfish grin. 'Can't stand the sight of sardines to this day. So perhaps that's the great man's legacy to me.'

The conversation drifted off, moving on to tales and reminiscence of a century and more of excavators, scholars, archaeologists and adventurers, Belzoni, Champollion, Lepsius and the man who had held the permit to dig in the Valley immediately before Carnarvon: the millionaire American lawyer, Theodore Davis – for whom Carter had excavated some years before Carnarvon hired him, and with whom Winlock had also done battle.

'A rank amateur, with amazing luck,' Winlock was saying, 'and a barbarian when it came to the actual dig. Theodore Davis was a treasure hunter, pure and simple – which makes his numerous and important finds all the more galling. Still, *nil nisi* et cetera.'

'Remember Ayrton? Excavator for Davis after I escaped his

clutches?' Carter put in. He'd gulped a glass of champagne and one of wine, and seemed more at ease now. 'Good archaeologist, had the training, had the nose – but Davis soon ground him into the dust.'

'Indeed I do. Alas, poor Ayrton!' Winlock said. 'Did you ever meet him, Lord Carnarvon? Very young, very bright indeed. Spent his boyhood in China. The Valley gave him nightmares – at the Davis dig house, no one would share a room with him. He'd scream out in his sleep, you see. In fluent Chinese.'

'Dead now,' Carter said. 'Joined some archaeological expedition in Ceylon, and drowned a few years later. Can't have been much more than thirty.'

'And Jones – you remember Harold Jones, who came after him? Welshman, sweet fellow, trained as an artist – Davis finished him off too. Or the dust in the Valley did.'

'What happened to Mr Jones, Daddy?' Frances put in.

'Tuberculosis, darling. It was very sad. A nice man – witty, and a good artist too. He used to drink quarts of milk every day; it was thought to keep the disease at bay. I remember meeting him once, sitting outside the dig house, staring at the hills – it was a glorious evening, the most magnificent sunset, but I could see how exhausted and miserable he was, so to cheer him up I said, "Evening, Jones – on the lookout for a new tomb?" And he gave me this puzzled look and said, "In the Welsh valleys? Why would I do that? No, I'm admiring my nan's little house. See it, Winlock? That's it, over there, beyond the chapel, on the edge of that green field." Poor man. I knew it couldn't be long after that – and it wasn't.'

'Some bread, Miss Payne?' Lord Carnarvon said, making me jump. The conversation, to which I'd been listening intently, had taken me off into a dream of valleys and ill-fated excavators; now I returned from them with a snap, to find Carnarvon turning in my direction, and the servant called Abd-el-Aal proffering a basket. Miss Mack was looking the other way, so I took some bread, broke off a small piece and ate it. It was excellent. Before I knew it, I was telling Lord Carnarvon about Hassan and our trip to the pyramids.

'By Jove!' he exclaimed, having listened with grave attention. 'He actually warmed it up on the Sphinx's paw? Most ingenious. What an admirable fellow.'

'He was a very kind man,' I replied. 'When we said goodbye, he gave me an *ankh.*'

'Did he *indeed*? How absolutely splendid. You must show me that one of these days.'

'I can show you now,' I said, fishing the *ankh* from my pocket – I carried it everywhere, wrapped in my handkerchief; it was my talismanic equivalent to Frances's scarlet lipstick.

Carnarvon took the small fragile piece of tin from me and examined it scrupulously; had it been some priceless *antika* he could scarcely have given it closer scrutiny. 'That is a *very* fine present,' he said, returning it to me. 'It signifies life, of course – you'll know that? And what better gift could anyone receive?'

'I also have a bead – a very ancient bead that Mr Carter gave me,' I said. 'Might you like to see that too?'

'My word, what treasures you carry around with you! I most certainly *would,* Miss Payne.'

I handed him the bead, and with similar care and seriousness Carnarvon examined it. I was being taught a lesson – in charm, and the deceptions that charm conceals. But I didn't know that then; Carnarvon was a fine actor; it did not occur to me that his fascination might be feigned.

He took his time inspecting the lapis lazuli bead, and, as he was now wondrously near, I took the opportunity to inspect him. I knew he was in his mid-fifties, roughly the same age as Miss Mack, and only some six or seven years older than Howard Carter. Close to, he seemed much older, his evident frailty and ill-health in marked contrast to their air of well-being and vigour. His face bore the traces of smallpox scars and his complexion was a sickly grey, with tired blue shadows beneath his ice-pale eyes. His breathing was laboured, and he had an odd mannerism – a continual pressing of his hand to his chest – that I thought must be a legacy of the many operations endured since the motoring accident years before that had rendered him an invalid.

His clothes were those of a dandy or an aesthete from an earlier era: they looked old and slightly shabby, but were exquisitely tailored – my father, who was fussy as to dress, would have admired them, I knew. According to Frances, Howard Carter so admired Carnarvon's *fin de siècle* style that he copied it religiously, favouring the same Savile Row tailors, the same exclusive shirt-makers and hatters as his patron. When I examined the two men now, however, the differences between them were marked: Carnarvon's shirt was darned, his bow tie was frayed, yet his elegance appeared effortless. Carter, portly and sleek, with a silk pocket handkerchief that matched his florid bow tie, looked overdressed and faintly preposterous by contrast.

Carnarvon seemed unused to children's eating alongside adults; he solved this puzzling American difficulty by ignoring it, and by treating me as if I were a woman of age and experience. He returned my lapis bead to me, and, as fresh plates were brought, ensured I took some figs and some little Egyptian pastries, oozing honey. He said with solemnity: 'Now, Miss Payne, you simply must tell me – what do you think of our Valley?'

That 'our' made me blink. 'Well,' I began, carefully, 'I've only had a glimpse so far—'

'Nonsense. You are an observer – Carter confirms that. In which context, and remembering your – *observations* – at Shepheard's, Eve and I and our mutual friend Mrs d'Erlanger are grateful to you and to Frances as well.' He slowly closed one keen grey eye, and then opened it again. 'So, as an observer of the Valley, fresh from your first view of it, tell me your impressions.'

I hesitated. My impressions were a muddled series of images that had not yet had time to lie down, let alone be assimilated. I thought of the approach path we'd taken that morning: it wound up towards the hills on a rough incline, and I'd caught my first glimpse of Castle Carter as we passed, not a castle at all, but a small, white, domed house, sited like a sentinel post near the incisor rocks at the mouth of the Valley. Lord Carnarvon's hired car was parked outside it, I saw; a young boy was busy polishing its gleaming coachwork.

We'd passed into a long, narrow defile that curved ahead of us like the blade of a sickle, its track glittering with broken flints, and at once the heat had intensified – coming at us in a rush, as if someone had thrown back the door of a blast furnace. As we rounded a massive fluted outcrop that seemed to bar our path, a great ravine suddenly opened up before my startled eyes, a place of terrible beauty, tumbled with rocks and mounds of shale – a place that looked as if it had recently suffered a catastrophic earthquake. I realised that this vast slashing gash through the hills was the Valley of the Kings.

Staring at the spillage and debris, at the rockfalls caused by flash floods and the mountains of spoil left by man, I'd begun to make out the black gaping caves that were the tomb entrances – scores of them, some cut into the Valley walls, some into its floor, some facing the main path and others, just visible, secreted in the smaller wadis that snaked and bifurcated between the hills. Winlock, knowing the Valley and its ways, had raised a hand and brought us all to a halt. Frances, who'd been chanting Tennyson, and had just reached 'Half a league onward/ Into the Valley of', stopped speaking; the donkey boys ceased their chattering, and moved to calm their animals. 'Listen,' Winlock said – and when the donkeys finally stopped their head-tossings and pawings, I heard what clever Mr Winlock meant me to hear: a hot, fearsome and resonant silence.

It was broken in due course, inevitably. We were not alone in the Valley, whose clear air carried every sound and magnified it. I heard the mew of a kite far above, the jingle of a harness, then, in the distance, the voices of tourists entering a tomb, and the shrill call of their dragoman. But that experience of silence remained: it was still in my mind at this table and I knew I should never forget it.

'Your impressions,' Carnarvon prompted.

'The silence. It made me feel – like a trespasser,' I began. 'And the number of the tombs, I think. There are so very many. I wished . . .'

'Don't be shy. Tell me what you wished, Miss Payne.'

'I wished the tombs had been left undisturbed. I wished no one had ever come here, so the kings could – wait out eternity in solitude as they meant to do. That's why they made the tombs here; that was *their* wish. I was sad their wish hadn't been granted.'

I said this earnestly, but in a blurt. The instant the words were out, I saw they were tactless. For a moment I thought Lord Carnarvon was affronted, or in pain: his face contracted and his gaze became sombre. Then, with a grace that was characteristic of him, he gave me a wry smile. 'My dear,' he said, 'you know, I don't disagree with you? However . . .' he glanced around the table, 'here we are, Carter, Winlock and I – three ardent trespassers, three disturbers of the peace, all guilty as charged, and, I'm afraid, woefully unrepentant. Are we to leave, according to your doctrine?'

'No, it's too late,' I replied. 'The tourists are here now. And the tomb robbers arrived centuries before you.'

'And if we weren't here now, their thieving modern counterparts would be only too quick to replace us,' Carter put in, somewhat aggressively.

'Alas, they *would*,' cried Miss Mack. 'Oh, if only the kings had seen fit to have a modest burial . . . if they hadn't believed in the need for huge tombs, for great statues and paintings and sarcophagi and gold and jewels. I'm sure no one would have disturbed them then.'

'A nice, sober, modest, Episcopalian burial,' said Winlock, with a grin, helping himself to figs. 'That would have saved them, eh, Myrtle?'

'Now, now, Herbert,' she corrected him, good-humouredly. 'I'm from Princeton and of Scottish descent – modest and *Presbyterian* is of course what I had in mind.'

'Maybe a funeral pyre,' Eve suggested in a dreamy voice. 'If they'd simply been burned. A spectacular conflagration. You know, like Shelley—'

'Very poetic, Eve,' said Helen. 'But no Lord Edward Trelawny figure to steal the heart away from the embers, mind – they'd have to bury it in the Valley tomb, so it would be there for the Weighing of the Heart ceremony.'

'Complete tommyrot,' Carter interrupted irritably. 'Their bodies had to be preserved – that's fundamental to their beliefs. The Egyptians didn't just believe in the immortal soul, they believed in the immortal body. You're all forgetting that. You're also forgetting beauty: these burials and these tombs are incomparably beautiful. What about the art they contain – the art *we* uncover?'

'Carter's right. We might put in a *little* word for the science of archaeology,' Winlock interjected in a mild, amused tone. 'Before we go totally off the rails, might we be pious for a second? Think of what we learn from the tombs, about the Egyptians' way of life and death. Of their history and religion. Think of the art we save – and take to museums, make available to thousands of people every year. All right, I'm biased because I practically grew up in the Smithsonian, but even so . . . Museums change people's lives – they certainly changed mine. They're powerful.'

'Well, that is true of course, Herbert,' Miss Mack put in. 'And

I wouldn't presume to argue with you or Mr Carter. But I still feel I have a point. The very opulence of the tombs was precisely what defeated their purpose. If the kings had been modestly interred, they would never have been disturbed, and their poor bodies would never have been rifled. You must admit, their burials were vainglorious——'

'I can't believe this,' Frances suddenly burst out, her eyes bright and her cheeks flushed. 'A *modest* funeral? A wooden coffin? Dust and ashes? That is so mean and dreary. Who wants to lie under a stone in a mouldering old churchyard, or in some horrible overcrowded cemetery, with an inscription that just gets worn out, so no one can read it or remember you? No – I think the Egyptian kings got it exactly right: in the Valley, in a huge rock tomb, with a magnificent gold coffin, and a vast sarcophagus, and priceless . . .'

' . . . Treasure?' suggested someone.

'Yes, treasure!' Frances cried, ignoring her mother's semaphored attempts to silence her. 'Powerful spells on the walls, and heaps of jewels and glorious paintings. The pharaohs wanted their names to live eternally, they wanted to defeat death – and they've succeeded. If they'd just been bundled up in some old sheet and stuck under a rock, no one would bother to dig here – and no one would remember them either.'

A silence followed this outburst, broken by a barking laugh from Carter: 'Well, that hits the nail on the head,' he said. 'And it's honest.'

'Don't encourage her, Howard,' Helen said quickly; two bright patches of colour had risen in her cheeks and I could see these comments had upset her. 'Frances, that's more than enough. We are not here to be lectured by you.'

'Have you been drinking water, Frances, or did you filch some champagne by any chance?' her father put in. 'What are you thinking of? Seen and *not* heard, please——'

'Pups, darling – are you all right?' Evelyn interrupted and, with a sudden cry, half rose from her seat.

We all turned towards the head of the table; Carter and Winlock leapt to their feet and there was a moment of panic. Lord Carnarvon, silent for some while, had taken no part in this argument. Now he had slumped back in his chair, his lips blue, his eyes closed and his face ashen.

'Smelling salts!' cried Miss Mack, 'I have some in my purse . . .' An instant later, just as Miss Mack was producing a small brown bottle, Carnarvon gave a start and a sigh and opened his eyes again.

The collective alarm took a moment to register, and then with a smile, and a waft of the hand, he reassured us. 'Good grief, how disgraceful – I must have drifted off for a second. The penalty of age and an excellent lunch . . . Forgive me, everyone. Eve, perhaps if we had our coffee now? And then, you know, my dear, I think we might wend our way back to Carter's place, pick up our motorcar and return to the hotel—'

'You can't leave now. We planned to show everyone our workings,' Carter interrupted, with a scowl. 'You wanted Winlock to see our latest finds.'

'Well now, our latest finds are not so very exciting,' Carnarvon replied. 'A few pottery shards, a couple of ostraca – I feel you'll explain them better than I shall. Another time, my dear fellow, another time . . .'

He half turned to the four Arab servants behind him and, addressing the air, said: 'Send word back to the house. I'll need the car ready. The donkeys in fifteen minutes.' His eyes rested briefly on the four men and he added: 'Boy, take the chairs outside.'

He turned back to us. 'We'll have our coffee there, shall we? I need some fresh air. No, no – I'm perfectly fine, I assure you . . . Eve, my puss-cat, no need to fret. If you'll all forgive me, I'll stay for a brief while, and sun myself – and then I'll leave you.'

14

Lord Carnarvon was as good as his word: he sat with us outside the
tomb, sipping coffee and conversing amicably; he seemed interested
in the desultory conversation and completely restored. The chairs had
been arranged in a semicircle in the shade, with two folding stools for
Frances and me. Having served the coffee, Abd-el-Aal and Hosein
returned to the tomb, from which drifted the sound of men's voices
and the faint clatter of crockery. I watched the kites circling on the
updraughts above us; beside me Frances, flushed and mutinous, still
smarting from the reprimands earlier, sat scuffing at the sand. Even
in the shade it was stiflingly hot; rivulets of sweat were running down
my back. I looked at my watch: time in the Valley had come to a
standstill.

Carnarvon smoked half a cigarette, inserting it into an amber
holder that matched the one Howard Carter was using that day; he
seemed so relaxed and at ease that I wondered if he'd change his
plans. But no; exactly fifteen minutes after he'd sat down, two boys
and their donkeys appeared. Carnarvon mounted without assistance;
Eve was helped into the saddle by Carter, who said something to her
in a low urgent tone. 'No, no, not tomorrow,' I heard Eve reply, 'I
have to . . .' The rest of her words were inaudible. Without further
delay, father and daughter rode off. No one spoke until they had
rounded an outcrop of rocks and disappeared from sight.

As soon as they had gone, Carter began to pace up and down, then
wrenched off his tweed jacket; he looked flushed and belligerent.
'Christ, it's hot,' he said, tossing the jacket aside. 'Damnable flies.' He

batted at the air. '*And* that champagne wasn't cold enough. I gave Abd-el-Aal strict instructions, damn it. What's more, the bread was stale.'

'The bread was delicious, Howard,' Helen said in a pacifying tone. 'Really, it couldn't have been fresher—'

'I tell you it was *stale*,' Carter replied, with a rudeness and aggression that startled everyone. 'Hard as a board. Cracked my teeth. Carnarvon didn't touch it – he scarcely ate a thing. And that clown Hosein, slopping chicken onto Eve's plate, like being in a blasted soup kitchen. Well, I won't stand for it. I pay their wages, it's a simple enough task – cook the damn bread, wrap it, bring it up here – am I supposed to do everything? *Christ*, I turn my back for ten seconds, and the whole meal's bloody ruined. I've a good mind to send them packing right here and now.'

Miss Mack, allergic to profanities, had blushed deeply; she began on low polite squeaks of protest. Seeing this, Winlock rose and said in an easy tone: 'Come on now, Carter. Cool down, old sport. It was an excellent lunch. Your men managed it perfectly and we all thoroughly enjoyed it. There's really no need to—'

'Need? *Need?*' Carter interrupted, rounding on him, his face now sneering and furious. 'What would you know about my needs, *old sport*? Don't patronise *me*, Winlock. We all know you grew up with servants and I didn't – that doesn't mean you can lord it around here. They're my staff, damn it, and I won't tolerate sloppiness. Did I ask you to poke your nose into my affairs? Mind your own bloody business.'

He gave the chair on which he'd been sitting earlier a violent kick, pushed past us and strode into the darkness of the tomb. 'Abd-el-Aal, where the hell are you?' we heard him shout. There was the sound of glass smashing, and then of raised voices, Carter's and another man's, both speaking rapid Arabic. 'Heavens *above*,' said Miss Mack as the voices rose in pitch and then receded into the depths of the tomb.

'That's torn it,' Winlock said, sharing an expressive look with his wife. 'Don't upset yourself, Myrtle,' he continued. 'Abd-el-Aal has worked for Carter for twenty-five years. He's used to the tantrums – and he can give as good as he gets. There'll be no bloodshed, no firings and in about, let's see . . . ' he glanced at his wristwatch, 'fifteen minutes, twenty at the outside, Carter will be back out here, being as nice as pie. Nicer, probably, because he'll be penitent . . . That's if he doesn't decide on one of his mammoth sulks, of course. Which is also on the cards. Meanwhile, my apologies.'

'It's not *your* apology, I require, Herbert,' Miss Mack replied, with asperity. 'Mr Carter said nothing I haven't heard before – I have worked as a nurse, if you recall. But in front of the children: such loss of all control, such a display of temper! And after such a pleasant lunch too – I'm at a loss to understand what provoked it.'

'Carnarvon's remark about their finds, for one thing.' Winlock shrugged. 'His early departure – that won't have pleased him. Carter has a bit of a chip on his shoulder too . . . he's on a short fuse at the best of times. He likes to be in control, Myrtle. He has these fixed plans, and he can't stand it if they're altered.'

'But poor Lord Carnarvon was *ill*. He may have made light of it, but he hadn't just dozed off, that was obvious. His lips were blue. It might have been a stroke – I was seriously alarmed – really quite fearful for him. And now he has that journey back to the hotel. Having to ride in this terrible heat, and then driving all that way on that appalling track. He shouldn't be here in my view. He's a sick man. Surely Mr Carter can see—'

'Oh, he can see, all right, Myrtle,' Helen said gently. 'Howard's well aware of Carnarvon's precarious state of health. That's another reason why he lost his temper.'

'He's *afraid*,' Frances said, jumping up from the stool next to mine. 'Oh, for heaven's sake, Miss Mackenzie, can't you see? He's afraid Lord Carnarvon will be too ill to carry on in the Valley, and afraid they'll lose their chance to find a glorious tomb, when it might be just inches away, and he's spent half his life looking for it and he *knows* it's there. And he's afraid we all despised the lunch, because Mr Carter didn't know how to get the details right . . . He's afraid we'll be sneering at him because that stupid champagne wasn't cold enough – a thousand things! That makes him furious with himself, so he starts shouting and cussing—'

'Hold your tongue, Frances, please,' her father said curtly. 'We've heard enough from you for one day. I've already warned you—'

'It's so unfair!' Frances cried. I could see she was close to tears. 'Now he'll be ashamed and embarrassed, and that will make him even worse. And it shouldn't. What does cussing matter? I'm used to it. Daddy cusses every morning, when he's trying to shave and the water isn't hot, or he's late for the dig, or—'

'My father does too,' I said, suddenly fired up by Frances, the words spoken before I could think. 'And when *he* loses his temper, which he does for no reason at all, when I haven't said a word, scarcely breathed, it's *much* worse than Mr Carter. It's hateful.'

'Lucy!' Miss Mack gave a cry of outrage, and rose to her feet. 'You will be silent this instant. What in heaven's name has come over you? How dare you speak in that way?' Advancing upon me, and angrier than I had ever seen her, she took hold of me by the wrist, hauled me to my feet, propelled me aside and backed me up against the rocks. 'One more word of that kind,' she said, 'just one word, Lucy Payne, and I'll take you straight back to the hotel, do you understand me? How can you be so disrespectful and disloyal? To speak of your own father in that way.'

'It's *true*,' I cried, now furious and beside myself. 'You *know* it's true. You've been there, you've heard it. He shouts and curses, and then he goes for days and days without speaking at all and I know it's the war that makes him do it, but he bullies me – and he bullied my mother as well.'

I burst into tears. Miss Mack seemed to have been rendered speechless, and my head swirled with all the heat and consternation exploding like ordnance in the Valley. Behind me, I could hear Helen's voice raised in angry reproof, and Frances's tearful protests. Above me, in the high blue air, the kites were shrieking alarm, and from inside the tomb, amidst crashing and smashing, came Arabic wails.

'Holy *Moses*,' said a voice that I realised was Winlock's. 'Who or what unleashed *this*? Has the world gone completely mad? Right, that's it: I've had enough. Helen, I suggest you get out your water-colours and paint, as you planned to do. Myrtle, if you'd be kind enough to keep her company? You, Frances, and you, Lucy, come with me. *Now.*'

He spoke in a tone that brooked no disagreement. He marched Frances and me away, towards the main section of the Valley. After a hundred yards, he handed us a handkerchief, telling us brusquely that we'd darn well have to share it. Frances and I mopped our wet eyes and our hot faces, and struggled to keep up, for Winlock was walking at a brisk pace, apparently oblivious to the burning heat of the afternoon sun. After a long interval, Frances began on some muttered speech, in which I joined her. Winlock held up his hand, paused briefly, glared at us both and said: 'I don't want to know. I don't want to hear. I've seen the Valley have this effect before, and no doubt I'll see it again, but that's *enough*.'

He walked on a little further, and then, coming to a halt by a spillage of rock, he said, on a kinder note: 'Okay, let's get this over with. You two have just defended your friend Carter: that was loyal and we'll let it pass. But at lunch, you inflicted your opinions concerning Egyptian tombs on a group of people who've forgotten more than you'll ever know on that subject. I can sympathise: I had opinions in spades when I was your age. I was opinionated at Harvard, and nearly got thrown out for it. I still am excessively opinionated, I'll admit that, but then a world where people didn't have ideas and opinions would be a very dull one. However, as I finally learned, opinions are valueless unless they're informed – and neither you, Frances, nor you, Lucy, are well informed on that subject. In fact, you're conspicuously and lamentably *ill* informed.'

He paused, frowning along the Valley, removed his panama and mopped his forehead. 'So,' he continued, 'out of the goodness and generosity of my heart, and in a spirit of self-sacrifice, because there are more important things I could be doing right now, working, for instance . . . I intend to educate you just a little. We may as well rescue something useful from the wreckage of the afternoon. Lucy came here to see the Valley, and see it she will. I'll give you two hours of my precious time, and during those two hours, we will explore some tombs of my choosing. I will speak, you will listen. Then we'll go home and have tea. How does that sound?'

'It sounds good,' Frances said in a small voice. There was a pause and then she added: 'I'm sorry, Daddy.'

'I'm sorry too, Mr Winlock,' I muttered. 'I shouldn't have said that. I don't know why I did.'

'Oh, I'm sure you do,' Winlock replied, with a sharp glance. 'These things will out. And if ever there was a place to bring them out, it's this one. The Valley can be disruptive and this infernal heat doesn't help, but it can also be a calming place – trust me. You'll see.' He patted my shoulder, and in a quieter voice continued: 'You can come here feeling pretty terrible, Lucy, really churned up with anger and misery and heartache, and then you enter one of the tombs and – it kind of slips away from you. It's happened to me many times. I call it the three-thousand-year effect.

'Now,' he looked along the Valley, towards the wider, bellying space where the most-visited tombs were located, 'I don't intend fighting our way past a hundred tourists, and dragomen and hawkers and charlatans, so we'll avoid the main drag for the moment. We'll start with Frances's favourite tomb, which is also my favourite and, in my view anyway, the most beautiful in the Valley. It was made for a king called Seti I, Lucy. He ruled Egypt roughly one thousand three hundred years BC. He was a warrior king, inevitably, though nothing on the scale of his son and successor, Ramesses II, who was the greatest of the pharaohs, long lived, all powerful, a ruthless imperialist and a pitiless dictator – a monomaniac who bequeathed us some of the most glorious monuments in Egypt. We'll visit him later. This way, Lucy.'

Frances took my hand and we followed her father. Turning aside from the central section of the Valley where scores of tourists and donkey boys were milling about, and hawkers were noisily over-charging for candles and magnesium flares, he led us to the right, into a narrowing wadi where the rocks either side protected us from the sun; within a few yards, the tourists became inaudible and silence enclosed us.

'It's the longest, deepest tomb in the Valley,' Frances whispered. 'It's pitch dark and terribly hot. You won't be afraid, Lucy? It goes down and down for ever.'

Winlock came to a halt. Squinting up at the sun, he said: 'Lucy, I want you to listen – and Frances, given your remarks at lunch, it won't hurt if you listen too. You spoke of treasure – now, I want you to think about the implications of that word. I want you to think about this place. Try to put aside all preconceptions and consider what it signified to the man for whom it was made.' He gestured towards the dark gape of the entrance, and said: 'Right, lecture begins.

'Seti chose this wadi as the site of his tomb, I expect because he wanted to be buried next to his father, Ramesses I – that's his tomb, Lucy, over there. You see how secluded it is now? Try to imagine how remote and hidden it was then. Work on Seti's tomb would have begun long before he came to the throne and it continued throughout his reign. He employed the greatest architects, goldsmiths, painters and sculptors of his era. The most powerful spells known to his priests were recorded on the tomb walls – and there was a reason for that. These tombs are not about death, Lucy: never make that mistake – they're about *conquering* death. Everything in them is designed to ensure safe passage through the underworld and an afterlife that would never end. Seti would have been buried inside three magnificent coffins, Lucy, with a solid gold portrait mask covering his face, and with the flail and the crook – they were the symbols of his power – in his hands. Inside the mummification bandages, his priests secreted jewels, weapons and amulets to protect his body eternally. And on his chest, they placed a single, huge scarab: that was there to protect him during the Weighing of the Heart ceremony, as Frances knows: its weight prevented his heart from crying out, you see, and confessing its sins . . .

'His three coffins would have been installed inside a vast calcite sarcophagus – we know about that sarcophagus for sure, because it's in London now, at the Soane Museum, Lucy: you should go and look at it one of these days. And that sarcophagus would have been surrounded by four protective wooden shrines – we know that from descriptions on papyri – each of them panelled in sheet gold. But that's just the bare details of his funeral chamber, the Holy of Holies: as you'll see, the approach to it goes three hundred feet deep into the rock. There are seven corridors leading to the Burial Chamber, and ten ante-rooms off them. In those rooms, his priests piled treasure upon treasure: there were magnificent things – golden chariots, weaponry, thrones and jewels – but also practical, useful things, like linen and looking glasses and tools; they left board games and musical instruments, so, in the afterlife, the pharaoh might never be bored . . . And there were *shabti* figures, of course – hundreds of them, so every task in the afterlife could be performed for Seti by his servants just as they had been in his lifetime.

'People think these burials were all about glory and display, as Miss Mackenzie claimed over lunch,' he went on. 'And that's true to a degree, of course. But they were also thoughtful, Lucy, when they supplied these tombs: thoughtful – and loving too. The priests wanted to ensure the pharaoh's happiness and well-being in the afterlife, so they left him with food and grain and meat and wines. They provided him with medicinal ointments and sweet-smelling oils, and left him lamps so he need never endure the dark. Those who mourned him decorated his tomb with flower wreaths, just as we do now . . . ' He hesitated and his voice caught. 'I've seen examples of such wreaths, in fact we have some at the Met, and it always moves me to look at them . . . They're beautiful, Lucy, woven from olive and palm leaves, interlaced with beads, decorated with blue lotus, cornflowers and nightshade berries. They're joyous things – not like the funereal tributes we send now. The ones we have at the museum are in a near-perfect state of preservation, yet it's three thousand years since the funeral for which they were made.'

He fell silent and looked along the wadi, his face clouded and his eyes sad. Frances reached for my hand and clasped it tight. I wondered if they were thinking of other, much more recent funerals, as I was; perhaps the burial of the little son who died when his father was on a different continent, fighting a war – and maybe they were, for Frances wiped her eyes, and Winlock remained quiet, his gaze averted.

After a while, he gave himself a shake and said in a newly hesitant way: 'Where was I? Ah yes: the death of kings . . . Lucy, all those things I've just described, are you imagining them? The Burial Chamber, the shrines, the treasures – can you see them?'

When I nodded, he said in a new brusque way: 'Good. Go on imagining. Imagine very hard – because they've gone. None of it is here. Not the chariots or the shrines or the golden coffins . . . there's not one stick of treasure left. All the loving tributes disappeared long, long ago. That's true of this tomb – and, to a greater or lesser degree, of every single one ever found in the Valley. There isn't one that wasn't rifled. The spells, the amulets, the goddesses and the guards, even the slow, hideous process of execution by impaling that was inflicted on all tomb robbers who were captured – *none* of it could protect Seti from human avarice. All that is left of him – and a poor forked creature he is – you saw in a glass case in the Egyptian Museum in Cairo.

'Meanwhile, I've come prepared,' he added, turning towards the dark entrance to the tomb. 'No candles for us, and none of those infernal magnesium flares either. The smoke and the chemicals damage the wall paintings – and the ones here are magnificent, as you're about to see, Lucy. Also, the flares and the candles can go out and then you're left in the dark. That's unpleasant: it once frightened Frances badly.' He turned with a smile to ruffle Frances's hair, then handed us the torches. 'New flashlights and new batteries, and I'm with you, so there's nothing to fear. Are you ready? I want you to use your eyes: the two eyes you've been blessed with and your mind's eye as well. You'll need all three. The dead await us. In we go.'

And down, down, down we went, descending flight after flight of crumbling steps, negotiating a rough wooden bridge over a deep black well-shaft; into one great subterranean hall, and then on again down more steps and along more hot dark corridors until I felt we must be a mile underground . . . and then forgot distance, because every step of the way we were accompanied – by depictions of the dead king himself on his journey to eternity, and by an escort of gods and goddesses, Ra, Aten and Isis, her green protective kite wings outspread in the beams of our flashlights.

The deeper we went, the quieter my mind became – Winlock had been right about that three-thousand-year effect; all the turmoil of the day seemed to slip away from me. I could recognise only some of the painted gods that lined the corridors, but I could feel the reassurance of their power. I could sense something else too: I took it for fear at first, and then decided it was holiness. It was the first time I'd ever experienced such a thing. I've sensed it on many occasions in the long decades since – it's caught me unawares, surprised me in the hush of an English country church, stolen upon me in a mosque or a temple. But the first time I ever truly felt *that* breath on the back of my neck was in Seti's tomb, when we reached the last room, three hundred feet into the rock, the final space that Winlock had called the Holy of Holies.

When we came to that last chamber, her father hung back, and Frances took my hand. She switched off my flashlight, and then her own, and we stood side by side in the absolute dark. 'Now, look up, Lucy,' Frances whispered.

She switched on the torch again, training its beam across the high vaulted ceiling of the Burial Chamber. It curved over us, I saw, so wondrously beautiful and strange that I gasped: a blue night sky of planets, constellations and their ruling deities, still protecting a dead king whose body now lay five hundred miles away in a glass case in a museum. The gods' hands were spilling stars and their eyes were eternally watchful; the paint was as fresh as if it had been applied yesterday.

We stayed longer than intended in the underworld of the tombs and visited more of them than perhaps Winlock had first planned. When we finally emerged from the last, the sun was beginning to set in a sky stained the purple of blackberries. The tourists and their guides had long gone: just three boys were waiting for us in the distance, at the donkey shelter where the two branches of the Valley divided. We began to walk back, Winlock striding ahead, Frances and me lagging behind. None of us spoke. The heat of the day was already being sucked back into the sky, and the air was chill. I shivered.

My donkey was docile, old and reluctant to move. I stroked the coarse cross of fur on her neck and whispered words of encouragement, while the boy in charge of her, skipping behind, gave her an assortment of slaps and barefooted kicks, all of which she ignored. She proceeded on, at an obstinate arthritic pace, and gradually the gap between me and the Winlocks widened. By the time I approached the soaring rock spur that marked the throat of the Valley and its exit, I was fifty yards behind, and Frances and her father were already out of sight. I looked back – knowing the Valley would be deserted, yet sure I'd glimpse the spirits who reclaimed it when darkness fell. In the velvety creeping dusk I did see a man's shape and, for one second, took him for a ghost. Then I realised that it was Howard Carter; perhaps waiting for the Valley to empty of people, he had now returned to occupy it.

He was standing in the belly of the Valley, at the navel point marked by the tomb of Ramesses VI. I watched him clamber up a high mound of scree by the mouth of that tomb. Hatless and in his shirtsleeves, he started off at a run, but it was a reeling, ungainly climb; he missed his footing several times, whirling his arms to get his balance. When he finally reached the summit, he stood there, scowling at air. The declining sun silhouetted his figure, and as I looked back, I saw him stoop, pick up a stone and hurl it against the rock face behind him. First one stone, then another, then violent handfuls of them in rapid succession – in the clear air, I could hear their ricochet, like a spatter of gunfire.

My donkey, tired and refractory, had come to a halt at the mouth of the Valley; the boy gave her a hard smack on her rump. She kicked out at him and shied, nearly dislodging me from the saddle. By the time I'd regained my balance and she'd been persuaded to move on again, Carter had flung himself down on the shale, with his back against a rock.

Looking back one last time, I saw him take a flask from his pocket; there was a flash of silver as he raised it and drained its contents. We rounded the rocks, and set off at a sober pace for the American House, leaving Carter alone, in possession of the Valley.

The next morning, when we were at breakfast at the American House, a handwritten note was delivered to Helen. We were coming to the end of our meal: Frances and I were sitting at the foot of the long refectory table; most of the working archaeologists, including the amiable Harry Burton, had left by then. Minnie Burton remained, seated near the table's head. She had eaten a large breakfast, helping herself to bacon, eggs and pancakes, kept warm in chafing dishes on a sideboard. Now she was delicately munching toast and marmalade, with her head bent over a book that she'd continued to read through-out the meal. She looked up and watched the delivery of this note with close interest, I saw -- but then Minnie kept an eye on all activ-ities at the house, and very little escaped her scrutiny. Helen read it, smiled, shook her head and showed the note to her husband, on his way out of the door and late for his dig.

'Astonishing.' Winlock laughed. 'That's the nearest thing to an apology you'll ever get from Carter. Consider yourselves honoured.'

The note was handed to Miss Mack, who raised her eyebrows but made no comment; finally, since we were also addressed, it was passed to Frances and to me. It read:

My dear Helen, likewise Miss Mackenzie, Frances and Lucie,

I shall be at my dig in the Valley today and you are welcome to visit it should that prospect be of interest. If it appeels I can offer you tea afterwards at my 'Castle' hoping it will,

Sincerely yours,

Howard Carter

'He can't spell, Myrtle. Never could.' Helen sighed. 'Or punctuate. Or, indeed, bring himself to apologise. In fact, he's impossible
and an unmannerly bear, but—'

'It's a charming note. Touching in its way.'

'Shall I accept? I'd love you and Lucy to see Carter's house. We
could go this afternoon? His boy Hosein is waiting for an answer.'

'Can we rely on his temper this time, do you suppose?' Miss Mack
asked, in a dry tone.

'Not in the least. But let's risk it, shall we? Come and help me,
Myrtle – I think I should write a *very* ceremonious reply, don't you?'

The two women left us. Minnie Burton ostentatiously turned a
page of her book. 'Well, well,' she said. 'Lunch with Carnarvon and
Carter yesterday. Castle Carter this afternoon. Aren't you popular
little girls?'

'I guess we must be, Mrs Burton,' Frances replied demurely, her
tone a precisely judged one millimetre away from insolence. 'I
wonder why?'

'I wonder too.' Minnie looked up and gave us both an appraising
stare. 'One thing you can be sure of – Howard Carter never bothers
with people unless they are useful to him. So either you two have
been useful to him already, or he plans to make use of you very soon.
Which would you say it was, my dear?'

'Gee, I can't think,' Frances answered, in an innocent tone. 'I guess
it's just that he *likes* us. He says Lucy has remarkable powers of observation.'

'Does he indeed? How flattering. And do you share her abilities?'

'What, me, Mrs Burton? Gosh, no. I just goof around. I make him
laugh, maybe.'

'Well, I can't say I share his sense of humour.' Minnie's cold blue
eyes rested first on Frances's face, then on mine. 'In my day, children
spoke rather less than you do, Frances. They endeavoured to be seen
and *not* heard.'

'Then we go one better,' Frances smartly replied. 'We try not to
be heard *or* seen, Mrs Burton. We endeavour to be *invisible*. And we
often succeed.'

There was a silence, and it was not a comfortable one. 'And so I
am beginning to realise,' Minnie replied at last, colour mounting in
her cheeks. She rose to her feet, frowning. 'Most amusing. All I will

say, Frances, to you and your little friend, is that your private jokes may entertain you, but they do not entertain *me*. You may smirk to your hearts' content, and no doubt consider yourselves very clever – but you know the expression "He who laughs last, laughs longest"? You'll discover the truth of that one of these days.'

She picked up her book, marked her place in it with an old envelope, tucked it under her arm and left us. Frances made a face at her departing back.

'Oh well done,' I said. 'Brilliant, Frances. Now she knows we're spies.'

'She knew anyway. She must have worked it out – she's not stupid. She must have seen us on the terrace at Shepheard's and now she's put two and two together. What do I care? There's nothing she can do anyway. She wouldn't dare say a word about Poppy, not after that dressing-down Lord Carnarvon gave her . . . except, what did that last remark of hers mean? Could you see the title of that book she was reading?'

'No. I looked, but she kept her hand over it. Could you?'

'I tried but she was too quick. It was too fat to be a novel – Queen Min doesn't stoop to fiction anyway, she's a snob about books *and* people. A biography? Some reference thing? You saw the way she kind of flourished it and hid it at the same time?'

'I did. Was it one of the books from the library here, maybe? I thought I could see some kind of stamp on the cover.'

'I'll check. Anyway, it's a clue, Lucy. We'll keep a watch on her – she's up to something.'

Burton-watching was a fine game; we tried hard to keep it up after breakfast, but our spying activities were thwarted time and again. Frances checked the American House library, stacked with works of archaeological reference in the main, but the results were inconclusive. For the rest of that morning, we were kept occupied. Neither Helen nor Miss Mack approved of idleness, so we were banished to our room to practise our ballet steps, then spent an hour over hieroglyphs and Egyptian history on the veranda; finally, easels were set up for us outside the house, so we could paint industrious watercolours of the Theban hills.

Minnie Burton reappeared as Frances and I were embarking on our watercolours, remarking acidly to Helen that it was good to see the children occupied for once. 'Maybe Frances will inherit your talents, Helen,' she said sweetly. 'I was saying to Harry the other day, *such* a pity you never trained – for an amateur, you really do paint so charmingly. You must do a little sketch of me, one day – just as a keepsake, you know.'

'Beyond my powers. I know my limitations.'

'You're too modest. I don't mean a full-scale portrait, nothing ambitious, dear.'

'Minnie, I'd never do you justice. The result would be unflattering. You must excuse me – I need to get the girls organised. Now, where did I leave my spectacles?'

Helen extricated herself, and, once Frances and I were engaged on our paintings, retreated to the far end of the veranda to sit in peace with Miss Mack. Minnie Burton, watched carefully by Frances and me, settled herself in a planter's chair and opened her book. She studied it minutely, turning its pages back and forth, while Frances and I concentrated hard on being invisible. I painted a tight circle of toothed rocks, but my sky-paint ran down and ruined them. Frances painted a route through the rocks that was purely imagined: no such view was visible from this vantage point. Then, bored with the inanimate, she added a figure in an unlikely hat, which she claimed was Jones, the sad tubercular Welsh archaeologist, gazing at the Theban hills and seeing his homeland. When the luncheon gong sounded from the depths of the house our opportunity finally came. The adults were scarcely through the doors before Frances was on the veranda, the suspicious book in her hand.

'KV,' she said, as I reached her side. 'Quick. She's forgotten it at last. Sit on it. If she comes looking for it, say you haven't seen it. Give me two seconds, Lucy. Don't move.'

The weighty book, its leather cover stamped with the Met's insignia and, as suspected, borrowed from the American House library, proved to be *Burke's Peerage and Baronetage*. I sat on it. Minnie Burton, fond of food, always punctual for meals, querulously eager to find fault with Mrs Lythgoe's menus, must have been distracted. She did not return in quest of the book – but a few minutes later an excited Frances reappeared; she had a cut-throat razor in her hand.

'I knew it!' she said, snatching *Burke's* from me. 'It's Mrs Lythgoe's copy. She keeps tons of this stuff, umpteen volumes of the Social

Register, and the *Almanach de Gotha* as well – they help with all the precedence and placement nonsense when she gives a big dinner here. And we're in luck – just in time! Queen Min's reached page 250 – she's halfway through the "G" section. She's working her way through it alphabetically, because she doesn't know the exact name to look up. But I do. Thank goodness she hadn't got as far as "H", then we'd have been in trouble . . . Wait a second, let me find it – now hold the book steady. Oh, perfect, I can cut it here, and here, and the whole section will come out cleanly. Unless she looks at the page numbers, *which* she won't, she'll never know.'

With an unwavering hand, Frances flicked the razor open and sliced through the paper. She handed me the two-page section she'd removed, inverted the book, shook it to ensure no other pages had come loose, and replaced it on the table. This surgical operation took less than a minute. We raced back inside the house, and were chattering in the hall, when Frances hissed 'KV' again as Mrs Burton emerged from the dining room.

'Did I leave my book outside?' She glared at us as she passed. 'What a mess you're in. Paint all over your faces – you look like two little savages.'

'I didn't notice your book, sorry, Mrs Burton. Just going to wash,' Frances called over her shoulder, and dragged me down the corridor. She nipped into her parents' bedroom, replaced her father's razor on the washstand, then pulled me into the American House's bathroom, bolting the door.

'Old witch,' she said, leaning against the doors. 'I knew she was looking for something – and that's it, near the beginning of the "H" section, right there.'

She jabbed a finger at the second page she'd extracted. I peered at the small print, trying to make sense of the peculiar abbreviations *Burke's* employed. The meaty section Frances was indicating spelled out the lineage of a family of Hampshire baronets named 'Hallowes'. At the end of the long list, I came to the last of their line, a Captain Sir Roland Hallowes, MC, DSO. No issue; he had died five years previously, unmarried, aged twenty-one, in 1917 at the Battle of Arras.

'I don't understand,' I said. 'Who are these Hallowes people? Why would Mrs Burton be trying to look them up?'

'Go up a line.'

I did as she bid. I saw that Captain Sir Roland had two sisters, named Octavia and Poppea; all three were the children of one Sir Quentin Hallowes, deceased 1912. I stared at these sisters' names, dates of birth and marriage details: a familiar sick, smoky unease began to swirl around in my mind.

'Tell me it isn't. Frances, it can't be . . .'

'Of course it is. This edition is out of date, so it only cites Poppea's first marriage – but that would have been enough: as soon as Mrs Burton saw that, she'd know she was on track. Poppea is Poppy, of course – and Roland was her brother. Poppy told me about him once, he nearly got a posthumous VC. He was stupendously brave – well, Poppy's brave too, in her way. He was in a cavalry regiment. They charged their horses straight at a German machine-gun emplacement and every single man was—'

'That can't be right. Frances, look – this Poppea's father is dead. He died ten years ago.'

'I know. Poppy adored him. She talks about him all the time.'

'But he *can't* be dead. He's at his villa in France, he fell ill very suddenly, the doctors thought it was pneumonia, Poppy's with him now.'

'Oh, Lucy – don't tell me you believed that!'

'Of course I believed it. Lord Carnarvon explained it. He was as clear as could be.'

'I know – wasn't he brilliant? I wish I could tell lies that well. But it was a white lie, and told for honourable reasons to protect Poppy, so it's just a fib, anyway. Queen Min must have suspected and she was trying to make sure – well, she won't now!'

I turned away to the washbasin. The tap gushed rusty water. I washed all the yellows and scarlets and blues from my hands. My watercolour had been a runny mess: I couldn't paint, I couldn't detect lies, I was useless as an observer, truth eluded me. I thought of Rose and Peter; of a small boy waving from the hotel balcony. After a long pause, I looked up. Frances was drying her hands. 'So if none of that was true,' I asked carefully, 'if Poppy isn't in France with her father, where is she?'

For the first time I saw doubt and anxiety betray themselves in Frances's eyes. 'I don't know. I don't think *anyone* knows. No one will tell me anything, Lucy – I'm as much in the dark as you are.'

'But Rose and Peter think she's on her way back now. What lies have *they* been told? Rose must know their grandfather's dead, even if Peter doesn't understand.'

'I don't *know* what they were told. Maybe that Poppy is with friends. No one wants them to worry. You mustn't tell them, Lucy — promise me.'

'I won't say a word — of course I won't. But it's so cruel and wrong to let them think she's coming back any moment — Frances, anything could have happened, Poppy could have gone anywhere, it might be *months* before she deigns to show up again. Oh, this is horrible! I can't think why I liked her, why I was taken in by her. I don't believe she cares for them at all — if she loved Rose and Peter, she'd never put them through this. No mother would. She's nothing but a selfish, vain, stupid woman.'

'She isn't. She isn't. Don't *say* that.'

Frances, bright-eyed, flushed, was angry, defensive and close to tears. I forgot sometimes that she was younger than I was. Not that those years made any difference: I felt hot and choked and close to tears too. I knew we'd quarrel if I pursued this, so I bit back my words and said nothing more. We went into lunch, and all through the meal these well-intentioned deceptions swirled around in my mind. Frances and I were caught up in them, and no doubt they'd prove harmless, but they left me with a sense of guilt and creeping unease. Frances, as always, recovered more successfully. Her quick inventive mind was already jumping ahead; by the time the meal was over and we'd been allowed to leave the table, she was already planning what to do with the purloined pages of *Burke's*. Our next task was vital, she said: we had to get rid of the evidence.

On the way back to our room, I suggested umpteen, simple, practical methods of achieving just that, but Frances, in a lordly way, dismissed them all. I began to suspect that, liking ceremonies as she did, she already had some solemn ritual, some hocus-pocus, in mind.

Before we left for the Valley, we just had time for the initial preparations. As soon as we were safe in our room, we tore up the stolen pages of *Burke's*: Frances would not rest until we'd reduced ancient lineage to unreadable confetti. She produced a small leather doll's purse, and all the confetti was stuffed inside. I could tell it hurt her to part with this, for Frances loved gaudy things — always plainly dressed by her mother, she could not resist anything brightly coloured. The purse, heart-shaped, rose-pink, fashioned from soft glove leather, was clearly much cherished; even I could see it was an appropriate container for Poppy's secrets, so it was agreed the little purse would be hidden and 'sacrificed'. I think Frances, with her queer imagination, felt that if sacrifice were involved, Poppy would quickly return and all would be well. She was, to her fingertips, her father's child, an archaeologist's daughter: she had reason to know how capricious the gods could be, and how essential it was to propitiate them.

Frances secreted the purse, and took it to the Valley that afternoon, but if she had some specific ritual or hiding place in mind, she refused to divulge it. The site of Carter's dig proved to be deep in a remote arm of the Valley; it was near the tomb of a pharaoh called Siptah, first discovered about seventeen years before. I'd seen Siptah's broken body at the Egyptian Museum: he had a pitifully deformed, withered foot, perhaps the result of polio, Frances's father had suggested. When we arrived at the site of this crippled king's tomb, the scene was so bewildering that I soon forgot Frances's secret plans. True to his scheme, Carter was removing the tons of spoil in front of Siptah's burial place; until I actually witnessed it, I'd not realised how gargantuan a task that was. The floor of the Valley resembled the interior of a vast quarry – indeed, much of it *was* a quarry, a place where thousands upon thousands of tons of limestone and flint chippings had been dug out of the hills for centuries, to be discarded at random.

Tall plumes of white dust billowed up from the site, gusting and swirling in the burning air; they were visible from afar and chokingly thick when close. Carter himself was white as a ghost, smeared in dust from head to foot, as were his Arab basket boys and workmen. There must have been forty men on the site, digging, hoeing, sifting and shovelling, and there were even more boys, perhaps a hundred of them, some of them my own age and many much younger, fleet of foot, nimble and acrobatic, dodging among the rocks, removing the spoil in rush baskets. It was being sieved, inspected, then loaded into open crates on a manually operated railway system – a Decauville track, Carter explained, jumping down from the heaps of spoil, and striding forward to greet us.

'Cost Carnarvon a pretty packet,' he announced with a wide grin.

'Worth its weight in gold. Can't think how we ever managed without it – cuts the labour time in half, means we can shift the spoil well away from the Valley floor, and dump it where it can't do any harm. The men fill the crates, push them the length of the line, then lift the rails at the back, refix them at the front, and off we go again! Clicks together like a Meccano set – best toy I ever had! We can shift the stuff half a mile, more, in next to no time – Helen, Miss Mackenzie – you don't mind the dust? Come and see the progress we're making. Frances, introduce Lucy to Girigar, he's looking forward to seeing you.'

I'd never seen Carter in such ebullient spirits; he seemed immune to the dust, and unaffected by the cacophony of noise, the clamour of voices. Miss Mack and Helen lowered the veils they'd pinned to their hats, and began to pick their way gingerly through the treacherous spoil. Carter strode ahead of them, laughing and gesturing. No reference to the ugly scene after lunch the previous day, no trace of the man I'd glimpsed, alone in the Valley, hurling stones at the rock face.

'This way, Lucy,' Frances said, 'follow me.' She led me up a narrow path, skirting the area where the men were labouring. We mounted a small rise some distance away, where the dust was a little less choking. There we discovered a peculiar structure that resembled a cage; its roof was shaded with canvas, its sides constructed of finely pierced metal, like a fly screen in a pantry. It had muslin curtains and contained a single chair, well padded. The cage was unoccupied.

'Lord Carnarvon's,' Frances said. 'Protects him from the flies. And the dust. He's stayed at the hotel today: some people are arriving from Cairo, officials, I think – bigwigs, anyway, and Eve said they had to see them. But when Carnarvon is at the dig, which is most days, that's where he sits.'

'In that?' I stared at the cage. 'But what does he do?'

'Well, he can keep an eye on things, of course – it's a good vantage point. And then he reads, I guess. Dozes off, I expect. Thinks about his ancestral acres and his stud and his racehorses. Dreams of discovering treasure, maybe.' She grinned. 'Who knows? You don't expect an English lord to get his hands dirty, do you? If they find anything – which mostly they don't – Mr Carter sends an emissary, and Lordy ventures out, and then they examine it together, and

Carnarvon looks at some bit of old pottery, or an ostraca if they're lucky, and he says, "Oh I say, well *done,* my dear fellow, jolly interesting." And then he goes back to his cage again.'

The imitation of Carnarvon's drawling tones was exact: Frances was a pitiless mimic.

'But doesn't he get bored?' I asked.

'Bored to tears, I should think – wouldn't you? Eve's always here with him, and she tries to keep him entertained – she's so saintly and sweet-tempered, she really *works* at it. I guess it was all right in the early days, before the war, when he and Mr Carter first excavated together. They weren't in the Valley then, and they made lots of good finds. But since they came here – years of work, and almost nothing to show for it, think of it, Lucy! Lordy must be losing heart. He enjoys the Winter Palace, I think, the dinners and parties and his friends visiting – and he enjoys *buying* things, of course . . . '

She gave me a narrow look. 'Thanks to Mr Carter, he's built up a wonderful Egyptian collection, you know – Daddy says it's one of the best private collections in the world. Lordy has a very good eye, and Mr Carter has an even better one, so there's that consolation. But it must be dawning on him that it's easier to buy beautiful things than it is to dig them up – I mean, look!' She gestured to the army toiling below us. 'All that labour, and they could still miss some glorious tomb by a foot, two feet.'

'If it exists. If it hasn't been rifled.'

'That too. Come and meet Girigar.' Pointing out a small tent, she drew me towards it. 'He's been Mr Carter's *reis* for decades now – before that he worked for the Welshman, Harold Jones. Mr Carter says Girigar has the sharpest eyes in the Valley . . . Oh, it's so hot. Aren't the flies awful?'

Reaching the tent, we retreated into its stuffy airless shade. There I was introduced to Girigar, Carter's foreman, a thin, elderly man, who greeted us with great ceremony. He lit a primus stove, plied us with tea and opened a tin of Rich Tea biscuits. Taking me to the mouth of the tent, he courteously explained the system of excavation being used. I had the impression that he expected few discoveries at this particular site. Meanwhile, he took pride in the fact that this was, in part, a family endeavour: two of the overseers were his brothers, he said; the tall man supervising the Decauville track was his eldest son, and the very small boy – the one carrying the water flask – that was his grandson, six years old tomorrow, a bad boy, up to a thousand tricks.

'What is his name?' I asked.

'Ahmed.' He rolled his eyes. 'Years he's been pestering me, "Grandfather, let me come to the Valley, let me work like the other boys, look how strong I am!" Finally, I talk to Mr Carter and I say, "Mr Carter, sir, this year, let us find work for my grandson, who bears my name, and is a good, industrial, hard-working boy, and will do you pride," and Mr Carter says, "Ahmed Girigar, since it is you who ask, I agree," and so the boy comes . . . and what does he do? He falls asleep. He plays. One ambition this boy has and one only: to ride on the railway, bouncing along, falling off and getting his skull bashed in. I have told him: do that once, I forgive. Do it twice, and I beat you so bad you fall down.' Girigar smiled mournfully. 'A lie, miss. I'm an old fool, who dotes on this naughty grandson too much. But he doesn't know that: watch.'

Issuing from the tent, Girigar shook his fist and bellowed a stream of vituperation. His little grandson, who had slunk off to a shady corner where he'd been engaged in a fine game, making stones skip, leapt to his feet and scurried off to refill his leather water flask. He nearly collided with Miss Mack and Helen, now covered in white dust, who were retreating to the refuge of the tent. Girigar at once busied himself boiling fresh water for tea. Frances, who had been silent and thoughtful all this while, scanning the rocks below, grabbed my hand. 'Quick,' she whispered. 'Now's our chance, Lucy.'

Telling her mother we were going to inspect the Decauville in all its splendour, she drew me from the tent into the rolling clouds of white dust below. When she was sure that we were safely out of sight, she led me aside, into the confines of a narrow wadi on the opposite side of the Valley. We ran up it, until we were well away from the workmen and hidden from prying eyes. We came to a halt, flushed and sweating, in a space encircled by tall, fluted rocks. The heat was intense, the baking air sullen and unmoving. From her pocket Frances produced the small pink purse with its confetti of evidence. 'Now we dig,' she said. 'By this stone here. It's the perfect marker.'

I looked uncertainly at the stone. Weathered, rounded, deeply fissured, rose-red, it was taller than a man, sculpted by sand and wind into a suggestion of a female shape. It had stony breasts, curves that might have been thighs and hips and, if you squinted, blind eyes in a beautiful, passionless face. I reached up to stroke the stone's long tresses, which lay in limestone rivulets about its slender, vulnerable neck. Something moved in those tresses. I drew sharply back. 'What about scorpions?' I said.

'Oh, for goodness' sake, Lucy! We're only digging a little hole. Get on with it.'

We both knelt down and dug into the sand and soil at the base of the stone. This proved difficult, for it was heavily compacted: the crumbling lime, soaked by floodwaters after rains, had formed a substance that was unyielding, like half-set cement. We removed a sandal each, and dug with them. Stoutly made, and of tough leather, these were a good tool: after fifteen minutes' sweating labour, with torn hands and broken nails, we had achieved a hiding place about a foot deep. Frances hauled me to my feet, told me to bow my head and concentrate, and embarked on what she claimed was a sacred prayer to the powerful sisters Isis and Nephthys: it would ensure a swift return for Poppy, preserve her secrets eternally, and cause confusion to her enemies — Mrs Burton being top of the enemies' list. I suspected this prayer was more of Frances's made-up mumbo-jumbo, but she uttered it with such conviction, and on such a weird imploring keening note, that it took effect. I too began to believe. I closed my eyes and offered up a silent invocation: I felt it eddying out from me, into the hot still air, up, up, up into the blue empyrean where the kites circled and the gods awaited.

'Beloved and revered goddesses,' Frances chanted, switching to English. 'O Isis, O Nephthys, may your wings enfold and protect the secrets of our friend, Poppy d'Erlanger, and may they carry her back to us and Rose and Peter without delay.' Frances paused. Then she added: 'Now, Lucy: give me your *ankh*.'

'What?' I took a step back. 'You never mentioned that. I will not.'

'I know you've got it on you. You always have. We *both* have to make a sacrifice, or it won't work.'

'That *ankh* was a present. It's special.'

'I *know* it's special. That's the whole point. It has to be something you really love. I'm sacrificing Poppy's lipstick. Look.' She produced the lipstick from her pocket, and examined it sadly. 'Come on,

Lucy – give me that *ankh*. Hand it over. No grumbling. When you make an offering, you have to do it with a glad heart, surely you know that?'

I thought this was pushing it, but in the end I gave in. With great care, we placed the *ankh* and the lipstick in the hole; we each gave the pink purse a ceremonial kiss and gently lowered it on top of them. We knelt down again on the hot sand, joined hands, and refilled the burial place. As we did so, we felt a sudden change in the air: the faintest of breezes shivered across our skin – Frances said this meant the twin goddesses were responding. When we had finished stamping on the sand, all trace of our excavation had disappeared; the soil looked as it had before: mute, undisturbed for millennia.

We turned back to the main Valley and, as we reached it, saw to our surprise that the workmen were already downing tools, although it was still only three in the afternoon; one of them greeted us with a warning gesture and a grimace; he shouted something in Arabic and gestured upwards. Tilting my head back, I saw the sky was changing colour with astonishing speed – air blue, darkening to a bruised mauve. Above the summit of el-Qurn in the distance there was now a spreading stain of dark purple, as if the sky had begun bleeding.

'Storm coming,' Carter shouted, striding towards us. 'The wind's getting up – can you feel it? Rain any minute . . .'

As he spoke, the hot dry air, so motionless for days, came alive: it tugged at my hat, and scraped a razor down my arms. The sand at my feet begin to crawl away from my shoes, as if shifting on a tide of thronging invisible insects.

'I've sent for the donkeys – they'll be here soon.' Carter came to a halt, and shouted up at the tent: 'Girigar, tell the ladies we need to leave at once. If we go now, we'll make it back to my house before the rain starts.' He shouted some last instruction in Arabic, then swung back to us: I'd never seen him look more exhilarated – almost exulting.

'About time the Valley put on one of its shows, eh, Frances? Don't be scared, Lucy – we'll be back at Castle Carter before the worst of it hits.' He turned and pointed to el-Qurn, where the swirling clouds were now black, torn into rags and tatters. 'Feel it?' He yelled the question. 'Feel the electricity?'

As he said that, I suddenly felt the charge: *KV, KV* – the hot air pulsed with energy, thousands of volts, fizzing, incendiary. Frances and I ran for the donkeys, but before we reached them, the first stinging squall of rain came in. We ducked our heads, clung on to our hats, and ran faster. I heard the wind come hissing along the Valley; as we reached the donkeys and clambered astride them, I looked back. Above the hills, over the high pyramid point that was the cobra-goddess Meretseger's domain, the clouds coiled. The sky simmered and swirled, cracked wide, and spat out the first forked tongue of lightning.

16

By the time we reached the shelter of Castle Carter, the sky was black and afternoon had become night. At the house gates, there came a huge, deafening thunder clap and the sky released a deluge. Carter, who had escorted us out, had ridden ahead for the last hundred yards to alert Abd-el-Aal; we found the servants were waiting for us. They came running out into the yard, splashing through pools of water, holding lamps, grabbing at the reins of the nervous shying donkeys, and urging us inside. 'Quick, miss, quick,' the boy Hosein said, pulling me down from the saddle. 'Fire lit, dry off, tea soon – good storm, English rain – run now, yes?'

Frances and I ran: there was a car parked outside Carter's entrance, and we had to dodge around that; it was less than ten feet to the shelter of the veranda and yet in that short distance we were soaked. We hurried inside, swiftly followed by Miss Mack, wringing out her old-fashioned voluminous skirt, and by Helen, who was laughing and excited. 'Oh these Valley storms,' she cried. 'Wasn't that spectacular? Did you *see* that lightning, Myrtle? Look at my poor hat – silly thing, it's completely drowned. Lord knows how we'll get home in this. Frances, Lucy – are you all right? Heavens, you're both soaked to the skin. Abd-el-Aal, do you have some towels – some rugs, perhaps?'

'Warming by fire, this way, please,' Abd-el-Aal replied, ushering us ahead into a hall. From behind us came the sound of running foot-steps, of shutters being slammed against the storm. Hosein, bringing up the rear, swung the entrance door closed and barred it – and I suddenly understood why Carter's house had acquired the name 'Castle'. It might not have battlements, a moat or a drawbridge, but it had its defences all the same. The storm was now shut out, the wail and the thump of the wind diminished to a whisper – and I could imagine how these defences would slam shut to protect Carter from anyone he regarded as an enemy. Given Carter's character, there'd no doubt be numerous candidates. 'This way, this way,' Abd-el-Aal, was saying. 'Hosein, more firewood, tea double quick – through here, honoured ladies.'

He threw open a door, bowed, and stood back to admit us. Helen entered first, then we all bundled into the sanctum of Carter's sitting room. I found myself in a square, pleasant space, lit by oil lamps and the flames of a huge banked fire. Removing my wet hat, rubbing rainwater from my eyes, I had a quick glimpse of bookcases, of maps, of plain plastered walls, a bright woven rug, and of welcoming chairs grouped around the fire; of a place where a man could be comfortably alone, and perhaps often was.

'What a marvellous fire! Quickly, girls, come and dry off,' Miss Mack was saying, extricating herself from the huddle we'd formed by the door. Leading the way, she was advancing towards the fireplace, her hands held out to the warmth of the flames, when she came to a halt so suddenly that we all cannoned into her. She said, 'Gracious, Mr Carter – I didn't see you. Oh, I'm sorry, we're interrupting you—'

Helen, who had been blocking my view, took a small step backwards; she appeared nonplussed, perhaps embarrassed. Peeping around her, I saw to my surprise that Carter was indeed already there – and that he had a guest. He'd been bending forward over a wing chair to the right of the fire, and had been speaking to its occupant in a low voice as we entered. Somehow he'd contrived to wash and change his clothes in the short interval since he'd ridden off ahead of us: he was now dust-free, improbably sleek and spruce in clean country tweeds. The occupant of the chair remained hidden from where we stood – but as Carter straightened and hastily stepped away, I realised that the tall back of the chair was concealing someone female. I could see two slender silk-stockinged legs, the pleated edge of a skirt that was inches shorter than any that Helen, let alone Miss Mack, would have countenanced, and a pair of exquisite snakeskin shoes, with little heels, a strap across the instep and gold buckles.

I stared at those shoes. Frances gave a low gasp. The same idea entered both our heads at the same moment; our eyes met, hers alight with triumph. Her offerings and prayers had *worked*, I thought; I should never have doubted her. Isis and Nephthys had brought Poppy d'Erlanger back to us – and with astonishing speed. My heart lifted.

Miss Mack and Helen had also registered the woman's presence; they too had noted the haste with which Carter stepped back as we entered. Both now seemed rooted to the spot. I saw them exchange a quick interrogatory glance. A silence fell; it was broken not by Carter, who appeared incapable of speech, but by the occupant of the chair. The woman gave a muffled sound of distress, stood up and revealed herself: she was hatless, and her hair was dishevelled; her face was smudged with tears – or could it be the rain, had she been caught in the storm, as we had? I stared at this small, agitated stranger – I caught a drift of her scent. With a lurch of dismay, I recognised her. Not Mrs d'Erlanger.

'Oh, Helen – Miss Mack, thank God you're here,' Eve said, holding out her hands in an odd imploring way. 'I came over in the motorcar, I've been looking for you everywhere, I went to the American House, but they said you were in the Valley, so I started off for there . . . and then this awful storm came in out of nowhere, and everything was so *dark*. It was so *hellish* – the track turned into a river bed in seconds. I tried to turn back, and then I skidded, and the car got stuck and some natives pushed me out and I thought if I came here, Howard would—'

'Eve, Eve, sit down, dear,' Helen said, exchanging a quick anxious glance with Miss Mack. 'My dear, you're dreadfully overwrought – whatever has happened? Is it your father?'

I could see her thoughts, racing ahead: she was thinking of Carnarvon's collapse of the previous day, as I was. Frances was staring at Eve, white-faced. When Eve began crying, Helen took her hand.

'Eve, dear – try to explain. Is your father ill? Has he—'

'No, no – Pups is at the hotel now – he can't leave. But we thought, I thought, perhaps if you and Miss Mack . . . I don't know what to do. It's all so terrible. I need your help. I must talk to you . . . '

'Tea. I prescribe sweet tea.' Miss Mack advanced, helped Eve into her chair and with that air of quiet authority I remembered from my own sickroom in Cambridge, she turned to Carter. 'Mr Carter, it isn't for me to take charge, when we're guests in your house – but I think, if Lady Evelyn could have something to eat, and a quiet talk with Helen and me? The children must be hungry after this adventure of ours, but I wonder . . . is there another room, where they could sit while we have our talk? Just until Evelyn feels calmer?'

I expected Carter to demur. There was something I'd glimpsed between him and Eve as he'd bent over her chair, an intimacy that was unexpected, quite unlike their usual friendly, bantering demeanour. I felt he'd take affront at being effectively banished from her and his own hearth – but he gave no sign of it, and even seemed grateful for Miss Mack's intervention. 'Certainly,' he replied. 'Of course. Yes . . . very sensible. We'll have our tea across the hall in my study. Frances, Lucy – come with me.'

He ushered us quickly from the room – so quickly that I felt he was glad to escape. Encountering Abd-el-Aal and Hosein outside the door, both carrying laden trays, he gave a series of quick commands in Arabic.

'Well, you two look like drowned rats,' he said, in a cheerful way, leading us into a room opposite, a small, spartan space that contained a desk, some armchairs and bookshelves. 'Right, now let's get organised, shall we? Frances – the fire's already laid, here's some matches, will you light it for us? And Lucy, you see that chest over there? That's full of plaids and picnic rugs, I don't want you two dying of pneumonia, so get those out, and wrap yourselves up and sit by the fire. How pale you both are! I expect the storm shook you up a bit. Tea will be here in a second – and while we have that, I'll – let's see, I know! I'll show you my maps and my photographs and my notes, and – and we'll discuss where I should dig in the Valley next autumn, how about that?'

I could see Frances was as cold, as ill at ease and as miserable as I was: we both nodded wanly and did as instructed. Carter began bustling about, lighting oil lamps and arranging chairs. Once the fire caught and began to warm the small room, and once the lamplight banished the gloom, I felt a little reassured. Outside the wind was still moaning, and I could hear the distant wash of rain, but the shutters softened the sound, and the thunder was now diminishing, reduced to low growls, the intervals between them lengthening. Carter installed us in chairs either side of the fire, ensured we were well wrapped in rugs and, with the air of a magician, produced a toasting fork.

'When I was a boy in Norfolk,' he said, 'I lived with my two aunties, in a little cottage on the outskirts of a town called Swaffham. I was ill a lot – that's why I never went to a proper school – and there wasn't much money around, and not many treats. But one treat we *did* have, and that was hot buttered toast, made on the fire. We'd sit round it and put our feet up, and get a nice fug going – there's nowhere colder than Norfolk on a winter's day – and then we'd have a slap-up tea. My aunties would knit and gossip and I'd sit there drawing and reading, and we'd have toast made on the fire, and some good strong Indian tea. Then we'd tuck in to my aunties' famous fruit-cake . . . and that's what we'll have today. I've taught my cook to make it – well, given him the family recipe, he's done the rest. But he's a smart boy, and cooks up good grub . . . Ah, Abd-el-Aal, there you are.'

Carter paused to ask some questions and to listen to Abd-el-Aal's lengthy and animated replies. Taking the tray from him, Carter glanced into the hall: from the room beyond we could just hear the low sound of women's voices. Shutting the door firmly, he said: 'Good. Eve's calming down now, by the sound of it. Women's work: I expect Helen and Miss Mack will sort things out in no time.'

'Will they?' Frances turned her pale face from the fire and looked at him intently. 'Something's happened, Mr Carter. What is it?'

'Well, you know, I'm not really too sure, Frances. I'd only just that second got in. Eve didn't have time to explain. And then she was very upset, as you could see – been through a bit of an ordeal, driving over here, the storm, getting the car stuck—'

'But she wouldn't have *done* that unless something was badly wrong. And she was crying too – I've never seen Eve cry before.'

'Well, I have,' Carter replied, unexpectedly. 'Eve has a very soft heart, she's highly strung, and she's easily upset. Good Lord, I remember one terrible occasion at Highclere—'

'At Highclere? With Eve? Why – what happened?' Frances asked, looking at him eagerly. She had taken the bait, I saw, and I knew that had been Carter's intention.

I stared at the fire and said nothing. Whatever had happened must have been sudden, had perhaps occurred at the Winter Palace, since Eve had come from there. Had there been some accident? I thought of the hotel's balconies – and the sheer drop from them.

'Well now,' Carter replied, busily pouring tea, 'Lord Carnarvon is a superstitious man in many ways: you may not know that, but you should see him at Newbury races, when one of his horses is running! What's more, he has an extraordinary weakness for fortune-tellers, spiritualism, mediums, seances . . . I have no truck with such claptrap, but Carnarvon believes in it, so I stay mum and I go along with it – start toasting this bread, will you, Frances? And you, Lucy, you're in charge of the buttering.'

He plied us with hot sweet tea, and once we were engaged in the toasting process, settled himself in a chair and, with every appearance of enjoying himself, continued his story. 'So, as I say, I go along with his superstitions and when I stay at Highclere Castle, which I do most summers for a few weeks, helping Lord Carnarvon catalogue his Egyptian collection . . . well, during that time, there's always at least one seance. One evening last year, we all assembled in one of Highclere's gloomiest rooms. There were twelve of us, seated around a table in the dark, and Carnarvon's medium was trying to get through to her spirit guide. Nothing happened at first, then, without warning, she went into a trance, a really deep trance, I'd never seen anything like it in my life. Her eyes rolled back and her whole body went rigid. She began to speak, but in a guttural man's voice, and a foreign language . . . Poor Eve was petrified. Out it came, sentence after sentence, and it was a language not one person at that table could understand.' He paused. 'No one except me, that is. It made absolute sense to *me*. I recognised it at once. And I said so, to everyone's amazement. It was Coptic. How d'you explain that, eh?'

'Gosh,' Frances said, on cue, with a tired wan glance in my direction. 'What did she say, Mr Carter? Was it a prediction . . . a terrible warning, perhaps?'

'My lips are sealed.' Carter gave us both a dark penetrating glance. 'I can say nothing. More than my life's worth to reveal it.'

There was a silence. From the hall came a thin dry whistling sound, like the wind through a keyhole. Frances seemed disinclined to question Carter further, which surprised me. Could she have heard this tale before; was it perhaps part of Carter's repertoire? Something in this tale did not fit, and it made me uneasy.

'I wonder, did the medium woman speak Coptic herself?' I asked earnestly, after a pause.

'Of course she didn't,' Carter said, with scorn. 'The woman didn't speak Arabic, let alone Coptic. It's a dead language. *No one*'s spoken it since the sixteenth century.'

'But if no one speaks it,' I said, ignoring Frances who was making a face at me, 'if no one's spoken it for hundreds of years, how did you recognise it, Mr Carter?'

'Because I can *read* it,' Carter replied brusquely. 'Seen it on papyri a thousand times.'

'But reading is different,' I persisted. 'It's not at all the same as knowing how it sounds. My father can read Homer, but he says no two scholars agree as to how Homeric Greek actually sounded when spoken. They really have no idea. So if Coptic is as dead as you say, I still don't see how you could possibly—'

'Well, I did.' Carter, his manner curt, interrupted me at exactly the moment that Frances gave me a warning kick. There was an awkward silence, then Carter, who had seen the kick, gave his bark of a laugh. 'Well, that's *my* story anyway . . . and it went down a darn sight better at Highclere Castle than it has here. Lord Carnarvon has never forgotten it.'

He gave us both a dark considering look. 'I can see I'll have to watch my back with you two girls – you're as sharp as needles. Wouldn't do to reveal any more. I might have been tempted to . . . but no, better not. Let's see: what started me off on all that? Ah yes, Eve . . . Well now, you may quibble, but this much is one hundred per cent true: Eve was so upset by that experience that she's never attended one of her father's seances since. She had sleepless nights for months afterwards. She's of a nervous disposition, and can get far too worked up about things – women are like that, I have a sister just the same. If Eve's upset, it's nothing to worry about. Let's have some more of that toast, shall we?'

And so, with tales of his childhood, buttered toast and a ghostly story, he set about distracting us – I can see that now. I was half aware

of his tactics, as was Frances, I think. At first, his success was intermittent: I kept straining to hear the voices from the other room, and
I could see Frances, pale and tense, was still puzzling over Eve's
behaviour; but we were tired after the heat of the day and the hasty
retreat from the Valley through the storm. It was warm and peaceful in the small room; as time passed, Carter's attempts to divert us
became more successful.

Oddly enough – he was not in the least a paternal man, nor was
he avuncular – I think Carter was enjoying our company: he seemed
at ease in a way he rarely was with adults. Perhaps he felt we were too
young and inexperienced to criticise him; maybe he was aware of the
hero-worship Frances felt for him, and found it flattering: whatever
the reason, he was as unguarded and confidential that afternoon as I
ever saw him. I thought of Minnie Burton's accusation – her claim
that Carter never bothered with anyone unless that person could be
useful to him. How wrong and mean-spirited she was, I told myself:
Carter could gain nothing from Frances and me. I was beginning to
believe that Frances had been right: put simply, Carter *liked* us, and
that liking was completely disinterested.

It is always reassuring, and flattering, to believe that one is liked,
of course. Warmed by this feeling, lulled by toast, tea and fruitcake,
and encouraged by Carter's ebullient spirits, I forgot my unease. I
forced all thought of accidents, of balconies, from my mind. Once
our tea was finished, Carter dumped the crockery unceremoniously
on his desk and, having cleared the small table in front of us, produced a pile of notebooks and maps. Unrolling one of the latter,
which proved to be a large-scale plan of the Valley covered in neatly
pencilled marks and notes, he said: 'Right. Time for you two to advise
me. Examine it closely. Where do I dig next autumn?'

He moved away to some bookshelves, from which he took down
a glass, a half-empty bottle of whisky and a soda siphon. 'Sun over the
yardarm now,' he remarked, as Frances and I bent studiously over the
map. 'Cheerio,' he said, raising his glass to us, and then added after
a brief pause: 'Come on, get a move on – we haven't got all day, you
know.'

The prospect of a treasure map was exciting and I inspected it
intently; but it wasn't easy to see the details in the light from the oil
lamps; Carter's marks and notes were writ small and virtually

149

unreadable. It might as well be a map of the moon, I thought, for all the help I'd be. Frances, who seemed to revive when the maps appeared, who knew this territory and was familiar with the similar maps her father used, traced some of the pencilled lines with her finger. 'Well,' she began, 'this doesn't show the whole Valley. It doesn't show where we were today, for instance. But it does show your famous triangle.'

'Good. Go on.' Carter sat down at his desk, a few feet away. He lit a cigarette.

'I can see which areas in the triangle you've already cleared – they're the shaded squares. So I can see you've almost exhausted that whole area. You've done this wadi here, the one that leads up to Merneptah's tomb. And you've cleared the area over there. So there's very little left unexplored, except here, by the tomb of Ramesses VI … Daddy pointed that out to us yesterday, remember, Lucy? There are some ruins of workmen's huts, ancient ones – but I thought you'd cleared most of those, Mr Carter?'

'A year ago.' Carter flicked ash on his desk and took a swallow of whisky. 'January '21. Didn't finish the job, too late in the year, height of the tourist season – dig any more and I'd have been obstructing the entrance to Ramesses VI's tomb, which gets scores of visitors. Same problem this year: if I could have started back in November, fine; but I was delayed by that blasted operation in London. Now it's February, and the Valley's infested with tourists again; if I blocked that entrance off with my diggings, it wouldn't go down too well with the Antiquities Service, especially its esteemed Director. I'd have our dear friend Monsieur Lacau on my back – any excuse to nit-pick and interfere. Can't stand the man – and he's not too enamoured of me either.'

He made a restless gesture, stubbed out one cigarette and lit another. In his odd, brooding, way, he said: 'That area will have to wait until next autumn. Let's try another tack. We'll play a game: imagine you're a king, and one fine day you've ridden out to select your final resting place in the Valley. What would influence your choice?'

'It would depend on my dates,' Frances replied, smothering a yawn. 'If I was an *early* king, I'd be looking for a potential tomb in the cliffs, somewhere well hidden. A few hundred years later, and I wouldn't be worrying about hiding my burial place, because there's a system by then, and the Valley is well patrolled and guarded by the Medjay. So I'd make my tomb lower down in the *talus* – digging in through the mounds of scree to the cliff behind. And if I were later still, an eighteenth-dynasty king, say, I'd dig straight down in the Valley floor, and tunnel underground from there.'

She raised her head from the map, and gave Carter an appraising stare. 'Which is why I'd guess that right now you're looking for a particular tomb, belonging to a particular king, and he's eighteenth dynasty at that. *That*'s why you're concentrating on the Valley floor, Mr Carter, and *that*'s why you're levelling down to the bedrock.'

'You're your father's daughter. And you're no fool – I'll give you that, Frances.' Carter took a swallow of whisky. 'Lucy, your turn. You're choosing the place for your tomb: how do you select it?'

'Well, I wouldn't have thought of any of the things Frances has mentioned. I don't know about them. I suppose I'd do what people have always done – I'd want to be buried near my family. Grandparents, father . . . ' I paused. 'My mother.'

'I agree. Human instinct.'

Carter drained his glass, tossed his cigarette into the fire, and crossed to the table. He bent over the map. 'So, bearing in mind what you've both said, supposing I told you that your father's tomb is . . . around about *here* . . . ' He jabbed at the map with his forefinger. 'And suppose I *also* told you that items relating to your funeral rites had been hidden a short distance from your burial place, somewhere around *there* . . . ' He jabbed the map again. 'And finally, that a very beautiful cup, bearing your name, and perhaps stolen from your tomb, had been found *here* . . . where do you think your actual tomb is located?'

I bent over the map obediently, though my vision had blurred and I couldn't see the triangulation points he'd indicated. All I could see was the grey stone in a Cambridge churchyard bearing my mother's name and dates. Frances, like me, gave Carter no answer. Looking up, I saw she had fallen fast asleep, curled under one of those plaid rugs; her face was pale, and her eyelids flickered, so I knew she was dreaming. There was a silence. Carter, frowning into the fire, gave no sign that he was awaiting an answer; I felt he'd forgotten us.

'I'm sorry, Mr Carter,' I said at last. 'I'm afraid we're not much help – well, I don't expect you thought we would be, not really.'

'No matter.' Carter began to roll up the map. 'I work to a *system*,' he went on, staring at the fire. 'I don't go out there and dig at random, though plenty of people have done just that in the past – and it served them well enough. But oh no, I *work* at it. Every tomb, every cache, the smallest find that's ever been made in the Valley – it's in these notebooks and I've mapped it. In that notebook, you'll find the details of every king that's buried there, the ones that have been found so far, which is virtually all of them, and the few – the one or, at very most, two – whose tombs *should* be there, but remain undiscovered. In this, I note the tomb robberies described in antiquity: they give me valuable clues. This records conversations with natives, men I've taken the trouble to cultivate, men like Girigar who know this place like the skin of their own hands . . . I *know* I'm on track. I *know* it's there. Give me time, and I'll find it—

'I'm actually *digging* in the Valley for – what?' He threw the note-books onto his desk. 'Weather permitting, four, at best five months a year. And how do I spend the other months, when I'm back in England, when I'm having a high old time at Highclere – with Carnarvon at the racetrack, at one of his shooting parties? I enjoy it, don't think I don't: but I never escape. I never shake the Valley off, it's *always* in my mind. Thousands of miles away, a world away, and I'm always *there*, in the Valley, poring over its maps . . . I dream the damn place contour by contour – until sometimes I'm so sick of its tricks I swear I'll never set foot in the accursed place again. Only I know that won't happen. It's got me by the throat. And one of these days, I'll just drop like a dog and die there.'

He was wrong in that prediction – but of course neither of us knew that then. I said nothing; his manner frightened me, and besides, it seemed wiser to remain silent for Carter wasn't address-ing me, I could tell. He was speaking to himself and seemed scarcely aware of my presence. I shrank back under my rug and half closed my eyes, so when he came to himself he could believe I'd been asleep like Frances and had heard nothing – I thought he'd prefer that.

Watching covertly, I saw him roll up the last of the maps and gather the scattered notebooks that he'd tossed down as he spoke. I heard the gurgle of whisky as he refilled his glass. I heard him slump down in his desk chair and mutter something to himself. There was silence after that, and exhausted by the day, by too many things happening too fast, I began to drift into a troubled sleep. I was half under, somewhere in a tomb, I think, when I heard the door across the hall opening, then the sounds of footsteps and women's voices. I rubbed my eyes and peered dazedly at my wristwatch. It had stopped.

Carter rose and quietly left the room. I heard him say, 'They're both asleep. Worn out, the pair of them.' Then he closed the door. Straining my ears, I caught murmurs from the three women, forceful interjections from Carter, but no actual words. By the time Miss Mack and Helen came in to wake us, a plan had been decided upon, it seemed – though there was no further explanation.

'Now, my dears,' Miss Mack said gently, and I could see that she was anxious and Helen had been crying. 'Now, children, we want you both to do just as we say, no questions and no arguments. It's too late to ride back to the American House on the donkeys, and we're all far too exhausted. So Eve is kindly going to drop us off in her motorcar, and Mr Carter is coming with us. Then he'll escort her back to Luxor and her father—'

'But why?' Frances protested, struggling with her rug and sitting up. 'Why can't Eve come and stay with us? She could go back to the Winter Palace in the morning.'

'Darling, what did Miss Mack just tell you?' Helen said, in weary tones. 'Eve's father is expecting her back at the hotel, and she can't drive there on her own when it'll be dark any minute – that's out of the question. Just do as you're told, Frances. And when we get home, both of you will go straight off to bed. Now, come along, please.'

We trooped out to the car to find that while we'd been inside the fastness of Castle Carter, the Valley's mood and its weather had altered once again. It was now dusk: a still, calm and beautiful evening. The last of the evening sun lay along the Theban hills, a sickle moon hung low over el-Qurn; the acacia trees by Carter's house were unruffled by wind, and the air, refreshed by the storm, was sweet with their honey perfume. We climbed into the car, Carter seating himself next to Eve, the rest of us cramped in the back; the boy Hosein ran out and cranked the engine.

'Now please don't be nervous,' Eve said in a shaky voice, as the car started. 'I've been driving since I was twelve.' No one answered, and we began bumping along the rutted track to the American House. After we had gone a hundred yards or so, Eve said in a sudden distracted way: 'Oh, I've just remembered something – the canary! I never bought you that canary, Howard—'

'Never mind that now,' Carter replied. 'Calm down. Concentrate on the driving, Eve.'

The car hit a deep rut, tilted, juddered and then righted itself. I saw Eve struggle with the gear lever; we careered forward as she accelerated.

'Watch out . . . the visibility's going,' Carter said. 'You just missed that boulder – put the lights on, damn it.' Reaching across, he flicked switches, and the headlights came on.

'The canary would have brought us luck,' Eve said. I saw a tear fall from her cheek. In a bright vacant tone, she added: 'That's *much* better. I can see the way perfectly now.'

I saw them exchange a glance, Carter's piercing and interrogatory, hers placatory. Eve then concentrated on the track, and her driving steadied. We continued bumping along through the hills towards the American House. It was not far – a mile at the most; for the duration of the journey not one further word was spoken by anyone.

We watched as the car accelerated away; Eve and Carter disappeared in the direction of the Nile and the ferry, and we were quickly ushered indoors. We were given hot baths – in tin baths in our bedroom – then we were brought glasses of warm milk, and put to bed: 'Like infants,' Frances said bitterly, when the lights had been switched off, and the door closed. She sat up in the dark – I could just see the outlines of her white nightdress, her pale face and her wide eyes. She leaned across towards my bed. 'What time is it, Lucy?'

'I don't know. My watch has stopped. It's dark outside now.'

'What's happened, do you think?' she whispered. 'Oh, why aren't they telling us?'

'I don't know,' I whispered back. 'But whatever it is, it must be serious.'

'Mr Carter didn't say anything? While I was asleep?'

'No. He just talked about the Valley, and his searches there and—'

'His demons? He does have demons – I've heard Daddy say so.'

She sighed and fell back on her pillows. We both lay there in silence, while the ceiling fans revolved with a soft rhythmic swish. 'Did you notice, Lucy,' she said, 'Mr Carter and Eve? When we first walked in? When we thought she was Poppy?'

'Yes, I did notice. They were different together. In the car too.'

'Do you think *that* could have something to do with it? Was that why Eve was so upset?'

I considered this. I wasn't at all sure what it was we had witnessed; all I knew was that I'd sensed something concealed – and powerful, like an undercurrent. 'I don't *think* it was that,' I said. 'Maybe it sort of contributed. But there was another reason too. Miss Mack knows what it is. And your mother. And they're not telling us.'

'Maybe they'll explain in the morning,' Frances said in a forlorn voice, but she did not sound convinced. We lay there in silence again. I looked at the shadowy scorpion nets across the windows, at Frances's shrine of photographs, lit by a faint, flickering night light; her grandparents, her parents, her little drowned brother, lost to the cold waters off Maine.

I closed my eyes and found I was in a tomb again, Frances leading the way, guiding me by the narrow beam of her flashlight. Deeper and deeper we went, our route twisting past doors and beckoning passages. Frances darted ahead, taking first this turn, then that one. I hastened to catch up with her. I knew we were in search of her brother, and our task was to bring the little boy back from the underworld, but I could hear the gates of night slamming shut behind us, and that frightened me. I wanted to ask Frances how we'd ever escape this labyrinth, but I knew that, to make her understand, I'd have to speak Coptic. Then her flashlight went out. I could see nothing, but my hearing was sharpened. I could detect the sound of rushing water, and, echoing along the passages, came the piercing cry of a child.

'*KV*,' Frances said, as sleep finally claimed me.

The next morning, Frances and I were woken early and told there was a change of plan: Miss Mack and I would be returning to the Winter Palace as arranged, but Herbert, Helen and Frances would accompany us. We were informed we would be meeting an important official from Cairo, who wished to speak to us. There was no cause for alarm: he simply wanted to ask us some questions, and when he did, we must answer him clearly and truthfully.

No further explanation was forthcoming, though a great fuss was made about our clothes: both Frances and I had to wear dark dresses, jackets, gloves and our best panama hats. Miss Mack and Helen were sombrely dressed; Herbert Winlock wore a grey suit and a black tie. We waited for the official upstairs at the Winter Palace, in one of the hotel's private rooms, where we sat without speaking. Helen and Miss Mack gazed at their laps and their kid-gloved hands; Herbert Winlock, grim-faced, stared into the middle distance. I stared at the room's glass doors, which led out onto a balcony.

Eventually, the official, who proved to be a tall Egyptian, wearing a black suit and a scarlet fez, poked his head around a door and, with wide smiles and an air of great benevolence, asked Miss Mack to be so gracious as to spare him some of her time. She disappeared into the room beyond, where she remained for some five minutes. Herbert Winlock and Helen were ushered in next, and their stay was longer. Finally it was our turn: Frances and I rose, and with trepidation entered the room. There, the benevolent official sat down at an ornate Empire desk, adjusted a bronze paperweight in the shape of the Sphinx, and invited us to sit opposite him.

He was not alone in the room, I saw to my surprise: loitering next to a less splendid desk a few yards behind him, and looking profoundly ill at ease, was a young man I recognised. He had fair hair, a fresh pink complexion, and round blue eyes; he was wearing a British officer's uniform. 'Don't mind me,' he said. 'I think we were introduced once, actually, in Cairo, at the Gezira Sporting Club? Tea that time, with Lady Evelyn? After the polo match? Ronnie Urquhart – well, Lieutenant Urquhart, I suppose I should say . . . here in my official capacity, request of the Residency and – er, so on.'

'Also at *my* request,' the Egyptian murmured, with a small glance in his direction.

'Oh, gosh, yes – absolutely.' Urquhart blushed and sat down. 'So just ignore me, Miss Payne and Miss Winlock,' he went on. 'In fact, pretend I'm not here. Have to do all this by the letter, you see – bit tricky at the present time. Sensitive, you know. Adjustments, handover and so on.'

'Perhaps we should commence?' the Egyptian official said, with magnificent courtesy and the faintest hint of impatience.

'Right. Yes. Spot on. So if you two young ladies would just answer the questions from – my colleague here. Nothing to be nervous about. You should address him as—'

'El-Deeb *effendi*,' the official said crisply. Urquhart subsided, picked up a pencil, and said nothing further. Mr El-Deeb settled himself in his impressive chair, and gave us a toothy benign smile. He remarked that it was an honour to meet us, albeit under difficult circumstances; he hoped we would forgive him, but he had certain questions that he must put to us. They concerned someone he understood was our friend, a most beautiful and accomplished woman, of the highest social standing in England, an intimate of princes and sundry other illustrious personages, a lady well known and much admired in Cairo. Her name, he said, frowning at us in a sudden fixed way, as if he suspected us of some heinous hidden crime, was Mrs d'Erlanger.

He paused, and then informed us, as if it were an afterthought, that perhaps we should know he was a senior officer in the Egyptian police force, here today as an investigator . . . somewhat in the manner of the immortal Sherlock Holmes, a character whose deductions he was sure we enjoyed as much as he did.

'Has something happened to Mrs d'Erlanger?' Frances asked, interrupting him. We had both been transfixed, trying to make sense of this.

I leaned forward: 'That's what we both want to know, El-Deeb *effendi*,' I said in an imploring rush. 'I thought – you see, no one has told us anything, and we'd like to understand. What has happened? Is Mrs d'Erlanger safe? Is she in Egypt? Has there been some accident?'

The detective raised his hand, its palm towards us. He remarked, with less benevolence, that *he* would ask the questions. He asked us to think back to the last occasion on which we had seen Mrs d'Erlanger, at Shepheard's Hotel, Cairo. He consulted a notebook: 'Today is 21 February. That would have been 7 February – two weeks ago. You can remember that occasion?'

'Yes, *effendi*,' Frances said meekly.

El-Deeb was not a man to be rushed. He explained that he had already spoken to Lord Carnarvon, to his gracious daughter, and to several other people who had been present in Shepheard's dining room that night. He had also spoken, at length, to Mrs d'Erlanger's maid, Miss Wheeler, who had provided him with a description of the clothes Mrs d'Erlanger had been wearing on the night she disappeared. Since he understood we had been present in her room when these clothes were selected, he would like to confirm certain details. 'Dress?' he said, so suddenly and with so little benevolence that both Frances and I jumped. 'Describe to me, please, what dress Mrs d'Erlanger was wearing?'

'It was a pink dress,' I replied, in a small voice.

'Shocking pink,' Frances added. 'A friend of Mrs d'Erlanger's designed it especially for her. It was made in Paris. Poppy – Mrs d'Erlanger liked it because it was fast.'

The official wrote this word down, then frowned at it.

'Look, I say, El-Deeb,' Lieutenant Urquhart burst out in an anxious tone. 'Don't want to interfere, but that doesn't mean a thing, old man. It's just the way Poppy – Mrs d'Erlanger – it's just the way she talked.'

'Thank you, my English is fluent. I have been told it is Oxford irreproachable.' The Egyptian gave Urquhart a quelling glance and, when he had subsided again, turned back to us. 'So,' he said. 'A dress. Fast. Pink. Shocking. Made in Paris. What else?'

'She had a fur with her,' I said, anxious to be helpful. 'A dark fur, a sort of wrap. I remember that, because Eve — Lady Evelyn — said she couldn't possibly be needing it, it was too hot. But Mrs d'Erlanger said . . . ' I hesitated.

'What did Mrs d'Erlanger say?'

'She said, yes, it *was* a hot night — but she needed the fur because she might be — she said she might be "trotting on somewhere". After dinner, I think she meant.'

'I see. And did you subsequently witness her with that fur, in the hotel dining room?'

'Yes, we both did,' Frances confirmed eagerly. 'She was carrying it, then she put it over the back of her chair during dinner, and then she—'

'She sort of tossed it over her shoulder, and took it with her when she left the dining room,' I said. Should I mention the two men, the altercation between them and Poppy's response? Better not, I decided.

'Excellent. I commend your sharp eyes and your good memories.' Benevolence restored, El-Deeb beamed at us again. 'We will continue. Think very carefully, please. Was Mrs d'Erlanger wearing jewellery, and was she carrying a bag that evening?'

'She was definitely carrying an evening bag,' I replied. 'It was very small, a tiny thing, like a doll's almost.' I stopped. I'd been slow but suddenly I'd understood the reason — the only possible reason — for these questions. 'It was . . . very pretty.' My voice faltered. 'It had embroidery on it, something that sparkled and — and — I can't remember if she was wearing jewellery.'

'I can.' Frances reached for my hand and squeezed it. 'I remember exactly. She was wearing earrings made of priceless Burmese rubies, and a beautiful ring that matched, a square one. They came from Cartier. I recognised them because I'd seen them before, and she'd told me they were a wedding present from her husband, Mr d'Erlanger.'

'Most interesting.' El-Deeb made a small note. In a casual tone, he added: 'Wedding ring? Was she also wearing her wedding ring?'

'Oh, for Christ's *sake* ...' Urquhart burst out. He threw up his hands and turned to stare mutinously at the wall opposite.

'A small point,' El-Deeb said, with a cold glance. 'It is the small points that speak. I pay them the closest attention, always. I advise you to do the same. So, Miss Payne, Miss Winlock: the wedding ring — was this a detail you noticed?'

'Yes, it was,' Frances confirmed, as I shook my head. 'When we were in her room that evening, I noticed her wedding ring. Mrs d'Erlanger wanted to give us presents when we left and she asked us to choose something pretty from her dressing table. The ring was there, lying on the table, next to some scent bottles, and under—'

'Was that unusual? Did Mrs d'Erlanger not make it a habit to wear that marriage ring?'

'She hadn't worn it while she was in Cairo, no. But she put it on that night — and I saw her do it. She gave us our presents, and then she noticed the ring. It was underneath a swansdown powder puff and when that was moved, she suddenly saw it. She gave a little cry and said, "Oh — so *that*'s where you've been hiding!" She snatched it up and put it on, and she — she winked at Wheeler. And then we left.'

I stared at Frances in astonishment. How observant she was. How much she noticed that I missed. I wasn't sure if she'd understood the purport of these questions: her expression was unreadable. El-Deeb bent over his notes and wrote. A silence ensued, during which Lieutenant Urquhart showed signs of mounting consternation. He wriggled in his seat, coloured hotly and eventually burst out: 'Look here, I'd just like it on the record: in my opinion we're galloping straight down a cul-de-sac. This ring, that ring — what difference can it possibly make? Poor Poppy wasn't—' He broke off. 'I just jolly well don't see any possible relevance. I object to this line of questioning. And I want that formally noted on the files, El-Deeb.'

El-Deeb made a mark in the margin of the page. 'Duly noted,' he replied. 'And — let us agree to disagree, Lieutenant Urquhart — the information is germane. Miss Winlock is an excellent witness. Truly an archaeologist's daughter,' he continued, with a bow of the head to Frances. 'She understands the importance of the substrata. She does not just examine the surface, oh no, she examines the information that lies hidden beneath. She examines it,' he paused magisterially, 'and then she allows it to speak to us.'

He looked intently, first at Frances and then at me. His expression became less severe, and for a moment I thought he might relent and explain; the possibility seemed to cross his mind. He hesitated and then said: 'This is hard for you both. You are young, and I can see you find these questions alarming. I apologise. I am doing what I came here to do, and I hope in due course you will understand that.

'As you will have gathered,' he continued in a cautious way, 'there are – concerns as to where Mrs d'Erlanger went, and what happened to her after she left Shepheard's Hotel that night. I should stress, no time has been wasted, no stone left unturned. Lord Carnarvon informed the Cairo police of Mrs d'Erlanger's absence within a day. He also alerted his friends at the British Residency . . . and initially no one was greatly alarmed. Mrs d'Erlanger had a history of such sudden and unexplained departures, it seemed. Enquiries were made, and this took time, cables had to be sent, letters written . . . When none of the many friends and family Lord Carnarvon contacted proved able to explain her whereabouts, and when police enquiries met a similar blank wall, it became clear that Mrs d'Erlanger's disappearance might, after all, give cause for alarm.

'In recent days,' El-Deeb continued, exchanging a glance with Urquhart, 'there have been certain developments – I will say no more than that. They indicate Mrs d'Erlanger may possibly have met with an accident. That possibility remains to be confirmed. At the present moment, we continue to hope that your friend will be found safe and well.' He flashed a reassuring smile. 'Meanwhile, the details as to what she was wearing, and her – demeanour that night are vital to establish. So if I may just be completely certain: in your recollection, that was the *only* jewellery Mrs d'Erlanger was wearing? No necklace or brooch? No bracelets? No wristwatch?'

'No, none,' Frances replied in a flat voice.

'And, finally, was there anything else that was notable about Mrs d'Erlanger's behaviour or appearance that evening? Anything, however small, that struck you?'

'She was very worried about what to wear that night,' I said, after a pause. 'It seemed to matter a great deal to her. She was nervous. Excited.'

'She was wearing scarlet lipstick,' Frances said; she cleared her throat. 'Bright scarlet. Might that be important?'

'Ah. Lipstick.' El-Deeb exchanged a glance with Urquhart, and for once both men seemed in accord: it was a glance of understanding and sympathy. Urquhart buried his face in his hands. El-Deeb shook his head and bent over his notebook. 'A very valuable piece of information,' he said gently, and without looking up. 'I shall certainly make a note of it, Miss Winlock. And now, I need detain you and your friend no longer.'

That was the end of our interview. There were no further questions or reassurances – and no further explanation was proffered by either El-Deeb or Urquhart. By then, neither Frances nor I was expecting one.

When we left, we found Frances's parents were waiting for us. They sent us ahead to Miss Mack's room, where they said they would join us. Halfway down the stairs, which were crowded as always with hotel guests, Frances caught me by the hand, and drew me aside; we fled into a quiet, deserted corridor. We came to a halt in a window embrasure overlooking the Nile; below, the ferryboat was about to depart; a whistle sounded.

'When did you know?' Frances said fiercely.

'When I began describing Poppy's handbag. Then. As soon as I said how small it was.'

'I knew then too. That exact same moment.' She turned away.

'They've found her, I think. That's why he asked all those questions about her clothes.'

Frances did not reply. She was staring out of the window at the river below, her face chalk white and her expression fixed. I still wasn't sure how much she'd understood, so I said quietly: 'Poppy's dead, Frances. I think she must be dead. Cairo isn't safe, especially at night. Everyone said that. There must have been some terrible accident. Maybe they haven't confirmed her identity yet, but—'

'I know she's dead.' Frances continued to stare fixedly at the river below. 'We'll never see Poppy or speak to her again. When she left the dining room that night, when she gave that toss of the head and walked out – that was the last time. And neither of us knew.' She took a deep breath. 'She was magnificent then, Lucy. All those hateful people in the dining room staring at her – and she was so brave and defiant. I shall always remember her like that. I'm glad they've found her in that dress, with her wedding jewels and her red lipstick. Looking beautiful. As she always did.'

I couldn't bring myself to reply. I was thinking of the two weeks that had passed, of the fierce Egyptian heat. If Poppy had died that same night, or the following day, and, given the questions as to her clothes, I thought she must have done, then this image of her was sadly wrong. How strange that Frances, so knowledgeable as to embalming, the preservation of bodies and the ancient ways of death, should be mistaken now. I could imagine, only too well, why it might be taking time to confirm Poppy's identity.

'We'd better go back, Frances,' I said gently. 'Otherwise they'll come looking for us.'

Frances did not move, or look around. 'Our spells worked too. I knew they would. I asked Isis and Nephthys to bring Poppy back. Without delay. And they did it that very same day . . .' She hesitated. 'Just not in the way we expected, Lucy. But then I guess the gods are like that.'

I was thinking that if Frances's gods were given to that kind of trickery, I'd avoid them in future: they'd get no more sacrifices from me. How stupid to get caught up in Frances's schemes: to steal pages from a book, to bury them in the desert; to invoke the powers of gods who'd never existed, gods I didn't believe in anyway. Frances had made these actions seem meaningful, but now I saw them for what they were: a foolish game, childish delusions. I thought of the story Carter had told us the previous day, of Carnarvon's seance, and a stream of words that might have been a warning. There could be no such warnings, I decided, because there were no gods to make them. I'd felt the presence of gods, of *something*, when I'd explored the tombs, but that too was an illusion.

I knew it would hurt Frances and provoke a storm of tears if I said that, so I stayed silent. After an interval, Frances stepped away from the window and gave herself a queer little shake. Looking at her bright, set face, I realised that, as always, she was moving on to the next challenge, the next task; and, as always, she was leaving me behind her, sick at heart, in a maze of uncertainties.

'I guess we'd better go, Lucy,' she said. 'They'll be waiting for us. I wonder what half-truths they'll come up with next? They're letting us down gently. They *mean* well, I know that. We all *meant* well, you and I, Lord Carnarvon and Eve and Mr Carter – we all acted for the best. It doesn't matter what they say to us now, anyway. By hook or by crook, we'll discover the truth, won't we, Lucy?'

'I expect so. Eventually.'

'Oh, sooner than that. *I* shall find out – or you will. And whoever does it first has to tell the other at once. Promise me, Lucy.'

'Of course – if I can. But I'm leaving next week, Frances.'

'Oh, for heaven's sake! As if that matters! I shall write you every week, and you'll write me. Look how close we are!' She grabbed my hand and pressed it between hers. '*That* close. Distance won't make the least difference. I love you dearly, Lucy. Maybe not quite as much as my mother and father, but next. Even more than Poppy – and I loved her a lot. So whatever we find out, we *share it*. From now on until the day we die, there will be no secrets between us. Give me your solemn word.'

I looked at Frances's intent, urgent face. Her bright gaze held mine. I was wary of her schemes, of her capacity to recover and move on, but how could I refuse her? Only one person had ever expressed love for me before then, and she was gone. And so, hugging her to me, I told Frances that she was my dearest friend too. I promised, as she did, that we'd never keep a secret from each other and would share all truths – including the truth as to Poppy d'Erlanger, should that emerge. We clasped hands and thus what Frances called the sacred 'pact' was made.

'Why do we have to call it a *pact*?' I protested belatedly, as we returned to the stairs; Frances's heightened language, her love for high-flown terms, both thrilled and alarmed me. We turned along the corridor to Miss Mack's room. Faint voices were audible behind its closed door. 'Why can't we say something ordinary, like "agreement"?'

'Oh, Lucy, has Egypt taught you *nothing*? "Pact" sounds *much* better,' Frances replied. 'And it means more.'

Knowing Frances's skills, I expected she would be the one to discover the truth, but I was wrong. I discovered it, a week later.

By then, the arrangements for our journey back to England had been adjusted. Miss Mack had learned that Rose and Peter's father was demanding their immediate return home. They had been told, as we had, that their mother might have met with an accident, that there were reasons to be anxious on her behalf. Small hints had been dropped that Poppy might not be returning for a long, long time, and that therefore they must travel back to England without her. Their father had sent wires to Lord Carnarvon in which he made it clear he expected them to set forth at once, on the next available boat, with Wheeler as escort; he would meet them at Dover.

When Miss Mack discovered this, first from a tearful Eve, then from an indignant Wheeler, she was outraged. 'Lord Strathaven' became a name she refused to pronounce; from then onwards, he was *that man*. Outwitting that man, compensating as best she could for his deficiencies as a father and his abject failures as a human being, became her obsession. She could speak of nothing else – and I had never admired her more than the afternoon on which she returned triumphant from yet another skirmish at the Cook's travel bureau to announce that the matter of Rose and Peter's return was now settled. Their departure would be delayed by two days; our departure would be moved forward two days; as a result we would all leave Egypt together. We would take the same boats, the same trains, and with the assistance of Lord Carnarvon, who'd wired contacts at the train and shipping companies on our behalf, we were all to be accommodated in comfortable berths, at every stage of the long journey.

'And I hope that teaches *that man* a lesson!' she declared. 'Alexandria to Marseilles – a four-day crossing, and he expected Wheeler to travel third class! Imagine: those two poor bewildered children, all alone on one deck, and Wheeler down in the bowels of the ship somewhere. I can tell you, Lucy, I've learned a very great deal on this journey of ours, and never again shall I be taken in by an English gentleman. Some merit that title, and some, my dear, do *not*. And I've had just about enough of his American counterparts too. At first I'd felt that you and I might economise, dear. But then I thought of those high-handed, hard-hearted Emersons and Stocktons – and I remembered you'd need to be near Rose and Peter, because you're a comfort to them, Lucy, and little Peter adores you . . . and, well, I just decided, there and then. I threw caution to the winds, and did it.' Coming to a halt, inspecting my face, she hesitated: 'I did do the right thing, didn't I, Lucy?'

'Absolutely the right thing. Truly, Miss Mack. You've done everything, and more, that I could have wanted.'

'And you won't mind leaving a little earlier, Lucy? You're sure?' She
looked at me intently. 'I know you're reluctant to leave. I know how
close you and Frances have become – and I expect there are many
uncertainties, even anxieties in your mind about returning home, and
how it will be, there in Cambridge, without your dear—'

'No, no, no,' I said, knowing I must stop her at once. 'Two days
makes no difference. And anyway, Frances and I were prepared – we
shall write to each other.'

'Sure you will.' Miss Mack was attuned to me now: she planted a
kiss on my brow, and with no further mention of Cambridge or my
father or my future, for which mercy I silently blessed her, announced
that the sooner we started packing, the better.

We took the night train to Cairo two days later; Lord Carnarvon and
Eve, Frances and her parents came to see us off. They all kept saying
how much they would miss us, how we'd meet again soon, how we
must return to Egypt . . . Fortunately there was no need to reply:
Peter, overwhelmed by yet another departure, burst into tears, so
Rose and I could be occupied in soothing him.

From Cairo, we took a train straight on to Alexandria and
embarked on the *Berenice*, an ageing but still glamorous *paquebot*. We
sailed at noon, Miss Mack pointing out the sights she remembered
from her time there in the war, and the hospital where she'd nursed
the wounded men evacuated from Gallipoli. There was a strong
onshore wind, and as soon as we were beyond the harbour, the seas
became choppy. Within an hour, Miss Mack, greenish of complexion,
announced that it was undeniably *rough*, and she would retire to her
cabin. She was followed, soon afterwards, by most of the other passengers; the decks emptied. Wheeler, Rose, Peter and I held out
until, unwisely, tea was risked. Peter took one look at the cakes, hic-
cuped, and was copiously sick; through clenched teeth, Rose
announced she might be dying.

Wheeler whisked them away, and I was left alone. I wandered
through the staterooms, which were deserted, and out onto the
empty decks. From the stern, Egypt was invisible, left far behind;
from the bows, I could see nothing beyond a wall of cloud. I did not

feel seasick, or dizzy; no smoky typhoid uncertainties clouded my mind. I just felt alone, on a brilliantly lit ghost ship, sailing to nowhere.

I walked the port deck, then the starboard, and after a long while, when it was absolutely dark at sea, without stars or moon, I sat down on one of the steamer chairs and stared at the invisible horizon. Someone had left the *Morning Post*, an English-language Cairo news-paper, on the chair; I picked it up. The wind kept riffling the pages, so I took it back to my cabin with the fixed intention of reading every word of every column: then, as now, reading was the best cure I knew for affliction.

I lay on my narrow cabin bed and continued reading where I'd left off: a long account of the declaration of independence for Egypt, issued on behalf of the British government by Lord Allenby the pre-vious day, 28 February. As the ship rolled and pitched, I read through the comments from English diplomats and Wafd Party nationalists, beginning at last to understand that uneasy scene between Lieutenant Urquhart and Mr El-Deeb – when that interview took place, the transfer of power had been just a week away. I turned to the second page, and the third, which seemed to suggest that this transfer was partial at best, attended by scores of muddling provisos. The British would retain control of the Canal Zone, the army, of the Sudan, of . . . I turned the page, and there opposite was a large photograph of Poppy d'Erlanger. It was a recent picture, one that captured the woman as she was then, and as I still remember her. A speaking glance straight to the lens: unforgettable eyes, a half-smile, and an air of hastening away somewhere.

The inquest had been held in Cairo the previous morning. Interest in this sensational death of a society beauty was so great that it had been standing-room only in court. I bent over the close columns of print, and that was how I finally learned the truth as to the death of Mrs d'Erlanger.

She had been discovered among the rushes and papyrus of the Nile marshes three days before El-Deeb's arrival in Luxor. It was an English subaltern who happened upon her body. Newly posted to Egypt, he had joined one of those pre-dawn, duck-shooting parties favoured by members of the Gezira Sporting Club. The shoot was over by then, the catch had been good; he and his fellow officers were about to leave for the traditional hearty English breakfast at the Mena House Hotel, when the hum of flies, a sweet stench in the air and a patch of vivid colour amidst the reeds caught his attention.

'Flamingo pink' was how he described it. Intrigued by its brilliance, ignoring his friends who were urging him to hurry up, he waded towards it along the marshy foreshore. The reeds were alive with birds, dragonflies darted across the water. He found Poppy d'Erlanger lying at the edge of the river, concealed by rushes, beside a patch of blue lotus flowers. She was still wearing the remnants of her shocking-pink dress. It was dawn when he found her, and in the warmth of the rising sun the blue lotus flowers were unfurling.

An iridescence of insects had obscured Poppy's face; the young subaltern, overcome and turning aside to vomit, was uncertain who or what he had found, but he could see this broken creature was female, was dead – and, judging by her clothes, was a white European; the Residency was contacted, the police were summoned. It was quickly established that it was murder: the woman's throat had been savagely cut. It took longer to establish that the dead woman was Mrs d'Erlanger. How she came to be there by the river, what had become of her jewellery and fur, and what had happened to her after she left Shepheard's remained a mystery.

Poppy's husband Jacob d'Erlanger and a British officer named Carew, the two men who had quarrelled over her that night at Shepheard's, had been interviewed at length: both had British friends who provided unshakeable alibis. An Egyptian taxi driver alleged to have driven Mrs d'Erlanger that night was then charged with her killing. He too had an alibi, but it had been provided by 'natives' and could thus be dismissed by the British authorities as a tissue of lies – a verdict with which the British-owned newspaper I was reading concurred. A few years, it trumpeted, even a few months previously, and this man would have faced the death penalty; but his arrest occurred on the eve of independence, at a time of great political sensitivity. When it provoked nationalist outrage and violent street protests, the man had been quietly released.

The verdict of the inquest was 'murder by persons unknown' and the newspaper saw this as an injustice with the very gravest implications. SAVED BY HISTORY! declared its headline – and, since there was no risk of being sued for libel by an Egyptian too poor to afford lawyers, it devoted many column inches to proclaiming the taxi driver's evident guilt, the breakdown of law and order these events presaged, the glimpse they gave of the corruption that would inevitably follow independence, and the proof they provided that Egyptians were manifestly unfit to govern their own country.

I read this account from beginning to end. Then I tore it up. I found a pen and *Berenice* writing paper, and, as the ship rose and fell, at once and according to our pact, wrote to Frances. When the letter was complete, I sealed it in an envelope, and then carried it around with me for days.

Perhaps I had a superstitious fear it would go astray if I consigned it to the ship's mail. Perhaps I felt that, if the letter remained unposted and its news unshared, its contents would prove untrue. I'm not sure what my reasoning was, or even if there was any reasoning: I was numb at that time. I put the letter aside and throughout the voyage spent my days on deck with Peter and Rose. A rough crossing: I was unable to tell them the truth; I was forced into comforting evasions and shaming lies. I'd decided to send the letter when we reached Dover, but the parting there with Peter, who clung to me, whose small hands, clinging desperately to my coat, had to be prised loose by Wheeler, drove all thought of it from my mind. Still I delayed: I finally relinquished my letter when, having said my farewells to Miss Mack in London, I was back in Cambridge at last.

Escaping for half an hour from the rigid programme of lessons that had been lined up for me, a regime that had begun within a day of my return, I stuffed the letter in the pocket of my warmest coat, and trudged into the town from our tall grey house in Newnham, on the city's outskirts. I walked across the Backs, crossed the swollen muddy-brown river, and inspected the few wan daffodils poking through the wet earth; they were being battered by that vicious east wind I remembered of old – the one my mother Marianne used laughingly to claim came straight in from the Urals, from Siberia.

It was early March. In Egypt, Howard Carter and Herbert Winlock would soon be closing down their digs for the season; the remorseless heat would be intensifying. In Cambridge, the temperature was one degree below zero. Pacing my way past the colleges,

I felt I'd imagined Egypt, had never truly been there – and would certainly never return.

The letter in my pocket felt like a last, precious link with Frances: I was still reluctant to let it go. I counted to ten, then consigned it to a red pillar box in King's Parade. I stared numbly at the fantastic roof of King's College Chapel. Two gowned male undergraduates passed by me, arguing loudly about Nietzsche. My heart hurt. I began the walk home. *Mal de mer*: two days since I'd been on a boat, and the pavements still felt unsteady.

Grey buildings, grey skies, grey rain: I was late for my next lesson (Literature: Miss Dunsire) and an explanation, an alibi, would be required. By the time I crossed the Cam on my return journey, I had a lie in place. It was an intricate lie, one even Frances might have admired, but on reaching home, I found I was too angry to employ it. 'Posting a letter,' I replied to the quiet insistent questions.

Miss Dunsire sighed. 'I see.'

Across the room, her level gaze met mine; the clock ticked, the fire crackled, and a secret intense rebellion, sparked during my months in Egypt, stoked and fed ever since, blazed up in my mind. I had no doubt then, and have none now, that Nicola Dunsire noted that emotion, recognised it, and filed it away as information to be used another day. On that occasion she said nothing beyond the fact that our lesson would be extended to compensate for the missing forty minutes. She folded her long-fingered hands and waited for the mounting hostility in the room to reach the precise pitch she desired.

'Open your Shakespeare, Lucy,' she said, when the atmosphere between us was sharp as knives. I obeyed her, without comment. I'd learned from my sojourn in Egypt. We had the measure of each other by then, Dunsire and I.

'*Twelfth Night*. Act I, Scene II,' she prompted, as I riffled the wafer-thin pages of my mother's *Complete Works*. 'We shall pick up where we were interrupted. As you will learn, or may already know, there has been a shipwreck. Viola has survived it. She has been washed ashore in an unknown land. Such incidents, sea voyages, storms, wreckage and its consequences, recur in Shakespeare. His imagination dwelled upon them, as we will discuss in due course. I shall read Viola. You will take the other parts.'

She waited in silence until I found the correct page. I stared at the swimming words.

'*What country, friends, is this?*' she enquired.

'*This is Illyria, lady,*' I answered, after a long pause.

FOUR

Antique Land

I met a traveller from an antique land
Who said, 'Two vast and trunkless legs of stone
Stand in the desert. Near them on the sand,
Half sunk, a shattered visage lies, whose frown
And wrinkled lip and sneer of cold command
Tell that its sculptor well those passions read
Which yet survive, stamped on these lifeless things,
The hand that mocked them and the heart that fed.
And on the pedestal these words appear:
"My name is Ozymandias, King of Kings:
Look on my works, ye mighty, and despair!"
Nothing beside remains. Round the decay
Of that colossal wreck, boundless and bare
The lone and level sands stretch far away.'

P. B. Shelley, 1818

The sonnet was inspired by a colossal statue of Ramesses II,
removed from Egypt by Giovanni Belzoni two years earlier.
Belzoni gave it to the British Museum, where it remains.

18

'How you've *grown*, Lucy! Your father won't recognise you – two inches taller, I could swear,' Miss Mack had said, as the boat-train drew away from the station at Dover. She'd settled herself into her seat opposite and was inspecting me with worried eyes. The prospect of meeting my father was making her anxious; I sympathised.

Miss Mack felt that once we reached London, there would be ample time for a leisurely farewell: perhaps my father would take us out to lunch? And then we'd discover what arrangements he'd made for my new Cambridge life. All I knew was that I'd be returning to the house in Newnham, purchased at the time of my parents' marriage, the house in which, two years later, I'd been born. I'd never lived anywhere else, but I associated it solely with my mother: since returning from the war, my father had chosen to live in college, coming home only at weekends.

'He's said nothing of his plans in his letters,' Miss Mack confided fretfully, as the boat-train puffed through the bleak landscape, while I stared out at leafless trees, at black, freshly ploughed fields. 'Your father writes in such a terse way – well, men do, I suppose. But I feel sure he will have thought the matter over very carefully, and your welfare, Lucy, will be uppermost in his mind. He'll need a woman's assistance. Perhaps one of his Norfolk cousins might help out, or your Aunt Foxe? Your dear mother was fond of her.'

Aunt Foxe was my father's elder sister, from whom he was estranged. My mother had indeed liked her and had attempted to heal the breach; it was on a visit to Aunt Foxe in Norfolk that my mother and I had taken that last walk together. I stared fixedly out of the train window. 'I don't think so,' I replied. 'He doesn't speak to his cousins. Or his brother. And he detests Aunt Foxe — he never sees any of his family if he can help it.'

Miss Mack, still recovering from the pain of our parting with Wheeler, Rose and Peter at Dover, and increasingly nervous at the prospect of meeting my father, said nothing further. I knew she cherished a lingering hope that she'd be invited to delay her return to America, come to stay in Cambridge and — at least for a while — take care of me. I'd tried to dissuade her; I knew it would never happen, not while my father lived and breathed.

And, as things turned out, the lunch we'd imagined never happened either: there was no lingering farewell, no discussion as to past travels or future plans. My father, spruce and businesslike, was waiting for us on the platform at Victoria. Miss Mack was courteously met, courteously thanked, courteously escorted to a taxicab, beseeched to write once she'd returned to America — and courteously dispatched to the London hotel room booked for her. The entire transaction took fifteen minutes. One second I was clinging to her in a final embrace; the next she had gone.

'Better hurry. We'll just make the two o'clock train from Liverpool Street. What a mountain of luggage, Lucy.' My father regarded my cases and trunk narrowly.

'I have been away for months, Daddy,' I said, 'the whole of January and February.'

'Have you really? How time flies!' He gave me a cool, satiric glance, weighing my cases, weighing me. He tipped the porter sixpence, then climbed into the waiting cab.

'One suitcase is full of books.' I climbed in after him. 'And I've brought presents too. For Mrs Grimshaw, and Aunt Foxe, and for you, of course . . .'

'Dear God. Not one of those appalling scarabs, I hope. If you inflict one of those on me, I can assure you it will go straight in the rubbish bin.'

I blushed. A scarab was precisely what I'd bought for him, bargaining for it in the souk at Luxor with Frances and her mother. I'd thought it a beautiful thing, carved from golden-veined lapis lazuli — it was genuine and not a tourist fake, Helen had been sure. That present-buying expedition had been an ordeal: Frances had scores of gifts to buy for her large family, for their numerous friends. I'd been able to drum up only four candidates: my father; Aunt Foxe, whom I rarely saw; Dr Gerhardt, an elderly don and friend of my father who'd taught me German and French in the past; and Mrs Grimshaw, who was our charwoman in Cambridge.

I was fond of garrulous Mrs Grimshaw, a fixture throughout my childhood; I liked my Aunt Foxe, and Dr Gerhardt, who dozed in a companionable way through my lessons with him, but I now saw these gifts would have to be re-allocated. I'd bought a small *shabti* figure, of dubious provenance but the best I could afford, for Dr Gerhardt: perhaps I could give him the scarab instead and present the *shabti* to my father. Would that be destined for the rubbish too – or might it pass?

I worried about this all the way across the din of London from Victoria to Liverpool Street station. I was still worrying about it – *shabti* or scarab, scarab or *shabti* – when we boarded the Cambridge train. The entanglement of gifts, once bright with promise, now dulled and stupid-seeming, would probably have preoccupied me for the rest of the journey; I was extricated from its coils only when my father, leaning forward to examine me, suddenly said, 'Lucy, you've grown.' It was the first remark he'd made since we'd boarded the train: it might have been a compliment or an accusation. With my father, there was often this uncertainty.

I fixed my eyes on the strings of the luggage rack opposite, on the framed sepia photographs of Cambridge colleges. The seats were scratchy red moquette: there were white starched antimacassars on each headrest. We had the compartment to ourselves. I suffered his scrutiny.

'Yes, definitely taller.' He frowned. 'And you've filled out, less scrawny than you were, your hair has grown a little ... you look reasonably well. The Orient must have agreed with you.'

'You look well too, Daddy,' I replied timorously. He was wearing a new overcoat and a well-cut grey suit I'd never seen before. He'd abandoned the black tie he'd worn in mourning for my mother for one made of patterned silk foulard. He looked handsome and youthful – even pleased with the world; less thin and strained than I remembered. 'Yes, well, time passes,' he remarked, and opened his newspaper.

With this broadsheet wall between us, it felt safe to look at him. All I could see was his thick springy dark hair above the opened pages, and the quizzical arch of his eyebrows. His eyes, of a light hazel colour, their habitual expression one of disdainful mockery, were mercifully hidden. I tried to reacquaint myself with him, this man who was my father, but it was difficult – I knew so little about him; I could see him only through my mother's stories, through her eyes. He *was* a handsome man, I thought. My mother always claimed that she had loved him from the first instant she set eyes on him at a party in London: Robert Foxe-Payne, an Englishman unlike anyone she'd ever met in America: vigorous, incisive and iconoclastic; a young Cambridge classicist who'd taken a double first, a golden boy of twenty-two, predicted to do great things.

And so he had – at first: a smooth progression to his doctorate, to a fellowship at Trinity College, to his first publication, a translation of Books 1–6 of Homer's *Iliad*. That had caused a great stir: 'In academic circles *and* beyond, Lucy,' my mother would say with pride. He had his detractors, of course, she'd add, but with such a brilliant man, that was inevitable. There were those who took exception to his politics, those who mocked his decision to remove the 'Foxe' element of his surname; some even suggested that, had he been the heir instead of the younger son, he might have been pleased to retain both the full name and the ancient, if reduced, Norfolk estate that went with it. Certain astringent critics claimed that a private income, even a relatively small one, was a pleasant cushion for a man of such advanced left-wing views – one Dr Robert Payne had no inclination to forgo, despite his preachings on equality for all.

Those factions, my mother said, spread malicious untruths about my father: they suggested he'd married her because she was an Emerson and an heiress, that he hadn't foreseen the severance with her family the marriage would cause, that he'd believed her family would come round, if not when the marriage took place, then surely when the first child was born? The Emerson clan's stony-faced refusal to do so, these factions claimed, caused difficulties between husband

and wife, who were incompatible from the first, one a gifted scholar, the other an impetuous, ill-educated society girl.

'And that is a lie, Lucy,' my mother would say. 'It's so hurtful. Robert and I married for love. Neither of us cared a straw about money. It's just envy that makes them say these wicked things.'

Envy *was* rife among Cambridge academics, so perhaps that was true, I thought, as my father turned a page of *The Times* and, attacking the crossword with a silver propelling pencil, began filling in the answers at speed. Perhaps that explained why my father had so few friends among his fellow dons . . . On the other hand, were there really so many reasons to envy him? His much anticipated translation of the next six books of the *Iliad* had never appeared; interrupted by the advent of war, it had since been abandoned. He had published nothing in the past decade. His health had been impaired by his time in the trenches. His marriage to an American heiress had not brought him a fortune, but had brought him a child. Now my mother Marianne was dead – and what was he left with? A daughter whom he scarcely knew, one who required housing and teaching: I must be a burden, I thought. My father entered another answer to a clue; the flat fields passed; the train wheels revolved.

It took him until the next station, finishing the crossword in the half-hour he always allowed it, before he looked up and began to ask me about Egypt. He listened to my halting replies.

'Ah yes, *ballet*. You mentioned that in one of your inimitable postcards,' he remarked. 'You must cure yourself, Lucy, of this predilection for exclamation marks.' My description of the Winlocks elicited a dismissive, 'Oh, *Americans*,' and an incautious reference to Lord Carnarvon was an error: ever emphatic in his Socialist views, my father detested and despised aristocrats. He despised the working and middle classes too, but this fact was less often canvassed. I switched tack fast, but my earnest account of the Valley of the Kings caused immediate irritable mirth: his lips thinned.

'Mummified kings, cats, baboons, bulls – even crocodiles, I understand. There's a civilisation for you! One so advanced it failed to produce a shred of literature. Why any archaeologist worth his salt should choose to dig there, rather than Greece or Italy, I can't imagine . . . except for the *gold*, which they unearth with monotonous regularity, though less so of late, I observe. They impressed you, did they – those Egyptian gods, with birds or dung beetles for heads? They seem preposterous to me.'

'Those beetles symbolise rebirth, Daddy,' I replied. 'I liked the gods. And the goddesses.'

'Ah, so you have opinions now, do you?' He raised an eyebrow. 'Forgive me: once you've seen the Parthenon, perhaps I'll bow to them; not before. And the famous tombs? How were they? I seem to remember their prospect excited you a good deal – and Miss Mackenzie too, though, as we know, it takes precious little to excite *her*.'

'The tombs were the most astonishing thing I've ever seen in my life, and I shall never ever forget them.'

'Two "evers" in one sentence! My dear, your eloquence is such that I dare ask no further questions. Your replies would overwhelm me.'

He returned to *The Times*; I turned to the window. Fields scudded past; it had begun to rain; it was still only three in the afternoon, but the light was fading fast. We were one hour into the journey: another hour to go. I'd forgotten my father's talent for withering any enthusiasm betrayed by others; I was dying by inches again. I wished I had my *ankh*, and for want of it fingered the lapis lazuli bead Howard Carter had given me. Folded around it was the note with her address on it that Rose had given me that morning.

The two of us had been standing on the deck of the Channel steamer, watching the cliffs of Dover approach. 'My mother's dead,' Rose had said suddenly, in a sensible tone. 'I do know that, Lucy. I may not know how, or where – but I've worked it out, and I know she's never coming back. You know it too – I can see it in your eyes. But you don't have to pretend any more. You must still protect Petey – but not me.' She gestured towards her brother; hand-in-hand with Wheeler, he was further along the deck, feeding gulls. Rose gave a small cough. 'You've been jolly good at it, an absolute *brick*,' she went on, stealing her small gloved hand into mine. 'No, don't argue – you *have*. So you've got to promise me: you'll write, won't you, Lucy? You'll come and visit Petey and me?'

'Of course I will,' I replied.

There would be no difficulty in writing, but a visit? I couldn't see my father's agreeing to that, but now was not the moment to say so. I looked down at Rose's small, plump, resolute figure: she was glaring at the white cliffs as they inexorably approached. Both of us had been given the Wheeler treatment that morning: my hair had been disciplined in honour of my father; Rose, prepared for a similar reunion, was wearing a smocked woollen frock, a double-breasted green tweed overcoat with velvet collar, kid gloves, and a bottle-green velour hat with a turned-up brim, fastened under her chin with elastic. This garb did not meet with her approval.

'For two pins, I'd chuck this hat in the Channel,' she said, sensing my gaze. 'Hideous thing! *And* the elastic itches. Can you imagine what Mamma would say, if she could see me now? She'd say I looked bloody awful. But then everything's bloody awful, my entire life's going to be bloody awful, and Petey's too, so I suppose a bloody awful hat doesn't matter much. In the general scheme of things.'

'It might not be *so* bad, Rose.' I was startled by the forbidden swearword and trying to inject conviction into my voice. 'Wheeler will be there. Eve will come and see you as soon as she's back in England. You and Petey will have each other—'

'Eight years,' Rose interrupted. 'That's my sentence. I worked it out last night, Lucy. I thought, I can manage that, it isn't so long – the second I'm eighteen, I shall just snap my fingers and *flit*. I had it all worked out: I'd set up house with Wheeler, learn typing and that shorthand stuff and become a tip-top secretary. I think I'd be good at that: Mamma always said I was a whizz at organising. Only I won't be able to flit – I realised that one second later. Because I can't abandon Petey. So I'll have to wait until he's old enough to escape from Father too. And that means fourteen years of hellishness – maybe more.'

She pinged the elastic on her hat. 'Unless my father *dies*, of course,' she added, in a reflective tone. 'And there's not much chance of that, worse luck, because he's fit as a fiddle and he's thirty-two, which isn't terribly old. Still – my mother was only twenty-eight, so accidents *can* happen. That gives me hope. Meanwhile, here's my address.' She handed me a crumpled piece of paper, turned her droll face up to mine and fixed me with her blue piercing stare. '*Write*, Lucy. You have to swear you will. Say: "Rose, I bloody well give you my word".'

'I bloody well give you my word, Rose,' I'd replied. It was the first time in my life that I'd said the word 'bloody' aloud.

I began composing a letter in my mind as the Cambridge train rattled onwards. But I'd never attempted to describe my father to Rose or discussed my mother's death with her, and Rose – trapped in the cocoon of her own grief, fear and bewilderment – had never asked. My imagined letter wasn't much of a thing: it was so veiled, so disguised, so pumped up with fake optimism that you could tell it was hollow one sentence in. I made up two lines for Rose, then two for Peter, then remembered his tears at Dover and gave up. We were approaching our destination. My father consulted his pocket watch, roused himself and put down the paper at last.

'We shall take a taxicab,' he announced. 'I'd prefer to walk, but as it's raining and you have such an encumbrance of luggage, that seems sensible. Miss Dunsire said she'd have tea waiting for us. I don't want to be late. I must be back in college well before Hall.'

'Who is Miss Dunsire, Daddy?' He'd shown no inclination to tell me, so I finally risked the question as the taxicab turned into the bleak familiar road to the town.

'Miss Dunsire is the answer to my prayers. She will be looking after you.'

'But I thought——'

'You surely didn't imagine I'd be performing that onerous task?'

'Of course not. But I'm eleven now – I'll be twelve quite soon. I thought, if Mrs Grimshaw still came in, as she did when Mummy was – was there, and if I——'

'Lucy, please. Mrs Grimshaw is the wife of a Trinity College porter. She is a retired gyp who can make beds, deal with laundry and scrub floors. She's hardly the person I'd want supervising my daughter. Nicola Dunsire is a gentlewoman. She grew up in England, but is descended from a long line of Scottish lawyers and lairds – there's even a distant connection to Sir Walter Scott, I believe. She has a Cambridge degree – insofar as any female *can* hold a degree, of course. She completed her course in English Literature at Girton College two years ago, and passed Tripos with distinction. So she——'

So she's young, I thought. 'So she's to be my governess?' I asked.

'Certainly, up to a point.' His tone became testy. 'She will take charge of some of your teaching at least. She will also fulfil the necessary role of housekeeper – something she's perfectly willing to do, I may add, which is a great weight off my mind, given that most governesses these days are morbidly sensitive as to their status, expect a houseful of ancillary servants, and demand to be waited on hand, foot and finger. I'd remind you that I am not one of those millionaires you seem to have been consorting with in Egypt: I'm a Fellow of Trinity, on what one can only describe as miserly remuneration. This discussion is otiose. You'll be meeting Miss Dunsire shortly. She's an intelligent, resourceful, modern young woman.' He paused. 'In fact, she has what one might call *advanced* views. I find that stimulating. As you will, Lucy, I feel sure.'

She was also beautiful: he forgot to mention that. Had he noticed? I wondered, as I was ushered into the drawing room once marked with my mother's imprint, and now so changed; as Nicola Dunsire rose with restless grace from the chair by the fire where she'd been reading, put down her book, and advanced, both hands held out to me. My father was not a man who noticed women; he claimed to dislike all the dons' wives included in our small circle of acquaintance. Women made him nervous and irritable; finding their voices shrill and their views vacuous, he much preferred the company of men. In the past he'd seemed never to notice their conversation, their appearance or their dress, let alone any claim they might have to prettiness or charm; yet even he, surely, could not have failed to be struck by the young woman who was now clasping my cold hands in her warm ones, and saying, in a low, pure voice: 'Lucy. How glad I am to meet you. At last.'

She was tall — about five foot nine, almost my father's height. She was slender and composed, leaning down to place a gentle dry kiss on my cheek. Not flamboyant, like Poppy d'Erlanger — and as different from her as it was possible for a woman to be, yet equally arresting. Very pale skin; a camellia complexion; a profile as perfect as a Grecian statue, the nose straight, the lips carved. Not a trace, not a hint of make-up — not even of the discreet kind a woman like Eve allowed. Extraordinary eyes, large, blue-green, thickly lashed, with an expression that was clever, appraising and serene; and astonishing hair, thick, lustrous, bronze in colour, intertwined with copper, with gold. She was plainly dressed, in a fine-spun white shirt, and a knee-length grey skirt; she wore no jewellery beyond the smallest of wristwatches. I examined her white skin and the luxuriant flame of her irrepressible hair; it was cut boyishly short in the modern way, and in the firelight resembled pagan armour. Grave, beautiful and austere, I thought; a helmeted virgin goddess: Pallas Athene come down from Mount Olympus to serve tea in a Cambridge sitting room.

She said little at first: as I'd learn, Nicola Dunsire was a woman possessed of well-honed patience. She concentrated her will – and I could already sense the power of that will, feel its beating pulse in her long silences – on putting my father and me at ease. The tea was Lapsang Souchong, his favourite; as were the small triangles of toast, spread with Gentleman's Relish, and the cucumber sandwiches, each the size of a postage stamp. The cake, made by her own hands, she ruefully confessed, was Madeira. My father and she sparred a little as to whether this cake were a success, she claiming failure, he insisting it was the best she'd yet made.

How long has she been here? I was thinking. How long had it taken this Miss Dunsire to ascertain my father's tastes and practise such homely skills as cake-baking? Averting my eyes from the spectacle of their teasing argument, a protracted witty dispute they clearly both enjoyed, I examined my mother's room. Who had removed her paintings? Where were the cushions she'd embroidered? Where were her sewing baskets, her books, her photographs? Not even the dusty outlines remained where the pictures had hung. The room, once papered in William Morris's willow design, had been painted a pale blue; the furniture had been rearranged. My mother had vanished; her presence here, once so vibrant, had been eradicated by an unknown hand.

Perhaps my face betrayed my feelings: it was at exactly this moment – when I was realising the extent to which my mother had been exorcised, wondering whether my father had organised it, and if so when – that Nicola Dunsire altered course. Ending the dispute as to her cooking skills with a small reproof to my father, she turned her attention to me. I must be exhausted after my journey, but even so she longed to hear . . . And then began the interrogation: had I seen this, had I been there? Pyramids, temples, tombs: she'd done her homework; she knew all the right prompts, and when they failed to elicit much by way of reply, she shifted ground with skill, a silky segue from Egypt to Rome, from Rome to Greece – thus giving my father the facility he most enjoyed: a platform.

Off he went. Fifteen minutes, twenty, thirty, ticked by – and he was somewhere in Plato or Aristotle when she cut him off. She performed this act of daring, one that astonished me, with assurance: mid-sentence, her gaze of rapt attention changed to a frown; she rose to her feet, and tapped her watch. 'Enough!' she said. 'Dr Payne – you're making me forget the time, as you always do. I could listen for another hour, as I'm sure Lucy could. But you're too enthralling for your own good: two more minutes and you'll be late for Hall. That I cannot permit.'

I waited for the irritable outburst that always ensued whenever my father was interrupted or chivvied. It never came. Flattery – even gross flattery, it seemed – could produce a response that my mother's timid reminders had never achieved. My father rose to his feet like a bashful, obedient little boy. Giving Miss Dunsire a dark sidelong glance, he remarked that the fault was entirely hers: she was such a good listener, he forgot the time when in her company. They laughed together at this, and there was a brief, queer spurt of excitement between them – ignited in their gaze, which had locked. I felt it enter the room with a poltergeist's zeal.

Then it was gone, and my father was searching fussily for the gown he'd need for dinner in college, and Miss Dunsire, grave, amused, had it immediately to hand. The door banged shut behind him. From beyond the new curtains came the sound of Cambridge bells. Miss Dunsire returned to the chair opposite me. It still wore its old cover; also a Morris design, it was called 'Strawberry Thief' and depicted a thieving thrush, in faded pinks and jade greens. Miss Dunsire sat down.

'When will my father be back?' I asked.

'We can't expect him until the end of the week, Lucy,' she replied. 'Saturday, perhaps – or Sunday. He's been living in college since you left for Egypt. I'm sure you understand. Your father has a tremendously heavy workload: lectures, supervisions . . . And at last he's begun his new book, did he tell you that? On the plays of Euripides. I rather bullied him into it, I'm afraid. He needs constant access to libraries.' She paused. 'Shall you mind?'

'Only seeing him at weekends? No. My mother and I were used to that.'

'Of course you were,' she said quietly.

I think she was considering a more intimate approach, another clasping of the hands, but seeing me shrink back in my chair, she changed her mind. To my surprise, she reached for a small box, and took a cigarette from it. She lit it with a match, inhaled, and blew the match out. I caught the faint scent of brimstone.

'I was on five cigarettes a day in the lead-up to Finals, Lucy,' she announced, in a wry confessional way. 'I gave up after the last exam, just like that.' She snapped her fingers. 'When I came here, I hadn't touched them for two years. But your father smokes on occasion; he offered me one the other week – and here I am, addicted again.'

Some comment seemed required, so I said: 'In Egypt, everyone smoked, women as well as men. Well, practically everyone,' I added, as the ghost of Poppy d'Erlanger briefly entered the room. 'Oh, *hellishness*,' the ghost remarked, and disappeared. Silence fell.

'You'd noticed the alterations here, hadn't you, Lucy?' Nicola Dunsire ventured, after a pause. 'They must upset you, I think? May I explain? At our interview, when your father hired me, I could see he was in a pitiful state, worried about your return, unsure what would be best for you, and he was still – lacerated by grief. I do not use the word "lacerated" idly. I never use words in an idle way. It was becoming an ordeal for him, returning to this house, with its many reminders of your late mother's presence . . .

'You don't know me, Lucy, so I'll come clean!' She tossed the cigarette into the fire. 'I detest secrets. All those prudish Victorian evasions – no one ever daring to say what he thinks or she feels! This is the 1920s, it's a new era, and I believe in bringing things into the open – *dragging* them into the open if need be. So, when I saw the effect this house was having on your father, I came right out with it, Lucy, and I told him frankly that he needed to make a break with the past. No one can live in a *museum* – nor should they. I told him: stay in college for two weeks, don't set foot in this house for that time, and leave everything in my hands. *I* will make the necessary changes. They will be radical. They may shock you at first. They may pain you initially: I'm prepared for that. Leave it to me, I said – and dismiss me if I'm wrong.'

'And he agreed?'

'Of course. Your father is a scholar; men like him, with busy professional lives, have a horror of domestic detail. Why should they concern themselves with cooking and curtain materials, with laundry lists, with deciding where pictures should hang? Things like that bore them to distraction – and, I may as well admit it, they bore *me* to distraction too. I much prefer to study. I'm a bluestocking, Lucy.' She gave me a mocking half-smile. 'On the other hand, I like to live in a place that looks pleasant and runs efficiently, and I'm a well-organised person – I'm a fiend for order, always have been. So I could effect the practical, simple changes that were needed here very easily and quickly. I knew that in your father's case they'd be *therapeutic*. And so they have proved.'

'He likes it? He approves?'

'Lucy, I'll be frank: he scarcely notices! *That*'s how well I've performed my task.' She laughed. 'Before, it was a little – how shall I put this – overcrowded? Its effect on your father was oppressive; not everything here was to his taste, you know.' She paused; the flicker of amusement vanished and her face became grave. 'However, I'm not a fool, Lucy, as you'll realise when you know me better. So please understand: when I made these little changes, moved a few things here and there – I wasn't thinking only of your father, I was thinking of *you*. A young girl, whom I'd never met – a girl who'd been subjected to sudden, tragic change. A child who was far away, experiencing the excitements and uncertainties of a foreign country. A traveller from an antique land.'

She waited to see if I'd pick up the Shelley quotation, made in a testing tone; when she saw that I did, she continued in a warm, confiding way: 'I knew that this girl would be expecting to return to a familiar place. And I was torn, yes, *torn*, Lucy, between your father's needs and yours. So in the end, I decided to take the middle way: I made changes, yes – but I also *preserved*. Everything belonging to your late mother, all her bits and bobs, her paintings and books and little trinkets: I've packed them up with the greatest care, Lucy, and I've kept them for you.'

I think she was expecting thanks. I think she actually was expecting thanks. If so, she was not as clever as she imagined herself. At that moment, I'd sooner have thrust my hand into the fire than utter one syllable of gratitude.

There was a long, lethal silence. Less than a year since my mother died: I was imagining Frances's reaction, the outburst that these actions and this explanation would have provoked from her. A part of me longed to speak out as Frances would have done, but there were other ways of dealing with a woman like Nicola Dunsire, more indirect ways, as Frances had also shown me. Besides, old habits die hard.

So I rose and merely told her that I was tired from the long journey, and thought I'd go to bed now. The flatness of my voice, maybe some mutiny in my eyes, disconcerted her momentarily. She was a woman who was rarely flustered, as I'd learn – but she was flustered then. She rose, fiddled with the cushions on her chair, began suggesting that I should have something to eat: she'd prepared a light supper. I took the opportunity to glance at the book she'd put down when my father and I entered the room; both title and author were unfamiliar to me: Sigmund Freud, *The Interpretation of Dreams*.

'I'm not hungry, but I am tired. I'd really prefer to go straight to bed. If you don't mind.'

'Of course. You must be exhausted – all those ferryboats, all those trains. May I bring something up for you? Warm milk? Hot chocolate? I make the *best* hot chocolate.' She gave me a conspiratorial smile. 'It was our great treat at Girton. The food in women's colleges is vile, Lucy – not like the men's. We undergraduates were always starving, we used to meet up in one another's rooms in the evening, and make cocoa and chocolate on a little gas-ring. Then talk about books until the wee hours!'

The sudden girlishness was unconvincing. 'No, thank you,' I replied. 'I don't really like hot chocolate. Or cocoa. Where have you put my mother's things, by the way?'

'*By the way*, I have put them in a spare room,' she answered, with emphasis, and after a fractional pause. Her gaze met mine. With three small words, a gauntlet had been thrown down – and instantly picked up. When she could see from my face that I understood this as well as she did, Nicola Dunsire turned away.

'In the spare room next to your own bedroom,' she continued, her tone hardening. 'The overspill is in the loft. It can be brought down for you, should you wish it. Breakfast will be at eight o'clock sharp – I should warn you, I'm a fiend for punctuality, Lucy. We'll begin our lessons, and I'll show you the curriculum I've drawn up for you, the day after tomorrow. You'll need twenty-four hours to rest and adjust, and I've allowed for that. Meanwhile, is there anything else you need?'

Not that you can provide, I thought.

'No, thank you,' I replied and, resisting her attempts to help me with my overnight case, went upstairs to the top floor.

My attic room was unchanged. There were the same sprigged curtains at the dormer window, the same brass bedstead and rosebud-patterned eiderdown; the wallpaper, blowsy with faded poppies, the pattern that I'd pleaded for and my mother had smilingly allowed, was unmolested. When I'd last seen this room, I'd been ill; now I was cured. I lit the small gas fire and, shivering, unpacked and undressed in front of it; but I had become used to the heat of Egypt by then, and the room remained breath-catchingly cold.

I huddled under the blankets and at once fell asleep. When I woke, it was three in the morning. I wrapped myself in my woollen dressing gown, and stood at the window for a while. There was a full high moon and a sharp frost outside, and my breath kept misting up the window-panes. I rubbed the mist away, then pushed up the sash – and there Cambridge was, bright and bone-white from this high vantage-point, its glittering spires, towers, turrets and pinnacles: that palace of knowledge to which I'd returned.

I made a vow then – and all these long decades later I can claim that I kept it religiously. Then I padded next door to examine my mother's archaeological remains. They filled the spare room from floor to ceiling and from wall to wall: box upon box of them, all painstakingly sealed, stacked and labelled in the italic script that I would come to recognise as Nicola Dunsire's hand. Here my mother's diaries, there her dresses; here her hats, there her paintings and jewellery. *China ornaments, assorted*, said one label; *Emerson family letters*, read another; *Photographs: USA and England,* read a third. There was a box for official documents, passports, visas, birth and marriage certificates. There was a box labelled *Final illness and death of*; there was a box labelled *Stockings and undergarments*, and another for *Condolence letters: family and friends.*

No archivist could have taken greater pains. The room itself deserved a label: *The Museum of Marianne Emerson Payne*. It felt as if my mother had died a second time.

I returned to bed, fell asleep and entered a nightmare – a nightmare that recurred for years. I was back in the Egyptian Museum, compelled to walk past that fearsome line of mummies again. Rose and Frances were with me, all three of us clasping hands. Alongside the dead kings lay my mother and Poppy d'Erlanger and a small shape that Frances recognised as her little brother, lost in the waters off Maine. All the mummies were in a state of distress, protesting at the labels describing them and their lives, insisting the Museum officials were mistaken: it hadn't been like that, *they* hadn't been like that; their identities were confused, or distorted; subverted, or just plain wrong.

Their anguish cut us to the heart, but in our dream state we were impotent to help. We glided silently past them – and then, at the end of the row, in a special case of their own, we came to a new exhibit: three mummified women, who were regarding us cunningly, who whispered to each other and moaned. When we tried to creep past them, they became very agitated; they began to rip the bandages from their faces, they shook out the snaky locks of their dust-encrusted hair and, to our horror, they called out our names: *Don't you recognise us?* they cried. *Don't you see who we are?*

Mesmerised and afraid, I bent to read the labels that recorded their names and lives. In a shaky voice, Frances said: 'Don't, *don't*. I know who they are. That's you, Lucy, with the fountain pen. That's Rose, in the hat. And the one with scarlet lipstick is me.'

'That can't be! We're alive – and they're dead. That's not possible!' I cried.

'That's ridiculous,' said Rose, beginning to weep. 'That horrid old hag? Look at that hideous hat of hers! I wouldn't be seen dead in it. How can that possibly be me?'

Sick with fear, I bent to the labels again. They informed me that the dark-haired woman on the left was indeed Frances; the fair-haired woman on the right was Rose; the pallid cipher of a woman between them bore my own name. Pen in hand, she'd begun to scribble frantic words on her bandages. I stared at them: I could see no resemblance to Frances, Rose or me – yet the Museum labels, which were printed, authoritative, as readable as the clean pages of a new book, made their identities only too clear.

'Wait, wait, wait. Let me *read*! Let me see what the labels say,' I cried, as Rose and Frances tried to drag me away. 'There must be some mistake. Let me check the dates when they died. Then we'll know for sure—'

'*That information is classified. Access denied*,' boomed a terrible voice from the dark recesses of the Museum – and I woke, shaking with fear, to an attic bedroom and a new Cambridge day.

'What's happened to that Wong fellow, the one who was interrogating you?' Rose asked, adjusting her new hat. She closed the glass division between us and her chauffeur. We had been inching our way west out of London and had now reached the motorway; before us stretched the M4.

'*Fong*,' I corrected, absently. '*Dr* Fong.'

It was April; there had been a fortnight of fine weather, and spring might, or might not, have arrived. I was on my way to stay at Rose's house in the country, as I did every year once winter was past. We were installed in Rose's car, a vintage Bentley originally bought by Rose's husband; it had been cherished by him until his death thirty years later, and by Rose ever since. This was its last ceremonial outing. It was soon to be sacrificed. Rose, who had always liked causes, had recently embraced a new one, sustainability; she was newborn, reinvigorated; she had become, she'd informed me, *eco-aware*.

It was months since I'd seen Rose and we had a lot of catching up to do, I thought, gazing out of the window as the Bentley, its great engine soundless, picked up speed. I had spent a cold winter looking back at the past; Rose had passed those months looking forward. She had been overhauling the large, draughty, seventeenth-century manor house in which she'd lived for sixty years. It was to become *carbon-neutral* — or so she claimed. The massive upheaval necessary had been seized upon with zeal. Once the floors were up, once her house was crawling with 'legions of plumbers and electricians', Rose had embarked on a 'massive clear-out'. She'd spent the entire winter on this archaeological task, as she'd explained to me in numerous phone calls. Attics had been raided, cupboards gutted, cellars cleared: the accumulated possessions, all the records of Rose and her large family, had been examined, saved, discarded, consigned to Oxfam, passed down, sold off, burned or conserved. For various reasons, these activities had caused me alarm.

Now, apparently, this act of clearance was complete, but – bringing back the past as it inevitably did – it had reminded Rose of certain obligations, such as 'making calls', 'cheering up ancient chums' and 'staying in touch'. As a result, this journey west along the M4 was to include a brief diversion: en route to Rose's home near Bath, we were to pay a visit – to someone Rose described as a dear old friend. 'Fifteen minutes,' she'd said. 'Half an hour at most. Haven't been there in ages. We've neglected our duty. Has to be done.'

I'd been reluctant to agree and was regretting this diversion. I didn't want to discuss Dr Fong either, and hoped Rose would not pursue that subject. She was now fumbling in her ancient crocodile-skin Hermès handbag. I continued to gaze out of the window; a peculiar double vision afflicted me now. I saw a lost Egypt as we passed green English fields.

'What's happened to Wong? What did you say, Lucy?' she enquired. 'I do wish you'd speak up.' She might deny it, but I felt Rose was becoming deaf: a hearing aid wouldn't do any harm.

'Fong,' I said irritably. 'He's American, and his name's *Fong*, Rose.'

'Fong, Wong, Wrong – whatever.' From the recesses of her handbag, Rose extracted a powder compact. She patted pink powder on her nose, peered at her own reflection and sighed. 'Until recently, I thought I was quite well preserved, you know, Lucy,' she remarked in mournful tones. 'Not beautiful, obviously, I was never destined to be that: Ma's genes all went to Petey and passed me by. And never pretty either, but I always told myself I was *presentable* – and I thought I'd stayed that way. It was the cataracts, of course. The mercies of soft focus. Then that damn doctor *insisted* I have the op. Now I can see again and there's no escaping the appalling truth. I look in the glass and think: what a terrible old hag – who in hell are *you?*'

Rose's assessment of her own appearance was characteristically harsh: she'd retained her English-rose complexion; age had not

withered the acuity of her gaze. She was looking well, I thought –
but I'd save the compliments for later. I said, 'Join the club, Rose.'

'Thanks. I knew I could rely on you for sympathy.' She laughed,
and settled herself more comfortably in the Bentley's deep leather
seats. 'Remember this?' She held out the compact to me. I took it
from her, and examined it: a period piece, fashioned in rose gold,
decorated with vivid blue enamel, with the initials 'PdE' in a diamond
scroll.

'I do. It was Poppy's. I remember her powdering her nose with it –
and I remember when, too. We'd just had tea at Shepheard's, after our
ballet lesson with Madame.'

'Gosh, you've got an amazing memory. Nowadays, of course,
"powder" and "noses" have quite different associations. Or so my
grandchildren tell me. They think it's a hoot.'

Rose took the compact back and squinted at it critically. 'I suppose
one would remember it – it's awfully flash. Very *goût* Rothschild. But
then Jacob d'Erlanger gave it to her, and he *was* a bit Rothschild.
Poppy adored that in him, she never stopped teasing him about his
taste. Well, she adored *him*, of course . . . I found it in the back of a
drawer when I was doing the great clear-out. Hadn't laid eyes on it
in years, and then, suddenly, there it was! Oh, so *that*'s where you've
been hiding, I said to myself . . . I've started talking to myself now,
incidentally, which *cannot* be a good sign, I feel. Do you ever do that,
Lucy? No, of course you don't. Far too strong-minded. It still has the
powder in it that my mother used. What a relic! But then I found all
sorts of interesting *relics* during my clear-out.' She gave me a sly considering glance, replaced the compact, snapped her bag shut, and
turned to the window with a frown. 'Look at this traffic! Where on
earth are all these people *going*? It's ten-thirty on a Wednesday morning, for heaven's sake.'

'They're going about their business, I imagine. They're *working*,
Rose.'

'If you say so. I think they're just gallivanting. The instant the sun
comes out in this godforsaken country, every man, woman and dog
says, Let's head for the M4 and cause the mother of all jams. It's the
English disease. So, let's catch up. You're not looking well, you
know – how's the hip? Where's the Fong fellow gone?'

'The hip's hell. But less bad now it's spring. And Dr Fong's finally left for Egypt. They've begun filming his documentary at last, so I imagine he's in Luxor.'

'Staying at the Winter Palace?' She grimaced. 'Oh, Lucy — I had nightmares about that place for years. Eve taking Petey and me into her room to explain, everyone trying to pretend it was going to be all right, when I knew it wasn't. It was a palace of tears for me. Misery HQ. Still, it must be very different now. I expect your Fang's having a whale of a time. You must be relieved to have him off your back. Frightful man.'

'Very clued-up. Sharp. And he's not so bad. In some ways I rather liked him . . . '

'That's not what you said on the phone. You said he was pestering the life out of you, came to see you twice, stayed for hours, kept phoning and emailing, and was driving you round the bend. You said you couldn't wait for him to bugger off to Egypt.'

'I expect I was exaggerating. I don't like being interrogated.'

'So I've observed. You were always like that. *Close*, Wheeler used to say, and she was right. I can't think why you're so allergic to imparting information. I *love* being cross-questioned. I positively jump at the opportunity. After all, one doesn't often get it, not now one's old. Absolutely no one, in my experience, has the least interest in anything one has to say. And as for one's *memories*, they just bore everyone to tears. "I once met Herr Hitler, as a matter of fact," I said to my grandchildren the other day — you'd have thought *that* might have grabbed them. But did it? Two sentences in, just hitting my stride, and there they were, smothering these huge yawns. It was *mortifying*.'

'Hitler?' I gave her a startled glance. 'I never knew that. You actually *met* him, Rose?'

'No, of course I didn't. I just threw it in to liven things up. And it was *almost* true. I mean, given my father's political views, it was on the cards. He was always buzzing off to Germany before the war, and then coming back and going on and on about parades and discipline and trains that ran on time. *Alles in Ordnung*. That was his watchword. Vile old fascist. Petey was in his teens by then and very left-wing, longing to go off and fight in Spain — you remember how he was, Lucy. So Pa only had to say it, and Petey would go white and clench his fists and—'

Her voice caught. 'Don't, Rose,' I said gently. 'Don't go there. Not now.'

'Not ever,' she replied. 'I do know that, Lucy. I'd willingly forget him, but sometimes he intrudes. Up he pops from his tomb, and starts on the inquisitions . . . a bit like your Dr Fang, I suppose. Only *he*'s alive, of course.'

I gave up. 'Dr Fang' had a certain ring. 'Safely in Egypt, though,' I said. 'He kept telephoning when I was hoping it was you. But I don't think he'll bother me again, not now. I was just a minnow – he has bigger fish to fry.'

'So what did he ask you?'

'Oh, you can imagine – describe Carnarvon and Howard Carter – *with* anecdotes. What game was the Met playing? Did Carter *know* that tomb was there? Was it true he was looking for Tutankhamun from day one, as he claimed afterwards, or was that one of his fairy tales? Carnarvon's death, of course. Oh, and the fabled Curse – inevitably.'

'Crikey. Did he ask about Eve?'

'Not much. She didn't really interest him.'

'Helen Winlock? Minnie Burton? The other Metropolitan wives?'

'Below his radar. Bystanders, and female ones at that. Supernumeraries.'

'Written out – and written off. *That* has a familiar ring. I hope you corrected him?'

'No. Life's too short. Besides, he wasn't altogether wrong: the men did make the running, it was 1922 – what else would you expect?'

'You have an argumentative nature, so I'd expect you to argue. Why didn't you?'

'Because I felt old and ill. This bloody arthritis was half killing me.'

'What a liar you are, Lucy,' she said comfortably. 'Don't worry, *I'm* not going to cross-question you. In the first place, I don't need to because I know the answer anyway. In the second, you'll only get grumpy and clam up. And in the third – look,' she gestured at the motorway signs. 'That's us. Exit thirteen. It's only twenty minutes from here. I've brought lilies – horribly florist, but I panicked – they're in the boot. What did you bring?'

'Spring flowers. Masses of them. Jonquils and narcissus. I picked them in my garden.'

'Oh, how clever! Her favourites. She'll love that.'

Rose's face lit. For a second, the lines on her face vanished, the grandmother and widow vanished, and I saw her as the indomitable child I'd known. The effect was weakening; it brought tears to my eyes. This happens occasionally now and very tiresome it is; I assume it's a symptom of age. I brushed them away quickly, but not before Rose had noticed them. Her face softened.

'Ah, Lucy,' she said, resting her hand on mine. 'I know. How many decades has it been?'

'A great many. We've been friends now for—'

'Most of our lives. Let's just say that. *Good* friends. And long lives too . . . though, of course, I'm just a stripling compared to you,' she added, as the small country church that was our destination came into view. This was a familiar tease: Rose's landmark birthday was still some distance away; she had not yet passed ninety; I had. She liked to remind me of my greater decrepitude.

'Well, we're not likely to make this trip again, so we'd better get a move on,' she remarked, on a firmer note. She opened the glass partition. 'Wheelie, park over there, would you? Get as close to the lych-gate as you can, then it's less far for us to hobble. No, no, don't fuss, we can manage the flowers perfectly well. You just stay here and smoke a cigarette. We shan't be long. Then we'll trot on home and have lunch.'

Wheeler, who was the great-nephew of the original Wheeler, had been driving Rose since he was eighteen. After some thirty years, he was used to her vagaries; he assisted us gallantly from the car, opened the lych-gate and obediently retired. Removing his cap, he leaned against the vintage Bentley's gleaming bonnet, and lifted his face to the sun. 'Wheelie *claims* to have given up,' Rose hissed, as we began to negotiate the churchyard path. 'But I know differently. He's cut down, that's all. The second we're out of sight, he'll light up a Silk Cut. I like him to know *I* know – keeps him on his toes. Now, where are we? Is it left or right, Lucy? It all looks different. I'm not sure.'

It was ten years since our last visit, so I wasn't too sure either. The warm weather had brought the grass on, and with it a thick spring burgeoning of weeds and wild flowers. Leaning on my stick, I peered about the graveyard short-sightedly: the small church was fifteenth century, and many of the tombs were almost as old; we were in this ancient sector now, where lichens and the weathering of stone made the inscriptions virtually unreadable. *Who wants to lie in some mouldering old churchyard?* Frances's voice enquired from a long-distant past. This might convert her, I thought: it was a serene and lovely place, isolated, quiet, with a matchless view across the north Hampshire downs.

'We need the modern bit, Rose,' I said. 'I think it's over there. No – not that way. You should never walk around a church anticlockwise. It's widdershins. It's unlucky.'

'The hell with that, it's quicker, *and* there's a path. I'm not risking that long grass,' Rose replied. Ignoring superstition, she set off to the left; I turned to the right. The hip started complaining immediately, so it took me an age to negotiate the bumpy surface and limp my way between the stones. I passed into the shadows to the north of the church, and emerged into sunlight the far side; the hawthorn hedges bordering the churchyard were coming into flower and I could smell their heavy, peculiar, vixen scent; from their depths, a thrush burst into song. I found Rose standing by Poppy d'Erlanger's overgrown grave, clutching her florist's flowers.

Jacob d'Erlanger, who had selected this burial place and commissioned this ornate and magnificent headstone, was buried next to his wife; he had shot himself on the anniversary of her death, three years later to the day. Rose, who had turned to his grave, gave a sudden moan of distress. 'Got it wrong,' she said. '*All* wrong. We should have brought him flowers too. How crass I am. He was always really good to me . . . Now what are we going to do? *I* know – we'll give Poppy your lovely jonquils, and I'll give him my lilies. They're absolutely Jaco's style.'

We laid the huge swath of pink-throated lilies on d'Erlanger's grave and the loose bunch of spring flowers on Poppy's. Neither of us was sure what to do next: I felt I couldn't utter an agnostic platitude, and Rose, who went to church regularly in the same devout spirit as, when younger, she'd ridden to hounds or opened her gardens to charitable causes, seemed moved, but reluctant to risk a prayer. 'Well, God bless you both,' she muttered, crossed herself with a practised gesture, and turned away.

'He chose well, Jaco,' she remarked as, arm in arm, we made our halting way back towards the car. 'He chose the right wife – and, when she died, the right place to bury her. People thought all Poppy cared about was parties, and rushing about and being fashionable – but really she hated that life. It made her hectic and miserable. Jaco understood that. They used to live near here, you know, Lucy, in this absurd mansion he bought for her – it was sold eventually, after he killed himself. It's one of those spiffy country-house hotels now, Poppy would *rock* with laughter if she could see it.'

Rose came to a halt, shivered and drew her fur coat more tightly around her. She peered across the graveyard towards the church, as if she expected someone to emerge from its entrance porch – her mother, perhaps.

'That night at Shepheard's,' I said, finally voicing a question that had perplexed me for decades: ask it never, I thought, or ask it now: 'When Poppy set off from the hotel – was she on her way to meet Jacob?'

I wasn't sure how Rose would react, but she seemed unperturbed. 'Oh, I think so, don't you?' she replied. 'That's why she was making such a fuss about what to wear that night. That's why she wore those rubies Jaco gave her, and put her wedding ring back on. I knew they'd never divorce. They'd quarrelled, but that meant nothing. Those weeks in Cairo, she was just fretting about Jaco, waiting for him to turn up and tell her not to be so damn stupid. The second he did, we'd have been on the next boat home.' She paused. 'I couldn't say that then, Lucy. No one could. Wheeler was brilliant, so careful what she divulged, but that policeman, the Egyptian – can't remember his name—'

'El-Deeb. It means "the wolf" – Herbert Winlock told me afterwards.'

'Does it really? Well, the wolf prowled around, as you know, and eventually he found out which rings Poppy had been wearing, and their significance. Who the fool was that gave him *that* information, I can't imagine – Wheeler and Eve certainly never let on.'

Rose gave a puzzled frown. I said nothing – Frances's involvement was safe with me.

'That detail was fatal. It *convinced* him my mother met Jaco that night, and planned to do so; by then he'd heard all about Poppy's flirtations and the fight at Shepheard's with that ghastly Carew man, of course. So he put two and two together, made eighty-eight and decided the solution was obvious: it was Jaco who killed her, in a fit of jealous rage.'

'He wasn't the only one who came up with that solution, Rose,' I said. The d'Erlanger case, a cause célèbre resurrected to this day, had attracted the attention of numerous writers over the years, and new solutions were regularly propounded. Five books had been published – the two that came out in the 1930s being especially virulent.

'Indeed. But then Jaco was a Jew, Lucy. His family might have been Church of England for three generations, but he was Jewish by descent. So certain factions couldn't *wait* to point the finger. After he died they really let rip – but even before that they made his life hell. Cut him, ostracised him, blackballed him from their stinking clubs – and some of them were so-called friends, people who'd sponged off him, sucked up to Poppy, stayed at their house. Christ, it was vile. I learned a lot from that.'

Her hand, resting on my arm, had begun to shake. 'Don't get upset, Rose,' I said. 'I'm sorry – I shouldn't have raised it. Let it rest. Let them rest. Come back to the car.'

'Very well. Just as long as you know – Jaco didn't do it, Lucy. He adored Poppy. He was a kind, gentle man and he wouldn't have harmed a hair on her head.'

We turned and continued down the path to the lych-gate. I wondered if Rose had heard about the latest book on the d'Erlanger case; my publisher, knowing my interest in Egypt, had sent me a proof copy some months before. Its thesis was new: Poppy had been killed by her lover Carew, a British officer then notorious throughout Cairo; obsessed with Poppy, he had intercepted her when she left Shepheard's and persuaded her into his car, where they had quarrelled violently. Known for his drinking, his womanising, his brutal temper and his prowess on those shoots in the marshlands where Poppy's body had been found, Carew had strangled her, the writer claimed – citing medical evidence not revealed at the inquest. In an effort to suggest robbery as a motive, he had then slashed her throat and taken her jewellery. His brother officers provided alibis, and the British authorities connived in the cover-up.

The writer made out a strong case; she'd pursued a lengthy paper trail, helped by government papers released under the thirty-year rule but long ignored. Carew had been swiftly posted to India, she'd discovered, where he'd conveniently drunk himself to death – and it was there, a year later, she claimed, that Poppy's missing rubies had surfaced. Following this lead in an attempt to clinch her case, she found that in 1924 they'd been purchased from a Delhi dealer by a Milwaukee millionaire untroubled as to their provenance. A footnote claimed that, recut and reset, they'd been sent to auction by the millionaire's widow in the 1960s as 'The Property of a Lady' at Sotheby Parke Bernet.

Should I tell Rose this? The past is an unruly place. Rose was no reader; with luck, the book would pass her by. There was no cause for me to bring it to her attention, I decided, especially now. *Let it be.* Rose was frailer than she'd been when we last met, as I was.

'How beautiful it is here,' I said, as we reached the end of the path and glanced back one last time across the quietness of green hills. Beech hangers, blossoming hedgerows, England in spring's bridal array. 'Look at those fields, those woods. Such light! I'd forgotten there were still views like this. I thought they'd all been built over. Destroyed.'

'I know.' Rose followed my gaze. Her hand was steady now. 'The image of England all those men in the trenches fought for. I always think heaven must look like this – English fields, on a spring day. But then I would: I have England in my bones.' She sighed and shook herself. 'So peaceful – and unspoiled,' she continued, in a stronger tone, 'and that's astonishing when you think how close we are to roads and towns and urban sprawl. But there's a reason for that. Ancestral acres, Lucy.'

'Really? Whose?'

'Carnarvon's of course. I thought you'd know. His land. As far as the eye can see from here. Passed on now – to his son and grandson, et cetera. I've lost count of those earls, but the estate's still huge. That's Beacon Hill over there, where Carnarvon was buried when they brought his body back from Egypt – where he asked to be buried. All alone. Overlooking his domain.' She turned and pointed. 'Highclere Castle is north of here, beyond those beech woods. And that house Ma left me, where Petey and I spent the summer after we left Egypt, such a heavenly place – you must remember that, Lucy?'

'I do.'

'Well, that's not far either. We could visit it, if you like, on the way to my house.' She glanced at me, and seeing my expression, changed her mind. 'No. Enough memories for now. Time for lunch! I'm starving. Graveyards always have that effect on me.' We had reached the Bentley, and with Wheeler's assistance, climbed back into it.

'Put your foot down, Wheelie,' Rose commanded. Wheeler obeyed.

We reached Rose's house with admirable speed. Here, Rose had spent her long married life and her long widowhood; here she had given birth to and raised four sons; a fifth, born disabled, had died in infancy. In the distant kitchen regions, Wheeler's wife was cooking lunch. Rose led me into a graceful drawing room with a view of the gardens that she and her late husband had created, a room that, in all the years I'd known it, had never changed. Apart from the new eco-efficient radiators it appeared unaltered: it was thick with belongings – no trace here of the 'massive clear-out'. Her three springer spaniels came bounding to greet us, and with the sense of pleasure this welcoming house always brought, I allowed myself to be settled on a huge sagging chesterfield, close to a log fire. Rose made me a dry Martini; she took a childish delight in all cocktails, and made them unapologetically strong. I sipped it cautiously.

'I've got a present for you,' she announced, to my surprise, turning to a tall walnut bureau and opening one of its many drawers. 'Something I found during my clearance activities. It will interest you, I think. I was feeling a bit seedy this winter,' she continued, rummaging around, 'down in the dumps. Nothing to worry about, the doc said, but I *am* getting on. That's really why I embarked on the clear-out. I don't want my poor boys to have to cope with a whole heap of rubbish once I go.'

Rose's eldest son was in his sixties; the youngest was at least fifty: I said mildly: 'I'm sure they'll manage, Rose.'

'Even so . . . had to be done! I was dreading it – this house is stuffed to the gills. But actually, I enjoyed it, Lucy. I dug up all sorts of glorious treasures – darling Bill's love letters to me in the war and mine to him – very racy *they* were, I was shocked. Lots of sweet pictures the boys drew for me when they were little. Souvenirs from Egypt, things I'd squirrelled away, I even found that bead Howard Carter gave me once . . . that brought the past back! D'you remember how rude Carter was to us that day? Such a *bully*. He intimidated people, even Carnarvon, I used to think, and definitely poor Eve . . .

'Bother, it's not here, where did I put it?' She shut the first drawer and began to rummage in a second. 'Of course, my Bill always said Carter's belligerence cost him his *gong*,' she continued. 'And Bill was in a position to know, being friends with those fusspots at court who fix these things. He said Carter put too many backs up, not just in Egypt, in London too. So when it came to the crunch, there was no one to lobby for him, which you *need*, of course. Result: not so much as a piddling decoration, let alone a K. No knighthood, Lucy, *despite* making the archaeological find of all time.'

Rose abandoned the second drawer and opened a third. I was listening with only half an ear, always an error in her case. Rose had worked as a volunteer prison visitor for decades, and had been a ruthless committee woman, fighting long campaigns for penal reform. She had served on the local bench as a magistrate for thirty years: anyone deceived by her twinsets and pearls, her unaltered upper-class accent or her manner of speech; anyone who assumed she was a pushover, a privileged relic of a lost era, or a fool, soon learned their mistake. 'Once you've *disarmed* them,' she'd say, 'you go straight for the jugular.' Rose's favourite disarmament technique, as I should have remembered, was the inconsequential chatter I called Rose's *riffs*, and she called 'rattling on'.

'Also, the *King* was fearfully sniffy about Carter, I gather,' she was saying now. 'And the courtier contingent considered him a *bounder*, of course. They didn't care for him at all. When Carter did that lecture tour of America, you know, he was given an honorary degree from Yale, and he was invited to the White House *twice*. Eve was so thrilled for him. She said President Coolidge was really fired up about the whole Tutankhamun thing, simply *had* to hear all about it from the great discoverer himself . . . But in England? Fobbed off with one invitation to a Buck House garden party! Poor Carter. I never liked him much, but even I think that's a pretty damn poor show.

'A grotesque injustice, actually,' she went on, bending over, rummaging, keeping her back to me, and sounding cross. 'I don't like injustice, Lucy, as you know. And in Carter's case, the reason was just plain old *snobbery*. Carter wasn't a gentleman, and it didn't help that he pretended he was — but who cares? Does that alter what he achieved? If he'd been Eton and Oxford, they'd have given him a knighthood like a shot. Mind you, my darling Bill didn't agree. *He* maintained it was all that dealing Carter did: people thought it bad form. Well, *that*'s a joke, Lucy, as you know. Bill was such an innocent! I told him: eliminate dealers, and you can kiss goodbye to half the contents of the British Museum, *and* the Met *and* the Louvre, because where d'you think *they* came from?'

I made no comment. I too thought Carter had been treated shabbily by the British powers-that-be; in view of the historic nature of his find, he'd expected, and deserved, some honour. Several archaeologists contemporary to him *were* knighted, including Flinders Petrie, Evans of Knossos, and Woolley of Ur: for Carter, nothing, not so much as an OBE. I found it hard to care. Rose attached importance to the honours system; I did not. But then Rose and I differed in many key respects: she was a staunch monarchist, a lifelong Tory activist, a churchgoer, a faithful wife; I was none of those things.

I turned to look at the silver-framed family photographs clustered on the table next to me, and they led me back to a past where Rose's chatter became inaudible. Rose as a debutante; Rose in uniform, arm in arm with the young officer who would become her husband. Her brother Peter as a small boy, then as a thin, beautiful, ferocious young man. An older Peter, in wartime uniform. Rose's husband again, in his later incarnation as Lieutenant Colonel Sir William Hicks, MC, DSO, CVO, equerry to some royal. A kind man, I was thinking, and a good husband: why had Rose chosen well and I so badly; why had her life been tranquil, mine otherwise?

Rose abandoned the drawer she'd been searching, and slammed it shut. 'Dammit, *where* did I put your present?' she said. 'And where was I? What set me off on that rant about Carter? Oh yes, archaeology, that's the link: my massive clear-out, my very own dig! I can't tell you, Lucy, how much stuff I unearthed. Tons of it. Treasures and trinkets and trash. Ration books. Medals. Baby clothes. Boxes and boxes of *letters* . . . mine, Petey's. Blurry old photographs of you and Petey and me in Egypt — and later of course.'

She bent down to the lowest of the bureau's drawers and gave a small cry of triumph: 'Ah, *here* you are at last!' Turning to face me, her face flushed from her efforts, she tossed a bundle into my lap. It was a bulky thing, tied up with scarlet ribbon. I looked at it in silence, alert too late. 'I got shot of almost all the letters I found,' she went on, avoiding my eyes. 'I had a huge bonfire. I don't want my boys discovering my secrets – or anyone else's for that matter. But those I kept.'

My hands had begun to tremble. I put on my spectacles, and the contents of the bundle swam into focus: a clutch of fat treacherous envelopes. *KV, KV* . . . Then I saw the name and address, saw they were written with a schoolroom dipping pen, in blue-black ink, saw the looped handwriting was neat and pinched. I felt a flood of relief: nothing revealing here, surely? Just early letters, schoolgirl letters: written in an attic bedroom, at an old desk, with a drawer that locked. There was only one key that had fitted that drawer. I used to wear it on a chain around my neck.

'Your Cambridge letters.' Rose hesitated. 'They were a lifeline to me then, Lucy. I found them at the back of a cupboard. I read them again last week. So many things I'd forgotten – your father, that bloody governess.'

'I have your letters too. And Frances's. All of them. I was reading them last night.'

'I'm glad. Then we're quits.' Rose crossed to her drinks tray, and waved the cocktail shaker about. 'Still a smidgen left. Have a top-up – we can't waste it. Ages since I've seen you. I've missed you badly, Lucy. Let's celebrate.'

She replenished my glass and her own. She sat down next to me on the sofa and turned to face me. I'd picked up the hints by then, and knew what was coming, so I said: 'I know where this is leading. Are you trying to get me drunk, Rose?'

'Might be. Anything to loosen your obstinate tongue.' With great gentleness, she laid her hand on mine. 'You *can* talk about it, Lucy,' she said, her eyes searching mine, her expression troubled. 'You shouldn't store things up the way you do. I knew some of it anyway – and what I didn't know I'd guessed. *Years* ago. Long before I found those boxes of letters . . . and those, I promise you, have now gone up in smoke.'

She leaned closer towards me. '*Please,* Lucy. Why hide things from me, of all people? I know you loved him – and where's the shame in that? Why do you lock things away like this? I know it hurts – but if you'd only share it, it might hurt *less*.'

'It isn't a question of shame. And it doesn't hurt. Nothing does any more. You know that.'

'I know nothing of the sort. Why must you pretend to be invulnerable? I know you, Lucy. I know you inside and out. Dear God, you're *obstinate*. Right, one last time, and remember: given your age, and mine, there might not be another opportunity.'

'A low blow. Stop it, Rose. Back off.'

'Last chance. Yes or no. If you want to talk, we can. If you don't, more fool you.'

There was a silence. The fire sputtered and hissed. I love Rose and the temptation was strong, but there are some things I never have, and never will, discuss. Eventually, I said '*Pass*,' and, knowing Rose's skills, I said it firmly. She sighed and then smiled in resignation. 'Very well. Have it your way for now. But I'm warning you – I shan't give up.' Giving me her hand, she helped me to my feet.

'Watch your step, Lucy,' she continued, drawing me towards the door, making sure the dogs and the rugs did not trip me. 'Time to eat. Mrs W has made us a feast … Rereading those Cambridge letters has made me think, you know – there are *lots* of questions I want to ask you. So, no forbidden topics, I swear, but let's be wicked, let's talk about Cambridge and that Dunsire woman instead. I want the full story over lunch. None of your endless evasions and artistic nips and tucks. You may slide things past your editor when you write your books, and I'll bet you danced rings round that Fong fellow, but that won't wash with *me*. I want the truth.'

'If you like.' I shrugged. We began to inch our way slowly towards Rose's dining room. 'But where's the point? You never liked Nicola Dunsire. You never understood her.'

'Yes, I did. I've met scores of bitches in my time: she was in a class of her own. When I think what that woman did to you – Dunsire was an arch-bitch, an *arch-demon* actually.'

'Oh, really? Demons are fallen angels. Anything else you'd like to accuse her of?'

'Plenty. I'm just getting started. I'm hardly revved up yet. Wheeler couldn't stand her, and Wheeler was always right. She thought Dunsire was a vampire. One of the undead.'

'And you believe in vampires, do you? Stop this nonsense,' I said, as Rose grasped my arm and led me the last few steps. The delicious scent of roast lamb drifted along the corridor. My hip was aching badly. I felt sick and dizzy with fatigue. That route I'd taken through the churchyard, the graves, that long grass, all that *undergrowth* . . . unwise: now I was paying for it.

'Believe in vampires? Once I'd met *her*, I did. I'm telling you, Nicola Dunsire was an unholy influence. Dazzling, I grant you, but a fiend incarnate.'

'Make your mind up,' I said crossly. 'Demon or vampire? Even Nicola can't be both.'

'Can't she?' Rose gave me a glance of triumph. 'She still has a hold on you, even now. Dead these sixty years — and you *still* use the present tense whenever you mention her. Case proven, I think.'

'Two letters,' my father said. 'Two *invitations*, no less.' He slipped his hand into his inside jacket pocket, and in a fastidious way, as if they might be contaminated, drew out two white envelopes. He was not in a good temper. 'My daughter is much in demand, Miss Dunsire – were you aware of that?'

He laid the pair of envelopes on the garden table in front of him; one bore American stamps, the other a dark blue coronet on its ivory flap. 'I assume not,' he continued, when Miss Dunsire made no reply. 'I doubt Lucy takes you into her confidence any more than she does me. My late wife had identical tendencies: evasive, tight-lipped—'

'*Reticent.* That might be *le mot juste.*' Miss Dunsire cut across him, her tone cool. She was leaning back in her wicker chair, her eyes resting on the rose arch at the end of our Cambridge garden. The branches of our birch trees shaded her from the hot sun, and their leaves imparted a greenish pallor to her face. Earlier, before our luncheon guests had arrived, she'd complained of a headache; after a difficult, antagonistic meal, they had departed some ten minutes ago. Now she might have been tired – or bored or irritated.

'*Secretive,*' my father corrected her, giving Miss Dunsire a savage glance that she ignored. 'Secretive is the apposite term. And that is merely a variant on deceitfulness.'

'Secrecy. Deceit. How very astute, Dr Payne.' With a restless movement, Miss Dunsire rose and stood for a moment, still pondering the rose arch. 'I'd always seen those two qualities as distinct,' she continued in a pensive voice. 'I'd felt someone could guard secrets, while *scrupulously* avoiding deceit. But now I see – you're right: why, they're as close as sisters, virtually twins. How dangerous! How lucky I am not to have skeletons in my closets. How fortunate I have this odd *obsession* with the truth. Will you excuse me for a moment, Lucy? I must take some aspirin. My headache is worse. I'll be back in – two ticks.'

She turned and drifted towards the house, leaving me to wonder how she contrived to say one thing and imply its opposite – she was a mistress of that art. There had been no trace of satire in her face, yet I sensed she'd been mocking my father while appearing to agree with him. I'd sensed irony and insolence too; he might also have suspected this – certainly her comments did not improve his mood, which had been worsening since our lunch guests had first arrived. I could calibrate his temper with precision: repressed while they were there, it was now approaching explosion point. *Am I afraid?* I asked myself, staring at the two envelopes.

My father ignored me, staring after Miss Dunsire's slender figure, as, taking her time, she meandered her way down the garden, pausing to smell a rose here, pausing to pluck some lavender there. She was wearing a white dress of pleated linen; the sun beat down on her brazen hair, her bare white throat. In those days, knowing nothing, nothing, I did not understand that this dress and her languid unhurried movements could be erotic in their effect. I didn't perceive that Miss Dunsire's equivocal tone and the uncertainty it engendered could be sexually provocative. I thought of her, quite simply, as my enemy. I resented her for looking so enviably cool, in this hot town garden, in her white dress.

My father seemed unwilling to continue the conversation he'd instigated. He sat there, scowling into the middle distance, tapping his fingers. 'Dear God, it must be eighty degrees. This heat is insufferable. Did that blasted poet leave *any* wine, or did he wolf the lot? Ah, a drop left.'

He poured himself a glass from the bottle of hock that had remained on the table after lunch, glowered at a bowl of leftover strawberries, moved his chair into the shade and, tilting his head back, closed his eyes. Valley of the Kings heat. I was trying not to move or breathe. *We endeavour to be invisible*, said Frances's voice from that other world, a few months back. Not so easy now, I thought. Five minutes ticked past. I began to wish my enemy would return; it was Miss Dunsire who was responsible for the lunch party, I couldn't be blamed for *that*, surely? Given this transgression, perhaps she'd draw some of my father's fire – though I doubted it.

It was now 1 June, three months since my return from Egypt, and almost the end of the Cambridge Easter term; in a few days the long vacation would begin. Examinations were over, the university was *en fête*, and Nicola Dunsire, influenced by the heatwave, had persuaded my father to hold a lunch party in the garden. She'd thrown herself into this scheme with a strange nervy zeal, planning it for weeks: whom to invite, what to serve? Should it be poached salmon, or a chicken *chaud-froid*; a cold apple tart, peach Melba, or Cambridge burnt creams? How should we – it was 'we', for she insisted on my involvement – how should we decorate the table, what should we wear, what should we do if it rained that day, God forbid?

I thought her chief worries should have been the guests – my father had few friends and many enemies in Cambridge; and the expense, since he hated to spend money. I said so.

'Stop cavilling.' She snapped her fingers. '*I* run the household budget – and very clever I am at it too. If it can cover those ballet lessons you pleaded for, Lucy – *which* it does, so they're *our* secret, never breathe a word to your father – it can cover one lunch. Besides, Mrs Grimshaw and I have been plotting. We're in cahoots! She's had a word with her husband, and the college kitchens will help out. I may have learned to bake a damned cake, Lucy, but concoct a *chaud-froid*? Beyond even *my* powers.'

By then both Mrs Grimshaw and her husband were Dunsire converts: little gifts, confidences in the kitchen, visits to their home, pleas for help, reliance on their superior wisdom etc., etc. – these charms worked their effect. Besides, Mrs Grimshaw loved excitement, and Miss Dunsire certainly generated that. In anticipation of one small lunch party, the entire house had to be spring-cleaned, the garden pruned and groomed, the silver cleaned, all the table linen inspected . . .

Mrs Grimshaw was in her element. 'She's like a whirlwind, is our Miss Dunsire,' she'd said to me admiringly, as she bent over the ironing board. 'Three days of this blessed ironing I've done – *and* there's more. My Albert's been round, done the windows, done the lawns, tied in the roses – well, he'd do anything for her. Got him eating out of her hand, she has. A lovely job he made of it too – and *still* she's fussing. She's worked herself up into a right tizzy about this lunch: I told her, you want to take a rest, dearie. Put your feet up for five minutes. Who's going to notice a smear on the window, or a crease in the tablecloth? But will she listen? I thought *I* was thorough, Lucy, because I like a nice house and I have my standards. But I've got nothing on her. One of God's perfectionists. That's what she is.'

This was true – Nicola Dunsire *was* a perfectionist; or, to be more accurate, she had *fits* of perfectionism, weeks when she would drive herself, and me, at breakneck speed, cramming our days with projects. Then, as suddenly as these periods had begun, they would cease. They would be followed by a week, sometimes ten days, of moodiness and irritability, during which time and for no apparent reason she would lose interest in all the tasks she'd set herself. Our long walks, our visits to libraries or the Fitzwilliam Museum would cease. Her appetite would dwindle, then fail; she'd complain of headaches and fatigue; she'd retire for long periods, setting me a mountain of tasks and leaving me to negotiate them alone. There I'd sit, as the days grew longer and the spring evenings stretched, working, working, at my algebra, at my maps, my Shakespeare sonnets, my Tudor kings, my translations, my *Jane Eyre*, my *Middlemarch,* my arithmetic.

At such times, I grew to fear her temper: 'How can you be so backward, so slow, so *stupid?*' she would cry – and then she might slap my hand in vexation, or tear up some exercise. '*Read*, Lucy, learn to *read*,' she'd said once, white with anger, as I halted my way through the long periods of George Eliot, toiled through Dorothea and Casaubon. 'You read like a fool. Can't you see *inside* the sentences? Under them? Behind them? Beyond them? Christ in heaven – I'm wasting my time on you.'

At such times, nothing I could do was right: my map drawing was clumsy, my handwriting was unreadable, my failure to grasp the simplest mathematical principle was infantile. I especially feared French: within weeks of my return from Egypt, Dr Gerhardt's services were dispensed with – it would save money if Miss Dunsire taught me languages as well as everything else, and Dr Gerhardt, though a fine scholar, was too lazy and good-natured to teach such an obstinate, unresponsive child. Besides, he needed more time to work on his book: this masterwork, on his fellow countrymen Zwingli and Calvin, had been in preparation some fifteen years. In Cambridge, this was scarcely unusual: on the same staircase in Nevile's Court as my father lived a don who, in 1872, had written the definitive and ground-breaking study of shellfish and their digestive systems; he had published nothing in the fifty years since – and no one thought the less of him. Miss Dunsire had no sympathy with such attitudes: swift in all things, she detested procrastination. My father, once given to delaying tactics, now agreed with her. His book on Euripides was progressing well, he'd report, eyeing her; he expected to finish it within eighteen months, to be helped by his forthcoming twelve months' sabbatical.

'*I* shall take over from Dr Gerhardt,' Miss Dunsire had announced, and, since she could twist my father around her little finger when she chose to do so, he'd quickly concurred. Out went the vocabulary lists and the irregular verbs Dr Gerhardt and I had laboured over: in came magnificent floods of Goethe, Racine and Baudelaire, not a word of which I understood. During her gentler periods, Nicola Dunsire could make these passages speak, so I began to grasp their meaning, thrill to their use of words; but during those black spells when her mood altered and she became so unpredictable, anything might happen – she might smack me around the ears, throw the book across the room, or pull my hair. '*Listen*,' she would cry. '*Respond*. I won't let you inch your way through this like some blind worm, do you hear me? I'll make you *run* before you can walk – I'll make you *dance*, damn you, you stupid girl, if it kills me. Again, like this, listen: *C'est Venus toute entière à sa proie attachée* – no, no, no. Get rid of that hideous accent. You're not English, you're *French*. Read this speech of Phèdre's and remember – you're not some plain little schoolgirl, you're a *queen*.'

How could I have seen her as serene that first day I met her, I thought, as – having remained in the house for twenty minutes (twenty minutes? to take an aspirin?) – Nicola Dunsire emerged at last, and began to make her way slowly down the garden with an air of queenly unconcern. I fingered the key to my desk: I'd taken to wearing it around my neck on a chain. My letters and my diaries were in that locked desk – if Nicola Dunsire had used her aspirin absence to spy among my things, as I was certain she did, she'd have been thwarted this time.

My father, who might or might not have been dozing, opened his eyes, looked up and watched her approach. She took her time, delaying by the lavender again, lingering by a rose, her slim white dilatory figure the only cool thing in the crucible our garden became in this weather, the heat enclosed, reflected, intensified by its high brick walls. The slowness of her advance did not improve my father's temper: the longer he gazed at her, the deeper his scowl became. Miss Dunsire, having reached us at last, sat down without a word, confident in the knowledge that however much my father might want to ask why it took twenty minutes to swallow a pill, such a remark was immodest, impossible. Even in this brave new post-war world, a lady's disappearances could not be enquired upon.

She leaned back in her wicker chair and gazed dreamily at the rose arch again. Those who did not know her (that group included my father, I felt) might have imagined she was calm. I knew better. Attuned to her now, sensitive to the slightest perturbation in her unpredictable nature, I knew we were in the midst of one of those monthly black spells. I could sense a seething disquiet in her – just as you can with a cat, who will sit, kneading its paws, betraying agitation with the merest flick of the tip of its tail.

I doubted Miss Dunsire's claws would come out in my father's presence. I waited. My father had picked up the two envelopes again and was examining them with a frown. I could smell incipient punishment in the air and felt the axe was likely to fall on my neck; yet I had the sensation that, even if it did, his ire was not truly directed at me, but at the silent, languorous, abstracted Miss Dunsire.

'*Secrecy*,' my father said, as if there had been no interruption to the conversation earlier. 'Twin sister to deceit. Qualities I abhor in a woman and, Lucy, find unacceptable in a child. I have here two letters, one from Boston, one from Hampshire. It is obvious you *knew* these letters would be written and encouraged their sending. Your laments and complaints to your little friends from Egypt, you'll be glad to learn, have borne fruit.'

'I haven't complained to anyone about anything,' I muttered, staring down at the grass. 'Why would I complain – or lament?'

'And these children, in turn, have whipped up others on your behalf,' he continued, pressing on as if I'd said nothing. 'As a result, *two* invitations.' He picked up the American envelope: 'Let us deal with this first. Here I have a letter from someone signing herself *Helen Chandler Winlock*. Why Americans feel this need to embroider their names with matrilinear flourishes, I cannot comprehend, but let us move on . . . Mrs Winlock informs me that she and her family plan to spend the summer at their holiday cottage, a *cottage* with twenty bedrooms by the sound of it. Why do our transatlantic cousins infallibly over- or under-state? Where was I? Ah yes, *et in Arcadia ego:* Mrs Winlock and her rustic *cottage*. I understand it's on some island, Lucy, yes?'

'North Haven,' I said. 'It's an island off the coast of Maine, Daddy.'

'Excellent: Miss Dunsire's attempts to impart *some* understanding of geography have clearly had effect. Now – how she writes, this earnest friend of yours! Four sentences, where one would suffice . . .'

'And not alone in *that* vice,' came a low murmur from the wicker chair beneath the birches.

I started and looked up. I wasn't sure if I'd heard the words, or imagined them. Imagined them, I decided; Miss Dunsire's lovely eyes were closed. She was possibly asleep.

'Finally, Lucy my dear, we come to the crux.' My father sighed; his anger seemed to be diminishing, I thought. His expression was faintly amused: 'Mrs Winlock seems to feel the summer vacation at the University of Cambridge is protracted. Through June to October, she understands. Now who, I wonder, told her *that*?'

'No one. She doesn't *need* to be told, Daddy. Her father taught at Harvard University, he was Dean of the School of Architecture there. Her brother and her husband Herbert, the – the splendid archaeologist I told you about, they both studied at Harvard too. So Mrs Winlock *knows* how long university vacations are.'

I was hoping the mention of Harvard would help; I had faith in Harvard. In my father's opinion, it was not at the peak of academe's pinnacle – that sublime summit was reserved solely for Cambridge, with Oxford allowed grudging space on a lower ledge. But Harvard was an august institution, it was Ivy League – and even with him, so finicky and critical, that must surely count. And maybe it did, I thought, with a sudden spurt of renewed hope: his expression had warmed; there was now a twinkle in his eye.

'She also knows – or has been given the impression – that my daughter may be *at a loose end for some of that time* and as *Frances is missing dear Lucy so much*, Mrs Winlock proposes to reunite you. She invites you to join her family for a month or even a generous six weeks, on this romantic island. Off Maine. In the United States. There, you'll be able to go for long *hikes* – can she mean walks? And, to add to these delights, her daughter will teach you to sail. First it was *ballet*, then *hieroglyphics,* now it's *sailing*. Gracious me, this Frances child is a prodigy – is there no end to her accomplishments?'

He chuckled, shook his head in amusement, and then, looking up from the letter, smiled at me in an indulgent way. Miss Dunsire stirred in her chair. 'So tell me, Lucy,' he went on, 'should you like me to accept this kind offer?'

'Before you answer, Lucy, might I trouble you for a glass of water?' Miss Dunsire said. I stood up and fetched the water jug. I handed her the glass and, as I did so, her cool fingers brushed mine. She pinched the back of my hand lightly, then swatted at some insect invisible to me, murmuring, 'A *wasp*, I think, Lucy. The warm weather has brought them out. Take care, dear.'

'A very generous invitation,' my father continued in a reflective tone, as I returned to my chair. 'But then Americans *are* generous. We have them to thank for your trip to Egypt, Lucy, remember. So tell me, my dear, would you like to do this?'

'I'd love – like to do that more than anything, Daddy,' I replied, on a wild surge of hope.

'As I feared.' He gave a profound sigh. 'I thought that would be your response. That makes it all the harder for me to tell you that it's out of the question. I wish it were otherwise, Lucy, but there are your studies with Miss Dunsire to consider, and there's also the question of *fares*. My means will not stretch to transatlantic crossings. The answer, therefore, must be "No". I wrote yesterday to Mrs Winlock to explain that.'

I felt the blood rush up into my face, then drain away. Silence fell upon our garden and then the Cambridge church clocks began to chime: it was four o'clock; the air rang with bells. I stared fixedly at a bed of blue lupins; after a while, they disappeared, and I found

I was watching a carefree girl jump from a car, run across the sand and perform a cartwheel. I stared hard at this pyramids' girl until the first sharp stab of pain began to ease. When the bells finally ceased tolling, Miss Dunsire, her manner still languid, roused herself from her chair. Leaning forwards, shading her eyes from the sun, she said in her cool pure voice: 'And the *other* letter, Dr Payne? Have you also replied to that?'

'I haven't. Not as yet.'

'May I read it?' She held out her hand.

'If you wish it, Miss Dunsire . . . ' He hesitated.

I marvelled at this capacity she had, to place him on the defensive. He was clearly reluctant to hand her the envelope and yet he did so. He leaned back in his chair and lit a cigarette. Miss Dunsire extracted the letter, which was brief, a single page, and began to read. My father took out his pocket watch, examined it, frowned, played an arpeggio with his fingertips.

'Lady Evelyn Herbert,' she said, after five long minutes had passed. 'She writes, Lucy, in her capacity as godmother to your friend Rose. Rose and her little brother Peter are spending the summer at a house in Hampshire, under Lady Evelyn's auspices, and in the care of their nanny, Wheeler, while their father travels abroad. She asks *your* father if you, Lucy, might be allowed to join them for a month . . . You would be collected by car, the dates are flexible. What a very kind letter! What a charming way she has with words.'

'You admire her style, Miss Dunsire?' My father snorted. 'It passed me by, I fear.'

'Slangy.' Her smile was imperturbable. 'I like that. We can't all achieve your high standards, Dr Payne. Lady Evelyn is young. She writes as she speaks, no doubt. See how kindly she describes the little boy's devotion to Lucy. I'm sure you'd have expressed it differently, and you'd certainly correct her grammar . . . but her affection for the children is evident: this is a letter written from the heart.'

'All the sadder then that this heartfelt invitation will be refused.' My father rose to his feet. 'Lucy has better things to do this summer than waste it in the company of empty-headed idlers. She needs to *work*. Her standards have improved, I acknowledge that. I expect them to improve further by the start of next Michaelmas term.'

'You don't feel, perhaps, that a holiday . . . ?' Miss Dunsire also rose.

'I don't believe in holidays. I don't take them, and I fail to see why Lucy should. I haven't time to discuss this now, and I haven't time to answer letters like this either – you take care of it, Miss Dunsire. A few lines of polite refusal is all it requires. Reply this evening, please. I must be getting back to college. I need an hour or two in the library before Hall.'

'Of course, Dr Payne. But if I might just ask, before you leave – once I've refused this invitation, what arrangements would you like me to make for the summer? You'll be away for much of June, for the whole of July and August. Research, guest lectures, conferences, all that travelling; you really need a secretary. I'm afraid you'll be exhausted, though of course you do have such energy . . . such stamina.'

She paused on the word *stamina*. My father looked at her furtively; for a moment he seemed to forget the demands of libraries. 'Yes, yes,' he said, 'a heavy programme. And you're to blame for some of it, Miss Dunsire. It was at your – urging that I embarked on this book. But that does involve additional work, long hours . . . into the night sometimes.'

'*Late* into the night,' she said with warmth, taking a small step closer to him. 'I admire that so much. Your powerful resolve, your capacity to plunge to the *depths* of scholarship.' She frowned. 'Do you know how I imagine you when you're at work, Dr Payne? I imagine you plunging – down, down to the very depths of the ocean, and then surfacing, gasping for breath, with the pearls of knowledge cupped in your hands. I see them so clearly: round, milky, glistening . . . ' She gave him a sidelong, considering look. 'Ah, I know that expression of yours! I can see you think I'm being absurd.'

'No, no, not at all – well, not the simile I'd have used perhaps.' He gave her an uncertain glance. 'Charming, charming – but a scholar's work can be dry as dust and—'

'*Dry?* That's *not* the adjective I'd use. Describe you as dry? Never! Let me see, I'd say . . . ' And she leaned closer to him, lifting her face to his. She whispered some word into his ear. My father's face crimsoned. He stared at her; he appeared thunderstruck, appalled, disbelieving, fascinated – he had, I think, no recollection that I was there.

'I'm making you late,' she said, breaking the silence, moving a few steps away. 'Before you go: there's the small problem of *dates*. You realise you'll be responsible for Lucy for the whole of September? You plan to be in Cambridge then. But I shall be away.'

'Away?' He was still staring at her. 'What are you talking about? Away where?'

'Ah, you've forgotten. Our agreement, Dr Payne, was one month's holiday for me every summer. In return, I would forgo most weekends, even breaks for Christmas and Easter. You put that agreement in writing – and I must hold you to it.' Her manner became stern. 'I shall be in France for those four weeks, at a chateau in the Loire. A reading party – a number of my friends are going, we'll be quite a crowd. The arrangements were finalised weeks ago. I did tell you. I even entered the dates in your desk diary.'

'Impossible. Out of the question. Responsible for Lucy for the whole of September? Delightful as that prospect might be, I'll have work to do. My sabbatical is coming up.'

'Precisely my own view,' she said, in unruffled tones. 'Which is why I suggest I accept this invitation. For those four weeks, Lucy would then be safely in Hampshire. That seems convenient for everyone, Dr Payne. It kills several birds with one stone. Shall I write this evening and accept? I dislike arrangements to remain unsettled, if you recall.'

'I don't *recall* any of this,' my father burst out, suddenly enraged. *Now we're in for it*, I thought, inching backwards from his wrath while Miss Dunsire coolly held her ground. 'Reading party? What damned reading party? Who's attending this reading party? That so-called poet you invited to lunch today, I suppose? Dear God, imagine it, listening to *him* prosing on for an entire month. I never met such a blasted poseur in my life, preposterous hair, affected manners, opinions about everything under the sun, a damned insinuating manner too – who in hell does that young man think he is?'

'Rupert Brooke?' Miss Dunsire sighed. 'There *is* a Brookeian epidemic in Cambridge, and the disease is very infectious; that iconoclastic tone could well be a symptom. I so agree with you, Dr Payne, he's a pest – and a bore. I invited him today at the last minute to make up the numbers and regretted it the second he arrived. And he won't be in France, I can assure you of that! It's *strictly* a women-only reading party. Which I much prefer.'

She paused, and then in an altered tone went on: 'Ah, this is all my fault! I blame myself. I should have reminded you again – you have so much on your mind! But I did inform you, Dr Payne – shall I fetch your desk diary? I can show you the entry I made.'

'No, no – no need for that.' My father hesitated, looking down at Miss Dunsire's face. Her expression was now penitent; his temper seemed on the mend. 'I know how efficient you are, Miss Dunsire. And I didn't mean to suggest – of course you are entitled to your holiday. A reading party in the Loire . . . delightful! A very beautiful part of France, too. A "crowd" of you going, I think you said? Your friends from Girton, I expect?'

'Indeed. We remain very close. What's the collective term for us bluestockings? A covey of bluestockings . . . a chattering, a charm, a cabal?' She smiled demurely, and my father, who liked wordplay, smiled in return. 'My friend Dorothy whom you met today will be there and her sister Edith. Evadne and Winifred, Meta of course – and my very dear friend Clair, who shared supervisions with me. There will be twelve of us, I think, perhaps thirteen . . . I'm looking forward to it *immensely.*' She lowered her eyes.

'Excellent, excellent.' My father seemed to find this chaste roll-call reassuring. 'You will be missed here, I hardly need say. I shall be looking forward to your return, as will Lucy. Very good. Fine. The whole of September . . . that's settled then. Oh, and accept that invitation from Lady Evelyn, if you'd be so good. Now I really must go.' With that, he set off across the garden, humming to himself, his spirits restored.

Miss Dunsire and I watched him depart. The heat of the day was diminishing now, and in the cooling air the scents of the flowers intensified. Silence fell. I kept my eyes on the garden; I gazed at the roses pinned to wires on its high walls: *Edith Cavell, Lady Hillingdon, Grace Darling, Mrs Herbert Stevens.* My mother had planted them; I'd never noticed that all our roses were named for women. I examined them studiously. Well trained and tied in, branches expertly crucified to maximise flowering: displaying an abundance of blooms.

'Are you going to thank me, Lucy?' Miss Dunsire spoke so suddenly she made me start. 'You don't like me,' she went on. 'You make that abundantly clear. But be honest and admit it: it was *I* who won you a month with your friends. Shall I tell you why I did that? Please do not imagine I was motivated by compassion or sympathy. No — I did it *because I could.*'

This was true, I realised. I didn't doubt it for one second. After a pause, I said in an obstinate way: 'That was the main reason, perhaps. It wasn't the only one, though.'

'Well, well, well. *Not* such a simpleton, after all. But then I never made the mistake of thinking you were.' She gave me a long glittering look. 'Sharp. Quick. A subtle child. You repay teaching, I see. Come with me.'

Catching me by the hand, she began to walk back to the house at a swift pace, coming to a halt in the cool shadows of the hall. 'One of my migraines is coming on,' she said. 'I shall go and lie down. But there's something I need to do first — come in here.'

She threw back the door to my father's study — the Holy of Holies; infrequently used, since he preferred to work in college, it remained sacrosanct. It was a place I revered, feared and rarely entered. I hesitated, then with reluctance followed her inside. I saw to my surprise that the *shabti* figure I'd given him, a present he'd rejected as more loathsome than a scarab, had been retrieved and reinstated; it now stood on his desk.

'*I* rescued it, Lucy.' Miss Dunsire followed my gaze. 'I persuaded him of its virtues. It isn't genuine, I'd say, though I have no expertise in such matters. Ah, I'm right, I can see it in your eyes.' She looked at me curiously. 'How can you tell it's a fake?'

'You need to look at lots of them, and you have to know *how* to look,' I replied. I couldn't understand why she had brought me in here, especially now. She was leaning across the desk and had picked up the *shabti* figure. 'Go on, Lucy,' she said. 'I want to know.'

'Mr Carter, that archaeologist I met,' I began, cautiously, 'he said the best way to tell if an object was genuine was to look at it every single day. By the end of a week or a month, the quality of the genuine object would become obvious. It would — sing out. Whereas the coarseness of the fake would gradually reveal itself. Its flaws would become evident . . . That's what *he* said, anyway.'

'A useful technique. I'd always thought I could spot a fake at forty yards. Maybe I have something to learn.' She frowned. 'I read up on these *shabti* figures. Their name – it means *answerer*, doesn't it?'

'Yes. That's what they are – answerers. In the afterlife, when a king needs them, he only has to call out, and there they are, ready to do his bidding, answering all his needs.'

'Every man's dream. The perfect present for your father. Now – where's that diary of his?'

She began to move the books on my father's desk back and forth. Having found the diary, she flicked through the pages, plucked up my father's fountain pen and unscrewed its cap: 'September. You'll observe those pages are blank. Astonishing! I could have sworn I entered my holiday dates. I must have dreamed it. Still, that's easily rectified.'

In her neat italic script, she made the requisite entries, blotted them, closed the book, replaced the pen, and turned to face me. She leaned against the desk and gave me a challenging stare. Her hands were trembling. 'Tell him if you like,' she said. 'I really don't care.'

'So you lied,' I said, after a pause. 'Were you lying about the reading party as well?'

'Maybe. It's happening. I may go. I may not. It depends on my mood.'

'Why did you lie?'

'Who knows? You were being bullied and tricked. I disliked that.' She shrugged. 'If I could have spited him and pulled Maine out of the hat for you, I would have done. But he'd already written, and besides, think of the expense! He could afford it – just as he can afford to travel to Greece and Italy this summer for his all-important *work*. But his tendencies are economical. *Tight*, as we say in Scotland – does your father have any Scottish blood in his veins, Lucy? No, no, he may have the Scotsman's reluctance to part with money, he fits that stereotype – but his blood is of the thin, blue, English sort.'

Her voice had risen, and the taunt in it was obvious. For the first time – how slow I'd been – I realised her dislike of my father was intense. I could see contempt, even loathing in her eyes. 'You shouldn't say that,' I began haltingly. 'Not about Daddy. Not to me. Not ever. It's not right.'

'No, it isn't. You're correct. Disrespectful. Disloyal. I apologise. I told you, I have a migraine. The light hurts my eyes. When that happens, I'm not myself. I say things I later regret.'

At that, she gave a curious gasp and pressed her hand against her face. I couldn't tell if she was in sudden pain, or strangely excited, or both. Her breath was coming fast, and the dark pupils of her eyes were dilated; her hands were now trembling violently – and, as I stared at her, this infirmity seemed to increase, passing up her arms and into her body until she was visibly shaking. For a moment I feared she might be about to collapse, perhaps suffer some fit.

I was unsure what to do. Into my head rushed a comment Dr Gerhardt had made some weeks before, when I went for my last lesson with him: 'I shall miss you, my dear – but Miss Dunsire is more than competent. Her German is good and her French is very pure. My sister Helga taught her at Girton, you know – she was sorry to hear of her illness, as I was. Most distressing. We're delighted to learn she's made a full recovery.'

No mention of this illness had been made by anyone else. I'd assumed it was minor; now I felt less sure. I took a step forwards, but before I could reach her Miss Dunsire regained physical control. She had been gripping the edge of the desk so tightly that her knuckles stood out white; now, she pushed herself free of it and stood upright.

'I shall go and lie down,' she said. 'But I must be sure of one thing first. I taught you a lesson this afternoon, Lucy – do you know what that lesson was?' Snatching at me, she grasped my wrist painfully tight and said in a low, angry, voice: 'I taught you power, Lucy. I taught you *how to get what you want*. If you prefer not to go through this life getting trampled underfoot; if you wish to avoid being thwarted at every turn; if you wish to prevent your deepest desires being ridiculed or dismissed – then *learn* from it.'

She walked out. I lingered, then followed her. As I reached the hall, she was already on the stairs; she had come to a halt five steps up and was leaning against the banister, head bent. Looking up at her, fearful she might faint, I realised there was a spreading stain – scarlet bloodstains on the back of her white skirt. They had not been there earlier. I stared at her, dismayed and shocked. Could she have somehow cut herself, and wiped her hand? The stain seemed too large for that . . . So she *is* ill, I thought. Could she be bleeding? Could she be *haemorrhaging*? I knew the word for this condition, but not its causes nor its cure. I knew it could be fatal; it had once happened to Mrs Grimshaw, and she had given a vivid, vague, and horrible account of it. It had mysteriously prevented her from increasing her family of six children, and she had 'bled like a stuck pig'. Miss Mack, deep in the subject of nursing and Gallipoli wounds, had also described the phenomenon, so I knew it could affect men as well as women. But surely Miss Dunsire couldn't be wounded? And if she wasn't injured, why would she bleed?

'Miss Dunsire, are you ill? May I help you?' I called.

She had begun to climb the stairs again. She did not look back or reply. I heard her steps pass along the landing to her room on the first floor; its door slammed behind her, and its key turned in the lock.

I mooned about the house for a while after that, anxious and at a loose end. I tidied away the party things and washed them up. Several wasps had drowned in the sweet leftover strawberry mush; I tipped it and their stripy corpses into a flower bed. I thought of the cruel expertise with which Miss Dunsire had boxed me in: if I told my father the truth, I'd not only be telling tales, a despicable act, I'd also be ensuring my visit to Rose and Peter was cancelled forthwith. Was there a way out of this moral maze she'd constructed? I couldn't see one: damned either way; guilty if I spoke out, guilty if I did not. But nothing would make me sacrifice the visit to Rose and Peter, so there was no point in agonising; I'd keep my mouth shut.

I tried to untangle the many mysteries of the day, the lunch party, the ill assemblage of guests, the fact that three of the dons invited had refused, and the two married dons who *did* honour us with their presence had turned up without their wives, each of whom sent a curt, last-minute and inadequate excuse. I thought of Dr Gerhardt, who had loyally attended and brought his sister Helga with him; of the way in which Helga had praised the food; of how they'd both tried to prevent the flickering antagonisms at the table from flaring up into confrontation – peace-making overtures that met with little success.

I couldn't understand why Nicola Dunsire, clever in so many ways, could also be reckless and obtuse. Why propose the party, when my father detested such gatherings? Why, knowing my father's dislike of women in general and opinionated women in particular, had she invited no less than three of her Girtonian friends? It was bound to cause trouble and duly did. Dorothy Lascelles – *Just call me Dotty, Dr Payne, everyone does* – was now training to be a doctor at the Elizabeth Garrett Anderson hospital in London. A cheerful forthright woman who described dissections across the lunch table, she had bristled when my father, seconded by the two dons, insisted that medicine was not, never could be, a woman's profession. 'That's just guff,' she'd said. 'I'm sick of that refrain, Dr Payne. Tell that to the women I treat, the women from the King's Cross slums, in labour with their tenth child. Frankly, they'd laugh in your face.'

My father expected to be spared contradictions at his own table, as he was swift to point out. The warning went unheeded; the second of Miss Dunsire's friends, a scornful classicist called Meta, now reading for her doctorate, dared to dispute his translation of some Homeric epithet. She did so between the iced soup and the *chaud-froid*; over the salmon in aspic, she moved on smartly to the sacred ground of Euripides. 'I can't agree with you there, Dr Payne,' she said in her sharp voice. 'You're entirely missing the point. In his *Hippolytus*, the warring forces central to the play – a woman's violent sexual desire versus a man's prudish chastity – are present on stage throughout in the persons of Aphrodite and Artemis. Do you *understand* the effect of that device?'

The two dons bridled; the third Girtonian friend, the 'Clair' Miss Dunsire would mention later, found this exchange hilarious. She laughed so much at Meta's analysis, and my father's horrified expression on hearing it, that she almost choked. It was the only moment during the lunch that she showed the least animation – but then she was a strange, brooding, unresponsive creature, who sat next to Miss Dunsire, sometimes muttering to her in a low voice, but otherwise maintaining a sulky silence.

One hour ticked by; too much wine was being consumed, and the conspicuously handsome poet Miss Dunsire had invited at the last moment appeared drunk. I had not caught his full name – it was Eddie something – double-barrelled; he was rumoured to be an Apostle, and therefore one of the Cambridge elect. The heat was intense; it was hard to keep track of the fizzing hostilities at the table, as I was pressed into service, hastening to and fro, ferrying plates.

By the time I fetched the burnt creams, the atmosphere was curdling fast; everyone was arguing about Mount Everest, exactly how high it was, and whether Mallory's expedition would succeed in conquering it . . . everyone except Eddie-the-poet, who had just dealt Tennyson's reputation its death blow and was now intent on Wordsworth's scalp. By the time I cleared the strawberry plates, it was babel: Irish Free State to my left, new divorce bill and its iniquities to my right; whether the Italian fascists would take Bologna and if so, where next . . . Meta and my father had locked horns again and were fiercely disputing the next eclipse of the moon, while poet Eddie, who'd mutilated Keats meanwhile, then diverted to the curious subject of tom-cats, was now launching a pincer attack on Coleridge.

Returning with a laden tray – gleaming silver coffee pot, fragile cups – I found a violent squabble concerning Schopenhauer and his essay on womankind, *Über die Weiber*, had broken out. Dr Gerhardt, I knew, revered this philosopher, but Meta was dismissing his misogyny as infantile, while Dorothy declared Schopenhauer's aversion to women was so extreme it suggested psychological *abnormalities* . . . At these two offensive words, the dons decided they'd had enough. Declining coffee, off they marched, gibbering to each other; a distressed Dr Gerhardt and his sister followed them soon afterwards.

The poet watched them leave, his eyes narrowed; he downed another glass of wine in one gulp. Not sober when he arrived, he was now intoxicated – and the only person at the table enjoying himself. Having decimated the ranks of dead and buried greats, he scented a new quarry. Prompted by a mention of my travels, and perhaps by this lunch's events, he began to tell us about Egypt – a country he had never visited. Within seconds he'd pounced on Shelley's sonnet 'Ozymandias', fourteen familiar lines I'd come to dread.

'"*I met a traveller from an antique land.*" Poor mad Shelley! Hits the wrong note in his very first line.' He sighed. 'Does the word "antique" suggest desert monuments to anyone here? Not to me, it doesn't. To me it irresistibly suggests furniture – nasty, wormy, outmoded, unnecessary bits of furniture: chiffoniers, escritoires and vile knickknacks. In fact, now I think about it,' he gave my father a waspish glance, 'it suggests my spinster Aunt Agatha's drawing room – or the Senior Common Room at Trinity. It suggests a damned great pile of pointless outdated belongings and similarly antiquated petty beliefs. I appeal to *you*, my beauteous Nicole.' He winked at Miss Dunsire.

'Does "antique land" evoke Egypt to you? Because I'd say it evokes somewhere *much* nearer to home.'

My father did not give Miss Dunsire the chance to reply. In a loud unequivocal voice, he said, 'Christ in heaven, will this ass ever shut up?'

The three Girtonians could take a hint: Dorothy and Meta departed at once, dragging the offending Eddie with them. The odd, silent Clair was the last of them to leave. She had arrived by bicycle from the station, and went to fetch this bicycle now. She wheeled it across the lawns and came to a halt in front of us. 'Thanks,' she said, shaking hands all round.

'Is that *your* bicycle, Clair?' Nicola asked.

'How could it be? I've just come up from London,' she replied, in faintly irritated tones. She inspected the bicycle and I inspected her: very small, very thin, her black hair cut in a bob, and a straight fringe above her brows; tiny monkey hands, an urchin face, an unyielding dark-eyed gaze. She was wearing a peculiar dress of patchwork colours that gave her a harlequin air. Nicola had said she was a painter and a bohemian – I noticed she had paint ingrained beneath her bohemian nails. Her expression was hostile: she seemed to dislike us, the garden, the house, the town of Cambridge, possibly the world.

'I stole it at the station,' she went on, mounting the bicycle. 'I suppose I'd better return it before it's missed. Not that I care two hoots. Salmon in aspic! The most interesting lunch I've attended in a *very* long time. Goodbye, Dr Payne. *Au revoir*, Nicole.'

She rode off along the garden path, ducked beneath the rose arch, exited the gate onto the lane to the Backs and, without a wave or backward glance, disappeared.

I considered these happenings – and those that came after them. I felt there must be a thread that connected all these events. Why had my father accused me of deceit? What word had Nicola Dunsire whispered to him? But I couldn't perceive the links; it was as if there were some key information I lacked. I gave up the attempt, made myself a sandwich, and took up a tray with toast and scrambled eggs for Miss Dunsire. She made no reply when I tapped at her door. I listened, and thought I could detect the sound of her breathing: she couldn't have bled to death then, she was alive and probably asleep . . . I left the tray by her door. It would be there for her when — if — she awoke.

I retreated to my attic and in the cool decline of the evening began on my letters. I assembled the writing paper, the blotter, my dipping pen. I filled the inkwell with blue-black ink. I'd wait until I was sure of our holiday before writing to Rose, so decided to reply first to Frances. But what to say? Where to begin? What to censor, what to express? *I can't come to Maine. No news from Cambridge*, I scratched.

The pen, as usual, was giving problems. I was sworn to tell Frances the truth at all times. I inserted a new nib. I wrote: *I learned something today.* I found the ink flowed after that.

Twelfth birthdays were momentous events for a girl – or so Nicola Dunsire said. She did not explain why; my own twelfth birthday at the end of July passed uneventfully. My father sent a postcard from Greece that arrived three days late. Miss Mack sent me a volume of Rudyard Kipling's short stories, and my Aunt Foxe a manicure set containing many surgical tools, sharp and of obscure function. 'Maybe that will persuade you to stop biting your nails, Lucy,' Miss Dunsire remarked acidly, from the depths of another black mood. Later she seemed to repent, and took me out to Fitzbillies, her favourite of Cambridge's many tea shops.

'Why is a twelfth birthday momentous?' I asked, munching one of their famous Chelsea buns. We were both sipping Gunpowder tea. 'You'll find out. In due course,' she replied. 'Have you finished? May we go? My head aches.'

She led me along King's Parade, complaining at my slow pace. 'Why don't you go ahead, Miss Dunsire?' I suggested. 'It's such a lovely afternoon. I'd like to walk back the long way through the colleges. Look at some bookshops, perhaps.'

'Oh, very well. As it's your birthday.' She shrugged impatiently and glanced at her watch. 'I'll expect you home in one hour. Don't be late.'

She set off at a swift pace towards the Silver Street bridge; I ducked into a side street where I was safe from sight. Miss Dunsire was an efficient watchdog, but over the summer she'd occasionally become careless. Perhaps she resented the fact that curtailing my freedom meant curtailing her own; perhaps she simply grew bored – and who could blame her – at yet another long day in my company; maybe, now my father was abroad, she felt less inclined to zealousness.

Whatever the reason, I'd begun to steal an hour here, an hour there, and when there was no sign that these stolen hours resulted in any mishap, Miss Dunsire grew even more lax. I learned I was more likely to get my way when her black moods gripped her, or if she herself wished to be elsewhere. In June, she had left me in the care of Mrs Grimshaw for an entire day, while she went to London to see some art exhibition at the Tate. A few weeks later, she went to London again and stayed overnight; her friend Eddie, the poet my father had so disliked, was giving a reading that evening, and she wished to attend it. Again, Mrs Grimshaw was pressed into service – and she, an amiable gaoler, was easy to escape. Now I had one whole hour of freedom, just enough for my purposes.

I hurried along, into the maze of Cambridge's alleyways and backstreets, and, ignoring the bookshops for once, came to a halt outside Mr Szabó's shop. *Jewellery and Curios,* it announced, in gilded curlicues above the bellying shop-front. I inspected its display window beadily: silver snuffboxes, pairs of candlesticks, a Russian icon so ancient – or so doctored – that one could scarcely discern its blackened saint; fat velvet pads displaying rings and bracelets, some rubbishy-looking, some good. Stirrup cups, a stuffed owl, drinking flasks, stock-pins, dress studs, cufflinks. The locket and chain had gone, I saw to my relief.

I climbed the steps, jangled the bell, and, teacups already in hand, Mr Szabó, a Cambridge institution for decades, of late my friend, emerged from the dark recesses of his shop. 'Dealing *again?*' he said, in his richly accented voice. I could hear in it his native Hungary, but also hints of Vienna, Italy, France and London. Mr Szabó was much travelled; he described himself as a wandering Jew, an eternal émigré; I loved the foreignness, the layers, the history in his voice. He dropped one sugar lump into my cup and three into his. 'And what are we peddling this time, Miss?'

I'd learned from the souks of Cairo and Luxor, so I said, 'You've sold the locket. I told you you would. Did you get a good price for it, Mr Szabó?'

'Enough, just enough.' He waggled his hand. 'I have to make a *leetle* profit, you know. I have to subsist, *meine liebe junge Dame*. When a customer drives a cruel bargain, the way *you* do, I'm lucky if I make sixpence to spare. Look at me! Skin and grief!'

I looked at him. Mr Szabó, sixtyish, white-haired and wily, was rotund; one might say *fat*. I suspected his margins were generous, but felt his dealings were fair; besides, I liked him. Delving into my pocket, I produced a handkerchief. Inside were two more objects purloined from the spare-room boxes, from the museum of Marianne Payne. Once my mother's: left to me in her will and now mine to sell or keep. Her collection was large, much of it bought as gifts for her by her parents, given prior to her marriage and the severance that caused; so far Mr Szabó had taken five pieces off my hands. Today, I'd brought him a narrow bangle and a brooch set with glittering stones. I was pretty sure they were diamonds, good ones. Having a mother born an Emerson had its advantages.

I placed them on a velvet pad, then sat down and sipped my tea. *Show no emotion. Make it clear you're ready to walk away*, Frances's voice counselled, and her mother chimed in: *Never, never take the first price they offer, Lucy — or the second, or the third. You absolutely* must *haggle — then honour's satisfied all round and everyone enjoys it.*

Their advice had related to buying: when selling, the same rules applied. Dealing was universal the world over, and I felt the techniques that worked in a Luxor souk worked extremely well in Bene't Street, Cambridge. Mr Szabó adjusted his jeweller's spyglass and with intense concentration began scrutinising the stones in the brooch.

'Not bad,' he said at last, in a grudging way. 'A nice little trinket. Before the war, I could have sold one of these the second it went in the window . . . but now? Tastes change, women are fickle. These flapper girls in their strange dresses — they want platinum and silver, not gold; they want clips, not brooches. Pretty stones, these — but the setting is dated. The bangle? Gold again, alas. Could I find a taker for them? Oh dearie me — I doubt it. I might just stretch to . . . ' And he named a figure. 'But that's a special price for *you*, young lady! Ah, I'm a foolish old man. Too soft-hearted for the harsh world of business: my problem all along.'

'Mr Szabó, the brooch is a Tiffany piece. From Fifth Avenue. My grandmother bought it, and Tiffany's was her favourite place on earth. In Paris, she liked Van Cleef & Arpels . . . ' I hesitated. Hearsay evidence, but true: sort of.

'A woman of discernment.' Mr Szabó made a snickering sound.

'That bangle is Van Cleef: it's twenty-two carat. Those are fine diamonds in the brooch – look, that one's a whopper. But never mind, I was thinking of taking them to London to sell anyway. I'll be sure to get the right price there.'

We exchanged a combative glance. Mr Szabó said: 'Not so fast, no need to be hasty, are you catching a train, young lady?' And with these essential preliminaries over, we set to.

It took three-quarters of an hour. Both Mr Szabó and I enjoyed every minute. *Caveat venditor*: I was rooked, as I later understood, but not as badly as I might have been, and not as much as I merited. Clutching the banknotes, I ran to the Post Office, entered this deposit in my secret savings' account book, and handed it all in. Adding up the entries, I saw I'd almost reached the total I needed – and that I'd calculated carefully. One more piece of jewellery should do it. Frances and her parents would be returning to Egypt in December; Miss Mack planned on a return journey there in November; I intended to go too. There were still minor obstacles in the way of this escape plan – my father, for instance, and Miss Dunsire. I'd deal with them in due course. *Money* had been the chief of my problems – and that was almost solved. Money was power; it bought freedom.

I ran home to Newnham and danced into the house only ten minutes late. Miss Dunsire was in the garden. She inspected my flushed face in her cool assessing way – and for one intoxicating moment I wanted to flourish my savings book under her nose: *Remember that lesson you taught me?* I'd say. *I've learned it, and I've learned it well.*

I resisted the impulse: I didn't trust her; I wasn't a complete fool. I went upstairs, hid the savings book in my locked drawer. I examined my presents, counted the Kipling stories, puzzled over the surgical tools in the manicure set. I washed, tidied my hair and came down promptly for the evening prep.

'What a very *birthday* face you have, Lucy,' Miss Dunsire remarked – and for some reason this birthday face of mine seemed to unsettle or annoy her. She handed me a set of geometry problems and told me brusquely to get on with them. While I fiddled with protractor and compass, she moved restlessly about the room, then announced she was going out for a walk: she needed air. 'Oh, and when you next go upstairs,' she added, in an irritable way, 'you'll find something from me. A token. I'll leave it on your bed.'

I discovered the token hours later. It came in a large white box, exquisitely wrapped. *Happy 12th Birthday*, said the attached card, in neat italic script. Inside was a dress, exactly the right size, the most beautiful dress I'd ever possessed.

'Is it *silk*?' I asked Miss Dunsire in awe, next morning, when I was able to thank her.

She shrugged and lit a cigarette. 'Who knows? You tell me – real silk, or fake?'

'It *is* silk.' I stroked it reverently. 'I can tell. I learned a lot about clothes in Egypt.'

'I'm sure you did – rubbing shoulders with so many fashion plates. Well, put it on – let's see how it looks.' I turned to go upstairs to change, but Miss Dunsire shook her head impatiently. 'For heaven's sake, child – you can put it on here. There's only the two of us. I shan't be shocked by the sight of you in a petticoat.'

I hesitated prudishly – we were in the sitting room; but in the end I complied. Miss Dunsire remained in her chair – my mother's chair, with its faded cover of 'Strawberry Thief'. She watched me as I drew the dress over my head, leaning back, her eyes half closed, the room aromatic with the scent of tobacco smoke, as I managed the tiny buttons, all twenty of them, smoothed down the skirt, and wriggled the bodice into place. 'Does it fit – does it fit?' I said, tense and excited. 'Do I look all right in it?'

'Oh, it fits,' she replied in a slow, measured way, and I saw a shadow pass across her face. 'But then it comes from Paris, where they understand such things. You are . . . ' She hesitated. 'You are a *jeune fille en fleur*, Lucy.'

'Is that good?' I asked uncertainly. I knew the meaning of the words, but her expression seemed to contradict it.

'I believe so. It's preferable to more predictable terms I could use. The colour suits you, and the cut. You remind me of someone I used to know.'

'One of your friends? Someone I've met?'

'No one you know. And she's dead, in any case.'

With a restless gesture, she extinguished her cigarette and rose to her feet. She stood for what seemed a long time, staring at me from across the room, then her face contracted. 'Well, well, well – who would have thought it? I'm quite moved. No, don't do that—' she added sharply, as excitement took hold and I performed a sudden impromptu pirouette. 'Save that for your dancing classes. I can't bear to watch it.'

She turned away, so I could not see her face, and a silence fell. I wanted to speak, but didn't know the right words: they were there in my mind, but stuck in my throat. In the end, I said: 'I'm sorry I remind you of your dead friend, Miss Dunsire. I can see that's upset you. But I want you to know: it's beautiful, this dress, and I'm very grateful. Thank you. It was awfully kind of you.'

'Kind?' She swung around. 'Kind? I detest that trite anodyne word. I'm not a kind woman, Lucy – as you should know. And I didn't buy that out of kindness either. I saw it that day I went down to London. There it was in a Bond Street window, and I thought: *why not?*' She shrugged. 'Besides, you need some new clothes for your visit to Hampshire. Your father may not care how shabby you look, but I do. Oddly enough.'

I coloured: I did not know much about London, but I could add up the equation even so. Bond Street + real silk + 'Made in Paris' = expensive. I had no idea how much my father paid Miss Dunsire, but I doubted it was generous. Miss Dunsire read my mind – as she often did.

'Housekeeping,' she said briskly, 'and don't even *think* of enquiring further. Just be prepared to subsist on bread and cheese for the next month.'

I thought that claim was untrue – I might not yet read her as well as she read me, but I was beginning to discern when Miss Dunsire told the truth and when she did not. I said nothing, but I was puzzled: on occasion, and always unpredictably, Miss Dunsire *could* be both kind and generous. This dress and my secret dancing lessons were evidence of that: she was similarly generous with her time, with her teaching, with her *mind* – why pretend she was not? Especially to me when it was I who reaped the benefit?

I still disliked her, I still thought of her as my enemy, I'd tell myself – but we'd been alone together in Cambridge for the past two months; I knew my hostility to her was lessening by the week, and that alarmed me. It felt disloyal to my mother, whose place she'd usurped – and feeble too. I had no intention of being manipulated and won over as Mrs Grimshaw and even my father had been; I was made of sterner stuff. She exerted a fascination, true, but that was for one reason only: it was because I could not understand her, because, dangerous, unpredictable, moody and mysteriously wounded as she was, she remained a puzzle I could not solve, one whose pieces would not fit.

You're not trying hard enough, Frances had written in her latest letter. *Remember what Mr Carter said? You're supposed to be good at observation, so watch her. What can you see? Ask her some really cunning questions – she's bound to let something slip.*

I tried. I tried during the long hot month of August, when Cambridge, deserted en masse by dons and undergraduates, reverted to a villagey somnolence. And what did I learn, from these cunning interrogations? I learned Miss Dunsire was twenty-four, and would be twenty-five this coming November; that she was born under the sign of Scorpio; that she was an only child, like me. That her Scots barrister father was dead, and her widowed mother, whom she rarely saw and with whom she had little in common, was French: now living in Provence, she was a lifelong hypochondriac who'd elected to become an invalid. At her mother's behest, I learned, she'd been christened 'Nicole', pronounced in the French way, but only a few old friends used this name; she'd changed it to 'Nicola' while at Girton, and preferred that. I learned Miss Dunsire's two dearest friends were shrewish classicist Meta and bohemian bicycle-thief Clair, now living in Chelsea and studying art at the Slade. I learned that Miss Dunsire's favourite colour was black (which didn't even count as a colour) and her favourite composer was Bach.

No progress. Or so I felt then. I made one last attempt, the day before I was to leave for my holiday with Rose and Peter. Nicola Dunsire and I were in my bedroom, packing my suitcases – a task she undertook with her customary perfectionism. New crisp tissue paper, muslin sachets for underwear, every garment washed, starched, ironed and irreproachable. Miss Dunsire was more

234

amenable to questions when her hands were occupied, so I waited until we were packing the last item, my as yet unworn silk dress; then, proud of my casual tone, said: 'By the way, that friend of yours, the one you mentioned to me, the one who's dead . . . '

'Yes?' Miss Dunsire arranged protective tissue paper in the folds of the dress.

'I was just wondering when she died. Was it a long time ago?'

'Two years ago. Maybe it's three now. I forget the exact date. Long enough . . . How awkward this is to pack! The silk *will* slip.'

'Was she young when she died?'

'She was. She was my own age – we grew up together, went to the same dancing class. Help me fold this in half, Lucy.'

'And why did she die? Was it an accident? Had she been ill?'

'She killed herself.' With an expert twist of the wrist, Miss Dunsire flipped the bodice over the skirt, smoothed it and placed it on top of the clothes in the suitcase. 'All done,' she said, on a note of triumph. 'Will it close? Yes, it will! Excellent.'

'Oh . . . how sad.' I was taken aback. 'Was she – why did she do such a terrible thing?'

'She wanted to die, I believe. She'd threatened to kill herself, and finally she succeeded.' She shrugged. 'There's nothing one can add to that: it's over, it's done, I've put it behind me. I mourned her deeply for a while, now I mourn her less and one of these days I shan't mourn her at all. That's the pattern to grief – as you should know, Lucy.'

She gave me a venomous look as I recoiled from these words. How quick she was to retaliate! She knew that sting in the tail would silence my questions – and it did. She lined up the three leather suitcases we'd packed, fastened them securely and lifted them onto the floor. One smaller case, empty, remained on the bed.

'Almost done,' she said in her crisp way. 'I'll leave you to pack the little attaché case, Lucy. I thought you'd need that for your diaries and your letters. You'll want to take them with you, I'm sure. And I can hardly help you there – not when they're in a locked drawer and the key to that drawer is on a chain around your neck. I hope it won't take you long: you have an early start tomorrow, so early supper and early bed tonight.'

And then, having ensured that she was fully reinstated as my enemy, she left the room. *Beware Scorpions*, I thought. I watched her serene departure with fresh hate.

At ten the next day, punctual to the minute, the astonishing car Eve had sent for me pulled up outside our house.

'Well, well – a Hispano-Suiza, no less.' Miss Dunsire examined the car's glorious coachwork with a satiric eye. 'And the driver in *such* a smart uniform. What a tragedy our neighbours are away and missing it: they'd disapprove so deeply; they could have dined out on this for weeks. And what a pity your father can't see it, Lucy. He'd have forty fits. How high-minded they all are! *I* think it's thrilling . . . Ah, your friend's come to escort you. You must be Lady Rose? How do you do, my dear?'

Rose bounced out of the car, and shortly afterwards bounced back into it. 'Crikey,' she said, when we were safely settled inside, 'I've never had a governess who looked like that, Lucy. Mine have all been the most frightful old sticks. She doesn't look like a bluestocking either, I'm sure they're all plain as a pikestaff – and she's *stunning*.' She frowned. Rose, well schooled by her mother, was far more worldly than I and a merciless judge of female appearance. 'That auburn hair and those eyes! And that frock of hers was fearfully clever. *Masses* of SA. I thought she was quite *it*, actually.' She paused and gave me a narrow glance: 'When is she off on that boring reading party?'

'In a day or two – that's what she said anyway.'

'And when does your father get back from Greece?'

'The end of this week, I think. Why? What difference does that make?'

'Absolutely none, let's forget them!' Rose inserted her small gloved hand in mine. 'Oh, Lucy – what fun we're going to have! Petey's missed you so much. He can't *wait* to see you, he's drawn you a picture of a rainbow and caught you a newt! Wheeler's really looking forward to it too, she's *wild* with excitement.'

'I can't imagine that.' I was touched, especially by the newt – but I'd never known impassive, formidable Wheeler betray any emotion; her reticence was exemplary.

'Well, you're right, she hides it, of course, and stumps about being sensible – but even so, she is. And Eve's coming over to see us, and we'll have lots of wonderful picnics. If we're good, Eve says she'll take us over to Highclere, and her father will show us his Egyptian collection – Howard Carter's going to be turning up at some point to work on it. There's something brewing there, Lucy, some kind of row, I think . . . Oh, and Eve's brother was married in July, did you see the photographs in the *Tatler*? Heir to the whole lot and he's married some American who hasn't a penny, they say – Eve wore the most divine dress . . . There's tons to tell you, Lucy. Oh, I'm so glad to have you back!'

She chattered on; I was only half listening. I was wondering what 'SA' could be; Rose's questions had made me uneasy. If perfectionist Miss Dunsire *was* leaving for France in the next two days, how odd that she hadn't begun to sort through her clothes and books, let alone pack. She'd given me no address for the Loire either, I realised – and that was odd too; in such matters she was always punctilious.

'Meanwhile,' Rose was saying, 'I haven't told you yet about the brilliant *plot* Wheeler and I hatched. I've been dying to tell you, but I had to wait until I was sure we'd succeeded. We'd worried and worried what to do, all the way home from Egypt. You see, as far as Papa was concerned, Wheeler was a lady's maid – and Mamma's maid at that. We knew he'd dismiss her the second we got home – and I'd have *died*, Lucy, if he'd done that; she's the only reliable thing in Petey's life – and mine, come to that. We had to persuade him to let her stay and be our nanny – and the chances of him doing that were zero. Wheeler and I were in *black* despair; then I remembered what a skinflint he is, and it came to us!'

On their arrival home, Rose explained, Wheeler had requested a brief interview with Lord Strathaven. At this interview, she informed him in her stolid way that she would like to be considered for the position of family nanny, that she could assume that role at once, on a trial basis, and was prepared to do so on half-wages for a period of six months. If, during that time, she failed to provide satisfaction, she would leave at once. If, on the other hand, she *did* provide satisfaction, perhaps Lord Strathaven would consider employing her as the children's nanny on a formal basis, once those six months were up. Having made this proposal, Wheeler had simply stood there, large, plain, forty-something yet ageless, a Lancashire woman as impassive and immovable as an Easter Island statue.

'Didn't she explain how close she is to you and Peter?' I asked. I was trying to concentrate on this ploy, but I was still worrying about the Loire, and the chateau for which I had no address. 'How much you and Peter love her – did Wheeler emphasise that?'

'Of course not, idiot!' Rose gave me a look of scorn. 'If he'd known it was what *we* wanted, she'd have been out the door in a blink. No, she said we were thoroughly spoiled children who'd played her up the whole way home from Egypt. She said we needed a strong hand and firm discipline, and she could provide it. Papa lapped that up: *discipline* is his favourite word – well, next to *fillies* and *bitches* it is . . .

'Then Wheeler made herself indispensable,' Rose giggled. 'When she saw Papa, which wasn't often, she began to boss him a bit: he adores that because it reminds him of his own sainted nanny – she looked like Wheeler and she used to spank him with a hairbrush. So Wheeler came cheap and suddenly he was five years old again, and if he didn't behave Nanny would punish him: "No supper for *you*, young man!" and then *whisk* him upstairs to bed.' She turned to look at me. 'What on earth's the matter? Are you listening, Lucy? You *do* look peculiar! Are you feeling car-sick?'

I was listening all right. I said: 'I'm fine. I'm – just admiring her methods. Go on.'

'Well, that was six months ago – and now he's hired her. It's official. Now she wears a brown uniform instead of a black one, and she's Nanny Wheeler and rules the roost.'

Rose paused for breath. 'Isn't Wheeler *brilliant*? She manages my father so well, and he's so conceited he never notices. Poor Mamma could *never* do that, she hadn't the knack. There wasn't a peep out of Pa when the idea of us staying in the country came up. He wanted to forget us and trot off to America for the summer, you see, so all Wheeler had to do was remind him how convenient our absence would be, and he agreed at once. Pa's in Newport. Sailing, or so he said . . .

'He's thinking of marrying again, I expect.' Rose sighed. 'He'll be chasing after some heiress, or one of his chorus girls – there'll be a *woman* behind it anyway, there always is. Papa thinks all women are fools, he says his dogs are more intelligent, but,' Rose lowered her voice, 'but he can't *resist* anything in a petticoat. One sniff and he's after it. He's always been that way, Lucy – as poor Mamma discovered inside six months.'

How airless the car felt. The word 'petticoat' reverberated. I stared at Rose. 'I don't understand . . . six months? How did Poppy find out?'

'Oh, women can always tell,' Rose said in a small voice. 'When he's up to something, there's a look he gets on his face. Furtive. Shifty and greedy at the same time. You know how dogs look when they smell something delicious in the kitchen and they're working out how to slink in and steal it? Like that.'

I'd never owned a dog. My father did not approve of pets. I tried to imagine this – how the dog, how the man might look.

The car felt so stuffy and hot; it was making me light-headed. I wound down the window a crack and examined the flat passing landscape: how parched, how *dry* it was.

'Anyway – let's not talk about him,' Rose went on, brightening. 'The point is, our scheme worked. Wheeler really has got Pa right there in the palm of her hand – she can make him do almost *anything* if she sets her mind to it.' She nudged me. 'So, come on, stop daydreaming – tell me what you think. Weren't we clever? Aren't you impressed?'

'Very.'

The smooth swift passage of the Hispano-Suiza *was* affecting me, I decided. A few miles further on, and the car had to be halted. I just made it to the roadside, where I was violently sick.

22

The house where I was to stay was called Nuthanger: an old farm-house, with some hundred acres, it had passed down the female line in Rose's family. Poppy d'Erlanger had inherited it from her maternal grandmother and had often visited the farm as a child; she had always loved the place, Rose said, but never lived in it. After this grandmother's death, it had been let for years on a farming tenancy. Now it belonged to Rose, who had been left it in Poppy's will; it was being administered for her by her mother's trustees, who were currently seeking a new tenant. Meanwhile the house was a place of romance to Rose who, from her earliest childhood, had grown up with her mother's stories and memories of it. 'Look, Lucy,' she said, as at last, after our long, hot, giddying drive, the Hispano-Suiza turned into a narrow twisting lane descending into a hidden valley: 'Look – you can just see the chimneys. Beyond the hedges, below the beechwood.'

Rose wound down the window, and sweet fresh air filled the car. Craning my neck, narrowing my eyes against the sun's dazzle, I saw the rising curves of the chalk downs on the far side of the valley, and, directly below us, clusters of chimneys, a trail of blue smoke drift-ing up, and a huddle of roofs, thick with mosses and lichens. I caught one tantalising glimpse before the high impenetrable hedges hid it from view again.

We bumped on down the steep track, past banks with tangles of ripening blackberries, into a tunnel shaded by elms, and out again into sunlight. I couldn't see the farm; I could see no other houses.

Then the driver hauled on the wheel, we passed through an invisible gap in the hawthorns, a cluster of hens squawked and scattered and I found we were there, in a huge yard, protected on three sides by an old brick house and its attendant sheltering barns; to my left, green fields still thick with clover fell away to the valley and the distant windings of a small river . . . I would revisit that house again, much later in life; its lineaments remain sharp in my memory. I loved it, at first sight.

At the door of the house, as if guarding the entrance, stood Wheeler, unchanged, impassive, suppressing a smile of welcome, wearing a new brown uniform; and next to her, clasping her hand, jumping up and down, jiggling from foot to foot in excitement, was a small boy, an unknown boy. Blond hair bleached almost white by months of summer sun, brown-skinned, bare-legged, clad in old shorts and a muddy shirt. It wasn't until I'd climbed out of the car, and Wheeler released him, not until he came hurtling across the yard and, almost knocking me down, flung his arms around me, that I realised who he was. His dark blue eyes were unmistakable, as were those of the mother from whom he'd inherited them.

I said *Peter, it's you*, in the same second that he said *Lulu*.

I was taken on what Rose called the tour, within minutes of arrival. My cases were dragged up to an attic room and unceremoniously dumped there; Wheeler disappeared to the kitchens to make tea and with Rose gripping one of my hands and Peter the other, I was propelled outside into the sunshine. 'No servants. Just Wheeler and us. For weeks and weeks. Isn't that glorious?' Rose said. 'What shall we show Lucy first, Petey?'

They couldn't agree: the orchard, or the barns? The pond or the river? The tree platform; the hen that had chicks, twelve of them; the hayloft where they'd made a den? And so I discovered the place in the turmoil of arrival, rushing in one direction, doubling back, pausing to pick apples, discovering some freshly laid eggs, mounting into a loft sweet with the scent of hay, and then out again, up the steep winding lane behind the house. The hay fields high above it had been newly cut by a neighbouring farmer, and there, finally, we halted. The air was filled with birdsong – but I could see no birds.

'Larks,' Rose said, 'so high they're invisible. Hundreds of them, Lucy. They'll wake you in the morning . . . '

' . . . No clocks in this house,' Peter carolled. 'Not one . . . '

' . . . so the larks are our alarm clocks.' Rose flung herself down on the grass.

'And we know when it's bedtime,' Peter added, flinging himself down next to her, 'because it's dark and the owls hoot.'

He put his small brown hands over his mouth and made a hooting sound that was startlingly convincing. I sat down next to them on the grass, inhaled its rich scent and lifted my face to the sky: an *exultation* of larks, I thought: I'd been learning collectives.

Reaching across, Rose tapped my wristwatch. 'Take that off,' she said. 'Leave it in your bedroom, and don't wind it again until you leave.'

I saw that my watch had stopped; its hands were stuck at ten-thirty, so it had wound down somewhere on the long drive from Cambridge. I still felt dazed from that journey, from my shaming episode of sickness by the roadside. 'I've no idea what time it is anyway,' I said, 'it's all happened too fast. I'm not even sure where I am.'

'You're in *our* house,' Rose said. 'And *our* valley,' Peter added. 'And now it's yours too,' they carolled in unison.

Sitting up and pointing, Rose then explained the geography. The river below was a tributary of the Test, a clear chalk stream famous for its sweet-tasting brown trout; Peter had once seen something lurking in its shadows that he thought was a pike, but Rose thought was just river-weed. On the crest of the downs opposite, which could be reached by a footbridge, there were rides, and sometimes you'd see horses from the Carnarvon stud being exercised, or hear in the distance the thunder of their hooves as they galloped. On those downs you could walk for miles, walk all day, without seeing another person, and there were thousands of butterflies. '*Millions*,' said Peter dreamily. There, back in July, high up on Beacon Hill, they had seen thirty-five Adonis Blues and, once, a Monarch, a great rarity.

'And that? Is that a *castle*?' I pointed across the valley to where, a long way away, in the far hazy distance, half-hidden by intervening woods, rising up from a declivity, I could just discern the fairytale pinnacles of a tower, a suggestion of fortifications, a glitter that might have been leads under sunlight and something that fluttered, a flag perhaps.

'That?' Rose followed my gaze and shrugged. 'Oh, well, it's a castle of sorts, I suppose. That's Lord Carnarvon's place, Lucy. That's Highclere.'

It wasn't until after tea that day that I was alone and truly able to get my bearings. Peter was inside, being bathed by Wheeler and Rose, and so, in the cool of the evening, I set off to explore on my own. Wandering around the farm-yard, I began to understand the complex of buildings that at first had been so confusing. I found that Nuthanger was a long, low house, built of roseate brick; its oldest part, its core, dated back to the sixteenth century, or so I was informed by the stone above its entrance, which bore the Armada date, *1588*. Cradled and protected by the chalk downs, it was a house of adjustments and accretions; over the centuries it had grown an arm here, a wing there, extra rooms to house children, another byre for animals, another barn to store the land's riches.

It had many gables, many hiding places, passageways that doubled back on themselves, and a bewildering number of winding, creaking elm staircases, some concealed behind doors, masquerading as cupboards. It had many windows; those in the oldest parts of the house were small and secretive casements; others, added later, were tall, wide sashes that filled their rooms with light. Attached to the house, grafted to its walls and roofs with joinery ties and linked by complex masonry umbilicals, was a massed range of barns, byres and stables, treasuries for hay and grain. They were piled to their rafters with the artefacts of farming, with an archaeology of ploughs, carts, harvesters: with enigmatic machines, devices for sowing and reaping, maybe; for winnowing and baling. Many looked long discarded, superseded by more recent inventions but still preserved, paying silent rusting testimony to the work of long-dead farmhands.

I stood in the yard for a while, listening to the laughter from inside, and the sounds of bathtime splashing. I counted the swallows swooping above my head and, when I reached fifty, went inside again. I wandered through peaceful shabby rooms downstairs; there, on a capacious armchair, Wheeler's knitting lay, spiked by its needles. I examined a jigsaw puzzle Rose and Peter had left unfinished, and inserted a missing section of sky. Not one clock, as Peter had said: no ticking, no hours chiming. I wandered through to the huge, flagstoned kitchen and explored the warren of pantries, larders and still rooms that led off from it. I found myself in a gunroom, its racks emptied of guns – and then in a dairy: white-tiled, cool, every surface scoured scrupulously clean, white muslin cloths still hanging on hooks, earthenware bowls, a butter churn, instruments for sieving and skimming. It was in perfect order, as if the dairymaids who'd once worked in it had been there that very day, and would return the next morning. Like the barns, this space and its implements told a story – and the same one: it was eloquent of past industry.

When I'd explored downstairs, I knew this house spoke to me – and that it made me sad. A great melancholy washed over me, and the doubts and uncertainties, the alarms I'd felt on my journey, came rushing up on a tide. Choosing one of the many doors at random and discovering yet another staircase concealed behind it, I followed it up, and found to my surprise that it led into my own bedroom: that room had two approaches, one obvious, and one hidden. There my Cambridge suitcases were, packed with the aid of Miss Dunsire. They were reproaching me. I removed my stopped watch and slowly began to unpack them. I was halfway through this task when Wheeler tapped at my door, said, 'Ah, *there* you are,' and then – seeing my expression – came into the room, closed the door firmly and, making no comment, began to assist me.

We opened the case of books, and put my Egypt ones, a little library that was growing, on the nightstand by my bed. 'Extra candles in the drawer, and matches,' Wheeler said. 'If you want to read all night, that's *your* lookout. It won't worry me. Like this stuff, do you?' She picked up Belzoni's account of his exploits in the Valley of the Kings.

'I do, Wheeler. You can learn a lot from it. And I find it takes me back there.'

'That must be a comfort.' She lifted out a stack of work and exercise books. 'And whatever's this lot?' she enquired, dumping them on a table by the window.

'It's my homework, Wheeler. Miss Dunsire has set exercises for the whole month. I have to do some every day. She doesn't want me to fall behind.'

'You could do with a rest from all that. You're looking peaky. It's not for me to say, but I will: is she here, this Miss Dunsire of yours? Here to check up on you and your homework, is she? Turning up – this week, next week? Not to *my* knowledge.'

'No, Wheeler. She's going to France for a month. At least, that's what she said. Only, when we were in the car coming here, just something Rose said . . . I thought maybe she *wasn't* going there, and she might have lied. She does lie – sometimes.'

Wheeler considered this information. I could tell her mind was working it over. 'If she has told an untruth,' she asked, 'and she's *else-where*, this Miss Dunsire of yours, where might that be?'

'I don't know. London . . . or I thought – it crossed my mind, she might stay in Cambridge.'

Wheeler considered the paltry evidence I then gave. 'What non-sense,' she said eventually. 'Stay in some stuffy old town in England, when she could be free as a bird in France with her friends? Doesn't sound likely to me. You come up with some funny ideas, you do. As for that address – it's obvious: she'll write from France and send it . . .

'Right, let's get the rest of this unpacked,' she went on, 'then you can go and read Peter a bedtime story. Stick to treasure hunts or knights, avoid witches: I don't want him having nightmares. You remember how he was, in Egypt? I'm not having *that* starting up again. He's over the nightmares now, thanks to this house – it has curative powers, this place, as I expect you've seen because you're quick that way.' She gave me a sharp look. 'He's healing, and Rose too. He turned four back in April, and that makes a big difference. You can see how he's come on. But I still have to stay on my guard, and so do you. Don't mention his mother – not unless he does.'

We unpacked the rest of my things. We hung up my cotton dresses and blouses; put jumpers and underwear into a chest of drawers. 'Well, *someone* knows how to pack,' Wheeler remarked, unfolding tissue paper. 'Couldn't have done it better myself. Suffering saints – what's this?'

'It's my birthday present, from Miss Dunsire. She saw it in a window in Bond Street and she thought – I'd like it.'

Wheeler shook the dress out and inspected it. I thought of those exquisite clothes of Mrs d'Erlanger's that Wheeler had looked after, of the decades she'd spent as a lady's maid, her deep knowledge of the mysteries of dresses. I wanted her to approve my own dress, wanted it passionately, with an eagerness and trepidation I couldn't have explained. I suffered as, like a scholar inspecting a rare book or some precious artefact, she silently examined the hand-sewn seams, the construction of the lining, the set of the sleeves, the alignment of the bodice darts, the fall of the skirt and the pure geometry of the neckline.

'Now *that* is a treasure.' She was trying to hide it, but I could see she was moved. 'That is a lovely, lovely thing. Someone's *cared*, when they made that – and they knew what they were doing too. Look at those stitches, all done by hand – see how tiny they are? And the material – there's silk and then there's *silk*, I always say. This is pure – you won't find better than this, not even in China . . . Did you know, the secret of silk was so precious that anyone caught trying to smuggle the cocoons out of China was executed on the spot? Take a strand of steel, Miss Lucy, and a strand of silk the same thickness – and the silk is the stronger of the two: think of that! So when you write to your Miss Dunsire, *which* you'll be doing in due course, you tell her from me: Wheeler approves! You can tell her this too: when a dress passes muster with *me*, that means something.'

I blushed with delight. 'I know it's a party dress, Wheeler, so it probably won't be needed here. But I couldn't tell Miss Dunsire that. I didn't want to disappoint her.'

'There might be a call for it. There's Rose's birthday coming up, towards the end of the month, just before you leave.'

This caused immediate consternation. Rose had never mentioned this birthday, I had no present for her . . . 'What a worrier you are!' Wheeler interrupted. 'If it's not one thing, it's another. I'll manage something. I always do. Now run off and read that story.'

I read Peter a story about Galahad, sundry other knights and the powers of Excalibur. There were enchantments in it – but no witches. Outside, darkness was falling, and an owl – 'That's a *tawny*, Lucy,' he said sleepily – had begun to call from the beechwoods. Next morning, when the sun – or the larks – woke me, Peter came padding into my room with the presents he'd forgotten to give me in the rush of my arrival.

There was the newt, in a jam jar, to be admired for a short while and then returned to the pond: a fine creature he was, with pads on his hands and a dinosaur crest — watery first cousin to the lizards I'd seen in Egypt.

'And I done this. For you. All by my own,' Peter said, scarlet with pride, handing me the rainbow drawing Rose had mentioned.

I have that drawing still. At the top, in careering purple crayon, it said *weLcOm lUcY*. At the bottom, in red, it said, *LOvE froMm PeTeY*. The rainbow, an elaborate one, with many kinks in it, made a jagged arch over a house. This house, bright orange, with a green roof, a path to it like a ladder, and next to it something that might have been a tree or possibly a chicken, was extremely small; it had one window and no discernible door; a flock of tick-marks flew over its roof, and below it flowed a powerful navy-blue squiggle. It was blessed by the protective rainbow; also by a red sun, a blue moon, and two bright stars, made of gold foil. 'It's *our* house, Lucy,' Peter explained anxiously.

I could read the drawing's marvellous perspective, and hadn't doubted it for one second, so I said: 'Peter, I can see that. I knew it *at once.*'

His face lit up; he gave me a bear-hug, and I kissed him.

We spent my first week at the farm outside — at least, in my remembrance we did; but then in my remembrance, the sun shone every day, rain and clouds were banished and I was inhabiting a place without shadows. Sometimes, on the rare occasions when I was alone, a hint of a shadow might fall, and I'd start to fret at the fact that Miss Dunsire had failed to write from her Loire chateau. Or I'd dwell on Rose's birthday and the necessity of a gift. But Wheeler had developed a sixth sense for these anxieties — and always had a cure for them. Sometimes she'd take them on directly and say, 'Do you *know* how long a letter from France takes? Those Frenchies don't hurry themselves — I've heard it can take weeks — more! And that's if they don't lose it this end,' she'd add darkly.

Sometimes she'd divert me — at which she was expert: and that was an easy enough task, in this place where, every day, there was somewhere or something new to discover. Sometimes Eve's maid Marcelle would come over to see Wheeler and bring us news of events at Castle Carnarvon. Sometimes we'd be dispatched to the farmer along the valley for freshly churned butter and cream, or sent to find field mushrooms, or pick apples and blackberries for a pie – or, since Wheeler had discovered Miss Dunsire's lessons left yawning gaps in my education, I'd be whisked off to the kitchen with Rose and Peter and taught to cook: cakes, and gingerbread men, and tarts with home-made jam in them. When the anxiety as to Rose's birthday present was noted, I was taught to sew. 'Something you've made yourself,' Wheeler said. 'That always makes a suitable present.'

I doubted this. The sewing did not go well: I hadn't inherited my mother's needle skills. 'Maybe we'll try knitting,' Wheeler announced, showing rare signs of uncertainty. 'We'll have a practice run first.'

The practice session could take place in public, she felt, so an old jumper was found; Rose, Peter and I unpicked and then rewound it. 'No point in wasting new wool, not for the first attempt,' Wheeler said thriftily, producing fat knitting needles for all three of us. She cast on the stitches, showed us how to do plain and purl, and then sat back and watched. Peter couldn't master it at all and ran out in search of a hen's nest. Rose got into a tangle two rows down, tossed it aside as the most annoying thing ever and ran out to join him. I laboured on, frowning and fretting, dropping stitches, picking them up: first the tension was too tight, then too loose: I had ambitions for it, but it grew very slowly. It started life as a scarf, then shrank to a pot-holder; after a week of intermittent toil Wheeler inspected it and said she thought it might make an egg cosy.

Fortunately, I was able to abandon it the very next day, when the two last problems afflicting me were resolved, by the arrival of the post, and by the advent of Eve, who had been away in London with friends, but had now returned to Highclere Castle. It was Eve who arrived first, at the wheel of her own car, a dashing open-topped marvel in British racing green, with a leather belt around its bonnet. It was a Lagonda 11.9 coupé, she explained airily, and her favourite little runabout. 'Rosebud, my best beloved – how *brown* you are!' she cried, stooping to kiss her. 'And who are these two little savages?' she enquired, as Peter and I ran out to greet her.

'We're *pirates*,' Peter corrected, and Eve said: 'Darlings, of *course* you are. What an idiot I am – I hadn't noticed the cutlasses.'

She was looking very pretty, I thought, in her floating dress, with her nut-brown hair and nut-brown eyes; at first I was shy of her, but that wore off as she stayed all morning and chattered away. Wheeler had tipped her the wink, I suspect, because when she was readying herself to leave, she drew me apart from the others, and taking my hand in a solemn way, said: 'Lucy, shall you mind if I ask you a *huge* favour? I need to trot over to the shops one day and find a gift for Rose's birthday – and I need help choosing it. I'm so bad at making up my mind, and bound to pick the wrong thing. I get *frantic* with indecision . . . You wouldn't be an absolute angel, and come with me and advise me?'

I said I would like that very much, and asked if I might buy a present for Rose at the same time. 'Daddy gave me pocket money for the month before I left,' I explained. 'Sixpence a week, so I have a florin. Do you think that will be enough, Eve?'

'*Enough?* Lucy, it's munificent! What fun! We'll make a day of it, shall we? We have so much to catch up on – I want to hear all about Frances and her island. You *must* tell me about Cambridge . . . I'll fix it all with Wheeler – maybe next week? *I* know, I'll pick you up in the morning, and we'll buzz off in my little car to Alresford, and shop like mad things, and have a slap-up lunch. Then I'll take you over to see Highclere, and our Egyptian treasures – the others can meet us there and we'll have tea. Howard Carter will have arrived by then, and he'll love to see you all. Right, that's our secret plan, Lucy.'

I was still reeling at this prospect hours later, when the young boy who delivered our letters arrived with the second post of the day. I watched him come toiling down the steep hill with his leather satchel, and while he was being tended to by Wheeler, given lemonade and cake, fuel to propel him back up the hot hill and on the further two hot miles to the next farm, Rose, Peter and I sorted the offerings he'd brought with him. They included items for me, the first mail I'd received since arriving. There was a postcard from my father in Cambridge, the flowing copperplate informing me that the weather was changeable there and Euripides was progressing. And there was a letter – a fat letter – from Nicola Dunsire.

I inspected its envelope closely: French postage stamps and – no doubt about it, no possible ambiguities – a legible French postmark. The last lingering shadows that had threatened disappeared in a mirror-flash. Now I had the envelope in my hand, I found I wasn't that eager to read its contents; I went fishing with Rose and Peter instead. But when I went to bed that night, the letter reproached me – it was kind of her to write, after all; so I opened it and read it by the flicker of candlelight.

Description of Loire and chateau; address of said chateau, which she'd clean forgotten to give me ... account of trains, drains, weather, local beauty spots. Books being read by their party: Nicola Dunsire discovering the world of someone called Marcel Proust. Dorothy doing this, Meta saying that, Evadne in charge of meals, Edith deep in Hume, Clair bicycling off to paint landscapes ... Thirteen earnest, industrious, high-minded and, I felt, rather boring bluestockings ... I yawned and skimmed to the last page; the poet from our Cambridge lunch party had turned up – out of the blue apparently: Eddie something – double-barrelled, surname unreadable in candlelight. Eddie sent on his way ... *The most beautiful evening, such a view from my room. Back to Monsieur Swann's tomorrow,* she wrote, and with that the letter ended abruptly.

Amusing in places but a plod through predictable territory, I thought. She had signed off: *Voila! Ecrivez-moi, ma chère Lucy. Je vous embrace, Nicola.* There was a postscript: *How are your Egyptologists? Have you worn my dress yet?*

I tried on her dress the next morning: I was reminded of it by that postscript, and I wanted to be sure it would fit me for Rose's birthday. At the end of July, it had fitted perfectly; only six weeks ago, but since coming to the farm I felt as if I'd grown – my body felt different. I blamed Wheeler's excellent cooking, the sharpened appetite that came from running about all day; those cakes and pies and biscuits we consumed, the eggs and bacon breakfasts, the pints of milk we drank. I locked the door, removed my nightdress, and peered down at my own nakedness. I was taller, but my legs and arms were still thin, my hip and collarbones stuck out; you could count my ribs. Wheeler said both Peter and I were too skinny, and I was built like a boy – since I'd have liked to *be* a boy, I took that as a compliment. No change, no change, I thought with relief, and eased the silk over my head. The twenty tiny buttons ran up the side of the dress; the ten lower ones fastened easily; the ten above did not.

What had happened? I *had* grown; I'd put on weight, but only in one small area of my body. What was wrong with my *chest*? I tried breathing in and out; when I was gasping for air, I could manage six more buttons. The final four simply would not do up. I ran weeping to Wheeler. 'What's happened? Oh, what's happened, Wheeler?' I cried. 'If I starve myself for the next two weeks, will it fit again?'

Wheeler might have explained: looking back now, I can see she considered that possibility and rejected it; perhaps she saw that the issue might lead on to other biological inevitabilities, and such difficult topics were best avoided. I saw something – a wariness – flash across her face, but it quickly returned to Easter Island impassivity. 'What a great fuss about nothing,' she said. 'You see those darts in the bodice? Let them out and it'll fit again right as rain. No problem there!' She made the adjustments and returned the dress to me that night. I tried it on. It fitted.

I didn't mention these difficulties to Nicola Dunsire when I answered her letter. I told her I'd be wearing her dress for Rose's birthday. I told her how lovingly it had been inspected by an expert in the field: *Wheeler approves!* I thought that would please her. I told her Mr Carter was arriving soon, that I had seen Lady Evelyn and might visit Highclere, that Peter and I had caught two trout, that I'd seen a sparrowhawk, was doing my homework, and – as instructed – had been learning some poems by heart.

Rose and I had chosen Tennyson's *The Lady of Shalott*: we both loved its rhythms, its rhymes, its tale of enchantment and love's appalling fatalities. It was long, but we mastered it all, and used to chant it as we climbed the high blue hills beyond the farm. Even Peter learned some lines, and would join in at key points: *She left the WEB, she left the LOOM/ She made three paces through the ROOM/ She looked down to CAMELOT*. Looking down at the distant towers of Highclere Castle, we'd shout these lines from the hilltops. We also liked, *Out flew the web and floated wide/ The mirror CRACK'D from side to side/ 'The CURSE is come upon me,' cried/ The Lady of Shalott . . .*

Tennyson's best line, we agreed, and the proof of his sublime genius, was our favourite: *The CURSE is come upon MEEE*. We yelled that, and sometimes wailed it, banshee-manner, clutching our sides, rolling on the ground; once, we howled it, all three of us in unison, so loudly that Lord Carnarvon must have heard us in his castle three miles away.

We overdid it that time, and Peter, who didn't understand curses, began to tremble. 'But what *is* it? What did it *do*?' he asked in a little voice. 'Oh, Lucy – does it dead you?'

Had Frances been there, she'd have told him curses were terrible things: inescapable, irreversible and eternal. Six months later – by which time Carter, Lord Carnarvon and tales of Egyptian curses would be on the front pages of newspapers worldwide; by which time my own life would be changed in ways I'd never foreseen – I might have felt Frances had a point; I was certainly considering the nature and origin of curses, and I still do. But that day Rose and I were anxious to prevent nightmares, afraid Peter might begin asking about his mother again; and so, improvising fast, we explained curses were nothing to fear. They were a passing affliction. They were quickly cured – like chickenpox. And anyway, they didn't happen, they belonged to fairy tales, they were the stuff of fiction.

'I don't expect your poet friend Eddie would approve our taste in verse!' I wrote to Nicola Dunsire, describing this episode. 'Given his views on the immortal Alfred!' I did try to be sophisticated when I wrote; I thought this was a passable witticism. Miss Dunsire could not have agreed; nor did my other news seem to engage her, for she never commented on anything I told her, and she never answered any questions I asked. I received many letters from her over the next weeks, they flew in with astonishing regularity, on the dot, one every three days. She kept me up to date with her own activities and those of her bluestocking friends. She kept me posted as to her deepening fascination with M. Swann . . . and what a disappointment there! I'd finally realised that Swann was not a real man, as I'd half hoped, half feared – he was merely a character in a novel.

But not once, not once, did Nicola Dunsire respond to anything I wrote in my letters. Maybe she just tossed them aside unread? Maybe Rose, Peter, Wheeler and I were of no interest to her? I was wounded by this deafening silence. I confessed that.

'Miss Manners could teach her a thing or two. *Self-centred*,' pronounced Wheeler.

23

'Eve, may I ask you a question – what does SA mean?' I asked as Eve and I were having our 'slap-up' lunch.

It was market day at the small Austenish town of Alresford, and as we could not, of course, enter a public house, Eve had made other arrangements. We were eating a Highclere Castle picnic, sitting by the river below the town, overlooking the watercress beds for which it was famous. We'd had foie gras sandwiches and slices of partridge pie. We were munching apples and sipping cold lemonade. Eve had been staring dreamily at the river for some while – in a Lady of Shalott manner, I thought: *Tirra lirra, by the river/ Sang Sir Lancelot.* Now she roused herself.

'SA stands for sex appeal, Lucy,' she replied – the great thing about Eve was that if you asked her a question, she answered it. 'It means you're madly alluring to the opposite sex. A man can have SA, or a woman. And it doesn't mean that they're handsome or pretty – not necessarily. It just means they have this irresistible, magical power to *attract*. Poor darling Poppy had it, for instance . . . ' A shadow passed across her face. 'I *don't* have it – and I used to mind and wish I did. But now I think I'm safer without it.' She stuffed the last things back in the picnic basket. 'Right, one final try for these presents. We're not getting on very well, are we? Before we head for home, shall we try the market?'

We did so. The shops at Alresford had proved a disappointment: had we wanted to buy Rose some ironmongery, a teapot or a whale-bone corset, they might have helped, but not otherwise. The market looked more promising. We wandered between the stalls, admiring the bowls of eggs, the hand-made cheeses, the wooden toys whittled on farms as a sideline industry, the hand-knitted baby clothes being sold by farmers' wives for pin money. I was considering the nature of SA, the fact that Miss Dunsire (according to Rose) had it, and Eve (according to her) did not. Eve, wearing a pale pink frock, pretty, smiling and courteous, recognised and greeted on all sides with doffed caps and curtseys, was as charming that day as I could imagine any woman's being. The differing appeal of Mrs d'Erlanger and Miss Dunsire remained mysterious. When I was a grown woman, would I ever resemble Poppy or Nicola? I couldn't imagine that. I'd have to settle for safety, I decided.

Clutching my money, I inspected the stalls. It did seem that Eve had been right and my florin was enough: it would easily have bought a wooden train or a knitted doll or a crocheted shawl – objects someone must have laboured over for days; but none of these things would appeal to Rose. We walked on, past the gypsy women selling lucky heather, the gypsy fortune-teller reading palms – Eve scurried past him, and I remembered Howard Carter's story of Carnarvon's seances and how much they had frightened her. Eve bought some little things – a rose-pink sash, a corn dolly. I couldn't find anything suitable, until, as we reached the outskirts of the market, I saw a man with two large mewling baskets; one contained puppies, the other kittens. Rose loved animals.

I drew Eve aside and we debated: cats versus dogs, possible prices. Eve recognised the man, who'd once been a ditch-digger on the Carnarvon estate and a beater on shoots; he had been dismissed, she said, and was now famous in the district as a drinker, poacher and general ne'er-do-well. We returned to the stall. Eve asked about price. 'Kittens, a tanner apiece. Dogs ditto. As it's your ladyship . . . Got to get rid of 'em.' The man heaved a sigh. 'Otherwise it's into a sack, and into the water-butt with 'em.'

'What nonsense, Fletcher,' Eve replied coldly. 'We both know you'll be taking them on to Winchester market in two days' time, and if you don't sell them here you'll certainly sell them there. What do you think, Lucy?'

I was inclining to the dogs; I asked what kind they were.

'*Kind?*' He scratched his head. 'Well, that's 'ard to say, miss. My bitch got out, and I couldn't rightly say as to the father. There's terrier in there, good blood, a fine ratter their ma was – but as to their *pa* ... Foxhound? Collie? Bulldog? Got a foreign look to 'em, a lapdog look. Bit of French poodle maybe? They look kind of woolly, see?'

He plucked a puppy from the basket and held it up by the scruff of its neck; it squealed. It had dirty matted black and white fur and terrified milky-blue eyes. 'For goodness' sake, Fletcher,' Eve said, 'those puppies are virtually newborn – a few days at most. They should be with their mother for *weeks* yet.'

'Died.' He grimaced. 'Ten of 'em, see, milady. Too much for 'er. Gettin' on, the old bitch was, and when the last one come out dead, covered in blood, no bigger than your thumb, I knowed what was coming, and—'

'Yes, yes – that's quite enough, Fletcher.'

'How much are the leads and the collars?' I asked – there were several of these on sale too, and I had my eye on the red ones. Red was Rose's favourite colour.

'Ah, now you're talking, miss,' Fletcher said, brightening. 'Tip-top leather, nice brass buckle – two shillings for the collar and one shilling for the lead, which makes three and sixpence *with* one of these fine little dogs 'ere, but as I knows 'er ladyship of old, miss, let's say three shillings.'

'No, let's say one shilling all in,' I replied. Eve coughed.

'Are we talking dog or bitch, miss? The bitches is more valuable, see? But 'arder to train. In my experience.'

'That one, please, Mr Fletcher.' I pointed to the one he held. 'And how does one feed it?'

'Baby's bottle and milk, miss. Guzzles it down. You knows your dogs, I see. A fine bitch. Two and ninepence – *with* the collar and lead, and I call that generous.'

'One shilling and sixpence,' I said, trying to hide my mounting desperation. 'I only have two shillings, you see, and I'll have to buy a bottle as well. That's – my final figure.'

I showed Fletcher my florin. By then I wanted to rescue the dog badly and, disobeying the international laws of dealing, I was making that only too obvious. To my surprise and relief, Fletcher gave in with alacrity. He winked, spat on his hand, shook mine, and bundled the puppy into a brown paper bag. With my remaining sixpence Eve and

I bought a baby's bottle and teats and then set off for Highclere in her car, top down, wind blowing in our faces. The little dog lay in my lap, trembling.

'I can't believe you did that, Lucy,' Eve said. 'What an adventure — wait till I tell Pups! Fletcher has twelve children and lives in this disgusting filthy shack — you can't begin to *count* the pheasants and rabbits Pups has lost to him. He's up before the magistrates for poaching every other week, and the sob-stories he tells! "Who'd begrudge me one little rabbit, Your Honour, when my kiddies ain't eaten in weeks."' Eve, who was a poor mimic, did a whining, clown-like Hampshire accent. 'The truth, of course, is that he drinks — and that's where your one and sixpence will go . . . He's *such* a rogue.'

I considered this analysis. According to Rose, Lord Carnarvon expected to bag a thousand birds a day on his pheasant shoots. Ditto rabbits. I said nothing. The puppy whimpered.

One of Highclere Castle's lodges and castellated gates came into view. Eve accelerated up the winding drive: it was a mile long, Rose had told me. The parkland through which it passed had been laid out by Capability Brown; the great cedars I could see ahead of us had been planted in the 1790s by a previous earl, one with botanical inclinations.

'What's more,' Eve continued, changing gear, 'Fletcher's obstinate, and he usually drives a *very* hard bargain. He must have liked you, Lucy. I was fearing the worst. Daylight robbery, but I thought he'd be *sure* to stick at two and ninepence.'

By the time we reached the house itself, and I saw it for the first time in all its vastness and grandeur, I realised that I'd created a problem. By then, the little dog had peed on my dress, woken up, scratched and, trembling, gone to sleep again. Its vigorous scratching was as infectious as a yawn — it made me itchy too. I was supposed to be joining Rose and Peter inside for tea, for the tour of Lord Carnarvon's Egyptian treasures. Glancing up at Highclere's massed façade, its towers, its ranked windows, I realised belatedly that this puppy did not belong in this palace, and I didn't either — not with the spreading wet stain on my skirt, and the powerful smell that was now emanating from me, a smell that was part pee and part unwashed dogginess. This odour became obvious the second Eve stopped the car. 'Oh Lord,' Eve said. We had a hurried consultation.

We'd already agreed that the puppy would be given to Rose today, with the lead and collar kept for her birthday. But what to do with it now? Eve felt the dog could be whisked away to the kitchen quarters or the stables until the time came for us to leave – 'Streatfield will deal with it,' she said, indicating a stately man who was descending the steps and advancing upon us. Scarlet with embarrassment, I vetoed that; the thought of the little dog peeing on Carnarvon's butler was humiliating; besides, it was frightened and I didn't intend to be parted from it.

In the end we agreed I'd be parked outside with the dog, and Eve would go in quest of Rose and Peter and resolve matters. 'If you insist, dear,' Eve said, and I could see that even her good manners were failing her. I could detect a faint but fatal note of impatience at my obstinacy. Escorted by a liveried footman summoned by Streatfield, I was led to a table and chairs beneath a cedar, and asked if I required tea. I said I'd like that.

'China, Indian or Ceylon, madam?' the man enquired.

'Indian, please,' I replied, redder than ever and snatching one choice at random.

'Milk or lemon, madam?'

'Milk.'

'Jersey or Shorthorn, madam?'

Minutes later a maid appeared with a silver tray on which was tea, and an array of tiny sandwiches and cakes. Realising I'd left the bottle in the car, I poured some of the milk into a cup, dabbled my fingers in it and allowed the puppy to lick them. Its small pink tongue was sandpaper rough. It seemed to like the milk, licking off the drops that adhered to its whiskers; it went to sleep again. This was soothing, as was the absence of further servants, or indeed any people.

Feeling calmer, I inspected the house – how huge it was, a momentous high-Victorian pile, square as a dice, surmounted by towers and pinnacles, solemn yet fantastic. Replacing earlier houses on the same site, it had been commissioned by the third earl, and finally completed during the lifetime of his son, the fourth earl. This last, the present Lord Carnarvon's father, had been a celebrated classicist and a distinguished statesman, Eve had said; serving in three Cabinets and appointed Lord Lieutenant of Ireland, he had made Highclere into a Conservative Party outpost: politicians of the day had gathered there to shoot and to plot. Disraeli had taken the same approach we had that day, Eve said with a smile, and, passing the lake, the temple to Diana and the deer park, had cried out in an ecstasy of admiration: 'How scenical, how scenical!'

Highclere's architect had also designed the Houses of Parliament in London – and, thinking back, I can see the resemblance. It had the same assertive air and the same spurious suggestion of romance; architectural allusions to some mythic Arthurian past, as if a brother-hood of knights occupied it, ready to ride forth and conquer the forces of darkness. It suggested gravitas, government, a domain where a kingdom and a great empire were administered. Did it look like a country house, someone's home – even someone as rich as Lord Carnarvon? No, it didn't. Too many Camelot towers. I gazed at the flagpole on the main tower. The air was hot; no breeze: the flag drooped motionless.

Inside, Rose and Eve had told me, it was regal and masculine, resembling Pugin's House of Lords, or one of the gentlemen's clubs in St James's. Lord Carnarvon's wife, Almina, had tried to tame these male tendencies and put her own mark on the house, Eve said. Aided by the fortune of her father, Alfred de Rothschild, an indulgent man – *'Another ten thousand pounds, puss-cat? But what have you done with last week's?'* – Almina Carnarvon had thrown money at Highclere. Almina's upbringing was French – she'd grown up in Paris – and her taste was Louis Quinze or Louis Seize; to her, the Puginesque flour-ishes, all that pomp and circumstance, all those heraldic beasts, were anathema. And so, with her, had come an attack of femininity: Hepplewhite, Boulle, pretty Aubusson and Savonnerie carpets, flow-ered Meissen porcelain – and a jewelled flask, kept in Almina's boudoir, that was said to contain five precious drops of Marie Antoinette's execution blood. 'But it's hopeless,' Eve had said with a sigh. 'The house resists it. You might as well plant a rose on the slopes of Mount Everest.'

It was the east face of this mountainous house I was examining now – and to my consternation I saw that there were figures emerg-ing from it. I squinted at them, hoping they would not be strangers; Eve had said, in a negligent way, that only twenty people or so were staying at present. One of those guests was Howard Carter – but it was not his welcome figure that I saw now. A wispy young man in plus-fours, carrying a golfing bag, advanced across the lawns, and came to a halt at the tea table.

'I say, you haven't seen Biffy by any chance, have you?' he enquired, addressing the sky above my head.

I told him I hadn't seen anyone; this seemed to make him cross.

'Well, honestly! Four o'clock I said, four o'clock we agreed, four o'clock it *is*. Typical! If you see him, tell him from me, will you – I've gone on.' He frowned. 'And he can put that in his bally pipe and smoke it,' he added, and walked off again.

Shortly after this, I thought I did spy Howard Carter in the distance – a familiar bulky figure, who issued from the house, surveyed the lawns as if searching for someone and then, in a purposeful way, strode off towards the stables. Not long after this sighting, a tiny man with bandy legs ambled across the grass towards me. He came to a halt and inspected both me and the puppy with sharp electric-blue eyes.

'Let's be having a look at this beast then,' he said, and crouched down next to my chair.

He had very small hands and handled the puppy in an expert way. As soon as he touched it, its trembling ceased. He felt along its back and around its muzzle; he lifted the little dog's head, and examined it in a squinting manner. 'Never look them in the eyes direct,' he said. 'Dogs don't like that, not on first acquaintance. Bide your time: when they're ready to look you in the eye, they'll let you know it.'

The puppy gave a small shudder, then licked his hand. He smiled, made a crooning sound and fondled its ears. 'There's Jack Russell in there for sure,' he said, 'and lurcher. So she'll be fast, and a rare little hunter – give her a few months and you watch her go.'

'You don't think bulldog? Or sheepdog? Mr Fletcher, the man who sold her to me, said there could be French poodle.'

'Did he just? Don't you be listening to fairy stories like that. There's gypsy dog for sure. She's in a state – look at her fur, poor thing! She needs a good groom and a bath – and what's more, she's hungry.'

He bounded to his feet, fetched the jug, tipped some milk into his cupped palm and held it out. 'Jersey, my little darling,' he murmured. 'Nice and creamy.'

The puppy lapped inefficiently, splashing most of the milk on the sleeve of the natty brown suit the man was wearing; this did not appear to concern him. After a while he rose, and announced a bottle was needed and he'd organise it.

'Too young to be parted from her mother,' he said, giving the little dog one last caress. At speed, he departed in the direction of the house. The puppy went to sleep again.

I was left alone for a while after that. I was beginning to think my next Wonderland visitor would be a white rabbit consulting his pocket watch, or a mad queen crying, '*Off with their heads!*' Eventually two visions of loveliness wandered across the lawns, and came to a halt at the tea table. Both were tall, elegant, older than Eve, and clad in exquisite tea dresses. 'Eve said we'd find you here,' said one of them, sharp-featured, with a chignon of thick dark hair wound about like a coil of cobras. 'How do you do, my dear. I am Dorothy Dennistoun, and this is Lady Cunliffe-Owen ... oh, look, Helen,' she went on, 'this must be the famous puppy! Isn't he *adorable*? What a little *scamp*.'

Both women bent over my lap, cooed, wrinkled their noses and rapidly retreated. They sit down on the far side of the table. I muttered an apology and, clutching the puppy, removed myself, wandering a short way across the lawns until I was out of their line of sight. Thinking the puppy might like to walk a little, I lowered it very gently onto the grass and released it. It tottered a few steps, then tumbled over and yelped. Open space seemed to terrify it; it peered about and began to shake violently.

I wasn't sure what to do, and felt I couldn't go too far in case Eve returned for me. So I bundled the little dog up and returned to the vicinity of the tea table, sitting down on the grass at a safe distance behind the two women. Tea had been brought them and they were deep in conversation. I glimpsed the figure of Carter again in the distance; he still seemed to be in search of someone. I saw him scanning the lawns; he glanced towards the tea table but then, to my disappointment, struck off at a swift pace in a different direction.

I regretted that; the previous day a letter from Frances had arrived, forwarded from Cambridge by my father. It brought exciting news about Carter and his quest in the Valley of the Kings. I'd been hoping I'd encounter him today; hoping that he, or Carnarvon, or both of them, would discuss this latest development. I'd have to wait. I leaned back against the trunk of the cedar and stroked the puppy until it was calm again. Snatches of the two women's conversation drifted across on the still afternoon air.

I was paying little attention to the women's talk until I heard the one called Helen Cunliffe-Owen mention Carter's name, and realised she was discussing the famous seance at Highclere that he had described to Frances and me. 'And then, Dorothy dear,' she said, 'Howard Carter finally admitted it: he'd recognised the language the instant the voice began to speak through me. It was Coptic! Imagine! A dead language no one's spoken for *thousands* of years.'

'Helen, *darling* – how positively bloodcurdling! Was it a *warning*, do you think?'

'Carter wouldn't say. He clammed up . . . but there *have* been warnings.' Her voice dropped, then she said something about Carnarvon's consulting a palmist in London: 'It was back in July, Dorothy . . . the great Velma took one look at his hand and said: "Lord Carnarvon, if you value your life, you must *never* return to Egypt. No matter what the temptation or circumstances."'

I heard that clearly – and I heard her friend's reply too.

'Well, he *won't* be returning, I know that for sure,' the woman called Dorothy Dennistoun said in her assertive voice. 'Almina confides in me – we're like *that*, darling. So I can tell you, she's put her foot down at last. She's had just about enough of Egypt! It's her money that pays for that little hobby – and it doesn't come cheap! So they've decided: no more Valley of the Kings. No more excavations, time to call a halt! Besides, dear, strictly *entre nous*—'

'Now, Dorothy – we mustn't tittle tattle.'

That rebuke made Mrs Dennistoun lower her voice too, so although I was listening unashamedly by then, I caught only scraps . . . *Even their money not inexhaustible . . . already got through the millions Rothschild left Almina – inside four years, darling . . . Son-and-heir's new bride, not a penny to her name . . . Carnarvon's health . . . if the worst happened . . . Death duties . . . cruel wicked taxes.*

'That terrifies Almina,' Mrs Dennistoun concluded on a dramatic note. 'She says death duties could wipe them out. The horror of it! Imagine, Helen – if all *this* had to be sold.' She waved a hand in the direction of house, lawns, cedars and undulating acres.

'I'm sure it won't come to that, Dorothy.' Lady Cunliffe-Owen rose to her feet, as if anxious to curtail her friend's gossiping. 'Shall we go back to the house now or watch the croquet?' With a regretful shake of her head, she added: 'Major economies and no more Egypt, then? That seems sad. Carnarvon loves it there so much. Whatever will he do about Howard Carter?'

'Give him his marching orders.' Dorothy also stood up. 'He's nerved himself to do it and it's slated for tonight. After dinner, Almina says. A man-to-man talk. Expect rages . . . Carter won't go down without a fight.'

'No, indeed.' Both women laughed; linking arms, they strolled off together.

I stared after them. I wondered if it could be true, that the expeditions to the Valley were over, that Carnarvon was pulling out of Egypt, that Howard Carter would have to abandon his life's work.

I could not believe it: that was *not* the information Frances had given me in her letter. She claimed Carter was keener than ever – and with very good reason. Before her family left for Maine, she'd explained, her father had been in New York, tying up his work at the Metropolitan Museum. There – possibly at Carter's behest; Frances left this unclear – Winlock had re-examined some artefacts found in a pit in the Valley of the Kings years before, in the days when Theodore Davis had been digging there. This find included numerous large pottery embalming jars, much rough linen material and papyrus wreaths. When they were first unearthed, Davis, the avid treasure hunter, had angrily dismissed them as worthless. He had handed them to Herbert Winlock – it was either that, or dispose of them. That had been fourteen years earlier; the collection had been languishing in the Met's storerooms ever since, with many of the jars still unopened.

Examining them again, Winlock realised he was looking at funerary material: natron, embalming vessels, mud-seal cartouches and linen bandages – the two latter bore hieroglyphic inscriptions. Experiencing a sudden stab of excitement and triumph, Winlock recognised the throne name of a little-known king, Tutankhamun – and that changed everything.

They were found in the Valley, Frances wrote, in high excitement. *And if his funeral artefacts were buried there, it means Tutankhamun is buried there too — it's a virtual certainty. Yet his tomb has never been found! Daddy wrote Mr Carter to tell him. It could mean Mr Carter was right all along, and the Valley isn't exhausted. It doesn't tell him exactly where Tutankhamun's tomb might be, of course, though it's likely to be somewhere close to the funeral cache — and it could have been robbed anyway. But it must give Mr Carter new hope. This is top secret! Don't breathe a word to anyone.*

I considered this evidence: gossiping Mrs Dennistoun must have been wrong, I decided. In view of this breakthrough, it was impossible that Lord Carnarvon would end his quest now. Surely Carter would be dispatched to the Valley post-haste . . . I closed my eyes. Even in the shade of the cedar it was hot. The puppy had peed on my skirt again. Everyone seemed to have forgotten its existence — and mine. I felt myself drifting off; Highclere and the Valley began to blur in my mind, and the heat of the lawns became the heat of the desert. From the depths of the Valley, someone was calling to me. The voice was insistent: *Lulu, Lulu, Lulu.* I opened my eyes and saw Peter standing in front of me, jiggling with excitement. He was holding the hand of a very tall and good-looking young man; a man with a Lancelot look, I thought, staring at him.

'This is Mr Bee — Mr Bow . . . we've come to see the puppy,' Peter said.

'We've come to *look after* this infernal puppy,' the young man corrected, in an affable way. 'You are Lucy, and I am Brograve Beauchamp. Staying at Highclere for the first time and now, at long last, of service. You, Lucy, are to put on this apron, which Eve feels you may need. Then you are to go and admire Lord Carnarvon's Egyptian treasures. Peter and I are to tend this charming beast. We have a bottle. We have milk. We have several towels, and I fear we'll need them.' Bending down to the puppy and grimacing, he ruffled its head, parted its fur, and nipped something between thumb and forefinger. 'Off you trot,' he said. 'Eve's waiting for you. I wish I could say she was waiting for me, but that's life — one cruel blow after another.'

I put on the white apron; it covered the pee-stains, even if it did nothing to alleviate the pungent, vixenish smell that still hung about me. I hastened towards the house; now was my opportunity; Eve would certainly know her father's plans. If a fateful conversation *was* to take place between Carnarvon and Carter that night, Eve would tell me. Reaching the house, I found she was waiting for me; she took my hand and drew me into an enormous, cold and echoing entrance hall, and then into a further hall beyond, double height, Arthurian, rife with statuary, paintings and heraldic devices.

'I hope people have been looking after you, Lucy,' Eve said, in a distracted way, leading me along corridors and through rooms, until I'd lost all sense of direction. 'It's absolute mayhem here today. Howard's on the warpath, and Pups is trying to avoid him – he's exhausted, and he's gone to lie down, I think, or maybe escaped for a walk – anyway, I'm deputed to show you his collection. Along here, dear, follow me.'

We began walking along yet another corridor; we seemed to be in some remote part of the house; wherever we were, it was a silent as a tomb, the only sound Eve's chatter. 'And you met Mr Donoghue, I gather,' she went on, 'isn't he just a *marvel*?'

'I met *three* men. The first had a golf bag and was looking for someone called Biffy.'

'Really, dear? I can't think who that was.'

'I met Mr Beauchamp, who gave me the apron. And before that I met a very *small* man. Not even as tall as me. He was wonderful. He says our puppy has lurcher in her.'

'That's definitely Mr Donoghue – Steve Donoghue – you must know, Lucy, who he is? Why, he's one of the most famous men in Europe!' She glanced at my blank face and laughed. 'He's a *jockey*, Lucy – the best in the world. He won the Derby last year *and* this. He can ride anything. He's famous for his magical hands. Pups adores him – they're the closest friends . . . You *must* have heard of him! No? Gracious! Lucy dear, what *do* you all talk about in Cambridge?'

Saying this, she threw back a door, and we entered a large, dimly lit room; previously the Smoking Room, it was now known as the Antiques Room, Eve said. It was lined with dark mahogany-framed display cases. I passed from one to another, peering past the reflections on the glass at jewellery emblazoned with Egyptian enamels. There was a gold statuette of an Egyptian king; there were vases of iridescent glass, and alabaster bowls; there were hundreds upon hundreds of objects, all exquisite. They looked displaced; I felt the silent room sucked energy from them. I wondered how many visitors this private museum had, how often these objects were examined. Howard Carter would be working on their cataloguing during his stay, I knew, so there must be recent acquisitions to be added to those already here. I looked at the golden Egyptian king, striding forth into the afterlife, his gaze fixed on eternal glass doors in a cabinet in England.

Eve had moved to the windows and was looking out across the lawns. I was longing to ask her about the man-to-man discussion slated for tonight, but unsure how to raise the issue. I kept wondering how the puppy was, whether the feeding was successful. 'I hope Mr Beauchamp and Peter are managing,' I said eventually.

'Oh, don't worry about that,' Eve said. 'I can see them from here, and they're managing perfectly.' She turned away from the windows. 'Besides, Brograve can cope with anything. He's *such* a nice man, Lucy. He dances divinely. In the election, he's standing for the National Liberals, which makes Mother *fume*. Brograve is candidate for Lowestoft, which was his father's seat, so it ought to be safe. But *we're* all secretly hoping it will go Conservative.' She glanced at her watch. 'You're very silent, dear. Look, isn't this beautiful? It's a heart scarab – the kind they placed over a king's heart to prevent it confessing his misdemeanours during the Weighing of the Heart ceremony.'

I inspected the scarab, which was as large as a plate. That should weigh down the rebellious heart and shut it up, I thought. Eve began to consult Howard Carter's catalogue to help us identify the objects on display. I remember looking at it over her shoulder, pages of meticulous drawings, lengthy notes, with codes for prices paid, and I remember that – at some point – Carter himself burst into the room. He was clad in loud tweed, with a bright red handkerchief spilling from his jacket pocket.

'Ah, Eve.' He came to a halt and glanced at me, but gave no sign of recognition. 'I'm looking for your father,' he said. 'Hunting high and low. Can't seem to find him.'

'I'm not sure where Pups is – he had some estate business, I think, Howard. He's fearfully busy. He's probably closeted with Rutherford, or Maber, perhaps . . . Better not to interrupt him.' Eve gave her dimpling smile. 'You remember Lucy? From Egypt?'

'Of course.' He shook my hand. I could tell he hadn't the least idea who I was. I'd been erased, I realised: the lunch in the tomb, the buttered toast by the fire at Castle Carter, his praise for my observation skills – it was as if none of that had happened.

'Frances Winlock's friend,' Eve prompted. Carter's eyes remained blank. His smile widened. 'Ah yes, Frances. Smart girl, very quick on the uptake – I must be going. Rutherford, did you say, Eve? I might try the estate office then.'

He was out the door before Eve could speak. She raised her eyes to the ceiling: 'Oh, Lord! Now what have I done? If Howard tracks him down, my father will be *livid*. He's been hounding Pups for the last three days. He's here for two weeks, and if he keeps this up, he'll drive us all mad. He can't seem to accept – Pups isn't at *all* well, Lucy. He's been fearfully seedy all summer – colds, bronchial attacks – it's *so* miserable for him.'

'Will your father go back to Egypt again, Eve?' I asked, seizing my opportunity.

'Lucy dear, I think *not*.' She hesitated, frowning at the cabinets. 'The doctors say no, my mother says no. *I* think Pups has had enough, in many, many ways. So he's been thinking it over, weighing the pros and cons, and he's finally made up his mind: time to call a halt – no more excavating, no more Valley. I think it was a relief to him, Lucy, when he decided, but he still has to break it to Howard. Poor Pups! He's going to tell him tonight, after dinner. He'll be firm, of course, but he's dreading it. To give up now – when Howard's so certain he's on the right track . . . Except Howard's been certain for *years*, and he's always been wrong. And one really can't ignore that for ever, can one?

'Pups does expect *results*.' An indignant, faintly peevish note had crept into her voice. 'Howard's position – well, Pups does *employ* him, so Howard's situation is really not a million miles from someone like Maber's – he's our Head Keeper, Lucy, and he's a Norfolk man too, like Howard, oddly enough. At the start of the season Maber knows exactly what bag Pups expects on each drive, and he makes sure he gets it. If he didn't, he'd find himself unemployed – very rapidly! Of course, we all know Howard's role is a little different – and he's become a friend, a dear friend. But . . . '

Her tone hardened: 'But people should never *presume* on friendship, should they, Lucy? And I do get cross with Howard sometimes. He shouldn't be bothering Pups now, and that was made perfectly clear to him.' She consulted her watch. 'My dear, will you forgive me? Let's go and find Rose – she's with my mother, I think. Then I'd better run off and find Pups and warn him!'

She gave me her sweet dimpling smile, and — *how slow, how slow* — I realised I was a nuisance who was in the way. I'd caused enough complications for one day. I too was in danger of presuming on friendship.

I didn't encounter Lord Carnarvon as I was leaving, and, given the apron, the state of my dress and my vixen smell, I was hoping to escape his wife too; I almost succeeded, meeting her only briefly on the steps outside, where she and Dorothy Dennistoun, deep in conversation, were waiting for a car to be brought round. Both women were wearing duster coats, large hats and motoring veils.

'My dear! Eve's told me *everything*!' Lady Carnarvon said. She seemed unaffected by the powerful doggy odour emanating from me — perhaps she had no sense of smell, I thought hopefully. 'The sweetest little puppy, Dorothy tells me. I adore dogs! I have three — or is it five now? *So* clever of you, dear — I've told Rose, if she has the *slightest* problem with it, she must telephone at once and I'll send a man round to dose it . . . So glad to see you here, Laura. You *must* come over again . . . ah, here's the motor at last. Goodbye, my dear.'

I didn't correct my name or inform her there was no telephone at Nuthanger: I was reluctant to be seen, let alone to speak, and there wasn't time anyway. Lady Carnarvon, so tiny — five feet of beaky-nosed, buzzing, compressed energy, a marvel of furbelows, scarves and milky, glistening pearls the size of a wren's egg — was there and then gone. Five minutes later, Wheeler emerged from the servants' quarters, another car appeared, a French Panhard, with Rose, Peter and puppy in the back, and we could leave at last.

The little dog had been tightly swaddled in a towel. It looked like one of the mummified babies I'd seen in the Egyptian Museum. 'This is the best present ever, Lucy,' Rose said, cradling it, then scratching herself. 'I'm going to call her Bluebell. Mr Beauchamp says she drank a whole bottle of milk—'

'And a *half*,' said Peter, also scratching.

'Did Mr Beauchamp mention *fleas*?' Wheeler sniffed. 'Keep that filthy thing wrapped up. This car will need fumigating. You'll all need fumigating. No one sets foot indoors when we get home — not till I've dealt with it.'

'Where *were* you, Lucy?' Rose went on. 'You missed all the fun. We had tea with Lady Carnarvon, and she showed us that Marie Antoinette blood, which was still bright red, as if it spouted from her chopped-off head yesterday . . . And then Lord Carnarvon took Peter to admire his cars, there's twenty-three of them, and the Bugatti can do *well* over sixty. Then he showed us his wireless set! I've never seen one before, and it's *huge,* with an aerial like a crucifix, and we were allowed to twiddle the knobs and listen.'

'A man *talked* out of it, Lucy,' Peter said, putting his hand in mine. 'A man I can't see. A ghost man.'

'And then we came outside and had a *long* talk to Mr Carter. I told him the story of how Wheeler and I outwitted my father. All the details! Half-wages and everything! He was mightily impressed, wasn't he, Petey?'

'*Jolly* impressed. He said we're conning little beggars.'

'He gave us a tip to share. A whole *sovereign*,' Rose cried, triumphant.

'What *is* a beggar, Wheeler?' Peter asked.

'Nothing you need worry your head about,' said Wheeler, with finality.

I turned to the window; we were halfway down the drive. In the distance, striding across the lawns from the direction of one of Highclere's follies, I saw the familiar figure of Howard Carter. He was walking rapidly, a stooped and weary-looking earl at his side. Lord Carnarvon was limping and keeping up with difficulty; he was wearing his Tennysonian hat and leaning on his stick.

Carter was gesticulating and speaking with emphasis. So he *had* tracked Carnarvon down, I thought; he might not yet know the fate that awaited him, but he had, meanwhile, found his quarry.

24

That night, I wrote to Frances to describe the events at Highclere: perhaps that man-to-man conversation was happening as I wrote, I thought. It was dark outside the farm; at Highclere, they would be coming to the end of dinner. I imagined the women withdrawing, the port circulating among the male guests, and then Lord Carnarvon taking Carter to one side. I wondered which of the many, many rooms at Highclere he'd select for their interview. I tried to imagine what he might say, and how Carter would respond. I felt sure that Carter would now inform him of Herbert Winlock's discovery. And once given *that* key information, once Carnarvon knew it was not just *a* king they were pursuing, but a named king, whose tomb must be there, it was obvious he would relent – he couldn't abandon the Valley now, surely?

I left the letter to Frances unsealed: sooner or later, I would hear the results of these after-dinner discussions, and I planned to add the final details as to Howard Carter's fate in a postscript, the instant I heard them. I was impatient for the latest news – and I did not have long to wait.

The following morning, as hoped, Eve's maid Marcelle turned up for her weekly visit to Wheeler. She came over by bus, looking very chic in a handed-down dress of Eve's and a new hat. She strolled along the lane, paused in the yard to admire the puppy – now bathed and flea-powdered – and then wandered into the kitchen for her regular gossip. Marcelle was sure to tell me what had happened; unlike Wheeler, she was rarely evasive, tight-lipped – or reticent.

My chance finally came when Wheeler called us inside for biscuits and lemonade at eleven o'clock. Once we were all settled at the kitchen table, Marcelle launched herself on an interminable description of the dinner at Highclere the previous evening, a description that focused on dresses and jewels. This delighted Rose, but not me. Lady Evelyn had worn this, Lady so-and-so had worn that, Lady Carnarvon had dazzled in her famous emeralds . . . Then she switched to the menu, the soufflés sent up, the chefs' tantrums, the ongoing rivalry between the senior chef, who was French, and the pastry-chef, who was Austrian – and the sulks of the Ceylonese chef, hired solely to cook Lord Carnarvon's curries, whose services were not required on this occasion. Such politics were dear to Marcelle; I knew that if I failed to tilt the conversation quickly, we'd be in for hours of below-stairs analysis. But I'd learned from Nicola Dunsire's techniques, and at last managed to steer Marcelle in the direction I wanted. Within minutes, she was off and away. The events of the night before, she said, were a puzzle – a surprise to everyone.

'We think Mr Carter must have sensed what was coming,' she said. 'Streatfield said he was in ever such a twitchy state all through the dinner. There were thirty at table, and Lady Evelyn made sure he had ladies he knows either side of him. But he barely ate a thing. His hands were shaking – all the footmen noticed that. His face was grey, they said, and he never uttered one word from the consommé onwards. Drank very little, which is unusual for him, because he's fond of wine, Mr Carter. Refused the port too, I hear – and when someone, it was Mr Donoghue, I believe, took pity on him and asked him about Egypt, he gave a start, and knocked over his glass . . . Then, after the port, Lord Carnarvon took Mr Carter to the Antiques Room – just the two of them.

'His lordship laid it on the line, Miss Lucy. I know that for sure because he told Lady Evelyn afterwards: she'd waited up to hear – and she told *me* when I was doing her hair for bed. No *ifs* or *buts*. No, "Let's think this over." His lordship knew *that* wouldn't work: give Mr Carter an inch and he'll take ten miles, he's well known for it. No, his lordship broke it to him gently but firmly. He wouldn't let him fetch out his maps – which Mr Carter was dead set on doing. And he made it clear there'd be no discussion or argument. He said to him:

"My old friend, the Valley of the Kings is finished as far as I'm concerned. The end of the line has been reached at last."'

I suspected this quote was apocryphal, but made a mental note of it. Marcelle was polishing this story, I felt; when I recounted it to Frances, I intended to polish it further.

'But you know the extraordinary thing, Miss Lucy? Mr Carter took it like a lamb! We'd all been expecting one of his outbursts. Lady Evelyn was afraid he'd keep her father up half the night, arguing and haranguing him the way he does. But no: not one word of protest apparently. He took it on the chin like a gentleman, shook his lordship by the hand, got a little emotional at one point . . . but he pulled himself together. He said he understood the reasons for the decision, and he owed his lordship a great debt of gratitude for his unfailing generosity, for the years they'd worked together side by side. He said he believed they were friends – and they'd *remain* loyal friends for the rest of their days. Lord Carnarvon was touched by that.

'Isn't that strange?' Marcelle looked around the table at her audience. 'To give in so easily? No one expected that – and last night Lady Evelyn was ever so worried. She thought there'd be a delayed reaction, one of Mr Carter's tantrums this morning. But there's no sign of any trouble so far. He was sunny over breakfast, I'm told, and he must have got his appetite back, because he wolfed down the devilled kidneys *and* the kedgeree. Streatfield says he was a bit distracted at first, not saying much, but by the end he was nattering away as if nothing had happened. He was going off to the Antiques Room to do some cataloguing when I left. I passed him in the south corridor. Quieter than usual, perhaps, and looked tired, so maybe he hadn't slept too well, but—'

'How well would you sleep, if you'd just been told your services were being dispensed with?' Wheeler gave her friend a look of scorn. 'Sixteen years he's been working for Lord Carnarvon. Took it like a lamb? My eye, he did. Mavis Marcelle, you're a fool.'

'Well, if I am, I'm not alone,' Marcelle retorted, with spirit. 'Lady Evelyn says Mr Carter has had enough of that godforsaken Valley and those nasty dirty tombs, and he'll be glad to escape the place. She says he may *claim* he loves that Valley, but actually he's quite ambi—' She hesitated. 'What's the dratted word? Ambigous? No, that's not right.'

'Ambivalent?' I suggested. Marcelle nodded. 'That's it, it was on the tip of my tongue. Ambivalous about that Valley, that's what he is. *I* think Lady Evelyn may have hit on it. What do you think, Miss Lucy? You've seen him working there. Do you think that could be the truth of it?'

I did not. I escaped from the kitchen as soon as I decently could, hastened upstairs and added a postscript to my letter to Frances. *I can't understand it*, I scratched. *No more funding, no more digs – and apparently Mr Carter's accepted that, despite your father's discovery. But I think he must be devastated, don't you? I asked Marcelle straightaway whether Lord Carnarvon will now give up his permit to dig in the Valley of the Kings – but she didn't know. I'll ask Eve when I see her.*

There was no need to interrogate Eve: the following day both she and Howard Carter turned up at the farm in her car, and he – to my surprise – showed a marked inclination to discuss the subject. He came into the farmhouse looking subdued. He'd come armed with a present – a dog basket for Rose's puppy – and in the intervening hours, it seemed, he had remembered who I was. There were several references to my observation powers, smiling reminders as to lunches in tombs, buttered toast, his aunties' famous fruitcake.

He spent some time exploring the farm with Rose, Peter and me, admiring the orchard, counting the swallows and their nests. He told us about the various animals he'd kept in Egypt over the years: the pet gazelles; the donkey so devoted it would try to follow him indoors; the horse that died of a cobra bite; and various pet dogs, none of which had long survived the dangers of a desert environment. He described his birdwatching expeditions by the Nile, and the water-colours of birds he'd painted. He began digging around in the barns and examining all those enigmatic farming artefacts, many of which he recognised – and I saw another side to Carter, hidden before: the countryman, the lover of birds, animals and wildlife. Yet when we sat down outside for tea, this side to his character vanished. He reverted to archaeologist – and he raised the subject of Egypt at once.

I thought the topic of the Valley made Eve uneasy, but Carter seemed calm: he had seen it coming for months, and he understood. He respected Lord Carnarvon for not mincing his words. 'What I can't stand,' he said, 'is diplomacy and double-speak. I'm not one of nature's diplomats myself. I like to give it straight and *hear* it straight.

Now I know where I stand.' He blew on his tea. 'And I can plan accordingly.'

'Will you be going back to Egypt, Mr Carter?' Rose asked.

'Certainly. I do *live* there, Lady Rose. No fixed abode in England. I'm a bird of passage. My home is in Egypt, and I'll be returning as usual this winter. Next month, late October, that's the plan. My place needs some repairs – I'll look into that. See my old friends from the Met, catch up with Winlock and Lythgoe.'

My chance had come. 'What will happen to the permit to dig in the Valley of the Kings?' I asked. 'Will Lord Carnarvon give that up now?'

'I imagine so.' Carter looked pleased at this cue. He glanced at Eve, who was inspecting the tea things with great concentration. 'The permit is coming up for its annual renewal, Lucy,' he continued. 'Lord Carnarvon will resign it in the next few weeks, I expect. No point in him hanging on to it now. It's our difficult friend, Monsieur Lacau, who decides who gets it next, and he does *not* favour what he calls "amateur gentlemen" excavators. So the Valley permit will go to some learned body – most probably, one of the great museums.

'The Metropolitan will get it. That's my belief. They want it, I know that. They have the expertise, and they have the backing: virtually inexhaustible funds – or so I hear from my good friends Lythgoe and Winlock. The Met already has an excellent base near by: the American House is half an hour's ride from the Valley, if that. Of course,' he continued, in a meditative tone, munching cake, 'none of the Met team is that experienced when it comes to the Valley of the Kings. Harry Burton's dug there in the past, but it's new territory for them even so. They'll need to recruit some outside expertise. They'll need the guidance of someone with a ready-made team of trained local men; someone who knows the Valley, who's endured its tricks and its traps for decades . . . ' He left the sentence hanging. 'Well now, that was a fine tea,' he said. 'Thank you. I like it here. Such a beautiful day. I wonder, Eve, should we be thinking of getting back now?'

'Have the Met actually *said* they're after the Valley permit?' Eve asked sharply.

Carter appeared to give this simple question considerable thought. After a long pause, he said: 'They've been *circumspect*, Eve: let me put it that way. They have the greatest respect for your father, and they know my unshakeable loyalty to him. Lythgoe and Winlock wouldn't dream of stepping on anyone's toes. But once they hear your father's pulled out, they'll make their move. In my view, they'll go after that permit immediately. The possibility your father would give up on the Valley *was* something they'd foreseen, I'm afraid: the decline in his health was noted back in February, and they'd drawn their own conclusions, made contingency plans. Inevitable, alas. You know how people talk, Eve. And archaeologists gossip like girls.'

'Have you *told* the Met what's happened, Howard?' Eve's tone became sharper. She had risen to her feet and was looking at him in consternation.

'Good grief, no! Well, not *yet* . . .' He sighed. 'I began writing a letter to Winlock this morning, as a matter of fact – after all, it's no secret now, is it? All open and above board. I was pretty shaken after my talk with your father, Eve – I can admit that to you. I needed to get it off my chest to *someone*, so I thought it would help to write to my old friend Winlock. He and I are close, we've always got on well and I respect him.'

He frowned. 'I could *cable* Winlock, of course,' he went on. 'Maybe I should do that – he'll be anxious to hear the news. On the other hand, maybe I should let things settle for a day or two, wait till I'm calmer. What d'you think, Eve?'

'I think you should wait. And I think you know that perfectly well, Howard.'

'I'll give it a couple of days, then. I'll be guided by you,' he replied, his tone humble, and turned away to inspect the view across the valley, the narrow ribbon of river below us, the blue-shadowed hills beyond. He sighed. 'Absolutely right, Eve, as you always are. No point in my rushing things. I'll let the dust settle. For a few days. What a restful place this is,' he went on, in stronger tones. 'I tell you what, Eve, why don't you drive back to Highclere and leave me to find my own way home? Would you mind? I'm in the mood for a good long walk. Give me time to think things over.'

Shortly afterwards, this plan having been agreed, he put on his tweed countryman's cap, straightened his tweed jacket, and strolled off across the fields. Eve left at once for Highclere, driving at speed.

*

The next report from the castle was that Lord Carnarvon had been told of the Met's pressing interest in the Valley of the Kings' permit – I felt sure Eve must have driven straight back to the castle that day to tell him. On being given this news, her father had laughed and said the Met men were welcome to it – more fools they, and he hoped they were contacting their millionaire donors right now, because they'd certainly need to.

I felt this reaction must be a blow to Carter, but it was he who reported it to us some days later, and he did so with no sign of dismay; on the contrary, it seemed to amuse him. He'd begun to visit Nuthanger quite often by then, usually on his own, strolling across the downs and taking the bridge across the river. On every visit, he appeared unconcerned as to his altered future. He said it made a change to be here, away from the smart pace of affairs at Highclere; he enjoyed the castle, of course, very much so – but it was good to get away, to clear his mind. He'd stay for an hour or so at the farm, sometimes chatting to Wheeler, sometimes to us. He would join in our games and was even prepared to play I Spy or Dumb Crambo with us. He liked card games too, we discovered, and was happy to play two-pack Patience with me, Snap with Peter, and poker with Rose, a game to which he introduced her.

Carter taught Rose the techniques of bluff and double-bluff, and how to retain a poker-face, useful techniques that she imparted to Peter and me. He taught her some amusing methods of cheating too, dealing from the bottom of the pack and so on, and we all spent many hours trying to perfect these tricks. Rose hadn't the patience for sleight of hand; Peter's small fingers weren't yet deft enough, but I became quite adroit.

'Not bad,' Carter said, giving me a considering look, when I showed off the results of hours of card-sharping practice.

'Better than your knitting, anyway,' Wheeler pronounced sourly.

Carter claimed that he liked being at the farm because it took him back to his childhood in rural Norfolk; he'd also grown fond of Rose's little dog, he said, but he feared it was the runt of the litter and would never thrive – and in this he was right. The little creature was never strong. But during the puppy's happy weeks at the farm, Carter brought it several more gifts, and one afternoon, he drew it as it lay snoozing on its back in the sun, in sprawled surrender to sleep. He presented this clever lightning sketch to Peter, and Peter gave it to me, many years later.

Caring for the little dog, meanwhile, was becoming exhausting, as both Carter and Wheeler had warned it would be. The puppy was so young and frail that it required feeding every three or four hours, all day and all night. Wheeler refused to have anything to do with it; it was our problem, and we'd have to cope with it. She said she'd brought up four brothers and sisters, and nurturing a puppy was exactly the same as nurturing a baby, non-stop work, non-stop worry and no sleep. The little dog was greedy; if she drank too much milk too eagerly, she'd get colic, and would lie on her back, stomach distended, whimpering and whining. At first, Rose and I took it in turns to do the night-time feeds, but Rose was a heavier sleeper than I, and complained so vociferously that after a few days I took it on. I'd read my Egyptian books in my room until I heard Wheeler going to bed; when I judged another hour had passed, I'd creep downstairs, prepare the bottle, give the puppy her midnight feed, soothe her and return to bed again. She was confined to the kitchen regions, but she soon learned to make a babyish, plaintive, penetrating cry that echoed up to me through the floors and chimneys. Somewhere around three or four, this summons would wake me, and I'd pad down to her again. These expeditions made me sleepy during the day, but I came to love them. It was peaceful there, sitting on a cushion on the kitchen floor, close to the warmth of the banked wood range, one oil lamp lit, with the tiny creature cradled in my arms. I began to believe that she loved and trusted me — that I alone possessed the powers needed to soothe her.

After a week or so of this routine, the lack of sleep began to take its toll. I was down to three hours a night by then; the puppy was going through a fretful phase; sometimes she'd sick up the milk, then fall asleep, then wake demanding more milk just half an hour later. This made me anxious; I was so on edge, I'd wake long before it was time for a feed, and find I couldn't sleep once it was over. Wheeler was displeased. 'Look at you,' she said one morning over breakfast. 'Bruise marks under your eyes — you're exhausted. It's Rose's birthday in three days — and at this rate, you'll be sleepwalking through it. This afternoon you go to bed and you rest for two hours minimum, young lady.'

On another occasion I might have argued, but I felt so peculiar that morning, sick and faint, with an aching head and cramps in my stomach, that I gave in. I went upstairs after lunch and lay down on my bed in my petticoat: Wheeler drew the counterpane over me and rested her hand on my forehead. 'Well, there's no fever anyway . . . ' I saw wariness flash across her face: 'You don't have a pain anywhere?'

I denied it. She gave me an aspirin anyway. 'Growing pains,' she diagnosed. 'Get some sleep. I'm taking Rose and Peter to the river – and I'm taking that blasted puppy too, so there's nothing to wake you. We're in earshot, so you shout if you need me.'

I was asleep before she left the room. I closed my eyes and drowned: oblivion closed over my head like water.

When I woke, I had no idea how long I'd slept, or what time it was. I felt hot and sweaty; the house was silent. Opening the curtains, I saw the sun was still high and bright; there was neither sight nor sound of the others. I still felt dizzy and removed – that typhoid smoke seemed to have clouded my mind again, but the dull ache in my head and my stomach had gone. I washed, found a clean dress, then padded barefoot downstairs.

I was in the kitchen, making myself some tea, when I realised the farm had visitors. Parked in the corner of the yard was Eve's racing-green car. Eve must have walked down to the river to join the others, I thought, and then, moving to a window that overlooked the valley, I saw I was not alone at the farm after all: Howard Carter was sitting outside in the sun, gazing at the chalk downs opposite. He was so silent and unmoving that the swallows were flitting within a few feet of his head.

I made a cup of tea for him and took it outside. He thanked me but seemed scarcely aware of my presence. He fell silent again, and showed no inclination to speak when I drew up a chair and sat down at the table with him. I still felt light-headed and had no inclination to speak either, so I sipped my tea and debated what illness I might have; whether it was serious or a trivial passing affliction, from which I'd already recovered. The latter, I decided.

I stole a look at Carter's face: his expression was calm – as calm as I'd ever seen it. I turned towards the valley, where I caught a glimpse of Peter on the far side of the river, and of a woman in a pink dress. For a muddled instant I thought it was Poppy d'Erlanger – I often sensed her presence in this house; then I realised that it was Eve. 'There! A *pike*,' I heard Peter cry. The two figures vanished.

'Well, it's all settled at last,' Carter said, in a quiet voice. 'One last dig in the Valley. Lord Carnarvon agreed to it last night. He's changed his mind – or, to be more exact, *I* changed it for him.'

He still seemed almost unaware of my presence, indifferent to it, anyway, so I said nothing. I waited.

'I let it lie for a few days – always a good tactic,' he went on, after a long pause. 'Then I went to him with a new proposition. No maps, no arguments – we were past all that. I said: Give me one last chance. The permit's still in force. Let me dig that one last area by the entrance to Ramesses VI's tomb. It'll take me six weeks, probably less, to clear the rest of those workmen's huts. I have Girigar and my team ready and willing to work. It costs five Egyptian pounds a day to employ them, that's thirty-five Egyptian pounds a week. Add in ancillary costs and let's say a six-week dig will cost around two hundred pounds sterling . . . Not much, in the circumstances, when there's so much riding on it.

'I told him: that's what it will cost, and *I'll* cover all the expenses: my own salary, the men's wages. There's no need for you to risk your health or come anywhere near Egypt. I'll handle it. The dig can be finished before Christmas. If I find nothing, at least we know we've exhausted every possibility. If I find *anything*, however large or small, it's yours, just as it would be if you were funding the dig . . . I pointed out it was our last throw of the dice. Worth a punt. In my view, anyway.'

Carter fell silent then, and after a long pause I felt I could risk prompting him, so I said: 'And then Lord Carnarvon changed his mind and agreed?'

'Yes. He's a betting man. I knew he would. He might have been touched, or amused – it's difficult to tell with him. Oh, and he won't accept my offer. He's paying for it.'

We sat in silence while I considered this. Carter's suggestion that he should bear the costs of the dig reminded me of Wheeler's half-wages gambit, and I wondered if that ploy might have influenced him. I didn't mention this possibility, but I did ask whether Lord

Carnarvon had been swayed by the fact that the Met might be after his permit.

'Could be. The idea that they could make a discovery that had eluded him for years might have alarmed him – I hope it did. He'd never admit it, if so. The main thing, the *key* thing, is he knows I won't give up. If I don't find *him* a tomb, I'll damn well find it for someone else. It's there – and it's *mine*. This year, next year, ten years from now: however long it takes. I'll find it, if it kills me.'

Carter lit another cigarette, and drew on it deeply. He stared at the hills opposite, his face sullen and brooding. 'Does Lord Carnarvon know about Mr Winlock's discovery now?' I asked, after another long pause, during which Carter showed no inclination to say anything further. 'Did you explain to him what Mr Winlock found? Frances told me about it, in her last letter, and I was so glad! I *knew* Lord Carnarvon would want to continue your work once he knew Mr Winlock had made a breakthrough.'

I faltered and came to a halt. Carter, who had not looked at me once during this conversation, had now swung around sharply and was glaring at me. I saw that the mention of Herbert Winlock was a mistake and my question had made him furious. He gave me a long, hard, withering stare.

'I *knew* you were trouble,' he said, 'I knew it the first time I laid eyes on you in Cairo. Frances's little friend, who's been seriously ill, or so it's claimed. Who's so shy she can't say boo to a goose, who pretends butter wouldn't melt in her mouth. The girl with too many names – Lucy Payne from Cambridge, Lucy Foxe-Payne from Norfolk, Lucy-Christ-knows-what, with her American connections. The girl I look at and think: is she what she claims – or an imposter? The sad little invalid who turns up in Cairo, then Luxor, then the Valley. The girl I take pity on and include in a lunch invitation, who then starts a row with her ignorant comments and ruins the occasion for everyone. The girl who turns up at Highclere with a sick, flea-bitten mongrel in tow, and embarrasses Eve in front of her guests. The rude, obstinate girl who insists on seeing Lord Carnarvon's collection, no matter how much it inconveniences everyone else – and who then doesn't have the manners to disguise just how damn boring she finds it.'

He rose and stood glowering down at me. I recoiled. For one moment I thought he was about to smack me, but even he wouldn't have gone that far, however much his fingers itched to administer a slapping; he could probably see that his words were more effective than a smack anyway. I wanted to protest, to say this wasn't true, that it surely could not be true, but the words would not be spoken.

'Anything Winlock tells me and I tell him is between *us*,' he went on. 'It's none of Frances's business – and it certainly isn't yours. I won't be spied on – you hear me? So don't meddle with things you don't understand. Stay clear of me from now on, little girl, and keep that damned mouth of yours *shut*.'

He strode across to the gate. 'I'm going back to Highclere. Tell Eve,' he said, over his shoulder; then he set off across the fields at a fast pace without looking back.

When he was finally out of sight, I waited a while and then walked slowly down towards the valley; there, I met the others making their way back. Both the puppy, who had ventured into the river, and Peter, who had rescued her, were soaking wet.

Eve was radiant. 'Isn't it wonderful, Lucy?' she said. 'Did you see Howard – did he tell you? I'm so happy for him, and for Pups. It's worth just one last try, and I told Pups that. Even if Howard finds nothing, his plans will be complete, so honour's satisfied, and besides,' she took my arm, 'he's such a *good* man, Lucy. Kind-hearted, utterly loyal, a true friend – look how he's been this last few days, coming over to see you children, helping with the puppy: I was very touched by that, and Pups was too. Howard had just suffered a terrible blow – but he'd put that behind him, not one word of reproach . . . He's so *generous*, Lucy. Howard has a heart of gold: I don't know why people can't see that.'

I said nothing. Peter had been carrying the puppy, but she was proving too heavy for him. Halfway up the hill, I took her from him and cradled her damp fur against my chest. She whined; she was cold and shivering and forlorn, so I wrapped her in my cardigan and held her tight. I set my face to the farm and walked on steadily. In the distance, I saw that the postboy was toiling down the hill, carrying his leather satchel, kicking up the dust. It was late for a delivery. When the boy glimpsed us he hallooed, jumped up and down, and began semaphoring.

'What's that daft boy doing?' Wheeler asked. 'Why is *he* back again? He brought the post earlier. There's a letter for you, Lucy, I left it for you in the kitchen, did you see it? From Miss Mackenzie – I recognised her writing.'

I hadn't seen the letter – and I had no opportunity to read it that afternoon. The postboy, with great excitement and an air of massive self-importance, met us in the yard. He announced he was delivering telegrams – the first ever entrusted to him. He handed them across: two small brown envelopes, one for me and one for Wheeler. The boy bustled into the kitchen, accepted his usual lemonade and cake, sat down at the table and looked from face to face expectantly – he was anticipating a death, I think; something juicy anyway.

I inspected the telegrams. I knew they couldn't bode well – telegrams never did. Mine read: YOUR FATHER UNWELL + URGENT YOU RETURN CAMBRIDGE IMMEDIATELY ++ NICOLA

Wheeler's read: LUCY'S RETURN IMPERATIVE + UNFORESEEN EVENTS + WIRE SOONEST RE HER ARRIVAL TIME CAMBRIDGE ++ DUNSIRE

'Heavens, whatever can have happened?' Eve said. 'Could it be an accident? Oh, Lucy, don't be upset, dear – I'm sure it will be all right, how lucky that I'm here – leave *everything* to me.'

No one seemed interested in the question of why Nicola Dunsire, still in France as of her most recent Loire letter, should now be back in England. No one enquired as to my father's state of health before I'd left – and perhaps that was irrelevant, I thought; perhaps some accident *had* occurred. I felt concussed. I stared at the telegrams. It occurred to me that I was *inconveniencing* people again. I was a *nuisance* yet again – why did that happen? I was very afraid Eve might think I was presuming on friendship, but when I muttered something to that effect, she gave me a hug, made an urgent face at Wheeler, and told me not to be silly.

'We'll get you back home in no time, Lucy, dear,' she said. 'And meanwhile, you mustn't worry.'

Before I could say a word, Wheeler was hastening upstairs to pack my cases. The Carnarvon machine swung into action, and its efficiency was impressive. We couldn't telephone my home, because there *was* no telephone; domestic phones were still comparatively rare then and my father regarded them as unnecessary, intrusive, new-fangled extravagances. He no more approved of phones than he did pet animals, holidays, Americans, aristocrats, scarabs, disobedient children, or deceitful women who concealed secrets from him. Accordingly, within an hour, no *ifs* or *buts* and no '*Let's discuss this,*' a telegram was sent in return, confirming my arrival home later that night. Half an hour after that, I was inside one of Highclere Castle's fast cars, its most reliable driver at the wheel. As it drew out of the farmyard, Peter and Rose, in tears, ran after it. I heard Peter call *Lulu* one last despairing time as the great machine turned and accelerated; then the farm – which I loved, which I'd return to, briefly, later in my life – was hidden behind its sheltering hawthorn hedges.

The time, the driver informed me, was 4 p.m. Four o'clock it *is*, I thought. I felt as if I were sleepwalking. I strapped my neglected watch around my wrist, adjusted the hands and wound it.

25

It was a long slow drive to Cambridge, and it took us through several counties. Periodically, the driver, a kindly man whose name was Frobisher, would look over his shoulder and inform me of our progress in an encouraging way. 'Well, that's Hampshire under our belt,' he'd say, 'now for Berkshire.' I think he could see I was in a wan, muddled state, so after a while he gave up on the confusion of counties. 'Twenty more on the clock,' he'd announce, 'I'll top her up soon,' or 'Another half-hour and we'll be seeing signs of civilisation . . . You all right there, in the back, miss?'

I'd assure him I was. By the time we'd reached the top of the lane behind the farm, I'd resolved to forget what Mr Carter had said to me. It had happened, I couldn't change it. I must concentrate on my father. Could he have suffered an accident – could someone, perhaps Mrs Grimshaw or the college or even a friend like Dr Gerhardt have summoned Nicola Dunsire from France? What did 'Your father unwell' *mean*? It must mean ill enough to send a telegram, ill enough to summon me – did that mean he was dying? Could it mean he was *already* dead – was I being gently prepared, as Rose and Peter had been with Poppy?

Somewhere on the edge of two counties, Frobisher pulled over to the roadside verge. He unstrapped two large petrol cans from the back of the car and filled up the tank. I opened the little attaché case I had with me. Inside it was the letter from Miss Mack. I left that unopened and took out my book. It was Charlotte Brontë's *Villette*: over six hundred pages of holiday homework; I was halfway through it. As Frobisher started the car again and pulled away, I found my place at the end of Volume I. How the car jolted, how the words bounced on the page! I read: *I was left secretly and sadly to wonder, in my own mind*— I lost track as the car cornered sharply and had to read back. The heroine and narrator of the novel, Miss Snowe, had seen a ghost, which might have existed, been faked or been imagined; it might have come from a realm beyond the grave, or was perhaps *only the child of malady, and I of that malady a prey.*

I turned to the next page, new volume, new chapter, and read: *A new creed became mine – a belief in happiness.* I wondered distantly if you *could* adopt that particular creed: could you decide to be happy, as you might decide to become a Roman Catholic, a Hindu or a Muslim?

'Skirting London now,' Frobisher announced – and I saw to my surprise that we were: I'd been in a Brussels convent school and had looked up expecting to see its garden, its *allée défendue.* Instead here were houses, shops, other vehicles. There was even a garage, where we pulled in and the thirsty car was refilled. London huddled on the grey horizon. I got out and stretched my legs on the dusty forecourt. I walked back and forth, back and forth. It was beginning to rain hard. I climbed back into the car, and we set off again. The windscreen wiper swished a rhythmic semicircle. I replaced *Villette* in my case: the light was now too poor to read by.

We reached Newnham some four or five hours after leaving the farm – it was difficult to be sure of the time: my watch, unwound for weeks, seemed unreliable; it would tick, stop, tick again. I stared at the tall grey house as we drew up outside it: every light in the rooms facing the road was on. Frobisher waited until I'd unlocked the door with my latchkey, and then lifted the cases into the hall for me. He asked if he should wait, but when I thanked him and told him I'd be fine now, he wished me good evening and left. I closed the door behind me.

Frobisher had been reassured by the lights in the house, I think – but I was not. My father disliked rooms to be lit unless they were in use, and Miss Dunsire always observed this economy. As soon as I'd seen lights in the drawing room, in my father's study, upstairs in the front bedroom, my heart had begun beating fast: they signified trouble. I was nerving myself for evidence of emergency, a doctor or a nurse emerging from a room upstairs — Nicola Dunsire, distraught, summoned from France, running to greet me.

The house was silent. No sounds from upstairs or down, only the faint hiss that came from the gas-lights — my father had always refused to install electricity. I dragged my cases to the foot of the stairs and listened. I called out. No answering footsteps or voices. I ventured into the drawing room, where I saw that a fire had been lit but was almost out. I went into my father's study, in which the gas-lights were hissing and blazing. The *shabti* figure I'd given my father had suffered an accident, I discovered. It had been smashed, and its fragments lay scattered across his desk. Apart from this isolated damage, the house seemed in perfect order: it looked exactly as it always did. I crept from room to room. Two wineglasses had recently been used and washed; they were the only signs of recent occupation; they lay resting on the kitchen draining board.

I was afraid to go upstairs, but when I'd called again and again, and no one replied, I did so. The bedrooms on the first floor, with the exception of Miss Dunsire's, were never occupied. I looked into my father's room at the back of the house: unlit and unused as always. I opened the door of my mother's bedroom next to it. That room was dust-sheeted. The white sheets around the bed billowed and beckoned in the wavering light from the landing. I slammed the door shut on them. I looked into the empty guest rooms and then, summoning my nerve, tapped on the door to Miss Dunsire's room.

When I'd tapped three times and there was still no answer, I opened it. All the gas jets were burning brightly. I stared around it in dismay. I rarely entered this room, but whenever I had, it had been immaculate. Now clothes and underclothes were tossed on the floor; a stocking snaked over the bedpost, a petticoat had slithered under a chair, and the bed itself, a double one, was tumbled. One pillow lay on the floor and the eiderdown was humped over the bed end. A white silk nightgown lay on the bare white undersheet. I gazed at this disorder — and saw that on the table next to the bed there was a telegram. It was unopened.

I picked it up — surely this must be the wire sent in reply to Miss Dunsire's cables? Why should it lie here, and why had she not read it? I stared at the objects scattered next to it, the painkiller aspirins, numerous bottles with pharmacy labels, the book by Marcel Proust that Miss Dunsire had been reading – *À la recherche du temps perdu*, lying open and face down, its spine broken. I hated books to be mistreated: I picked it up and closed it, and saw the letter beneath that it concealed. It was written in Miss Dunsire's neat, italic script. It bore that day's date. *Dear Lucy*, I read. *It's such a beautiful day here at the chateau. We had a picnic lunch by the river, then Clair, Meta and I walked to the market in town. Now we're back, and I'm sitting on the terrace overlooking the valley. I have a tranquil hour, my dear, in which to write to you …*

There were pages of it. I dropped the one I was holding and let it flutter to the floor. I backed out of the room and fled upstairs. No one there either: the whole house was unoccupied. In my attic the bed had not been made up; none of the gas-lights had been lit. I went to the window, opened it and leaned out. It was raining heavily, it was dark, and the Cambridge church bells had begun tolling. I counted ten strokes. As the echoes of the last bell died away, I glimpsed a woman walking along the lane towards our back garden. She was caught for an instant in the pooling light from a street lamp; she was walking swiftly, my view of her obscured by the umbrella she held. She passed into the shadows, was hidden from view by a patch of trees, then stepped into a circle of lamplight again. She was dressed in black – and she was not alone.

Two figures approached the gate that led into our rear garden. I could hear voices now and they were raised as if in disagreement. They were women's voices, I realised, and one of them was surely Miss Dunsire's – but whoever was with her, it could not be my father. The two shapes disappeared beneath the rose arch, took the path between the lavenders and came to a halt on the terrace directly below me. The light spilling from the house illumined their faces. The taller of the two women – and it *was* Nicola, I saw – gave an exclamation of annoyance and lowered her umbrella. I realised that the person with her was her artist friend Clair. As they came to a halt, she was clasping at Nicola Dunsire's arm with her small hands, and Miss Dunsire was closing the umbrella and attempting to shake her off. She said: 'Let go of me. Let go. It's done, Clair.'

She tried to prise her friend's hands free, and for a brief moment the two women seemed to struggle. Then Clair released her, and took a step back. Her white face flared in the light. She said: 'This will finish you, Nicola. We both know that.'

Miss Dunsire made some reply that I couldn't hear – though I recognised the familiar taunting tone in her voice. Then she seemed to reconsider, or falter – I wasn't sure what happened, but it was swift. She made a low sound, and the next instant Clair's arms were around her. The two women clung to each other; they embraced and kissed – it happened swiftly, in a swirl of agitation. Then they broke apart. Clair turned away down the path without a backward look. The gate slammed shut behind her. Miss Dunsire turned to face the house. Her expression, caught in the light, assumed a fixed serenity. She walked inside, and when I heard her moving in the drawing room below, pacing back and forth, then pausing to put coal on the fire, then pacing again, I went downstairs to her.

She must have seen my cases in the hall, but if she had, she'd not taken in their import, I think. I made sure to come downstairs noisily, but even so, I startled her. She wheeled around from the fire, her face bloodless, and stared at me. She said, 'Oh – it's you, Lucy. For a moment I thought—'

'You haven't been in France,' I said. 'You lied to me. Who posted those letters?'

'Such a greeting! My letters? Does it matter?' Her gaze dropped. 'Meta. My friend Meta. I gave her a batch of them before she left. I told her to send one every three days.' She frowned and I saw her make a quick calculation. 'What happened? Was there a gap? Maybe I underestimated how many she'd need – ask *her* when you next see her.'

'Why are you wearing black? *Is* my father ill? Where is he?'

'No, he's not ill.' She took a breath, and I could see that – swiftly as always – she was asserting her will and regaining her self-control. 'He's well – he's remarkably well. He was here earlier, now he's back in college. I'm sorry for that deception . . . no, actually, I'm not. I needed you here and that seemed the quickest, most effective way.' She paused. '*Too* effective: I wasn't expecting you until the morning.'

'If you'd opened the telegram that's lying next to your bed, you'd have known I was arriving tonight. Why didn't you?'

There was a silence. For the first and the only time in all the years I was to know her, she blushed. I watched the blood course up into her pale neck and stain her face. It was painful to watch; then she brushed at her wet jacket with a black-gloved hand, and said, 'Don't look at me like that. I've acted wrongly: I accept that. As for that telegram — I must have forgotten it ... I was distracted ... your father was here, then Clair arrived. First *he* wouldn't leave, then *she* wouldn't: such a scene — I took her for a walk to calm her down. Clair doesn't approve of what I've done, you see. She came here to persuade me *not* to do it. But by then it was too late. I've told her. The matter is settled.'

In a resigned way, she drew off one of her gloves and extended her left hand towards me. I stared at it, not understanding at first. Then I realised that she was wearing an engagement ring. A narrow gold band, a small stone; her hand was unsteady.

'The wedding is in two days' time,' she said. 'A register office. It will be a stupid, ugly sort of ceremony, but very quick and efficient, I expect. We decided two days ago. And the instant we *had* decided, I found I wanted you back at my side. So I summoned you. I needed you, Lucy. To celebrate. Or commiserate.'

Her tone, as it often did, veered between mockery and gravity. She had begun to tremble. I gazed at the ring, then her face, in incomprehension. I was trying to work out this husband-to-be's identity: was it someone unknown to me, or could it be the poet Eddie, whom I'd met at her luncheon party? She'd gone to that reading he gave in London, I remembered, and had stayed there overnight. She'd mentioned him in one of the letters from France; perhaps not everything in those letters was fiction. Then I raised my eyes to her pale set face — she couldn't hide the expression in her eyes, not from me, not by then — and I understood at last. I said: 'My father? You're going to marry my *father*?'

'Yes. I am. He needs a secretary, and since an unmarried woman can't travel with him on his sabbatical, he needs a secretary-wife. I am over-qualified for such tasks.'

She gave a small impatient toss of the head as she said that. Her face had become a mask of arrogance, and she was attempting to stare me down; the trembling in her hands, as before, had now spread to her whole body.

'But you don't love him,' I burst out. 'You don't even *like* him. I've seen the contempt in your face when you look at him. How could you do that? Why — *why* would you do that?'

'I did it because I *could*.' She turned away. 'Because I don't want to be governess to some girl for the rest of my life, not even yours. Because I don't want to go on – and on, and on, scratching a living, moving from place to place, buried alive, taking orders from fools. Because people won't talk once I'm a married woman. Because your father was available and one fine day I thought – *why not*? Because I'm angry, and it gets me nowhere. Because I'm exhausted and I gave in. Because I once wanted to do great things and now I know I won't—' Her voice caught and she covered her face with her hands.

'How many reasons do you want? Am I *so* intolerable as a step-mother? I had thought you might be pleased. How stupid of me. Now I see I was wrong.'

I was staring at her as she spoke these words, but I couldn't see her very well; tears had come to my eyes. I thought her distress was acted, then I thought it was genuine, that it sprang straight from her heart. Fake or real? Fake or real? I thought how much I hated her, then I pitied her and thought I could love her, and then I found I'd crossed the room, flown across the room and put my arms around her. She bent her head and rested it against mine. I held her until her trembling ceased, until my own tears dried.

When we were both calmer, she drew back a little and gave me a sidelong, glinting glance. 'It wasn't difficult, Lucy,' she said. 'You've seen him. I had two weeks to work on him before you returned from Egypt. And six – nearly seven months since then. Once I decided not to go to France, I knew . . . *Well* within my powers.'

I looked at her uncertainly. 'Your bicycle-thief friend thinks it will finish you. I heard her say so.'

'Clair?' The fact that I'd overheard this perhaps disconcerted her. 'Oh, Clair is so intransigent and demanding,' she said quickly, in a negligent way. 'She's possessive and she talks nonsense. Who cares what *she* thinks, Lucy? I certainly don't.'

Some while later – considerably later, when I'd made something to eat, and she'd poured us glasses of red wine, and insisted I drink – she sat in my mother's 'Strawberry Thief' chair and I sat on the rug at her feet. I was calmer now, but I could sense agitation in both of us. The room was quiet, the fire warm on my upturned face; its flames lit the bronze, gold and copper of Nicola Dunsire's hair. After some time had passed, she took off her engagement ring, held it delicately to the firelight, examined its small stone – and told me it had been chosen at a shop in Bene't Street, owned by a Hungarian by the name of Szabó.

'How many pieces of your mother's jewellery did you sell that man, Lucy?' she asked quietly and, accepting that she'd always be a hundred yards ahead of me however fast I ran, I told her. I also told her what the money was for. I described my escape plan, how much I yearned to return to Egypt, to the Valley of the Kings, to Frances – and why. Maybe the wine loosened my tongue, maybe she did. Because, I said, beginning to cry; because, because, *because*.

I spoke at length; once I began speaking, I found I couldn't stop. Somewhere in the midst of this blurt, this *cri de coeur*, Nicola Dunsire took my hand in hers. She listened intently, without interruptions or questions. Nothing I said seemed to surprise her – it was as if I were describing a state of mind long familiar to her. When I finally ceased speaking, she said: 'You've let me into your secrets. In return, I shall let you into mine. You remember that friend I spoke of, the one you remind me of, the one you resemble so closely?'

'The one who killed herself? Yes, I remember her.'

'That friend was me. She and I are one and the same. Her name was *Nicole*. She turned on the gas in her room at Girton one night, and she died. The next morning, *Nicola* – the Nicola you know, was born. You and I are as alike as can be, Lucy. We are two sides of the very same coin.'

I stayed silent, watching the firelight play across her face. I thought through this revelation and wondered if it were true and, if it were, what had brought her to that pass. Were we alike? The idea bewildered me.

'But I wouldn't have done that, Nicola,' I said gently. 'I would never try to kill myself.'

'Don't tempt fate.' She snapped her fingers. 'And don't argue. Like as like, even so. You and I are twins, Lucy – and I knew that within an hour of meeting you.'

We returned to Mr Szabó's shop the following morning and sold him the last necessary item of jewellery: Miss Dunsire and I selected it together from the museum of Marianne. I wrote to Miss Mack, confirming I could accompany her to Egypt again – the dates, as Miss

Dunsire pointed out, would be convenient for us both, leaving her free to travel with my father for part of his sabbatical. And, a few days later, we gave a small supper party to celebrate the surprise wedding: no Girtonian friends present, no waspish, hard-drinking poets; several carefully selected dons – all those invited, and their wives, attended. Everyone brought presents. Dr Gerhardt made a kindly speech. My father, the unexpected bridegroom, looking suave, handsome and pleased with himself, a man who'd pulled off a complex conjuring trick to the amazement of his friends, proposed numerous toasts.

At some length, and with a gallantry and eloquence everyone remarked upon, he explained his new wife had transformed his life. He felt as if the roles of Orpheus and Eurydice had been reversed, he said; as if it were Nicola Dunsire who had risked that journey to the underworld to rescue him from the shadowland of bereavement – and had done so, unlike ill-fated Orpheus, successfully. She had changed his name, he said, with a flicker of amusement – he would revert to his old surname from now on. She had changed his life – and his work: it was thanks to her promptings that he'd finally understood the form his book on Euripides must take, he added. He raised his glass, and we drank to the successful completion of this book, to him – and to Nicola Foxe-Payne, the wife who would soon be accompanying him to Athens and Paris for research purposes, the wife whose devotion, intellectual support, acuity and secretarial skills he could now rely on.

Miss Dunsire – I still thought of her by that name and always would – then proposed a toast to me, and my forthcoming stay in Egypt: '*Life! Prosperity! Health!*' she said, raising her glass, using the salute I'd taught her, the salute traditionally given to all Egyptian kings. She was happy that night, I think. It was an evening of gaiety and good fellowship. We'd filled the house with white lilies with pink throats, and their scent was intoxicating. I drank a glass of champagne for the first time in my life. I wore Miss Dunsire's silk dress for the first time. It was greatly admired by everyone present.

'You promise you'll write to me from Egypt, Lucy?' Miss Dunsire said. We were alone by then. Our guests had left, and my father, seeing no reason why marriage should alter by one iota the habits with which he was comfortable, had returned, as always, to college.

The house was quiet again. Miss Dunsire and I climbed the stairs to bed. She kissed my cheek, as we reached the first landing.

'Oh, I'll write punctually. One letter every three days,' I answered, with a small sidelong glance.

'Wicked girl. Goodnight then.' She laughed as I turned to the stairs to my attic.

FIVE

Oliver No. 9

AT LAST HAVE MADE WONDERFUL DISCOVERY IN THE VALLEY.
A MAGNIFICENT TOMB WITH SEALS INTACT. RECOVERED SAME
FOR YOUR ARRIVAL. CONGRATULATIONS. CARTER

Telegram from Howard Carter in Luxor to Lord Carnarvon
at Highclere Castle, 5 November 1922

26

'Curious, that famous telegram of Carter's,' Dr Fong said.

He settled himself in his chair on my Highgate terrace and surreptitiously switched on his tape recorder. I poured him a cup of Gunpowder tea and kept my eyes on the graves of Highgate Cemetery below my back garden walls: that long, long view over a wilderness of ivy and brambles, over crucifixes, obelisks and angels. A party of volunteers was clearing the undergrowth in this, the oldest, most neglected section of the burial ground. Their shouts as they uncovered another overgrown monument interspersed with the whine of their chainsaw.

A hot afternoon in May: I had recently returned from my stay in the country with Rose; Dr Fong, driven out of Egypt by temperatures that made filming impossible, had just left Luxor. This meeting was the first we'd had since his return. I wasn't sure why he had pressed for it, or why I'd agreed. Perhaps I welcomed company: since leaving Rose's house, my days had been solitary.

The first two episodes of Dr Fong's Tutankhamun documentary were complete, the remaining two would be filmed the following autumn, he said, and the programmes would be ready for transmission by next January. But filming had disagreed with him: the technical wizardry took days to set up, the helicopter shots used up half the budget, the script kept altering and the producers had decided too many scholars were involved. 'Too many "talking heads",' Fong explained in an irritable tone. 'First they wanted to cut half the interviews, then they had a panic attack and said we needed *drama* ...

Intercut scenes from the life and death of King Tut. Costumes. Actors, God help us. Tut's mourning sister-widow, villainous viziers.'

That insurrection had been successfully put down, but the political infighting of prime-time television had taken its toll. Dr Fong was looking tired and dispirited; there'd been a noticeable ebbing of confidence; his former youthful bounce was gone. He'd been ill while in Egypt, he'd told me: one of those feverish Valley colds, the ones that could fell you for weeks. I wondered whether these factors explained the change in him; not entirely, perhaps. I noted that his wedding ring had disappeared, though he said nothing of its absence and neither, of course, did I. Fong's manner was chastened, less impatient than it had been; he'd greeted me with surprising warmth and a kindly concern: 'You've lost weight since I last saw you, Miss Payne,' he'd said gently. 'You're looking exhausted, you know. You haven't been ill, have you?'

I brushed these enquiries aside. I'd endured similar cross-questioning from Rose, who was urging me to see some Harley Street specialist she favoured; under pressure, I'd made an appointment to see this man. A waste of time: even top consultants can't provide a cure for age. I was able to give Dr Fong the same answer I'd given Rose: I'd been sleeping badly, that was all. I blamed the months spent poring over letters and journals, re-exploring my past . . . A trivial complaint, I told him crisply: nothing that the latest sleeping pills couldn't cure.

Having made that remark about Howard Carter's famous telegram to Lord Carnarvon, Fong lapsed into silence. He seemed unwilling to pursue that subject, but sat frowning at the cemetery below. The scent of the wisteria on my house walls honeyed the air and a faint breeze riffled the pages of his notebook. 'To tell you the truth, Miss Payne,' he said suddenly, 'I found it kind of dislocating, being back there, in the actual places where it all happened – the Valley, the American House . . . I had hoped a friend would be there with me, but in the end he couldn't make it, so I was on my own a lot. I had time to kill while the crew did their endless set-ups. I was kind of losing faith in the whole documentary, so I'd wander around the Valley for hours at a time. And that's a strange place, as you know. It doesn't exactly lift your spirits when you're feeling low – buses, car parks, exhaust fumes, a damn great tarmac road, restrooms, guards and touts everywhere. A million visitors a year – and counting. The toxicity of tourism. The Valley you knew is lost for ever – all that's left of that is photographs.'

'And memories.'

'Memories don't survive – not unless they're recorded. And besides, who's to say what's memory and what's myth?' He made a restless gesture. 'I met this old man while I was in Luxor, Miss Payne – he must have been ninety or more. He used to hang around the hotels, yarning to the tourists. He waylaid me one day, wanted us to film him, I think. He told me he'd been one of the water boys on Carter's dig. He claimed it was he who found that famous first step that led down to Tutankhamun's tomb. Said he was six, maybe seven years old, and was just kidding around, delved about in the sand with a stick, suddenly hit stone, brushed the sand aside – and, abracadabra, there the step was . . .

'That information cost me five Egyptian pounds – not that I minded *that*: the man was blind. Thin as a reed, eyes bandaged, could scarcely walk – he was pitiful; if he made some kind of living spinning tales for the tourists, I'm glad. We didn't film him, of course – Luxor is filled with charlatans making similar claims. But true or false, Miss Payne? Howard Carter gave two versions of how that first step was found, if you recall. In the first version, his *reis* Ahmed Girigar and the workmen uncovered it, early one morning, before Carter turned up on site – and just three days into the dig too: 4 November 1922. In the second version, it was the water boy at play who uncovered the step by chance . . . kind of a quaint detail, yes? But that boy was never mentioned until Carter was on his triumphant lecture tour in America two years later, by which time extra colour was getting added in by the day.'

'The old man was blind?' I turned to look at Dr Fong, but it was not him I saw; it was Girigar's grandson and namesake, that six-year-old imp of a boy pointed out to me in the Valley, the boy whose one ambition was to ride on Carter's Decauville rail-carts . . . a boy who'd be in his eighties now. 'Did the old man tell you his name?'

'Oh, sure. He claimed he was called Ahmed Girigar. As in, Carter's *reis*. That name wouldn't mean a thing to ninety-nine per cent of tourists, but who knows? Maybe he figured it added to the authenticity.'

'Maybe he did,' I replied.

I watched the little boy of eighty years before dash back to work as his grandfather shouted a reprimand: he leapt, sure-footed, among the stones of Carter's excavations, then disappeared into its billowing dust, leaving a familiar ache about my heart. I watched two small girls run through those dust clouds, escape into a narrow wadi, come to a halt by a tall wind-carved stone and bury a pink purse at its foot. *Let it pass.*

I turned my eyes back to the graveyard; the volunteers had taken a tea-break and were beginning work again. I watched them advance on an angel swathed in ivy and hemmed in with sycamore seedlings: the angel's head, the arch of a wing, and a warning upraised hand were all that were visible; the chainsaw spluttered into life, and whined.

'So – that famous telegram of Carter's,' Fong said, returning at last to the issue he'd been fretting over from the moment he arrived. 'I can't let go of that telegram, Miss Payne: it's a foretaste of all the puzzles to come. Think about it: Carter sent it one day after they found that first step. At that point, they'd cleared the stairway, sixteen steps down – and they'd got as far as a wall at their foot. All he'd found at that point were the necropolis seals on that wall's plaster: no identifying king's cartouche, or so he claims – and worrying evidence of forced entry in antiquity too. So Carter couldn't have been sure he'd made a "wonderful discovery" when he sent that cable. He couldn't have known it was a tomb he'd found – let alone a "magnificent" one. It might easily have been a cache, or a minor burial. Even if it *did* prove to be a tomb, the probability was he'd find it rifled and emptied – and he, of all people, *must* have known that. Yet he sent that cable to Carnarvon at Highclere, in the certain knowledge that the earl would then hightail it out to Egypt on the next available boat . . . Then he filled in the staircase and halted excavation until his patron arrived. All very proper – but a risk, even so. Suppose Carnarvon arrived – and they found an empty hole in the ground?'

'A risk Carter was prepared to take, I imagine,' I said absently. Below us, the angel was slowly emerging from its cloak of ivy. 'He was a showman. As you know.'

'A showman – and a fabulist,' Fong said, his tone bitter. I turned to look at him, surprised. 'I've reached the point, Miss Payne, where

I don't trust a word that man wrote,' he went on, his agitation now perceptible. 'How he found the tomb, what he and Carnarvon did next . . . Looking into the tomb for the first time by candlelight . . . the "glint of gold", the "wonderful things" he saw. Then, turn the page, and what do we find? Secrecy and deceit. A cover-up. You could say, a pack of lies.'

'Effective lies, Dr Fong. It took decades for the truth to emerge.'

'If it has emerged – even now. There are still unanswered questions. Too many of them.'

A silence fell. The sunlight glinted on the lenses of Dr Fong's spectacles; a mauve petal from the wisteria fell onto his notebook and he brushed it aside. 'Questions I'd like to answer,' he went on. 'I'd like to know whether the secrecy ever got too much for him. Did lying and subterfuge take its toll? Did he ever reveal the truth to anyone? Imagine it, Miss Payne: Carter makes the greatest archaeological discovery of all time – but he disguises the circumstances of that discovery. He lies – and he goes on lying. He pulls off an act of deception, aided and abetted by Lord Carnarvon and his daughter, by his Arab workforce and by a clutch of internationally distinguished scholars and archaeologists . . . And he does it in front of the world's press. The assembled journalists never noticed a damn thing. They were taken in by an act of theatre.' Dr Fong paused. 'Were you?'

The question was as sharp as it was sudden; I was unprepared, and it disconcerted me. I looked away. Silence fell, broken only by the occasional whine of the chainsaw below. In the distance the towers of Docklands pierced the heat haze and the bluish pollution clouds; the lights at the summit of Canary Wharf winked and blinked, two ever-watchful eyes. Egypt, my Egypt, felt close yet impossibly distant, here inside me, vanishing fast.

I closed my eyes: clear on the evening air came the eddying wash of the Nile. For our second stay in Egypt, Miss Mack had hired a *dahabiyeh*. It was moored on the west bank of the river at Luxor, and at night the music in the Winter Palace ballroom drifted across the water from the opposite shore. Frances and I danced to that music one night, a Viennese waltz: we traversed the decks in a series of dizzying spins. '*Weren't we just fine, Lucy?*' Frances cried, clutching on to me for balance, as we hurtled to a stop and leaned against the boat's rails. Catching our breath: there were two moons that night, one sailing the sky, and the other, a sister moon, in the river water below. An instant later, on a riffle of breeze, the sister moon shimmered, fragmented and was gone.

'I can't answer that question, Dr Fong,' I replied, after a long pause. 'I am old and you're too sudden for me. My memories are too freighted . . . and with people who mean nothing to you. For your purposes, they're marginal. They're not marginal to me.'

'I apologise.' Dr Fong switched off his tape recorder. Below us, the party of volunteers were packing up their tools and departing. We both listened as their voices receded and silence fell; the excavated angel, freed from the undergrowth that had obscured it, now stood revealed. Blind eyes in a beautiful passionless face. She had a wise, if punitive, air.

'I wish you would tell me – what you saw, what you learned, what you *felt*,' Dr Fong said, on a sudden note of appeal, laying his notebook aside. 'I'm in no hurry, you know. I have nowhere to go, no one to see. I can stay here and we can talk, Miss Payne, or I can go back to my room for yet another long evening and wrestle with all the questions I thought I'd answered when I started in on this project of mine. That's what I did in Luxor. That's what I do in London, these days. Stare at a wall, order a take-out, ask myself questions about a tomb – and watch the answers I thought I had slipping away from me.

'You're my only witness, Miss Payne. Everyone else is dead. But you were there. Those crucial three days when the tomb was found, when Carter breached the wall into its antechamber, looked through and saw his "wonderful things" . . . You were close by. You knew all the people involved. You witnessed the events after that, you watched the story unfold.' He paused. 'To me, your memories are like a treasure house. And you won't admit me. You're always blocking the entrance, standing on guard . . . A sort of watchdog – no, a Cerberus. Why is that? Don't you trust me? All I want is the truth, you know.'

'The truth? I certainly can't give you that, Dr Fong.'

'A variant would do. Your variant. Your version. I'd settle for that.'

He was looking at me in a sad, regretful way – and I took pity on him. The man had changed, as I had: we had something in common – we were both grappling with the past, if for different reasons and in differing ways. I too was facing the prospect of another evening alone.

The light was fading, inside the house my ever-present ghosts would be circling; perhaps it would do no harm to talk, just a little, just for a while.

I hesitated, then sent Dr Fong into the house to find whisky, water and glasses. When he'd returned, poured drinks for us both and settled himself in his chair again, I said: 'I tell this my way or not at all. Without interruptions and questions from you.'

'I'll be as silent as the grave.'

'Very well.' I paused, then began. 'I was in Egypt with the friend I once mentioned to you, Miss Mack. She was a good woman – one of the few truly good women I've ever known. She had rented a houseboat for our stay. It was called the *Queen Hatshepsut*. It was moored at Luxor, on the west bank, just below the American House and within sight of Castle Carter. The track to the Valley of the Kings passed right by it – so as the story of the tomb unfolded we had what Miss Mack liked to call a ringside view.

'We arrived there the day after Lord Carnarvon and Eve reached Luxor, when the excavation was about to begin. By then, over two weeks had passed since Carter sent his telegram, and the secret was out: everyone knew that Carter had found *something*, which might or might not prove to be a tomb. When Miss Mack and I were in Cairo, the city was ablaze with excitement; by the time we reached Luxor no one could talk of anything else. What would they discover when they breached the wall at the bottom of the staircase Carter had found? So we were in the right place, at the right time – and that wasn't entirely accidental. My friend Miss Mack was writing a book, you see.'

'A book?' Dr Fong looked at me sharply.

'Yes. A book. Within a very short time, *everyone* began writing books, Dr Fong. Howard Carter himself, several of the journalists who came out to cover the story – there was a positive *outbreak* of books. But Miss Mack was ahead of the game. She had been planning to write her memoirs for some while, you see, and once we were in Luxor, those memoirs – evolved. She was writing on a manual typewriter – an Oliver No. 9. I can still hear it, Dr Fong: she liked to write at night, so she'd be rattling the keys until midnight and well beyond. It kept me awake, but I didn't mind that: I was twelve years old, I was in love with Egypt. I'd go out on deck, and sit there in the dark: star-gazing, thinking.' I paused. 'Why, sometimes I'd stay out there for hours at a time.'

'Night vigils. A houseboat within sight of Castle Carter. Well, well, well. So you really were in the key place. At exactly the key moment. You're full of surprises, Miss Payne.' Fong gave a low laugh, but he was quick on the uptake, as I'd noticed before, and I could sense a new excitement in him. Reaching for the whisky bottle, he topped up my glass and then his own. 'That won't loosen my tongue,' I told him.

'I live in hope,' he replied, reaching for his notebook. 'Go on.'

A book was not the term Miss Mack used, and in deference to her I didn't use it either; it was The Book – and it had an imperialistic nature, I learned. As Miss Mack would explain our first evening on the *dahabiyeh,* The Book made constant demands.

'It's a most peculiar phenomenon,' she said, leading me into her cabin, indicating a stack of onion-skin typing paper and carbons, stroking the Oliver No. 9's round metal keys; it was painted olive green, weighed as much as a small child, and had terse instructions stamped on its front: *Keep machine cleaned and oiled at all times*. 'The Book leads me into the most unexpected places,' Miss Mack said with an authorial sigh. 'It's taken me over. And it's most dictatorial, even tyrannical, Lucy. It has Napoleonic tendencies. I feel it's changing my whole outlook, even my character. Truly, dear, I'm putty in its hands.'

I wondered if this could be so: it seemed unlikely – and unwise. Could a book, even The Book, have such an effect? But I had noticed changes in Miss Mack on our voyage out to Egypt, so perhaps it was true; these alterations in her outlook became more apparent that first evening by the Nile. Obtaining the use of this boat was a coup of which Miss Mack was proud: she had pulled it off with the assistance of the Winlocks as well as every other contact ever made in Egypt and beyond. It belonged to some New Englanders, cousins of acquaintances, who had planned to use it this winter, but changed their minds. Mounted above the upper deck was a flagpole, from which the Stars and Stripes bravely fluttered in the breeze from the Nile.

There was a saloon, with books and an out-of-tune piano; there were two bedrooms, with dark panelling, awnings and louvre shutters; there was a bathroom of sorts, where we'd bathe in Nile water.

It was romantic *and* economical, Miss Mack claimed. She went on an inspection tour of the galley areas within seconds of our arriving and pronounced herself fully satisfied: the kitchen was spotless, the Egyptians who'd be looking after us were most obliging, spoke excellent English and kept everything shipshape; the boat might be old, but it had immense charm. 'One can't *fuss* too much, Lucy,' she said breezily. 'If one's going to have adventures – as I certainly hope we shall – then there's no time to fret about the finer details of hygiene, don't you agree?'

This startling emancipation extended to our meals, I discovered, when we sat down under the awning on the upper deck to eat supper. The cook, whose name was Mohammed Sayed, served us grilled fish freshly caught from the river, *shamsi* bread, a salad of onions, herbs and cucumbers . . . A feast, Miss Mack declared, tucking into everything with a keen appetite. She had brought her binoculars to the table, and at intervals, trained them on the desert beyond. 'Birds, dear – maybe a *jackal*,' she said; but I noticed it was the area around Castle Carter on which she focused her gaze. When the failing light made the binoculars useless, she abandoned them and, in her new spirit of adventurousness, poured us both a glass of wine – mine diluted with Evian. We sat back to admire the numberless stars and their reflections, leaping like silver fish in the wash of the Nile.

To crown my astonishment, Miss Mack lit a fat Egyptian cigarette, puffed at it in a professional way, and explained that tobacco helped to provide *inspiration*. 'Just the one after dinner, dear,' she said. 'I find it gets me in the writing mood. I like to write at night, you see. I hope you won't mind.'

I assured her I wouldn't. Her colour had deepened as she made this confession, and I wasn't sure whether that implied that discussion of The Book was taboo. I finally risked a shy question – might she, perhaps, tell me what her book was about? Miss Mack, scarlet with emotion, was at once launched.

There was a lengthy preamble – how she'd been *deeply* affected by two sermons her minister had preached while she was home in Mercer Hill, Princeton: one relating to the parable of the *talents*, and the other to *hiding your light beneath a bushel*. 'I'll be sixty in two years, Lucy, dear,' she confided. 'Of course, I shall never be able to leave my dear mother, but it's time to grab life by the scruff of its neck even so. A bit late, you'll say – but better late than never, don't you agree? I always wanted to be a writer – I wrote poems as a girl, you know, and my, oh my, how I fussed over the scansion and the rhymes! Then, somehow, I lost the habit, and all my splendid ambitions went underground. Never, *never* let that happen to you, Lucy, dear . . . '

She paused. 'Then, this summer, I decided to bite the bullet, stiffen the sinews, screw my courage to the sticking point and take the plunge! So I bought my beloved Oliver, and off I went. And once I started, I discovered it was surprisingly easy. I can't think why I imagined writing would be hard, dear – it isn't at all. You simply sit there and talk to the page. Sometimes you know what's coming and sometimes you don't, in fact, all sorts of things just *pop* up out of nowhere and astonish you.'

I listened to this intently – it continued in similar vein for some while. When Miss Mack finally drew breath, I reminded her that she still hadn't told me what her book was about. At this, she shifted in her seat and gave me a sibylline look that, over the next two months in Egypt, I would come to recognise.

'Well, dear, it's called *An American Amidst the Tombs*, but that will have to change. You see, Lucy, it started off as a family memoir: I wrote a great deal about my first visit to Egypt with my father, the pyramids, the pelicans, and so on. I did *so* want to do the flora and fauna justice . . . ' She frowned. 'But The Book soon began to make its wishes known. It reminded me of everything that happened to us on our last visit: meeting Mr Carter and Lord Carnarvon – that lunch in the tomb, the storm in the Valley, the political upheaval, a new nation in the throes of being born. And *then* I heard the rumours that Mr Carter had found a tomb. That's when I realised I was an eyewitness, Lucy, right there on the spot when history was being made.

'I can see now how *slow* I was,' she continued, 'but The Book knew which route I should take – and once I listened to it, all became clear. What I need to write, Lucy, isn't some fusty memoir. I need to *report what's happening in the Valley right now*. A detailed blow-by-blow account by one who was there. What do you think, dear?'

I made encouraging noises. I asked her if she was writing to a plan, an authorial scheme.

'No, no, *no*!' she cried, throwing up her hands. 'A scheme would have a very *cramping* effect! The Book itself will decide that – and where it leads, I'll follow. A bit like Ruth and her mother-in-law in the Bible. You remember, Lucy? *Whither thou goest, I will go.*' She paused. 'However, I have given considerable attention to the far more important issue of *style*. I've never written *reports,* as such. They need to be crisp, concise and *informed*. But I've rewritten my first five chapters now, dear, and I've found my voice, I'm hitting my stride. I have a model in mind, obviously.'

I could see she wanted me to press her, so I asked who this model could be.

'Mark Twain, who else?' she replied, on a triumphant note – and shortly afterwards we retired to our rooms. 'Stout shoes and an early start tomorrow morning, Lucy,' she announced from her bedroom doorway. 'It's time to explore the Theban hills. We'll do some investigating; the view of the Valley from there is superb. If anything is happening at Mr Carter's site, we'll soon know. The Book needs *material*, dear. Mohammed will pack us a picnic. Some rugs – binoculars, obviously – and off we'll go!'

She gave me a speaking look, then firmly closed her door. From beyond it, within minutes, came the rattle of the Oliver No. 9 keyboard, the screech of the return carriage, the ratcheting sound as she inserted a fresh page. The Book must have had her in an iron grip: it was two in the morning before the Oliver fell silent at last.

I'd gone to sit on the deck by then, to breathe the air, to drink in Egypt and remind myself that at last I was there. I gave silent thanks to my mother and to Miss Dunsire, the two women who had made my journey possible. The crew had left one kerosene lamp alight; I extinguished it and wandered the boat in the starlight, back and forth. At a distance, on the east bank of the river, the windows of the Winter Palace glowed. It was still early in the season, but even so I could hear hotel dance music, drifting its seductions across the water – blues, a tango, ragtime; another drift of blues. I lay down on the deck and gazed up at the heavens, the arching stars. I could hear the shift and lap of the Nile, a sussuration as it stroked the *dahabiyeh*'s hull. The boat's timbers creaked and moaned as it moved on the water, tugged against its mooring ropes; the reeds whispered and rustled; from the desert came the hooting of an owl.

Sitting up, and turning towards the hills that hid the Valley of the

Kings, I could just make out the American House, its dark crouching bulk backed up against the rocks; the Winlocks were not due in Egypt for some weeks yet, so perhaps it was still closed up, awaiting their arrival; it was unlit, I saw. At Castle Carter, however, someone must have been keeping a vigil similar to mine: lights blazed from its windows – and I wondered if a wakeful Howard Carter was there, planning his next day's work in the Valley; if so, was he alone, or were Lord Carnarvon and Eve with him? What would they find tomorrow?

I returned to my cabin and, still wakeful, wanting to share the excitement I felt, I began on the first of my promised letters to Nicola Dunsire. I wrote: *Luxor, aboard the good ship 'Queen Hatshepsut', Friday 24th November 1922. Dearest Nicola ...* My handwriting was improving: I had nearly mastered italic script, and, as a parting gift, Miss Dunsire had given me a fountain pen. It fitted my hand perfectly. *Now Lord Carnarvon and Eve have arrived*, I wrote, as I reached the letter's end, *Mr Carter can recommence excavations. They begin tomorrow, which is very exciting! Miss Mack and I are making an expedition to the hills in the morning, in the hope of watching them at work.*

Meanwhile, the great news is, Miss Mack has decided to become a reporter. She has begun a book about Mr Carter's work. In the style of Mark Twain. If you'd been here, we might have laughed together about this – but you aren't, so I did so alone. Such a night, so many, many stars ... I'll send this letter to Athens, where you should have arrived by now.

Pour mon père, félicitations. Pour toi – à bientôt et je t'embrasse, ma chère Nicole.

'Can you see anything, Lucy?' Miss Mack asked. She was pacing restlessly back and forth between the rocks high on the barren Theban hills. 'Surely you can see *something*, dear?'

I could see dust. My binoculars were focused on clouds of billowing white dust. Occasionally, when these dust clouds dissipated, I could see below us the figures of Carter's workmen; some seemed to be resting, but a few were still plying their way back and forth from the dark square that must be the entrance to the putative tomb. Standing on a rise from which he could direct operations, was the thin bearded figure of Ahmed Girigar. It was ten minutes to four in the afternoon of Sunday 26 November – and this was the second of our reportorial expeditions to the hills.

At the behest of The Book, we'd spent much of the previous day in the same way, exploring the hills, selecting a suitable vantage point, picnicking and reading, while watching the events in the Valley below – historic events, or so local rumours claimed. When Carter had removed the infill protecting the stairs, he had discovered seals on the wall at their base – and they bore a king's name. The discovery, which suggested this was a royal tomb, even if it did not prove it, had given the excavators new heart. They'd pressed on at speed: the previous morning, they had demolished the wall and discovered behind it a tunnel of unknown length. That tunnel proved to be blocked off, packed to its roof with rocks and chippings.

Both yesterday and today, Carter's workforce had been excavating this barrier – or so we'd heard. And it seemed to be true: for two days, Miss Mack and I had watched huge quantities of flint debris being carted from a shadowy hole in the ground . . . not the most exciting of views, I felt. As I'd pointed out several times, there could be more tunnels and, for all we knew, they could *all* be blocked. They might extend two or three hundred feet into the rock, as those leading to the tombs I'd visited with Frances had done. Carter's workmen could be engaged on this task for the next week, the next month, *longer* . . . in which case, Miss Mack was in for a tedious wait – and so was I.

'I think they're slowing down now,' I said. 'Maybe they're taking a break. Not much seems to be happening.'

'Oh, for heaven's sake, child,' Miss Mack said, losing patience, 'give *me* the binoculars.'

I retreated to the shade of a rock, ate an apple, stared at the air. I was thinking of the meeting in London, which Miss Dunsire had described as 'the handover' when I passed from one protectress to another. 'Ah, *that* must be your guardian angel, Lucy,' Nicola had remarked, spotting the anxious figure of Miss Mack on the boat-train platform at Victoria. Nicola had looked her up and down, eyebrows arched, and then advanced, with me scurrying beside her. 'Don't tease,' I was muttering. 'Be nice. I told you, she's very kind – and she isn't stupid, either.'

'Miss Mackenzie. At last!' Nicola clasped Miss Mack's hands, kissed her in the French fashion on both cheeks. Miss Mack recoiled sharply and then, as I'd known she would, over-compensated. She talked. On and on, while Nicola stood by, appraising her, a bemused smile on her face: *So taken aback when she'd heard of the wedding ... Gracious! Didn't mean that, quite the wrong way of putting it. Sincere congratulations, overjoyed for everyone, the best thing that could have happened ... so kind of Mrs Foxe-Payne to entrust her new stepdaughter to a woman she'd never met and didn't know from Adam ... Rest assured, vigilance, best possible care, old Egyptian hand, firm friends, would ensure Lucy wrote regularly, and kept up with her homework ...*

I could sense Nicola Dunsire's amused derision, her deepening scorn. I crimsoned with embarrassment, praying she'd see beyond that torrent of words to the essential good-heartedness of the woman who uttered them. She gave no sign of doing so. She glanced at her watch, smoothed the lapels of the exquisite suit she was wearing, allowed her beautiful satiric gaze to dwell on Miss Mack's crumpled tweeds, her flushed complexion, her untidy hair escaping from its pins; she cut in on the word 'homework'.

'Indeed. Lucy must not let her standards slip. She must keep up with the work I've set her. I intend her to be intelligent.'

There was a tiny pause: the word 'intelligent' hung in the air like a sword. Miss Mack lowered her eyes. 'But Lucy *is* intelligent. At least, I have always believed so,' she said in a quiet tone. 'However, no doubt there is room for improvement, as there is for us all.'

It was the gentlest of reprimands – I wasn't sure whether Nicola even noted it. She gathered me in her arms for a farewell embrace. '*Improve each shining hour, remember, Lucy,*' she instructed, in a teasing tone, over her shoulder – and then she was gone.

In the heat of the Theban hills I considered the nature of shining hours. My plans were specific: I meant to return home and dazzle Miss Dunsire with the amazing progress I'd made while away. Accordingly – one poem, by heart, every day. I leaned back in the shade of my rock, opened the collection of Coleridge I'd brought and made sure I now knew *Kubla Khan* by heart. I did . . . *Caverns measureless to man*: would Carter and Carnarvon discover such caverns? Should I next learn sections of *Christabel*? I read on for a while, then closed the book and turned back to examine the Valley. From here, the view of it was magnificent: I could see its every twist and turn, trace the routes I'd followed with Frances, identify the tombs to which Herbert Winlock had taken us. The site of Carter's excavations lay close to the ramped entrance to the burial place of Ramesses VI. So the tomb he'd found – if it *was* a tomb – was situated, as he'd believed, beneath the workmen's huts, in that last unexplored section of his celebrated triangle.

A few of his men had been posted to keep any tourists at bay – though I'd seen very few visitors and the Valley was now deserted. The only activity had been centred on Carter's workplace, next to which a small white tent had been erected; but even this work seemed to be winding down. The noise of digging was intermittent, and the number of basket boys carrying spoil much diminished: perhaps Carter's workforce was making ready to down tools for the day.

My guardian angel was still on the alert, but I was beginning to lose faith in her reporting skills. So far, the gathering of information had consisted of these walks and a shameless attempt to interrogate our cook Mohammed, who, according to Miss Mack, would convey the all-important reactions of a man born and bred in this area. She had then discovered that he could be an even richer source of material: Abd-el-Aal Ahmad Sayed, Howard Carter's major-domo, encountered on our previous visit, was his uncle.

Mohammed, grilled at length that morning, had proved richly informative. It was universally known, he said, and had been for over two weeks, that Mr Carter had *already* uncovered a tomb. This discovery had been predicted by his uncle Abd-el-Aal and by all the other servants at the Castle, the instant Carter arrived from Cairo to begin his dig. Carter had brought with him a cage containing a bird unknown in Egypt, a canary; the servants instantly understood that, *Inshallah,* this golden songbird was a good omen – so they were not surprised when that first step was found, only three days after its advent. They'd been sure that the stairway then revealed must inevitably lead down to a tomb filled with treasures, and had at once christened it 'The Tomb of the Golden Bird'.

Unfortunately, and in circumstances that were opaque, this bird had been eaten by a cobra some days later. A cobra decorated the crown of all ancient Egypt's kings, so the snake's sneaking into Carter's compound and snacking on the canary was *not* a good omen; quite the reverse. However, Mohammed continued more cheerfully, the cobra had subsequently been shot by Mr Carter's good friend, Mr

Pecky Callender, on whose watch the disaster had occurred: he had dispatched the snake with two blasts from a shotgun. And this *first* golden bird had now been replaced with a *second*, brought by Lady Evelyn from Cairo; so perhaps the ancient gods would be appeased and all would be well.

In any case, Mohammed went on, in a more confident tone, it was well known throughout Qurna and Luxor that the current activities of Mr Carter and El Lord in the Valley were a blind: fabulous treasures, tons of bullion, had *already* been removed from the tomb and spirited away. This booty, which included a mummified king and his gold coffins, was on its way to England right now and would never be seen in Egypt again; it had been looted weeks ago, then collected from the Valley by a fleet of aeroplanes.

Miss Mack, who had been taking rapid notes, stopped him at that point. 'Now, now, Mohammed,' she said, 'you *know* that can't be true. Land an airplane in the Valley? That's just plain ridiculous. Besides, it may not even *be* a tomb, and they're still in the first stage of excavating. I watched them with my own eyes yesterday.'

Mohammed stuck out his lip and regarded her in an obstinate way. As I'd learned on my previous visit, the Egyptian notion of truth was often elastic and imaginative; it differed from Miss Mack's somewhat hard-line, narrow-minded Yankee approach. It did not always admit the concept of facts and, given the choice between two versions of events – one likely, unvarnished and dull; the other *un*likely, glittering and resonant – it went for the Homeric alternative. Miss Mack, who never appreciated such distinctions, became fretful at Mohammed's stubborn refusal to recant. 'Fairy stories like that,' she said reproachfully, 'are of no use to me whatsoever, Mohammed. The canary I like. The canary I can *use*. Thank you. But airplanes? I shan't waste a single *piastre* on *them*, I assure you!'

Mohammed pledged immediate reform, a newly industrious approach. Thus, while we we'd been up here in the hills, our binoculars trained on Carter's excavations, he'd also been working on the case. This very afternoon he was visiting Castle Carter, where he would cross-question his esteemed uncle Abd-el-Aal on Miss Mack's behalf. He would report back this evening. I sighed: I really could not understand why Miss Mack needed such a go-between. Why couldn't she walk up to Carter's castle and do her own investigating?

I had suggested this; several times. Miss Mack reacted with scorn. 'Lucy, I'm sorry, but you don't grasp the *methodology* of journalism,' she said. 'That approach would be premature – even fatal. No, dear – by indirection, find direction out. I'm laying the groundwork. I shall move on to *interviews* in due course.'

I stretched lazily in the warm sun and looked up at her with affection. The Book and its needs had her in their grip, I felt. We'd been up here in the heat of the hills all day. Miss Mack's hat was askew; her grey hair was dishevelled; runnels of sweat ran down her face, yet here she still was, untiring, dedicated, remorseless as destiny, binoculars trained on the Valley below. As I watched her and smiled, she gave a start; she adjusted the glasses and said: 'I *knew* it, Lucy. Something's happening.'

Turning to look at the dark entrance of the tomb below us, I saw she was correct. Excavations had finally stopped. Carter's workforce, some standing, some hunkered down, were gathered silently together a short distance from the mouth of the dig. His *reis*, Girigar, was now standing at the top of the sixteen steps, peering down, his attitude expectant. There was no sign of the excavators, who must still be underground. The westering sun lit the peaks above the Valley and washed them in gold; below them, the shadows were lengthening fast. As always, the kite birds circled the updraughts and broke the silence with their cries. I felt the first flutterings of excitement, but for a while, ten minutes, perhaps more, nothing happened; below us, no one spoke or moved. I glanced back the way we had come: it was almost five o'clock – we'd have to leave soon, before the light began to weaken and the long, steep descent through the hills became treacherous.

'Lucy, *look*,' Miss Mack said, and I turned to see the unmistakable figure of Howard Carter emerge at last from underground. He was walking unsteadily; he paused to mop sweat from his forehead, and then looked about the Valley with a blind man's gaze. Without a word, Miss Mack handed me her binoculars; by the time I had focused them on Carter's white distraught face, two other figures were emerging from the dark: Lord Carnarvon, who seemed similarly dazed, and Eve, who was shivering violently.

Eve wiped her eyes with the back of her hand and, in a sudden, impetuous way, embraced her father, then clasped Carter in her arms. Her father grasped both their hands; he seemed to be deeply moved and was saying something with emphasis. Carter made some reply and covered Carnarvon's hand with his own. He gestured to one of the boys, who came running with stools, and Carnarvon sank down onto one of them, burying his face in his hands. Eve bent over her father. Carter crossed to the thin alert figure of Ahmed Girigar. The two men, who had worked together so long, spoke briefly; Girigar, turning to his workmen, said a few quick words. Their reaction was immediate: first one man, then another rose to his feet; they lifted their faces to the sky and tilted back their throats – and in unison they released a haunting sound, that long guttural ululation peculiar to Arab ceremonies, that whooping cry that can signify rejoicing or lament; the cry that, in Egypt, accompanies births, deaths, weddings and funerals.

The unearthly howl swooped, echoed and re-echoed around the Valley like the voice of the long-dead; it pricked the hairs on the back of my neck, closed a cold hand around my heart – and if I shut my eyes now, I can hear it still, echoing down the decades: the crying out that told me Carter and Carnarvon had finally found their tomb.

27

The great discovery was confirmed for us later that day when, in a state of ebullient excitement, Mohammed returned from his fishing expedition at Castle Carter. He had hung around, he said, until seven o'clock when El Lord and his party finally returned from the Valley; he brought much news. Miss Mack at once retrieved her notebook and sat waiting expectantly, pencil poised. At once, words spilling over each other, Mohammed launched on his account of what had happened when, late that afternoon, the tunnel had at last been cleared of debris. The excavators had found themselves facing a second wall. Mr Carter had then, with the greatest care, made a small peephole in that wall, and thrust his arm through it, holding a candle—

'A candle?' Miss Mack interrupted. 'Why not a flashlight, Mohammed?'

'Foul gases, miss!' Mohammed cried. 'The air in the tombs is dangerous! If the candle extinguishes, take care . . . if it doesn't, Mr Carter can proceed.'

The candle had not been extinguished, it seemed. 'There is a little rush of air, miss,' said Mohammed. 'It is the spirits breathing out as they awake. After three thousand years, they are disturbed for the first time. The candle flame wavers, then it grows strong. Mr Carter widens the hole, just a small bit, the merest fraction . . . and he peers into the darkness beyond. What will he see? Another tunnel? More stairs? No, miss, he sees *gold*. Treasures beyond imagination. King Tutankhamun's treasures, lying there in the dark.'

He took a deep breath. 'Meanwhile, El Lord and his daughter are standing by Mr Carter's side, miss, filled with fears and excitements. They cannot breathe for the suspense. Minutes pass. Eventually, El Lord can bear it no longer and he says . . . Look, miss, I wrote down for you their very words. He says: "For God's sake, Carter. Speak, man. Can you see anything?" And Mr Carter makes a sigh and answers him. "*Yes*," he says, "yes. *Wonderful* things" . . .'

'Wonderful things? King Tutankhamun? Heavens above! Oh, Lucy!' Miss Mack clutched at my hand.

Mohammed then launched on a long description of these wonderful things, this unimaginable treasure, King Tutankhamun's gold, his jewels, and, gathering speed, he explained that today was a great day, but, *Inshallah*, tomorrow, Monday, would be a greater day still. In the morning, Carter's friend, the engineer Mr Pecky Callender, would tap electricity from an adjacent tomb. With the aid of electric lamps, El Lord and Mr Carter would then re-enter King Tutankhamun's tomb and explore it thoroughly—

'Re-enter?' Miss Mack enquired sharply. 'You mean they've *already* been inside it?'

'Yes, yes, yes,' Mohammed replied, with impatience. He did not like interruptions. 'Made the peephole bigger, then climbed inside. But there are two chambers, miss. Much to explore. Today, they only have flashlights. One quick look. Tomorrow, blazing electrics. Then they will certainly find the king's mummy. It eludes them as yet – but not for long!'

Miss Mack forbore to point out that, according to Mohammed that morning, the mummy had already been removed by aeroplane and was now in the Bank of England's deepest vault – or possibly at Highclere Castle. She waited. In a jubilant rush, Mohammed then explained that, such was the splendour of the discovery, the world would be beating a path to Luxor very soon. First, the officials would come, then the bigwigs, the High Commissioner, the Sirdar, the Mudir of Qena, the Maamor of Luxor, Wise Bey from the police, umpteen Pashas, a host of other excellencies . . . He paused for breath; Miss Mack, who had been writing rapidly, leapt in.

'Slow down, please, Mohammed,' she said. 'I need to get this straight for The Book. "Officials"? What officials?'

Mohammed, who had a taste for bureaucracy and its abstruse

ways, began to reel off details: the Antiquities Service in Cairo, he explained, would now be intimately involved. It was a solemn unbreakable rule that any excavator in the Valley must notify the Department the instant a discovery was made. Mr Carter and El Lord had done that; the Chief Inspector of Antiquities for Upper Egypt, an Englishman by the name of Rex Engelbach, had been summoned the previous Friday to examine the first sealed wall to the tomb. Having inspected it, he had enjoyed a convivial lunch in the Valley and had then departed for the city of Qena, where, unfortunately, he had an unbreakable three-day engagement. He would not return until Tuesday – and we'd be sure to see him when he did, as he always travelled on a motor bicycle, a much envied, locally famous machine. Meanwhile, under the terms of El Lord's permit, an interim inspection was essential, indeed belated, in view of the breakthrough today. In Mr Engelbach's absence it would therefore be made tomorrow, Monday – by his Luxor deputy, one Ibrahim Effendi, a local man, husband to Mohammed's cousin's half-brother's aunt.

'And this is somewhat a tragedy,' Mohammed remarked savagely. 'Ibrahim Effendi is a grossly fat gentleman. He does not respect my cousin's half-brother's aunt as a husband should. I have umpteen run-ins with him since our schooldays. He is a fool and a bungler. El Lord and Mr Carter will dance jigs around him, confuse him utterly, and pull the woolliness over his eyes.'

'What nonsense, Mohammed,' Miss Mack said firmly, while noting all this down. 'I'm sure Ibrahim Effendi is excellent at his job. They wouldn't have appointed him otherwise. You must never allow personal animosity to distort your judgement, you know. Though the timing is odd here: it seems *very* remiss of this Mr Engelbach to disappear to Qena for three days at such an historic moment – what *can* he have been thinking of? Still, on Tuesday, I shall look out for his motor bicycle . . . A nice touch, that, I may well use it. And tomorrow I'll be on the watch for this Ibrahim Effendi – a large man, you say?'

'Elephantous, miss,' Mohammed replied. 'Wearing a red tarboosh, riding a mule. A lazy man, puffed up with his own importance. He will stay five minutes, write two pompous notes and depart. The instant he's gone, El Lord and Mr Carter will remove all the treasures from the tomb. They will have the rest of Monday to loot it.'

'Now, now!' Miss Mack wagged her pencil at him. 'That is positively libellous, Mohammed. As if they'd dream of doing such a thing! And just supposing for one second that they did – I think Mr Engelbach might have something to say about it when he arrives on Tuesday, don't you?'

Mohammed stuck out his lip and became obstinate again. In his opinion the tomb was so crammed with treasures – many *portable*, many *pocket-sized*, he stressed – that hundreds, *thousands*, might disappear in the period between inspections, and no one would be any the wiser. However, he continued, brightening, there would shortly be an official opening of the tomb: that was the custom. There would be a splendid reception in the Valley. The British High Commissioner, Lord Allenby himself, would attend, with many other illustrious guests. And hotfoot from Cairo would, of course, come the great Director of the Antiquities Service.

'Gracious! Monsieur Pierre Lacau himself?' Miss Mack enquired. 'Have you ever encountered him, Mohammed? Can you describe him for me?'

Mohammed was happy to oblige. He had never actually met this famous man, he admitted, but he had seen him on his official visits to Luxor. And he was not the kind of man you forgot: 'Seven feet tall,' he said. 'Looks like a holy man, hairy white beard down to *here*.' He hit his heart region with his hand. Miss Mack scribbled fast. 'A very wise man,' he went on, 'and a wily one too. El Lord will not pull the woollens over *his* eyes, miss. And as for Mr Carter . . . Ah!' He sniffed the evening air and gave a sudden cry of consternation. 'The dinner chicken is burning, miss. I must go.'

He disappeared at a run to the galley regions where his wife's nephew, a boy my own age, was in charge of our meal. We never discovered what Carter's fate at the hands of Monsieur Lacau was to be, but the chicken survived its rough treatment and was delicious; we ate it with the keen appetite engendered by our long walk in the hills.

'Monsieur Lacau is known as "God the Father",' I told Miss Mack, as we ate, hoping this detail might be of assistance to her. 'That's what the Metropolitan Museum archaeologists call him, you know. Because of the white beard, I think – and also his character.'

I thought back to that conversation over dinner at Shepheard's, the night Mrs d'Erlanger had disappeared. 'Mr Lythgoe thinks Monsieur Lacau is devious,' I went on, 'and Mr Winlock said he was two-faced, that one minute he was smoothing his path with the powers-that-be at the British Residency, and the next he was sucking up to his new-found Nationalist friends. They thought he'd cause trouble.'

'No gossip, now, Lucy,' Miss Mack said in a reproving tone, noting this assiduously in her neat hand. 'What *kind* of trouble might he cause, dear – did you glean that?'

I fetched my diary, so I could be sure of all the details. I flicked through its earnest pages: a description of Mrs d'Erlanger and her fast dress, of the two Englishmen forced apart by waiters at the entrance to the dining room . . . Ah, here was my report of the conversation. I read it out. When I came to the end, Mis Mack shook her head disbelievingly.

'Change the rules of *partage*?' she said. 'But they've been in place for years. In the case of a *royal* tomb, Lucy, the truly important pieces, the *pièces capitales* – the actual mummy, its coffins, the sarcophagus and so on – they automatically go to the Egyptian Museum in Cairo . . . though no archaeologist has ever found an intact burial, so that provision has always been academic, of course. But that is the only exception. Everything else is divided in equal shares between the Museum and the excavators concerned. You say Mr Winlock feared that arrangement would change?'

'Yes. Monsieur Lacau believes that system is wrong. He takes the Nationalist view. He believes *everything* that's excavated is the heritage of Egypt and must remain here for evermore.'

'Are you *sure* of that, Lucy?' Miss Mack's eyes had widened in surprise. 'The Egyptian Museum is stuffed to the gunnels already. Under that system, it would run out of space very fast; they sell things off *now*, in a desperate effort to cram in new discoveries. Are foreign excavators to cover the costs of excavation without any recompense? Are museums abroad to be denied *any* share of the objects they've discovered – things that would never have been found without their expertise, their funding, their years of labour? I cannot believe such a system would work.'

'Neither can Mr Lythgoe. He intends to prevent it. And he's already made his preliminary moves, too. He said the Americans and the British would pull out and cease excavating here if the rules of *partage* were changed. And once the Egyptians and Monsieur Lacau realised that, they'd back down.'

'Gracious me – how *political* it all is: I had no idea. I wonder if these proposed changes will affect Mr Carter and Lord Carnarvon now? I can't see how they could. After all, they're excavating under the terms of his current permit – and that stipulates a fifty-fifty split. I can't believe Monsieur Lacau can change the rules *retrospectively*, can you?'

'Mr Lythgoe seemed to think Monsieur Lacau was capable of anything. And Egypt has been granted independence, Miss Mack. The Nationalists will surely bring reforms, won't they? So perhaps the Antiquities Department's rules *will* change.'

'*Independence?*' Miss Mack gave an angry snort of derision; I should have remembered that, to her, this word was like a clarion call. She mounted her republican war-horse at once, and was off and away before I could say another word. 'One can hardly describe Egypt as *independent*, Lucy,' she said in fiery tones. 'Not when there is still a British High Commissioner, not when the Residency still dictates every political decision that's made. The British control the army and the civil service, *and* the Antiquities Service. It may have a Frenchman at its head, but it answers to British officials in the Ministry of Public Works, or some such dead hand . . . I can't see that changing, even if they allow these free elections they're campaigning for now. The British will cling on to power, even then. So Monsieur Lacau may want to alter the system, but I feel he'll fail.'

She sighed and turned her republican eyes to the darkening hills. 'I think Mr Winlock must be overreacting, Lucy. I see little prospect of change.' She gave herself a small shake. 'Meantime, what a mine of information you are! The Book shall duly benefit. What a beautiful evening! Pour me some coffee, dear. I might have my cigarette now.'

She lit it, and lapsed into thought. The fragrance of strong Egyptian tobacco mingled with the scents from the Nile. We sat in silence for a while. I riffled through the pages of my diary, thinking of Poppy d'Erlanger and the last time I'd ever seen her; thinking of Peter and Rose. The silence was broken when Miss Mack gave a low cry and, scrabbling for her notebook, wrote an aide-memoire in large letters: *NB – The Division of the Spoils.* Shortly afterwards, she felt inspiration had come to her and retired to her cabin; her Oliver No. 9 began its clattering, so I knew The Book was in full flow.

I returned to my own cabin and wrote for a while. I brought my diary up to date, and wrote messages on the postcards I'd chosen for Peter and Rose: *Mr Carter has found his tomb!* I began another letter to Nicola Dunsire, from whom I'd not heard, as yet – but no doubt the post between Athens and Luxor would be slow. Writing to her made me miss her – and that made me restless. I returned to the upper deck of the boat and lay down on a bench under its awnings. I took with me one of the novels on the reading list Nicola had given me – Conrad's *Heart of Darkness*. I bent over its pages, deciphering its small print by the light of a kerosene lamp, pelted by the white fluttering moths that were attracted to its flame; lying above the waters of the Nile, but imagining the Congo river and another part of Africa. The hours ticked by; the gates of night slammed shut one by one. In the distance, as before, the crouching shape of the American House was dark and unlit and the lights at Castle Carter blazed.

The next day, the Monday, passed pleasantly – and rewardingly, as far as The Book was concerned. Miss Mack, accompanied by Mohammed, who had promoted himself to dragoman as well as cook, made an expedition to the local market held near the ferry landing that served the Luxor hotels. She returned with many bundles, everything from fly whisks to cucumbers – and told me that the rumours at the market concerning Carter's find were becoming more imaginative by the minute. Mohammed had translated for her. 'And Scheherazade herself couldn't have bettered their stories,' she said. 'By the time I left, Carter had found not one but several mummified pharaohs *and* their queens – a whole *hoard* of them.' She hesitated. 'And there were more rumours of *theft*, I'm afraid. There's a deep distrust of foreign excavators, Lucy. It's really quite alarming.'

I was sorry to have missed this. I'd spent the morning on the homework Miss Dunsire had set, calculating algebra, translating some speeches from Racine's *Phèdre*, while keeping an eye out for the promised passage of Deputy Inspector Ibrahim Effendi, en route to the Valley of the Kings. His advent, Miss Mack said, was of great importance to The Book, and must on no account be missed.

After lunch, Miss Mack and I were at last rewarded with a sighting of this man: he was immediately recognisable from Mohammed's description: large, wearing the coal-black suit of officialdom, sporting a red fez, mounted on a mule. He passed our *dahabiyeh* at around one-thirty, acknowledging Mohammed's shouted greeting with a lordly wave of his hand. He must have been more industrious than Mohammed had claimed: two hours passed between his disappearance into the mouth of the Valley and his reappearance.

Miss Mack had decided Ibrahim Effendi was a vital witness; accordingly, on his return trip, Mohammed lay in wait, blocking his path. Ibrahim Effendi reined in his mule and the two men proceeded to have a lengthy conversation in Arabic; baroque compliments and courtesies seemed to be exchanged. They parted with great cordiality. Mohammed then returned to the boat, his face fixed in a furious scowl.

'Quickly, Mohammed,' Miss Mack cried. 'What did he *say*? What did he *see*?'

'Pah!' Mohammed spat. 'Ibrahim Effendi is even more of a fool than I took him for, miss. He says they've found two small rooms only, stuffed to the roof with gold, as the whole world already knows . . . but no mummy. He tells me there is a sealed wall at one end of the first chamber, and the king's mummy may lie behind that wall. A *third* wall, miss! At once I could see that this *third* wall was a matter of the utmost importance! But El Lord and Mr Carter have not opened up this wall yet: they have not been *near* it, they have not touched it – or so they convince Ibrahim . . .

'"*Aha!* So, tell me, did you inspect this wall closely, Ibrahim Effendi?" I ask him at once. "Did you immediately go right up close and poke it about, the way *I* would have done? Did you ensure there had been no Britisher skulduggery, jiggery-pokus and mischief-making?" No, Ibrahim said to me, no, he damnation well did not: he is Deputy Inspector of Antiquities and he knows what he is doing – unlike some fool fellahins he could name. Besides, the path to that wall was blocked with treasures, golden thrones and marvels, miss – and he couldn't trample these priceless *antikas* underfoot. So he gives the vital wall the keen-eyed once-over from a distance. And then he leaves.'

Miss Mack wrote industriously. Mohammed drew himself up,

cast a venomous glance at the departing back of Ibrahim Effendi and raised a prophetic finger: 'So you see, it is as I, Mohammed Sayed, predict: Ibrahim is a testy man, quick to take offence. He is a buffoonery, who believes every rubbishy nonsense that is told to him. Trust me: the king's golden mummy is indubitable behind that suspicious wall, and by tomorrow morning Mr Carter and El Lord will have stolen it. That is the fact of the matter and I weep for my country. I weep also for my cousin's half-brother's aunt. Had circumstances been differing, she might have married *me*, and now she's saddled with that jackass.'

'Oh dear,' Miss Mack said, some while later; Mohammed had retreated to the galley, from which came the furious noise of rattling pans. 'I fear there is some *history* between Ibrahim and Mohammed, Lucy. I sense he is a little biased – what do you think? Still, he has made some extremely serious points. This three-day absence of Mr Engelbach is the nub of the matter. Mr Carter and Lord Carnarvon knew he'd be away. I feel they should have waited for him to be present before they entered this antechamber – yet they decided to press on. I'm not sure their permit gives them that right. People *might* say they were taking advantage of the Chief Inspector's absence . . . Gracious, how very difficult this reporting can be! One does not know whom to believe. I shall be glad when we see Mr Carter and Eve and her father – *then* we'll have the truth at first hand, don't you think?'

I did not reply. I was by no means sure such a meeting would elicit the truth: Howard Carter could be slippery, as I'd seen; Eve was open, but biased by the defensiveness she felt for her father, and Lord Carnarvon had the unpredictability of an aristocrat. With lordly disregard, he *might* furnish Miss Mack with the entire story of their discovery, yet he was equally capable of fine-tuning or disguising it. I did not want to crush Miss Mack's hopes, so kept these doubts to myself.

That evening, following our now-established routine, Miss Mack smoked her Egyptian cigarette, then retreated to her cabin to wrestle with The Book. I remained on deck, deep in *Heart of Darkness* – but that night my reading was interrupted by a strange and unsettling development.

As midnight was approaching, I heard the clatter of donkeys' hooves in the hills. I could hear voices, the jingle of harnesses, carrying clearly in the desert air. Looking up from my page, I saw lights from lanterns and torches, moving between Carter's house and the track beyond. I realised that a group of people were riding away from Castle Carter – several of them, to judge from the number of lanterns. Assuming they must be visiting guests, I expected them to take the track that led down to our houseboat, to the river and on to Luxor; to my astonishment, they took the opposite way, turning onto the track that led up to the Valley of the Kings. I watched them mount this path until they rounded the rocks at the Valley's mouth and disappeared from view. Shortly after the lanterns vanished, all the lights at Castle Carter went out.

I could scarcely believe what I'd seen: why would anyone risk the Valley in the dark, at night? I stayed on deck, watching for the return of the riders. The hours passed, tiredness crept upon me, and I fell asleep over my book.

I woke as dawn was breaking: my watch said it was half past four. I was cold and stiff. I sat up and rubbed my eyes, only to find I was not alone; Miss Mack had joined me. Wrapped in a flowered dressing gown, she was seated near by; her binoculars lay in her lap, and her kind face was pale and troubled. 'I couldn't sleep, Lucy,' she said, in an anxious tone, 'I was worrying about The Book. I tossed and turned – when the birds began singing, I decided I'd never settle, so I'd get up to watch the dawn. Now I wish I hadn't, Lucy. Look.'

She gestured towards the hills and handed me the binoculars. I focused them and saw what it was that had caught her attention: a weary party of four, mounted on donkeys: Lord Carnarvon, Eve, Howard Carter and a tall, bulky man whom I did not know. They emerged from the direction of the Valley, picked their way between the rocks at its mouth, then headed down the track that led them the short distance to Castle Carter. Servants ran out to meet them, and all four dismounted. There were cries of greeting, then the group entered the house and disappeared.

'I saw them leave for the Valley last night,' I said, after a long silence. 'I couldn't tell who it was then, Miss Mack. But I heard their donkeys and saw their lanterns.'

'What time was that, Lucy?'

'About half past eleven.'

'You're sure of that?' I nodded, and she looked at her watch. 'They've been away nearly five hours. How very, very strange. To go to the Valley at night, under cover of darkness. To return at first light. It does seem— I fear it seems clandestine.'

She rose and looked down at me sadly. 'We must never speak of this, Lucy,' she went on. 'You do understand, dear? I'm sure there will be a perfectly reasonable explanation – and perhaps we'll hear it in due course from Eve or her father or Mr Carter, though we mustn't *dream* of asking them, of course. But at the moment, with all these rumours of theft already flying about – you do see, Lucy, don't you, how badly this could look? It could be very damaging. We must never, never speak of it – not to anyone.' She paused.

'I want you to give me your solemn word, Lucy.'

I gave it to her – and I kept that promise for eighty years. I told no one what we'd seen, not even Frances. I finally broke my word late that evening in my garden in Highgate, when – knowing by then it could do no harm, all the participants being long dead, the events of that night having in the intervening decades gradually leaked out, though not, perhaps, in their entirety – I told Dr Benjamin Fong what Miss Mack and I had seen, from the deck of the *Queen Hatshepsut*.

When I'd finished my account of a sighting that had taken on a dreamlike quality, as if it had been an apparition, Dr Fong sighed. 'The Monday night,' he said. 'So it *was* then. I'd suspected as much. It had to be one of two days. It could have been the Sunday night, but the Monday always seemed the more likely to me. They had the advantage of electricity in the tomb by then. They must have decided to make their move between Ibrahim Effendi's inspection Monday afternoon and Rex Engelbach's at noon on the Tuesday – and they couldn't risk being seen, so they had only the hours overnight at their disposal. So that is when they did it. *That's* when the deceptions began.'

He rose, and stood looking down at me. 'Will you tell me one last thing, Miss Payne, before I leave? When you and Miss Mackenzie finally met up with Carter and Carnarvon, with your friend Eve, did any of them mention that expedition, explain why they'd gone to the

Valley that night in secret? Did they tell you why they went, and what they found?'

'No. We saw them some days later, at Castle Carter. Nothing was said on that subject. Miss Mackenzie and I kept our secret – and they kept theirs.'

I hesitated, and made to rise from my chair. 'Meanwhile, it's late – and it's getting cold. I'm very tired. No more questions, Dr Fong. You must leave me now.'

To my relief, he did not argue. 'Of course,' he said. 'No – please don't get up, Miss Payne. I can see myself out. I know the way now.'

28

Our meeting with Lord Carnarvon, Eve and Howard Carter took place later that week, some days after the official, ceremonial 'opening' of the tomb. Eve finally 'ferreted us out', as she put it. Radiant with happiness, excited and nervy, she called at our houseboat, reproached us for not letting her know we were there, and invited us to tea at Castle Carter. She and her father would shortly be returning to England, she said: they'd be there for Christmas, and would return to Egypt some time in January – there was so much to arrange regarding the tomb and the way its excavation should be handled, but her father was anxious to see us before they left.

'Prepare for a surprise,' she said, her eyes sparkling, 'you won't recognise him, Miss Mack – nor you, Lucy! Pups is like a new man – so much stronger than he was in the summer at Highclere. Discovering the tomb has revived him – he says it acts on him like a magnum of champagne. I shan't say a word now, because I know he'll want to describe it all to you – and Howard will too, of course.'

I was sure that amiable Miss Mack would be a welcome guest at Castle Carter; I was less sure of my own welcome, given what Carter had said to me at our last meeting at Nuthanger. When we reached his house that day, I hung back shyly, half afraid that Carter would order me to leave. But he gave no sign of animosity, or even of remembering that incident. Instead, he bustled us onto his terrace, where a tea table had been set up and where Lord Carnarvon, Eve and another man were waiting for us. In the burst of excited greetings that broke out, he drew me aside and to my great surprise said, in his brusque way: 'You're looking well. In at the kill, I see. Been here long? Heard from Lady Rose yet? How's that little dog of hers?'

The little dog was happy and fit, or so Rose and Peter had informed me in their last letter. I told Carter this, and then, summoning my nerve, offered my congratulations. 'Blessed by the gods,' he replied, 'three days into the dig – and there it was. Unbelievable, isn't it? Lord Carnarvon will tell you all about it. Let me get you some tea. And before you leave, you must admire my canary. Not the first one that brought us such luck, but the one Eve brought me from Cairo – the golden bird who'll ensure our luck continues.'

He placed me in a chair next to Eve, who smiled up at him, and told me this canary was called Fidelio: it was a sweet little bird that sang from dawn till dusk. 'The first one did that too,' said the other man present, a tall, heavily built stranger, to whom I'd not been introduced, but whom I recognised at once as the fourth member of that secret night-time expedition to the Valley. He was standing just behind Eve's chair, puffing on a cigarette, his expression sorrowful; he seemed uncertain whether to go or stay.

'Oh yes indeedy,' he went on, in a reflective tone, 'that first canary carolled away. Morning, noon and night. Relentless it was. Until the cobra got it.' He thrust a large hand in my direction. 'Haven't done the honours. I'm Arthur Callender. Call me Pecky: everyone does.'

'Mr Callender is a very old friend of Howard's,' Eve put in sweetly, and with a dimpling smile, as she introduced us. Mr Callender trapped my small hand in his large one, gripped it hard and shook it manfully. 'He's the most – brilliant engineer, with many years of experience on the Egyptian railways. It's he who contrived to light the tomb for us and – and a thousand other things.'

'Semi-retired,' Callender put in. 'Have a farm now. In Armant. Not far from here. On the river. Sugar cane ... and suchlike. Old Egyptian hand. Out here too long for my own good. Hail from Lancashire originally. Know Lancashire, do you? No? Neither do I, not any more. Left when I was three. Been to Australia, by any chance, Miss Payne?' He cocked a nervous, bloodshot eye in my direction. 'No? Pity. Great place. Marvellous country. Yes, indeedy. Opportunities aplenty. I spent time there. Years ago now, of course.' He took a gulp of breath, stroked his pencil moustache, smoothed back his gingery hair and, having given this lurch of biography, lapsed into musing silence.

He had not been handed any tea, I realised – and no cup seemed to have been provided for him. Eve, who noticed this in the same second as I did, leaned towards Carter and said something inaudible.

'Oh, Callender won't be wanting tea,' Carter said, breaking off the conversation he'd been having with Miss Mack, tantalising phrases of which had drifted across to me. 'He's off on a walk – he told me. Going for a stroll by the river, aren't you, Callender?'

'Wouldn't say no to a cuppa first, old boy, actually. If there's one going,' Callender said mildly, eyeing the teapot and a cake that was now circulating. He caught Carter's gaze and seemed to reconsider. 'Except – well, maybe not,' he went on, his tone resigned. 'Time calls. The river beckons. Better shift myself. Nice to meet you, Miss Payne, Mrs – er – Macpherson. Jolly exciting times, eh?'

He ambled away and was shortly to be seen ambling out of the gates to Castle Carter.

'*Lancashire*,' said Eve thoughtfully, with another dimpling smile. 'Does that explain it? I'd felt *sure* it was South Africa. But then I'm simply hopeless at accents.'

'Heart of gold,' Carter said in a forceful tone.

'Lord, yes. Absolutely,' Carnarvon confirmed, with a tiny satirical glance at Eve.

'Callender'd give his right hand for me,' Carter said, even more firmly. 'Bit of a rough diamond, but a damn good engineer, nothing he can't contrive. If we'd needed to shore up the roof in the tomb, Miss Mackenzie, he'd have been our man. And when we start bringing out the things we've found – we'll need his expertise then. It's going to be a difficult business: the entrance and the stairs are narrow, you see, and . . . '

That was Mr Callender: disposed of. Carter, Eve and her father then began to tell us about the tomb, how they had felt, what they had discovered. All three kept speaking at once and, once they began, couldn't stop. Miss Mackenzie was listening closely, as I was; she could not, of course, produce her notebook, but had resolved to remember everything we were told for transcribing later that day. I could see she was trying hard; but very soon we were both lost, dazzled and confused in a bewilderment of riches. There were several magnificent gilded couches, one with lion heads; there was a throne, the most beautiful object Lord Carnarvon had ever seen in Egypt, its workmanship exceptionally fine: it showed Tutankhamun as a young man, with his wife tenderly bent towards him; there were caskets, golden chariots; strange white oviform boxes whose contents had not yet been examined – all of it stacked, higgledy-piggledy, under, behind and above; treasures undreamed of, all infinitely precious, their position frighteningly precarious.

'It was like looking into the property shop of some ancient opera company,' Carter said. 'And in this first room, which we're calling the Antechamber, there was an opening into another small space – we're calling that the Annexe—'

'And inside *that*,' Carnarvon interrupted, 'the confusion and disorder were even greater. It's another storeroom – everything Tutankhamun could have needed in the afterlife. We just peered into it, Miss Mackenzie. You couldn't have risked entering it. There are thousands of objects there, heaped on top of one another, tossed onto the floor. One step inside and you'd risk breaking the most astonishing, exquisite things. We're facing a gargantuan task. We'll need expert help – we hope the Metropolitan may assist us.'

'We think the tomb was broken into twice in antiquity,' Carter put in. 'That accounts for the disorder. We may have to revise that view, but that's what we think at present. One party of thieves seems to have been after the perfumes and the anointing oils, the cosmetic creams and unguents – they were priceless then. We found the containers they'd left behind. Glorious things, finely carved, made of calcite, alabaster, but they left them – all they wanted was the face creams. We even found their fingerprints in the residue.'

'And the other party of thieves was after gold,' Carnarvon interjected. 'We could see the places where they'd snapped statues off their bases, and tried to prise the beaten gold from the chariots and the throne.'

'Howard found this ancient piece of cloth, Lucy,' Eve said, 'the kind of linen the natives still wind around their heads to this day. It was just tossed down – and bundled up inside it were some of the king's beautiful, beautiful gold rings—'

'So we think the thieves may have been disturbed,' Carter interrupted. 'Caught in the act. Then, when the necropolis officials returned to the tomb, to restore some semblance of order, they simply left the rings in the thief's turban, just as they'd found them.'

'Oh heavens,' Miss Mack cried, 'you think the thieves were caught in the act, Mr Carter? Imagine it, Lucy!'

'I do. That is my belief at present. And if they were, Miss Mackenzie, we know precisely what fate awaited them. Torture. Impalement. A slow and a hideously painful death.'

'Oh, please don't talk about thieves, Howard,' Eve said quickly, and I saw she had paled. 'Please don't let's think of that, or of them. We can't be sure that happened – they may have escaped.' She hesitated, with an odd pleading look at her father. 'The *important* thing, Myrtle, is that the robbers seem to have taken very little, hardly anything at all really, almost nothing – and – and they've left us so much. So many, many lovely things. When we first went inside the – oh, it was the day of days, wasn't it, Pups?'

'The greatest day of my life, my darling,' Carnarvon said quietly. He reached across and took Eve's hand in his. There was a silence. 'Though there may yet be an even greater one, Miss Mackenzie,' he continued, in a careful, measured way, as if rehearsing his words. 'We may have penetrated only *part* of Tutankhamun's tomb, you see. Beyond the north wall of the Antechamber, which is sealed, as the first two walls were, there may be another chamber. We believe we may find the king's burial place. The Holy of Holies.'

'A *third* wall? The king's actual *sarcophagus*? Mercy!' Miss Mack coloured.

'That wall is *guarded*,' Eve said, her voice unsteady. 'Standing either side of it there are twin statues, of the king and his *ka*, and they're like – sentinels. They're life-size, deathly black like Osiris, with eyes made of obsidian. Their eyes glitter. They've been keeping watch for over three thousand years, and I felt they were watching *us*. I wanted to explain to them – *we* hadn't come to rob or disturb. We came – reverently.' Her voice caught and tears sprang to her eyes. Carter immediately interrupted.

'All that's in the future,' he said briskly. 'We shan't know what's behind that north wall for weeks yet. We can't think of investigating it, let alone dismantling it, until after the Antechamber is cleared. That space is extremely cramped; we can't risk damaging the objects there. They have to be recorded, conserved, removed to safety. We have weeks of the most delicate, painstaking work ahead of us. When that's complete, and not before, we'll investigate what's behind that wall. Its wonders – if such they prove – must wait. Meanwhile, we'll *hope*.' He glanced at Carnarvon, who, meeting his gaze evenly, inclined his head. 'Eve, why don't you take Lucy to see our little canary?' Carter added.

Eve gave him a grateful look. Taking my hand, she led me indoors; the canary's song could be heard at once. Its cage had been placed on the windowsill of Carter's sitting room in full sunshine; the little bird fluttered from perch to perch, fluffed up its bright yellow feathers, opened its tiny beak and sang with an astonishing, sweet musicality.

'Ah, Lucy . . . ' Eve wiped her eyes. 'I'm so happy, but . . . Everything Pups and Howard dreamed of and prayed for and more – their wildest hopes: and now they've been granted. Somehow that frightens me. I'm sorry to be foolish. It's just that sometimes – it's lack of sleep, I think. Howard has been so marvellous and – oh, doesn't he sing sweetly? Poor little prisoner. I wish I could let him fly free – but I daren't, of course.'

I waited quietly, saying nothing, remembering that secret night-time expedition, of which no mention had been made. I listened to the canary's singing and, after a while, I asked Eve who had named him. I could see she was tense with some hidden distress, and I thought such an innocuous question might help to calm her.

'I did,' she replied, in a distracted way. 'My father loves opera, you see, Lucy – and *Fidelio* is his favourite, so I named him for Pups. My father can be superstitious – he was desperately upset when he heard what happened to Howard's first canary. He saw it as a bad omen. So I hoped – *Fidelio* is a joyous opera, you see. And this is a joyous moment – I do know that . . . And you're joyous too, aren't you, my sweet?' Breaking off, she stroked the bars of the cage.

We listened to the little bird's outpourings; its songs seemed to help Eve recover her equanimity. Apologising for her tears, she then led me back to the terrace. There her father and Carter were in the midst of describing the Antechamber's opening ceremony, explaining that Lord Allenby, detained in Cairo by demonstrations and the worsening political situation, had been unable to attend, but Lady Allenby had represented him; describing the reactions of the Maamor, Wise Bey – and Monsieur Lacau.

'Couldn't bring himself to attend the same day as everyone else,' Carter was saying. 'Had to have his own private view the next day. Typical Lacau! But when he entered the Antechamber, *that* took the wind out of his sails – it silenced him. That has to be a first.'

'Come on now, Carter,' Carnarvon said mildly, as Eve and I reappeared, 'we're going to have to work with the man, you know. Lacau was perfectly civil to me. I think he was genuinely moved – overwhelmed by what he saw. Give him some credit.'

Carter did not reply to that but rose to his feet and turned his back. Eve, in her capacity as peacemaker, was swift to intervene: 'And Howard's friend from Cairo, Mr Merton from *The Times*, was at the official opening too, Myrtle,' she said quickly. 'We'd decided that he was the best person to break the story and *The Times* published it yesterday – it was headed *"By runner from the Valley of the Kings"* – so exciting! Now the whole world knows our secrets! We haven't seen the paper yet, of course, but Mr Merton says it's caused a sensation: Reuters picked it up at once, all the papers have cabled Cairo and they're sending their stringers to Luxor post-haste. Mr Merton's given us a copy of his article. It's marvellous, Myrtle, *frightfully* atmospheric and really quite erudite.'

'It damn well should be. *I* wrote most of it,' Carter put in.

'And a *tremendously* good job you made of it too,' Carnarvon said in his urbane way. 'Missed your vocation there, my dear fellow. But your chance will come, Carter ... I'm planning a *book*, Miss Mackenzie,' he continued, rising to his feet. 'There will have to be a full scholarly publication in due course, naturally, but that's a long, long way off. Meanwhile, I think a more popular, less highbrow account of my find might be the thing. Why let these journalist fellows make all the running? Carter could write it, we'd need to get it out quickly, capitalise on the news while it's still fresh, obviously. Yes, a book. A blow-by-blow report – there'd be a pretty good market for that, don't you agree?'

'A blow-by-blow report?' Miss Mack echoed faintly. She swallowed hard and blushed crimson. 'My goodness! What an excellent idea, Lord Carnarvon. A *book*. Indeed. Yes ... Gracious, is that the time? It has flown by – all so fascinating. So moving ... privileged to have heard it ... Our deepest thanks, mustn't detain ... Now Lucy and I really must go.'

She rose, caught me by the hand and began propelling me towards the garden at guilty speed. Carter, who'd been staring towards the river, said, in his brooding, abrupt way, 'Before you go, take a look at something. Then perhaps you'll understand what this means to me. I brought it here for safe keeping. It was lying on the floor, on the threshold of the Antechamber. When we entered, it was the first thing I saw. I nearly trod on it.'

And it was then he showed us an object soon to become famous: one that can be seen in the Egyptian Museum now, one that has been replicated and constantly photographed over the years: Carter had given it the name that is still used for it, Tutankhamun's Wishing Cup. He fetched it from the house, carefully removed its linen wrapping and held it up to our gaze. A translucent chalice, cut from a single block of the palest alabaster, shaped like an opened lotus flower, that Egyptian symbol of rebirth; it was an object of serene, delicate beauty. Its surface was incised with hieroglyphs – and what I remember of that afternoon is not just the evasions that were contrived, or any lies we were told, but Carter's voice, steady at first, then hoarse with sudden emotion, as he translated those hieroglyphs: *Tutankhamun, King of Upper and Lower Egypt, Lord of the Two Lands, Lord of Heaven*.

'I think he was a child when he came to the throne,' Carter said. 'Until now, you see, we knew virtually nothing about him: almost all traces of his reign were destroyed by his successors. He disappeared from history. But all the images we've found so far show him as a child or as a very young man. A boy when he inherited and still little more than a boy, perhaps, when he died.' And then he translated the words etched around the mouth of this boy's wishing cup: *May your spirit live ... O, you who love Thebes, may you spend countless millions of years, seated with your face to the cool north breeze, with your eyes beholding happiness.*

A version of that wish would, years later, be inscribed on Carter's own grave in a London cemetery. That day, I could see how profoundly it moved him. Since Carter hated to betray his emotions, he disguised this at once. Breaking off, turning aside, he said that was an approximate translation; inscriptions were not his field, and more expert deciphering than his would be required. 'A young boy praying to rest his eyes on his homeland. An eternity with a sweet cool breeze on his face. That was his concept of heaven ...

I prefer it to ours,' he said in a gruff tone. Keeping his back to us, he rewrapped the chalice and walked away.

Miss Mack and I left shortly afterwards, walking in silence, thinking of all we had seen and heard; the inscription on the king's cup lingered with us. I was thinking of the dead boy's love of Thebes – and wondering where my own homeland lay. Miss Mack may have been considering The Book, even the threatened *outbreak* of books: I knew better than to ask and she didn't say.

Descending the track that led from Castle Carter to our houseboat, we were arrested by the sight of an exotic species new to the area, one that would infest the Valley within weeks and would soon reach plague proportions – a harbinger: it was the first of the journalists.

His long legs dangling either side of his donkey, sweating and red-faced, wearing a white pith helmet that did not fit him, swatting irritably at flies, and mounted on a saddle that was clearly paining him, he was toiling up the track towards the Valley – and still had a long way to go. He was escorted by his elderly dragoman and by an impudence of donkey boys; they were lugging his camera, its tripod and other impedimenta. All their faces bore an expression I recognised from expeditions with that soft touch, Miss Mack: excited, scornful, derisive but keen to please, it meant they'd scented a rich new source of *baksheesh*.

'Christ, it's sweltering. I'm on a deadline. I need to wire my report by six at the latest, and to do that I'll have to get back to Luxor. How much bloody *further* is this blasted Valley?' he demanded, glaring at his guide as we passed.

'Two seconds from here, excellency! Very close now – just past this damnation big rock,' his dragoman cried.

Encountering yet another rival so soon after the first proved too much for Miss Mack, who uttered a forlorn cry of authorial anguish. Within minutes of our return, she had stationed herself at the Oliver No. 9. She remained there, punishing its keys, for hours afterwards.

29

Shortly after this meeting, Lord Carnarvon returned with Eve to England; there, the press laid siege to him – and he did not take kindly to this *lèse-majesté*, we heard. Somehow, his telephone numbers had been obtained by the Fleet Street scavengers. They telephoned Lady Carnarvon in the middle of the night, demanding 'updates'. They accosted his daughter, pleading for 'quotes'. When he had an audience at Buckingham Palace – both the King and Queen were anxious to hear the full story of his historic discovery – there was a new flurry of insolent calls: what had His Majesty *said*; what had been Her Majesty's reaction? Reporters hung around his London house in Seamore Place, Mayfair; they skulked in the bushes outside the lodge gates at Highclere; he wasn't safe at his clubs, at the opera house – wherever he went, some impudent hack clutching a dog-eared note-book would emerge to buttonhole him.

The final blow came a few days before Christmas when, just as he was about to sit down to luncheon at Seamore Place with his good friend, Dr Alan Gardiner – one of the world's foremost experts on Egyptian inscriptions, whose assistance with the new-found tomb Carnarvon relied upon – his butler announced that he had an unex-pected guest: Mr Geoffrey Dawson, the editor of *The Times*, was downstairs and most anxious to see him. He did not have an appointment.

'Dawson? Never met the fellow. Damn cheek. Get rid of him,' Carnarvon said.

Dr Gardiner intervened. He suggested that showing the door to the editor of *The Times* was akin to barring the Archbishop of Canterbury. Carnarvon said he'd boot *him* out as well, should he come between him, the Dover sole and the sublime Montrachet '65 that were about to be served; but Dr Gardiner was persuasive, and Dawson was permitted to remain. He was left kicking his heels for an hour and a half, but the two men did, finally, have the conversation the editor had so importunately sought. What he wanted, Dawson explained, was a monopoly on all news relating to the tomb and Tutankhamun.

Howard Carter told us this story on Christmas Day at the American House, over a lunch of roast turkey, followed by a Fortnum's plum pudding, sent with Carnarvon's compliments. The Winlocks had just arrived in Egypt: Frances and I had been joyfully reunited, and Miss Mack and I had been invited for the feast. The dining room at the American House had been festooned with paper streamers, a large lemon tree decorated with stars stood in for the Christmas fir and the room was hung with lanterns.

It was a large group, sixteen of us; it included Arthur Mace, the English conservationist from the Met's team, and Harry Burton: both men had now been seconded to work on Tutankhamun's tomb. Several other Met archaeologists made up the party, and we'd been joined by Howard Carter, who had ridden over from his house to join us. Albert Lythgoe and his wife were not there; they were still in London, locked in negotiations with Carnarvon as to what further assistance the Metropolitan might provide him – or so Herbert Winlock had told us, somewhat irritably. Pecky Callender was also missing: he was spending the holiday with his sons at his Armant farm, he'd said, and intended to have a 'knees-up' and a 'bit of a beano'.

It wasn't exactly a beano at the American House – things remained decorous; but there had been red wine with the turkey, and then sweet wine with the pudding; after that, we'd played games – Dumb Crambo and Consequences. Minnie Burton had obtained crackers, and we were all wearing paper hats. Miss Mack had an approximation of a red revolutionary French bonnet; Howard Carter had a gold-foil crown, crammed down over his ears; he was chain-smoking and began drinking whisky after lunch.

Once the games ended, he seized the chance to talk shop with Herbert Winlock.

Clasping my hand, Frances drew me behind the chairs ringing the fireplace; we knelt down and began stuffing the hats and feather boas we'd used as accessories in our Crambo game into the large chest where they were stored. '*KV, Lucy: out of sight and out of mind*,' Frances whispered, putting a finger to her lips and, hidden by the chair backs, we listened. Frances's face was tense with concentration and concern – the conversation began amicably enough, but its underlying tensions were apparent to us.

'So – that's the latest news,' Howard Carter was saying to Winlock. 'According to Dawson, *The Times* did a similar deal with the recent Everest expedition. Paid them one thousand pounds for rights to the story worldwide. For exclusive rights on the tomb, we'd get much more: it could go as high as four thousand. The *Daily Mail* would trump even that, I gather, but *The Times,* as Lord Carnarvon says, *is* the first newspaper in the world . . . He'll consult me before he makes the final decision. What d'you think, Winlock?'

'The Everest expedition?' Winlock's tone was dry. 'Not *exactly* the same, is it, Carter? No reporter was going to hike off to the Himalayas to cover that story – besides, that expedition never made the summit. This is different: it's a massive story already, and if you *do* find an intact burial chamber, it will be front-page news, worldwide . . . The journalists are already on their way to Luxor; there were three sleuths on our boat over, and two more on the train from Cairo. The manager at the Winter Palace told Helen he's never had so many bookings – they're flooding in, from tourists and newspapermen. The latter might not be *too* pleased to trek all the way to Luxor, only to find *The Times* had stolen a march on them. They'd be expected to sit around, waiting for whatever scraps it deigns to pass on to them, would they? I can't see that happening – even if it *is* the first paper in the world. And it might be tactful to avoid that kind of remark, Carter – you know, if you're speaking to *The New York Times*, for instance. Or one of the Arab papers. Journalists just might take exception to it.'

'Tommyrot,' Carter replied, refilling his whisky glass. 'The truth of the matter, Winlock, is that it's put your nose out of joint, our discovery. You'll pooh-pooh any arrangement we make. It's sour grapes. You can't deal with us stealing your thunder.'

'Well, you're certainly stealing my *team*,' Winlock replied, lightly but with edge. 'You've already snaffled Burton and Mace. You have the loan of Hauser and Hall, as well.' He glanced across the room at these two men, both architectural draughtsmen previously working for him, now redeployed to map and record the artefacts in the Antechamber. 'However, needs must. No doubt I'll learn to live with it.'

'Not much choice in the matter, old sport,' Carter replied, with a sneer. 'Like it or lump it. Your boss Lythgoe's orders. *I* found the tomb – and *I* take priority.'

'And *I* wish you all joy of it,' Winlock replied, in a tone that silenced even Carter.

The party broke up shortly afterwards. Frances's face was flushed with indignation; her love for her father was intense, and her loyalty to him absolute. I think her hero-worship of Howard Carter began to diminish from that day onwards.

'Oh dear, oh dear,' Miss Mack said, when we'd returned to our *dahabiyeh*, 'Mr Carter can be so *graceless*, don't you find, Lucy?'

'Not always. But he is when he's been drinking,' I replied. 'And he was knocking it back today.'

'Knocking it back?' Miss Mack gave me a reproving glance. 'Lucy, really! Where do you pick up these phrases? Though I fear it is accurate. On his third stiff whisky, dear – I'm afraid I counted. He was not sober – and he was unpardonably rude to Mr Winlock. It soured the whole atmosphere. Should I mention all that, Lucy – in my current chapter? The Book feels I should, but I'm not sure. It *is* Christmas. I don't want to be uncharitable.'

'Charity has nothing to do with it. You should write the truth,' I flashed back, flinging myself down on a bench on the upper deck.

Miss Mack's moral haverings often made me impatient; I could imagine how mercilessly Nicola Dunsire would have dealt with them. In honour of the Christmas lunch, I was wearing the dress she'd given me, and although it still fitted, the bodice felt tight and restricting. I'd had two long letters from her by then, letters I knew by heart, and she'd sent a Christmas present from my father and her: a single string of seed pearls. I knew it was she who had chosen them. I fingered them now, milky, glistening pearls.

Miss Mack gave me a long, silent look. 'Well, no doubt you are right, my dear,' she said at last, in a quiet tone. 'I shall bear your views in mind. I am sorry to have inflicted my uncertainties on you.'

I could see that she was hurt. She retreated to her cabin, but inspiration could not have come, for the Oliver No. 9's keys remained silent. I repented almost at once. I changed out of Miss Dunsire's frock, and after half an hour's deliberations, wondering why these sudden moods and rebellions seized me without warning, I knocked at Miss Mack's cabin door. When I entered, I saw that she had been crying. Flinging my arms around her, I apologised for being rude; I said I didn't know what had come over me.

'Say no more about it, Lucy dear. I've already forgotten it,' Miss Mack said, wiping her eyes and returning my embrace. She hesitated, and then, blushing painfully, continued: 'I'm very fond of you, Lucy; deeply so, as I hope you know – you've become like a daughter to me, and, and – the truth of the matter is this: it must often be tedious for you, spending so much time with a fussy old woman. You're a bright girl – coming on in leaps and bounds, whereas I can be slow and indecisive. Of course that makes you impatient. I'm no longer young, but I haven't forgotten what it *is* to be young, dear. You're growing up fast, Lucy – changing before my very eyes. So the fault is mine. You are no longer a child, and I must remember that.'

I did not deserve this generosity and I knew it: it filled me with shame. I kissed Miss Mack and brought her some tea, persuaded her to go for an evening stroll along the river – she loved these gentle forays, and only too often over the past days I'd churlishly and moodily refused to accompany her. As we walked, I silently resolved to make it up to Miss Mack and decided the best way to do that would be to help her with The Book. I'd say nothing of this plan until I had results to show for it – and it was easy to remain silent on the subject for, that evening, our walk was interrupted by an unforeseen meeting.

'Why, it's *you*, Mr Callender,' Miss Mack said, with surprise, as we drew level with a great bear of a man mooching along by the water's edge; he was wearing a pith helmet and his once-handsome, now-ruined face was hidden until we came close. She held out her hand to him. 'Merry Christmas! But I thought you were at your farm with your sons?'

'Bit of a mix-up.' Callender turned his sad, bloodshot eyes towards us, then back to the reed beds. 'They'd made other plans. Sent a cable cancelling. Got the dates confused. Young men do that, you know. So I celebrated Christmas on my ownio up at the Castle. Pulled a cracker. Toasted the King. At a loose end after a bit. No sign of Carter. So I thought a nice stroll along the river might be just what the doctor ordered.'

'My own feelings exactly!' Miss Mack was struggling to conceal her consternation. 'But Mr Callender, you should have said – you'd have been very welcome to join us at the American House, I'm sure. One more wouldn't have made any difference, you know.'

'Carter said if I went, there'd be thirteen at table. Can't have that at Christmas, can we?'

I was about to correct him – sixteen at lunch, as Carter knew full well. Miss Mack gave me a warning glance and I stayed silent.

'What a great shame,' she said gently. 'We'd have been so pleased to see you . . . What a beautiful evening it is, Mr Callender. So lovely and peaceful here by the river. Are you on your way back to the Castle? I think Mr Carter must be home by now.'

'No hurry. Just between you and me and the gatepost, Mrs Macpherson, it can be a bit iffy up there. I'm living at the Castle for the duration, you see. Well, I'm short of the readies, so there's not a lot of choice. And I don't know if you've spotted it, but Carter's a nervy sort of chap. Highly strung. Gets het up. Used to living alone. Used to working alone. Sometimes he likes company. Sometimes he can't stomach it. Under a hell of a strain at the moment, too. So I try to stay out of his hair. Don't want to irritate him.'

'Oh, I'm sure you don't do that, Mr Callender.'

'Expect I do. I irritate a lot of people. Never have understood why. I tend to the doleful – that might be it. I try to hide it. Yes, indeedy. But I don't always succeed. The tomb gets me down – I think it's that. It gives me the willies. Can't say so, of course; wouldn't dream of it. I'm lucky to get the work. Jolly generous of old Carter to rope me in, Mrs Macpherson. I do know that.'

'*Miss*. Miss *Mackenzie*.' She drew in a deep breath.

I knew what was coming, for she could never resist extending a helping hand to lame dogs; sure enough, the shy and awkward Mr Callender was quickly invited back to our *dahabiyeh*. There, as dusk fell, he sat for an hour with us on the upper deck, sipping a beer Mohammed produced, nibbling dates and pistachio nuts, his mild eyes resting on the river. He told us about sheep ranches in Australia and prospecting in South Africa. A lesser woman than Miss Mack might have seized this moment to pump him for information about the tomb and any further secrets that might lie behind its north wall; but that action she'd have viewed as immoral, as taking unfair advantage of a vulnerable man. I knew she would not countenance questioning him – and so, having fewer scruples than she, even then, I did.

'Why does the tomb give you the willies, Mr Callender?' I asked him, shortly before he left. I thought this a cunning gambit, one that might provoke revelations as to night-time expeditions, their purpose and outcome.

It did no such thing. Callender turned his kindly eyes to me, gave me a puzzled look and with transparent honesty replied: 'Well, it's all about the afterlife, that tomb, isn't it? That's why it's there, Miss Payne. And I don't believe in afterlives. When you're dead, you're dead. That's it, over and out, farewell, my hearties. So I look at all that stuff they left there for that poor boy, the boats he could sail, the food he could eat, the clothes he could wear – and it gives me a pain round the heart, just here.' He rested his big mottled hand on his chest. 'Because he hasn't used them, has he, not once in three thousand years? Never did, never will. Dead as the proverbial doornail.'

Miss Mack, whose views on an afterlife were very different, gave a pious intake of breath. She opened her mouth to speak.

'Someone loved him, though,' Callender went on, before she could interrupt. He stood up and looked about him, perhaps admiring the rose sky, the tranquil air, the river's eternal flow. 'They'd kept his things. A glove he'd worn as a child – it's a tiny thing: he can't have been more than four when he wore it. Toys he'd played with. A reed he'd cut as a walking stick when he was a little kid – someone went to the trouble to keep that, even labelled it, recorded when he cut it and where. That's what we all do when we love someone, isn't it, keep mementoes? I keep all my boys' bits and bobs. So they speak, those little things of Tut's — loud and clear, right across the centuries. Or *I* think they do.'

He turned and, having thanked us, ambled away towards the gangplank. Miss Mack, who had taken a liking to him, I could see, followed him to say her goodbyes; I did too.

'Crikey, jolly good view of the Castle from here,' Callender said, on reaching the bank. 'Lights on, I see, so Carter must be back now. Better head home, I suppose. Can't put it off for ever. In for a penny, in for a pound. Yes indeedy.'

'You must call in and see us whenever you're passing, Mr Callender,' Miss Mack said.

'Pecky, Miss Mackenzie, please. Pecky . . . '

'Myrtle,' she replied, to my surprise. 'Myrtle. I insist.'

They shook hands; Miss Mack's was bruised for days afterwards. 'A very sound man,' she announced, as we watched him make his way up the track. 'A rough diamond, perhaps. But a good heart. One can always tell, can't one, Lucy?'

She sounded very sure of herself: I didn't reply.

How do you weigh a heart? I asked Nicola Dunsire later that night, as I wrote to her in the quiet of my cabin, her fountain pen snug in my hand. Had she met Mr Callender, whom I'd been trying to describe, I felt she might have found him absurd. But then such issues as good-heartedness made her impatient: what mattered, she always said, was the possession of a good mind.

Events in the Valley moved very swiftly once Christmas was past; I soon found there was no shortage of information for Miss Mack. News winged its way to the American House, and there it was instantly discussed, in fine detail. The best time to harvest it was over tea, when Frances's father returned from his work at Hatshepsut's temple, and his fellow archaeologists returned from Carter's tomb in the Valley. Before they bathed and changed for dinner, they would all stretch out in the common room, unwind and discuss the events of the day. An hour later I'd be dispatched back to the houseboat, but at teatime the presence of children was tolerated — and quickly forgotten, so Frances and I could sit quietly, be invisible and listen.

I couldn't reveal to Frances or anyone else that Miss Mack was writing a book — I was sworn to secrecy on that topic. But Frances was as absorbed by the tomb as I was, so no explanations were required. Pent up with excitement as to whether Tutankhamun's Burial Chamber would eventually be uncovered, whether it might have been robbed or whether it remained intact, she was irritated by the discovery's numerous, and increasingly apparent, side effects. 'Well, I can tell you one thing about it, Lucy,' she'd said. 'It doesn't improve anyone's temper. All they do is squabble, morning, noon and night. That tomb is having a really *evil* effect.'

She made that remark to me one day in the Valley, to which we'd begun to make frequent expeditions. Miss Mack, ever alert, notebook and camera at the ready, made visits there almost daily, noting the increasing numbers of tourists and journalists, often sitting encamped among them, recording the procession of marvellous objects now being removed from the Antechamber for conservation and packing. The escape techniques I'd perfected in Cambridge the previous summer stood me in good stead: Miss Mack was so absorbed in her task, her attention so riveted by the glories on display, that it was easy for Frances and me to slip away. First it was for fifteen minutes, then an hour, then, gloriously, an entire morning. Frances and I could walk and talk to our hearts' content – it was as if we had never been parted, never endured those long months of separation. There we were, just as we'd always been: attuned, knowing each other's thoughts before they were spoken.

'Like sisters,' I said to her one morning.

'No, like *twins*,' Frances countered.

We'd creep back from these expeditions reluctantly, expecting remonstrations. They never came: Miss Mack seemed unaware of passing time; her watchdog instincts were blunted. Besides, as she'd said, I was no longer a child. This new status bought Frances and me the freedom of the Valley.

So intense was the interest in Tutankhamun's new-found tomb, and the secrets it might yet prove to contain, that the other tombs in the Valley were now neglected; few tourists and no newspaper men ventured beyond the new site, now christened 'KV62', and marked by a stone painted with Carnarvon's monogram, a curious device of two interlocked initials that resembled a skull and crossbones. Pushing our way through the crowds clustered at the mouth of the tomb, Frances and I could, in minutes, escape to the Valley's further reaches, and find ourselves alone in its heat and its silence. We re-explored the sites we'd visited the previous year and one day, it must have been early in the new year, we returned to the site of Siptah's tomb, where we'd watched Carter's excavations, on the day the storm struck the Valley.

It was Frances who proposed that route; I suspected she had an ulterior motive, and I was right. As soon as we reached the place where we'd stood watching the Decauville rail system at work, she caught me by the hand and drew me into one of the numerous small wadis that led away from the main track. How accurate her memory was! I doubt I could have found the correct place again, but Frances's instincts were unerring. Ignoring the snaking paths that led off right and left, increasing her pace, she led me around and between the hot bare rocks until, coming to an abrupt halt, I realised we'd reached the place where we'd buried our offerings to Isis and Nephthys – the *ankh* Hassan had given me, and the scarlet lipstick given Frances by Poppy d'Erlanger. There we were again, at the foot of the same tall rock, examining its blind impassive face and its scorpion-haunted tresses. With the toe of her sandal, Frances scuffed at the burial site we'd made.

'No one even mentions Mrs d'Erlanger now,' she said, frowning. 'In another few weeks it will be the anniversary of her death. Not even a year yet – and everyone's forgotten, Lucy. Well, we haven't.'

Frances inspected the stone. The heat beat down on my head: it was noon; I'd forgotten my sunglasses, and the sand dazzled painfully. 'Do you visit your mother's grave, Lucy?' Frances asked, poking at the stone. 'Does your father, now he's remarried?'

'I think he did for a while,' I replied. 'I went there last autumn before I left for Egypt.'

I hesitated; Miss Dunsire had accompanied me on that occasion; we'd taken a bunch of flowers from our Cambridge garden, rose-hips, the last Michaelmas daisies. I'd stood there looking at a name, at dates, trying to remember the timbre of my mother's voice. I thought: *I mourned her deeply for a while, then a little less, and one day I shan't mourn her at all. That's the pattern of grief, Lucy.* Miss Dunsire might have forgotten that remark of hers, but I hadn't. Now, standing by the rock, I traced the snaky fall of its limestone hair and tried to summon my mother. For a second she was vivid; then time began to occlude her. Frances and I sat down by the stone, and I told her all this. She listened intently, but with a frown.

'That's what she claimed, your governess? I thought you said she was so clever?'

'She is clever.'

'Well, she can't be so smart if she said that. She's totally wrong. That *isn't* the pattern to grief. It stays and stays. It worms itself deeper. And if she thinks it doesn't, she's never experienced it. You should tell her that, Lucy, when you write the next of your endless letters to her.'

I frowned at the sand, considering this advice. I wouldn't take it: I could imagine only too well the waspish rejoinder I'd receive if I risked it.

'Come on, Lucy, I suppose we'd better go back,' Frances said, hauling me to my feet. She patted the coiling limestone, then, taking my arm, drew me back the way we had come. 'I visit my little brother's grave once a year,' she remarked, as we retraced our steps. 'My parents take me. We go in August, on the day he drowned. It's a nice plain grave, Lucy, in a beautiful part of a beautiful cemetery, and his name's still as clear as can be. But it never feels as if he's *there* ... I often sense him in Maine, though, by the water. So does Daddy. And my mother. And I sense him *here*, which is kind of strange, because of course he never came to Egypt, let alone the Valley.'

She came to a halt. We were in sight of KV62 by then, though the tomb entrance was invisible behind the press of spectators. 'Look at all those people, Lucy,' she said, 'they don't give a dime for Tutankhamun, or who he was. All they care about is the gold they buried with him.'

I looked at Frances's small, intense and accusatory figure; she was wearing one of her irreproachable cotton frocks, a panama hat was jammed low on her brow, and she was scowling. Turning to follow her gaze, I saw a painted wooden manikin was being carried from the tomb on a tray; the crowds sighed and cried out as it passed, parting like the Red Sea before Moses, then closing in again. Camera shutters clicked. As we drew nearer, we could see the figure of Miss Mack on the edge of the crowd, fanning herself, and could just make out the spruce figure of Howard Carter, tweed-suited and Homburg-hatted, escorting the manikin to the conservation laboratory.

It was a depiction of the king as a small child, Miss Mack told us: a marvel of portraiture, why, it made the little boy so real, she felt she could have sat right down and had a talk with him. She began to make copious notes. The crowd, having taken pictures as the manikin passed, lost interest. Some clustered around the mouth of the tomb, in eager anticipation of the next object to be carried forth; some sought pockets of shade and unwrapped picnic sandwiches. There were complaints as to the heat, the lack of seating and the tedium. 'That statue was *chipped*,' a woman was saying to her husband. 'And I really do think they could speed things up a bit. Why does it all take so *long*?' From the conservation lab tomb came the sound of Carter's voice, raised in angry vituperation.

Frances made a face. 'I told you,' she said, 'the greatest find in the Valley ever made, and all anyone does is argue and complain. It's brought out the worst in everyone, that tomb . . . And there's no escaping it either,' she added, 'it's just as bad at Castle Carter, and it's even worse at the American House. It's like a disease, Lucy. Daddy calls it the Pestilence.'

Whether the tomb was entirely to blame for this state of affairs, I doubted; there were other irritants, especially within the American House itself. Frances's mother Helen had contracted a mild fever en route to Luxor, and she could not shake it off. She spent days in her room, resting. Mrs Lythgoe, senior wife, usually there to rule the roost, was still in London, where her husband continued to negotiate with Carnarvon.

In her absence, and with Helen Winlock too unwell to resist, Minnie Burton rose up in triumph, seizing her chance to reorganise the entire house, redeploy the servants and improve the menus. She had always felt, she said, that Mrs Lythgoe and Helen were unambitious: they simply didn't try hard enough and were far too indulgent with the staff. Yes, the head cook, Michael-Peter Sa'ad, was Nubian, and his experience of Western food was limited; yes, Sa'ad could be obstinate, but – using *her* recipe – he had cooked the Christmas turkey and, if he could do that, why baulk at shortbread? Or scones? Or fruitcake? Now that Carter's discovery was bringing a flood of the famous, the well-connected, the influential and the rich to the Valley, the role of the American House had changed. 'Sa'ad has to learn,' she declared. 'We are ambassadors. This house is now an *embassy*. This is *American* territory.'

I was with Frances at the American House constantly, so was able to sample Mrs Burton's reforms. Monday, the shortbread was burned; Tuesday, the cake frosting set like concrete; Wednesday, the scones were leaden. Frances and I spat them into our handkerchiefs; it was Sa'ad's revenge, she whispered. 'He can cook scones when he wants. But he *doesn't* want. And he won't – not with Queen Min bossing him about in his own kitchen.'

Sa'ad was a man of subtlety. He could hold his nerve too. The next day, he failed with a Victoria sponge. He went on to fail with cookies, meringues and brandy snaps. After some ten days of this, when he felt he'd tortured Mrs Burton almost enough, he went for one final turn of the screw: ignoring her orders completely, he sent out a tray of Egyptian sweetmeats. There were no guests that day, but the assembled archaeologists, exhausted by a day in the field, stared at these riches: crisp pastry, honey, raisins, nuts, a heady scent of cloves and cinnamon. Before Mrs Burton could say a word, they fell on them.

'Thank God. Something edible at last,' Herbert Winlock said, with a sigh of satisfaction. 'Pour me some more tea, please, Frances.'

'Delicious.' Arthur Mace stretched and smiled. 'I feel almost human again now.'

'Me too.' Harry Burton licked his lips. 'Sugar. That's what we need. In vast quantities and immediately we get home – our thanks to Sa'ad.' He turned to his silent, seething wife: 'And to you, Minnie. Can we have them again tomorrow?'

Arthur Mace was well into his conservation work by then. He was being assisted by an eminent chemist, Alfred Lucas, whom Carter had recruited. Fortified by sugar, Mace described to Frances and me the objects they'd tried to preserve that day. They'd opened up a casket, he said, which proved to contain exquisite beaded garments and sandals: the fabric was frail – one touch and the tiny beads scattered by their thousands. Lucas had suggested they pour liquid paraffin wax over them, then wait for it to solidify. It had taken them two painstaking hours to save one pair of sandals.

'How many more of them are there, Mr Mace?' Frances asked.

'God knows,' he sighed. 'We've only been through a few boxes, Frances. There could be hundreds more. Our next task is a walking stick, an exquisite thing. It's entirely covered in iridescent blue beetles' wings. *Loose* beetles' wings.'

Harry Burton was complaining about the problems of photographing inside the tomb, where there was never enough light, and the heat was near unendurable. He was working with a large-format camera, long exposures and large, heavy glass plates; he had a darkroom in a little-visited tomb, but it was some hundred yards from Tutankhamun's. The plates had to be wrapped, then transported fast to their developing bath: he had a minute and a half at most to sprint between the two tombs. At first, this had been easy enough – Burton was lean and fit, agile and fast on his feet – but as the number of tourists and reporters increased by the day, his task was becoming more difficult. The crowds *would* cluster around the mouth of the tomb, avid for the sight of treasures. They were supposed to stay behind the retaining walls Carter had built, and there were guards to restrain them, but even so Burton was now having to fight his way through the mêlée. 'Yesterday four plates got spoiled,' he said. 'Today it was six. It all had to be shot again – and that held Mace up as well. Carter was livid.'

'Bad news, Harry – it's about to get worse,' Herbert Winlock said. 'Take a look at this.' He tossed him the latest cable from Albert Lythgoe in London. 'Carnarvon *has* signed with *The Times*. Exclusive rights, worldwide. They raised their offer to five thousand pounds, plus seventy-five per cent of syndication profits, so they obviously believe a burial chamber *will* be found. Carnarvon signed yesterday – and he didn't consult Carter.'

'Oh God. That won't please him.' Burton read the cable, his face gloomy. 'But what does it all *mean*? I can't make head nor tail of all this exclusivity jargon.'

'It means that only *The Times* has access to the tomb, and to the excavators. All the other papers will have to buy their information and their pictures from *The Times,* and they'll get it a day late. So they'll get scooped on a daily basis – *if* they accept this monopoly, which they won't. Watch this little deal explode in Carnarvon's face. Lythgoe says it's already leaked, and Fleet Street's in an uproar. New York isn't exactly overjoyed either.'

'*All* the other papers?' Harry Burton asked sharply. 'Including the Arab ones?'

'The Arab papers get the information free – at least Carnarvon had the wit to ensure that. But they're as dependent on *The Times* as everyone else. They don't have access either.'

'Jesus wept. An Egyptian tomb – and they exclude the Egyptian press. What diplomatic genius thought *that* one up? Minnie, give me some more tea – two sugars, no, make that three. It's hell in the Valley now – can you imagine what it'll be like when this gets out?'

Minnie poured the tea. She was still smarting from her earlier defeat at Sa'ad's hands, and it was clear she did not share her husband's anxieties. With Mrs Burton, nothing succeeded like success, and any antipathy she'd felt for Carnarvon and Carter was now forgotten – they were the men of the hour. Lord Carnarvon was not due in Egypt until late January; in his absence, Carter controlled access to the tomb. If Minnie wished to obtain a visit for her fashionable friends, it made sound commercial sense to stay on the right side of him.

Minnie had been hemming curtains for Howard Carter, Frances had reported with disgust a few days before: 'And she got her reward too. That contessa friend of hers had a private viewing of the tomb the next day. Instant kudos for Minnie! She'd better watch it, though. Carter has no mercy, and Daddy says he *always* calls in his debts. He'll have her shopping for him next.'

'Five thousand pounds,' Minnie was now saying. 'Munificent. Quite a coup! I can't see why you're being so pessimistic, Herbert – or you, Harry. Why shouldn't Carnarvon make the most he can? He has to cover his expenses. The new car, the steel security gates, all the packing and preservation materials, his native workers, the extra staff he's taken on. He has Mr Lucas's services to pay for, as well as that lump Pecky Callender's. After all . . . ' She paused, giving a sidelong glance at Winlock, whom she did not like, as I was beginning to realise; perhaps the fact that he referred to her as 'Queen Min' had got back to her. 'After all, Herbert, Lord Carnarvon's outlay is heavy, and will be for a long time to come. We still don't know what marvels there may be if he finds a burial chamber. He could be looking at months and months of work, unending expenses.'

'How true. There's a difference between covering your expenses and profiteering, however,' Winlock replied evenly. 'That word is already being bandied around, Minnie, and you can expect to hear more of it. Money, money, money. Money for newspaper rights, photography rights – *and* a book, remember, which Carter is somehow supposed to cobble together in record time. Now Hollywood has been in touch, and the newsreels too; Lythgoe says Carnarvon thinks he can get at least ten thousand pounds from Pathé News alone. He's going all over London, spreading the glad tidings. He'd be well advised not to publicise sums like that when he gets back here. He's a millionaire many times over. And Egypt, just in case it's escaped your eagle eye, Minnie, is a poor country.'

'Fiddlesticks! It's his tomb. Lord Carnarvon can do exactly what he likes. He certainly doesn't need your permission or your approbation, Herbert.'

'No, Minnie. It is *not* his tomb. It belongs to the Egyptian government, and the sooner Carnarvon understands that, the better. He appears blissfully unaware at present.'

'I don't agree.' Minnie glared at her husband, who was making pacifying faces. 'It's all very well for you to preach, Herbert: you have the Met to cover the costs of your dig. Carnarvon is just one man, a private individual. His expenses are rocketing by the day—'

'Are they indeed?' Winlock said coldly. 'How lucky that he isn't paying for Hauser and Hall's work, Minnie. How fortunate he doesn't have to cover your husband's salary, or Mace's. Thank God he gets the services of the Met's experts for nothing. We wouldn't want dear Lordy bankrupted, would we?'

'No, we wouldn't,' Minnie replied, with spirit. 'And that remark is beneath you. The Met's generosity will be rewarded. There will be a quid pro quo: Lord Carnarvon has made that *perfectly* clear. When the finds are finally divided, we will get our fair share. Carnarvon has said he'll ensure the Met is *well* taken care of. We all know that.'

'Then you know more than I do,' Winlock replied acidly. 'If Monsieur Lacau and his Nationalist buddies get their way, the entire contents of that tomb will go straight to Cairo, down to the last ivory hairpin. It will all remain in Egypt and Carnarvon won't get a thing. What happens to your quid pro quo then, Minnie?'

Shortly after that difficult conversation ('You see what I mean, Lucy?' Frances had said. 'It's like living in a hornet's nest'), Winlock's predictions swiftly came true – or some of them. By late January the Valley was swarming with journalists, all bent on outwitting *The Times,* all dispatched by editors who had no intention of accepting its monopoly.

Their headquarters was the Winter Palace Hotel. They were spending money like water, Mohammed reported gleefully. The amount of *baksheesh* they were prepared to scatter around was astonishing; each one of them had his own dragoman, his own clutch of donkey boys, all doubling up as spies and informers. The rate for donkey hire to the Valley had trebled inside a week and quadrupled within a fortnight. Several of the reporters had fought in the war, or been correspondents on the Western front: they approached the story of the tomb with military zeal. At night, they spied, danced, drank, partied – the Winter Palace was enjoying the most glamorous season it had ever known, people said, so there was plenty of opportunity. Next day, these men bravely shook off their hangovers: Carter's team began work early, and so did they. At eight in the morning Miss Mack and I would see them, mounted on mules, wearing a strange assortment of headgear, riding full trot from the ferry landing. They'd pass our boat, their outriders and spies clustered around them, and make for the Valley. '*Early bird, first worm,*' they'd cry, and, '*Onwards the cavalry!*'

They'd then take up their positions at the tomb, where a pecking order had quickly been established, with the *Daily Telegraph,* the *Mail, Express* and *Post* taking the front row of the circle, as it were, opera glasses at the ready. There they would sit, on or next to Carter's retaining wall, as the sun rose higher in the sky, and the merciless heat of the Valley began to roast them. Since they could neither enter the tomb, nor interview anyone connected to it, all they could do was note the parade of objects being removed from it. That was the extent of their news.

By mid-morning, the press representatives would be joined by the tourists. Cook's were laying on extra steamboats from Cairo to cope with the unprecedented demand, and the number of visitors was increasing exponentially. The journalists found this displeasing: it was not helpful, they felt, nor did it befit their dignity as newspapermen to be elbowed aside and crushed by crowds of ignorant rubberneckers who failed to understand that the gentlemen of the press took priority. Scuffles began to break out, as tempers frayed in the heat.

'Perhaps you don't understand,' Bradstreet of the *Post* and *New York Times* had said to a party of tourists alleged to hail from Huddersfield, 'this is world news, and *I* am here to report it. My articles are syndicated to forty newspapers in England, ten in Australia, nine in Canada, twelve in India and one hundred and four in the United States of America. To the furthest reaches of the British Empire. From sea to shining sea, sir. So kindly do *not* stick your elbow in my ribs, and you, madam, kindly do not block my view with that infernal hat of yours.'

'Don't you take that tone with *me*,' the man replied, squaring up. 'Stand on my toes once more, you blighter, and I'll punch your fat snout. And watch it when you speak to my missus. Or I'll flatten you.'

This riposte was joyfully seized upon by Bradstreet's journalistic rivals; they broadcast it, with embellishments, around Luxor — Frances and I heard at least three versions of it. But that was in the early days, when they *were* still rivals. As time passed, and the news they were able to glean remained pitiably small — when they all began to receive crushingly sarcastic cables from their editors, pointing out the pathetic starved inadequacy of the stories they were filing; when the fact that from day one they were being scooped by Merton of *The Times* rankled, then festered — there came a change. A quartet of the leading journalists decided to pool their resources: they became sworn blood brothers, dedicated to uncovering the truth. They were calling themselves the Four Musketeers, we heard. Shortly this changed: they were now known as the Combine.

'And the Combine means business,' Herbert Winlock reported to Miss Mack one hot afternoon on our houseboat. Helen Winlock had almost recovered from her bouts of fever by then, and he had brought her and Frances to have tea with us. Helen's improved health had restored his spirits; he was enjoying the journalistic fray.

The press knew, he said, that once Carnarvon returned to the Valley, and he was due from Cairo any day now, things would hot up. Their daily pilgrimage to the tomb had given them one solitary but useful lead: they knew that the clearing of the Antechamber was nearing completion. Once it was emptied, the excavators would tackle that mysterious third wall; it would, at long last, be breached – and then the world would discover whether or not the first intact burial chamber of an Egyptian king ever found lay behind it. *That* story was the great prize – and the Combine intended to break it.

'Will there be another official opening, when they remove that wall, Daddy?' Frances asked, as she and I passed cups of tea.

'There certainly will. And it's going to be quite something.'

Miss Mack leaned forward. She never forgot the demands of The Book, even when the taking of notes was impossible. 'An official opening for the inner chamber? Do you know, Herbert, when – exactly when – this will happen?'

'I do, Myrtle. But my lips are sealed. Sorry, sworn to secrecy. *The Times* will cover the great day – but apart from that, it's a news blackout. Carter's terrified the date will leak. The Combine has eyes and ears everywhere.'

The ringleader of the Combine, he went on, was the special correspondent sent out by Reuters, one Valentine Williams. The handsome, dashing Mr Williams wrote books – spy stories, or 'shockers' – but was a seasoned reporter and an indefatigable newshound. Some weeks before, on discovering that Lord Carnarvon and Eve were about to return to Egypt, he'd booked a passage on the same boat for himself and his wife. Together they had approached Carnarvon and Eve in the bar of the *Adriatic*, and then stuck to them like limpets for the remainder of the voyage. This imaginative tactic had amused Carnarvon, but got Williams nowhere. He'd been getting nowhere in Luxor too – and that had made him all the more determined, Winlock said, grinning. 'Williams intends to break the story of the inner chamber. He says he'll scoop *The Times* if it kills him.'

Williams was backed up by three other senior reporters, we learned: there was a man called H. V. Morton from the *Daily Express*, a Fleet Street star, one of Lord Beaverbook's finest, author of several bestselling travel books. There was Mr Bradstreet, a tricky customer, stirring up trouble via *The New York Times*. And there was Lord Rothermere's secret weapon, special correspondent for the *Daily Mail*, one Arthur Weigall. Like those of his fellow Combine recruits, his reports were internationally syndicated.

'Carter and Carnarvon need to watch their backs with Weigall,'

Winlock went on. 'He writes romantic novels and works of popular Egyptology now. But he used to work in Egypt. He was an Inspector for the Department of Antiquities, back in the halcyon days before the war. It was Weigall who oversaw Carnarvon's first dig and ensured he was given a lousy unrewarding site to work on too. Weigall has no time for gentlemen excavators – and no time for Carter, either. They loathe one another and have done for years – which doesn't bode well.'

'At daggers drawn, Lucy,' Frances whispered. 'You remember: we saw Mr Weigall in the Valley. He's the short, fat, pink-faced one. Jovial, but kind of smarmy.'

There was a silence. Miss Mack was staring forlornly at the hills. 'What a great many books these reporters have written,' she remarked, in an unhappy tone. 'Do you think they'll be planning *more* books, Herbert – about Tutankhamun's tomb, for instance?'

'Books by the barrowload, I expect. Imagine the potential sales – there were five thousand visitors to the Valley yesterday, did you hear? "Tutmania", Myrtle, that's what they're calling it. And that's *before* we know whether Tutankhamun's actually buried there. If Carter finds an intact burial chamber . . . well, you can imagine.'

'Do you believe that Mr Carter *will* find an intact burial, Daddy?' Frances put in dreamily. She had been staring at the Nile and now stirred restlessly.

'What, the king himself, in all his funeral finery?' A shadow passed across Winlock's face. 'Well now, Frances, my hunch is that Carter just *might* . . . and I truly hope he does. I'd like to live to see that. Faustian stuff – I'd darn near sell my soul for it.'

'You should keep quiet about those hunches of yours, darling,' Helen said, quietly.

'So I should! I mustn't speculate. A couple more weeks and we'll all know the truth.' In his easy way, Winlock altered tack. 'Meanwhile, to return to Arthur Weigall . . . Carter and Carnarvon should take care with him. He's clever and unscrupulous – and what's more, he's a close friend of Rex Engelbach's. Engelbach is furious with the way things are being handled at the tomb: the secrecy, the difficulties created when he tries to make routine inspections. He'll pass on those concerns. In fact, I'd lay good money it's thanks to him and Weigall that the Combine is now taking a new angle.'

'And that is?' Miss Mack asked.

'Oh, causing as much trouble politically as possible,' Winlock replied, suddenly irritable. 'Cosying up to the Nationalists in Cairo. Stirring up the Arab newspapers. This deal with *The Times* was a disaster, Myrtle. It's ensured that the rest of the press coverage is hostile. Carter and Carnarvon need to build bridges fast. I've tried to get Carter to see that, but there's not much he can do: it's Carnarvon who makes the decisions. Infallibly the wrong ones. Lordy is so insulated by his wealth and his class that he just can't see how damaging those decisions are. He has nothing but contempt for bureaucrats; he resents Egyptian officialdom. He's been able to snap his fingers at the world for his entire life, Myrtle. Why stop now?'

'Maybe all this adverse publicity will change his ways?' Helen suggested. 'What they're writing now is pretty incendiary.'

'I doubt it. Carnarvon finds it amusing. One in the eye for all those grubby journalists he so despises. The ones who work for a living. The ones who aren't gentlemen.'

'I think you're wrong, Mr Winlock,' I said, finding my voice, speaking for the first time and surprising everyone, myself included. 'Lord Carnarvon might even *like* journalists. I don't think he minds whether someone's a "gentleman". One of his closest friends is a jockey, Eve told me. He doesn't care tuppence about class distinctions.'

'Really? You sure could have fooled me,' said Winlock.

Who do you think was right, Nicola – Mr Winlock or me? I wrote later that night, Miss Dunsire's fountain pen clasped tight in my hand. I inspected the paragraphs I'd already written: my italic script was near perfect now, as Nicola herself had remarked in her last letter to me. Let her be the arbiter, I thought – and imagined my pages winging their way to her. She and my father were renting an apartment in Athens, with a view of the Acropolis, she'd told me in her last letter, received six days before: *And I have never loved a place more than I do this. After your father leaves for the library, I sit on the balcony and wait for the maid, who is called Iphigenia and – even better – is married to a man called Achilles. She brings me strong coffee and little rolls and the letters – and if it is a very good day, there is one from you. I store up its contents and carry them about with me – and it makes me invincible.*

I need that because, in truth, I have one or two small worries: my mother has been ill, this time genuinely so, I believe, and is pestering me to go to Provence, and Clair (Clair the bicycle thief as you called her) writes to say — oh who knows? Some litany of misfortunes. So I am a bad woman, Lucy, and toss these complaints aside, and turn back to your letters. What an age they take to reach me! But we'll be moving on to Paris next week, where they'll reach me more quickly — and once I'm there, it won't be long until you and I are reunited. The end of February! I am counting the days, Lucy — are you?

Write to me at once, and bring me up to date with all these excitements at the tomb. Give me the latest instalment on Miss Mack. Poor lady! Not cut out to be a writer, I'm afraid. Writers need hearts of stone. And, just occasionally, the capacity to think is of assistance to them. Tell me, is she still pressing on with this absurd project, or has she realised that this silly Book of hers is doomed?

Miss Mack had not realised this; quite the contrary. My own loyalties were torn: I wished Nicola were less scathing on the subject of The Book — although her latest comments were mild compared to others she'd made. I wished I'd been more discreet when describing Miss Mack's writing travails. I hadn't meant to poke fun, let alone be malicious. I would watch my words in future, I decided; meanwhile, wishing Miss Mack nothing but good, even when she most irritated me, I wanted her project to succeed. 'Perhaps we haven't paid enough attention to the newspapers, Miss Mack,' I suggested, the day after our meeting with the Winlocks. 'If we went over to Luxor today to collect our post, we could stock up on all the latest editions.'

Miss Mack agreed at once: she *had* been ignoring the press coverage, she admitted. We made the trip to Luxor after breakfast. There were no letters awaiting us at the Poste Restante, but Miss Mack stormed the news kiosk at the Winter Palace without delay, and there was an unforeseen bonus to our expedition: we sighted the Combine.

They had forsaken the Valley for once and were plotting on the hotel terrace, waiting for Carnarvon and Eve who were now said to be arriving from Cairo later that day. Miss Mack felt an immediate need for refreshments: we were soon seated at a table next to the cabal, in earshot and able to inspect all four men closely. Miss Mack did so with zeal. I found it hard to take an interest — the recent dearth of letters was weighing on me and souring my mood. Nothing from

Nicola, nothing from Peter and Rose . . . The journalists were disappointing: four middle-aged men in hats, suits and ties. They seemed to relish the fact that many of the hotel guests crossed the room to avoid them.

'*Lepers*,' the one I recognised as Valentine Williams was saying plaintively to the short, fat man seated next to him. 'Social lepers, that's what we've become, Weigall. Carnarvon's packed the hotel with his friends and supporters. That's why they're all giving us the cold shoulder. Sassoon cut me at breakfast, and I've know him since prep school. Who's that old trout in the corner? She's got her beady eye on us.'

'Lady Pemberley, Carnarvon's cousin. She's a close friend of the mater's. She's bound to know something – and I just might have an in there, old boy.' Weigall lifted his hand in salute; the dowager raised her lorgnette, stared him down and turned her back on him.

Weigall sniggered. 'Oh, Lord. Won't be getting much info out of *her* by the look of it.'

'We're not getting much info out of *anyone*,' Valentine Williams replied tetchily. 'Now I really know how ostracism feels. It's giving me the pip. I might require medicine.'

The Combine reporters agreed that medicine was a good idea all round. As Miss Mack and I left, weighed down with newsprint, four large brandies had just reached their table. It was eleven o'clock in the morning. This eccentricity visibly cheered Miss Mack. 'Frankly, Lucy,' she said with asperity, 'the Combine is *not* impressive. I don't see any of *them* writing books. I'm surprised they can manage two-hundred-word articles.'

She revised this view rapidly when, on returning to our houseboat, she read the papers she'd bought. I sat there trying to fight the irritability and moodiness that had yet again seized hold of me. Miss Mack scanned the articles. With a sigh, she passed me the *Express*, *Mail*, *Post* and *New York Times*. 'Oh dear, they speak with one voice, Lucy. I have to admit, they do marshal their facts in a persuasive way. Also, they seem to have done quite a lot of *digging*.'

Indeed they had. The Combine might have been cold-shouldered by the well-heeled, pro-Carnarvon guests at the Winter Palace, but others, it seemed, had been only too keen to speak to them. These people were cloaked in anonymity, but reading between the lines I suspected that Rex Engelbach might have talked, and Ibrahim Effendi might have seconded him: *someone* had been singing – warbling away like Carter's canary.

The charges were uniform, and as follows:

1 Lord Carnarvon and Mr Carter had not observed protocol when first entering the Antechamber: a government inspector should have been present and was not. This contravened the terms of Carnarvon's permit. As a spokesman from the Antiquities Department confirmed, further breaches could lead to that permit's withdrawal, and all rights in the tomb reverting to the government.

2 Lord Carnarvon's agreement with *The Times* laid him open to accusations of profiteering. It had been an act of profound insensitivity to exclude Egyptian reporters; to exclude *all* reporters created the impression, no doubt erroneous, that the excavators had something to hide.

3 Among 'the native population' it was widely believed that the excavators had removed priceless *antika* from the tomb. Such rumours would be more easily rebutted if the government inspectors were allowed free access to it. These allegations of theft were without foundation, but were damaging to British interests in Egypt. As a spokesman confirmed, they were viewed with the very gravest concern, in government circles and at the British Residency.

4 Such issues must be urgently addressed before the formal opening of the tomb's inner chamber. Any discovery made then must be handled with a sensitivity and openness lacking thus far. If not, it could prove the spark that would blow the magazine that was Egypt sky high. Lord Carnarvon should heed this warning, which the newspapers concerned offered with all due humility.

'Do you think newspapers employ *lawyers*, Lucy?' Miss Mack asked. 'Some of it has that weaselly attorney sound, dear, don't you find? Did you see any positive comments?'

'There's a couple of mentions of the conservation work – and how exemplary it is,' I said. 'And one of them points out that Mr Carter couldn't have formed a better team to assist him than the Met's. But *The New York Times* is asking what recompense the Met expects in return — *and* who is authorising it . . . Maybe that's an angle The Book might want you to pursue, Miss Mack?'

She did not take this hint — most of my hints passed her by, as I was beginning to see. She picked up the four Arab newspapers she had purchased. Unlike the Western newspapers, which were days old by the time they reached Luxor, these were hot off the presses. Mohammed was summoned and asked if he would kindly translate. He did so. *Al-Balagh, Al-Mahroussa, Al-Akhbar* and *Al-Siyasa* — all spoke with one voice: Britain had already annexed Egyptian sovereign territory including the Suez Canal and the Sudan; now imperialistic British interests were annexing the tomb of an Egyptian king. By what right did an English peer deny Egyptians the right to enter the tomb and investigate these scandalous proceedings? By what right was he claiming half of everything found?

'What if an intact sarcophagus is uncovered?' *Al-Mahroussa* demanded. Was King Tutankhamun's grave to be plundered by foreigners? Or would the current government, a weak-willed tool of the British colonialists, have the courage to rule that the tomb's entire contents, not one whit less, belonged in Egypt, the rightful heritage of its people?

Seeing Mohammed's angry reaction, Miss Mack sought to persuade him that Carnarvon was now attempting to solve some of these problems. 'I hear he's been in Cairo for days, negotiating with the authorities,' she said. 'They *are* trying to make special arrangements, Mohammed, so the Egyptian journalists will at least be given a tour of the tomb once a week. I believe even the British Residency is pressing for that now.' Her voice tailed away; she was aware, I think, that this gesture was hopelessly belated and insultingly inadequate. Mohammed regarded her with stony eyes.

'And what of the king's mummy, miss?' he enquired. 'Is he to stay in his homeland? When El Lord takes half the treasures from his tomb, will he want his share of the king's body too? What will he do then? Saw King Tutankhamun in halves?'

Miss Mack was silenced. Mohammed left us, and we sat for a long while without speaking. I stared fretfully at the Nile. I counted the multiplicity of houseboats that had appeared since news of the tomb first broke. I'd been keeping a note of their flags: today the tally was nineteen Stars and Stripes, seventeen Union Jacks and one Tricolour.

Miss Mack remained chastened, saying nothing. The accusations of grave robbery in the Arab papers had struck a chord with her: she had always felt that the archaeology of tombs verged on the sacrilegious. Rousing herself at last, she said that Mohammed's image of Tutankhamun's body, sawn in two, had shocked her to the core. 'I fear it is all becoming like the Judgment of Solomon, Lucy,' she said sadly. 'And the wisdom of Solomon will be needed to solve it, dear, don't you agree?'

'Wisdom is in short supply, so there's not much hope of that,' I replied snappishly.

Miss Mack's frequent recourse to the Bible grated: *not on* my *reading list,* I longed to say.

Miss Mack made no reply. Shortly afterwards, she retired to her cabin, and began banging the Oliver No. 9's keys. The noise made my head ache. For the first time in Egypt, I longed to be elsewhere: a balcony with a view of the Acropolis; Paris; even Cambridge – anywhere but here. Feeling entombed, I took myself off on a walk through the hills. This did not cure my mysterious malaise, so I fled to the American House, in search of Frances.

30

It was February before Miss Mack and I entered the tomb for the first time. No doubt we could have visited it earlier, had she pressed for an invitation as others such as Minnie Burton certainly did, but Miss Mack would not have countenanced such an approach – she would have regarded it as ill-mannered and exploitative. As a result, we were forgotten or overlooked. I never discovered who procured for us this belated 'invitation to view'. It might have been the melancholy Mr Callender, who had taken to visiting our houseboat on his river walks. It might have been Eve, who often passed our boat and called in to see us. I always suspected it was Frances, who in her direct way simply told Howard Carter to invite us – though this she strongly denied.

Whoever was responsible, a note was delivered by Pecky Callender one hot afternoon. It read:

My dear Miss Mackenzie,

I shall be delighted if you and Lucie would care to visit our tomb tomorrow. I suggest you come to the Valley at four o'clock when with luck our Scourge the tourists and pressmen will have departed but no doubt Eve will be there. Messrs Mace and Lucas will be glad to show you our 'laboratory' and if I am not free Callender will look after you and explain procedings to the best of his ability.

Sincerely yours,

Howard Carter

PS Perhaps Frances might like to acompany Lucie?

Frances did like: she had viewed the Antechamber with her parents at Christmas, when all its glorious contents were still in situ; I suspected she had seen it several times since as well, but was too tactful to say so. But she was excited to see it in its denuded state. 'Now's our chance, Lucy,' she explained, as we rode our donkeys up the Valley track. 'I want to work out when this famous opening is going to be. We'll be able to tell when we see the Antechamber. It's pretty well emptied now, Mr Mace says, so they must be going to open up the inner chamber in the next few days . . . I think they're hanging on until Lord Carnarvon gets back from Cairo.'

'He's gone to Cairo *again*?' I asked in surprise.

'Just for a day or two. On his own. A flying visit. Intrigue and negotiations . . . Also, he had to see his dentist there.' She lowered her voice. 'Lordy's in agony, apparently – his teeth keep falling out, and Eve says he's feeling terribly seedy. Daddy says he's trying to get that Rex Engelbach man fired. I expect he's arguing about *partage*, and the arrangements for the opening too – they want King Fuad there, you see, and all the top brass, so it's complicated. Especially with the Combine breathing down their necks.'

'Has Eve not gone to Cairo with her father then?' I asked, as we rounded the rocks and entered the Valley. Eve rarely left her father's side, so this also surprised me.

'No. Eve says her father thinks it isn't safe for her there. There were two more assassinations last week – all British officials are armed now. You daren't go to the Mousky bazaar any more. Eve has stayed here because Luxor is safe – or so she claims.' Frances gave me a sidelong look. 'You remember how she and Mr Carter were last year when we had tea at his house?'

'I do.'

'Well, see what you think now. They're very *thick* together; everyone's talking about it. Thick as thieves, Daddy says. That's just one of his jokes, of course.'

I was familiar with Herbert Winlock's jesting remarks – by then I knew just how double-edged they could be. I said nothing. I felt I was in a better position to understand Eve's relationship with Carter than I had been the year before: I had watched Nicola Dunsire, watched my father and learned. I was twelve now; I was experienced.

There was no sign of Eve or Carter when we finally reached the tomb. It was very hot that day, over one hundred degrees in the shade, and, as Carter had predicted, the heat had driven most tourists and pressmen from the Valley. Numbers dropped in the afternoons anyway, as the excavators now worked in the tomb only in the mornings, concentrating on conservation work in the afternoons. A small group of people remained by the tomb when we finally reached it: three elderly women, sitting in the shade of a propped umbrella and knitting; a couple of excitable young men with box cameras; and an overweight, pink-faced man I recognised as the journalist, Weigall; he was seated on the retaining wall, scribbling in a notebook. As we approached and dismounted, Arthur Mace emerged from his laboratory and came across to greet us.

'*Les tricoteuses*,' he said with a smile, gesturing towards the three placid, knitting women. 'They're here every day, all day. As is that prince of cads, Weigall. If he starts pestering you with questions just ignore him.' Mace began to cough. 'Sorry. It's the sand,' he said. 'All the chemicals Lucas and I have to use – the fumes build up. But I've been inhaling mummy dust for the last fifteen years of Met excavations, which doesn't help. My poor lungs are shot . . . Come and see our lab when you're done with the tomb,' he added. 'Where's Callender got to? Ah, there he is – he'll guide you.'

Pecky Callender had emerged from underground and was bruising Miss Mack's hand. 'Not a *whole* lot to see,' he remarked, leading us towards the steps. 'But you'll get the feel of it. It's hot down here. Very. If you come over faint, Myrtle – or you, young ladies, just say. I'll whisk you out in two ticks. First aid. Yes indeedy.'

Frances, veteran of tombs, gave him a look of mild scorn. She led me down the sixteen steps, Miss Mack and Callender following. The steel gate Carter had installed was open, and the heat from the Antechamber beyond was fierce. It exhaled into our faces, then breathed in and sucked us along the approach corridor. Its damp intensity brought me to a halt on the threshold; even Frances faltered. The room beyond, so often described to me and so often imagined, was much smaller and more confined than I'd expected. The pale plaster that covered the walls was disfigured by a strange creeping pinkness, by blossoming stains. They had crept their way across the bare wall opposite, an area once piled, I knew, with treasures. Now these were gone; the mottled stains created patterns, the suggestion of watching faces concealed in the walls.

'Spores,' Callender said from behind me. 'Fungi or mould. Not sure what's causing it. Not sure what it *is*, actually. Lucas has run tests. It's the alteration in the humidity, he thinks.'

'It's spread since I was last here,' Frances said in an uncertain voice. 'It's spread a *lot*.'

'Well, it does. Every day. Too many people in here, perhaps. Or my lights.'

He gestured to my right, where two large arc lamps had been fixed. Frances and I took a step towards them, and the heat at once intensified. Beyond their dazzle, I saw two tall black and gold figures, and realised they were the sentinels Eve had described, still standing guard in the emptied tomb. Their obsidian eyes glittered at us. As we gazed at them, one of those eyes closed, then reopened. I gave a startled cry.

'Did he wink at you? He does that,' Callender said. 'It's the gilding – tiny fragments break off. They cling to his brows, or his eyes. Then they get dislodged again, and for a moment you think—' He cleared his throat. 'Optical illusion. Nothing to worry about. Take a close look, they won't hurt you.'

Frances and I hesitated, then approached. My nervousness began to abate: the statues were a little taller than I was, imbued with an eternal stillness; their faces were beautiful, and their expression profoundly gentle. If they had turned and spoken to me – and I felt that if I were alone with them, they might – I would have answered them without fear.

'This is the wall to the inner chamber, Lucy,' Frances said in a low voice, and I realised that of course it was: this was Mohammed's important wall, the one that might conceal the boy king's final resting place. Frances began to point out the seals on its surface: there were one hundred and fifty-one of them – she'd counted. 'You've moved the rushes and the basket that were here,' she said, in a sharp tone, glancing at Mr Callender. 'The ones at the base of the wall. You've put this boxing in. When did you do that?'

'Yesterday. Getting ready for the opening.' He gestured to the boxwork covering the lower section of the wall. 'Tomorrow I'll box the statues in too. Lord Carnarvon wants them in place for the great

opening. He insists they be visible and Carter insists they be protected. So they're staying and I'm boxing them in. It's called
compromise. Plenty of *that* at the moment.' He rolled his eyes.
'Myrtle, you'd like to look at the statues, I expect? Should have covered them up today. Disobeyed orders. I knew you'd want to see
them.'

Miss Mack was touched by that. She gave him a grateful glance and
stepped forward. In silence, she stared at the statues, meeting their
steady obsidian gaze. Before anyone could demur, she lifted her right
hand and rested it against the wall they guarded. She closed her eyes
and bowed her head. She appeared to be listening.

We listened too, and I realised that the tomb was not a place of
silence, as it had seemed at first, but an echo-chamber for the tiniest, most infinitesimal of sounds. The air eddied and sighed; there
were little creaks, wooden protests, easings and shiftings in the walls,
sounds like the trickling of gravel; the hot metal of the arc lamps sizzled and clicked. Miss Mack remained still and intent. Then she
straightened, removed her hand from the wall and turned. Her face
was bloodless.

'I shall go outside,' she said. 'It is – I feel – Pecky, if you wouldn't
mind helping me.'

For a moment I thought she was about to faint, but Callender
grasped her arm and she seemed to recover her poise. He led her
outside. Left behind in the tomb, Frances and I clung to one another
tightly. I think we both felt that we were not alone, that there was
another presence here. We waited: it appeared to tolerate us. After
a long eddying silence, Frances tugged at my arm. 'You must look at
this, Lucy,' she whispered. 'The last time I was here I had to crawl
under one of the couches to reach it, and Daddy kept telling me to
come out. He dragged me out by my heels in the end . . . but now it's
much easier to see in. Look, this is the little storeroom Mr Carter
calls the Annexe.'

I turned to see that there was a small opening low down on the
room's west wall; the beams from the arc lamps were not directed
that way, so it lay in shadow. Frances led me across and we knelt
down. The opening was a jagged one, made by the thieves who'd
plundered the tomb millennia before and left unsealed by the necropolis officials. I leaned forward and peered into the dusty space

beyond, Frances crouching beside me. This area had not been cleared: as my eyes grew accustomed to the darkness inside, I began to make out the tumbled shapes, the mountainous, precariously balanced pile of *things*: vases, chairs, boxes, rifled and rejected by the thieves, seized upon and cast aside. Some shapes I could identify, others not: I glimpsed an oar, a carved walking stick, an intricate boat, glints of gold, the faint phosphorescent gleams of alabaster. There was a strong scent emanating from the dark: unexpected, unnerving, the scent of ripeness.

'I can smell *fruit*,' I whispered. 'Surely there can't be fruit in here, Frances?'

'There might be,' she whispered back. 'They found fruit in the Antechamber, Lucy. In baskets and in those strange, white, egg-shaped boxes. Fruits and meat and grains and vegetables. In three thousand years, none of it had rotted – it was sort of desiccated.' She reached her hand into the dark space and felt around. Dust eddied. 'All those provisions, stored away for his afterlife. Do you think the dead get hungry, Lucy?'

I thought of my lost mother, of lost Poppy d'Erlanger . . . Did the dead have appetites? To me, they were sad, shadowy, irretrievable. 'I can't imagine that,' I whispered.

'Neither can I. But then I can't imagine being dead . . . and if I do, when I try, if I try now, I can't see anything. Just nothingness.'

She turned her face to me and fixed me with her dark bright gaze. 'Do you think people know when they'll die, Lucy?' she then asked. 'Do you think they foresee it?'

'No, no, no,' I whispered. 'I'm sure they don't. Don't say that, Frances. Not in here . . . '

'Sorry.' She grasped my hand tightly and began to cough. 'Oh, this dust – everything's covered in it,' she said, 'and the sand – it gets everywhere, it's choking. Maybe it's that horrid mould on the walls – I can't breathe. Let's go now, shall we?'

'Yes, let's.'

We both stood up and looked around the empty chamber one last time. A mischievous look stole onto Frances's face. Releasing my hand, she ran across to the sealed north wall and, before I could prevent her, tapped it lightly. 'Until we next meet,' she said. 'Farewell, King . . . ' Then she laughed softly, which made her begin coughing again. I dragged her away. We both ran towards the stairs and, terrified, elated, made quick our escape – up and out, into the blessed air, into the hot light of the Valley.

The three women had abandoned their knitting; they were folding up their camp stools and making ready to leave. The two young cameramen had gone. The journalist Arthur Weigall was pocketing his notebook. He nodded to us as we drew level with him. 'Beautiful evening. I think I'll walk back over the hills,' he announced, in a friendly tone. 'My favourite route. Keeps me fit as a fiddle. I can make it to the ferry in under two hours from here – pretty good, eh?'

He looked closely at Frances; recognition dawned and I saw him make a lightning-quick calculation. 'Miss Winlock, I presume?' He smiled broadly, edged closer, tipped his hat. 'Didn't I see you here with your father the other week? How's the clearance work going? Encounter anything interesting down there in the tomb, young ladies?'

We made no reply. Escaping fast, we ran to the tomb of Seti II, now used as the conservation laboratory. It proved to be deep, facing north and refreshingly cool. The only daylight came from the entrance, and it was dark in its furthest recesses – so dark that Miss Mack and Callender, who were examining *antika* there, were using flashlights. It was set up with an array of benches, tools, ranked bottles, burners, tiny bellows for removing dust, and porcelain crucibles. It smelled strongly, chokingly, of chemicals.

'Acetone. Ether. Pure alcohol.' Mace ran his hand along the bottles. 'Formalin and collodion – we're using celluloids and formaldehyde too. None of them nice. Horrible stink. I have to go outside for a breather, but Lucas seems immune, don't you, old chap?'

Lucas, his fellow conservationist, then came forward: a tall, thin man, a good ten years older than Mace, he was also English, and had worked for years as a government chemist in Cairo. Both men were somewhat donnish, I thought; Lucas was wearing a three-piece suit and brogues, whereas Mace, as usual, wore shabby, crumpled work clothes; Minnie Burton liked to say he dressed like an under-gardener.

Lucas shook hands and regarded us in a dry way. Glancing back to

Mace, he winked at him and said to us: 'So how was the tomb? Been admiring Callender's carpentry work?'

'Just following orders,' Callender interjected mildly, from the recesses of the lab. 'As per instructions, I'd point out. When he removes the wall, Carter wants a platform.'

'I'll bet he does,' Lucas replied. 'Don't we all?' And with that enigmatic remark, he and Mace began to explain their work, to show us their triumphs and recount their disasters.

The single most difficult task they'd faced, they said, was the chariots. Only two had ever been discovered in Egypt before; in the Antechamber, there were four. They had been too large to be manoeuvred whole into the tomb when it was originally stocked, so their axles had been sawn in two and their parts dismantled. They had been piled together in a corner, and there, over the millennia, their leather fittings had disintegrated, forming a black sticky resin, glueing all four chariots together. They had had to be disentangled, piece by delicate piece. It had taken weeks of work in the tomb before they could safely be removed from it. Their six-spoked wooden wheels had been bound with thin tyres of rawhide, fragments of which had survived: Mace and Lucas had experimented with seven different chemical solutions until they found one that kept these scraps intact.

Frances and I bent to examine the gold relief work – and there the boy king was before our eyes, mounted in the chariot's basket, bow aimed, his arrow about to fly, plumed horses at full stretch, a hound racing beside: galloping to a hunt one glorious morning three thousand two hundred years ago.

Mace and Lucas showed us the records of this work – and it was then I began to understand for the first time how prodigious a task this was, and how minutely Carter had organised it. Every object was numbered and mapped by the Met's draughtsmen Hauser and Hall and its position in the Antechamber recorded. Each object, small or large, was then photographed in situ by Harry Burton. Carter himself drew them and recorded their measurements, their materials, their smallest details. Once restored to a state in which they could be safely transported, they were recorded again; finally they were packed – padded with wadding, wrapped in linen bandages and shrouds, laid into special boxes made to fit their contours.

'The most precious things ever found by any archaeologist,' Lucas said, 'and we have the job of saving them. We're trying to do it, God help us, under the noses of these pestilential journalists and tourists—'

'In one-hundred-degree heat,' Mace put in.

'While being pickled in chemicals—'

'While being constantly interrupted by visitors with special access. Carnarvon's friends, Egyptian officials. Two US Senators and four Pashas yesterday—'

'One earl, two Honourables, a viscount, three ladies and a bishop the day before—'

'But we stay calm and even-tempered at all times. No matter the provocation—'

'No matter how fatuous the questions. Even when Carter shouts and rages—'

'Which he does. On occasion. Very, very rarely of course—'

'A mere five times today, for example.'

Both men laughed. Drawing Frances and me deeper into the tomb, they began to show us some of the objects that had been restored but not yet boxed for transport: a gold stick adorned with a tiny statue of the king as a child; an exquisite fan made of ostrich feathers – feathers that had survived three thousand years. We were standing in a small area, hemmed in on all sides by packing cases. 'Where is all this treasure *going*?' Frances asked; she'd been counting the containers and had given up at two hundred.

'Ah. Tricky question, that,' Mace replied. He and Lucas exchanged glances. 'Some of it will be destined for the Egyptian Museum in Cairo, Frances . . . but there's the question of Carnarvon's share. That issue – well, it's not resolved yet. Negotiations continue.'

'I understand,' Miss Mack said, seizing her chance, 'I understand that under the terms of his permit, Lord Carnarvon is entitled to half of everything found. Strictly speaking, and aside from the *pièces capitales*, of course. Is that correct?'

'Well – up to a point, Miss Mackenzie,' Lucas replied. 'But every object here is exceptionally fine. You could argue they *all* come into that category. You could also argue that a find such as this, unprecedented, of such beauty and historical importance, should not be broken up under any circumstances. I make no comment either way—'

'And it's not as simple as that anyway,' Mace put in. 'Had the tomb been completely intact, had there been no break-ins in antiquity, then *everything* would be destined for the Egyptian Museum. No argument. The permit stipulates that. But there *were* break-ins.'

'*Minor* break-ins,' Lucas interjected.

'So it's all bally well up in the air at the moment,' Callender muttered.

'And likely to stay there for some considerable time,' Lucas added.

Miss Mack digested this information and the manner in which it was imparted. She gave all three men a barbed look. 'I imagine Lord Carnarvon could *renounce* his claims? That might be a wise solution, perhaps, in the circumstances?'

None of the men seemed keen to express a view on that possibility. She pressed on. 'What is Mr Carter's view on the matter? Does *he* not feel these wonderful things should be kept together and should remain in Egypt? I myself feel very strongly that to split them up, to divide them like – like the spoils of war is nothing short of—'

Miss Mack never completed this crusading sentence. At that moment, deep in the tomb, hemmed in by those packing cases, we were interrupted. We heard a woman's voice, calling from the Valley. 'Howard, where *are* you?' it called. 'Where have you got to, dear?' I recognised the voice as Eve's a second before she entered the laboratory.

She came to an abrupt halt in its entrance, peering into its depths, catching the gleam of our flashlights, but unable to see us clearly in the shadows. As we came forward to greet her, I saw she was wearing a new and very pretty pink dress; she was clutching her hat and was bare-headed, her hair freshly washed and waved. She must have come straight from the Winter Palace and the skilled ministrations of her maid Marcelle, I thought – but I was wrong.

'Oh where has Howard *gone*?' she cried, on a shrill note of anxiousness, as we emerged into the daylight and she realised that Carter was not among us. 'I've been searching for him high and low – I've been to the Castle *and* the American House. I've been up and down the Valley *twice*. There's no sign of him anywhere.'

The three men looked at her awkwardly, and then at each other. They consulted. Where, indeed, was Carter? He'd been with them at lunch . . . Callender had spoken to him at around two o'clock.

Mace might have glimpsed him after that, but wasn't sure. Lucas said he had definitely been in the Valley at three – they'd had a brief word, Carter complaining at Weigall's presence. No sightings since. There was a silence.

'What time is your father arriving from Cairo, Lady Evelyn?' Mace asked, in a neutral tone. 'Might Carter have gone to Luxor to meet him?'

'Pups won't be here for hours yet. His train gets in late. I need to see Howard before he arrives. Why would he just disappear? He promised me that—'

'I expect he'll be in Luxor,' Lucas said. 'Some administration matter . . . some last-minute problem about the opening, Lady Evelyn? It wouldn't be the first time that's happened.'

'That's true.' Eve's face brightened, then instantly clouded. 'But why didn't he send word? I could have stayed at the hotel and met him there. I'm sure he can't have gone to Luxor – he'd have told me.'

Colour came and went in her face, and for one moment I thought she was about to cry. She must be very agitated, I realised, for her habitual good manners had, for once, deserted her: she had not greeted Miss Mack, Frances or me and seemed blind to our presence. Frances, standing next to me, gave me a small nudge – though she had no need to remind me of her earlier remarks: Eve's distress, and the embarrassment it was causing the three men, were only too evident.

The silence lengthened; Miss Mack was looking at Eve in consternation; the men shifted from foot to foot and avoided each other's eyes. Eve twisted her hat in her hands, and said in a low voice: 'You're sure he didn't leave a message for me? If I just knew where he was, I could . . . Howard isn't well,' she went on, addressing the air, 'he's under so much strain and – I know it's silly but I worry about him.'

At this, Pecky Callender slowly raised his eyes from the floor, inspected Eve with sympathy and cleared his throat. 'Crikey, it's just come back to me,' he said. 'Sorry, Lady E. Memory like a sieve. Carter took off, about four o'clock it would have been, just before *you* arrived, Myrtle . . . Said he needed a walk. Yes, that was it. Needed to be alone, I think. Hasn't been a good day, you see. Worrying about the opening, I expect. Needed time to – go over things. Gone off to the West Valley. Headed that way, certainly.'

'The *West Valley*?' Eve glanced down at her pale silk stockings, at her pretty shoes. It was painfully obvious to everyone that she was considering following Carter there, and was realising that, in these shoes, at this time of day, in that remote, little-visited and wild part of the Valley, such a journey was unthinkable. The blood rushed up her throat and suffused her cheeks. With a pitiable attempt to pre-serve her dignity and recover face, she said, 'I see. Thank you. In that case I'll have to abandon my search. If you'd tell Howard I was look-ing for him, Mr Callender, I'd be grateful. I'll go back to the hotel now.'

She turned and walked out of the tomb. The three men looked at one another guiltily. 'For God's sake, Callender,' Mace muttered, 'do you have to be that clumsy?'

'Well, *someone* had to say something,' he replied, in injured tones. 'Fat lot of help you and Lucas were. You could see how she was. And he *has* gone for a walk . . . I think. Stalked off about four. Beyond that – don't ask me because I don't bally well *know*.'

'Someone needs to go after her,' Lucas said, interrupting them both and taking a hesitant step forward. 'We can't let her go back on her own. She's not in a fit state.'

'Tea. Maybe we should offer her tea?' Mace said. The men exchanged helpless glances.

'Oh, for heaven's sake.' Miss Mack, suddenly decisive, shouldered her way between them. 'Girls, come with me. *I* will talk to Eve, and *I* will take care of it.'

Eve had driven over in her father's car, we discovered; she had left it parked at a dangerous angle in full sun at the mouth of the Valley. We caught up with her as she reached it – we could hear the sound of her sobbing by then. Frances and I let Miss Mack take charge. We watched her approach, take Eve's arm, and then, as Eve began on a storm of weeping, embrace her. Patting her shoulder, she spoke to her without preamble, in a way that astonished me. 'My dear . . . my dear, you are very, very young,' she said. 'Believe me, this will pass. One day, perhaps sooner than you think, it will vanish away – you'll even think you imagined it. I promise you that is true. I *know* it to be true. Meanwhile, Eve, have your cry. It will help you.'

'I'm such a fool,' Eve said in a choked voice. 'I could see they were laughing at me. I must be mad – driving up here, running around the Valley. I don't know what's happened to me. Oh, I'm so ashamed, Myrtle. I feel so utterly stupid.'

'You are wrong. Strong emotion is not stupid. You should not be ashamed of it. Now, come back with me to our houseboat, and we shall have tea. That will revive you. Then, when you feel better, you can decide what to do next. Mr Carter will return from his walk in his own good time. When he does, you can see him – or not. As you decide. Now, into the car – are you able to drive? You are? Good. Girls, hurry up. Eve is joining us for tea on the *Hatshepsut*.'

We climbed into the scalding-hot car, and, driving erratically, Eve took us back to our houseboat. She left the car half slewed across the track; a party of goats soon came to investigate it, nibbled at its fenders and, losing interest, moved on. Eve sleepwalked her way to the upper deck and sat in the shade of its awnings. Frances and I plied her with tea, which she drank without seeming to notice she held a cup in her hand. And it was there, sitting staring at the river, with the cool north breeze from the Nile on her face, having been silent a long while, that she suddenly, and without the least prompting, began to speak.

We had all been trying to keep a conversation going and to avoid awkward silences; we had all carefully ignored her obvious signs of distress, the nervous pleating of her dress, her deafness to everything we said, the curious blindness of her gaze, as if she watched something vivid that was to us invisible. We talked of somethings and nothings, and eventually of the visit to the Valley just made. Frances was speculating as to what the inner chamber would contain; of what glories might be found behind its concealing wall; whether there might be shrines, a sarcophagus——

'There *are* shrines,' Eve said, gazing at the river. 'I've seen them. The outermost one is gold and blue. It's the most beautiful thing I've ever – my heart stopped beating when I first saw it. I dropped my torch. That shrine has two doors and they were bolted, but their seal was broken. When we stood in front of them, Howard said, *Ah, dear God*. He took my hand. My father couldn't speak, he could scarcely stand. He knelt down – we all knelt down. Was it wrong to be there? It didn't *feel* wrong, not then.'

'My dear, you don't have to tell us this,' Miss Mack said, reaching

372

across and patting her hand. 'Hush now. You must not say anything you'll later regret.'

'No, no, no,' Eve replied. 'You're wrong, Myrtle. I hate these lies and these deceptions. They're unbearable. They're a horrible burden I've been carrying around for months. It seems so wrong to deceive people. I *want* to tell you . . . The thieves had broken through into the inner chamber as well as the Antechamber, you see. We could see where they'd got in, where that north wall had been resealed – and we couldn't rest until we knew for certain whether Tutankhamun was there, or whether everything had been rifled. *I have to know*, my father said, *I have to know*. So – we went back to the Valley one night, I forget which night – and we re-opened the hole the thieves had made. We only made a tiny opening . . . ' She turned pleadingly towards us. 'I went through first, because I was the smallest. But I was afraid, and I – I sort of froze. So Howard widened the hole a little and came through to me. I was all right then, I always feel safe with him. Then my father joined us, and . . . Mr Callender was with us that night, but he stayed in the Antechamber; he was too large to wriggle through, and he – he didn't seem to mind. He was very good about it. He said it was *our moment*. And so it was. Everything we saw, how it felt, it's all branded *here*, in my mind.'

She hesitated, and then, sometimes meeting our eyes, sometimes looking to the hills, the sunset, the river, the rising moon, she described what they had found on their secret night-time expedition to the Valley. It was evening by the time she began on her confession, and the orchestra at the Winter Palace had struck up. So we listened to her story in silence and against the drift of dance music; under Eve's words, and across the placid surface of the Nile: the blues, then a slow waltz; blues again.

It had been agreed Frances would spend that night on the houseboat with us; but it lacked a spare cabin, so Mohammed had produced hammocks for us, slung between the masts on the upper deck. Late that night, long after Eve had left us and returned to Luxor, Frances and I lay in these hammocks, swaying back and forth in the moonlight, listening to the Winter Palace music and the chatter that carried across the water from the other houseboats. It was a full moon, and a chill night; neither of us spoke for a long time; in the cabin below

Miss Mack's Oliver No. 9 was silent. I knew Frances was not asleep; her wakefulness transmitted itself to me. I knew she was thinking of Eve, and what she had told us, as I was.

I was thinking of the space in which she, Carter and her father had eventually found themselves. Beyond that north wall of the Antechamber lay wonders: a vast cedar shrine, entirely covered in blue faience and gold, so large it almost filled the Burial Chamber. So mesmerising was this, lit in the flickering beams of their torches, that it was some while before they had realised that this was the first of two rooms, and one more lay beyond it. Remembering her words, I watched Eve touch the heavy bolt on the shrine's two doors, and her father sink his head in his hands as he realised the seal on the bolt had been broken. I watched Carter summon his nerve and, gently at first, then exerting force, slide the bolt back. And I heard Eve's low cry, the men's sigh as the doors swung open. Behind them a second shrine and a second pair of gold doors was revealed: they too were closed, but they were fastened shut with rope bindings, and the rope's clay seal was unbroken. In silence they stared, then Carter said: *It's intact. The inner shrines are intact. He must be in there*, and Carnarvon slumped to his knees and said: *Christ in heaven — I've got him.*

From across the Nile came a burst of song, then laughter, then a door slamming, then silence. I turned in my hammock and lay looking at the moon. The sealed gold doors of the second shrine showed Tutankhamun greeting Osiris, god of the underworld. And between the two outer shrines, Eve said, were a multitude of offerings: alabaster lamps to light the king's way to the afterlife; a cluster of oars to row him across the underworld's dangerous rivers . . . The three of them had stayed there a long, long time, looking into the unknown; then they had turned and seen that the Burial Chamber contained one further space, a second shadowed room, one that they would call the Treasury. There in its entrance, they found their way barred by a statue of the jackal god Anubis, stretched full length on a bier, black as night, prick-eared, ever watchful, the god who supervised the Weighing of Hearts, Anubis the guardian of graveyards.

'Are you awake, Frances?' I whispered.

'Yes. I'm thinking of Anubis. Those gold doors. How they'd look, by flashlight, when your hands were shaking. I'm afraid to go to sleep in case I dream of them.'

'Should they have gone in?' I asked, sitting up and leaning across to her. 'Oh, Frances, should they have done that?'

'No. They should have waited for an inspector to be there. Carnarvon could lose his permit if anyone found out. There'd be an unholy row.' She sat up, and turned her pale face towards me. 'That's why they've covered their tracks, Lucy. They must have refilled the hole – then they disguised that area with rushes and a basket: I saw those the first time I went into the Antechamber. Now Callender's erected all that boxwork we saw today. So when they have the official opening, that part of the wall will be completely invisible. Carter's thought of everything.' She shivered. 'They've lied – and they'll have to go on lying. Imagine it, Lucy: a grand, formal opening, Monsieur Lacau and all those officials and scholars and archaeologists sitting there watching their every move – and they're going to take down that wall and pretend that they have no idea what's behind it.'

'Don't forget the journalists,' I said. 'Think what the Combine would do with this story.'

'I don't think they care about *them*. They hate them – they're delighted to mislead them. But their friends – maybe they care about lying to them. I think Eve does, anyway. She was ashamed to lie to Miss Mack. That's why she told us.' Frances tossed back her blankets and slid out of her hammock. 'Oh, I can't sleep,' she said restlessly. She padded across the deck to the rails and stood there in her white nightdress, like a little ghost gazing across the water.

I climbed down from my hammock, pulled a jumper over my pyjamas and joined her. We both stood looking out at the lights and listening to the music from the Winter Palace, watching the moon's radiance: two moons, one in the sky, its twin in the Nile water.

'Where do you think Mr Carter was today,' I asked her, after a long silence, 'when Eve was searching for him?'

'Somewhere he could be alone. He needs to be alone, I think, Lucy. Daddy says he's cracking under the strain – might even be close to a breakdown. Daddy thinks it's because of the papers, the politics, all the tourists, the heat in the Valley, the work in the tomb – and Mr Carter's demons. But I think it's the lies. The prospect of that opening ceremony, having to stand there and act, and then *more* lies. He'll never be able to tell the truth now. *That*'s what's done for him.'

'And Eve?' I hesitated, and then asked a question that was much in my mind. 'Do you think she's fallen in love with him, Frances? Is that what's wrong with her?'

'I don't know,' Frances replied, in a sad tone. 'I don't know what falling in love looks like. But you must know, Lucy, surely? Your father's just remarried. So you must have seen it. Did he behave the way Eve did today – did your governess?'

Her question shocked me. Looking away, I said stiffly: 'That was different. It was – an arrangement. A marriage of convenience. I told you – he needed someone to look after me, and someone to help him with his work. A secretary.'

Frances considered this in silence and let it pass. 'Well, I don't *ever* want to be in love if that's what it does to you,' she said in a fierce way, staring out across the Nile. 'And anyway, I don't think Eve is – not really. Stealing into the tomb at night – think how powerful that would be. It's bewitched her.' She paused, and then added in an impatient tone, 'In any case, what's the *point* of Eve being in love with Mr Carter? It's stupid. He may be fond of her as a friend, but nothing more. She's the daughter of an earl. He's the wrong class and he's old enough to be her father. She can't possibly marry him.'

'Things like that don't stop people falling in love, Frances,' I said, after a silence. 'It just happens,' I went on hesitantly. 'People just *do*. Miss Dunsire says that when it comes to love, there are no boundaries.'

'Oh, you and your Miss Dunsire.' Frances gave me a little push. 'You never stop quoting her, do you know that? If *she* says it, I suppose it has to be gospel?'

That remark hurt. 'Well, she knows a hell of a lot more about it than *you* do,' I replied.

'That's true,' Frances replied solemnly. 'Or *you*, Lucy,' she added, after a pause. 'The truth of the matter is, we are both of us horribly ignorant.' She began to smile; her quicksilver mood changed and her glance became mischievous. 'And I hope it stays that way for ever – for me, anyway. I *never* want to be in love and be frantic and silly. I mean to stay as free as a bird. I plan to paint glorious pictures and sail around the world – and wear red lipstick like Poppy d'Erlanger, of course.' She laughed and then caught me by the hand. 'Listen, Lucy – they're playing a waltz at the Winter Palace now. Isn't it lovely here, by the river? How I love boats! I wish you had come to Maine, and I'd taught you to sail. Can you waltz? Shall we waltz? It might warm us up.' She shivered. 'Oh, let's, Lucy.'

I could waltz, as it happened; I'd learned at my Cambridge dancing classes, and once, before leaving for Egypt, I'd practised the steps with Nicola Dunsire. So I held up my arms, Frances stepped into them, and I guided her around the deck in the moonlight, *one, two, three; one, two, three,* negotiating the benches and the chairs, risking a spin when we reached the clear areas. Frances danced gracefully; I was much the taller of us now, and Frances felt very small in my arms; she followed my lead, her hand warm in mine, her body pliant and responsive to my directions and guidance, her face pale and concentrated, her eyes sparkling, her black hair shining. Round and round we went, keeping time with the sweet rhythms of the music, weaving through the awning's shadows and then out into the astonishing glitter of the starlight. As the waltz approached its end, we launched ourselves into one last tremendous spin, the length of the deck, and came to a halt, breathless, against the rails. Frances broke from my grip, and sank down into a chair. 'Oh, weren't we just fine? You dance so well now, Lucy. Madame would be proud of you.'

I didn't reply – I was catching my breath; my mind was dizzied by the spins; waltzing saddened me. I couldn't have explained that to Frances, to anyone, least of all to myself. I stood leaning against the rails, gazing across the water, until my heartbeat slowed. It was late by then, past one in the morning, and the orchestra at the Winter Palace played no more tunes; a last waltz and then – silence, silence, silence.

After a while, Frances yawned and stretched and rubbed her eyes. She said she thought she might be able to sleep now; we climbed back into our hammocks. Both of us tossed and turned for a while, then settled. I listened to the lap of the Nile. Frances was asleep, I thought – but I was wrong. 'Tell me, Lucy,' she said, in a whisper, 'would you have done what they did? Would you have broken into the inner chamber?'

'Perhaps.' I reached across and clasped her hand. 'Maybe. Definitely not. I don't know.'

'I *would*. I'd have been so burned up with curiosity, I couldn't have resisted. Besides, what difference does it make? It's not as if they took anything, Lucy. Is it such a sin to look?'

I did not reply. I couldn't answer Frances's question then – and I still can't, all these long decades later.

The long-awaited, much anticipated opening of the inner chamber to Tutankhamun's tomb took place three days later, on Friday 16 February, 1923. This was a great relief to Miss Mack, for we were approaching the end of our stay in Egypt and she'd feared she'd miss the occasion, one she felt was crucial to The Book. And, in a sense, we *did* miss it, for it was a quiet affair, kept secret until the last possible minute, conducted with stealth, to outwit the journalists. Even if Miss Mack had been in the Valley that day, armed with her camera and notebook, she'd have seen little, for everything was happening inside the tomb, and, excepting Eve, no women were admitted there. But she and I were not in the Valley that day – we were with Helen and Frances, at Herbert Winlock's dig at Deir el-Bahri.

'We're banished,' Helen had said, arriving at our houseboat that morning. She gave Miss Mack a speaking glance: 'Strict instructions from Herbert: not allowed near the tomb today, mustn't go near the Valley – so we're escaping with a picnic to Hatshepsut's temple, Myrtle, and we're hoping you and Lucy will join us.'

Miss Mack gave her a speaking glance in return. 'My dear, I understand *absolutely*,' she said. 'We'd be delighted.'

'Well, the famous opening ceremony is obviously happening right now, Lucy,' Miss Mack remarked to me after lunch, as she and I explored the temple ruins, 'and to tell you the truth, I don't mind missing it anyway. The Book did tell me to be there, and you know how dictatorial it can be. But I'm not in the writing *mood* at present, dear. I was most upset by what Eve told us the other day. I wouldn't dream of breaking her confidence and recording it. But it does weigh on me.'

I'd already guessed that was the case. Since Eve's confession, the Oliver No. 9's keys had been silent. Miss Mack sat down on one of Winlock's excavated temple walls and surveyed the scene around us, her expression perplexed. Hatshepsut's beautiful funerary temple, backed up against sheer three-hundred-foot cliffs of rock, facing into the afternoon sun, was magnificent, and punishing. It was huge – inexhaustibly huge in archaeological terms: Herbert Winlock had already been working it for twelve years at the time of this visit of ours, and would continue to do so for another eight in the future. That day the site was empty of tourists. The heat was shrivelling. There was no shade. I put on my dark glasses. Miss Mack raised an umbrella and mopped her face. She glanced across to the temple's massive colonnade, where Helen and Frances were sketching.

'I'd like your opinion, Lucy,' she said. 'How many other people know what Eve told us the other evening, do you think? Have Mr Carter's fellow archaeologists been told the truth? Would you say Herbert knew – and Mr Burton, Mr Mace, Mr Lucas? Are they part of the deception too? And it *is* a deception, dear, let's be clear about that.'

'I think Herbert Winlock has guessed, if he hasn't been told,' I replied. 'As to Mr Burton and Mr Mace, I'm not sure – though the Antechamber is very small, and they were both working inside it for weeks, so you'd expect them to have noticed *something*. I'm sure Mr Lucas knows – that's why he made those jokes about boxing-in and carpentry. And Pecky Callender definitely knows, because he was there with them that night.

'I think they probably *all* know, Miss Mack,' I went on, glancing across at Frances: she'd abandoned her drawing and was now practising cartwheels. 'Frances says they wouldn't be shocked, anyway – they'd probably have done the very same thing Carter did. She says no one wants to go through a ceremonial opening with all the officials assembled, and then knock down the wall and find there's nothing behind it. She says that has happened in the Valley and elsewhere – many times, even to Mr Carter in the past – and it's horribly humiliating. Herbert Winlock says archaeologists should never knock down a tomb wall in public without being damn— without being sure what's behind it.'

'I see.' Miss Mack sighed. 'Well, if Herbert says that, I'll bow to his judgement. I expect I am old-fashioned and narrow-minded. I should not like to be in Mr Carter's and Lord Carnarvon's shoes today, however. Standing up in front of all those people – including Monsieur Lacau himself, for he's bound to be there – and dismantling that wall, feigning astonishment, acting a *lie* … and in such a sacred place too. No, I shouldn't like to have to do that . . . And how am I to deal with what Eve told us in The Book, Lucy?' she added.

'Why not just hint at it?' I suggested. As I'd learned from my letter-writing, there were things that were best left unsaid, things it was wise to edit out – and contriving this was easier than I'd expected. 'Surely you can bury things, so only people who dig deep and read between the lines notice them? Or leave it out. Just forget it. You could write about our visit to the tomb, then cut straight to the opening ceremony. No one will notice a gap.'

'Well, I can't *forget* what Eve said – obviously I·can't. But I see what you mean. Hide it and swiftly cut elsewhere . . . Perhaps that *would* be the solution.' She gave me a considering look. 'How crafty you can be, dear! I shall put it to The Book and see what it thinks. I shan't be in the least surprised if it agrees with you. Just between you and me, I fear The Book's morals are somewhat lax. It is often less than frank. I expect it will be only too delighted to conceal certain events. In fact, it has a *tendency* to conceal things, as I've begun to observe. It even hides things from *me*, Lucy . . . I must confess it is constantly tempting me away from stern factual objectivity towards – well, towards what I can only describe as *romancing*.'

'Romancing?' I looked at her in astonishment; this admission had been made with great reluctance, and she had coloured. 'I don't understand. Do you mean Eve and Mr Carter?'

'Good heavens, no. I shouldn't dream of touching on that matter, dear. No, no, I meant that The Book seems to have developed a fondness for certain characters. To be exact, *a* character.' Her blush deepened. 'It wants a hero, you see.'

'A *hero*? But why? I thought it was supposed to be a blow-by-blow report, Miss Mack?'

'I know. It's very strange, isn't it? But it's insistent. A hero it wants and a hero it's determined to get. I do not intend to give in, Lucy — and I'm holding my own thus far. But it's becoming progressively difficult. You see, The Book feels it *already* has a hero, and it's been concealing him from me. Now it wants him brought forth into the light.'

How puzzling this was. I considered the candidates: Lord Carnarvon? Howard Carter? Herbert Winlock? None of them seemed an obvious hero to me, but perhaps my concept of that breed, honed by Nicola Dunsire's taste and her reading lists, differed from Miss Mack's. A suspicion began to steal into my mind, and so I asked when this heroic problem had first manifested itself.

'Chapter Eight: *A Wishing Cup*, as I called it,' she replied. 'And I had to be *very* firm with Chapter Nine: *A Game of Consequences*. That described our Christmas lunch at the American House, and related events . . . You know, dear — this and that.'

This chronology narrowed the field. I had my answer, I felt; the identity of Miss Mack's nascent hero was becoming clear. It became clearer during the afternoon, as I thought the matter over while exploring the ruins with Frances. It became clearer still that evening when we returned to our *dahabiyeh*. There were candles on our supper table, and three places, not two, had been laid. Miss Mack bathed and changed into her best frock; she came up to the deck in a state of high nervousness, smelling of lavender water and mothballs.

She paced up and down; she fetched binoculars and scanned the river, the hills. She consulted her watch ten times in the space of ten minutes. I was kind: I asked no questions, made no comments. At seven, Miss Mack gave a cry and leaned over the rails: 'Why, goodness gracious, it's *you*, Pecky,' she called. 'What a pleasant surprise! You're just in time for supper — I know you won't have eaten yet. I *insist* on your joining us.'

When we came to the end of this meal — Mohammed had pulled out all the stops and served a feast — Miss Mack poured coffee, offered Callender a glass of brandy, which he refused, and then plied him with Turkish Delight. 'Now, Pecky,' she said sternly, 'the time has come for you to sing for your supper. Lucy and I want to know every detail of what happened at the famous opening today, and *you* are the person to tell us.'

Callender seemed surprised at this – not too many people requested his feedback, I think. He demurred, ate three pieces of Turkish Delight and was finally persuaded. Carter and Carnarvon had laid a *plan* for the opening ceremony, he said; it was cunning, required careful timing and was tailored to confound the pressmen. By eight-thirty in the morning, he explained, all four members of the Combine had been at their customary perch on the retaining wall above the tomb's entrance. They were suspicious that the opening was imminent, so for the last three days not one of them had shifted from that damn wall: they were lined up there from dawn to dusk, like so many vultures.

At twelve, as usual, the entire team of excavators broke for lunch. Carter locked the steel gates into the tomb and, joined by Mace, Lucas and Burton, strolled off for their midday meal in KV4, the cool 'canteen' tomb they used for that purpose. The Combine, unable to escape the Valley's heat, crept under the shade of a rock, where they drank warm beer, consumed dry, curling sandwiches and grew dispirited. By twelve-thirty the temperature was one hundred and ten degrees: this swiftly sorted the sheep from the goats; most of the tourists fled, as did the less determined journalists. The Combine sat it out . . . but they were beginning to despair: if anything newsworthy *did* occur that afternoon, they needed it to happen soon. Their dead-line for cabling their papers was 3 p.m. at the latest: in order to send those cables, they had to ride all the way to the ferry, a six-and-a-half-mile journey, then cross the Nile, then ride a further mile to the telegraph office. Time was running out on them.

At about one-fifteen, the excavators, Carnarvon and Eve emerged from their luncheon tomb where, according to Carter's plan and unnoticed by the reporters, they had been discreetly joined by their invited guests. This select group included Monsieur Pierre Lacau, Rex Engelbach, Ibrahim Effendi, Albert Lythgoe, Herbert Winlock, several important government Pashas, and two extremely eminent Egyptologists, namely Carnarvon's friend, Dr Alan Gardiner of Oxford, and Dr James Breasted, of Chicago. As they appeared, Carter's workmen unlocked the steel gates to the tomb, and began ferrying chairs inside, also tools such as picks and shovels. Seeing this, spotting the white-bearded Old Testament presence of Lacau, gal-vanised by the spectacle of Doctors Breasted and Gardiner – two plump august figures ambling across the sand arm in arm, resembling Tweedledum and Tweedledee and resplendent in matching pith helmets – the Combine realised the great moment had come at last. Zero hour. They shot back to the retaining wall and fumbled for their cameras and notebooks.

Leading the way into the tomb, Carnarvon glanced back over his shoulder and smiled at them. 'Just popping down for a little concert,' he said. 'Carter's going to sing to us.'

Humming a tune, he raised his hat in salute and sauntered down the steps. Arthur Weigall swung around to his fellow Combine journalists and said: 'If Carnarvon goes down to the tomb in *that* spirit, I give him six weeks to live.'

At this dramatic point in Callender's narrative, Miss Mack interrupted.

'*Six weeks to live?* What an extraordinary thing to say! How very unpleasant. Did he mean it in jest? If so, it is tasteless. Are you *sure* Mr Weigall said that? Would you mind if I made a note of it?'

'Feel free.' Callender concentrated: 'I *think* he said six weeks. It was definitely six *something*. Oh Lord, maybe it was six months . . . or six years? Does it matter?'

'Of course it matters! Six *years* doesn't have the same ring at all, Pecky – surely you can see that?' Miss Mack cried, becoming fretful. 'Which was it? *Think*.'

'I don't know. Weeks, I'm pretty sure. Blighter muttered it as Mace and I walked past. He was trying to put the wind up us. And we weren't falling for *those* little tricks.'

With reluctance, Miss Mack let this detail go. Later that night she told me she would not use it. She would revise that decision six weeks later, when Carnarvon lay mortally ill at the Continental Hotel in Cairo. 'Go on, Pecky,' she said now, and he did.

'Well, then they knocked the wall down,' he said. 'Carnarvon made a speech first – some rigmarole, went on and on for ever. Then Carter spoke for a bit. Then we got down to the nitty-gritty. Burton set up his camera, and angled his lights and reflectors and what-have-you. Carter stood on that platform I'd made – the one you saw – and he loosened the stones from the top downwards. He passed them to Mace, who passed them to me – and then the boys carried them out in baskets. That was it. Bob's your uncle.'

Miss Mack gave a cry of protest. 'Pecky, *please*. You're not trying. Don't be so *prosaic*. What did you *see*? Did the audience gasp? The tension must have been palpable.'

'Well, it was blood – it was hot,' he said. 'Boiling. Carter stripped down to his vest. We were all sweating.' He turned his mild eyes to the river; Miss Mack scribbled frantically. 'After a bit, he'd widened the hole enough and you could see blue and gold. I think Lady Evelyn cried out at that point, and there were gasps – yes, I'm sure there were. In fact, the tension *was* getting to us, now I think about it, because I nipped out to have a quick gasper, and Carnarvon shot out after me. Shot out like a rocket, Myrtle, and didn't look too good either. Pale as death, dripping with sweat, hands shaking. He lit his cigarette and took three puffs, then tossed it down and shot back in again.'

He paused thoughtfully. Miss Mack gave him encouraging nods and replenished his coffee. He continued: 'Let me think . . . Right, got it now: by the time I went back, the opening was large enough to enter and at about two-fifteen or so – Carter climbed through. Disappeared inside for a bit, not that long, then Carnarvon joined him. Then they *both* disappeared – for quite a while too. People started getting restive, twitchy, fanning themselves, and yes, Myrtle, the tension definitely was building . . . Lady Evelyn was saying, *Oh, what have they found, what's happened?* That Lacau man was muttering away – *Sacré bleu*, *mon Dieu*, *zut alors*, that sort of stuff, you know what the French are like, excitable. Finally, Carnarvon and Carter reappeared . . . then . . . I forget what happened then. Pandemonium. It was confusing. Everyone crowding around and asking questions—'

'But what did Lord Carnarvon and Mr Carter *say*? They must have said something, made an announcement, surely? Think, Pecky, *think*.'

'Can't remember. It's all a bit blurry. Carter looked ill, desperate – I thought he was going to pass out, I remember that. Carnarvon handled it better. He has nerve, you've got to give him that. *Noblesse oblige* . . . no sign of being rattled. Very solemn. Invited everyone to go inside. Two at a time. Carnarvon and Lacau first, then the others in turn. A bit like the animals going into the ark. And when they came out—'

'Yes, yes, yes?' Miss Mack leaned forward, pencil quivering.

'People wept. They were weeping. Winlock couldn't speak. Neither could Lythgoe.'

There was a silence. Callender shuffled his feet and squinted at the stars. 'I expect it was devastating,' he went on in a ruminative tone. 'I mean, it would be, wouldn't it? They've found him, you see, Myrtle. The shrines are there, and they're still sealed. They've found King Tut and he's intact and they've discovered – wonders beyond belief – things that take your breath away. The whole caboodle, in fact. Yes indeedy.'

Miss Mack wrote down the word 'caboodle' in neat copperplate. She then crossed it out, closed her notebook and looked intently at Callender. 'You didn't go in, did you, Pecky?' she said, on an accusatory note.

'Too tight.' Her hero gave her an evasive glance. 'The gap between the wall and the outer shrine is very narrow. It's a tight squeeze. You have to worm your way along the side of the shrine until you come out in the space at the front, where its doors are facing you. I'm six foot three. Forty-four-inch chest. Didn't want to get stuck like a bally cork in a bottle. Dr Gardiner's half my size and he nearly got wedged. So did Dr Breasted.'

'Piffle. Now tell me the real reason.'

'Too many people.' Callender sighed gustily. 'And it's going to get worse, Myrtle. The Queen of the Belgians is arriving on Sunday with Lord Allenby – so there's another big do coming up.' I could see his habitual dolefulness was creeping up on him, although he was trying manfully to resist it. 'When I go in,' he continued, 'I want to go in on my own. Have a bit of a think. Pay my respects to Tut. Explain what we're going to do to him. Make sure he understands, knows there's nothing to worry about and I'll look after him.'

He hesitated. 'I'll be working in there in due course, you see, Myrtle. It's me who's got to figure out how to dismantle Tut's shrines, how we'll get his sarcophagus open and handle his coffins. We won't be tackling any of that this season, we're buried ten feet under with the backlog as it is. So we won't even start on that until next winter. But I'm looking ahead, working out how the heck we'll do it, when the shrines are huge and there isn't room in that Burial Chamber to swing a cat.

'Oh, and speaking of *cats*,' his face, which had become mournful despite his best efforts, now brightened, 'the timing worked a treat, and the reporters all missed their deadlines, you'll be glad to know – but Carter had another little trick up his sleeve. He knew the Combine would be on the hunt for info – at it like madmen – *which* they were. And he knew they'd try to pump his workmen, *which* they did. So he planted a few rumours. Got his men to tell them there was a giant cat presiding over the Burial Chamber, the biggest damn feline ever seen in Egypt.

'We think they swallowed it too: hook, line and sinker.' He gave a wide, beaming smile. 'So we can all look forward to reading about a ten-foot cat in the newspapers.'

Callender's account of the opening ceremony seemed evasive to me – no mention of the dissembling involved, I noted. I also felt it was woefully dull and unimaginative. Miss Mack did not agree and brushed such comments aside.

'Wait until *I* write it up, dear,' she said. 'It may sound bald to you, but that's because you don't understand the first thing about reporting. Pecky has given me the bare bones, as I knew he would, dear man – now I shall wave my stylistic wand, Lucy.'

She disappeared to her cabin the instant Callender left, and the Oliver No. 9 keys were kept busy until three in the morning. This marathon session was followed by several more, all equally taxing, for the following seven days in the Valley were filled with incident: they were, as Miss Mack kept reminding me, historic.

The Times ran the first full account of the opening of the Burial Chamber, and the story told was the one Carter and Carnarvon had planned, much of it ghosted by them for the obliging Merton – or so the Combine was claiming. During the course of the week, the news spread worldwide – but in the excitement generated by the discovery, the duplicity involved went unrevealed. Frances was delighted by this: her sympathy was entirely with the excavators. 'So much for the Combine,' she crowed one day at the American House. 'Eve says there have been *acres* of coverage – but not one single journalist has come close to the truth. I *knew* Mr Carter and Lord Carnarvon would pull the wool over their eyes! Serves those reporters right for all that spying and lying they did at the Winter Palace.'

To its chagrin, *The Times* did not actually break the story: it was scooped by the newshound Valentine Williams, who went to the Valley that opening day armed with two pre-written, triple-rate, flash telegrams: one read TOMB EMPTY, the other KING'S SARCOPHAGUS DISCOVERED. Thanks to considerable cunning, forethought and expenditure, he contrived to send the second of these to Reuters within his deadline, and thus broke the news in London that same night – to the rage of *The Times* executives. His co-conspirators made the best of a bad job; when the English newspapers finally reached Luxor, Miss Mack, Frances and I fell upon them. We discovered that Weigall had not been deceived by those planted rumours of a giant feline; two of the Combine members, however, were. Our favourite strapline ran: GIGANTIC BLACK CAT FOUND IN KING'S BURIAL CHAMBER: WHAT CAN THIS SIGNIFY? ARCHAEOLOGISTS ASK.

The instant the news of the intact Burial Chamber reached Luxor, the number of visitors to the Valley doubled. Once the Queen of the Belgians, escorted by Lord Allenby, had made her tour of the tomb – a visit conducted with great splendour and maximum publicity – the numbers doubled again.

'Ridiculous!' Miss Mack said, with republican scorn, as we watched the Queen and her retinue make their slow procession to the Valley that Sunday. 'Why do they need royalty? What on earth has the Queen of the Belgians to do with it . . . though I'm sure she's a charming woman, of course.'

Frances and I counted an amazing seven cars, one motorcycle (Mr Engelbach), fifteen horse carriages and twelve donkey carriages. Mohammed, who watched with us from our houseboat, pointed out the Mudir of the province, Pasha Suleman, who was riding with the Queen, in a uniform so splendid it threatened to eclipse her grey fox stole and large, veiled picture hat. 'Observe the glory of the *ghaffirs*, misses,' he said – and we duly did.

It was difficult to miss these guards: on the Mudir's orders they'd been stationed every sixteen yards along the entire six-and-a-half-mile route from ferry to tomb, each in a magnificent parade uniform of red, green and magenta, with a glittering brass breastplate. As the Queen passed, each man came to attention and saluted with his *nabut*, or swagger stick. They saluted again for Lord Allenby and his wife, and a third time for the car containing Monsieur

Pierre Lacau, Lord Carnarvon and Eve; after that, they seemed to lose heart. It was one hundred and twelve degrees that day, so this was understandable.

The Queen of the Belgians had happened to be in Cairo, Helen Winlock reported – and had gamely stepped into the breach left by King Fuad; the political situation being as it was, *his* hoped-for visit had had to be abandoned. And very charming and indefatigable the Queen had been, removing her fox fur, descending into the Burial Chamber, and inspecting everything with interest for an impressive forty minutes before faintness came upon her.

'Poor Carnarvon,' Helen said, 'what he'd *really* have liked is a British royal – not the King and Queen, obviously. But given that two Englishmen discovered the tomb, I think he had cherished the hope that *one* of the royal brood would turn up – some HRH, a prince or princess, a royal duke – there are enough of them, in all conscience.'

'One crowned head is much like another in my view,' Miss Mack replied tartly. 'The effect will be the same, you mark my words, Helen.'

It was difficult to say whether the lure was royalty, the mystery of the tomb, the pull of buried treasure, the power of international front-page publicity, or a combination of all these factors, but the result was startling: on the following Friday, just a week after the opening, twelve thousand people visited the Valley; of the many tombs it contained, only one was of interest to them. Things had by then reached such a pitch, Frances said, that Carnarvon had decided they must close the tomb and concentrate on conservation for the remainder of the season. Everyone was about to take a short break, in an effort to preserve the team's sanity.

It was that Friday we went to the American House for tea to say our farewells. We were leaving for Cairo the next day, Miss Mack returning via England to America, and I to Cambridge via Paris, where my father and Nicola Dunsire were now renting an apartment. Our departure had been brought forward a few days; the New England acquaintances who owned our houseboat had decided to return to Egypt after all – they were reluctant to miss out on a ring-side seat for the archaeological event of the century, Miss Mack explained, frowning over their telegram. 'And I shan't mind leaving a little earlier,' she added. 'I do not like this hubbub. And besides, dear, I have all the material I need now. One last paragraph or so, and The Book will be finished.'

She extrapolated on this at length as we walked up to the American House that day. All she needed now, she told me, was an apposite sentence or two, a few wise words of summation. I nodded encouragement, but I was not really listening. I was thinking of my goodbyes to Frances – and of Paris, a city I had never visited, to whose delights Miss Dunsire was promising to introduce me. Would it feel like a homeland, a heartland; would Cambridge – or would the Valley still hold sway?

When we arrived, the Winlocks and Minnie Burton were already in the common room; Mrs Lythgoe, who had returned to Egypt with her husband for the ceremonial opening, was, to Minnie's fury, presiding. Carter, Carnarvon and Eve were outside on the veranda. Mr Callender had not been invited – or had simply been overlooked, as was often his fate; Mace and Burton arrived shortly after we did, both looking exhausted.

'Tutmania really has hit now,' Mace said, sinking down into a chair. 'They're saying there were twelve thousand visitors to the Valley today. It felt twice that. You can't move, you can't think. We can't go on like this – it's insupportable.'

'I blame the journalists,' Minnie Burton said irritably. She was examining with a critical eye the food Michael-Peter Sa'ad had sent in for Mrs Lythgoe: the offerings included cucumber sandwiches, scones of incredible lightness, a perfect Victoria sponge, a superb fruitcake and shortbread no Scotswoman could have improved upon.

'Those reporters deserve a flogging,' she went on. 'Apparently that Valentine Williams man procured a motorcar and hid it behind a rock in the Valley. He had a team of natives on hand to *drive* that wretched cable of his to the ferry, and that's how he scooped *The Times*. Can you imagine what that little escapade cost Reuters? They had to buy the car, at *least* three hundred pounds, *and* ship it to Luxor – just for one ridiculous cable. The malice of it! He's spent the entire week boasting about it.'

'The world's gone mad. You know they've turned the tomb's discovery into a dance tune?' Herbert Winlock said. 'The Tutankhamun

Rag. It's the most requested number at the Winter Palace ballroom, I hear. Is that right, Eve?'

'I wouldn't know,' Eve replied. She had just entered the room and was at the tea table with Mrs Lythgoe; her father and Howard Carter remained outside on the terrace. 'I avoid that ballroom, Herbert. All those journalists, eavesdropping on every word I say, writing these vicious lies about my father and Howard. I won't be in the same *room* with them.'

'Quite, quite,' Mace said in a peaceable tone. 'The Tutankhamun Rag? Absolutely disgraceful. Though these days nothing would surprise me.'

I knew the Rag in question – I listened to it nightly. I'd first heard it drifting across from the Winter Palace; a day or so later, one of the houseboats moored near us had taken it up. The young Americans there danced to the tune every night, thumping out its rhythms on a piano and a banjo. Its jagged syncopations lodged in the brain. I could hear it now, under the conversation and complaints in the sitting room:

Tut, Tut, Tutsie, at last!
Three thousand years-plus have shot past
I guess dying was hell but
Ain't resurrection just swell?
Now git out of that tomb, hand over your diadem
Wanna do, wanna do the Tut-strut again –
No putrefaction to fear, here's to mummification, my dear
Get the latest sensation
Watch that boy-king's gyration –
It's the Tut-tut-tut-HANK-HANK-HANK
It's the Tut-HANK-amun RA-AG …

'Reprehensible,' Miss Mack was saying, as I surfaced. 'Such delicious cake. I wonder – is Mr Callender not joining us?'

'Gone for a walk, I expect,' said Mace, who was sitting next to her; he lowered his voice. 'Things are getting difficult at the Castle, Miss Mackenzie. Carter's moods. The rest of us can escape at the end of the day, but poor old Pecky can't. It's been getting pretty bad – we all catch the edge of Carter's tongue, and it's not pleasant. Not even Lord Carnarvon escapes. Sometimes Carter dresses him down as if he's a naughty two-year-old.'

He broke off with an expressive glance as Carter himself entered the room; Eve immediately hastened to welcome him. Mrs Lythgoe and Mrs Burton clustered around him, pressing him to take some cake, some sandwiches.

'Lord Carnarvon will be joining us in a moment,' Carter said, settling himself in an armchair. 'He's just having a cigarette on the veranda. No, no, I won't eat anything, thank you. Just tea. Gyppy stomach, not feeling too bright today.'

'Oh, poor you,' Eve said, perching on the arm of his chair. 'You must be exhausted. How many people did you have to conduct around the tomb today?'

'God alone knows. Forty? Sixty? It took up the entire day. I've been at it all week. I'm a tour guide now, didn't you know that?'

That remark might have been a jest, but the tone in which it was said was not pleasant. Carter looked ill; it must have been at least two weeks, perhaps more, since I'd last seen him close to, and the alteration in his appearance was marked. He'd lost weight, and his face, puffy around the eyes, drawn around the mouth, had acquired a sickly pallor.

I saw Herbert and Helen Winlock exchange a warning glance; leaning forward, Helen said in a quiet tone: 'You need a rest, Howard. Everyone does. Things will get better once you close the tomb for the season – they'll quieten down then.'

'If you say so. I beg to differ. They'll improve when Carnarvon realises I'm not running some blasted salon, I'm running a scientific dig. When he realises I've got better things to do than escort Lord-this and Lady-that around the Burial Chamber – when he understands I have work to do, and can't spend all day every day answering damn-fool questions – yes, maybe then they'll improve. Not before.' He paused, glaring at Eve. 'You might like to tell your father that. Maybe he'll listen to you. *I'm* sick to death of telling him.'

Eve coloured and did not reply; everyone else began speaking at once. Frances gave me a small nudge in the ribs: '*KV*,' she whispered. She knew we were about to be banished from the danger zone of Carter's irascibility – and so we were. I saw Mrs Lythgoe and Helen exchange a few quick words, and in moments we'd been extricated, sent on an errand. We were dispatched to the veranda outside: Frances carried a plate with cakes and sandwiches, I carried a cup of tea with lemon. We found Lord Carnarvon, stretched out on one of the planter's chairs, feet up, and eyes closed. He was wearing his Tennysonian hat, a three-piece tweed suit and an ancient brown cardigan for extra warmth. The temperature was by then in the high nineties; he appeared to be sleeping.

'We bring victuals, Lord Carnarvon,' Frances said, as he opened one pale grey eye. 'I added an extra slice of fruitcake, because I know you like that.'

'Oh I say, how tremendously kind,' he replied gallantly, rousing himself. 'How uncanny. I was just lying here thinking how peaceful and quiet it was, and how nice, how very *restorative* a slice of fruitcake would be — and lo and behold, here it is. Brought by two ministering angels.' He inspected the plate, which Frances had piled high. 'By Jove — don't think I can quite manage all that by myself. You two had better help me out. Draw up some chairs. This *is* fortuitous. I was hoping to have a brief word in private with you two, and now here you are. Excellent.'

We sat down as invited. Carnarvon sipped his tea and ate one cucumber sandwich. He talked on in a desultory way, as we munched fruitcake. Unlike Carter, he appeared unruffled by that day's events — indeed, they seemed scarcely to have registered with him. Instead he lapsed back into the past. 'My doctors sent me to Egypt,' he said, his eyes on the river below, 'after I had that motoring accident in Germany. Years ago now . . . That had left me badly smashed up, as I expect you've heard. Even when the bones mended and the wounds healed, I got every infection going — couldn't deal with English winters at all. Too damp, you know. So they sent me here for the warmth, and the air — and the air is marvellous, don't you find? So pure. So dry. Never fails to restore me.'

Frances was not interested in the qualities of Egyptian air. 'I hear there were over twelve thousand people in the Valley today,' she said. 'That must have been terrible.'

'Oh, I don't know, Frances,' he replied, in his genial way. 'They're interested — and why wouldn't they be? It's the find of the century. Makes it tricky for Carter, of course — he doesn't like showing people round the tomb. I can't blame him for that, but one's friends turn up, and what is one to do? Naturally, they want to see what we've found, and one can't just turn them away. Don't want to be uncivil . . .

Anyway, things will quieten down now. We'll close the tomb next week, and then Eve and I are going to take a little holiday. A few days in Aswan. Get away from newspapers, escape the journalists.'

'Do you mind about them?' Frances asked. 'Mrs Burton thinks they ought to be hanged, drawn and quartered,' she added imaginatively.

'By Jove, does she really?' He smiled. 'Well, no, Frances – I wouldn't go that far. Some of those reporter johnnies are quite amusing – resourceful too. I just wish they'd stop painting me as this arch villain.' He gave us a perplexed look. 'It's awfully rum, reading about yourself in the papers. I can't say I like it. I look at some of the stuff they write, and I think – *That's not me, they must be mixing me up with some other fellow.* D'you know the latest accusation? They're saying I want to remove poor old Tutankhamun and take him back to the British Museum – or maybe post him off to the Metropolitan; they can't seem to decide which.'

He shook his head in bewilderment. 'Why are they saying that, d'you think? I just can't understand it. I can't seem to grasp the way their minds work. It's not true, and they know that, so why do they go on repeating it? We'll have to open Tutankhamun's sarcophagus and examine him in due course, but that won't be for at least another year. And when all that gruesome business is over, I want Tutankhamun returned to his tomb in the Valley. That's where he rightly belongs. I don't want him in *any* museum, not even in Cairo. I don't intend him to be a public spectacle. I've made that very clear to Lacau, to Allenby, to everyone. And I shall ensure it happens.'

He paused, his eyes resting on the Valley, and then, after a pause, he asked Frances if she'd bring him some more tea. She left us, and he continued to gaze out across the river for some minutes until, rousing himself, as if suddenly remembering I was there, he said: 'So, Eve tells me you and Miss Mackenzie are leaving us – I'm sorry to hear that. Where are you off to, Miss Payne? Back to England – Cambridge, I think it was?'

I explained I was going to Paris first, because my father and step-mother were there.

'I've never been to Paris before,' I said, trying to fill the silence. 'My father is writing a book. It's about Euripides, and his influence on French dramatists. He's working in the Bibliothèque nationale at the moment.'

'Excellent. Writer, eh? Hadn't realised. Good for him. Wonderful city, Paris – you'll like it. My wife and I go there every year – she grew up in France, prefers it to England, I often think. We always stay at the Ritz and they look after one jolly well, we find, Miss Payne. I recommend it. Charming rooms, excellent breakfasts. I always like guava jelly at breakfast, funny habit of mine, don't know where that came from – and they get it in especially for me. Might you be staying there?'

'I don't think so. No.'

'Pity. Bit stuffy, of course. I'm sure there are many livelier places. Goodness, yes. Places where painters and writers go, Left Bank, Montmartre, that sort of thing. That might be more your father's line, maybe. I've always thought *I*'d like to be an artist, Miss Payne, dabbled with it a bit. I have a good eye, or so I like to think – well, you need a good eye to *collect* things, and I've always done that. I take photographs too, you know: pride myself on those – not just your common-or-garden snaps. I'm not in Harry Burton's league, of course, but I try to be artistic.' He paused.

'Hollywood's interested in our tomb – did you hear? So I had a go at writing a cinematic treatment, thought I might as well give it a try. I could see it so clearly in my mind's eye, but it was a bit tricky to get down on paper, I found. Don't know why, but I'm not always too comfortable on the writing front – I expect your father could teach me a thing or two there. But I plan to help Carter out with this book of ours. I thought I might write an introduction to it. Nothing too wordy, just a modest contribution – what do you think, Miss Payne?'

'I'm sure that would be a help, Lord Carnarvon.'

'Well, I hope so. Not too sure if Carter welcomes the book idea. Difficult to tell with him at present. Under a lot of strain, you know. Eve says he finds it hard to cope with that . . . ' He let the sentence tail away and turned his eyes back to the river.

There was a silence during which I tried to think of something to say, and failed. I suspected Carnarvon's predicament was similar; after an awkward interval, he turned to me, his eyes bright with inspiration, with information lost and now recalled.

'Rose . . . ' he said. 'Rose and little Peter – heard from them, have you, Miss Payne?'

'Yes, I had a letter last week. They're – very well.' That letter had contained the news of Rose's birthday puppy, its illness and demise. I wasn't sure whether to mention this.

'Delightful children – very fond of them. Devoted to their poor mother. A sad business, that. I still miss Mrs d'Erlanger. A beautiful woman and one of the kindest hearts I've ever known. I can't believe that door is forever closed . . . It's been a year now, you know. Terrible for Rose and Peter. I hear their father is remarrying. An American.'

'I didn't know that.' I looked at him uncertainly; the ghost of Poppy d'Erlanger rose up before my eyes; I caught the drift of her scent. '*Oh, hellishness*,' she remarked. I think perhaps Carnarvon also sensed her presence.

'Well, that's what I've *heard*, Miss Payne.' He turned his cool grey eyes to mine. 'I know I can rely on your discretion. Say nothing to Rose and Peter – I may be misinformed. Probably rumour and sur-mise – probably nothing to it, like all this stuff they write about me in the papers. Ah, Frances, there you are. Thank you.'

He drank the tea Frances brought – I think he was relieved at her return, as I was. Poppy's ghost sighed and vanished. Carnarvon rum-maged in the deep pockets of his elegant, shabby jacket. 'Now where did I put them?' he said, patting one, then another. 'Ah, here we are . . . '

He extracted two small parcels, wrapped in newspaper and tied up with string, and examined them with a frown. 'The thing is,' he began in a hesitant way, 'you two girls have been very kind to Eve recently, and I'm grateful. It's far worse for her than it is for me, all this guff in the newspapers. I can shrug it aside, water off a duck's back – but she tends to brood on it. Eve is sensitive, imaginative – and she has me to look after on top of everything else. Not always in the best of health, which is a worry for her and – well, never mind all that. No man could have a better or a more loving daughter, or a more loyal friend and ally, that's my point. The apple of my eye. Eve told me how you came to her aid in the Valley the other week, how kind you were – and how discreet.' He paused. 'These little things are our way of thanking you for that.'

He handed the two parcels across. 'To be opened when you get home to England, Miss Payne — and you, Frances, when you're back in America. Not before, agreed? And no need to discuss them. Just a small memento. Our little secret, eh?'

With that, he shook hands with us in turn and strolled into the American House. He left not long afterwards with Carter, the two men setting off for the Castle. Eve kissed Miss Mack and me goodbye, then left in the opposite direction for Luxor. Frances and I escaped to her bedroom and said our farewells there, in front of the small shrine of photographs: her little brother, lost in the waters of Penobscot Bay, watched over us.

'I think our presents are identical,' Frances said, examining her parcel and mine in a covetous way. 'Same size, same shape, same weight . . . Oh, what can they be? Shall we open them now, Lucy?'

'No, no, no, no,' I said, though I could tell from the wicked glint of amusement in her eyes that she'd probably open hers the second I'd gone.

'Oh, very well,' she replied, and then held up her hand and pressed my palm against hers.

'Eternal truth, for ever and always, remember,' she said fiercely, and when we'd solemnly renewed our pledge, we hugged, kissed goodbye and then I left. Miss Mack descended the track to our houseboat slowly. I ran all the way to the Nile.

It didn't take me long to pack. My standards would have disappointed the perfectionist Nicola Dunsire, but I was torn by grief at leaving and excitement at where I'd be next, so I dispensed with tissue paper and just stuffed my clothes into cases. I packed my prize possessions more carefully, the little Egyptian library, all my letters and diaries, Peter's drawing of a rainbow, the books on my reading list . . . I could tick them all off except for one, a translation of Flaubert's *L'Éducation sentimentale*, which Nicola had told me to save for my journey. In half an hour the task was complete — and throughout that half-hour the keys of the Oliver No. 9 clattered away without pause. They fell silent as I left my cabin to go on deck, and not long afterwards Miss Mack joined me there, her face pale, her brow concentrated. Sinking into a chair, giving me a dreamy, seraphic smile, she broke with routine, lit her daily cigarette two hours early and inhaled deeply.

'Lucy, my dear,' she said, 'it is done.'

The solemnity with which she spoke could mean only one thing. I said: 'The Book?'

Miss Mack inclined her head in assent. 'It suddenly came to me, dear, walking back from the American House. There the ending was, as clear as could be. It was like taking dictation, like being a *medium*, Lucy dear. Most extraordinary. I simply sat there, and my fingers *flew* over the keys. Two paragraphs – well, maybe four; five or six at the most – and it was over. I do hope I have done it all justice. I have tried very hard, you know. Triple-spaced. Four hundred pages, Lucy, imagine that! I have wrapped it in my best silk scarf, the one Mother bought me in Florence all those years ago, and the second I get back to Princeton I shall take it to a publisher my dear father knew. He's a little elderly now, and retired of course, but he will know *exactly* where I should place it.'

Tears had welled up in her eyes. I embraced, kissed and congratulated her. This was wonderful news, a fitting climax to our stay – perhaps, I suggested shyly, we should drink a toast to it? Miss Mack thought that an excellent idea, so Mohammed was asked to fetch wine, and two glasses were poured. The Book, which had been rechristened several times over the course of the past two months, now had its final title: *In Search of a Lost Tomb*.

We drank to its success, and, as the light began to burn red over the Theban hills, Miss Mack, in an act of great daring, poured us both a second glass, diluting mine very heavily with Evian. We were sipping these when we were suddenly interrupted by halloos, huffings and puffings from the river path; seconds later, pale, sweating and deeply agitated, Pecky Callender appeared.

Miss Mack, rising in surprise to greet him, took one look at his expression and sent me below. I lay in my cabin and read the first chapter of the Flaubert, wondering what could be happening on the deck above, from which the sound of Callender's voice, but not his words, drifted down to me. He spoke, with brief interjections from Miss Mack, for half an hour. Then I heard his footsteps descend the gangplank and set off on the track along the river.

Could it be – was it possible? I hastened back to the deck: one look at the consternation on Miss Mack's face and I knew my surmises were wrong.

Callender had come to say his goodbyes to us, but his chief reason for visiting was not as I'd supposed. He'd been escaping from the Castle, Miss Mack explained — and from a bitter quarrel that had broken out between Carnarvon and Carter, only minutes after they'd arrived there. Callender had quickly made himself scarce and fled to his own room — but he'd still been able to hear their voices, especially Carter's. It had gone on for a good hour and had left him shaken. It had ended, he'd related unhappily, when Carter ordered Lord Carnarvon to leave his house that instant and never return.

'He banned Lord Carnarvon from his house?' I stared at Miss Mack. 'I can't believe that. Did Mr Callender explain why they quarrelled? Lord Carnarvon seemed perfectly calm when Frances and I were speaking to him.'

'Lucy, I truly don't know — and I don't think Pecky knows either. He said Carter was shouting about *partage*, about what should go to the Egyptian Museum and what shouldn't — he and Lord Carnarvon differ in their views on that issue, I think, though I can't be sure. At one point,' she lowered her eyes, 'at one point, Mr Carter must have poured himself a drink, and Pecky thinks Lord Carnarvon told him he should ease up on the amount he drank, that it wasn't good for him . . . One can imagine, can't one, dear: that would be like waving a red rag at a bull. Beyond that—'

'Was it about Eve?' I interrupted.

'My dear, I'm not sure. I feel Eve is already coming to her senses in that respect. She is very fond of Mr Carter, that I don't doubt — but she is a young woman of spirit, and she does *not* take kindly to that bullying tone he can use. That was very evident this afternoon, Lucy. He spoke slightingly of her father, in front of everyone, as you heard. Eve let it pass. But while you were outside, he did it again. Eve reprimanded him, quite lightly, but the line was drawn. When he crossed it a *third* time, she snubbed him — and most effectively too.

'My own opinion, Lucy, is that Mr Carter sometimes attempts to drive a wedge between father and daughter, for reasons I don't begin to understand. Possibly because that is his nature — he is quarrelsome. Possibly because he seeks to influence her father through Eve. Mr Carter, I fear, does not understand one simple rule: *never* attempt to come between two people who love one another. Anyone who does that will always and inevitably lose.'

Miss Mack spoke with authority; I listened closely to her words — and would remember them.

We ate our last meal on the *Queen Hatshepsut* and the quarrel was not mentioned again, except once, when we glimpsed Callender, returning to Castle Carter.

'Will you need to alter anything in The Book, Miss Mack?' I asked. 'In view of what's happened tonight – will you need to make changes?'

'Certainly not, Lucy,' she replied crisply. 'I have no doubt that this quarrel will be mended, and it is a private affair. Besides, The Book has done with me. I have served its purposes. It is now writ in stone.'

As it turned out, that was far from the case – but I wasn't to know that then. I went to bed for the last time on our *dahabiyeh* and dreamed of The Book. It harried me all night, taking different forms: one minute, fragile leaves that I was trying to retrieve and rescue as they fluttered into the sky; the next, oppressive Old Testament tablets, tumbling down on me like a collapsing wall. I woke very early, glad to see the first light, glad to be rescued from *In Search of a Lost Tomb* at last.

I went out on deck to watch the beauty of the Nile at dawn: the rose sky reflected in the river water, the slow eclipsing of the stars, the humming of insects and the cry of birds as the light reached the reeds and made their black shapes emerald. I was still there an hour later, as the light strengthened, and it was then that I saw a small swift figure, running down the track from the American House. It was Frances, and she sped straight to me. 'I crept out,' she said, catching her breath. 'I'll have to get back before they notice I've gone, so we must be quick. Fetch that parcel from Carnarvon, Lucy — fetch it now.'

I retrieved it and returned. 'Open it,' she said. 'I opened mine after you'd gone.'

Something in her expression told me not to argue, so I did so. I unwrapped the string and newspaper; inside it, padded in cotton wool, was a small blue faience *shabti* figure. Without speaking, Frances reached into her pocket and drew out its twin. We held the two figures next to each other: they were almost exactly the same size and colour; their glaze was identical – there was a slight difference in the expressions of our answerers' faces but beyond that it was hard to tell them apart.

'Look.' Frances pointed to a band of hieroglyphs that ran down the front of the statues. I recognised some of them from the seals I'd seen on the Antechamber's north wall; I could make out the oval cartouche with Tutankhamun's throne name. I stared at the little figures in excitement and dismay.

'Oh, Frances, have these come from the tomb?'

'Of course. There are hundreds of *shabti* there – and these aren't especially good ones, there are others much, much finer. But they're lovely, aren't they?' She stroked the band of hieroglyphs. 'Look, this is a spell from *The Book of the Dead* . . . Oh Lucy, such a face! You mustn't be shocked. Everyone knows Lord Carnarvon's taken a few things from the tomb, nothing too valuable, mostly little objects, choice items that caught his eye – it's on account, as it were! Even if he's denied his half-share of the tomb's contents, *masses* of things will come his way sooner or later. Meanwhile, he's picked out a few beauties. Daddy's always said that Lordy keeps a "pocket collection". And he has deep pockets in those jackets of his, as you've seen.'

Frances smiled. An archaeologist's daughter, she was neither shocked, nor greatly concerned: such transgressions were commonplace in that era, of course. I *was* shocked. I looked uncertainly at my *shabti* figure, remembering Mohammed's accusations of theft and pilfering. I knew that if Miss Mack saw it, she would be appalled. She would regard it as plunder, as grave-robbing; she would insist on its immediate return. No doubt she was right, but the little figure was speaking to me; I felt it wanted to stay in my care.

'Which part of the tomb do you think they came from, Frances?' I asked.

'Who knows? I told you – there are hundreds. These might be from the Antechamber or the Burial Chamber. Maybe Carnarvon picked them up the night they broke in there – and I hope they *are* from there, Lucy: that would make them super-powerful.'

She leaned forward, planted a kiss on my cheek and turned to go. 'They're twins – wasn't that thoughtful of Carnarvon? I expect he knows how close we are, and now we'll be closer still. These will bind us together. Whenever I look at mine, I shall think of you,

Lucy — and you must do the same. Always remember: *where you go, I go.*'

She gave me one last quicksilver glance, thrust her *shabti* figure back in her pocket and ran for the shore. Halfway up the track to the American House, she turned and waved. I watched her small figure recede, then disappear. I returned to my cabin and looked at my answerer hard and long: it was stern-faced, compact; packed with three thousand years-plus of power. Covetousness gripped me: no matter how wrong it might be, I couldn't bear to relinquish it. This wasn't some tourist fake: it was unquestionably genuine —unlike the one I'd given my father, the one broken in circumstances that remained unexplained, the one whose shards and fragments Nicola had swept up and thrown away. *How do you tell the difference between the real and the fake, Lucy? Tell me, I want to know.*

Now I shall show her, I thought. When a king called upon one of his answerers in the afterlife, it at once rose up to do his bidding: *Here I am*, it would say. I wondered if this little figure would obey me in the same way. I wrapped it in layers of cotton wool and tissue paper. I hid it inside a petticoat and buried it in the folds of my birthday dress.

There it stayed, for the duration of my journey back to Europe, its existence concealed. Its powers were increased, I felt, by this secrecy.

The day I arrived in Paris I gave it to Nicola Dunsire. I'd attached a label to it by then, in the italic script I'd perfected; it read: *For Nicola, from Lucy, with love. The real thing! Egypt—Paris, 1923.*

SIX

The Book of the Dead

... the growing good of the world is partly dependent on
unhistoric acts; and that things are not so ill with you and me
as they might have been, is half-owing to the number who lived
faithfully a hidden life, and rest in unvisited tombs.

George Eliot, *Middlemarch*

32

'Mary Cassatt,' Dr Fong said, 'Berthe Morisot . . .'

He was moving slowly along the north wall of my Highgate sitting room, where most of my paintings hang – it's the only space available to them, all the other walls being book-clad: a rainy day in July, the morning light silvery but thin – a heterogeneous art collection. Dr Fong was examining it minutely. He bent to examine the small Degas of a ballet dancer, lingered by Sargent's portrait of my mother Marianne, attempted to read Helen Winlock's signature on a still life, and failed. He briefly examined an unsigned pencil sketch of a small puppy lying on its back in the sun and returned to the Cassatt, which seemed to be his favourite. A lovely thing. It depicts a mother and child.

He had his back to me, and seeing that the paintings gripped his attention, I edged closer to my desk, picked up the small blue faience *shabti* figure that stood upon it and quickly slipped it inside a drawer. If Dr Fong was going to inspect my belongings, I did not want him inspecting that. From a distance yes; but not close up. I did not intend his expert eyes to read its king's cartouche, and I had no intention of answering the awkward questions that would ensue if he did. Stolen goods. I eased the drawer inwards; it creaked as it shut.

Rose, seated across the room, here for lunch to celebrate my birthday, saw this manoeuvre and, sympathising with the motives that lay behind it, raised her eyebrows and smiled. Loyal friend that she is, she embarked on diversionary tactics, at which she is skilled. 'Lucy's spoils,' she remarked. 'All this — and she's not even *alarmed*! Disgraceful, isn't it, Dr Fang?'

Waving a vague hand at my paintings, she rose and crossed to Dr Fong, who, gracefully, did not correct her version of his name. He'd attempted to do so twice in the hour that had passed since he arrived (out of the blue; without so much as a phone call) and had perhaps decided Rose was stone deaf; now he had given up. Side by side, they both inspected my wall.

They made an unlikely pair, I thought, sinking down into my old chintzy chair by the front windows, and moving the piles of Egypt books that encircled it. Rose, a diminutive white-haired figure, wearing a red suit of light wool made for her by Norman Hartnell some thirty years before, scarcely reached to Fong's shoulder. Fong, over six foot, lanky and laid-back, was wearing his usual hideous trainers, blue jeans and a T-shirt with the unlikely message: *Fond Greetings from Silicon Valley*. A large watch was strapped to his thin wrist, with a Mickey Mouse figure pointing the hours. He was wearing his wedding ring again — that had reappeared since a flying visit he'd made to Berkeley in June. I wondered what, if anything, this told me. Considering the nature of such clues — how *tiny* clues can be, how they flit past like pipistrelles on a summer evening — I turned my eyes to the window. In the square opposite my house, a young woman in a tracksuit was slumped on a bench, staring into space, rocking a baby-buggy back and forth. I could just hear the child's wails; its mother looked exhausted, or possibly disconsolate.

'Most of Lucy's paintings came from her mother, who was American,' Rose was saying. 'And she was an Emerson — you know, *steel*, Dr Fang. Some of the others are Stockton leavings, because Lucy's connected to *them* too, don't ask how, it's all far too complicated . . . They left her some of their loot. The Morisot came from them, I think, and the Degas ballet girl — she's *so* lovely. Lucy and I took ballet classes together once, you know. In Cairo. A hundred years ago. That always reminds me of our lessons there. She looks like Frances, don't you think, Lucy? You remember how exquisitely she danced?'

'*Emerson?*' Dr Fong said, before I could reply. He gave me a weighing glance. 'I didn't know about that connection. Stockton too . . . As in railroads?'

An expression of surprise and distaste crossed his face. Rose who did not like her riffs, or her chattering-on as she called it, to be interrupted, answered him before I could. 'Yes, yes, railways — and later, planes and armaments and bombs and guns and heaven knows what. Lucy didn't tell you? I'm not surprised.'

'Me neither,' said Dr Fong.

'Which do you like the best?' Rose continued, slipping her arm through his and giving him one of her little-old-lady smiles. 'My favourite is this tiny sketch of a puppy — but that's because she was *my* dog, and she died, poor thing. It's valueless, of course, just a drawing some friend dashed off one summer's day — but it's charming, don't you think?'

'Apt,' Fong ventured.

Since he did not know the identity of the artist, Howard Carter's sketch did not engage him long. Rose whisked him back to the Berthe Morisot — an eternal summer's day, two young girls in a sailing boat. She dallied by Sargent's version of my mother, exclaimed over Helen Winlock's still life — wild flowers and berries in a blue jar — threw up a great deal more flak and misinformation, and finally drew him to the last of the paintings, a portrait of Nicola Dunsire. It had been painted by Nicola's friend, bicycle-thief Clair, the summer she moved into our house in Cambridge. Clair came to stay for a month and remained for seven years. My father, rarely there in any case, had never seemed to object to her presence; I had. I called her 'the cuckoo in the nest', usually behind her back, once to her face. This antipathy had failed to dislodge her.

It was entitled *Newnham Garden, Summer 1928* — the summer I turned eighteen and won a place at Nicola Dunsire's former Cambridge college, Girton; the summer I moved out and Clair moved in. Most of Clair's paintings had titles that were similarly opaque; they were informative, specific — and told you nothing at all. It was a large canvas: wearing a novitiate white dress, Nicola Dunsire stood next to our rose arch, her eyes appearing to rest on someone, or perhaps respond to someone, who was behind the artist's shoulder, outside the frame.

'It's a Lennox,' Rose was saying. 'And Clair Lennox is *unbelievably* fashionable now. My granddaughter works at a gallery in Cork Street and she's mad about Lennox's paintings. I can't see it, can you? I can see the colours are glorious – they do *sing*, don't they? But I hate the way she stabs on the paint. That's Lucy's stepmother, Nicola Foxe-Payne. It's a very good likeness. She and Lennox were bosom friends. They died in the Blitz together. Nicola was terribly beautiful, wasn't she?'

'Very,' Fong replied. 'Troubling, though. It's unsettling – can't put my finger on it.'

'All Lennox's paintings are like that,' I said, interrupting before Rose could say more. 'They point you in one direction – and then in its opposite. The more closely you look, the more that's so.'

Taking pity on Fong, I gave him a glass of wine, poured Rose a gin-and-it. I made a face at her: *Cut it out, Rose: no more biography*, it said. 'Fifteen minutes while I cook the chicken,' I announced. 'Then I'm going to shoo you out, Dr Fong.'

'Happy days, chin-chin, Dr Fang,' Rose said, raising her glass. 'Isn't this fun? Now you simply must tell me *all* about your book and your documentary – but you must speak up: I'm the tiniest bit deaf, or so Lucy complains. I can't promise to read your book, because I'm not a great reader. But I can't wait to see your telly programmes. I shall *record* them,' she added, beaming. 'I've just bought one of those DVD whatsits.'

I left them to it and escaped to the basement kitchen. I fiddled with the birthday lunch, a recipe by Elizabeth David: she found it simple and straightforward; I did not. I leaned against the ancient butler's sink, washing lettuce leaves for a salad. I chopped herbs from my garden. The knife slipped in my old hands and I cut myself.

How copiously fingers bleed, from the smallest gash! I ran cold water until my hand felt numb, then dried it and slapped on an Elastoplast. A quiet day in London town. I could feel the ghosts gathering in the kitchen, murmuring by the fridge, protesting from the pantry region. They had been stirred up by that discussion of my paintings, and today, this happens, their mood was not benevolent. *Leave me alone, bugger off*, I told them – and that was a mistake. Spectres don't like it when you take that tone with them. Trust me, this is true. And if you don't believe me, if you think perhaps that I'm being fanciful, see how you feel when – if – you get to my age. Just you wait.

I poked at the chicken pieces in the pan, then gave them a pall of crème fraîche. I returned to the stairs – the arthritis was in summer abeyance, so I climbed them slowly but without any great pain. As I approached the hall, I could hear that Rose and Fong were now getting on like a house on fire. They were deep in the subject of Lord Carnarvon's death, and its aftermath.

'Two in the morning – at the Continental Hotel in Cairo,' Fong was shouting. He had clearly not twigged that this small, deaf, inconsequential old woman had known Carnarvon and was familiar with all these events. 'Bitten on the cheek by a mosquito while on a visit to Aswan with his daughter Lady Evelyn, that February. He nicked the bite with a razor, and blood-poisoning set in shortly after they reached Cairo. Followed by pneumonia, which spelled the end – but then he was a sick man, his immune system was shot, and this is pre-penicillin. It was 5 April 1923 – almost six weeks to the day from the opening of Tutankhamun's Burial Chamber. As predicted, allegedly, by some hack from the *Mail*. I've checked, and there's no record of that remark of his until *after* Carnarvon died. Which makes me just a *tad* suspicious.'

'And when Carnarvon died – at that exact moment,' Rose chimed in, 'all the lights in Cairo went out. At least, I believe that's what everyone *claims.*'

'That could be true, amazingly. There are records of a power failure that night.'

'Meanwhile, back in England, at Highclere Castle, his little dog suddenly woke up—'

'Oh, sure. Like, at exactly two in the morning Cairo time. It gave one piercing howl—'

'And dropped down dead.' Rose paused and sighed. 'I have to admit, I do *slightly* have my doubts about that. Gilding the lily. I can see it helped to get the Curse story off to a *very* good start, but frankly, it's complete rubbish. At Carnarvon's funeral, no one mentioned the doggie's timely demise, I can tell you.'

There was a silence. 'You mean you were *at* that funeral?' Fong said, his tone startled.

'Of course I was,' Rose replied. 'Eve was my godmother. I'd known Carnarvon all my life – he was very good to me and to my brother after my mother died. And very moving and strange that funeral was – up there on the downs, overlooking his house and his domain. It was spring, you see. A perfect English spring day. Hundreds upon hundreds of larks, singing their hearts out.'

I pushed back the door and re-entered the room. 'An *exultation* of larks,' I said, with finality, as polite Dr Fong rose to his feet. 'And now I'm afraid you must go,' I added, showing no mercy.

Fong gave me a plaintive glance, then turned to look sadly at Rose. He was kicking himself, realising he'd missed out on a source – that was evident. He fumbled for his card. 'Hey, I'm sorry,' he said. 'There I was, holding forth – I hadn't realised you knew Carnarvon. I'd like to ask you – I didn't quite catch your name, Lady, er—'

'Oh how nice!' Rose exclaimed, accepting the card, and tucking it into her ancient Hermès handbag. 'I *do* hope you'll be kind about dear Lord Carnarvon, Dr Fang. He was a charming man, you know – perfect manners. So delightful to have met you at last.' She shook his hand. 'I wish you *every* success with your labours.'

Rose had had many decades to perfect the act of dismissal: Fong accepted defeat. He drank the last of his wine and gave the room one final, keen inspection. 'I see you've moved your *shabti* figure, Miss Payne,' he remarked. 'Pity. I liked that.'

I led him into the hall, making no comment. 'I like your *shabti* too,' Rose said, when I returned. She had retrieved the little figure from the drawer where I'd concealed it, was holding it up to the light and turning it this way and that. 'It has an alert look – ever-watchful eyes. One of those enigmatic Egyptian smiles – the ones you see on so many of their statues. Just a small curve of the lips. An air of wise benevolence . . . If you call, does he answer? Have you ever tried it, Lucy?'

'No. He was made to answer to a king, not me. Disappointing if he didn't answer my calls. And alarming if he did.'

'Is this the one Carnarvon gave you – is that why you hid it?'

'No. I gave that one to Nicola Dunsire. She kept it for years. And then, during the Blitz . . . it disappeared along with everything else. There was nothing left of her house, Rose. It took a direct hit.' I hesitated. 'This is its twin – its near-twin. It's the one Lord Carnarvon gave Frances.'

'And Frances gave it to you?' Rose looked at me closely. 'I didn't know that.'

'It was at Saranac Lake. It was the last time I saw her.'

'Oh, I *see*.'

There was a silence. Rose gave the little answerer a last considering look, then gently replaced it on my desk. She and I are attuned to each other. 'How hard it is, being old, too many memories,' she said softly, catching my expression, lacing her arm through mine. 'How glad I am you're still here, Lucy. What would I do without you? I'm sorry, this is my fault – I started it, didn't I, rattling on about your paintings? And now I've been clumsy again. What a fool I am. I didn't mean to trespass, truly. Don't, Lucy, darling, oh, please don't cry – we mustn't be sad: not today. It's your birthday, remember.'

Rummaging in the pocket of her jacket, she produced one of her handkerchiefs: starched, monogrammed, lace-edged, relic of a lost era. I dabbed at my treacherous eyes, and she said: 'Stiff upper lip. England and empire and backbone and all that tosh. Dearest Lucy – deep breath. That's better. Well done. Now tell me – what have you made for us?'

'It's a sort of chickeny thing.'

'I *love* your chickeny things. Let's go and have lunch.'

As we ate, I could tell Rose was casting about for a subject that was neutral and unlikely to provoke waterworks. We were eating in my kitchen, which is large, comfortable and dilapidated. The table is an old one of scrubbed pine, rescued from some scullery region, and a trophy from one of my marriages, I forget which; the first, Rose always says. Rose, expert since childhood at meaningless social conversations, her art honed by decades of dinner and cocktail parties, was very good at talking about nothing, to anyone, and at length. We had reached the pudding before she risked any subject beyond the charming objects on my kitchen dresser, the charming view of the garden beyond the rear window and – to liven things up – the latest escapades of her sons, one of whom was divorcing his errant wife. They'd been married some three years, and now she'd flitted.

'And about time too,' Rose said. 'Naturally, I haven't interfered, and I've been as silent as the grave on the subject, but I knew she'd be trouble. I disapprove of divorce, but in this case . . . Oh, poached peaches – *and* they're delicious. What a good cook you are, Lucy – do you remember, at Nuthanger, those cookery lessons Wheeler used to give us? How I loved that house! This kitchen *so* reminds me of the one there — making pastry! Petey and I were cack-handed, but you had a light touch, even then . . . I'm just thinking, Lucy, dear.' She paused, and I braced myself. 'Is it good for you, digging around in all this Egyptian stuff? I can see why you embarked on it, when Dr Fang showed up — but aren't you getting buried? I saw those bundles of letters, those book mountains. You're looking exhausted. Slightly haunted. It's not *healthy*. Why not give the past a rest?'

I made some non-committal remark. It seemed effective — though with devious Rose, one could never be certain. She diverted.

'Mind you — I *did* like Fang,' she announced. 'And he certainly knows his stuff. He had some ingenious theories. *He* thinks one of the reasons Carnarvon decided to give up on Egypt that summer — before Carter changed his mind for him, of course — was the knowledge that naughty Almina Carnarvon was straying. She'd almost certainly strayed before, but this time it was serious. That last year she was in Paris with that frightful Dennistoun man for *months*. Your Dr Fang thinks the Carnarvons did a deal: I give up Egypt, and you give up that creep Dennistoun.'

'Possible,' I said. Almina Carnarvon, subject of marital gossip before Tutankhamun's tomb was even found, conspicuous by her absence once it *was* found, had been summoned by Eve, and had flown to Cairo when her husband lay dying. She reached him in time; her inconsolable grief then and at his funeral had been remarked upon by everyone. She married her lover the following November, a scant eight months later.

'*Or ere those shoes were old,*' Nicola Dunsire had remarked tartly, on seeing the reports of the sparsely attended Register Office wedding. Lady Carnarvon's action caused affront, as did her choice of bridegroom, 'Tiger' Dennistoun, louche ex-husband of her friend Dorothy, the woman with coiled-cobra hair whom I'd briefly encountered that day at Highclere. Scandal ensued; there had been some notorious court case. I wondered why Rose kept harping on divorce and marital infidelity. I changed the subject.

'Did Dr Fong ask about Eve?' I asked, making coffee.

'Not much — and I was *hyper*-careful what I said. I reminded him Eve married lovely Brograve Beauchamp six months after her father died. You remember him, Lucy? He and Petey fed my little puppy that day at Highclere. He and Eve were tremendously happy, you know. I emphasised that to your Dr Fang – I thought it might help scotch any rumours he'd heard about Eve and Howard Carter, and he *had* heard rumours, I could tell . . . So ridiculous! Carter was cantankerous, ill bred and old enough to be her father. As if Eve would have given him a second glance.'

'She did give him a second glance. Even a third. I saw it.'

'A passing infatuation. If that. How you exaggerate, Lucy.'

'You weren't *there*, Rose,' I snapped. Rose's ability to detect other people's feelings had always been unreliable. Sometimes she could be sharp, at other times, obstinately blind. 'After they found the tomb – there *was* something. You could sense it. Frances thought—' I hesitated. 'Frances thought it was the experience of discovering the tomb with him that caused it. She thought it had – bewitched Eve.'

I was expecting pragmatic Rose to dismiss that word and that suggestion; to my surprise, she didn't. '*Bewitched?*' she said in a tart way, eyeing me. 'How clever of Frances. She often hit the nail on the head, didn't she? All right, I can imagine that. I've seen women bewitched, Lucy. *And* I've seen the consequences.'

She did not expand on that acidic remark – and I did not invite her to do so. It was followed by a few uncomfortable moments, *un mauvais quart d'heure*. But the awkwardness that had fallen between us passed, as it does with those who have known one another as long as Rose and I have. With our coffee, Rose produced a box containing a miniature birthday cake, adorned with a single candle for simplicity's sake. We lit it, and I solemnly blew it out. Rose wished me Many Happy Returns – which, as we both knew, was a triumph of hope over realism.

At three, she made ready to leave. Wheeler was collecting her in her new eco-efficient car, a baby Mercedes – she was going on to visit the divorcing son, in deepest Kensington. I think she truly was anxious on my behalf, for she said I shouldn't be on my own, and tried to persuade me to join her. I was touched, but I refused. I wanted to be alone with my importunate ghosts. The time had come, I felt, to propitiate them.

At the far end of my back garden, there is a gate that leads out into a lane, and that lane winds behind houses towards a verdant park and, adjoining it, to the two sections – ancient and less ancient – of Highgate's famous cemetery. By the time Rose left, the thin rain of the morning had ceased, and a watery sun had emerged. I decided to go for a walk, to take my phantoms for a walk. The arthritis re-awoke and began to nag, inevitably, but it's fatal to give in to its arguments: if you do, it exhibits those same Napoleonic tendencies once so evident in Miss Mack's book. It takes you over and it does you down. *I'm going for a walk*, I told it. *Get used to it.*

I set off, grasping my stick, and took the route through the park. I passed the tennis courts where numerous *sportive* enthusiasts were grunting and banging balls within millimetres of the baseline – Wimbledon fortnight always has this effect. I passed the disused bandstand that's redecorated with new graffiti each week, and sur-veyed the duck pond. One white swan traversed the dark mirror of its surface, and my mind drifted to a swansdown powder puff hiding a wedding ring on Mrs d'Erlanger's dressing table, then to a *Swan Lake* girl in a Cairo ballet class: *Maintenant, on essaie le ballon, mademoiselle*, said a voice – so I knew my ghosts were assembling.

By then, I'd reached the southern section of the park, and through its boundary hedge could glimpse from the rear the great granite head of Karl Marx that marks his burial place. As I had come this far it seemed faint-hearted not to continue, so I left by the lowest of the park gates and turned immediately left, into the eastern section of the cemetery. It is large, wild and beautiful; it contains old graves, but it is still in use. I have purchased a plot here – one must look ahead and be practical.

The park had been crowded with children, with sunbathers, with dog walkers, though I'd scarcely registered their presence. I became aware of them only once they were absent. There was a cluster of German and Japanese tourists paying homage to Marx, but once I was beyond his colossal Ramessid head, there were few visitors. I passed into the winding leafy avenues of the cemetery, choosing my route at random, passing a huddle of angels, of crosses, and (the tombs here are eclectic) paused at a pyramid. I was in one of the more overgrown sections now, deep in the blue shade of trees, the tombs necklaced with ivy. I debated whether I should go in search of famous graves, George Eliot's, for example: she lies here, beneath an Egyptian obelisk. I could hear Miss Dunsire's voice, sharp with reproof, black in mood, reprimanding me for my failures with Eliot's *Middlemarch*. Learn to *read*, you stupid obstinate girl, she said. Can't you see under the words, behind them, beyond them?

Had I ever learned that difficult art? Perhaps not – though it was not for want of trying. I decided against searching for Eliot – too far; might get lost. So I sat down on a memorial bench by a tangle of dog roses, inhaled their fugitive scent and closed my eyes. A certain constriction around the heart, an incipient faint breathlessness: I'd walked further than was wise. I closed my eyes and the spooks, who are patient, who had bided their time, were on me in an instant.

The Egyptian ghosts are the wiliest and they came first, as they usually do – or perhaps, knowing them to be less dangerous than some of their accomplices, I offer them less resistance. They caught me by the hand, pushed and propelled, until they had me where they wanted me, deep in the Valley of the Kings. Back to its heat and its silence, the only sound the murmur of rock doves and the sharp cry of the kites skimming the updraughts. I watched as Frances and I buried a pink leather purse below a guardian statue, a purse containing a confetti of lineage; I watched Miss Mack scan the Valley with her field glasses from the hills high above, Lord Carnarvon tip his hat in ironic salute to a cluster of journalists as he strolled into a tomb, and Howard Carter, thinking himself alone, pick up a handful of stones and fling them at the rock face. The dead await us, Herbert Winlock said, and taking Frances's hand, following the beam of our flashlights, I stepped out of the heat of the sun and into the dark world tunnelled into the hillsides.

'Do you believe in the famous Tutankhamun Curse, Miss Payne?' Dr Fong asked me the other day, on one of his visits. 'Did you ever believe in it?'

I had told him 'no', which is the answer I generally give when asked – and I've been asked that question many times over the intervening decades: the concept of Tutankhamun's Curse, for some reason, exerts a continuing undimmed fascination.

'Oh, I don't believe in it either,' people usually reply to my denials, 'of course, it is all nonsense.' And I wait for the 'but', the 'even so', and it almost always follows. 'But, even so, one must admit – it *is* odd, macabre . . . That cluster of deaths, some of them seriously *nasty*. I'm sure it's nothing more than coincidence, but—'

In the past, I used to argue. My questioners would cite their evidence: the cluster of deaths in the years after the tomb was opened: Lord Carnarvon, and his two much younger half-brothers, all dead within a few years; kindly Arthur Mace, returning to England an invalid after his second season in the Valley, never able to work again, dying six years later. They'd cite the sudden death of Albert Lythgoe and the unpleasant, premature death of the journalist Weigall, deaths that occurred within months of each other. They'd add other names: a secretary who'd briefly worked in the Valley for Carnarvon, who'd died in mysterious circumstances; that man's father, who contrived to jump to his death from a fourth-storey window despite being bedridden; and a little boy who'd been knocked down and killed by the hearse at the father's funeral. On and on that list went: out would come the names of more marginal figures – those who were *said* to have visited the tomb and *said* to have died within weeks, having been in perfect health until . . .

Once upon a time, when more combative than I am now, I'd point out that Howard Carter, discoverer of Tutankhamun, opener of his coffins, had worked on in the Valley for ten long years without mishap, and had died of natural causes in his own bed in London in 1939, seventeen years after first breaking into the tomb. I'd remind them that Eve, present when the tomb was opened – and one of the four people who broke into the Burial Chamber in secret too, though I'd never reveal that – had lived into serene old age, and had died in England at the age of seventy-nine, which did not suggest the forces in the tomb were too punitive or selective. Now I say nothing. People have this unassuageable appetite for supernatural influence; they *want* to believe in shadowy powers, ancient taboos – and who am I to argue?

Now I stay quiet and do not admit the truth, though I could admit it to myself, sitting in the quiet of the cemetery. I believe in the power of chance – and have good reason to do so. Beyond that, the truth is I *do* believe in curses, but I believe they emanate from within, are the fruits of our own nature and upbringing. Why should we need to believe in supernatural malevolence, in ills that are fated to strike us down from outside, when we are all more than capable of contriving them, bringing them down on our heads without the least external interference? *The curse is born within me, cried / The Lady of Shalott.*

The first book I wrote was called *Deserts.* I began work on it in 1931, immediately after graduating – though, as I was female, my degree had limitations: it would be another seventeen years before Cambridge would permit female graduates to be full members of the university. I was twenty-one when I began the book, twenty-three when it was published. Eager to leave England, and with the carelessness of youth, I selected almost at random the two deserts that would be its subject. The first was an area of the Sahara – that chose itself, for I could begin my journey in the Valley of the Kings, then, with Arab guides, explore further and see what happened. The second was the Mojave – which I selected for no better reason than it was in the right continent, and I could visit Frances after my journey. Many of my subsequent books, which are inevitably classified under 'Travel', have involved exploration of remote, inhospitable places. By the time I came to write these later books, people accepted my periodic vanishings: 'Oh, Lucy's taken off again,' they'd say and, obligingly, forget my existence until I reappeared. But that first book, and the journeys it involved, did cause remark and argument – even protest.

Those close to me flatly opposed the project and ridiculed the proposed title. 'The whole idea is foolhardy and ridiculous. Just when I believed you'd be coming home at last. Three years at Girton, never here – last year, an entire *summer* in Princeton with your beloved Miss Mack – and now you're going to *desert* me, Lucy?' Nicola Dunsire cried.

That remark angered me, as she'd intended: the summer spent in Princeton was Miss Mack's last. Her elderly mother had finally died some years before, and Miss Mack was living alone when illness gripped her. She had needed me, and I had stayed for those last months at her side . . . My so-called 'desertion' of Nicola was unlikely to affect her too grievously, I felt, given that bicycle-thief Clair Lennox was planted in our house, had already been dug in for the three years I'd spent at Girton, and still showed no inclination to uproot herself.

'You'll have the cuckoo in the nest to keep you company,' I snapped – at which Nicola gave an impatient sigh and the cuckoo concerned laughed unashamedly. She was sprawling in our sitting room, lounging in that old chair of my mother's with its 'Strawberry Thief' cover. A summer's evening: she and Nicola, as was their custom, were drinking glasses of red wine. Clair was smoking, dressed as usual in filthy old trousers and a smock, both paint-encrusted.

'Christ, you can be a pain in the arse, Lucy,' she said. 'Sod off to your desert. It should be right up your street.' Clair never minded mixing her metaphors – or mixing *it*, as we'd say now.

Nicola remained venomously and vehemently opposed to my deserts project: it seemed truly to frighten her – though whether on my account or her own was hard to say. When her opposition and threats failed to move me, she embarked on an outflanking manoeuvre. She raised the issue with my father, asking him to inter-vene – she did appeal to his authority, oddly enough, on occasion. In due course and in his presence the question of my journey and my book was canvassed one last time; his visits to our Newnham house were regular by then, always taking place on a Sunday, for lunch; he'd stay precisely two hours before returning to college.

The resulting argument lasted throughout one of those Sunday lunches. I said little. As had become my practice, I closed my ears to the discussion and let my mind drift away. I was thinking of those final weeks with Miss Mack: sometimes alert, sometimes high as a kite on morphine, she liked me to read the Bible to her in the morning, and Shakespeare in the afternoon. 'I am the resurrection,' she'd mutter. 'Must be *absolute* for death.'

Her funeral was already planned in fine detail; she had decided she wanted a blue lotus flower, Egyptian symbol of rebirth, on her tomb-stone. I'd helped chivvy the mason who was creating difficulties. I'd watched her browbeat the local Presbyterian minister, who, incensed at this heresy, was forbidding it – she soon put paid to *his* objections.

Upstairs in my attic room, where my suitcases were already packed for the journey Nicola was even now disputing, was my copy of The Book: it had never been published, and Miss Mack had spent much of the last nine years rewriting it. She had presented it to me the week before she died. The typescript was still in a manila envelope, on which, in Miss Mack's loopy handwriting, was the enigmatic inscription, *To the Lucy I once knew . . .* I hadn't been able to bear reading it.

With an effort, I returned to our Newnham dining room, where Nicola's appeals and arguments eddied. She was reaching the end of her dissertation, and her hands had begun to tremble; her voice had risen. Finally, the appeal to my father was made. 'Robert, surely *you* can make Lucy see sense? *Deserts?* It's just an excuse to run away from home. Within a week, she'll be running back to England. Or America. Taking shelter with her precious Rose and Peter. Rushing off to see that little prodigy, Frances. Write a *book?* Where did *that* idea come from? Lucy hasn't the will-power. She'll never see it through.'

'Oh, she'll see it through. I don't doubt that for a moment,' my father remarked, in an even tone. He had already pointed out that attempting to argue with me was futile. Along the length of our dining table, he inspected first Nicola, then a silent Clair Lennox, then me. Still handsome, his dark hair springy but greying; his light, faintly mocking hazel eyes rested on my face. He patted his mouth fastidiously with his white linen napkin, then tossed it aside. I could tell that he found the discussion tedious, that the atmosphere in the room, sharp as knives, merely served to irritate him. The library, as usual, called to him. His mind was on the book he had begun that summer. It was to be on Aeschylus, on the implacable nature of Aeschylean tragedy.

Now he glanced at his watch. '*Deserts*. A foolish, ill-considered project and, in my opinion, a preposterous title,' he remarked, with a tight smile. 'Surely it could be improved? Have you considered *Just Deserts*, Lucy, my dear?'

That was his final word on the subject. It took me years to realise how apt his punning was, but then my father, blind when he chose, could also be uncannily, and painfully, accurate. Sitting in the cemetery now, alone on my bench, hemmed about with gravestones, I caught the sound of laughter. Its mocking note was faint, but inescapable. It was visitors', no doubt – but I thought of it as my father's, dead these many decades, amused and delighted to be proved right at last.

Get lost, I said sharply and out loud, the sound of my own voice startling me. Obligingly, the ghost of my father bowed from the depths of the undergrowth and retreated. My mind drifted away to that *Deserts* journey I'd made: the crossing to Egypt, my stay in Cairo, travelling on the White Train, express to Luxor and the Valley . . . *He slipped past me in the darkness*, said a familiar voice. Difficult to say where it came from; perhaps the tangle of dog roses behind me.

33

I met Howard Carter during the course of the journeys for my desert book. It wasn't the last encounter I had with him, but it was the penultimate one – unless you include attendance at his funeral, which I do not. It was January 1932, exactly ten years on from my first visit to Egypt with Miss Mack: I had planned it that way. En route, and in Cairo, I visited the Egyptian Museum and spent many hours examining the 'wonderful things' Carter had unearthed from Tutankhamun's tomb over the decade that had passed. I had read about them, in numerous articles and books, by then, including those accounts Carter himself wrote, the first of which – written with the help of Arthur Mace – is untruthful in many respects, yet powerful and curiously honest, even so. I had seen them before too, in photographs – but pictures do not prepare you for the astonishing beauty of the objects themselves, nor for the force they exert when inspected closely, alone, and in silence.

I gazed at these wonderful things, with which almost everyone is familiar – the blue and gold outer shrine; the gold coffin; the gold face mask; the golden canopic chest, with its guardian goddesses glancing over their shoulders as if in protection or warning – and that is one of the greatest works of art I have ever seen, in Egypt or elsewhere. I looked at the golden throne, on which Tutankhamun is portrayed with his young wife-sister Ankhesenamun: she is tenderly anointing her husband-brother with some oil or ointment. I turned to the less famous relics, those that do not glitter but which speak, the things some visitors pass by: the hank of hair belonging to his grandmother, which, presumably, the boy king wished to have buried with him; funerary wreaths, with intricate weavings of papyrus, olive leaves, beads, berries and cornflowers; the child's glove Pecky Callender once spoke of, which someone had lovingly preserved. I wondered what these objects told one about the dead king: had his grandmother reared him? Had he been especially close to her? And who had chosen these wreaths? They were resonant, these clues, but the questions they raised remained unanswered and unanswerable.

I knew there were ugly realities behind the timeless serenity here. Carter, together with the chemist Lucas and the pathologist who had assisted them, had extricated the dead boy from the shell of his magnificent innermost coffin with the greatest of difficulty. The ritual libations, the resinous oils poured over his mummified, en-coffined body, had, in the space of three thousand years, become bituminous. They had solidified; as a result, the famous gold mask had fatally adhered to the embalmed face beneath it, and the king's remains were stuck fast inside their solid gold carapace.

The archaeologists had laid the coffin outside, in the fierce sun of the Valley of the Kings, in an attempt to soften this hard, black substance. When that failed to melt it, hot knives and burners were used, until at last a combination of gas jets and brute force freed the king's body and released it from its protective gold casings. When the autopsy took place, and the mummifying bandages were cut open with scalpels, a piteous shrunken body was finally revealed, in a poor state of preservation. Wrapped and concealed within the bandaging were astonishing artefacts. Tutankhamun's body had remained in his tomb, as Carnarvon had wished (and is still there, the sole king left in the Valley), but the riches found on his body were on display here in the museum.

I examined the gold dagger and the iron-bladed one, the amulets, the dazzling pectorals, collars, rings and bracelets, all masterpieces of the goldsmith's art. They glittered with inlays of blue faience, orange carnelian, green feldspar and that yellow Libyan desert glass whose origins remain mysterious. These sacred jewels, over one hundred of them, many decorated with spells from *The Book of the Dead*, had been placed to protect Tutankhamun's throat, his groin, his heart, his wrists . . . It was for this kind of booty that the thieves in antiquity had ripped their kings' mummies apart. In the case of Tutankhamun, uniquely, these sacramental jewels were saved. But damage had been caused. 'They broke his neck,' Frances had written to me. 'They broke his neck when they removed the gold face mask.'

I turned to inspect that mask once more. Oblivious to such indignities, it looked into the future with the absolute serenity of art. I hesitated in the face of its youth, beauty, sadness and stoicism, then turned to go. One last glass case stayed me: it contained the two tiny mummified bodies of Tutankhamun's and Ankhesenamun's stillborn children, who had been found in the room Carter called the Treasury. I wondered, as everyone who sees them must, whether they died as a result of their parents' brother-sister union, some fatal genetic defect. I wondered, as everyone must, what the interval was between their deaths and that of the father buried with them. Not long, perhaps, given his age at death – which was probably eighteen. And I wondered, as everyone must, what became of their mother, who, after the death of her younger brother-husband, disappears into oblivion's echo-chamber, swallowed up in the maw that is history.

I was in my twenty-second year that day in the Museum. I had yet to bear a child and was still a virgin. Even so, ignorant and unscathed as I then was, I'd mourned those tiny mummified babies in the heat of the Museum that day. Today, I mourned them again, and I mourned my own lost child too – no passers-by to see, I'm glad to say. What a spectacle: a foolish, fond old woman sitting on a bench in a north London cemetery; waterworks yet again, amid a scattering of rose petals.

Perhaps it would be wise to return home. I rose and turned back along the cemetery path I'd taken earlier, still thinking of Howard Carter and of the last two occasions on which I'd encountered him. The first, a few days after that visit to the Egyptian Museum, took place in the Valley of the Kings. Carter's long decade of work was almost over by the time I made that fleeting visit: only a few objects from the little Annexe room that Frances and I had peered into remained to be packed and sent to Cairo, then his ten years' toil would be ended. I'd timed my visit for late afternoon; the journalists had long departed, and the influx of tourists was much reduced, but I wanted to see the Valley as I remembered it from my childhood, when it was quiet, the domain of the cobra goddess whose name means *She who loves silence.*

I took the route over the hills; by the time I reached a vantage point from which I could look down into the Valley, there were only a few last straggles of tourists. Examining the tomb area with field glasses, I recognised the photographer Harry Burton and the donnish chemist Alfred Lucas, who were packing up to leave. They were the only members of the original team still working with Carter: Arthur Mace, alleged victim of the Curse, was four years dead, and Pecky Callender, who had fallen out with Carter and resigned, had disappeared – disappeared off the map, or so Miss Mack had said. Her letters to him had long ceased to be answered. I could hear the distant murmur of the men's voices in the Valley below: Carter, keys to the tomb's steel gates in his hands, was seated on the retaining wall, where the journalists had once clustered. The Valley's shadows were lengthening as I began the long trek downhill, thinking as I walked of Carter's travails since I'd last seen him here in his moment of triumph, when Lord Carnarvon was still alive; there had been episodes of bitter controversy in the ten years since.

'*I'm not one of nature's diplomats,*' Carter himself had said to me. Once he was no longer protected by Carnarvon's influence, he had swiftly proved the truth of that assertion, and his many enemies, including Pierre Lacau, were equally swift to exact retribution. They'd made their move within months of Carnarvon's death, and a vicious struggle had then ensued, whipped up by journalists, complicated and intensified by the forces of Egyptian nationalism. Shortly after a new constitution was agreed and democratic elections in Egypt at last took place, the Wafd Party-dominated parliament moved to take control of the tomb, a task in which they were assisted by Lacau – and, in equal measure, by Carter's own intransigence and litigiousness.

For an entire year, he and his team had been barred from the tomb, and the Antiquities Service annexed it, though they left it untouched, there then being no Egyptian archaeologists sufficiently experienced to take it on, and no foreign ones prepared to risk the tomb's viperous politics. This situation did not last. In the wake of continuing unrest and a series of political assassinations, the British had once more taken a hard line: they ejected the Nationalist prime minister and his cabinet, seized the political initiative once more, imposed martial law and installed a pro-British government. Within weeks of this reversal, Carter was back in possession of his tomb.

Those events had taken place in 1924. Carter had remained here in the Valley, winter season after winter season, ever since. Eight long years, I thought, as I reached the rocky floor of the Valley and turned along the track that led me towards the tomb, and Carter's seated, unmoving figure. The shrines had been dismantled, the sarcophagus opened, the coffins extracted, the autopsy performed. Thousands of exquisite objects, large and small, had been removed, recorded, conserved, photographed, packed – and in an exemplary manner: even Carter's most vociferous detractors admitted that. They had then been consigned in their entirety to the Egyptian Museum in Cairo, as Herbert Winlock had foreseen. In this respect, Lacau and the Nationalists won the battle – and changed the ethos of archaeology, in Egypt and elsewhere, for ever.

Almina Carnarvon, inheriting her husband's interest in the excavation, had received nothing from the tomb, let alone half its contents as her husband had anticipated – but then, as Frances had pointed out, this was no hardship, since such artefacts did not remotely interest her. Officially, nothing found in the tomb had made its way back to a display case at Highclere Castle or to foreign museums; its entire contents would remain in Egypt for ever, down to the last ivory hairpin. Other than any small objects that had been spirited away, of course: any 'beauties' Carnarvon had 'taken on account' as Frances had put it – or, to put it another way, anything which Carnarvon had (tick your preferred term) secreted, smuggled, nicked, pilfered. There were rumours that Howard Carter had been similarly light-fingered.

'Mr Carter?'

Nerving myself, walking towards him, I held out my hand. I startled him; he had neither heard nor observed my approach. He swung around and inspected me blankly, as a sleepwalker might. He had put on weight and was portly now, his hair thinning, his complexion grey and his face puffy. He regarded me in a glowering, suspicious way. He'd last seen me as a child, now I was a grown woman. I knew he had no reason to recognise me. He ignored my outstretched hand and remained seated.

I explained who I was. When, as anticipated, my name meant nothing to him, I reminded him of Frances and my connection to her. His face brightened at once, the latent irascibility disappeared and he seemed eager for news. The Depression had halted the Met's excavation programme in Egypt, and Herbert Winlock was now based in New York, soon to be appointed Director of the Metropolitan Museum. Frances's annual visits to the American House and the Valley had ceased five years before, when she had been sent to a boarding school near Boston. I knew she had not seen Carter in that time, nor heard from him; neither had her father.

'And how *is* Frances? How's my old friend Winlock?' Carter said, and his demeanour changed – swiftly, as it always did.

I told him Frances would be leaving school in the summer and planned to study art. I brought him up to date on Herbert and Helen's activities. He showed little interest in Winlock's elevation to Director, but became hospitable at once; I was invited back to his house and stayed there an hour, being plied with drinks, nuts and dates by Carter's major-domo, Abd-el-Aal, and his younger brother Hosein – the boy, now a man, whom I remembered from our lunch in that Valley tomb.

It was a beautiful, still evening. I sat there on Carter's terrace, looking down at the stretch of the Nile where Miss Mack and I had stayed on our *dahabiyeh*. There were numerous houseboats moored there, but none that resembled the *Queen Hatshepsut*. I wondered what had become of the boat and Mohammed; I wondered what Pecky Callender's fate had been. Carter, uninterested, brushed all my enquiries aside. 'Callender? No bloody idea. Took off – could be dead for all I know,' he said, and changed the subject. He wanted to tell me about his work – and did so.

'The great sadness was, no papyri,' he said. 'I had Alan Gardiner on call, ready to work on anything we unearthed. Mace had found a box, filled with what looked like rolls of papyrus – but when we investigated, they turned out to be bundles of old linen. I'd hoped for *words*. Words that told us about Tutankhamun himself, his parentage, how he became king, his life, his wife, his children, what he believed, who he was.' He turned his eyes to the river. 'And there was nothing.'

He remained silent for a while, and then said: 'I thought I was bringing him into the light. But while I've been there in the tomb, all these years, uncovering Tutankhamun's belongings, trying to preserve and understand them – he slipped past me into the darkness. The more I searched, the less I saw him.' He paused. 'And when I finally looked at his face . . . Despite all I know, all my experience, I was still expecting him to look like his face mask. He didn't.'

He took a swallow of whisky. 'More fool me,' he said, with a bark of laughter – and returned to his more usual tone. Like a man settling down in his club for an evening's jaw with friends, he began winding his way back and forth in the past. He told me new stories – how, just the other evening, he'd seen a black jackal in the hills above the Valley: 'A veritable Anubis. Not one of your common-or-garden brown jackals. Black as night. Twice the size they usually are too – saw him with my own eyes.' With equal relish, he went on to recount old tales: I think they were by then a fixed part of his repertoire, perhaps shielding him when other memories intruded.

He described again that séance at Highclere – *Coptic! Recognised it at once! More than my life's worth to tell you what was said* – and, his manner briefly bewildered, then becoming firm, he spoke of Carnarvon's death. 'I was there at the end. At Carnarvon's bedside. And the next day, every single one of the Cairo newspapers, even the Arab ones, were printed with a black border, in honour of him. What d'you think of that?'

The fact was clearly of importance to him. I murmured some reply, though I could see it was unnecessary.

'Never happened before, hasn't happened since, will never happen again,' he said. 'Carnarvon was the last of his kind. And I've looked after his interests ever since, made a point of it, will continue to do so. My duty. Oh yes.'

This statement, fiercely made, seemed to be a prompt, and so, rising to leave, I asked Carter whether he still visited Highclere Castle every year as he'd formerly done, if he'd be going back there this coming summer to mark the fact that his decade of work on Tutankhamun's tomb had ended. Eve had never returned to Egypt,

I knew, but I thought she and the Carnarvon family would be certain to celebrate this occasion.

A closed expression came upon his face. 'Don't visit regularly, no — not now,' he replied in a brusque, dismissive tone. 'I simply don't have the time. Infernally busy, tied up, constant demands to lecture, write. Not a moment to call my own. It never lets up. And once I'm finished here, I'll be starting on the definitive account of the tomb and its contents. Beyond that, I have *plans.*'

He gave me a sidelong look. 'Can't reveal them. Like to keep my cards close to my chest. But watch the newspapers, because I have a few surprises in store, and our journalist friends would give their right hands to find out more. I knew where Tutankhamun's body was buried and I know where some other bodies are buried too. Illustrious ones. Ones that will make this discovery pale in comparison. I'll give you a little clue . . . *Alexander the Great.*' He bared his teeth. 'Believe me, there's a few tricks in the old dog yet.'

I could hear his voice, as I turned out of the cemetery gates today, re-entered the park, and began the long, slow and increasingly painful ascent to the sanctuary of my home. The arthritis was back with a vengeance: I'd stayed too long, come too far, and the spooks were now in full clamour — they always know when you're weakening. I set my face towards the wavering outline of my house, which I could just see in the distance beyond the thick dull July green of the trees ahead. As I'd learned on the journey that gave me my *Deserts* book, and had relearned on subsequent ones, the secret to walking distances over difficult terrain, in circumstances that are less than ideal, imperfect health, for example, is — don't stop. Don't pause. Don't allow yourself to rest.

So I pressed on, and Carter came with me and I saw him as I had the last time we met. That final meeting took place in the winter of 1937; it was some five years after the encounter in the Valley that I've described, and two years before Carter's death. My own life had changed in the interim: I had married. On the occasion of that last meeting, I was in flight from my first husband and taking refuge in Egypt. The Carter sighting took place at the Winter Palace Hotel, where I was staying for a few nights. I was sitting on the hotel terrace one morning, contemplating the Nile, thinking of the time I'd spent here as a child with Frances, with Rose and Peter . . . If I thought about them hard enough, it might block other memories of Egypt and this hotel: my honeymoon here, for instance.

I'd brought with me the bound typescript of Miss Mack's book that she'd given me the week before she died, and I'd determined that, while I was here, I'd at last make myself read it. *To the Lucy I once knew*: that dedication, written in a wavering hand, distressed me. I sipped coffee and turned the onion-skin pages; I could quickly see that Miss Mack's years of rewriting had effected an act of censorship. Entire episodes, lengthy conversations that I knew she'd recorded, had disappeared; Pecky Callender, her hero, had been virtually erased. I had once featured in The Book as a fellow bystander – now I found I too had been cut, cut comprehensively; there was nothing left of me.

Into the gap had sprung a new character, I saw. Her name was Tragedy. Hitting the Oliver No. 9's keys too hard, Miss Mack had punched the 'e' key with such violent authorial emotion that it had punctured the paper whenever this new protagonist appeared. Closing my ears to the voices on the terrace, I read: 'The discovery of the hidden tomb was attended by Tragedy, as the world now knows. Tragedy stood, waiting in the shadows, a veiled and unseen spectator to the events in the Valley of the Kings. I will not stoop to speak of a Curse, but . . . '

My vision misted: the sun made reading painful. I closed The Book, replaced it in its envelope and turned my eyes to the river below. Past visits made to this hotel sprang into my mind, a flutter of snapshots: waving to the small figures of Rose and Peter from the ferry; the interview Frances and I had with the police officer, El-Deeb. I was remembering the zeal with which Miss Mack had inspected the Combine on this very terrace, when, drifting across the tables, I heard the boom of a familiar voice. Turning, I realised with shock that the speaker was Howard Carter, that he was the elderly, besuited and behatted invalid whom I'd glimpsed in the distance several times, a fixture of the hotel, visiting it every day, planted at a far table by the balustrade. Most visitors gave this elderly man a wide berth, for he was known as the hotel bore – though whenever I'd seen him he'd been alone, and, judging from his demeanour, uncommunicative.

He'd been accosted by a group of tourists, to whom he'd been identified by one of the hotel's *safragis*; having introduced them, the man scurried away. None of the hotel staff had given me this intelligence, but then I'd scarcely spoken to them; I hadn't spoken to anyone. As I turned to look at Carter, he was in the act of signing a book – his own 'popular' account of finding Tutankhamun's tomb, I saw, as I rose and moved closer. In the past five years, there had been no sign of the long-awaited scholarly account of this work. Carter had been haranguing the tourists for some minutes.

'Yes, I still return here every winter,' I heard him say, as they glanced furtively at each other and began to edge away. 'I have *plans*, you see. Plenty of people only too ready to write me off – but there's a few tricks in the old dog yet. The burial place of Alexander the Great: one of the enduring mysteries of archaeology . . . starting work any day now. Alexander the Great! What d'you think of *that*? Quite a prize! Can't say any more . . . Mum's the word, eh?'

The tourists extricated themselves and left. Speak, or not speak? Carter had sunk back in his chair, and at ten yards I could see he was a sick man – almost unrecognisable. His formal clothes were those of a City banker, and old-fashioned – no one visiting Luxor dressed in that way any more. His figure was bloated by ill-health and perhaps by medication; his face bore a stricken expression. His eyes were fixed on the Theban hills opposite and his hands, which were trembling, constantly fiddled with the objects in front of him – as old men's hands do. He picked up a teaspoon; fumbled with his coffee cup. Remembering his former deftness and vigour, I pitied him. Crossing to his table, I quietly told him my name. I knew it would mean little; that he would no more remember me now than he had on many past occasions, and so – as he stared up at me uncomprehendingly – I tried to explain who I was.

'Who? Who?' He glared up at me. 'I'd remind you, madam, that I must have shown ten thousand people around that tomb – twenty! And I can't recall *one* of them, not their names or their faces.' He paused and bared his teeth in that smile I remembered. 'No disrespect, dear lady,' he added, with aggression.

I should have left it there. 'Lucy. Frances Winlock's friend,' I said. That form of identification had worked in the past with Carter, and I said it by rote.

'Frances?' Recognition sparked somewhere in his eyes, and his expression grew gentler. 'Oh, I remember *Frances*. Smart girl. Always liked *her*.' His gaze clouded and again became suspicious, as if I might be lying, might be an imposter. I'd begun to retreat, murmuring excuses, when in a stronger tone, he said: 'Years since I've seen her. She'll be grown up now. In her – let me see – in her twenties? How is she?'

'Frances is dead, Mr Carter.'

I spoke quietly, with reluctance, and for a moment thought he hadn't heard me. Then, as an expression of confusion and ire etched itself upon his face, I saw that he had. He fumbled with his coffee spoon again, and shook his head.

'I didn't know,' he said, gazing past me, into the distance. 'Winlock didn't let me know. A bit out of touch recently. Haven't kept up as I should have done . . . ' His gaze hardened and he turned to peer at me closely. 'Should I believe you, that's the thing? Who in hell are you?'

I did not reply and the suspicion vanished from his eyes as swiftly as it came. He reached for his Homburg and jammed it on, picked up his cane, pushed back his chair, his manner suddenly impatient. 'I must write to Winlock,' he said. 'Without delay. That's what one does. Those are the formalities. One needs to observe them – that's what my dear friend Lord Carnarvon always said. A condolence letter. I shall send it at once. I shall go home now and write it. I shall tell Winlock my plans too – Alexander the Great, I know he'll be interested to hear about that. Envious, I expect . . . Frances. Sweet child. Smart. Didn't make old bones, then.'

He tossed some coins onto the table, walked past me as if I were invisible – which, indeed, I'd become, and for him perhaps always had been. He set off at surprising speed in the direction of the ferry. I watched him bustle aboard, watched the beggars who haunted that area shrink back and avoid him.

It was the last sighting I ever had of him. A whistle blew, the Nile eddied, the ferry eased away from the shore – and in London, I finally reached the northern gates that led out of the green park, into the green lane, and into the green sanctuary of my garden.

The pain in my hip was acute by then. All my old bones ached. My breathing was fitful, my heart was rattling and my vision was smudgy.

I dragged myself inside the house, into the sitting room, and sank down in the nearest chair. It was early evening, and the light had thinned to late-summer silver, making the room, its furniture, its paintings, its books and its many accumulations, insubstantial. They were as transparent as air – as familiar to me as my own skin, yet frail as a dreamscape. Why, I've imagined you, I thought, and, closing my eyes, waited for these trappings softly and silently to vanish away. After an interval, opening my eyes, I saw they were still obstinately *there*. They asserted themselves. The room steadied.

I picked up the small *shabti* figure, and held it tight in my palm. *Where you go, I go*, Frances said from the room's airy recesses – and I understood that the surest of my spirits was here and had been faithfully waiting for me.

34

Saranac Lake, and the small town of the same name that grew up around it, is situated in the mountains and forests of upper New York State, not far south of the Canadian border. Frances lived there from June 1933 onwards.

In the March of that same year, I'd stayed with Frances and her parents in New York. During that visit, she had taken me to the Metropolitan Museum. 'Something I want to show you, Lucy,' she'd said, coming to a halt at a group of glass cases, filled with exquisite Egyptian jewellery. 'Remember these?' I shook my head: I'd never entered this gallery before; I was wondering why she'd chosen to bring me here. 'Read the labels,' Frances said, turning away. I did so, and found these jewels were – *The Treasure of Three Princesses*.

'The princesses' names were Menhet, Menwi and Merti,' Frances said. 'They've disappeared from history. This jewellery is all that's left of them, and I wanted you to see it. Just think: it took Mr Carter six long years to acquire their treasures, and then, just when he'd finally secured the very last pieces, I spoke out of turn. You remember: that day you and I and Rose and Peter had tea with him at Shepheard's?'

I remembered. 'I've learned to guard my tongue since then,' Frances said. 'You always knew how to do that. Now I've caught up with you.'

After that March visit, I was constantly travelling, and it seemed that Frances and I could never contrive to meet. We wrote as we'd always done, and meetings were planned, but Frances would always pull out of them. I wrote to her New York address, or to her family home in Boston. Throughout that time, Frances was in neither of those places: she was at Saranac Lake, but the fact that she was there, and the reason she was there, were kept secret. Frances hid her whereabouts from me – and from many of her friends, I suspect; as did her parents. Perhaps they hoped the reason for this secrecy could, in time, be put behind them and erased, so there need never be cause to discuss it. Perhaps it was simply too painful to discuss. I can't answer those questions.

It was Frances herself who finally explained where she was and why and asked me to visit her, but it was October 1935 before she did so. I was still unmarried then, and was returning from the pro-tracted journeys undertaken for my second book, *Islands*. En route to England, I'd washed ashore in Manhattan. I was given her letter late one afternoon, on my return to the hotel where I'd told Frances I'd be staying. Shock slows the mind: I was trying to understand why Frances had kept this from me so long; the address on her letter was 153 Park Avenue, and it took me a while to realise that this was not the opulent Park Avenue of New York City, where her parents then had an apartment, but a different one: a Park Avenue in a remote town I'd never heard of. There was a one-word postscript: *Come*. A bright, fall day. By that evening, I was at Grand Central station.

There was a queue at the ticket booth: I asked for a return to Saranac Lake, and the man waiting in line behind me laughed. He was thin, ill-kempt, threadbare. I'd seen many men like him, haunting Grand Central's levels – it was then the depths of the Depression and such sad figures haunted many parts of the city. This man had a half-bottle of bourbon in a brown paper sack and he'd already been hassling me.

'No *returns*. One way only,' he said. 'You don't know that? You wanna single, honey. Hey, you, buddy.' Shouldering me aside on a sickly waft of alcohol, he leaned in close to the grille and addressed the ticket clerk. 'Do the Limey kid a favour – switch that to a single, pal. Plenty of folks *going* to Saranac Lake. Ain't none of them coming *back*. Leastways, not outside a box, they ain't.'

I elbowed the man aside: after some of the journeys I'd been on, and some of the situations I'd encountered, I wasn't going to argue with a New York bum who was half-seas over. I bought a return. It was a long slow journey on a stopping train. A glorious warm evening when I left the city; by the time darkness fell, we were still rattling northwards and I could see no lights or signs of habitation. My watch stopped and refused to restart, so I don't know what time it was when, somewhere en route, the train came to a halt at some tiny remote station.

I had to change trains at the Lake Clear junction and take the branch line to Saranac Lake itself, but we surely could not have reached that yet? 'Do you know where we are?' I asked the woman who shared my compartment – she had brightly dyed hair, a raddled, rouged face, tangerine lipstick and looked a bit of a floozie; she was pleasant and kindly, if talkative. She lit a cigarette, inhaled and blew a smoke ring. She gave me a gaudy smile. 'Search me, kid,' she said amiably. 'Kind of *be*yond the back of *be*yond. But it won't be Lake Clear – no way, honey, not for hours yet.'

I went out into the corridor and pressed my face against the glass. Somewhere further down the train they were loading freight: I could hear the shouts of the porters. Doors slammed, the train shuddered and the voices receded, becoming faint, then inaudible. I hadn't seen the name of the tiny station and it wouldn't have told me much anyway – I'd left in a hurry, had little idea of the route and had no map with me.

What country, friends, is this? I peered out at the blackness beyond the glass: acre upon acre of Hansel and Gretel forest closing in on a small wooden station building, its platform and its single lamp; a huge sky, smeared with stars; a sickle moon hanging crookedly over the trees. From further down the train came the sound of a fretful child, sobbing. Something was wrong with the sky, I thought – and then realised it was snowing.

It was still snowing when I reached Saranac Lake early the following morning. I'd sent Frances a cable, telling her I'd be arriving – but perhaps it hadn't reached her or had gone astray: there was no one to meet me. I lifted out my small case and set off along the platform, shivering. The air was ice. The town was set down in the shallow bowl of a valley, ringed with snow-capped hills. I could see clusters of wooden buildings with gables, turrets and flourishes, many of them surprisingly large for such a remote town. Beyond them, more forests, black pine forests, the steel glint of water, and a blind white sky. Reaching the station building, I halted: there was a freight yard next to it, stacked with wooden boxes under a thin pall of snow. I'd been staring at them for some minutes before I understood they were coffins.

The station clock informed me that it was six in the morning — too early to turn up at Park Avenue, especially if my cable had not arrived and no one was expecting me. I needed to kill time. The ticket clerk suggested I leave my case at the station and make for the hotel that, he assured me, would serve breakfast even at this hour; it would also sell me a map — and a guidebook, he added. 'Not taking the cure? Visiting? Grandpa — Ma, maybe? You fixed up yet, ma'am — where you staying?'

I told him the Park Avenue address and he whistled. Looking me up and down, he said: 'That's Highland Park — swell area — plenty of swells living there.' He reeled off some names and, disappointed that they meant little to me, elaborated; one was a baseball star, another a famous magazine editor; there was a composer, a newspaper magnate, Wall Street bankers and numerous millionaires. I wasn't thinking too clearly: I became afraid that he'd go on to list some of the Emerson or Stockton clan — but he didn't.

I turned to go, then turned back and asked him about the coffins. Nothing to worry about, he said; they were the empties, ready for the next batch. The occupied ones left the town discreetly, he told me, on the 9.55 p.m. train, under cover of darkness.

I left the Union Depot and walked into town. I found the Berkeley Hotel that the station clerk had recommended at the junction of Broadway and Main. It was one of many hotels I'd passed; as I reached it, it stopped snowing. The streets were still quiet, but the town was waking up, shopkeepers were already opening their shutters. I was passed by several horse-drawn farm wagons, a logging truck and a jitney. As I reached the hotel, a Cadillac swished past: white-wall tyres, huge chrome headlamps, driven by a uniformed black chauffeur. I glimpsed a woman in furs bundled in the back, an imperious face, a gloved hand and the improbable glitter of a diamond bracelet.

The Berkeley proved to be a clapboarded, many-gabled edifice, with verandas and turrets. Inside, I was in a cluster of pioneer, log-cabin rooms, hung with moose heads on wooden shields. Log fires blazed; the receptionists seemed familiar with dazed, disorientated passengers from the night train. As promised, they provided a map, a guidebook and information. Flattening the map on the counter, the youngest desk clerk jabbed at streets with his finger; he was smartly dressed, in brown suit and vest, stiff collar, shiny patent-leather shoes; his hair, parted in the middle, was greased slick to his skull. I felt ice-cold, cold as a camera that day, so I can still see him. *Click*, and I'm looking down seventy years at the silver ring he wore on his little finger.

He was anxious to emphasise that Saranac Lake was not some hick town; whatever folks needed, it could supply. The skiing season would be under way soon, but meantime I'd find Saranac Lake understood entertainment. Too late in the year for canoeing, but I could ice-skate or hike up the trails through the Adirondacks; there was one fine view from Mount Pisgah, and that was close to where I was headed. The Winter Carnival was coming up: then there'd be ice-trotting races on Moody Pond and——

'Ice palaces,' he said, startling me, and reaching for an album. 'Famous for them. Take a look here, ma'am.'

I gazed at the transparent palaces with fixed attention: *Winter palaces* – and they were vast: some had ice battlements. Saranac Lake had its very own wireless station, he went on; there were three movie-theatres; there were glees, a barber-shop quartet and Negro minstrels; fancy-dress parties *and* dances – every week, regular as clockwork. The town boasted one library, two newspapers, four speakeasies, five drugstores, eight general stores, fifteen hotels, twenty pharmacies – and four hundred and fifty-six cure cottages. I must not miss out on the number one sights: these were the Trudeau sanatorium, the Franklin Falls and the Robert Louis Stevenson cottage.

'You're looking kind of *white*, ma'am,' he added, folding the map. 'Didn't sleep on the train, I reckon? Sit by the fire and I'll get them to rustle up some breakfast. Not here to cure? No, I guessed not. I can spot a curer at a hundred yards. English? You jest make yourself right at home now.'

I sat by the fire. A moose head looked down upon me, its glass eyes squinting and doleful. After a very brief interval, coffee arrived and a huge plate of pancakes, syrup and bacon. I managed to eat a little.

I turned the pages of the guidebook. *At sea*. I needed bearings, compass readings; Robert Louis Stevenson was one of my literary heroes, so I turned to him first – pages were devoted to him.

He had come here, I read, in 1887, and quickly formed a close friendship with the doctor who founded Saranac Lake's famous sanatorium, Edward Livingston Trudeau. For six months he had lived in one of the town's cure cottages and followed the strict regime Trudeau had initiated. Like the many other patients brought here by the curative powers of Saranac's dry pure air, and by the proven success of its treatment methods, RLS spent much of each day in enforced rest, even sleeping in the open air on the uniquely designed porch that was a feature of all cure cottages.

He had eaten the small, frequent and nutritious meals prescribed, and had drunk the daily quarts of fresh milk stipulated. He was instructed to avoid all stimulation – that category included writing – and to eschew all strife: Trudeau believed that a state of psychological equanimity was essential to the well-being of his patients. When Stevenson's condition improved, he was encouraged to take brisk exercise by the lakes and in the pine woods. He obeyed all these dictates ... up to a point: he had recently published *Dr Jekyll and Mr Hyde*, and while at Saranac continued both to write and to chainsmoke ferociously. Even so, when he left in the spring of 1888, his health was restored and his pulmonary tuberculosis was in full remission. He lived on for six years, and it was not TB but a cerebral haemorrhage that killed him, the guidebook stressed – this despite the fact that Stevenson was by then living in Samoa, a place that, unlike Saranac Lake, had a climate inimical to consumptives.

Some time later, a taxi took me to the Highland Park district. *Consumption*, *consumptive*, I thought. I could see what the ticket clerk meant when he said this area was swell. Set a little outside the town centre, it consisted of a few long streets. Park Avenue, the largest and evidently the most prestigious of them, curved along the base of pointy Mount Pisgah; it overlooked the saucer of the valley and the icy rush of the Saranac river. I wound down the window as we began to drive along it; the antiseptic air smelled of pines and, wafting towards me – crisp as new dollar bills – came the unmistakable scent of money.

The houses, well distanced from each other, surrounded by cropped lawns dusted with snow, fine gardens, graceful plantings of sugar maples and aspens — all leafless, for fall came early this far north — were imposing and architecturally surprising. We passed a Gothic mansion, then a French chateau, then a Scottish baronial.

'No cure cottages allowed up *here*,' the driver said, jerking a thumb as we passed a *schloss*, then a Cotswold manor house. 'Exclusive. The cure cottages back in town rent rooms by the week, see. No saying as who might rent the room next door: could be Polacks, Jews, Eyetalians, Greeks, Hispanics — we get us a whole lot of Hispanics, ma'am, up from New York City, the Lower East Side factories send them, they got a big problem with it, it's endemic . . . But this district, single occupancy only. Someone in the family gets the disease and they'll hightail it up to Saranac, home in on Park, build them a house and settle in for the cure . . . Strict regulations, though. Only so many houses per acre.'

He pronounced the word 'disease', as 'die-sease'. He was slowing and finally pulled up outside a very large, clapboarded, colonial-style house.

'Used to be called Talbot-Aldritch Cottage, after the family as built it,' he said, and from out of the past came the unwelcome sound of my father's voice, that Cambridge scholar's voice, thin and high-pitched, peevish and irritable: *A cottage with twenty bedrooms by the sound of it . . . Why do our American cousins infallibly under- or overstate?* I climbed out of the car. I thought: the hell with you, Daddy.

The house was a beautiful one, elegant in its proportions, harmonious in this landscape. A large open veranda ran around two of its sides; a Stars and Stripes fluttered from its flagpole. On the first storey, I could see the porch area used for treatments, with its distinctive floor-to-ceiling windows: they were wide open; I could see nothing beyond them but a flutter of white curtains. I walked up the path — the snow was already melting. As I reached the front door, it was thrown open and Helen Winlock held out her arms to me. I stepped into her embrace, and neither of us spoke for some while. When Helen was calmer, she drew back, and held me at arm's length.

'We got the cable this morning . . . Lucy, you shouldn't have come.

Frances shouldn't have asked you. You mustn't see her. She's — it's contagious.'

I told her I didn't care — which was the truth — and she began to cry. 'How obstinate you are. You always were, Lucy. And Frances too — such obstinate little girls. Frances is resting. We mustn't disturb her — it's a very exacting regime. So strict, so many rules and regulations. But they *are* working. She's much stronger. Her appetite is good, most days it's good. When it's sunny, she can go for walks. You remember how you used to walk to the Valley?' Tears spilled down her face. 'Come inside. You must be tired. We need to talk before you see her.'

She drew me into a large hall. It had the same pure tranquil light as a Vermeer — it was like stepping into the pearl dusk of a Vermeer painting. The house hummed with silence. We looked at one another without speaking. The guidebook at the hotel had not confined itself to details of buildings and amenities: it had also contained information as to the disease that was Saranac's *raison d'être* and prime industry. I'd read that section with close attention.

I said: 'What stage is the TB at, Helen?'

'Advanced.' She lowered her gaze. 'It was already advanced when they admitted her.'

I was allowed to see Frances later that day, after she had eaten lunch alone in her room, and had had the regulation one hour's sleep. Helen capitulated: I was to be allowed to stay — but I had to be careful.

'You mustn't excite her,' she said. 'Excitement *must* be avoided. It can bring on an attack. So you must be calm and quiet and show no emotion. Just talk to her gently — and if she wants to talk, let her. But not too much. If she gets agitated — she does get agitated — you must leave her room at once, and I'll go to her. If she coughs, make sure she can reach her gauze squares, there's a stack of them on her bedside table, they must be folded so they're four layers thick. Once Frances has used the squares, don't touch them. You must not embrace her. Don't kiss her. You can stay half an hour. Then the nurse will be arriving, to give her the daily massage — it opens up the breathing passages. It's very effective.' She paused. 'You'll need to lie. Can you lie, Lucy?'

'I can lie with the best of them.'

'Ah, you've changed. Well, we all have.'

I went upstairs and found Frances lying in the spacious porch that led off from her bedroom, the porch I'd glimpsed from below. Its windows were still wide open. She was propped up on one of the special day-beds Dr Trudeau had pioneered, designed to rest the limbs but promote ease of breathing. The air was bitterly cold, but crisp and dry; the porch was unheated. Frances was wrapped in a dark fur bedjacket, her thin hands lying on a white coverlet. Her face was thin too, but her complexion was clear and radiant. Two patches of scarlet stained her cheeks. Her hair dark shone. Her gaze was brilliant. When her eager eyes sought mine and her face lit up in greeting, her smile was unchanged – it spoke to me with the same immediacy that it always had, from that first moment when I met her at Madame's ballet class in Cairo.

'You came.' She held out her hand to me. 'I'm not dreaming you? Lucy, you came.'

'I'd have come sooner if I'd known. I'd have come at once, Frances.'

'I know that,' she said – and there we were, as we'd always been, two pieces that fitted, our understanding exact and unchanged: no words and no explanations needed.

'I've brought you a present,' I said, some while later – I'd just heard the sounds of the nurse arriving, and knew my half-hour would soon be up.

I had been quiet; Frances had been quiet – only once had she betrayed agitation. 'I'm *so* much better,' she'd said in a gay, merry way, fixing me with her bright gaze. 'Daddy came up last weekend – he comes most weekends, you know, when he can get away from the Museum. And I was telling him – how much stronger I am, how well I'm eating – and *twice* he left the room, crying. Isn't that silly of him? He says it's because I talk too much and that's bad for me – but I always did talk too much, you remember that, Lucy. It makes Daddy so stern – such a long face! But I just laugh at him.'

She laughed then, and the laughter made her cough a little. She pressed one of the thick gauze squares over her mouth. When the coughing eased, she turned her bright face away from me, towards her pillows, and then told me that as soon as the weather was sunny we would go for a walk together.

'We can go along the valley, and I'll show you the river. It's my favourite walk. I went there every day that first summer I came to Saranac, but I haven't been there so often . . . not recently.' She hesitated. 'I wasn't in this house, Lucy, when I first came here. Daddy only began renting this when we realised I might have to stay a little longer than we'd thought. I was in one of the cure cottages when I first came – over there on Kiwassa Road, the other side of the river.'

She waved a thin hand in the direction of the windows. 'A Mr and Mrs Erkander ran it – she used to be a nurse, and he came from Michigan. I wasn't so happy there – they were very kind, of course – she was *so* house-proud! Everything as clean as a whistle, you had to take off your shoes when you came in from outdoors. The rooms were disinfected every single morning. She'd bleach the sheets and the drapes and the chair covers – the whole house stank of carbolic. And the other people there, the curers – none of them stayed very long. You'd just get to know them, and we'd chat on the porch, and then they'd disappear. Mrs Erkander would say they'd moved to a different cottage, or maybe got better and gone home – but *I* think some of them went home via the funeral parlour. Mrs Erkander got pretty mad when I said that.'

'Hush, Frances. You mustn't talk too much. I promised Helen.'

'Oh – that's the doctors speaking! Such a fuss about nothing. I long to talk. I've been longing to talk to *you*. Well, I *have* talked to you, of course – such conversations we've had! But I imagined them – and that's not the same, is it? It's hard, Lucy – lying here in silence day after day. All sorts of silly gloomy thoughts creep in, and I can't seem to drive them away. But now they've all gone – they've fled! I'm so happy I could dance.' She turned her face away. Her breath caught. She fell silent.

I bowed my head and stroked her wrist. Her skin felt hot and dry; under my fingers I could feel the rapidity of her pulse. Helen had already told me about the spell at the Erkanders' house – and the circumstances that had led to Frances's admission to Saranac. It had happened *fast*: Frances had been nineteen, fit and well. She had left school, had come out, had rushed from one debutante party to another . . . had boyfriends, was planning to enrol on art courses in

442

New York, or study in Europe, perhaps at the Beaux-Arts in Paris, or the Slade in London – but, that winter, she kept getting colds and developed a thin, obstinate cough. Within weeks of our meeting in Manhattan, and that visit we'd made to the Met, she had begun to lose weight; Helen had suspected she was secretly dieting. Their doctor prescribed cough linctus, said there was no cause for concern – but that May, when the fevers and night sweats first developed, he suggested seeing a specialist. This man confirmed the disease, and advised treatment at Saranac Lake; its reputation in America was unrivalled.

'January to June,' Helen said. 'Six months, from the first little cold to the day she was admitted here. That was almost two and a half years ago. The doctors say that if it had been caught sooner, it would have made no difference. TB makes its own rules, Lucy. Sometimes it's fast, sometimes slow, sometimes latent.'

I thought: *so she was already ill that day in the Museum*. I said: 'Do they know how Frances caught it, Helen – or where?'

'No.' She turned her face aside. 'They call it the white plague. It's everywhere. The doctors say you need prolonged exposure – but what does that mean? A day? A week? Ten minutes? When you ask them that, they don't answer. She could have caught it in a restaurant. A movie theatre. At the opera. On the uptown bus. On the subway.'

I looked down at Frances's flushed face. Her eyes were still closed and her breathing had become gentle. I thought she might be sleeping, I thought I should perhaps steal away, but as soon as I moved, Frances stirred and clutched at my hand.

'Don't go – not yet,' she said. 'If you go now, I'll think I dreamed you. What was I saying? I've lost track – ah, I know. Our walk by the river. You will do that, Lucy? You'll stay for that? Promise me you won't leave until we've done that?'

'I promise. I'll stay as long as you want. I won't walk by the river until I can walk there with you.'

At that, she grew calmer again. She remained calm when I gave her the small present I'd brought, purchased in a Fifth Avenue store, on my way to the station. The assistant had gift-wrapped it. I could hear the nurse talking to Helen in the hall below as I helped Frances undo its pretty ribbons, its shiny white paper. Inside was a lipstick in a gilded case. It was a clear true scarlet, the closest match I could find to the one of Mrs d'Erlanger's that Frances had chosen, and sacrificed.

Frances gave a little cry of surprise and turned her brilliant gaze to mine. 'You remembered,' she said, turning it in her thin hands. 'You remembered.'

'That and everything.' This was true: the curse of a good memory. 'When you were grown up, you were going to wear scarlet lipstick all the time – even at breakfast.'

'So I was. And Rose said I'd never dare.' She laughed, which made her cough again.

'Well, I'm a grown woman now – and red lipstick isn't as wicked as it used to be, but even so – *I'll* show Rose. Give me that looking glass, Lucy.'

I handed her the small glass and, with concentration, Frances applied the lipstick, smudged her lips together and examined her reflection. She put out a pink tongue and licked her red lips, making the paint even brighter, more glossy. 'It's glorious. I feel as vain as a peacock. It suits me. I knew it would. It's the colour of rubies, Lucy. It's the colour of blood. It's the colour of heartbeats.'

The lipstick proved controversial: when Herbert Winlock visited, he was amused, but Frances's doctors frowned, her mother tut-tutted, and the nurses were annoyed – this disapproval, which Frances had predicted, delighted her. She had been obedient to the cure regime for so long, that this gesture of rebellion seemed to give her strength. It was like hoisting a defiant banner in the face of the enemy – and we all knew who that enemy was: you could sense him, prowling around the house, stalking up the drive, peering in at the windows. I knew him of old: I could remember how he'd hung out in my room at Shepheard's Hotel on my first visit to Egypt; how he'd hidden himself in its fearsome catafalque of a wardrobe. *Go away*, I used to mutter then. *Find some other prey*, I'd think here, closing the curtains as night fell. Frances wore that red lipstick every single one of the days that I spent with her in Saranac.

There were thirty of them. Most were spent at the house, as the weather remained cloudy and inclement. In the mornings, the visiting nurses would give Frances a sponge-bath in the cold water the regime stipulated; they'd remake her bed and supervise her breathing exercises. In the afternoons, once her meal and obligatory rest period were past, I would sit with her and talk or, at her request, read to her. She made out a list of books and I fetched them from the Free Library on Main. Frances would tire quickly and grow restless, so I read as she bid: a fragment here, a favourite passage there. We read *Little Women* and *The Secret Garden* and *Huckleberry Finn.* 'Ah, I love that,' she'd say. 'Read me that again, Lucy.' So I'd return to the same paragraph until her restlessness was quieted, and her eyelids began drooping.

She had a passion for news too, and when allowed would listen avidly to the wireless set. 'I have to know what's going *on*, Lucy,' she'd say. 'When I get back to the big bad world I must know what's been happening – people will think me a fool otherwise.'

And so I'd fetch the local papers, or bring up *The New York Times* and *The New Yorker*, to which Helen subscribed, and read out selected columns: the society pages, the lead news stories, reviews. In a careful, uninflected tone, I'd recount details of Mussolini's invasion of Abyssinia, the continuing suffering of Oklahoma sharecroppers, the latest logging prices, the dinner and dance Mrs Edgar P. Van der Luyden had given for her daughter Lavinia at the Pierre Hotel. Coming once upon an obituary of that legendary prima ballerina we'd known as Madame Masha, I turned that page quickly. I read accounts of Nuremberg rallies, and who had attended some dazzling first night at the Metropolitan Opera. Frances would lie back against her pillows, her bright eyes fixed on the open windows, her lips parted and her expression rapt – as if she were watching some marvellous film, the windows a cinema screen. All events, tiny, trivial or tumultuous, held an equal fascination.

Sometimes she liked to hear about people she'd known but had not seen for years such as Rose, or Peter – and I would read out the letters from them that Nicola Dunsire had forwarded from Cambridge. Rose was now living in a flat in London, bought with the inheritance from her mother Poppy that had come to her on her twenty-first birthday. Wheeler lived with her; the set-up was much as Rose had described to me that day on the ferry to Dover, returning from Egypt. Her brother Peter had recently joined them there, having contrived to get expelled from Eton and having severed all contact with his father. 'Expelled?' Frances gave me a doubting look. 'Peter? He was such a sweet obedient little boy. Timid. He wouldn't have said boo to a goose.'

'That was then. Now he's grown up. He's nearly seventeen, tall and strong and a hell-raiser. He's been working on expulsion for years. I knew he'd pull it off. He's determined.'

'Does he still have Poppy's eyes? Does he still look like her?'

'Yes. The same eyes – but fiercer.'

I examined the two letters: Rose's was long and communicative. Peter's was short, witty and on the whole uninformative: *Dear Lulu, I've escaped. I'm a free man! When you next see me, you won't recognise me . . .* I replaced the letters in their envelopes.

'How strange. Sometimes I feel I know them – and other times, I think I dreamed them.'

Frances turned her brilliant gaze to mine. 'I think I dreamed it *all*,' she said sadly, plucking at the bedclothes. 'Madame's ballet classes, your Miss Mack, Eve and Mr Carter, Daddy's excavations, even the Valley and the tombs – did we ever really go there, Lucy?'

'You know we did, Frances . . . It's time for your rest now.'

I was learning the danger signals by then. So I'd say: it's time for your rest – or the doctor, the nurse, the massage, the regulation milk. I was often afraid when I soothed her in this way, for the setbacks could happen without warning. One second Frances would be calm, the next in feverishly high spirits, or afflicted with a sudden swoop of anxiety; then she would begin gasping for breath, be convulsed by a coughing attack. Once she had needed oxygen; once she had coughed up bright blood and tried to hide the red square of gauze from me; once her skin had gone white and her lips blue, and the doctors came racing.

They carried paraphernalia into her room: large bottles, gauges, rubber tubes, a long rubber tube connected to a needle. Helen and I were banished to the landing so I did not witness this procedure, which was called artificial pneumothorax. Standing outside Frances's door, gripping her mother's hands, I heard it. One long high scream, then a prolonged hissing and bubbling. A man's voice said, *Hold steady, Frances*. I said, 'Ah, dear God, what are they doing?'

Helen stared at the wall. They were collapsing Frances's left lung, she said, by injecting oxygen through the chest wall into the pleural cavity. Both lungs were infected, but the condition of the left was worse. The needle inserted had to be wielded with absolute precision. It was an ancient technique, first mentioned by Hippocrates. The doctors at Saranac Lake, performing this therapy on numerous patients on a daily basis, were expert. Once collapsed, the afflicted lung could rest and healing was promoted.

'How many times, Helen?'

'This is the seventh time this year.'

'What will happen?'

'We'll go back to the beginning again. Longer rest periods. Longer exposure to fresh air. Less stimulation. More frequent meals, more milk — maximum nutrition. Gradually, the breaches in the lung should heal a little and the adhesions may weaken.' She reached up to straighten a picture on the wall — one of her own watercolours, the view from the veranda at the American House, sand and rose rock, desert. She dropped her hand and left the picture crooked. She said, 'Perseverance, Lucy.'

That event came early in my stay — at the end of the first week I was at Saranac Lake. After that, as Helen had warned, the regime became stricter still. The periods of enforced rest became more protracted, the doctors, tweed-suited, moustached, swept in, emanating professional confidence. They visited more frequently; their conferences with Helen lasted longer than they formerly had.

At first, I'd ply Helen with eager questions when they'd left: what was their advice, what further treatments did they recommend? There *were* no other treatments, she said in a hopeless way. Seeing that such questioning was painful to her, I avoided it religiously after that. Instead, Helen and I entered a conspiracy in which we were always, at all times, optimistic; at the end of each day, and often during the course of it, we'd remind one another of the advances, the tiny but noticeable improvements: the hour of peaceful sleep Frances had enjoyed, the animation she'd shown and the determination. She had managed to eat this, she'd expressed a wish to do that, her temperature had remained normal for three days in succession, her pulse rate had slowed and was now steady. We counted these events like beads on a rosary.

Helen believed in time, rest, quiet, dry cold air, nutrition – or said that she did. I embraced these faiths too: you have to have a creed in such circumstances. We'd cook and shop for the right provisions with shared zeal. Helen would send me into town with lengthy shopping lists. 'Go to Gibneys' Market,' she'd say. 'Tell William and Mellie I sent you. They might have squabs by now . . . Oh, and then go to Barr's, Lucy, and see if they have the Providence River oysters – Dr Brown says he can't recommend oysters too highly, very nutritious and easily digested – and perhaps some fish, and tell them the eggs must be new-laid – see if they have the Malaga grapes, they're Frances's favourites.'

The recommended diet had to be high in protein and vitamins, and high in calories too, for the portions Frances ate were tiny. So I'd consult with the solicitous shopkeepers, and come back with laden baskets: yes, they did have the Malaga grapes and the eggs were laid that morning, and look how plump and tender the squabs were . . . And then Helen and I would retreat to the kitchen while the nurses did their work upstairs, and we'd chop and slice and roast and poach: we'd make fresh, light vegetable soups and beef tea; we'd contrive tasty casseroles and nutritious puddings. Helen had never cooked and my own experience was limited, but I bought a recipe book and, fiercely evangelical, we improved. 'Oh, that was delicious,' Frances would say, sinking back on her pillows.

She might have eaten one square inch of chicken, a spear of carrot, half a potato, three grapes. Sometimes, if I was quick enough, I'd contrive to hide the leftovers from Helen, run downstairs and scrape them into the kitchen bin before she saw them – and then I realised that she was performing the same pantomime for my benefit. After that we were more honest.

'Only a quarter of the chicken breast,' Helen would say, and we'd inspect what was left, and tell one another that it was better than yesterday.

'She's drunk *all* the milk,' I'd remind her and Helen would sigh and say: 'Milk's so nutritious. You can *live* on milk, Lucy. I'm sure I read that somewhere . . . You remember Harold Jones, that archaeologist in the Valley, Herbert's friend? He had TB, and all that milk he drank kept the disease at bay for *years*.'

I looked away quickly: across a luncheon table in a tomb light years before, I heard Frances's light childish voice: '*What became of Mr Jones, Daddy?*'

When, ten days later, the doctors confirmed that the artificial pneumothorax procedure had been effective and there were signs of healing: we gained new hope. It was then early November. Helen began to make eager plans for Frances's twenty-second birthday, which fell on 9 December – weeks away still, but it would be on us before we knew it, she said. Frances's younger sister, Barbara, whom I had never met, would be coming up from New York with her father that day: her visits had to be rationed, for they disturbed both her and Frances. 'She can't go upstairs, you see, Lucy. It isn't allowed. We daren't risk that. So she stands outside, and we bring Frances to the porch windows, and they wave, and call to one another.'

Reaching for an album, she showed me photographs of the two sisters: the resemblance between them was strong. This picture had been taken in New York, that one in Boston, and this at their holiday house in Maine, on the island of North Haven.

'Oh, I wish you'd come there to stay with us, Lucy,' Helen said. 'Frances loves it so much – she always wanted to take you there.'

I looked at the photograph she was indicating: it showed a place I recognised from Frances's little shrine to her dead brother in her bedroom at the American House: a dangerous jetty, the turbulent waters of Penobscot Bay. Helen had already lost one child. I stared at the picture: an eternal summer's day; at sea, two young girls in a sailing boat.

Helen snapped the album shut. 'Let's not think about that,' she said, suddenly restless. 'Let's plan Frances's birthday, Lucy – should I order a cake?'

'I'll make one, Helen. I'm quite good at cakes. My governess taught me.'

'Bless you, dear.' Helen pressed my hand. 'Bless you for everything. Will you make a chocolate one? That's Frances's favourite. Twenty-two candles.'

*

449

The next day, a ridge of high pressure came in — and the weather changed. There had been day after day of mild weather, which had brought mist and rain and depressed Frances's spirits. 'Oh, all I can see is *cloud*,' she'd say, propping herself on one elbow, straining to see the view from her porch windows. 'The mountains have disappeared, I can't even see the valley.'

'The forecast is good, darling,' Helen said, from one side of the bed.

'Sun for days,' I said, from the other.

And the sun *did* come, transforming the valley and unveiling its beauty. The light sparkled, glittered on the snow-capped Adirondacks, turning Saranac Lake itself from black mirror to gleaming mercury. The blue sky was unclouded; there was scarcely a breath of wind, and when I walked into town to collect the latest batch of books, the air was everything the guidebooks affirmed: cold, dry, curative and exhilarating.

Frances was allowed up that day for the first time in weeks. She walked from her cure porch to her bedroom, along the landing and back again. Two days later, Dr Lawrason Brown, the senior medic, said he was astonished by the progress she'd made. 'I wouldn't have predicted this,' he said. 'Significant improvements. The will-power is very strong, of course.'

She could now attempt the stairs, he decreed, provided she took them slowly. Flushed with excitement and triumph, Frances did so: she made it down to the sitting room, even out onto the veranda. Wrapped in coats, she insisted we should sit there, watching while her mother painted a watercolour. I'd picked berries, grasses, a few last wild flowers on my walk back from the town. Helen, whose eye was unerring, placed them in a dark blue jar that set off the sealing-wax red of the rose-hips, and Frances, her lips and cheeks as red as the berries, helped her arrange them. It is that watercolour that hangs in my Highgate sitting room now. Helen gave it to me, afterwards.

Two days after that, when the bright weather still held, we bundled Frances into coats, helped her into a taxi and took her for a drive — not far, just around the town, past the river and the skaters on Moody Pond; the ice sizzled and hissed under the speed of their blades as they shot past us. They bent into the corners, performed waltzing dizzying spins. 'Oh, how good it is not to be cooped up, how

I wish *we* could go skating,' Frances cried — and Helen cautiously agreed that she could take a small walk around the garden when we returned home. With her mother supporting one arm and I the other, she did so, lifting her eager face to the blue sky, sniffing at the scents of dry grass and autumn leaves. 'I can smell the *sun*,' she said, and then, after a little silence, catching at Helen's hand, 'When's Daddy coming?'

'At the weekend, darling. You know that. And he'll be here again for your birthday.'

'I wish he were here *now*. Look how glorious it is. When he comes, I shall go for a walk with him. Meantime, I need some practice. I'm so stiff and unsteady, like some ancient old woman . . . ' She glanced sidelong at her mother. 'I promised to walk by the river with Lucy — may we do it tomorrow?'

Helen demurred, the doctors were consulted. Frances nagged and fretted and finally, two days later, anxious to avoid the excitement dissent caused, Helen gave her permission. We would be driven to the start of the river walk in a taxicab, and it would wait for us. We could walk along the level path by the riverside for precisely fifteen minutes.

'Five minutes each way. We have to be quick, Lucy,' Frances said, clasping my arm tight as we walked away from the car, 'there's something I need to show you.'

'We can't be quick, and you're not to get excited,' I replied, in the firm dull tone that, imitating Helen, I'd adopted — *Can you lie, Lucy?* Yes: with the best of them. *Can you hide heartbreak?* Sure: when we need to, we all can.

'I'm not excited. I'm as calm as can be. I was never calmer in my entire life. And look how slowly I walk — a snail would be faster.'

She gave me one of her quicksilver glances, then turned her eyes to the path ahead: to one side of us, pines; to the other, the fierce smashing turbulence of the river. We walked on along the path at a slow pace: crystal-clear air, a heavenly blue sky, our breath coming out in small white puffs. Frances's thinness was disguised by layers of woollens and a dark fur coat that Helen had insisted upon. She was wearing a flowered scarf over her dark shining hair, and I knew it must be one she had chosen herself, for it was brilliantly coloured, embroidered with red roses. Frances had never lost her love for objects that were gaudy, and she craved bright colours. The roses on the scarf matched the roses in her cheeks, Helen had said, kissing her. I knew the flushed cheeks were misleading, a symptom of her illness, but they gave her an air of radiant health. Her bright eyes, glancing at me, then fixing on the path ahead, were resolute; her expression was tight with concentration.

'I'm sorry I lied to you, Lucy, in my letters,' she said suddenly. 'I wanted to tell you the truth – I'm pledged to tell you the truth always.'

'It doesn't matter. You told me as much of the truth as you could. There were reasons why you couldn't tell me more. Anyway, I'm here now.'

'Even before I was ill – I didn't always tell you the *entire* truth.' She hesitated. 'When I wrote from school – I wasn't always as happy as I made out.'

'You weren't?'

I looked at her closely, thinking of the rapturous letters I'd received from the famous school she'd attended, Milton Academy near Boston. I could remember descriptions of the beauty of its campus, the schoolgirl fun in its dormitories; games, rivalry – and then, later, the graduation ball, the dress she'd made for it, the beau who would escort her. I had been jealous, I think. I envied her this school, envied such normalities; taught by Nicola Dunsire from the age of eleven onwards, I had never experienced them.

'I expect I didn't tell *you* the entire truth either,' I said gently.

'I got used to it eventually.' Frances kept her eyes on the path ahead. 'And it wasn't their fault. It was a wonderful school, the teachers were excellent – it was altogether civilised. And I made friends there, in the end. But to begin with, I didn't fit in and they found me strange, I think, Lucy – this earnest little girl, a bit of a misfit, obsessed with Egypt, and tombs and pyramids. I gave a talk once, about Hatshepsut and Daddy's dig. I hadn't been there long then, I was thirteen, I think. It wasn't a complete failure, my talk. It had novelty factor, I guess . . . it was unusual. But that all wore off, and some of the girls would get impatient. They wanted to talk about lacrosse and basketball – and about boys, once we got older. I had to keep Egypt locked up inside my heart and my head. I learned not to speak of it. But I missed it so terribly. I used to dream of going back there. I'd lie in bed at night and plan secret voyages.'

'You *will* go back there. When you're better, Frances. I'll take you.'

'No. I shan't. I shall never go back to Egypt. You know that as well as I do. Please don't lie to me, Lucy.'

She spoke quietly, but there was a finality in her voice that silenced me. We walked on a little further, Frances glancing continually at her watch, and at last came to a halt by a large grey boulder. To our right, the river valley narrowed and there was a series of falls, the water rushing over them, churning in pools, then swooping to the next. The spray flung up a diamond brilliance, and the noise of the water was loud, almost drowning Frances's words when she next spoke, so I had to lean closer to hear her.

'That took us five minutes,' she said. 'We have five minutes here before we have to turn back. You're not to waste it, Lucy – not one second. I'm so watched over – we might not have another chance. Do you recognise this boulder?'

I examined the rock, which was taller than I was, damp with spray, its crevices containing tiny sproutings of ferns and emerald mosses. At first I couldn't understand – and then I began to see: a suggestion of female breasts, a slender waist, a curve on the side exposed to the prevailing wind that gave a fleeting impression of a blind, passionless face. Ivy for hair, not limestone rivulets, but even so. I knew Frances's ways. Yes, I recognised it.

'It's a truth place. Some places naturally are, some aren't – and this *is*. I knew that as soon as I found it. So, don't lie to me, Lucy, don't even attempt it. Not here. My father won't tell me the truth, neither will my mother or the doctors – but I know you will. How long have I? Six months? Another year?'

I dropped my gaze. I couldn't have met her eyes, not then. Helen had never discussed this issue with me and I would never have raised it. Taking me aside when he last visited, his face drawn with exhaustion and strain, Herbert Winlock had said: 'You'd better know, Lucy. We'll be fortunate if she makes it to the spring. That's what we're praying for: another four, perhaps five months.' I suspected that estimate had been revised downwards since the last pneumothorax procedure.

'Will I make it to the spring? I so want to see the spring. All the plants springing up, and the clouds racing . . .'

Frances turned her face eagerly to the river and then the blue arch of the cloudless sky. My vision had blurred and I couldn't have spoken. I felt the burn of Frances's gaze, as she turned back to look at me, though I still didn't dare meet her eyes. She gave a deep sigh, removed her glove and took my cold hand in her hot one.

'Ah, you can't lie, not to me. I thought as much. Three months, then? Two? Is that all? That's not so very long, is it? And I used to think I had all the time in the world . . . Will you come to my funeral, Lucy? Will you miss me? Will you mourn me?'

'You know the answer to that.' The tears began to flow from my eyes. Frances leaned forward, kissed the tears and then hugged me tight in her arms, with a strength that surprised me.

'Well, I hope I pass muster when I get to the Weighing of the Heart ceremony,' she said, speaking lightly and rapidly. 'I should think I will. I must have a good chance – I've always been light-hearted, haven't I? And I'm not old enough to have sinned too badly. I'm sure I'd have sinned with the best of them, given more time . . . Such a journey. I *am* afraid, sometimes. Not always. Dry your eyes, Lucy. If anyone sees you've been crying, they'll guess – and I don't want you blamed. I knew anyway. I've known for quite a while, I think . . . I expect that's why I wrote you. I just wanted to be certain. Here.' She passed me a gauze square. 'Now mop your eyes. Prove you can smile – ah, you can. How dear you are to me. I have something for you.'

Reaching into the pocket of her fur coat, she brought out a small and compact object. I couldn't see what it was, but I caught a kingfisher flash of blue and knew what it must be, even before she opened her hand, pressed the little *shabti* figure into mine and closed my fingers around it.

'Keep him safe for me, Lucy. He can watch over you. He can see all the things I won't be able to see – what becomes of you, who you marry, the children you have – I hope you have a boy and a girl, *lots* of children. My *shabti* will see them, and the work you do, the journeys you make, the life you live – all the joy ahead. I wish you so *much* joy and goodness and fulfilment, Lucy – and the wishes of the dying are powerful.'

So she had planned this, I thought: for how long? I bent my head.

Seeing I couldn't speak, she embraced me again and then clung to me, burying her face in my shoulder. I held her tight against my heart and there was a flurry of words and blind panic: all the things that had not been said were said then. I covered her face in kisses and she kissed my eyes in frantic haste. You taste of salt, she said, that's how grief tastes, Lucy. Then – time running out on us – we walked slowly back to the cab. We reached it exactly fifteen minutes after we'd left it.

Two days later, early on the Saturday, her father Herbert arrived from New York. He had planned to leave again the next night, but Frances's temperature had suddenly soared, her pulse rate was rapid and faint, and her breathing was deteriorating. Seeing Frances's feverish face, listening to her wild talk, he abandoned that plan. By the Sunday morning, the last time I saw her, I knew she could no longer recognise me: her eyes rested on my face, but looked beyond me. On 18 November, on the Monday morning, when both her parents were with her, there was a sudden change, a leakage of air from lungs that were, by then, too consumed by disease to recover. That caused a fatal pressure to the heart, a final rupture, then haemorrhaging.

Frances died at two o'clock that same afternoon. As promised, I attended her funeral. A bright winter's day, the air clear, the sun shining, a glitter of frost where the grass was in shadow. She was buried in Mount Auburn Cemetery near Boston, in the family plot, next to the small grave of her infant brother William, the little boy to whose picture she'd brought pebbles, *ostraka,* small treasured finds from the Valley; the lost boy drowned in 1918 in the waters of Penobscot – that bay where it gave her joy to sail. It's a place I've never seen, but which I revisit often in my imagination. I think of her now as I first learned to do in Egypt: reunited with her brother in that Egyptian afterlife that lies beyond heartache, a cool breeze on their faces, their eyes resting on the places they loved. That is where she is. I refuse to contemplate the alternatives.

Mount Auburn Cemetery, like my neighbouring Highgate, has many famous graves and many unvisited ones. They lie side by side, in the equality of death, the celebrated and the forgotten. Approached through a gate built to resemble an Egyptian temple, it is impeccably maintained, with verdant walks, pavilions, gardens and woodland. It is not, as Frances would have said, some 'mouldering old churchyard', and – when I last visited – the inscription on her plain gravestone remained as clear and readable now as it was when first cut. This always mattered to her, and for her sake matters to me also.

When the ceremony was over, I wished my friend the safest of journeys through the underworld. Then I packed the small blue figure she'd given me, booked a passage on the first ship available and sailed to England.

A cold crossing. Days of grey swell. I spent the days staring at the waves, trying to hear a voice that had been silenced. It was on the upper deck of that liner, somewhere in mid-Atlantic, that I met the man who would become my first husband. Being green in judgement and grief-stricken, a state that does not improve anyone's clarity of mind, I lacked the good sense to turn away when he approached me.

'I think we've met before.' He looked me up and down, examined the lineaments of my face. 'Yes, I'm almost sure . . . Let me rack my brain. Years ago. A Newnham garden, a truly appalling lunch. Salmon in aspic? You carried the trays. You worked your little socks off. Ah, got it! *I met a traveller from an antique land* – and *you* were that traveller. You've grown up. Hello again.'

I examined his clothes, which were flamboyant. I frowned up at his face, which was handsome. A gull shrieked and swooped low. The grey Atlantic heaved. I couldn't see him too well but some memory came swimming towards me, up from the ocean. The remorseless beads on my memory abacus clicked into place. Nicola's poet friend. Rumoured Cambridge Apostle. Met once, and once mentioned in her lying letters from France, read in my bedroom at Rose and Peter's farm, the room with two sets of stairs to it, one obvious, one hidden; read late at night, by the flicker of candlelight.

Ah, got it . . . The poet. The annoyer of my father. Eddie something – double-barrelled.

35

'There's going to be a war. *Another* bloody war. Sorry to intrude on your grief and all that, but look at *this*,' Clair Lennox said, mooching into the dining room at our Newnham house. She tossed the newspaper she'd been reading onto the table. 'Rallies. Rearmament. You'd have thought they might have learned. Doesn't history teach them anything?'

'Evidently not. Do you mind not doing that? I'm working.'

Two days on from my return to England: a Cambridge December: a misery of rain and, as my mother used to claim, the wind blowing in from Siberia. On the dining table – my attic desk space was too small – I'd spread out all the notes and photographs for my next book; I was staring down at pictures of islands. A small fire was dwindling and choking in the narrow fireplace; above it hung the portrait of Nicola Dunsire that Clair Lennox had painted the summer she arrived for a short stay: *Newnham Garden, Summer 1928*. Seven years on and here she still was, immovable as ever.

It was Clair who had greeted me when I arrived back from America. She'd announced that while I was inconveniently in mid-Atlantic, Nicola had been summoned to France; there, her invalid mother, ailing for years, had suffered some crisis.

'Probably another false alarm, alas,' Clair said. 'She likes to keep Nicola on her toes, does Madame Maladie. If she's okay, Nicola will be straight back. If she dies, it will take longer. Fingers crossed. I believe there's a nest egg.'

Staring down at my notes, I ardently hoped that Nicola's mother would recover, and recover fast; I could suffer a few days of Clair's company – any longer than that and I'd throttle her.

'Where's *that?*' she said now, advancing on the table, disarranging my photographs and pointing a paint-stained finger at rocks, sand and a pine tree.

'Nowhere *you* know, Clair.'

'Oh, for fuck's *sake.*' She left the room, slamming the door behind her. I breathed again. I breathed in and out, experimentally; no pain in my side; nothing; all normal.

I'd been waiting for a thin dry cough to manifest itself – waiting for weeks, waiting since those first days at Saranac Lake; so far there was no sign of it. I could begin work tonight, I thought, or tomorrow morning. If I worked and worked, wrote and wrote, perhaps I'd get through this. A clock ticked; beyond the closed curtains, the Cambridge church bells began to chime: six o'clock. I rearranged the patterns of notes and photographs three times and, when they still made no discernible sense, panicked and abandoned them.

The next day it stopped raining, and after fighting *Islands* all morning, I went for a walk. Clair Lennox had made a studio for herself in one of our garden outbuildings, and through the ice on its windowpanes I could just see her small intent figure, stabbing paint on a canvas: malachite, chrome yellow, cerulean, cadmium orange – she was a brilliant colourist, even I had to admit that. The admiration for her work that I studiously concealed increased the dislike I felt for her: it seemed unjust that someone so self-centred and rude should possess an angelic sensitivity as an artist. What translation took place when she took up a brush, selected shades, magicked something out of the nothingness of blank canvas?

I edged along the path, trying to remain out of sight – I had no wish to speak to her. But despite her concentration, which always seemed absolute – *A bomb could go off, and if Clair was painting she wouldn't turn a hair*, Nicola liked to claim – she must have glimpsed me, for she threw back the studio door and glared out at me.

'Good news. Nicola's mother *has* died,' she announced – no preamble, as usual. 'Snuffed it last night. Nicola rang earlier. I didn't bother you because I knew you were working. She says it'll take her two weeks to sort things out, maybe longer. So you're stuck with me for the foreseeable. Sorry about that.'

She lit a cigarette, cupped it in mittened hands, puffed smoke and frowned at the frostbitten rose bushes. 'And what's more there *is* a nest egg. Madame Maladie must have squirrelled it away – well, she was ever the devout *bourgeoise*. Thank God for that. Quite a nice little sum, I gather – even once the loony-bin is paid off. Freedom!'

'It isn't a loony-bin. It's a nunnery. They take in people with nervous complaints. Nicola's mother was there of her own free will. *De mortuis nil nisi bonum* mean anything to you? Clearly not.'

'Loony bin, lunatic asylum, nuthouse, nunnery – who cares? Oh, and there was another call. For you, Lucy. Eddie-bloody-Vain-Chance. I told him you were working. I told him to get stuffed, actually.'

'Thanks, Clair. Any message?'

'Yes. He said to tell you the Furies were after him. They've got their claws into him, but the instant they let go, he'll be in touch. He rang from a party in Chelsea – it was still going strong at nine in the morning. Very rowdy . . . so I think the Erinyes were poetic licence, but with him, who knows?' She flicked the cigarette stub onto the path at my feet. It smouldered, then damply went out. She gave me one of her sharp, speculative glances. 'I didn't know you knew our beautiful Eddie.'

'Plenty you don't know, Clair. And I'm not in a hurry to enlighten you.'

'Temper, temper,' she replied, and returned to her studio, slamming the door. She kept a wind-up gramophone in there, and as I walked on through the garden, I could hear the record she'd chosen: *La Traviata*, consumptive Violetta's last dying aria. Chosen for my benefit, I felt; she had it playing full volume.

I walked into Cambridge along the Backs and went into Trinity College. There I left a note at the porters' lodge for my father, asking if I might call in and see him on my return from my walk. It was his afternoon for supervisions, but there'd be a brief gap after that, before he'd scurry off to the library, or pre-Hall sherry with another Fellow. I knew better than to telephone; *notes* had always been the preferred method of communication in Cambridge, and my father saw no reason to change that civilised practice. I felt the one I'd written would pass muster: *Dear Father.* Neat italic script, two sentences, no exclamation marks.

'I shall make sure Dr Foxe-Payne receives it without delay, miss,' said Mr Grimshaw, now elevated to Senior Porter. I wasn't sure if he recognised me; probably not. I rarely risked turning up at the college gates; my father did not encourage social visits. Should I reveal who I was, tell Mr Grimshaw my identity? It seemed pointless, vain. Maybe I wouldn't keep the appointment anyway. I said nothing.

I walked purposefully out of the town, along the riverside. The water meadows had flooded. The path was deserted. I was trudging past Ophelia willows, growing aslant the Cam, and a sea of silvery fields, water an inch deep, rippling like silk in the keen wind from the Urals. *Take a strand of silk and a strand of steel, Miss Lucy — and the silk is the stronger of the two.* I considered those I was bound to: Frances, who was gone; Rose and Peter a world away in London; Nicola, in France, dealing with her late mother's effects. I tried to fix my mind on her predicament. The nature of her mother's malady had always remained vague; there were claims and counter-claims (tick your preferred choice). It had never been clear whether she was insane or merely suffering from some minor nervous affliction, whether she was incarcerated or free to leave.

Some details had emerged over the years, but Nicola blocked questions — perhaps she feared that, whatever the malady was, she herself might have inherited it. This inheritance might explain her menstrual descent into those black caves of depression, I used to think — her mother, she'd once confessed, had suffered similar episodes. It might also explain the attempted suicide she'd once described to me. She still could not speak of her mother without those violent tremblings and that loss of control that I'd witnessed as a child. How bound was Nicola to her mother? How bound was she to Clair Lennox? Never ask. Inheritance explains everything, and nothing. The ties that bind people are best treated with discretion.

I came to a halt at the river's edge; swollen by the heavy rain of the past few days, the Cam was transformed from the easeful sluggish nature it exhibited in summer. It looked quite deep, sufficiently deep, clogged at its edges with a mess of sedge and broken willow branches, but with fierce eddying currents further out. I measured those currents. I wondered if it were true that drowning people surfaced three times before finally going under; if their lives flashed before their eyes in terrible entirety before they surrendered. I placed one experimental foot on the soggy edge; mud sucked at my shoes, the currents pulled me. I put my hand in my pocket and closed it around the little *shabti*, the little answerer, that Frances had given me. I took a step further. Then another. Something stayed me – or someone. I turned around, clambered back to the bank, faced into the wind and walked back to Cambridge.

My father gave me tea in his rooms in Nevile's Court. A college servant arrived, bearing a tray: Earl Grey, with lemon; college biscuits. He tended to the fire, added coals, ensured it was burning brightly.

'Will there be anything else, Dr Foxe-Payne?' he asked, then left as discreetly as he came.

My father, who disapproved of servants on principle, liked to boast of those at Trinity: many were third generation and could not be bettered; the college kitchens and its cellars were similarly unrivalled. Certain elements in the university would sometimes claim preeminence for King's College, or even St John's, in such respects; my father had nothing but contempt for such foolishness. Once the man had left us, he took the chair behind his desk and regarded me in a quizzical way, as if trying to work out who I was. Given my *Islands* journeyings and Saranac Lake, it was eighteen months since I'd last seen him.

'To what do I owe this pleasure?' my father said, as I'd known he would. Then he remembered: snatching his mind back from his book's next paragraph and the intricacies of Aeschylus, he said, 'I was sorry to hear about your little friend. Frances, was that the name? My condolences.'

Fifteen minutes in, I saw him glance at his watch. How unchanged he was, I was thinking; how unruffled. Marriage – his kind of marriage – had suited him. He had a sleek look, these days; the look of a man whose star was in the ascendant – it had been on the up for years. His book on Euripides had been well received. Nicola's efforts on his behalf, her regular lunches and parties – her *networking*, as we'd say now – had borne fruit. He had fewer enemies, more allies at Cambridge these days; there were rumours he might become the College Bursar, should the current holder of that august position decide to die, instead of clinging on in poor health, as at present.

I glanced down at my father's desk — our conversation was taking place across his desk. He had been reading undergraduate essays; in the margins of the scrawl nearest to me were my father's neat, cold comments, written in green ink. *Define your terms*, read the first of them. They were always telling you to define your terms at Cambridge: it was the university's watchword. It could stop you in your tracks for days, centuries . . .

My father glanced at his watch again and cleared his throat. This heralded dismissal, so I said, fast: 'The thing is, Daddy — someone wants to marry me. He's asked me to marry him. His name is Eddie. Eddie Vyne-Chance.'

Mercifully, this name, this pompous name, rang no bells; my father, despising all modern verse, never read any poetry post-1880 — and that luncheon party *was* a long time ago. He made a steeple of his fingers. 'I see. And your reply was?'

'I said I'd think it over.'

This was not true. What I'd said was, *Very well. Why not?* The marriage proposal had come thirty minutes after our encounter on deck, by which time we were in the bar, on my first and his third brandy. If he'd proposed vaulting the ship rails and diving into the Atlantic, I'd have given the same answer.

'Very wise. I suggest you do so. Do I know his people? What are his means?'

I knew it wouldn't assist to explain the grand Vyne-Chance clan, or to mention poetry; I could imagine the scorn it would provoke. I said, '*I* have means, Daddy.'

'Indeed you do. I hope that is not an enticement. Are you asking my permission? In my day, that task was undertaken by the swain concerned. No doubt customs have altered. Perhaps you came here seeking my advice? A pleasant change, if so.'

I rose and began to back away. He added, 'Have you known him long?'

'I met him on the boat from America. But I knew him before that, sort of.'

I averted my eyes, fixed them on the glories beyond the

windows: Nevile's Court, the Wren Library; sublime architectural order, unchanged in two and a half centuries. An antique land, as my suitor had once claimed; he had not been sober on that occasion of course. Byron had once had his rooms on this same staircase. On the roof of the Wren Library were statues representing Divinity, Law, Mathematics and the Arts. Four wise men. When I was a very small child — it must have been before my father left for the war — he took my mother and me on a tour of that library; he had shown us a few of its great treasures: a Shakespeare first folio, the books Isaac Newton had bequeathed his college, and a precious medieval missal; I could still remember its blue and gold angels. One had held a pen in his hands — a recording angel.

'A shipboard romance. Dear God. You retain the capacity to surprise me, Lucy. I had thought you possessed *some* modicum of sense. My advice is — discuss the matter with Nicola when she returns. You will find that, in such affairs, she is entirely clear-sighted. Beyond that, my dear, what can I say? You are twenty-four—'

'Twenty-five.'

'Twenty-five, of independent means, in good health and, as far as I am aware, of sound mind. You were obstinate as a child and remain obstinate to this day. You will act as you choose, and I will only waste my valuable time if I seek to reason with you, let alone to dissuade you. Goodbye, my dear.' He kissed my cheek. 'Close the oak on your way out. I have work to do. I wish to avoid further disturbances.'

I closed both doors to his set, inner and outer, as instructed. My father: hermetically sealed in, safe from importunates. He returned to Aeschylus, I returned to Newnham.

It was dark when I reached the house. Clair Lennox had ferried her records inside, I discovered. On entering the sitting room, I found her sprawled on the sofa in her painting clothes, fur-booted feet propped on a cushion, two glasses of red wine on the table next to her. The record on the turntable was, again, *La Traviata*.

'Do you have to play that?' I asked, coming to a halt in the doorway.

'Yes, I do, as a matter of fact. I'm considering consumption.

Chekhov, the Brontë sisters, Keats, Chopin, Modigliani, poor pale Thomas Chatterton – and your poor little friend. Deathbeds in general. It's giving me ideas – something I can use.'

'Frances was neither poor nor little. And she isn't material for your paintings either. What a disgusting ghoul you are, Clair.'

Crossing to the gramophone, I lifted the needle, silencing Violetta's caterwauling. Then I snapped the record in half. Then I sat down in my mother's chair and stared at the fire. Clair was unmoved by this act, though she gave me an assessing look, so possibly it interested her. More material.

After a silence, she said: 'You look like hell, you know. You're soaking wet. Have you been swimming? Look, I'm sorry about your friend, all right? I can see, on reflection, *Traviata*, not tactful. You won't believe me, but I didn't set out to upset you. I wasn't even thinking about you. Have a glass of wine – it might help, it might not, but it's worth a try.'

She passed me the glass, then returned to the sofa and slumped again. She lit a cigarette, inhaled deeply and turned her sharp dark eyes to inspect me. She still looked much as she'd done that first day I'd met her at Nicola's ill-fated lunch party. Scarcely aged, a little Harlequin; deft monkey hands, black hair cut in a severe bob, an uncompromising fringe. She was wearing paint-encrusted trousers and three jumpers – she never cared how she looked; she rarely bothered to change her work clothes. No inclination to please or be liked; a measuring stare that was at best critical, at worst hostile. *You don't understand Clair*, Nicola liked to say. *You can't see why I need her.* I drank some of the wine.

'Why didn't they tell you your friend Frances was ill?' she asked, after an interval. 'Did her family think it was the famous Curse, claiming yet another victim, or were they just ashamed? People get like that with TB, I've seen it. One of my Slade friends had it. Galloping in his case. His parents sent him to Switzerland. He died two days after he got there. That was hushed up too. They didn't want *talk*, they said. Or they knew they'd be shunned perhaps.' She gave me a narrow look. 'It's infectious.'

'Contagious.'

'There's a difference?' She rose, prowled about the room and returned to the sofa. 'So, let's *try*. I'm going to *try*. Let's talk. Tell me, what are you going to do now? I thought — maybe you'd take off for London. Stay with your friends there.'

'Rose and Peter?' I'd considered that possibility and rejected it. I didn't want to inflict myself on them, not in my present state. 'No. I shall write my islands book. Work.'

'Here?'

'Yes, here. Sorry to dismay you. Where else would I go? I do live. here.'

'You don't have to. You have money. Unlike some of us.'

This was true — much of what Clair said was true, which was one of the reasons why I found her so disconcerting. I *did* have money; I kept inheriting it unexpectedly. First, when I was twenty-one, a trust from my mother; then more from my Emerson grandmother, who out of the blue left me investments and paintings; finally from my father's estranged sister, my Aunt Foxe, who had divided her legacy between me and the RSPCA. The investments had plummeted in the wake of the stock market crash; the paintings were in storage. I had an emergency fund and a small monthly income; my first book had brought in some money, though a tiny amount, and perhaps the second would bring some too. I had enough to support me and pay for travel. I'd had enough to take me to Saranac Lake on the first available train . . . Money buys freedom. In Clair's view, frequently canvassed, it could buy other things as well, a London flat, for instance, a house at Land's End — wherever: she couldn't wait to get rid of me.

She rose, prowled about the room again, and refilled her wineglass. 'You?' She held the bottle poised over my own glass and, before I could demur, refilled it. 'Drink it down — sometimes it's as well to get drunk, you know. Think of it as medicine,' she added, her tone as close as it ever came to conciliatory.

'I had an abortion once,' she continued, in the same tone, lying back on the sofa again. 'Christ knows how I got myself in *that* predicament. It was when I was at the Slade. The paintings weren't working, and that was making me desperate, so I got blind drunk at a party one night. The only time I've ever made *that* mistake. Do it once, and get pregnant — just my luck. *He* coughed up, which was gentlemanly. So it wasn't backstreet — not some cackling crone with a wire hook. Oh no, it was a Harley Street cove in a morning suit, a swish clinic . . . I drank a bottle of gin every day for a month afterwards. Then I was cured. I've never looked back. The painting improved at once. So: when in distress, I recommend drink – used judicially.' She frowned. 'On the other hand, it got me into the fix in the first place, so maybe I don't. Tricky, eh?'

I looked at her curiously: what a peculiar woman she was – blind and impervious to other people's feelings, entirely without shame or conscience. I knew what abortions were. They were illegal. I had never heard anyone discuss them, let alone admit to having one.

After a while, I asked: 'Did you see him again?'

'Who, the perpetrator? No. I couldn't stick the man. Why would I?'

There was a silence then; Clair stared up at the ceiling and I stared into the fire, watching the flames' flickering patterns.

'It's not the same,' I said, after a long pause. 'Your situation then, and mine now. They're different, Clair. Even you can see that.'

'If you say so.' She shrugged. 'You don't have a monopoly on grief, you know.' She yawned, and jumped up. 'Christ, I'm starving. There's no food in the house. I leave all that to Nicola. I think I'll bike off down to the chippie. Cod and chips for me – you?'

'Nothing, thank you.'

'Suit yourself. I'm skint. I need ninepence – a shilling if you're feeling flush. Then I can get a slice and a pickled onion as well.'

Most of my money was still in dollars. Having nothing smaller, I gave her a five-pound note. I knew she wouldn't return the change – she never did.

'Gosh, *thanks*,' she said. 'Very generous, milady.' She gave a rustic curtsey, a housemaid's bob.

'Oh, and if the phone rings,' she added, moving to the door, 'it'll probably be Vain-Chance again. He rang twice while you were out. Once to say he'd be on the train to Cambridge tomorrow and once to say, oops, change of plan, no he wouldn't.' She paused. 'He was at some party again. At Baba's, he said. Very loud music, the merry tinkle and crash of glasses. Some man kept yelling that Eddie had pinched the corkscrew ... Nicola rang too. I told her Vain-Chance was pestering you. She was *not* pleased.'

'What did she say?'

'The same thing I'd say. Run a mile. Charm the little birdies out of the trees when he wants. And beauteous, of course. But he didn't get that nickname by accident. Think about it.'

Nicola was delayed in France longer than expected; she returned to Cambridge a few days before Christmas. Fresh from her mother's funeral, from prolonged battles with *notaires*, she arrived flushed with excitement, trembling in triumph. Yes, all her arrangements had gone perfectly, despite the entanglements of French bureaucracy. Her mother's affairs had been settled; the nunnery's bills had proved negligible. Her mother's house was already sold. The *acte de vente* had required the mayor's seal, the *acte authentique* had required four witnesses, but her orderly approach – she had always been a fiend for order – had carried her through. I forget how many thousand francs she had wrested from the grasping fingers of French tax officials, maybe it was hundreds of thousands in those days of unstable currencies, but it was – sufficient.

'Sufficient for what?' I asked, the first time this word was used. I soon learned.

'It will buy us a London flat. Maybe even a house, depending on the area we choose,' Nicola announced in a dreamy way, as we came towards the end of our Christmas lunch. 'But *I* thought: Bloomsbury. And the houses there are absurdly large, so a flat would be the thing for us. In one of those beautiful squares, a view over London plane trees. Close to the theatres and the opera house. Within walking distance of the British Museum and the Reading Room. Right in the heart of things . . .'

I looked around the table, decorated with holly and candles. Outside it was dark. In a distant way, I was wondering who came into the 'us' category and whether it included me; wondering whether this possibility had been discussed before and when. Had it been mooted years ago, while I was studying at Girton? Discussed when I was absent on my travels? I began to see that it must have been: it was news to me, but evidently not to my father or Clair Lennox. Both were delighted.

'Thank Christ. Escape from this miserable backwater at last,' Clair said. 'A toast to Madame Maladie.' She raised her glass.

'Now, now. Let us remain decorous,' my father said, in mock reproof. 'But the advantages are obvious, so we owe Yvette Dunsire,

467

poor woman, our thanks . . . I must say, it will be a great relief to sell this house, and we'll have no difficulty – family houses are always in demand in Cambridge. It is far too large for us, and always has been. The outgoings grow more punitive each year. I should make a considerable monthly saving . . . and of course Bloomsbury would be convenient for *me*, Nicola, my dear, should you decide on that. Not far to the station . . . I could be back in college in little more than an hour. To be so close to the Reading Room would be a very great pleasure. I shall of course need a study there, my dear. And I must have accommodation for my books.'

'And I'll need a studio,' Clare interrupted. 'Don't forget that, Nicola. Doesn't have to be big. But I must have large windows. North light.'

Along the length of the table, in the flicker of the fire- and candle-light, Nicola's eyes met mine and held them. We had had our quarrels over the years, but none of the sometimes bitter words that had passed between us had broken the strong thread that bound us: she could still read my mind, as she always had. Rising from her chair, as my father and Clair began to elaborate on their respective needs, she came quietly to my side and, taking me by the hand, drew me into the silence of the sitting room. Closing the door, she leaned against it. I could see she'd begun to tremble – that disability she had never conquered and could never entirely hide. She was very pale and still very dear to me.

'And you?' she said, with a half-smile. 'Do you also have a list of requirements, Lucy? Did you think I'd forgotten you? Well, I haven't. *They* don't know yet,' she gave a dismissive gesture towards the dining room, 'but I've already found the perfect place for us. I went straight to the agents, when I came off the train from Dover. It was only the third property I viewed, but I knew it was for us as soon as I saw it. In Bloomsbury, a large flat, and it has the perfect room for you. It's next to my own, Lucy, with a view over the square. The instant I walked in, I knew you'd love it . . .

'It's on the first floor, Lucy.' Faint colour had risen in her cheeks and the trembling in her hands was increasing. 'Four bedrooms, three wonderful reception rooms. High ceilings, abundant light – *calm* light, like a Vermeer painting. And in *your* room, the one that will be yours, space for your books . . . and your mother's paintings. You could unpack some of her things if you wish. I know you will like it. You'll be able to work there in peace, Lucy – take off on your travels if you must, though I hope your strange need to travel may pass once we're settled. Clair wouldn't bother us – there's a studio for her, in the mews at the end of the garden. You know how she works! We'd scarcely see her. You and I would be together again, Lucy. We could explore London together, the way we did Paris – do you remember that? I know you remember *that*.' She faltered briefly. I think my expression made her falter. 'It's close to the Museum, Lucy – a stone's throw. We could visit it together, talk about Egypt and Greece as we used to do . . .'

She left the sentence unfinished. I think that she did believe in this future she was conjuring up for me – that it was one she'd imagined, dwelled on and planned minutely. I could feel the force of her will, as always, pliant and python-strong, patient and relentless. It would have been so easy to give in to that will, to be embraced by its coils as I'd been before. Yes, I remembered Paris. I remembered coming under Nicola's spell there, and how that spell had held me in thrall throughout the remainder of my childhood. I had escaped once. If I went to Bloomsbury, if I returned to her now, I would not escape a second time.

'Is it Clair?' Nicola said, with sudden sharpness. She took a step towards me. 'If it is, just say. I'll tell her to leave – she can find somewhere else to live. I know you dislike her. Lucy, dear, please tell me if it's that.'

She laid her long-fingered hand on my arm. I gently released it.

'No, it's not that,' I said, turning away from her.

I knew it would be useless to raise that objection, or any other; useless to prevaricate or argue. Sooner or later, by stealth, guile and loving persistence, she would wear down my resistance. Putting distance between us was the only way I knew of evading the insistent need she had to have me near her and under her sway. I hesitated and then, seizing on the one reason even she could not overcome, I said: 'Nicola, I can't. It's not possible. I'm getting married.'

I thought I'd kept no photographs of my first husband – the marriage itself and its subsequent dissolution were not as painless as people assumed; at some point, around the decree nisi, I think, I went through the albums and destroyed them. But I must have missed one picture – and I examined it the other morning, sitting in my chair overlooking Highgate's square. It had been taken by a *safragi* at the Winter Palace Hotel where, as I've mentioned, I spent my honeymoon. Egypt was my suggestion, quickly endorsed.

'I'd like to show you the places I love,' I said. 'But if you'd rather go somewhere else, Eddie, just say. Wherever you'd like. Truly. You choose.'

Eddie was low on funds, a bit short of the readies. I was paying, and so made the suggestion timidly. I didn't want him to feel coerced or – worse – obligated. The low state of his finances was, he said, a bagatelle, a purely temporary embarrassment.

'Darling girl. Egypt it shall be. I had thought, maybe Capri . . . ? But I've been there so often and it's perhaps a little— No. The Orient it shall be. Don't let's dwell *too* long at the pyramids perhaps, I feel they could pall. But Luxor does tempt me. Flaubert went there, you know, and a wild time he had of it, a wicked *surfeit* of prostitutes. Can we really Ritz it up, darling? Can we afford the Winter Palace?'

I couldn't – not really. But Eddie liked luxury and I didn't want to disappoint him, so I flogged one of my mother's pieces of jewellery – that stock was diminishing – and off we went. The photograph I was inspecting had been taken halfway through our stay at the Winter Palace, at the end of our first week there. February 1936: it was three months since Frances had died.

We are standing on the terrace, above the Nile. I am twenty-five, wearing sunglasses and a hat with a wide brim, which protect me from the sun and completely hide my face: this thin stranger could be me, could be anyone. This person has averted her gaze. She is looking away from the camera, across the river. Her dark glasses are fixed upon the Theban hills in the distance. *And the word for horizon is? Akhet.*

Eddie, thirty-five, hatless, in shirtsleeves, his thick hair tossed back, one arm carelessly thrown around my shoulders and the other around the shoulders of the Arab boy he'd hired as our guide, is smiling straight at the lens, as if daring it to take a bad picture of him. No camera ever did. Eddie was, from every angle, handsome and startlingly so. He embodied that era's masculine ideal of beauty: tall, athletic, golden-haired, blue-eyed, frank-faced; a Grecian nose, a witty mouth: *sui generis* – bohemian in his dress, but no doubt as to caste: unmistakably an English gentleman.

I inspected the photograph minutely. *Read, Lucy, learn to read*: an injunction that applies to images as well as words. By the time this picture was taken, even I was beginning to understand that, less than a month in, this marriage had problems. I couldn't understand why. Yet there the evidence is, in front of my eyes, in a snapshot.

How slow can you be? I tore it into tiny scraps, into confetti.

36

On our return from our Egyptian honeymoon, Eddie and I had to live somewhere; this necessity was one he had overlooked. His inclination was to continue overlooking it for as long as possible. He'd been of No Fixed Abode prior to our marriage, he liked to say – this meant that he stayed with a succession of rich friends until such a time as they chucked him out. He intended to continue this mode of life for the foreseeable future; why should marriage alter anything?

We spent March in his parents' chilly and monstrous house in Shropshire. We spent April at a friend's mansion in Kensington, and May in a palatial villa his cousin owned in the South of France. In June, his luck ran out: a writer he knew grudgingly lent us the keys to a grim little cottage in the middle of Bodmin Moor. It had no running water, but we only discovered that on arrival.

'*Moors*,' Eddie said, our first night. His tone was reflective; glass in hand, he was staring out at the blackened wilderness that surrounded us. 'Moors. There's your next book, darling girl. You must start it the *instant* you finish *Islands*.'

A week later I took the train to London and began house-hunting.

The cottage I subsequently bought was off the King's Road, in what was then a poor part of Chelsea. I was staying with Rose and Peter while I made the search and, as it happened, it was Peter who heard of the place, and he who first took me there. It belonged to one of his fellow activists – Peter was caught up in left-wing politics, in anti-fascist demonstrations at that point. I never discovered if the owner was a Communist or an Anarchist – indeed, I never *met* the owner, a comrade of Peter's who had had to leave England hurriedly.

'It's going cheap,' Peter said.

'It has definite *potential*, Lucy,' said Rose, in a faint tone, when called upon to inspect it.

Rose, who had escaped unscathed from the marriage market of her debutante years, was now a top-flight secretary, working at the Ministry of Defence, much loved by visiting generals, who remembered her mother Poppy with great fondness. As she'd said to me all those years before, she was a *whizz* at organising; she organised field marshals on a daily basis, so organising a house move was nothing. 'Yes, definite *possibilities*,' she went on, marching from room to room, inspecting the dry rot assiduously. 'It will need *work*, of course.'

'It suits you, Lulu,' Peter pronounced, having persuaded the doors to unstick, the windows to open and the taps to work. He leaned back against the cottage's distempered walls and surveyed me narrowly.

'But will it suit Eddie?' Rose asked – at that point, neither she nor her brother had met my husband.

'Only Lucy can judge that,' Peter said. 'How would we know? She's hiding the husband away. Full fathom five her husband lies . . . She's gone to extreme lengths to prevent our meeting him.'

I ignored that. I considered the cottage. I could afford it – an important point, for marriage seemed to have dented my funds severely. It was pretty, if primitive. Its brick façade was whitewashed; a rose had been trained around its front door; to the rear, beyond a damp scullery, there was a small yard, occupied by a territorial tom-cat. I felt plants could be persuaded to grow in that yard – I imagined it swathed in honeysuckle, as the courtyard had been at Nuthanger . . . I dislike indecision. I bought it.

Verdicts on this purchase varied. Nicola, driving over from Bloomsbury, where she and Clair were by then magnificently installed in the flat she'd described to me, said the cottage was a slum. I'd been expecting that; I knew she'd be determined to find fault. I was still not forgiven for my marriage, nor for refusing to join her in Bloomsbury. Showing me around that apartment of hers, she'd thrown back the dividing doors that separated her room from Clair's. 'This could have been yours, Lucy,' she'd said to me.

She inspected the cottage minutely. I knew one of her black moods was upon her before she was in the door; by the time her inspection was complete, her hands had begun trembling. She proclaimed it a nasty artisan's house, in an unfashionable area. My neighbours would be plumbers and bricklayers. And it was so *small*, so confining, so tomb-like . . . Why, you couldn't swing a cat in it.

Clair gave her a reproachful push when she made that remark. Had I not known her as I did, I might have thought she felt sorry for me. 'Don't be such a fucking snob, Nicola,' she said. 'What's the matter with you today?'

She made a face behind Nicola's back and told me the cottage had atmosphere – and the area was fun; half her Slade friends lived around the corner. Eddie was finally persuaded to inspect it that September; it was the day before we were due to move in. By then, I'd worked on the place, worked on it for weeks, cleaned it from top to bottom, painted it, even furnished it. I'd made curtains, found chairs and bookshelves. I rescued some of my mother's paintings from store and hung them. I placed the *shabti* Frances had given me in pride of place on the mantelpiece. Peter had found me an old scrubbed pine table in a clever junk shop he knew, and I'd laid it in readiness for our first dinner with plates and wineglasses and napkins and flowers.

'Darling girl, you *have* been busy,' Eddie said, having roamed from room to room, and come to a halt in the kitchen by the table.

He could see I was keyed up, and he liked to tease; he finally con-fessed he was a *little* disappointed. What he'd really been hoping for, he said, was something more, well, Pooter-ish. 'A red-brick villa,' he said, with a sigh. 'A nice squat villa, with "Mon Repos" in stained glass over the front door . . . *that*'s what I expect from a marital home, Lucy.' Eddie found such phrases amusing, so 'marital home' became the cottage's title. It was the 'marital nest' when he really got going.

A few weeks later, Eddie, restless and unsettled, said the cottage didn't feel *right*: he needed to set his seal on it, he needed to baptise it, and the way to effect this baptism was simple: we must give a party. I vetoed that suggestion; I knew Eddie's parties by then, and I didn't intend the cottage to get wrecked this early. I proposed a dinner instead – a small one, an intimate one, where people could actually *talk* to each other. My friends Rose and Peter still had not met my husband, I pointed out; and it was they who had helped find the cottage.

'If it wasn't for them,' I said, 'we wouldn't be here.'

'How very true,' said Eddie.

The dinner was organised for the first week of October. Rose attended, but Peter did not: he had been arrested the previous day at the 'They Shall Not Pass' demonstration in Cable Street, fighting a pitched battle against Oswald Mosley's Blackshirts, and was now in jail.

Rose and I bailed him on that occasion – and a second dinner was arranged. Again, Peter did not attend. It was December by then; our first Christmas in the cottage was approaching. 'Where's Peter?' I said to Rose, opening the door to her.

He'd left for Spain the previous day, she said, shivering, pushing past me and making for the fire. 'You know what he's like, Lucy. Once Peter decides something, you can't stop him. He's joined the International Brigade.' She drew her fur coat more tightly around her. 'Don't let's talk about it. If we do, I'll start blubbing. Where's Eddie?'

Eddie was at the pub on the corner of our street, the Jolly Hangman. He was fetching a jug of Guinness. When he returned, he mixed this with champagne – on tick – and, disappearing to the kitchen, then added a secret ingredient, possibly brandy, possibly curaçao, possibly both. Eddie loved cocktails as much as Rose did.

'Is it Black Velvet?' Rose asked, as Eddie passed us a foaming coal-black substance.

'Certainly not,' he replied, with indignation. 'I've named it in Lucy's honour. You know how she is about Egypt. This, Rose, is an *Anubis*.'

'Well, it certainly has *teeth*,' Rose said, having sipped experimentally. 'I like it.'

She and Eddie settled themselves by the fire and began talking nineteen to the dozen; Rose had succumbed to Eddie's charm at that first dinner, within minutes of meeting him. She'd never stopped singing his praises since, to me – to her brother, to everyone.

Anubis, guardian of graveyards. Undrinkable. Blasphemous. Ill-timed. Unwise. I left them to it, retreated to the kitchen and tipped the cocktail down the sink.

*

'How's your *Islands* book going, Lucy?' Clair asked me. 'It's been a whole year now – you must have finished it surely?'

Clair's instincts for mixing it had never deserted her, I thought. This was a question she asked me whenever I saw her. Occasionally she'd vary it in a helpful way, saying, 'Do you think you could possibly have writer's block?' or 'Maybe islands was the wrong subject? Why don't you switch to mountains? Or valleys?' On this occasion – it was three days before Christmas; I was at the Bloomsbury flat to deliver presents for her and Nicola – she added a corollary: 'Here's a tip, sweetheart. Marriage doesn't suit you. That was only too predictable. If you want to finish that bloody book, get yourself some *space.*'

Something in her tone alerted me: for once, she wasn't setting out to annoy me, I realised – Clair herself was on edge. We were in the elegant drawing room of Nicola's flat; Clair was prowling around, in search of a corkscrew, and I was alone with her. Nicola was out, late returning from a shopping expedition – and this was unusual. Nicola liked to control her friends' meetings; she preferred them to take place when she herself was present.

I wandered around the room, as Clair began to open a bottle of red wine. Nicola had made the space beautiful, bringing most its furniture from France and claiming it had belonged to her mother. She had brought elegance and understatement, Clair had brought colour: a cadmium-orange shawl, tossed across a pale-grey chair; a citron-yellow cushion against dark-blue silk upholstery. Her portrait of Nicola in our Newnham garden hung above a side table. On the table's polished surface stood the blue stolen *shabti* figure I'd given Nicola in Paris all those years before. *For Nicola, from Lucy, with love. The real thing!* Clair's recent paintings pulsed from the walls.

This room, Nicola's creation, bore no resemblance to our house in Newnham, to the rooms there she had transformed. But in Bloomsbury her ménage continued much as before; its habits had become ingrained within weeks of the move to London. My father visited once a week, arriving on a Sunday morning, staying for lunch, departing soon after for college; occasionally he would come down on a weekday and spend it at work in the Reading Room at the museum. Clair spent her days painting. Nicola . . . I was never sure how Nicola spent her days, weeks, months. She always insisted she never had a minute to herself, but sometimes I wondered if she missed her contacts, her university scheming, missed Cambridge.

Clair had just come inside from her day's work in her garden studio. Paint-scarred as usual, in filthy dungarees, pouring the wine, chain-smoking, she prowled around Nicola's large drawing room as if it were a cage. Clair's habits never varied: she worked from nine in the morning until six at night, every day, including weekends. Recently, hitting a productive patch, these hours had increased – and on my last visit Nicola had complained of that fact, amusingly at first, and then in a querulous way, at length. *Get yourself some space.*

'Is everything all right, Clair?' I asked, with hesitation.

'Fine and dandy.' She sloshed red wine into two glasses. She was fiercely loyal to Nicola; I had never doubted that. 'Top hole. Spiffing. Pick your superlative.'

'Nicola *is* happy here still? She's not – she isn't regretting the move to London?'

'She says not. But she frets. She doesn't like to be alone.'

'She never did.'

'It'll settle.' Clair handed me a glass, sprawled on the sofa, lit another cigarette. 'But I've had to make some rules. Nicola should understand that – *she*'s made a few rules in her time, God knows . . .' She laughed. 'So I've told her: no interruptions when I'm painting. It fucks up my concentration. If there's some crisis, real or imagined, Nicola has to cope. No knocking on my studio door. There's been quite a lot of door-knocking, recently.'

'She's lonely, I expect. Sometimes she needs company.'

'She *has* company. Mine. Every evening, from six o'clock onwards. Then, my time is hers. That's the deal, and it always has been. Meanwhile,' Clair's small sharp face puckered in amusement, 'meanwhile, I've had bolts fitted to the inside of the studio door. Two. Nice and stout. I took Nicola to inspect them yesterday.'

'That went down well?'

'Yes it did. Nicola laughed. She said I'd made a very neat little hidey-hole. She said it was a fine and private place.'

'The grave's a fine and private place/But none, I think, do there embrace.'

'What?'

'It's a quote, Clair. One of her favourite poets.'

'It is? Oh, Nicola and her bloody *quotes.*' She shrugged, then stiffened and sat up; she had heard something, something that was inaudible to me. 'That's her key — at the front door downstairs . . . Silence is golden — is that a *quote* too? Keep your mouth shut. Don't mention bolts. Change of subject.'

She threw herself back on the sofa, put her fur-booted feet on a cushion. As Nicola came quietly and gracefully into the room, flushed from the cold air outside, carrying little parcels, trophies of her Christmas shopping, Clair was saying in a loud tone: '— and so we're planning a party here to celebrate my birthday, and you might as well come, Lucy. Bring Eddie if you must, come alone, as the mood takes you. It's coming up fast. On 12 February 1937, I'll be three hundred years old, and I don't feel a day over twenty.'

We went to Clair's three-hundred-years-old birthday party, my husband and I. We went to the three-hundred-and-one party held the following year. On both occasions, we took a taxi and trundled all across London from our Chelsea cottage to the flat in Bloomsbury.

In the taxicab to the first of those birthday parties, married a year, Eddie and I sat side by side. I said, taking his hand: '*Please* try, Eddie. It means a lot to Nicola . . . We needn't stay long, darling.'

On the way to the second, 1938 and a year on (the same cab, I could swear to it), I sat on the rear seat while Eddie perched, scowling, on the jump seat. I'd returned from my flight to Egypt, that visit when I'd encountered Howard Carter for the last time, the previous December. On my return, my husband had said he couldn't manage without me, that he needed me, that I'd been mad to bolt: what was I running away from? The new year saw us reunited: back together in the marital home, in the marital *nest.*

Somewhere around Marble Arch, I said: 'We mustn't stay late. And stay off the hard stuff, Eddie. No brandy.'

'No brandy. No cocktails. I swear on my dear old mother's grave.'

'Your mother's alive and well. Flourishing.'

'What a stickler you are! On my grandmother's then.'

'Just don't *start* anything, Eddie. It's humiliating.'

'*Teeniest* bit bourgeois, darling one. You want to watch that.'

Parties were Eddie's natural element: he plunged into them headfirst, at high speed, like a hungry gannet diving into a shoal of herring;

he swam through them with the grace of a seal underwater. Entering them with eagerness, he was scarcely through the door before women were clustering around him, locking their arms about his neck, murmuring endearments, like mermaids luring a sailor. I never minded *that*: they could sing till doomsday – my husband was immune to their charms and cajolings, and some of the women present knew that, though not all. I provided cover, as I'd come to realise, and when sober, Eddie *did* disguise it very well. Most women were charmed as effortlessly as Rose had been; my husband always remembered their names and histories; he complimented their dresses, he'd send them flowers, write them a sonnet, tell them what old Eliot had said to him last week, and young Wystan the week before; he'd listen to women's stories, indulge their foibles, tease them and amuse – and all the while his eyes would be surveying the room, on the lookout for what he called 'talent' and sometimes 'adventure' and occasionally, when very drunk, 'perdition'.

One of the reasons he disliked Nicola and Clair's parties was that 'talent' tended to be thin on the ground; knowing his weaknesses for certain types, they weeded them out when planning their guest lists. But those parties were unpredictable affairs; sometimes invited guests brought friends with them, so I never felt entirely safe . . . But by that time I didn't feel safe anywhere with Eddie; so nothing new there, then.

At that three-hundred-and-one birthday party, the rooms were very crowded. I pitched up here and there: I was talked at by the vicar of the church across the square, High Church, smelling faintly of incense; he explained his understanding of the Eucharist. I was talked at by a Marxist whom Clair had known at the Slade; he kindly explained Joseph Stalin's reforms and how beneficial they were to Mother Russia. I surfaced by a woman who'd been my contemporary at Girton, who said: 'You haven't seen *Snow White* yet? Oh, but you must, Lucy! My children adored it.' She sang a few bars of Snow White's 'My Prince Will Come' for me, then eddied away on the party's mysterious currents. They carried me into the adjacent room and then back again.

I was looking for Rose and Peter, both invited at my request. Rose was now engaged to be married; Peter had returned from the civil war in Spain that week; he had been wounded, but not seriously,

Rose had said. I couldn't see either of them anywhere; but, as the room's currents floated me past Nicola, she said: 'Oh they're definitely coming, Rose telephoned and confirmed that. She can't stay long . . . she's going on to dinner at Lady Evelyn's. Howard Carter's one of the guests, she told me. Lucy, dear, where's your glass, aren't you drinking? I wanted you to meet—'

Some sudden wave of new arrivals separated us before I could discover who this was, and I ended up adrift somewhere, talking to a young army officer. He explained why war with Herr Hitler was now inevitable. 'First it will be Austria, but he won't stop there – rearmament, Mrs Vyne-Chance! Time is running out on us. If we don't rearm faster, then frankly we're sunk.'

Next, I washed up by an American diplomat, who said how much he always enjoyed Mrs Foxe-Payne's parties. He turned out to know the Winlocks, and he informed me that Herbert Winlock had recently had a stroke: 'At the Museum. He was just coming down the stairs there, poor guy. Yes – a full recovery. Not too sure how long he'll stay on as director, of course. Pretty demanding, the Met, big ship to steer . . . Is that your glass, Mrs Chance? Let me freshen your drink.'

I floated away to the edge of the crowd, until I washed ashore by the table on which the blue *shabti* figure I'd given Nicola had pride of place. Twin to the one Frances had given me: I was looking at him, the little answerer, I had just picked him up, I was holding him to the light and examining him closely, tracing with one finger his spells from *The Book of the Dead*, powerful spells those, when Clair sought me out. She placed one unusually clean hand on my arm and said with a grimace, 'Over there – north-north-west from where you're standing. Nicola hasn't noticed yet. I don't know who they are. You won't extricate Eddie, he's well away, but we could shift *them* out of harm's way. If you corral one, I'll waylay the other.'

I looked across the smoky eddying room: the crowded backs parted, made a narrow channel, and there was my husband, in full flow, attacking *The Waste Land*. To one side of him was a young man with long Shelleyan locks, wearing a velvet jacket; to the other was an older man of stockier build, with a pugilistic look, who was smoking a pipe. Both were Eddie's idea of 'talent', a category that was catholic. 'Adventure' usually implied a Guardsman. 'Perdition' meant a married man who, until he met Eddie, had believed, or pretended, that he was heterosexual.

How many times had I done this? Gone across, politely intervened, tried to save face?

Too many times. The laws were what they were, so I didn't blame Eddie, but I was sick of deceit. I replaced the *shabti* figure on the table with great care. Then I crossed to Eddie, whom I liked – and of whom I remained fond to his dying day. He would live to a great age and remain incorrigible to the last, I'm glad to say. I kissed his cheek.

'You off, darling girl?'

'I am, actually. Yes.'

I left the party. I returned to Chelsea and, having packed the only belongings I wanted, typewriter, notebooks, the *shabti* Frances gave me, I left the marital home an hour later.

'Where *were* you, Lucy?' Rose cried, when I next telephoned her. 'We only went to that wretched party for your sake. Peter says he saw you leaving, getting into a taxi just as we arrived. He just caught a glimpse – you might have stayed, you know.'

'I might have,' I answered. 'But I didn't.'

My departure from the marital nest gave Nicola new hope. I saw it flash in her eyes when, after delaying for several months, I finally confessed it.

'At *last*,' she said. 'I knew it was only a matter of time. You can move in here, Lucy.' She was already rising; she had coloured and her hands had begun trembling. 'I can get a room ready for you in an instant. The one at the back, with a view of the garden. If we move a desk in there, Lucy – I can have some bookshelves put up—'

I knew I had to stop her and stop her fast, so I did. I told her that I already had somewhere to live – and this was true. A friend of a friend had sub-let me a room in World's End, at the far, far end of the King's Road. The district's name had a certain ring. It wasn't a bad room. I could write in it. I could finish *Islands* there. The place was cheap – and that was useful; as I was beginning to learn, it might be quick and easy to leave the marital home, but to unravel a marriage, to dissolve it, was in many ways expensive.

'Something died in me when you refused,' Nicola would claim. 'Up until then – when I realised you'd choose some hideous little room in the back of beyond rather than come here, where you'd have everything you need, rent free, where I'd be there to help you – I could have typed your manuscripts for you, made sure you *ate* ... Up until then, I hoped.

'I did warn you,' she'd say. 'I warned you again and again. To my dying day, I shall never understand why you married that man. You never loved him. You knew he was profligate. You knew he drank.'

And then Clair would interject, giving her gloss on this mysterious action. Weeks passed, during which time the topic was scrutinised with vigour when I was present and, I suspect, with venom when I was not, until finally Clair hit on her solution to this conundrum. 'Some women can't resist pansies,' she pronounced, one fine spring evening. Three months down the road to divorce, an inevitable war inching closer, lilacs in bloom in the square outside. I could hear children playing in its gardens; joyful cries and laughter drifted in through the open windows. 'Some women are drawn to queers. Maybe Lucy thought she'd convert him. *Is* that what you thought? Didn't you realise, once a queer always a queer? Trust me: I do *know*. It's in the bones. It's not some creed you pick up then cast aside, you know, sweetheart.'

Across the room, Nicola swung around, white-faced. She said: 'Clair. Stop this.'

'Wrong on all counts,' I said, moving towards the door. 'Both of you. I'm going.'

I always went back, though – I continued to visit Nicola, since she refused to visit me. I was drawn to her by a continuing need and anxiety. Attuned to her moods as I'd always been, I could see that her fretfulness and her restlessness were deepening. Part of me still yearned for the closeness that had once existed between us, the intensity of understanding we'd shared when I was still a child, and malleable. On the rare occasions when guardian Clair was absent, I would sometimes try to reach out to Nicola – to discover who she was now, what she felt and thought; but those attempts always met with failure, with cold glances and a change of subject. Thinking my own reticence was to blame, I'd sometimes try to tell her where I'd been and what I'd done – who I *was*. Nothing I said could ever hold her interest for long, and sometimes, as she frowned into the middle distance, I could see she was not even listening, but was brooding over some other matter she would not disclose, some unspoken grievance.

Clair also observed this brooding abstraction, and when she joined us I'd watch her efforts to break through Nicola's inward dreamings. Sometimes she'd try to divert her by bringing the realities of the outside world into this quiet drawing room. She'd speak of incipient war, rant about the blindness of politicians – with good reason at that date, of course. When such remarks drew no response, she would switch tack. She'd begin to hymn the praises of London. 'Dear Christ – how did we put up with Cambridge all those years, Nicola?' she'd say. 'It was like being buried alive living there, stuck out in the Fens, I couldn't breathe, I couldn't think. Those petty, fluting dons. Always so cold and damp. If we'd had to stay there one month longer, I swear I'd have topped myself. It was like being *reborn* when we came here.'

That claim was true in her case, I thought, on one of the evenings when she made that or a very similar remark; conversations here, as I'd begun to see, took predictable routes. They went around and around, always returning to the same fixed points; sometimes I too ceased to listen. That evening, as Clair spoke of being 'reborn', I dragged my mind back to the room and looked at the two women, one silent and abstracted, one excited. Clair was in the midst of a 'golden interval', as she described it; she was working more intensely than ever and her painting had moved in a new, joyous direction.

Nicola did not dissent from Clair's claims to magical metropolitan rebirth, but as I met her eyes across her drawing room in the fading light that evening, her discontent was very evident. It was autumn by then, the autumn of 1938. Over the past spring and summer, her restlessness had increased; she'd taken up a series of projects and abandoned them one by one: piano lessons, singing lessons, even – briefly and painfully – painting lessons. She had tried her hand at a little journalism; she'd tried private coaching, French lessons – her French was very pure, she'd reminded us. She had given that up too – her pupils were dullards.

'Oh, *Cambridge*,' she said, 'don't remind me of that, Clair.' Then she gave me the news: my father had telephoned that morning to inform her he had hired a new secretary – a role Nicola herself had clung to, then gradually relinquished after moving to London. His Aeschylus book, six years in gestation, was finally completed. It required typing.

'Some dowdy graduate,' Nicola said. 'He claims he needs someone who's at his immediate beck and call. Ridiculous! He could perfectly well have sent *me* the manuscript. Now he's hired some child. I told him: this girl may be able to type and take dictation, Robert – any fool can do that. *I* did so much more – half the ideas in his Euripides book came from me, Lucy.'

All that power and energy, I thought, as I sat in silence listening to her: all that intelligence, all that edgy, unpredictable sensitivity – it was still there, balled up inside her, tight as a clenched fist, yet she could not find a use for it. In mid-sentence, I met her gaze. For once, I was too quick for her; before she could assume the mask of her customary serenity, I looked into Nicola's eyes and saw fury.

At once, she attempted to disguise it. 'Heavens, how dark it's getting.' She rose and lit one of the table lamps. She shivered. 'And it's getting cold too. Close the windows, Clair. It will be winter before we know it. This room is impossible, Lucy. Oh, *why* did I choose a flat with such huge windows? It's always too hot or too cold. And the traffic noise is insufferable. It makes my head ache.'

I rose to leave. Time to escape. Clair closed the windows, then slumped in her chair. We could both recognise the symptoms, we'd both heard the suppressed irritation, the angry lilt of familiar complaints. Another fifteen minutes and Clair would raise the subject of last resort, the one that never failed to revive Nicola: my marriage; my failure, nine months on, to push the divorce through. They could chew *that* over till doomsday.

'What do the lawyers say?' Nicola demanded, whenever the divorce came up. 'I *told* you it was a major error to leave the marital home. To compound your idiocy, you've given him the house. Possession is nine-tenths of the law. Surely the lawyers can retrieve something? Why is it dragging on in this interminable way? Cut the Gordian knot, Lucy.'

I would make some evasive reply. The divorce had stalled. During the past summer, things had, for a while, looked promising: Eddie had agreed to take the then-customary, the approved, the gentlemanly route. He would hire a woman, take her to some seaside resort and there, by pre-arrangement, be discovered in compromising circumstances by private detectives. Umpteen firms offered this useful service. 'That will give you the usual grounds, Mrs Vyne-Chance,' my solicitor said. 'Then we'll wrap this up in no time.'

Eddie had been keen on this ploy. He was fired up by it. 'I shall hire a floozie,' he said, when we discussed the details by telephone. 'I'll hire an absolute eye-popper. We might as well have some fun. Shall I do it next weekend? Brighton, I think. Maybe a suite at the Grand, a bottle of Bollinger. I see myself in silk pyjamas, a cravat and a Charvet dressing gown.' His tone was hopeful.

'No suite, no Bollinger and no Charvet,' I said. I was paying for this: the hotel, the floozie, the obliging detectives. I was damned if I was going to throw in a new dressing gown. Eddie became lachrymose.

'I love it when you're stern,' he said tenderly as the phone line crackled and hissed. I could tell he was tight as a tick. 'When you cry, it's even worse, Lucy. It undoes me. That's why I proposed to you. There you were by the rails of that ship, staring down at the sea, and you looked so . . . I knew what I must do immediately. You have tragic eyes. Electra had eyes like yours. So did Iphigenia. Did I ever tell you that?'

'Yes. Three brandies in, usually.'

'So precise! I need you . . . A passing thought: you *are* sure you want to do this?'

'Next weekend. That's agreed?' I rang off quickly.

That was July. The promised trip to Brighton was postponed. Eddie rescheduled it for August, then September. By November it became clear he was digging his heels in. A payment from his publishers had not materialised; Eddie had not delivered the promised collection of poems on time – but he couldn't write poems when miserable, lonely and *badgered*. 'I can't conjure pure gold from the *air*,' he said peevishly, when I telephoned for the fifth time in December. 'I have to dig deep for it. Right down into the bedrock.'

My solicitor translated: he wanted more money. 'He feels he's entitled to a larger settlement, Mrs Vyne-Chance,' he said. 'I fear he is being *very* recalcitrant. You do have grounds – grounds that any court in the land would recognise. As we both know there *are* other routes you could take. Unsavoury, of course. None of us wants a scandal, believe me. But if needs must.' He gave me a delicate glance.

'No. Just find out how much more he wants. If I can afford it, he can have it.'

'And if you *cannot* afford it, Mrs Vyne-Chance – what then?' That query was delicately put, too. I had no answer to it.

By the March of 1939: stalemate. When I visited Bloomsbury, Nicola and Clair were quick to remind me of that fact.

'Thirteen months, it's been.' Clair said. 'So, Lucy, what's the latest?'

'There is no latest. We're waiting to hear back from his solicitors.'

'You look ghastly,' she continued, in a robust tone, pouring red wine. 'You're thin and white and you look really peculiar. You look as if you haven't slept in weeks. Do you have a cough? Been to a doctor? You should. TB can be latent for *years*. Nasty little tubercle bacilli, poised to go forth and multiply. You don't think . . . ?'

'No. I don't. I've been working. I've finished the islands book at last. I'm fine.'

'Well, you don't *look* fine.'

'She should come *here*,' Nicola interrupted. 'Then we could look after her.'

And they were off, bickering away as they often did when I visited. First my situation, then politics, imminent war, the price of coal, the latest books, the new must-see play, Nazis and power cuts, Evelyn Waugh and the new curtains they needed. Might as well be invisible, I'd sometimes think – but that was a familiar state, and preferable to being the focus of their attention.

I frowned at the costume I was wearing, a suit that was a hand-me-down from Rose. Rose was about to marry; her father was banned from the ceremony and Peter was to give her away – if he could get leave. He'd joined the RAF the previous summer and had been posted to Scotland for pilot training. I inspected the suit dispassionately. It was grey. Even extensively altered, let down and taken in, it didn't fit me; it was a misfit – as I was. So this is how it feels, I thought: three years of mourning, two years of marriage, one year alone, months of solicitors. I'm wrecked. Washed up on foreign shores. *That's* the latest.

'Oh, and that reminds me,' Nicola exclaimed, turning to me. 'Howard Carter has died. The announcement was in *The Times* yesterday. Did you see it, Lucy?'

'Yes. I saw it.'

'I've read the obituaries – well, what obituaries there were. *The Times* hasn't done him yet, though no doubt it will. There was one in the *Telegraph* ... I see he never published that so-called scholarly account of his work. But then that's hardly surprising. Carter wasn't a scholar. He was an adventurer.'

'He was more than that, Nicola. Much more. You do him a disservice.'

'Oh, very well. How should I know? I never met the man.'

She paused, and I could see she was trying to fight the petulance that often afflicted her now – fighting to curb the sharpness of her tongue too. She was forty-one; her beauty remained almost unchanged. A few lines had begun to show around her mouth, but she retained her slender grace; her thick bronze hair was ungreyed, the pale classical profile was unaltered. Time and age had been kind to her face, but they had not sweetened her volatile temper.

'Well, Mr Carter always sounded a charlatan to me. Still, no doubt the great and the good will turn out for him – shall you go to his funeral, Lucy?'

'I haven't decided.'

A deflective, colourless answer. Nicola knew such replies were my stock-in-trade; she'd watched me growing up and perfecting them. She gave me one of her weighing looks. Perhaps she sensed something was wrong. But the moment passed. Clair made a remark about funerals: *Frankly, I don't want one. I'd like to go up in a puff of smoke.* And Nicola forgot the matter; once, she would not have done so.

Or did she? Maybe it was I who was blind. Not long afterwards, rising to leave, I realised that Nicola's spirits were as low as my own, and that something was troubling her. 'Oh, what a miserable conversation!' she cried. 'No, no more wine, Clair. How horribly bright this room is. It hurts my eyes. My head aches.' I saw that her hands were trembling violently. Clair must have seen this too; as I edged towards the door, she crossed the room at once, knelt down and put her arms around Nicola with a swift, surprising tenderness.

'Oh, *why* did you have to mention funerals? All evening – nothing but worms and graves and epitaphs,' Nicola said to her fretfully.

'I didn't start it, darling. *You* brought the subject up,' Clair replied gently. She glanced over her shoulder, and motioned me to leave; the gesture was both impatient and dismissive. I backed away.

Nicola made a small sound, murmured some words.

'My darling. My sweet love . . . Ah, don't, *please* don't,' Clair was saying, as the door closed on them.

Howard Carter's funeral was held in Putney in south London, four days after his death. Until the last moment, I still could not decide whether to attend: one of the numerous side-effects of my marriage and its dissolution was the indecision it induced. I was unravelling, I felt; my stitches had dropped off the needles, I couldn't find a way to cast them on again, I must learn to *reknit* myself. In a weak moment, I'd telephoned Rose and asked her if she'd accompany me, but she refused. Rose had neither liked nor admired Carter very much, and I was not in her good books either: she disapproved of the planned divorce; she said marriage was for keeps, and I should go back to Eddie ... No, she couldn't come to the funeral with me, she said sniffily; she and her fiancé had another engagement.

'Eve will be there, of course,' she went on, thawing a little. 'She's terribly cut up. It was Hodgkin's disease, you know — Carter's last years weren't easy. Eve wants him to have a good send-off, but the numbers are looking thin, so she's ringing around, trying to drum up attendance. She's not getting much luck. Too many people opting to send wreaths — the coward's way out. They think that gets them off the hook. You should go. You owe it to him.'

The coward's route tempted me at once: perhaps a wreath *would* suffice? Knowing it would not, feeling shabby in mind and body, I set off for the smartest florist's I knew, the one Eddie always used when trying to propitiate the many hostesses he offended — the hostesses who always forgave him and asked him back. In heavy rain, I walked the length of the King's Road, from World's End to the smart Cadogan Estate area of Chelsea. I avoided the marital nest down a side-street. I examined the designs on offer – and miserable ugly things they were, those crosses and weighty circlets of laurel. I told the young woman serving me that I didn't want anything like that. I knew papyrus was out of the question – I had *some* residue of sense – but might olive leaves be feasible? Interwoven with berries, with something fresh, like cornflowers.

'*Olive* leaves, Mrs Vyne-Chance?' said the assistant, who was pert. She raised her plucked brows and pursed her painted lips. 'Cornflowers? It's *March*. Regardless of season, we find we have no call for things like *that*.'

She looked me up and down: I was not looking my best. I was looking – well, let's just say, bedraggled and a trifle unhinged. She registered that fact with a small tight smile. *Wasn't much to write home about in the first place. Now she's let herself go and no wonder*, said her expression. Could she have heard the gossip about my marriage and its unravellings? Almost certainly. Eddie came here at least once a week, and anyway he was famous in Chelsea. Everyone took a keen interest in his exploits, even the shopkeepers – *especially* the shopkeepers, since he owed money to most of them.

I lost it a bit then, then – looking back, I can see that. I asked the girl what, in that case, she *did* have a call for. I said the wreaths on offer were ugly, unimaginative, and hopelessly *vieux jeu*; this last was Eddie's favourite term for anything he wished to disparage, whether it was another poet's work, or the style of someone's drawing room. In extremis.

'Via what, madam?'

'*Vieux jeu*. Old-fashioned. Out of date. Old hat. Unoriginal. Bloody frightful. Wouldn't put it on a cat's grave. Or a dog's. An insult to the dead. Is that clearer?'

That kind of reaction, that kind of talk, was another symptom of my unravelling, my malaise: I'm turning into Madame Maladie, I thought. I was saved by the owner of the shop who, hearing this altercation, which continued some while, emerged from a rear room, sent the assistant packing, and listened gravely while I explained what I needed and why. He was gay, as we'd say now, queer as we said then; he was camp and astute. He *certainly* knew about Eddie's exploits, I thought, as I apologised.

'*Too* marvellously exciting, Mrs Vyne-Chance,' he said, throwing up his hands. 'Something different *at long last*. Egyptian . . . they used beads, you say? Madly original – we shall start a new fashion. How if we were to use *this* – if I interwove it with *that*? I have a book on Tut somewhere, I shall consult it for inspiration. Leave it *entirely* in my safe little hands, my dear Mrs VC . . . Oh, and when you next see that naughty husband of yours, remind him he owes me five quid for the last lot of lilies. Penitence comes *so* expensive.' He winked.

He was as good as his word, and creative too; the circlet he made was not authentic, how could it be? But it was close in spirit.

My offering looked strange next to the other conventional funeral flowers, I felt, when I finally reached the chapel at Putney Vale Cemetery where Carter's funeral was to be held. I had steeled myself to go – as I knew I should, as I knew Frances would have wished. I am here for me *and* Frances, I told myself.

It was a cold, grey day, threatening rain. The cemetery, faintly municipal, lines of graves punctuated by yews, was enormous. As I arrived – late; lost in Putney – the other mourners were just filing in. I joined the huddle of latecomers bringing up the rear, crept in behind them and sat down alone behind a pillar in a pew at the back. When the coffin processed in, it was a bright shiny mahogany, with ornate silvery handles. Once the mutes had put down their burden and withdrawn, I counted the meagre congregation, but the huddled figures and the women's hats confused me – nineteen, fewer? There were two hymns, which I mouthed. The first was 'Fight the Good Fight', which Carter would surely have appreciated.

The address was awkward and ineloquent; I think the priest officiating had never met Carter, but someone must have primed him, and he did his best. He spoke of Carter's work at length, consulting copious notes. I heard 'great Egyptologist' and 'one of the most exciting episodes in the annals of archaeology' and 'find of the century'. After that, I gazed at the stained-glass windows, trying to conjure the Valley as I'd known it in childhood, and Howard Carter, the unreadable man, as I remembered him.

The memories flickered, came close, but eluded my grasp; they disappeared into the billowing white dust of Carter's excavations. I came to only when I realised that the coffin was being carried out –

and that many of the congregation were looking at their watches and murmuring. We filed out behind it, heads bent. Once outside, several of the mourners left, making for their cars in the way people do when they wish to disguise unseemly haste. I joined the black straggle of those who'd remained loyal and were escorting the coffin to the graveside for burial. I attached myself to the tail of this procession, and then hung back. I edged behind a yew; that gave some shelter. It had begun to rain and umbrellas were being raised. I had no umbrella.

Why Putney? Why here? I'd heard via Rose, who had it from Eve, that in later years Carter had owned a series of flats in central London; the last had been in Kensington, near the Albert Hall. Putney was a long way from there, the other side of the Thames. This cemetery felt wrong – but then where in England would feel right for such a man's final resting place?

Perhaps Carter's family had made the choice: some of the mourners were family, I thought. There was an elderly man, stooped and obviously unwell, who bore a passing resemblance to him and might perhaps be one of his brothers; there was a young woman, who also seemed to be related; she was neatly dressed, wearing what looked like a new hat, and was crying quietly into a handkerchief. As was Eve, I saw, recognising her after all these years as she stood, head bowed, by the graveside.

I stayed listening to the quiet and beautiful words of the Committal. I stayed until the end. It began to rain more heavily. Dust and ashes, sure and certain hope. Scatterings of earth on the coffin lid. People were turning to leave. I hesitated, then approached and spoke briefly to Eve, who clasped my hands and said: '*Gracious, Lucy, is it you? But of course I remember you. Howard would be so glad you came ... Isn't this terrible? He was such a great man – you remember that. He had the world at his feet once, and now ... Oh my dear, don't – we mustn't cry. Doesn't this bring back memories of the Valley? Do you remember the time when you and Frances—*' She broke off, gave me a sad ghost of her former dimpling smile, turned up the collar of her fur and sighed. 'Certain people conspicuous by their absence, Lucy. Isn't it hateful?'

Someone claimed her attention and with a *Bless you, dear*, and a kiss to my cheek, a press of her black kid-gloved hand, a brush of her fur coat, she turned away. A queue had formed by the young woman who had wept and, as I waited to shake hands with her, I heard her speaking, with simple dignity, to a small bent old woman. 'Poor Uncle Howard. He was so brave. Yes, Hodgkin's – and he was in dreadful pain for years. He never spoke of it. None of the treatments really worked. But he soldiered on, and it was only in the last year that he became . . . Well, no. It wasn't swift. I wouldn't say swift. But a quiet end. Mercifully quiet. The nurse and I were with him. He just slipped away from us, between one breath and the next . . . Thank you. That's very kind. Yes, we had hoped for a few more people, but his friends – many of them don't live in London, you see, and I think the journey was . . . Yes, *aren't* the flowers lovely?'

I waited my turn, shook the young woman's hand and said the usual formal things. I was agitated, and I could tell that the words were not coming out as they should. 'Thank you for coming,' she said. 'It's kind of you to say that.' I turned away and began to thread my way between the gravestones. The grass was wet and it was beginning to rain very heavily. Reaching the main path, I faced the cemetery gates and began to trudge towards them. I'd walk back to World's End, I decided. I missed the kind of walking I was accustomed to when working on books, but any walk, even through busy streets, cleared the mind and led to places that were often unexpected – led to *calm*, for instance, a calm that was not always a mirage.

I was perhaps halfway down that drive, yes, I think halfway down it, when I realised someone was behind me, hastening to catch up. I could hear a man's footsteps on the gravel. I increased my pace. I did not look round. I wanted to speak to no one – and, apart from Eve, surely no one here knew me? The man behind me also increased his pace. He caught up with me in three strides. He put a restraining hand on my wet coat sleeve and said, 'Lulu?'

I swung around: a tall man, wearing a dark overcoat with the collar turned up against the rain; broad shoulders, his hair wet from the rain, and darker than it had been in his childhood. No trace now of the injury he'd sustained in the civil war in Spain. When I'd last seen him, his arm, fractured by a bullet, had been in a sling. I wasn't sure when that brief encounter had taken place: a year ago? Now he was in the RAF and had been posted somewhere for training; I found I couldn't remember where. I had to tilt my hat back and look up to meet his eyes – his eyes I'd have recognised anywhere: inky blue, like those of the mother from whom he'd inherited them, but their expression very different. We stared at one another in silence. I saw him take in the details of my appearance. Perhaps they shocked him.

He said, 'Lucy? Are you ill? What's happened to you?'

And at the same moment I said, 'Peter? Where did you spring from? Why on earth are *you* here?'

'To see you. Rose said you'd be here. I was looking for you in the chapel, but you must have been hiding somewhere. I was beginning to think you'd changed your mind, that you hadn't come after all. I did glimpse you talking to Eve, but I thought – no, that *can't* be her.' He paused in a grave, considering way. 'I didn't recognise you, Lucy . . . I expect your hat confused me.'

'All right, it's a hideous hat. I do know that.'

'It *is* pretty bad. And the rain hasn't improved it.'

'I know it's not just the hat. I know how I look. Did Rose send you?'

'No. Rose did not send me. I came of my own accord. At the first opportunity.'

'I don't believe you. Rose arranged this. Well, you can tell her from me, I don't need her assistance or yours. I'm perfectly fine. Fit as a fiddle, never felt better, pick your superlative. I've been to the funeral, I've done my duty, I've paid my final respects and now I'm walking home—'

'The perfect day for a stroll. In that case, I'll walk with you.'

He glanced up at the sky; the rain was now torrential. Taking my arm, he tucked it inside his own. I resisted and then stopped resisting. Looking down, he examined my hand – my bare and very cold hand. Madame Maladie had forgotten to bring her gloves as well as her umbrella.

'You've removed your wedding ring, I see.' He drew me along beside him at a fast pace, pausing only when we reached the cemetery gates. Leading me into the street, into the noise, the sudden clamour beyond, he came to a halt.

'So – which way? Where are we going, Lucy?'

I can't remember what reply I gave . . . The other side of the river,

494

World's End? Whatever I said, it's immaterial. We both knew exactly where we were going: *that* knowledge had flashed between us the second we turned to face one another. It is always swift. No point in pretending otherwise.

We began walking northwards and, after various detours and on reaching a bridge, paused to look down at the Thames, sullen, dark, an incoming tide coursing through a transformed city. Peter leaned over the parapet to examine the water, and I did too. The rain was beginning to abate, but we were both drenched by then. My mind felt marvellously clear, rinsed of all impediments.

'I'm glad you've told me all that,' he said, after an interval.

'I haven't said very much.'

'Then your silences must speak, Lucy.'

That was that. He took my hand and we continued walking. The route we took that day was no doubt erratic; it was a long wind through the city, and afterwards neither of us could recall its details. 'I think we walked along *that* street,' he'd say, 'but why were we there?' I couldn't remember either – I don't think there was any reason behind our route beyond the surprise and joy of being on it.

'When did you know?' Peter asked me, as we walked.

'At the cemetery gates,' I replied. I don't think he believed me.

'I *always* knew,' he said. 'I finally decided to stop waiting.'

We walked on. I can remember certain places where we paused, where we lingered, and I know where we were when he took me in his arms for the first time. Outside a museum – one of the many in Kensington. Outside a bastion of learning – in a courtyard, soundless traffic, invisible passers-by, a spring day suddenly, and the clouds racing.

'You're not to tell Rose,' I said. 'I don't want us to tell anyone.'

Peter agreed: neither of us wanted this discussed, gossiped over, analysed, muddied.

'I'm still not divorced.'

'Unimportant.'

'I'm older than you are.'

'In certain respects. Not in others. You're catching up fast. Come

495

over here . . . You see? No age gap. No gaps of any kind between us. And never will be.'

We met in secret whenever Peter could get leave, sometimes in London and, when summer came, the last summer before the war, we'd go to Hampshire, to Nuthanger, which was empty of tenants and which Rose's trustees were trying to sell: not many takers in 1939.

'I expect they'll requisition it when the war comes,' Peter said. 'Meanwhile, we will.'

We were careful to leave no traces of these visits. I never spoke of them to anyone and I will not write of them now. But I knew they could not continue for long, that even our meetings in London might cease, certainly become briefer and more snatched, once the war came. So it proved: Peter was posted to Yorkshire for further training that November. His squadron moved and was briefly based in East Anglia, then it regrouped and was posted to Sussex in the spring of 1940. We went to Nuthanger for the last time that May, just a month or so before the Battle of Britain began. Two days' leave, the poignancy of stolen time, owls calling from the beech hangers, larks singing above the hayfields, the drone of planes at night. Our valley — and our house, which I always thought of as Peter had drawn it in childhood, protected eternally by a scribbled rainbow, by a red sun, a blue moon, two gold-foil stars: *weLcOm lUcY*.

Bare feet on old elm floorboards; a room striped with moonlight. I knew what would happen, and it did; how inward *that* experience makes you, how unstable and yet serene — I waited until I was sure. I told him, but apart from that, old habits die hard, I told no one.

I hugged the knowledge to me and took it back to London. I'd left the room in World's End by then, and we'd taken the cheap tail-end of a lease on a small flat in Marylebone — fifth floor, a view over the doctor-land of Harley Street and its environs, roofs, chimneys, church steeples — and from late August, when the nightly German bombing raids began, a view of the fires at the docks and in the East End; fires they said you could see from ten miles away, the whole sky-line red, London burning. When he had leave, Peter would join me there. When he did not have leave, we wrote letters. His commanding officer had my telephone number, in case of – emergencies.

It was a short walk from Marylebone to Nicola and Clair's flat. I visited them often, hiding my fears, which were acute, and concealing the joy that possessed me. I'd walk to their apartment and try to get back before blackout. I'd look up at the silver barrage balloons, flying high over Regent's Park. I'd walk past Warren Street tube, where mothers and children carrying cardboard suitcases and gas masks would emerge in the mornings, pale from sleepless nights underground. I'd pass them in the afternoons, as they began to queue again for another night's shelter. I was superstitious – well, everyone was. I'd avoid cracks on the pavement, touch my *shabti* figure before I left the flat and on my return. I counted the barrage balloons and if their number altered, it was a bad omen; if it remained the same, a good one.

The timing of my visits to Bloomsbury was difficult: sometimes I'd be at Nicola's flat, and the first wave of Luftwaffe bombers would come in earlier than expected. The sirens would begin wailing, and I'd be forced to remain there. Sometimes Clair would succeed in persuading Nicola to take refuge in the house cellars; sometimes Nicola – who hated being underground – would refuse and would pace her drawing room, listening to the crunch of bombs in the distance. As the days passed and the Blitz intensified, the crunch of bombs came closer, then closer still: proximity to railway stations, to King's Cross, to Euston, to St Pancras was no advantage now; mainline stations were targets.

Once the 'All Clear' sounded, Nicola would cease her restless pacing and sink down in a chair, and sooner or later she and Clair would resume the bickering of the pre-war period. That was their routine, their preferred habit. Once the iniquities of war and food rationing had been exhausted as subjects, they'd return to the ever-dependable topic, the one that never failed them: my divorce – and my lamentable failure to secure it. I took no part in those conversations; Eddie had sailed for America the week before war was declared. He was not answering any letters, especially those from solicitors – and I no longer cared. In my mind and heart, I was not married to him, never had been; the formalities could wait. I had other, more pressing priorities.

I made what would be my last visit to Nicola's flat that October. I know that the Blitz lasted from August 1940 to the following May, with fifty-seven consecutive nights of heavy bombing, but at the time it seemed much longer than that, a nightly bombardment that left me dazed and deafened in daylight, lost in areas once known well that had become, overnight, an unrecognisable wasteland. Where were the landmarks? I calculate that it must have been day forty-five of the Blitz when I made that visit to Nicola's flat. I sat there hugging my secrets to me, shivering by a miserable fire – their coal supply was running out. It was still only four o'clock when I arrived, but the blackout blinds were already drawn. Only one table lamp had been switched on: money was tight, Clair and Nicola were economising.

I was sitting next to a table piled with Nicola's current reading – light novels, borrowed from a lending library. The flat was looking neglected. Behind the books, relegated to a dusty corner, scarcely given space, was the blue *shabti* figure I'd given Nicola in Paris, all those years before. *For Nicola, with love, the real thing!* I wondered when she had last held the little figure, or looked at him.

I was hoping for tea, but as usual Clair produced some foul vinegary red wine – it was all they could get their hands on, she said. Nicola fretted; there had been bomb damage to Mecklenburgh Square the other night, and that, she said, was too close for comfort. Clair dismissed this; the damage there was not that extensive, Mecklenburgh was much closer to main-line stations than their square was and therefore more vulnerable. Their part of London was still safe, and if it wasn't, too bad . . . Nicola said the bombing frightened her: they should move out to the country.

'We can't. Do shut up about that, Nicola,' Clair said. 'We can't afford it. You've burned your boats. We're stuck in this mausoleum you insisted on buying. Who's going to take on the lease now? Who'd even rent it?'

They continued this bickering as if I were not there, as they usually did. I was five months' pregnant by then. My baby had begun to move in the fourth month, punctually, on schedule, as the books I'd anxiously consulted had assured me would happen. I'd felt stirrings, shiftings, a surreptitious assertion – new life, within me. Now, my baby, my he-or-she would often give me a fierce little kick, or perform some gymnastic manoeuvre in the womb, a gentle roll, a flexing, a somersault.

The alteration in my figure, not that evident anyway, had gone unremarked. Neither Nicola nor Clair noticed my hands laced across my stomach; no one noticed my dreaminess or abstraction, though I think they must have been very evident. The wine, which I shouldn't have touched, was making me feel sick. I pushed the glass aside. I was nauseous much of the time, and it was worst in the afternoons and evenings. I had cravings too, which would come upon me without warning – at that moment, sitting there by the reluctant fire, I had a fierce desire for salt and sweetness. Sardines. Peaches.

I had been given a new ration book now, the special blue one that all pregnant women received. It entitled me to one pint of milk a day and first choice of the fruit at the greengrocer's. I dreamed of peaches, the unobtainable tang of oranges, lemons, pineapples: first choice made little difference, since all they had on offer was apples . . . I closed my eyes. As my baby turned in the womb, lazily stretched, gave me a small punch, I slipped into a greedy reverie of salted almonds, of maple syrup and bacon, Egyptian honey cakes and the salted pop-corn Frances and I had once shared in some movie-theatre long ago. Sardines. Peaches. No, sardines *and* peaches. Together.

Clair rose to put a record on the gramophone: Mozart, *The Marriage of Figaro* – and the last act of that opera. She had the volume turned down low, and as the sequence of intrigues and hidden iden-tities of the opera's final scenes began to play themselves out with sweet, sharp melancholy, I gazed dreamily around the room. I saw it had grown shabby, its fine cornice yellowed: the abode of two women who spent much of their life indoors, one of whom smoked heavily. The walls were stained with pale rectangles where Clair's paintings had formerly hung; they'd been removed to her studio, where she was preparing them for a new exhibition at a small gallery. It was owned by a friend, who was giving her this show as a favour.

'A complete waste of time,' Nicola had said snappishly. 'Who's going to buy paintings in wartime? No one understands Clair's work anyway.'

'Give it a *rest*,' Clair had replied. 'One painting will buy two cases of this foul wine we're drinking. That's better than nothing. I'm *giving* them away. It breaks my bloody heart. Five guineas a canvas. A steal.'

Reaching across Nicola's library books, as they talked on and the music wound its delicate phrases, I picked up the little *shabti* figure and brushed the dust from his head. I replaced him where he was visible, where the lamp shone its light on him.

'Ah, how beautiful he is, such an *enigmatic* smile,' Nicola had cried, when I'd given him to her on my arrival in Paris from Egypt. When I'd confessed his dubious history, she'd laughed in delight. 'So he's stolen goods? Who cares – who will know? He can be our secret,' she'd said – and then, catching me by the hand, she'd rushed me outside: the moment had come to show me, for the first time, the beauty of Paris.

One fine day a million years ago. Weeks of fine, fine days: the Louvre, Notre-Dame, the Right Bank, the Left Bank, the Seine sparkling; the Comédie Française, where I heard the true power of Racine's alexandrines, understood for the first time how cold and remorseless was the advance of Corneille's tragedies. Nicola took me to the Tuileries, out to Versailles, out to the wooded walks of the Bois de Vincennes and then back to the Jardin du Luxembourg – we'd stopped for a *café noir* here, a *vin rouge* there; shopped for a length of silk in the Rue Saint-Honoré one morning when she felt extravagant, and for little rustic cooking dishes in the Rue Mouffetard one morning when she felt poor. To that day, I could not revisit those places without remembering them as Nicola Dunsire showed them to me.

Afterwards, I had wondered if these explorations were an attempt to rid me of Egypt and replace my fascination for that country with a new one. Were they a deliberate assault on those old loyalties? It was possible. Nicola could be jealous of interests she did not share; she could regard them as a challenge to her hegemony. So perhaps that stay in Paris *was* a campaign of attack, a series of persuasions. Perhaps it was designed to cement our confederacy. French was her mother tongue, she'd remind me, laughing, as she introduced me to further proofs of French civilisation, to the refinements of French hedonism.

'*Now* do you understand?' she'd said once – when, after a day of such dazzlements, we'd returned to the apartment by the Seine that she'd persuaded my father to rent. He was elsewhere. '*Now* do you see, Lucy?' she said, her eyes meeting mine across the glimmering river reflections of its salon, as the room's many looking glasses reflected us back upon ourselves, as the traffic outside fell suddenly silent. A long, level, appraising look. She waited for my answer before she moved towards me . . . And I did see, could Nicola not understand that? I could speak this silver tongue of hers. I'd abandoned resistance our first day here; the windings of the Seine had seduced me.

My baby stirred. I opened my eyes and found myself back in a room in Bloomsbury, a room that felt suddenly unsteady, freighted with the weight of the past, as unreliable as the deck of a ship in a storm. The Mozart had ceased and the gramophone needle was scratching back and forth, stuck in the black grooves at the end of the record. 'What's the matter with you, Lucy?' Clair was saying. 'You haven't touched your wine. You're white as a ghost.'

'Is she going to faint? What's wrong? Clair, quickly – fetch her some water.'

'No, no. I'm fine.' I stood up. 'But I think I should go now.'

'Oh, don't go yet.' Nicola rose and crossed to my side. 'Sit down again – you don't look well, truly. You're safe for another half-hour at least. Stay a little, dear. Are you hungry? Let me find something for you to eat – eggs – Clair, do we have any eggs left? It's only five o'clock, Lucy. Please don't go. The planes never come over before six . . .'

'Even so.'

I managed to extricate myself. At the door to the flat, Nicola gently embraced me. Clair escorted me downstairs. I ducked out into the square's gathering dark and walked home past blacked-out buildings. As I reached my own street, the wails of the sirens started up; shortly after, the planes began to come over. Wave after wave of them: one of the worst of the raids of the war, eight unbroken hours of bombs falling. I never saw Nicola or Clair again. Their Bloomsbury house received its direct hit during that raid, at around three that morning.

I went there as soon as I heard the news on the wireless. I found the remainder of their Bloomsbury terrace almost unscathed, but the house in which Nicola and Clair had lived had gone. I stood behind the barriers the wardens had erected, and there was nothing: no trace of lives lived, only singed air, lingering smoke, dying fires, smouldering rubble. The building had become vacancy. At attic height, a fireplace was still attached to a party wall; on the floor that had been hers, shreds of wallpaper remained, clinging obstinately; where the basement and cellars had been, there was a black hole, already filled with water from a burst main. I was standing in a litter of sharp glass, in pools of water from the firemen's hoses.

Clair Lennox's studio, in that mews building at the far end of the house's long rear garden, escaped the blast. I was allowed to inspect it eventually; after prolonged frantic argument, the ARP warden in charge agreed to escort me there. I think I had some unreasonable hope that, after I'd left them, Clair and Nicola might have gone to the studio, and that I would find them there.

That was not so. The studio was unlocked and empty – or so I thought at first. Its windows had been taped, but had shattered. There were two shiny, well-oiled bolts on the inside of its door. I inspected a sink, a gas-ring, a wind-up gramophone, orderly brushes and stacked tubes of oil paint. The air smelled of turpentine and smoke. Broken glass was scattered everywhere, but the small building was otherwise undamaged. So too were Clair Lennox's paintings. There they were, some packed, some unpacked, awaiting her new exhibition. I stared at one of them: Nicola Dunsire, in a white dress, standing next to a rose arch in a Newnham garden. Across the space between us her painted stare met mine and held it.

'No, wait – one more minute,' I said, when the warden tried to persuade me to leave. I went on staring at the past, at Nicola as seen by Clair Lennox, she whose vision differed from mine, whose artist's vision was no doubt more acute than mine. I could not read that painted stare of Nicola's, couldn't decide whether Clair had made it searching or lost, challenging or defeated.

The warden finally took my arm and led me outside. 'You're in shock, miss,' he said, closing the studio door firmly behind us. 'I see it every day.' He sighed in resignation. He was not young, and I could see how exhausted he was. Hanging on by a thread.

'Far to go, love?' he said. 'Forgive me asking, but – are you expecting? I'm a family man myself. Three nippers, and one more on the way. You don't want to be taking any risks – not in your condition. Nothing you can do here. On your way now.'

Some months later, in December, Clair's gallery friend invited me to the exhibition planned before her death. Her paintings had been left to Nicola, with this gallery as backstop. It was a small place, behind the British Museum, and the show of Lennox's work had been on view for several weeks before I went there. None of the paintings had sold; not one had a welcome red sticker.

'Hopeless,' said her friend. She lit a cigarette. 'Look at them – marvels. No one's interested. It's this bloody war, of course, but it's not just that. People can't *see* it. Poor Clair. I'm glad she's not around to witness it – knew her well, did you?'

'No, not well,' I replied – and that was true: inspecting her grouped paintings had made me understand that. I bought that portrait of Nicola, and in my will I've left it to the Tate Modern. The curators are delighted; they will hang it next to the three other Lennoxes now in their possession, they tell me, and they plan a major Lennox retrospective. Times change, of course, and what we value – the *way* we value, alters. How do we decide *this* is worthless, and *that* is a treasure? Unless the object concerned is of gold, of course, whose value never declines, whose glitter can never be resisted.

Clair's painting has travelled with me down the years, down the decades, from house to house, from youth to age, until it finally came to rest here on the north wall of my sitting room in Highgate. I look at it often, must have looked at it a million times. I've been looking at it every day this winter, and still I can't decide – is that painted stare resigned or rebellious? *What are you thinking?* I ask it sometimes, in those moments when I permit or cannot evade such weaknesses. What are you saying, Nicola?

And then I turn away from it. I examine Sargent's version of my mother Marianne, or turn to the Degas ballet dancer who, fleetingly, from certain angles and depending on the light, resembles Frances. And I think of those who were never portrayed: I think of Peter, whose plane was shot down over the Channel that winter, and whose body was never recovered. I think of our daughter, born a month afterwards. The delivery went well, and the two midwives assisting me marvelled at the lucky speed with which I, a first-time mother, gave birth. But I knew there was something wrong almost immediately: I heard my daughter's first cry – but from the midwives, silence.

A problem with the valves to her heart, they said. They operated. And I did hold her; I nursed her, for a week or so. I named her. Then, one evening, my child gave a small sigh, and her tiny face puckered in brief distress. Her eyes opened with that wide unfocused gaze of babies; she made a snuffling sound and waved her tiny starfish hand. The next second, between one breath and the next, she slipped away from me. I still think of her. I still think of her father – though many years lost, their sharp presence, and their terrible absence, remain with me.

For some reason – and I think I know exactly what that reason is – this concatenation of absence and presence has been particularly testing this past winter in Highgate. There have been days and nights when it came close to breaking me. I hadn't expected or foreseen that. I'd believed that passing years, age and resignation had put a barrier between me and grieving. How wrong. Grief's talons are never sheathed, and its patient capacity to wound is unremitting – but then, it has been a long harsh winter and so, by extension, solitary.

When the year turned and January came, the weather suddenly, capriciously, became gentler. I told myself that I'd endured these wintry siege conditions for long enough. So I telephoned Rose, and she arrived last night. I was inspecting the little blue answerer Frances gave me at Saranac Lake when I heard the baby-Mercedes draw up outside in the square. Carefully, I replaced my *shabti* on my desk and examined him. *Where I go, you go.* His smile has never seemed in the least enigmatic to me: the three thousand-year effect – a smile of absolute and unshakeable serenity, I'd say.

I went to the front door to greet Rose. 'I come bearing gifts,' she said.

For an instant I thought she was bringing me letters – my letters to Peter, the ones she had claimed she'd carefully fed to her ceremonial clearing-out bonfire. Then I realised my mistake: Rose was waving a pack of DVDs at me: Dr Fong's documentary; a photograph of a world-famous gold face mask and large title letters – *Tutankhamun: The Untold Story.*

'I'd better get on home now,' Rose said, this morning, rising from the battered sofa in my Highgate sitting room. 'Wheelie will be here soon to collect me. Wasn't that *marvellous*? I'm so glad we watched it together. I think your Dr Fang did a thoroughly good job. A truly excellent *meaty* documentary. Very sound on Carter, I thought – and Carnarvon. The Tutankhamun things were even more beautiful than I'd remembered – that gold face mask! The *politics* were a little muddling, but I expect that's just me, I always find politics boring . . . And, goodness, the *mistakes* everyone made . . . *Why* couldn't they see what was coming? The great thing was, one could hear every single word your Dr Fang said – I can't stand those presenter people who mumble. He made it all so tremendously *clear*! Don't you agree, Lucy?'

'Crystal clear. Admirable.'

I switched off the television set. I had watched these programmes, alone, when they were first broadcast a few weeks before, so this had been my second viewing. Two DVDs yesterday, two more this morning; Rose and I, bingeing on Egyptology. KV62 – the history. Magnificent swooping helicopter shots of the Valley of the Kings and the Nile; a dizzying panorama, all the bells and whistles of the latest technology. Computer imaging, volumetric reconstructions, nifty intercutting, sly and judicious editing. The talking heads the producers had feared were, to a man, succinct and erudite. The lighting for the sequences in the Egyptian Museum in Cairo was a marvel – for that place is murky. The past *spoke* . . . It's a year now since Ben Fong first came here, I thought: full circle.

I turned to the window as Rose began to gather up her belongings. A fine day outside, deceptively springlike: a blue sky, a high sun, frost-bitten roses in my garden, but signs of life even so, bulbs coming up, et cetera.

I went out into the hall with Rose, helped her on with her coat, helped her find her gloves, handbag, overnight case. It was chilly, and in the hall's silvery wavering light I could sense my familiar ghosts; they love to cluster there, whispering as one departs and another enters. They seem drawn to stairs, and the recesses under them. I wondered if Rose ever noticed them, these companions of mine; she seemed not to sense them or, if she did, ignored them.

'Of course,' she was saying now, pulling on her gloves, 'you and I could read between the lines, couldn't we, Lucy? We *knew* those people. So when *we're* watching your Dr Fang's version, we can remember what it was *really* like. He had to concentrate on the main players – but we remember all those on the fringes – don't we? They couldn't matter to him, why should they – but they matter to us, and always will.'

She wrapped a red scarf about her throat and sighed. 'It was so cleverly filmed, wasn't it, Lucy? It reminded me of how utterly beautiful it was, the Nile then, the water, the palms, the astonishing green fertility of it – and then beyond that, bare desert . . . Peter and I used to stand on our balcony at the Winter Palace every evening, you know, watching the sailing boats. He loved the feluccas. He loved watching the ferry. And he'd ask if you'd be on the next one, or if the next boat would bring our mother back – and I used to say, Maybe not this one, but perhaps the next . . . Ah, Lucy. What lies one tells!'

'Don't, Rose.'

'No, you're right. I'll only get upset.' She paused and adjusted her scarf. Averting her eyes, she said: 'Goodness, I almost forgot. I meant to ask you, before I go: you did see that doctor? The specialist I recommended?'

'Yes, I saw him.'

'What did he say? Did he run tests?'

'Innumerable tests. The diagnosis was old age. As I could have told him.'

'Nothing else? Still ticking over, then? Oh I'm so glad!' She reached up and kissed my cheek. 'I'd been worrying about you, Lucy, you know – all this winter. That's a great relief. Now I want you to promise me something. When the spring comes—'

'Yes, Rose?'

'When spring is here, you *will* come and stay with me, won't you? As you always do?'

'Of course, Rose.'

I opened my front door for her and there, punctual to the minute as always, was the baby-Mercedes. Wheeler climbed out and came round to help Rose into the car. I watched her negotiate the path with care – she was frailer this year than last, as I was. As the car drew away, she lifted her hand. I lifted mine in a mirroring farewell, then closed the door, and leaned against it. I closed my eyes and waited for my pulse to slow to normal.

Too much past. So many lost people. I returned to my sitting room, where Nicola watched me from the corner of the room; where berries, flowers and ferns I'd once picked at Saranac Lake still bloomed in the blue jar in which Frances and her mother had arranged them; where a small dog still stretched out in the sleepy abandon of a lost past, an instant captured in pencil and charcoal.

Not long now, I thought, later this afternoon . . . It will be spring before one knows it. I pulled on a coat and went outside, shuffling along the paths in my back garden. From three houses away, where a new family has just moved in, came the bright upraised voices of children, playing outside. I stood quietly, listening to their cries and laughter. I turned to the flower beds and inspected the bulbs, green and determined, blunt noses coming up from the hard black soil. Here crocuses, there daffodils, and over there snowdrops – these were well advanced, almost in flower, incipient white petals still shrouded in their green calyx.

To tell the truth, which on the whole I've tried to do here, I'm none too sure I'll see these crocuses in bloom, let alone the daffodils. But let's not dwell on that. Far more interesting, and far more significant, is what happened next, when I'd completed my bulb inspection. One moment, there I was in my chilly garden, the towers of the new London in the distance against the unclouded blue of the January sky, and my wintry view of Highgate and its graves unimpeded by foliage. I was standing at the end of the lawn, close to the boundary wall. Below it, the ground falls away sharply to the beautiful wilderness of the western section of Highgate's cemetery. I was admiring the angel I like best, the one with spread wings, a blind passionless face and an uplifted, pointing hand, when I realised that this area, empty of people a moment before, was now occupied. Standing near the angel, between it and a pyramid, her attitude contemplative, her head bent, was a woman.

There was a transparency to her, you could almost see through her, and at first I assumed I'd imagined her. But then I realised, no; it was my own vision, my eyes that were at fault; they had made this figure blurry and uncertain. Once I concentrated, I could see that she was real. She began to walk towards me, threading her way rapidly between the stones; on her face was an eager look of expectation that I recognised. Why, she was *young*, I realised – a young woman poised on the very cusp of adult life, her eyes brimming with the future, everything ahead of her, all life's infinite possibilities, there for the grasping. My heart lifted. I moved forward to greet her. As she came close, I recognised her.

Coming to a halt below my boundary wall, she looked up at me with laughter in her eyes and lifted her hand to me. I knew that wall was insurmountable. I feared I'd be unable to reach her. But she raised herself on her toes and with a smile caught my cold hand in her warm one. She began speaking, and an impulsive, eloquent speaker she was too. She showed no reserve. I replied with equal openness. When we had finished this rapid, heartfelt communication, she gave me a quick-silver glance, pressed my hand, turned and swiftly returned the way she had come. I lost sight of her among the crosses, obelisks and angels.

It was three o'clock. The light was fast fading. I went indoors. I closed the shutters, opened the hall door so my ghosts might have ease of access, encouraged the fire, settled myself in my familiar chair. I thought of Dr Fong's Egypt and my own, and the places to which my Egypt had taken me. I thought of voyages made, of the Valley I'd known in my childhood, and the way it had lain hidden behind the hills on the horizon.

I closed my eyes. In an hour or so, I'd resume those ordinary tasks, those little rituals of every day that serve to punctuate the passing hours for all of us. I'd make tea, switch on the lamps, banish the evening's encroaching dark. Meanwhile, in the silent dusk of the long afternoon, I waited in patient expectation. I knew it would come, must come; and at last I discerned it. Difficult to identify; hard to put a name to it, but from the shadows, the shadows by the bookshelves I supposed, came the faintest of sounds, a gentle exhalation, a plaintive stirring, a sigh and an appeal.

PEOPLE, PLACES, PROVENANCE

Howard Carter

Carter's account of Tutankhamun's tomb was published in three volumes: the first, co-written with Arthur Mace, came out in 1923; the final volume in 1933. He never progressed beyond notes for the proposed six-volume definitive account of his work on the tomb, and never pursued the burial place of Alexander the Great, although he spoke of this project to numerous people in his final years. Once the excavation in the Valley was over, he wrote a series of autobiographical sketches about his life in Egypt; these remain unpublished.

On his death in 1939, the bulk of Carter's estate went to his niece, Phyllis Walker; it included the contents of his London flat, where artefacts were found that without question came from the tomb of Tutankhamun. They included a headrest carved from lapis lazuli bearing the king's cartouche, and a *shabti* figure that Carter had always kept on his desk. His niece at once attempted to return these to Egypt, but the process was interrupted by the outbreak of war. Deposited at the Egyptian Embassy in London in 1940, they finally reached Egypt under the auspices of King Farouk in 1946. The King then presented them to the Egyptian Museum in Cairo. 'Nobody will dare to make inappropriate insinuations in . . . a matter in which His Majesty himself is interested,' wrote the then Director of the Antiquities Service.

Some commentators believe these London-apartment artefacts were taken from the tomb by Carter for himself; others that they were part of Lord Carnarvon's collection, removed from it by Carter when he supervised its sale, since he knew them to be identifiable. There is no definite proof either way. Other artefacts found in his house in Egypt after his death and bequeathed to the Metropolitan Museum of Art in New York *did* come from the tomb, however, so the sad fact that Carter removed artefacts and and kept them seems irrefutable.

Lord Carnarvon

Carnarvon, together with his daughter Lady Evelyn Herbert and Howard Carter (with the assistance of 'Pecky' Callender), broke into Tutankhamun's Burial Chamber on either Sunday 26 or Monday 27 November, 1922. That they did so remained a secret for decades – in fact, it was one of the best-kept secrets in archaeological history. The true story began to leak out among Egyptologists in the late 1940s; it was subsequently confirmed by an entry in the journals of Carnarvon's half-brother the Hon. Mervyn Herbert, in whom Lady Evelyn and her father had confided. Those journals have been held by the Middle East Centre, St Antony's College, Oxford, since 1966 and the secret came to light when they were examined in the 1970s.

The revelations reached a wider public with the publication in 1978 of Thomas Hoving's book *Tutankhamun: The Untold Story*. Hoving was Director of the Metropolitan Museum of Art in New York, 1967–77; there – in forgotten archives that included papers originating from Carter's home in Egypt – he found further evidence of the secret entry to the Burial Chamber, the cover-up afterwards and the illicit removal of artefacts. Hoving's account is flamboyant and much of it is persuasive, but it is marred by innumerable factual errors.

Lord Carnarvon's collection of Egyptian art, later sold by his widow to the Met, included a number of exquisite objects that, while unstamped, almost certainly came from Tutankhamun's tomb; presumably they had formed part of what Herbert Winlock, who coined the term, wryly called the earl's 'pocket collection'.

Highclere Castle is now owned by the eighth earl (great-grandson of the Lord Carnarvon in this book); in its cellars there is currently an exhibition that details the work of Carter and the fifth earl in the Valley. The final gallery, 'Wonderful Things', contains examples of Tutankhamun's greatest treasures – in replica form.

Almina, Lady Carnarvon

In 1926, Lady Carnarvon bypassed the British Museum and, with the assistance of Carter, sold her late husband's collection of Egyptian art to the Metropolitan Museum of Art for the sum of $145,000 (the equivalent of some $1.5 million today). In 1930, after years of litigation and vituperative argument, the Egyptian government awarded her and Carnarvon's trustees the sum of £35,867 (around £1.1 million today) partly in lieu of any artefacts and partly in recognition of expenses incurred in the excavation and clearing of Tutankhamun's tomb. In later life, Almina Carnarvon continued to spend money as swiftly as she had when chatelaine of Highclere; she was declared bankrupt in 1951. Her last home was a small terraced house in Bristol. She died there, aged ninety-two, in 1969.

Lady Evelyn Herbert

The evidence of an attachment between Lady Evelyn and Howard Carter rests in the main upon two letters and one note from her to him, and one letter from her father to Carter. Carter's diaries detail nothing beyond the dates of her comings and goings, though he does record her bringing him the second, replacement canary. In the first of these letters, written from Highclere at Christmas 1922 to Carter in Luxor, Lady Evelyn speaks of entering the 'Holy of Holies', and describes it as the *Great Moment* of my life'. She also says that she is 'panting' to return to Carter; she *was* twenty-one and (as Arthur Mace wrote of her) 'slangy'. He also noted, however, that she and Carter were 'very thick together', and he was not alone in such observations.

It is possible, but not certain on existing evidence, that Lady Evelyn's feelings for Carter contributed to the quarrel between him and her father in February 1923. If there was an infatuation on her part, it seems to have been short-lived: she married Brograve Beauchamp (later Sir Brograve Beauchamp, MP) in October 1923, some seven months after her father's death. She never returned to Egypt. In 1972, when the celebrated touring exhibition of the Tutankhamun treasures came to the British Museum, Lady Evelyn attended and was photographed with them. She suffered a stroke on the steps of the Museum when leaving. She died in 1980.

Herbert Winlock

Winlock was the author of many books; they remain the best accounts of excavating in Egypt in the period 1910–1930; he wears his erudition lightly. His sharp, witty correspondence gives an insider account of the circumstances surrounding the discovery of Tutankhamun's tomb and its aftermath. Insofar as Howard Carter had friends, Winlock was one of the closest, and most loyal. His account of Tutankhamun's funeral, published in 1941, nineteen years after he made the discovery that confirmed Tutankhamun's near-certain burial in the Valley, repays rereading, not least for its tone of abiding melancholy. Winlock kept a close tally of those associated with the tomb who had died and those who survived; he frequently attempted to demolish journalists' claims of a 'Curse'.

In January 1934, following the deaths of Arthur Weigall and Albert Lythgoe, when speculation as to the 'Curse' broke out anew, Winlock wrote to *The New York Times* in yet another attempt to disprove such claims – and when the 'Curse' is discussed, as it still often is, this letter's tally is almost always cited. When it was written, his daughter Frances had been seven months at Saranac Lake, which perhaps explains why he pursued the subject with such determination and seriousness. Winlock remained Director of the Met until 1939. He died, aged sixty-five, of a heart attack while on holiday in Florida in 1950 and, as a veteran of the First World War, is buried in Arlington National Cemetery in Washington DC.

Helen Winlock

Helen Winlock survived her husband; she lived to see her younger daughter married and to become a grandmother. She returned to live on the island of North Haven, Maine, where her family still owned the house that is mentioned in this novel. She died on that island, aged eighty-seven, in 1974. She is buried with her husband in Arlington.

Frances Winlock

Frances Winlock's death was scarcely reported, and she was spared speculation as to whether she too could be added to the dubious list of 'Curse' victims. It proved possible to retrieve traces of her life from the shadows: there are references to her in letters written from Egypt by her mother, and by Arthur Mace and his wife; there are extant photographs that show her as a child at the American House in the 1920s. She is mentioned, in passing, in the one surviving volume of Minnie Burton's diaries. Her maternal grandmother's diaries provide further information about her and about the death of her infant brother; these diaries, and one letter, written by Frances from Egypt in 1923, were found with other family letters in archives in Boston. Detailed records relating to her proved to exist: they include her schooling, her medical records at Saranac Lake, together with information as to where she lived and which doctors treated her there and, finally, the details of her funeral at Mount Auburn.

Albert Lythgoe

A respected scholar and former professor at Harvard, Lythgoe became the Metropolitan Museum's first curator of Egyptian art in 1906, at a point when that department had little of worth to display. For the next twenty-three years, until his retirement in 1929, he laid the foundations for the great collections that can be seen today, pursuing acquisitions for the Museum through excavation in Egypt, and via an aggressive, well-funded buying policy. By the time Howard

Carter discovered Tutankhamun's tomb, his friendship with Lythgoe was well established; Carter had been instrumental in the Met's acquisition of some of the finest private English collections of Egyptian art when they were sold off during the First World War; their relationship had been cemented by the help Carter and Carnarvon gave the Met in the purchase of the 'Treasures of the Three Princesses'.

Lythgoe volunteered the assistance of the Met's team of Burton, Mace, Hauser and Hall early in December 1922, in an exchange of cables with Carter. He did so in part for pure and scholarly reasons – also, as his correspondence makes clear, in the hope of a quid pro quo. He was not disappointed: within weeks, a grateful Carnarvon had assured him, in confidence and at a private meeting in London, that he would gift the Museum a share of the objects found in the tomb and would ensure the Met was 'well taken care of'.

Both men, at that point, believed Carnarvon would receive half of the tomb's contents. Both knew that the Director of the Antiquities Service wished to reform this system of *partage*, so that all finds from foreign excavations were retained in Egypt; both believed he could be outmanoeuvred. Lythgoe fought for years to prevent reform, enlisting *inter alia* the support of the American State Department, the British Residency in Cairo, lawyers, newspapers and leading Egyptologists. He won the battle, but lost the war: the reform of the *partage* system was delayed, but in the end implemented – the discovery of Tutankhamun's tomb made that outcome inevitable. Lythgoe died in 1934, at the age of sixty-six, in Boston.

Arthur Mace

Mace, educated at Oxford and a cousin of Flinders Petrie, was the Met's senior conservationist. He worked for two seasons on Tutankhamun's tomb, in 1922–23 and 1923–24. During his second season there, he was accompanied by his wife and his elder daughter, Margaret, then aged ten; she was recovering from typhoid. At the end of that season, Mace's health collapsed and he returned to England: he never worked or wrote again. He died aged fifty-four in 1928 and was for a long period virtually forgotten.

In 1989, a school exhibition relating to the lives of ancient Egyptians was being mounted at a local museum serving the tiny village of Lochwinnoch, near Paisley, Scotland: Mace's daughter Margaret (Mrs Orr), who lived in the area, suggested she might have papers that would be of interest. They proved to be Mace's diaries and letters from 1922 to 1924, together with his wife's letters from the American House. An invaluable source, giving a new insight into the work on the tomb, the personalities involved and the politics of excavation, the papers had been stored in an attic, unexamined, for some sixty years.

Alfred Lucas

Lucas was a distinguished government chemist and forensic scientist, based in Cairo, when Howard Carter recruited him to work on the conservation of artefacts from Tutankhamun's tomb. It is largely due to his work and Mace's (under Carter's direction) that the objects found there were conserved, saved and safely transferred to the Egyptian Museum. It was Lucas who (as Alan Gardiner put it) 'spilt the beans', and revealed that Carnarvon and Carter had broken through into Tutankhamun's Burial Chamber in secret. He saw nothing wrong in this action, nor the subsequent cover-up, describing it as 'most reasonable'. His revelation came via three unequivocal notes to two articles in the journal of the Egyptian Antiquities Service, *Annales du Service des Antiquités de l'Egypte* – the second published in 1947 after his death. It was a specialist journal, with a narrow readership; his revelations were noted by Egyptologists, but otherwise ignored for decades. Lucas died, aged seventy-eight, in 1945.

Arthur 'Pecky' Callender

Howard Carter's diaries record that he visited his friend Callender at his farm at Armant on 28 October 1922, immediately prior to the discovery of Tutankhamun's tomb. On 9 November, five days after the discovery of the first step that led down to the tomb, he wired Callender to join him in the Valley. Callender then worked for him and lived at Castle Carter for three seasons; the Oxford-educated Arthur Mace described him as 'a decent sort, but rough'. In April 1925, Carter and Callender fell out. The quarrel was caused by arguments over pay; it was bitter and it was final: the two men – Carter had claimed they were 'the closest of friends' – did not meet again.

Few facts are known about Callender, other than those provided by Carter; even his date of birth is elusive. He had two sons, and was an engineer with experience on the Egyptian railways – and it was this engineering expertise that was to prove invaluable. Callender played a crucial part in removing large objects safely from the tomb, the entrance to which was small; it was he who succeeded in dismantling the four huge shrines and lifting the massive granite lid of the sarcophagus concealed within them, using a system of pulleys. This was achieved without damage, despite the space and height restrictions within the cramped Burial Chamber.

Once he left the Valley, Callender disappears from view: the location, circumstances and even the date of his death are uncertain – it is usually claimed as 1936, but sometimes as 1931. It is probable that he died in Egypt; it is not known where he is buried.

Harry Burton

Burton was born in Lincolnshire and was the fifth of eleven children; his father was a cabinet-maker – a background similar to Carter's. He was one of the few people who could endure working alongside the difficult Carter for any length of time. He had previously worked as an archaeologist, digging under the auspices of Theodore Davis in the Valley of the Kings, and coming within a few feet of Tutankhamun's tomb – as he himself later recognised. But he was trained as a photographer, and it is for the brilliance of his photographic work, his artistry and his extraordinary recordation of the work in Tutankhamun's tomb that he is remembered.

Burton worked in the tomb every season for ten years, taking almost two thousand photographs and also filming the excavators with the aid of an early movie camera. Subsequently, he was one of Howard Carter's two executors. He died within a year of him, aged sixty-one, in 1940 in Egypt and is buried in the American cemetery at Asyut. His wife Minnie Burton, the daughter of a British army officer, survived him.

Abd-el-Aal Ahmad Sayed and Hosein Ibraheem Sayed

'I have sarved Dr H. Carter 42 years pass well,' Abd-el-Aal Sayed wrote in a letter of condolence to Howard Carter's niece in March 1939. It is a poignant letter, in which he speaks of the 'ill and uncontent' felt by him and Hosein Sayed at hearing the news of Carter's illness and death. The Sayeds had run the household both at Castle Carter, and at Carter's previous home near the Valley. Abd-el-Aal Sayed received a legacy of £E150 in Carter's will; what became of him and Hosein Sayed after that is not known.

Ahmed Girigar

Girigar, Carter's senior foreman or *reis*, was the man in charge when the first step that would prove to lead down to Tutankhamun's tomb was found on 4 November 1922. He reported the find to Carter when he reached the Valley later that morning. Girigar, born locally, had worked for most of his life in the Valley, and for some of its foremost excavators, including Victor Loret and Theodore Davis. Working with Loret, Girigar was involved in the discovery of eight tombs, including, in 1898, that of Amenhotep II, with its important and macabre cache of royal mummies. He cannot have been young when the discovery of Tutankhamun's tomb was made, but his name continues to be listed in Carter's accounts, so he must have remained working at the tomb for the decade 1922–32. Beyond that, nothing further is known of him.

The 'American House'

In the wake of the stock market crash of 1929, the Metropolitan Museum's excavation programme in Egypt was curtailed; it ceased for the duration of the war. From 1948 onwards the American House was the property of the Egyptian Antiquities Service and fell into disuse. Since 1961, it has served as the headquarters for the Polish-Egyptian Archaeological Association, who continue to excavate Hatshepsut's temple at Deir el-Bahri, the site formerly dug for the Met by Herbert Winlock.

In poor condition in 1961, this large building has been gradually restored, a process that continues. Original plans of it survive, as do photographs that show both its exteriors and interiors as they were when the Winlocks, the Burtons, Arthur Mace and other members of Winlock's team lived and worked there in the 1920s. There are many descriptions of the house, and the parties and dinners held there, in letters and diaries written at the time Tutankhamun's tomb was discovered.

'Castle Carter'

Howard Carter left this house to the Metropolitan Museum of Art on his death, together with its contents (which included artefacts from the tomb and correspondence; among the latter, the afore-mentioned letters from Lady Evelyn). Empty during the war, it was later used by the Egyptian Antiquities Service to house its inspectors. It fell into disrepair and was threatened with demolition, but has recently been restored. In 2009, it reopened as a small museum and rest house. Visitors can 'see' Howard Carter and hear him speak of Tutankhamun, by means of a holograph.

The Metropolitan Museum of Art

The 'Treasures of Three Egyptian Princesses' whose acquisition is described here remain one of the prizes of the Met's collection of Egyptian art, and may still be seen at the Museum. They are now known as the 'Treasures of Three Foreign Wives of Tuthmosis III' — 'foreign wives' meaning, in this context, minor wives or concubines. Earlier studies of the find, including Herbert Winlock's of 1948, have been superseded by new analysis, using modern technology.

The most recent findings were published by Dr Christine Lilyquist of the Met in 2003; some pieces of the jewellery are now known to be forgeries — albeit very good ones. The circumstances of the women who owned them remain as unknown now as they were in 1922.

Lord Carnarvon's collection of Egyptian art also remains on display at the Museum. In 2011, the controversy over certain objects in that collection and others bequeathed by Howard Carter was resolved when nineteen items were returned by the Met to the Egyptian Museum in Cairo. They include a little bronze dog with a gold collar (he is glancing over his shoulder, as if in response to his owner's call). Less than an inch high and a masterpiece, it is one of the loveliest objects found in Tutankhamun's tomb.

The Egyptian Museum, Cairo

The Museum owns over 3,500 artefacts from the tomb of Tutankhamun, ranging from the famous gold face mask to walking sticks, funeral wreaths and the silver nails that fastened the king's coffins: around 1,700 of these are on display, with the remainder in storage. During the January 2011 Revolution, the Museum was broken into: some items from Tutankhamun's tomb were vandalised and others stolen, including two superb gilded statues of the young king, found by Carter in the Treasury. Both were recovered and the damaged articles are currently in the course of restoration. There are confusing reports as to whether other small tomb artefacts, or parts of them, remain missing.

The Valley of the Kings

Ninety years on from Carter's discovery, KV62 remains the last king's tomb — and the only one in a virtually intact state — to be found in the Valley. In recent years, two further minor tombs, KV63 and KV64, have been uncovered. KV63, discovered in 2005 amidst great archaeological excitement, proved to be a simple pit, containing a cache of mummification materials. KV64, found on 25 January 2011, the day the Egyptian Revolution began, and excavated the following year, contained the intrusive burial of a 22nd Dynasty singer from the temple of Karnak. The small burial chamber in which she lay dated from the 18th Dynasty, but no traces of its original occupants – if there ever were any – remain.

Archaeologists differ in their beliefs as to whether the Valley is now 'dug out', as Belzoni claimed as early as 1820, and as Theodore Davis reiterated in 1914; they also differ as to whether further royal tombs await discovery. There is dissent as to whether Tutankhamun's family, including his unknown mother and his heretic father, Akhenaten, are buried in the Valley, and whether his father's coffin has already been found. There is disagreement as to whether Nefertiti, Tutankhamun's stepmother and his father's 'great royal wife', may also be buried there. The largest excavation in the Valley at present is under the direction of Dr Kent Weeks, of the American University in Cairo, whose team has been excavating the tomb of Ramesses II's sons since 1995; that pharaoh sired over one hundred sons, and their burial place resembles a labyrinth. To date, Dr Weeks has uncovered 130 corridors and burial chambers, none containing intact mummies.

In 1979, the Valley of the Kings became a UNESCO World Heritage Site, but this status has failed to protect the Valley from the toxicity of modern tourism. Revenue from tourism in Egypt, vital to its economy, is in the region of $11 billion per annum; sites in and around Luxor contribute a substantial proportion of that figure. In 2004, the last time a full survey was undertaken, 1.8 million people visited the Valley in the course of the year, an average of 5,000 per day. The Egyptian Ministry of Tourism then planned to increase these numbers rapidly, aiming at 5.4 million visitors to the Valley, an average of 15,000 per day, by 2014. They had been on course to achieving that until, in the wake of the 2011 Revolution, visitor numbers began to plummet.

Yet even at such reduced levels, the effect mass tourism has upon the fragile ecology of the Valley and its tombs is catastrophic; as archaeologists have noted, more damage has been done in the past ninety years than in the previous three thousand. The optimists among them believe that this damage can be remedied; the pessimists believe it is already irreparable.

The Tomb of Tutankhamun

Tutankhamun's small tomb, the most visited in the Valley, is now in a critical condition. Its walls are cracking and subject to water leakage; the plaster in the Burial Chamber, affected by condensation, changes in humidity, dust and salts, is lifting; the fragile paintings are flaking off the walls. Since 2009, the tomb has been the subject of a five-year conservation rescue programme under the auspices of Egypt's Supreme Council of Antiquities (SCA) and America's Getty Conservation Institute. As part of this programme, the tomb was due to close in 2010, or, at the latest, in 2011. But the tomb is one of the Valley's main draws, and – being separately ticketed – brings in additional revenue. In the face of falling visitor numbers post-2011, it remained open.

In an effort to resolve these problems, a full-scale replica of Tutankhamun's tomb was commissioned in 2009. High-tech Lucida 3D laser scanning equipment, the latest software and high-resolution printing techniques were used in its creation; it was made by the world's leading art-replica specialists, Factum Arte, based in Madrid, whose founder, Adam Lowe, is English. It took three years to complete, was paid for via funds raised by the University of Basel and others, and was presented as a gift to Egypt from Europe.

Factum Arte's recreation of KV62 is astonishing in its verisimilitude; it is also portable. Delivered to Cairo in packing cases on 4 November 2012, the ninetieth anniversary of Howard Carter's discovery of that first step to Tutankhamun's tomb, it was assembled and unveiled at a joint Egyptian and EU reception held at the Conrad Hotel, Cairo on 13 November. It was on view for two days. Press releases announced that the replica tomb would shortly be installed in, or near, the Valley of the Kings, at a location still to be determined by Egypt's SCA. The then-favoured site for the replica tomb was next to Castle Carter, Howard Carter's former home. Once it was in place, it was announced, the actual tomb of Tutankhamun would finally close to visitors.

In January 2013, the BBC reported these developments and canvassed the views of tourists visiting the Valley of the Kings. They proved suspicious of the replica proposal; they understood the need for it, but had not come all the way to Egypt, they said, to view a facsimile: what they wanted to see was – 'the real thing'. At the time of writing (June 2013), they can still do so. Tutankhamun's tomb remains open and the replica tomb is in storage at the European Union Embassy in Cairo.

ACKNOWLEDGEMENTS

This book is a novel. It has a framework and core that is fictional, but the chapters that relate to Egyptian archaeology 1922–32 and to Saranac Lake in the 1930s are based on fact and on the documented lives of real people: they are as accurate historically as I have been able to make them. When researching those parts of the book, I received tireless assistance from many sources, to whom I owe a great deal. Some of those who assisted me have asked to remain anonymous: they know who they are, and I thank them. I am grateful to the following:

The Griffith Institute, University of Oxford, is the single greatest source for material relating to the excavation of Tutankhamun's tomb, and to the events that preceded and followed its discovery; its archives include Howard Carter's diaries, correspondence, maps, autobiographical sketches and journals, together with the photographs of Harry Burton; there is rich material from other Egyptologists who witnessed or were involved in the work on Tutankhamun's tomb. I am deeply grateful to Dr Jaromir Malek, keeper of the archive, and to Elizabeth Fleming, archivist, for generous assistance with the Howard Carter, Percy Newberry and Sir Alan Gardiner papers.

For assistance with research into Herbert Winlock and his family, I am indebted to the Massachusetts Historical Society, Boston, Massachusetts, whose archives proved to contain Winlock letters and diaries never previously examined. I thank Andrea Cronin, librarian, for the hard work she undertook in locating them.

I am grateful to Diane Pierce-Williams, archivist, Cox Library, Milton Academy, Massachusetts, and Pam Rodman, registrar, Milton Academy, both of whom gave very generously of their time and provided significant information regarding Frances Winlock's later years.

The sections of the novel that relate to Saranac Lake could not have been written without access to the vast and fascinating archives of Historic Saranac Lake: they document the history of the town, its cure cottages, patients, medical records and treatment regimes in meticulous detail. I'm grateful to Amy Catania, executive director, Historic Saranac Lake, to Kareen Tyler, town clerk, Saranac Lake, and to Michelle Tucker, curator, Adirondack Research Room, Saranac Lake, for their guidance to the town and its records.

In a book much concerned with tombs, my thanks for assistance with one in particular: I'm indebted to Meg Winslow, curator of historical collections, Mount Auburn Cemetery, Cambridge, Massachusetts, and grateful to Caroline Loughlin, archivist, for the information she helped uncover.

My thanks must also go to the Egyptian Exploration Society, London; to the staff of the London Library; and to Rosalind Berwald, who owns and is the guardian of the last surviving volume of Minnie Burton's diaries.

My thanks to Joe Alexander, Tom Allardyce, Beata Allen, Clarissa Ballantyne, Julian Barnes, Freddy Bywater, Carmen Callil, Caroline Dawnay, Yasin El Haddad, Dan Ellis, Angus Gough, Louise Gravellier, Mimi Howard, Stephen Kidd, Ben and Natasha Marlow, Hugh Paige, Anthony Quinn, Frank Raccano, Gabrielle Rourke, Ronald Stern, Anna Webber, Nicholas Weir, Emily Wyatt and Ahmed Zaky: whether they helped with details or suggestions or brickbats, I'm grateful.

My thanks to my editor at Abacus, publishing director Clare Smith, to Ursula Mackenzie, CEO, Little Brown, and to my agent, Sarah Ballard of United Agents, for their input and encouragement. Last, my gratitude to Alan Howard. He discussed the minutiae of this book *ad infinitum* for more than two years – a long time to spend in the company of the long-dead. I thank him for his insight and imagination; also for his patience, which never wavered.

BIBLIOGRAPHY

Baines, John and Jaromir Malek, *Atlas of Ancient Egypt* (Phaidon Press Ltd, Oxford, 1984)

Belzoni, Giovanni Battista, *Narrative of the Operations and Recent Discoveries within the Pyramids, Temples, Tombs and Excavations in Egypt and Nubia*, 2 vols (John Murray, London, 1820)

Breasted, Charles, *Pioneer of the Past. The Story of James H. Breasted* (Charles Scribner's Sons, London, 1948)

Carnarvon, the [5th] Earl of, and Howard Carter, *Five Years' Exploration at Thebes. A Record of Work Done 1907–1911* (Oxford University Press, Oxford, 1912)

Carnarvon, the [6th] Earl of, *No Regrets* (Weidenfeld & Nicolson, London, 1976)

Carnarvon, the [8th] Countess of, *Lady Almina and the Real Downton Abbey: The Lost Legacy of Highclere Castle* (Hodder & Stoughton, London, 2011)

Carter, Howard (and Arthur C. Mace), *The Tomb of Tut.ankh.amen*, 3 vols (Cassell & Company, London, 1923–1933)

David, R. and Archbold, R., *Conversations with Mummies* (HarperCollins, London, 2000)

Davis, Theodore M., *The Tomb of Queen Tiyi* (Constable & Co. Ltd, London, 1907)

Davis, Theodore M., *The Tombs of Harmhabi and Toutankhamanou* (Constable & Co. Ltd, London, 1912)

Edwards, Amelia, *A Thousand Miles up the Nile* (George Routledge and Sons, Ltd, London, 1877)

Hankey, Julie, *A Passion for Egypt. Arthur Weigall, Tutankhamun and the 'Curse of the Pharaohs'* (I. B. Taurus & Co. Ltd, London, 2001)

Hoving, Thomas, *Tutankhamun, the Untold Story* (Simon & Schuster, New York, 1978)

James, T. G. H., *Howard Carter. The Path to Tutankhamun* (Kegan Paul International Ltd, London, 1992)

Lee, Christopher, *. . . the Grand Piano Came by Camel. The Story of Arthur C. Mace, Egyptologist, and His Family c.1890–1928* (Mainstream Publishing Company (Edinburgh) Ltd, Edinburgh, 1990)

Lilyquist, Christine, *The Tomb of Three Foreign Wives of Tuthmosis III* (The Metropolitan Museum of Art, New York, 2003)

Petrie, William M. F., *Seventy Years in Archaeology* (Sampson Low, Marston & Co., London, 1931)

Reeves, Nicholas, *The Complete Tutankhamun* (Thames & Hudson, London, 1990)

Reeves, Nicholas, *The Valley of the Kings. The Decline of a Royal Necropolis* (Kegan Paul International Ltd, London, 1990)

Reeves, Nicholas and John H. Taylor, *Howard Carter before Tutankhamun* (British Museum Press, London, 1992)

Reeves, Nicholas and Richard H. Wilkinson, *The Complete Valley of the Kings* (Thames & Hudson, London, 1996)

Reeves, Nicholas, *Akhenaten. Egypt's False Prophet* (Thames & Hudson, London, 2001)

Romer, John, *The Valley of the Kings* (Michael Joseph, London, 1981)

Weigall, Arthur E. P., *Tutankhamen and Other Essays* (Thornton Butterworth Ltd, London, 1923)

Williams, Valentine, *The World of Action* (Hamish Hamilton, London, 1938)

Winlock, Herbert E., *Excavations at Deir el Bahri 1911-1931* (The Macmillan Company, New York, 1942)

Winlock, Herbert E., *The Treasure of Three Egyptian Princesses* (The Metropolitan Museum of Art, New York, 1948)

Winlock, Herbert E., *Materials Used at the Embalming of King Tut-'ank-Amun* (The Metropolitan Museum of Art, New York, 1941)

Winlock, Herbert E. (the above, reprinted with an introduction and appendix by Dorothea Arnold), *Tutankhamun's Funeral* (The Metropolitan Museum of Art, New York, 2010)

Winstone, H. V. F., *Howard Carter and the Discovery of the Tomb of Tutankhamun* (Constable, London, 1991)

Online

www.griffith.ox.ac.uk – Griffith Institute, Oxford; online resources include many of Howard Carter's papers and Harry Burton's photographs recording the work on Tutankhamun's tomb

www.metmuseum.org – The Metropolitan Museum of Art, New York

www.thebanmappingproject.com – Database for the Valley of the Kings and the Theban Necropolis

www.ees.ac.uk – The Egypt Exploration Society

www.nicholasreeves.com – The Valley of the Kings and Tutankhamun's tomb; Egyptology

www.britishmuseum.org – The British Museum

www.oi.uchicago.edu – The Oriental Institute of the University of Chicago

www.tawy.nl – The history of dig houses in Egypt

www.hsl.wikispot.org – The online archives of Saranac Lake

www.getty.edu – The Getty Conservation Institute

www.factum-arte.com – Factum Arte, creators of the Tutankhamu replica tomb

www.sca.egypt.org – The Supreme Council of Antiquities, Egy information on the current state of the Valley of the Kings and tombs, including visitor information

ABOUT THE AUTHOR

A native of the United Kingdom, Sally Beauman is a *New York Times* bestselling author and journalist who began her career at *New York* magazine.
Her internationally bestselling novels, including *Rebecca's Tale*, her sequel
Daphne du Maurier's iconic work, have been translated into more than
enty languages. She has written for *The New Yorker*, the *Sunday Times* (Lon-
), and numerous other leading periodicals on both sides of the Atlantic.
ves in the United Kingdom.

A Treasury of North American FOLK-TALES

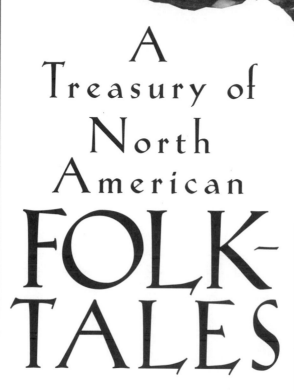

A
Treasury of
North
American
FOLK-
TALES

Compiled and Annotated by
Catherine Peck

Introduction by Charles Johnson

W. W. Norton & Company

New York   London

107931

Library of Congress Cataloging-in-Publication Data

QPB treasury of North American folktales.
A treasury of North American folktales / edited by Catherine Peck ;
introduction by Charles Johnson.
p. cm.
ISBN 0-393-04741-5
1. Tales—North America. I. Peck, Catherine. II. Title.
GR101.Q63 1999
398.2'097'01—dc21 99-17566
CIP

W. W. Norton & Company, Inc., 500 Fifth Avenue, New York, N.Y. 10110
www.wwnorton.com

W. W. Norton & Company Ltd., 10 Coptic Street, London WC1A 1PU

1 2 3 4 5 6 7 8 9 0

For Hannah and Ellie, with love

Contents

• CONTENTS •

2

TALL TALES, BRAGS, AND OTHER LIES 49

———•◦•———

3

LEGENDARY HEROES AND HEROINES 87

———•◦•———

•CONTENTS•

4

LARGER THAN LIFE 131

5

LIFE LESSONS 167

• CONTENTS •

Introduction

On the Nature of Tales
by Charles Johnson

A writer sampling the rich offerings in *A Treasury of North American Folktales*, hungrily reading each tale with an eye toward what he or she might learn about the craft of telling a good tale, comes away from this book at once humbled and reminded that folklore is the ancestral foundation for what we—as modern fiction writers—struggle mightily (and usually unsuccessfully) to achieve: a story worthy of being retold over and over for centuries. Like an old, old coin that has traversed continents, picking up something from each one, being passed down through centuries, and bearing the sweat and palm oil of millions who've handled it, these anonymous stories and yarns, legends and myths, distill the collective experience of mankind. They are unquestionably universal. They are timeless. They are, one might say, our human inheritance, for no single man or woman can claim authorship for "Opossum Steals Fire" or "The Yellow Ribbon." Yet modern storytellers as diverse as Vladimir Nabokov, *Twilight Zone* creator Rod Serling, Isaac Bashevis Singer, Alfred Hitchcock, Margaret Atwood, Robert Coover, Ursula K. Le Guin, Charles W. Chesnutt, George Lucas, O. Henry, and far more than I can cite here, have turned to the content and compositional strategies of the folktale to revitalize their own fictions. Reading these stories, carefully assembled by Catherine Peck, one easily understands why.

Tales usually deal with extraordinary events, and with fabulous characters (Brer Rabbit, Pecos Bill, Coyote) whom no one will assume is real. Strictly speaking, the Pecos Bill stories are *yarns*; the stories with animal protagonists are *fables*; and ones like "What Makes Brer Wasp Have a Short Patience" are *myths*. All these share elements of the folktale and are related to fairy tales, parables, and apologues; altogether, with their many variations, they comprise the ancient roots of the modern short story. Often, as in the wonderful story "Tom Dunn's Dance on Rag Rock," the characters are "things not of this world." But reality is never at issue in tales. They can never be "unrealistic" because tales have their own exuberant vision and interpretation of reality. Remember that what we call "naturalism," and sometimes refer to as "social realism," is a literary tradition that has its beginning in the late nineteenth and early twentieth centuries. The tale predates the arrival of these recent "scientific" approaches to fiction by five thousand years and can be found in the oldest African, Hindu, and Asian cultures. As the late John Gardner informed us in his first book, *The Forms of Fiction* (1962): "The laws governing the world of the tale may not be those of cause-and-effect, but even when they are not, they seem natural because they are psychologically and poetically true."

For example, in "Whickety-Whack, Into My Sack," the good-hearted protagonist Jack receives from a mysterious beggar an enchanted sack and drinking glass because it is imperative that he have these magical items later in order to save the king's daughter and capture Death. Or consider "The Haunted House," where a preacher attempts to exorcise a restless spirit and discovers it to be a young woman killed long ago by a lover who wanted her money. Her body, she tells him, is buried in the cellar. Following her instructions, the preacher properly inters her bones, gives her hidden treasure to the church and, with a macabre talisman—"the end joint of the little finger from her left hand"—succeeds in exposing her murderer. In these fantastic narratives, victims of murder walk among us, seeking justice beyond the grave, because—unlike our everyday reality—the dead must never go unavenged. And so phantoms walk. Angels intercede in human affairs (see Bernard Malamud's "Angel Levine"). The logic of the *heart* holds the tale together, fusing realism and fantasy in often profound gifts of the imagination.

Put another way, the reality of the world of the tale is that of a *moral* universe, a place where right and wrong are vividly dramatized, and time-honored ethical principles from the past are applied to present circumstances. Read "La Llorona Teaches a Hippie a Lesson." There, in this remarkable, Native American fiction, the spectral figure of an ancient Indian ghost-woman—La Llorona—appears in the 1970s to foil the stealing of her tribe's food by a hippie named "Bear" who "had some idea he was an Indian" but "didn't have any respect for people who worked hard." In fact, this disrespectful, lazy Californian from a rich family has stolen one of their totemic names ("Bear") as well as Indian dress and rides along the arroyo wearing "this little leather thing like Tarzan, with beads and feathers around his neck and moccasins." No one can catch him pilfering his neighbors' vegetables and fruit or drive him from the village he's plundering until La Llorona's banshee-like howling sends "Bear" scurrying away, terrified, on all fours.

In other words, La Llorona, Stackalee, Paul Bunyan, and Coyote do not have to be recognized as "real" people because they are infused with feelings we recognize in ourselves. More precisely, they are often the distillation of a single trait or emotion. Readers of naturalistic fiction expect writers to provide detailed, physical descriptions for each major character. We've come to expect, and rightly so, psychological realism, a biographical sketch ("back-story"), three-dimensionality, sociological and economic information about the protagonist, a conflict rooted in a performer's historicity, and crisp dialogue that sounds authentic. By contrast, characters in the traditional tale seem *flat*. Even one-dimensional. They are familiar *types*: kings, peasants, beggars, farmers, young men or women.

Notice how all we're told about the protagonist in "The Ghost of Jean Lafitte" is that he is "a young, war-weary Confederate soldier." The hero in "A Pretty Girl in the Road" is as featureless as a mannequin, as ahistorical as the Safe T Man dummies we place in our cars to fool would-be rapists and burglars. Yet there is more to these characters than initially meets the eye. In a haunting work like "The Grouse Girl," we are simply given "two men, the older lame and unattractive, the younger sound and handsome." They do not even have names. But from this spare description flows a complete, compelling "world." Although one man is young and handsome, he treats the Grouse Girl "roughly, and would not let her come near him" in her incarnation as a bird. However, the lame man "drew her fondly to him," and thereby weds his soul with hers, leading the first man to jealousy, then murder, and ultimately to the lonely fate of being "wifeless and partnerless."

Irrespective of their sketchiness, characters in tales do behave in ways we recognize because they are humanized, even supernatural beings like "Aunt Tucky," who "could slip out of her skin and become like a spirit or a ghost or a haunt" but who nevertheless must, after her nature is established, act in ways that do not violate that nature or the story's premise. Just in passing, I must mention that "Aunt Tucky" in particular is a folktale that has proven to be very influential on contemporary African American literature. Her skin-shedding talent is a trait I give to a witch in my first novel, *Faith and the Good Thing* (1974), a novel for which I read over eighty volumes of folklore, and it occurs again in Toni Morrison's third novel, *Song of Solomon* (1977). And how delightfully generous is the unexpected addition of rhyming dialogue in this tale—*Skin, my skin. Let me in* and *Skin, skin, always lucky. Welcome home your Aunt Tucky.*

From the tales in *A Treasury of North American Folktales* we see that in order to work their poetically compressed magic, tales must be terse, concrete, telegraphic, and must reveal character through action. (This, I assure you, is a virtue. The French have a word for needless literary padding, *le remplissage*, and you find none of that here.) The tale is *all* plot, like the epigrammatic story of Cain and Abel in Genesis (sixty lines in all), and just as bottomless in meaning as this famous biblical story. Despite this brevity, however, tales need not sacrifice "realistic" description when that is truly needed. We find a precise and terrifying description of the ghost in "The Haunted House" ("Her hair was torn and tangled, and the flesh was dropping off her face so he could see the bones and part of her teeth. She had no eyeballs, but there was a sort of blue light way back in her eye sockets. And she had no nose to her face"), and striking imagery in "The Weeping Woman" ("They always die with their eyes open like they were looking up at something and couldn't stop"), but in stories where such elaborately sculpted details appear the setting may be hazy and vague. The mysterious place of Rag Rock in "Tom Dunn's Dance on Rag Rock," where a demon crew keeps Tom dancing nigh unto death, is barely described at all, leaving us to conclude that the topography of the tale is deliberately ambiguous: moors, islands, wild mountains, dark seacoasts (or the "galaxy far, far away" in *Star Wars*), regions for which our only passport is our limitless capacity to dream. In point of fact, the landscape of the traditional tale shares much in common with and is surely sire of the numberless worlds of science-fiction—the Red Planet of Ray Bradbury's *The Martian Chronicles,* the ape-city of *Planet of the Apes,* and the Morlock/Eloi terrain in H. G. Wells's *The Time Machine.*

Added to the many splendors of these stories, and most important of all, is the authoritative voice of the narrator, which is largely missing in contemporary, naturalistic fiction. It is an oral, storyteller's voice, like that of an African *griot*, the keeper of his people's history, or the compelling voice of our own grandmothers. Often it begins, *A long time ago, all the animals in the jungle got along with each other, except for one* ("Tío Conejo and the Hurricane"), or, *There was once this stagecoach route in Texas* ("The Yankee Peddler"), or, *Well, once upon a time there was two people lived in the world* ("Bobtail and the Devil"), or yet again, *One time there was a fellow a-riding along . . .* ("A Pretty Girl in the Road"), and what we experience in each of these openings is that the very first sentence transports us from here and now to another world, usually in the past. Phenomenologically, these folktale openings force us to suspend for the duration of the story our immediate worries and cares and worldly involvements; they are—as powerful first lines—akin to the slow raising of a curtain in the theater, which quiets down the audience and brings their attention to the stage; or, if you like, the very frame that surrounds the "world" of a painting and sets it off from the rest of a room. Only a fully *voiced* fiction can accomplish this so swiftly.

Such a voice can conjure other delights of language too. In "A Pretty Girl in the Road," it can tell us how a character "hollered a boy out of the barn," for the region of the storyteller clings to his voice, texturing his vocabulary and grammar. And in "Aunt Tucky" it can soar, making a reader feel the teller of the tale is sitting right beside him when she says, "The child would break all four legs! Yes! Four legs. I said that to show you *double* bad luck!" Again and again throughout the folktales in this splendid anthology we encounter *pure* storytelling voices of this sort, confident speakers—sometimes humorous, sometimes moralistic, always compelling—who help us recapture the childhood wonder and awe that makes us hunger for good tales the rest of our lives.

Thus, *A Treasury of North American Folktales* is a book that, I believe, will thoroughly entertain as it enlightens. Whether one simply reads for pleasure, or is an apprentice writer hoping to unkey the technical mysteries of stories that, like the pyramids or Stonehenge, have survived the passage of time, this volume offers inexhaustible treasures. Read it to your children. And as you do, enjoy being a child once again yourself.

Preface

———

Who are these "folk" who tell folktales? The current definition of a North American folktale includes almost any narrative from the earliest Native American legend to the joke you told at the water cooler this morning. So the first person to tell a story in North America might have been a tribal elder living thousands of years ago whose purpose was to illustrate the origin of the world, and the latest folktale teller might be . . . you. Folktales are an ever renewable natural resource, conceived from the union between past and present human experience, and born of our natural longing to communicate our experiences, insights, and visions to others. Tales are instructive, funny, scary, fantastic, visionary, and factual. They celebrate romance, bawdiness, the hero, the fool, the ordinary, and the extraordinary.

The most important thing to know about folktales is that they are almost always originally *told*. In compiling *A Treasury of North American Folktales* my first goal has been to present versions of traditional stories whose tellers express the richness of our heritage with their distinctive voices. For no single voice can communicate a cultural heritage as deep and broad as North America's. Not only is the continent peopled by almost every cultural group in the world, it also has diverse regions whose traditions have evolved separately from those of other regions. On top of that, the history of North America is a history of rapid change in language, dialect, values, and technology. The wonderful thing about folktales is that, because they represent so many voices, they offer insight into the diversity of human experience among ordinary people on this vast continent.

This collection holds tales both ancient and modern. The voices here are Native American, Latino, African American, French Canadian, Native Canadian, and Mexican. They are also voices of the South, the Midwest, the Northeast, the Northwest, and the West. They are voices from the past, using dialects rarely heard in North America today, and they are voices of the present, with a little modern slang here and there. They are proof that in every era and in every region of North America, fresh voices always have been, and always will be, on hand to make the old stories new.

My second goal has been to provide readers with stories that will entertain as well as enlighten, which has always been the purpose of folktales. I was asked to choose one book's worth of stories out of thousands of possibilities. What a task! Decisions had to be made. My first was to choose primarily tales whose sources are traditional. So while a story might include the exploits of hippies in the Southwest, the purpose of the story is to remind people about the supernatural power of the region's most famous ghost, La Llorona. My second decision was to choose stories whose origins might be vaguely Old World, but whose tellers were firmly rooted on this continent to the extent that the details of the story make it unmistakably North American. Thus while the story of Cinderella is known to have originated in Europe, in the hands of an Algonquin storyteller details are transformed to make the story meaningful to the members of that tribe.

Another decision was to include a number of often-told stories, some of which, like Paul Bunyan, probably originated in print and then moved off the printed page into the rich oral tradition of the North American frontier and into the imagination of almost every American. Yet another decision was to tap into the fieldwork of folktale scholars for stories that have not seen the light of day in many years. There I found contemporary newspaper accounts that formed the basis of heroic legends, personal descriptions of supernatural encounters, and funny stories—brilliantly told—that were languishing in folklore journals on dusty library shelves.

Finally, I decided to call upon modern storytellers who have taken stories that in their original recorded versions had gaps in the narratives or were difficult to understand, and have smoothed out the rough spots in order to bring them to us now in such a way that they will be remembered and retold well into the twenty-first century. These folks are on a mission to keep the stories alive, and I have come to admire them enormously.

I hope you will approach this book as a celebration of voices. I hope you will discover your own voice and read the tales aloud, for they came from the spoken word and deserve to return there. Finally, I hope you will take these stories and continue the folk process; *tell* the tales as they have always been told, by adding, subtracting, multiplying, and dividing details until the stories become your own.

Catherine Peck
Princeton, New Jersey

I

How the World Was Made

Among the earliest North American folktales are stories that explain the phenomena that make up the natural world. Tales, especially among Native Americans, often revolve around godlike characters with mysterious origins, who appear suddenly to mortals, dwell on the earth for a while, and then disappear. As these culture heroes move through the world, and as they leave it, they create marvels such as celestial bodies or prominent features of the landscape. Tales that explain the peculiar attributes of particular animals sometimes make a culture hero of the creature who brings light or fire to people. More often such stories include a cast of characters whose exploits lead to a change in appearance that becomes a permanent physical feature for an entire species.

Some of the tales in this chapter are taken from stories heard firsthand by folklorists and anthropologists visiting Native American tribes during the latter part of the nineteenth century. Others have been adapted from various sources by contemporary storytellers for a modern audience.

The Boy of the Red Sky

This gentle Native Canadian tale presents an example of how explanation tales weave extraordinary details into a simple story. Many myths around the world have as their central character an unearthly being who appears in the lives of parents who have longed for a child. The magical being's time on Earth is almost always short-lived, and he or she always leaves a magnificent gift.

Long ago a young man and his wife lived near the Great Water in the west. They had no children, and they lived by themselves on an island, far from other people. The man caught deep-sea fish in the ocean and salmon in the rivers. He was gone for many days at a time, fishing. The woman was not afraid, but she was very lonely, looking each day at the gray sky and listening to the sound of the waves on the beach. Day after day she said to herself, "I wish we had children. They would be good company for me when my husband is far away."

One evening she sat alone on the beach at twilight, looking across the water. The sky was gray. Because she was so lonely, the woman said to herself, "I wish we had children to keep me company." At that moment, a kingfisher, with her family, was diving for food nearby. The woman said, "O Sea Bird, I wish I had children like you." The kingfisher replied by telling her to look at the seashells. The next evening a white sea gull was flying above the waves. The woman told the gull that she wished she had children. The sea gull replied, "Look at the seashells," and flew away.

The woman kept wondering about the words of the kingfisher and the sea gull. Suddenly she heard a strange cry coming from the sand behind her. When she came closer to the sound, she realized that the cry was coming from a large seashell lying on the sand. She picked up the shell and inside found a tiny boy, crying as hard as he could. The woman carried the baby home and took care of him. When her husband came home from the sea, he was very happy that she had found the baby. He knew that they would no longer be lonely.

The baby grew quickly. One day the child suddenly said to the woman, who was wearing a copper bracelet, "Please make a bow from the copper on your arm." She wanted him to be happy, so she made a tiny bow and two tiny arrows from the bracelet.

Every day the boy went out hunting. He always returned with his catch: geese, ducks, and small sea birds, which he gave to the woman.

As the boy grew older, the man and woman noticed that his face was becoming the color of his copper bow. Wherever he went, there was a strange light. When he sat on the beach looking toward the west, the weather was calm and there were strange bright lights on the water. His foster parents kept wondering about this unusual power, but the boy would not talk about it. When they asked about it, he was always silent.

Once the winds blew so hard over the Great Water that the man could not go out fishing. He had to stay on shore because the ocean waves beat so strongly on the beach. When the father, worried, said they needed to get fish to eat, the boy said, "I will go out fishing with you, for I am stronger than the Spirit of the Storm." The man did not want to go, but at last he listened to the boy. They went out together to the fishing grounds in the rough sea.

They had not gone far when they met the Spirit of the Storm. He tried hard to overturn their boat, but he could not. He had no power over them because the boy was rowing the little boat. All around them the sea was calm and the waves were still.

Then the Spirit of the Storm called his nephew Black Cloud to help him. But the boy said to the man, "Do not be afraid. I am stronger than he." When

Black Cloud came, he saw the boy, and he quickly disappeared. Then the Spirit of the Storm called the Mist of the Sea to cover the water, because he thought that the boat would be lost if the land could not be seen.

When the man saw the Mist of the Sea coming across the water, he was very frightened, but the boy said, "He cannot harm you when I am with you." Indeed, when the Mist of the Sea saw the boy sitting in the boat, he went away as quickly as he had come. Angry, the Spirit of the Storm also hurried away. And the sea became calm again.

The boy and the man reached the fishing grounds safely. The boy taught his foster father a magic song, which he could use to call fish into the nets. By evening, the boat was filled with fish. As they were rowing back home, the man said, "Tell me the secret of your power." But the boy said, "The time has not yet come."

The next day the boy killed many birds and took off their skins. Then he dressed himself in the skin of one of the birds and flew above the sea. The sea under him was gray like his wings. Then he dressed himself like another bird, a blue jay. This time, when he flew, the sea under him became blue like his wings. He returned to the beach and put on the skin of a robin redbreast. When he flew high above the sea, the waves in the ocean under him turned the bright color of fire, and the sky in the west was a golden red.

The boy flew back to the beach and said to his foster parents, "Now is the time for me to leave you. I am the Child of the Sun. Yesterday my power was tested and I succeeded, so now I must go away. I shall see you no more. But in the evening, I shall often appear to you in the twilight sky in the west. When the sky and the sea are red in the evening, like the color of my face, you will know that there will be no wind or storm the next day. Although I am going away, I shall leave you the power to call me when you need me. Let me know your wishes: make me a white offering, so that I may see it from my home far in the west."

Then he gave his foster mother a wonderful robe. He said goodbye to his parents and flew off to the west. They were left sad and lonely, but the woman still keeps a part of the power he gave her. When she sits on the island and loosens her wonderful robe the wind blows from the land and a storm begins on the sea. The more she loosens her robe, the stronger the storm is.

In the late autumn, when the cold mist comes from the sea, the evenings are chilly, and the sky is gray, she remembers the boy's promise to her. She takes tiny white feathers from the breasts of birds and throws them into the air. They float to the west, and fall to earth like snowflakes that blow westward in the wind. They come to tell the boy the world is gray and gloomy and wait to see his golden face. Then he appears in the evening and stays until the sun is gone. The twilight sky becomes red and the ocean in the west is filled with golden light. All the people know that there will be no wind the next day, as the boy promised long ago.

What Makes Brer Wasp Have a
Short Patience

———·+·———

Not all explanatory tales deal with the grand and sublime mysteries of nature. Some, with great humor, explain the smallest detail of some of nature's most ridiculous aspects. This African American tale was told in North Carolina.

———·———

Creatures don't all stay just the way God made them. No sir. With the mistakes made, and accidents, and natural debilitation, and one thing or another, they become different as time goes on, until sometime later they are hardly the same thing at all.

At one time, Brer Wasp looked very different from the way he does today. He was big on company, and he loved to talk, and joke, and cut the fool. He was one person that had to have his laugh.

One day, he was walking on a path, and he met up with Brer Mosquito. Now, Brer Mosquito and his whole family weren't very big at all, but they took themselves mighty seriously. Brer Mosquito and his pa planted a little patch of ground together, but they always called it the plantation. They talked so big about their crops and land and everything that you would have thought that they had a twenty-mile place. Now, Brer Wasp loved to draw Brer Mosquito out on the subject.

That same week, there had been a heavy frost, and all the sweet-potato vines died and turned black and everybody was forced to dig for the early potatoes. And Brer Wasp, after he had passed the time of day with Brer Mosquito, and inquired about his family, asked him about his pa's health and how he had made out with his crop. "We made out fine, Brer Wasp," Brer Mosquito said. "Just too fine. We had the biggest crop you ever have seen!" "The potatoes were big, then?" "I tell you, sir! They were huge! You have never seen such potatoes!" "How big are they, Brer Mosquito?" Brer Wasp questioned him. "My friend," Brer Mosquito said, puffing out his chest and reaching down and pulling his little britches tight around his little leg, "most of our crop came up bigger than the calf of my leg!"

Well, sir! Brer Wasp looked at Brer Mosquito's poor little leg, and as he thought about those "huge potatoes," he had to laugh to himself. Now, he tried to mind his manners, but his chest and face swelled up, and his eye water ran out of his eyes, and he burst out laughing right in Brer Mosquito's face. He laughed and he laughed till his sides hurt him. Whenever he thought he would stop, he looked at that ridiculous leg that stood there like a toothpick, and he laughed more than ever. His sides hurt him so much, he had to hold them in with both his hands and rock himself back and forth.

"What makes you have to do that?" Brer Mosquito asked him. "You had better explain yourself. That is, if you can act sensible!" Brer Wasp gasped out, "Good lord, Brer Mosquito, looking for the biggest part of your leg is like hunting for the heaviest part of a hair! How big those huge potatoes must be, if you say they are as big as that!" And he laughed again till his sides hurt so bad that it wasn't enough just to press them—he had to grab them in both his hands and squeeze.

Brer Mosquito was so annoyed that he felt like fighting Brer Wasp right on the spot. But then he remembered that Brer Wasp was kind of nasty when he got in a row. So he just drew himself up, and stuck out his mouth, and said, "Laugh, you no-mannered devil! Laugh! But take care that the day doesn't come when somebody laughs at you the same no-mannered way!" And he went away so blistering mad that his two little coattails stuck straight out behind him.

But that didn't stop Brer Wasp. All the way to his house he had been laughing so hard that he had to stop now and catch his breath. At last he got home and started to laugh some more and tell his family about Brer Mosquito. Just then his wife got a good look at him, and she hollered out, "For crying-out-loud, Brer Wasp! What's happened to your stomach?" Brer Wasp looked down where his waist had been and he could hardly see it.

He lost all notion of laughing right then. He looked again and he saw what all that shaking, and pushing, and squeezing had done to him. He was almost in two! Even his little hand could reach around his waist. He remembered how big it had been, and he saw how much he had shrunk up, and he was afraid to so much as sneeze.

Then he remembered what Brer Mosquito had said to him. He remembered all those people he had been joking about and laughing at so hard and for such a long time and he thought about how now the others were going to have their turn to laugh at that little waist he had now. He got so that he couldn't get that shameful thing out of his mind. And that is why he has such a short patience! Everywhere he goes he thinks somebody is ready to laugh at him. If anyone so much as looks at him, he gets so mad that he is ready to fight.

And that isn't the worst, because from that day to this day, he can't laugh anymore, because if he does, he will burst in two!

Opossum Steals Fire

Myths explaining how humans first got the use of fire often describe the journey of a culture hero who must steal the fire from a god or, more often, an old woman who hoards it for herself. In Greek mythology Prometheus makes this terrifying journey. His success is met with such anger from the gods that he spends eternity being punished for giving fire to humankind. In most North American tales, the theft of fire explains a feature of the animal who took it. Some describe the journey of a spider whose back remains forever stained red; others say a fox did it, and that is why the fox's feet are black. The following tale is from Mexico.

They say there was an old woman who managed to keep the fire when it had scarcely become separated from certain stars or planets. She was fearless and went to get the fire where it had fallen. She kept it a long time.

Then after a while, people decided that this fire ought to be for everybody and not just for the old woman. So they went to the old woman's house and asked for fire. But the old woman was ferocious. She would not give it to anyone.

Time passed, and word traveled that this old woman had managed to keep fire but would not share it. Then Opossum came along and said to the people, "I, Opossum promise to give you fire, if you promise never to eat me."

Then everyone made fun of the poor creature. But he remained calm and answered them: "Stop making fun of me, because you are only making fun of yourselves. This very evening you will see that my promise has been fulfilled."

When evening came, the opossum went visiting from house to house, saying he was going to get fire from the old woman, so that others might collect as much of it as they could.

When he arrived at the old woman's house, he said to her, "Good evening, Lady Fire. How cold it is! I'd like to stand next to your fire for a moment and warm myself. The cold is killing me."

The old woman really believed the opossum was cold, and she allowed him to come close to the fire. But this was a clever one, and he kept getting closer and closer until he could put himself into the fire. Then he put his tail down, and that's how he was able to catch it. When his tail had caught fire, he ran as far as he could, sharing the fire. And that's why opossums today have a bald tail.

Light

Similar to tales of how fire was brought to the world are stories of the culture hero's quest for sources of light. Like fire, light most often had to be stolen, according to origin stories of Native Americans. In this unusual tale, heard on Kodiak Island, Alaska, around the turn of the century, the hero is the raven, a well-known trickster among Northwestern American tribes. The following tale was recorded by F. A. Golder and published in The Journal of American Folklore *in 1903. Like most folklorists of his day, Golder translated the tale to fit the Victorian literary style of the period.*

Light was not so universal formerly as now. Its cheering influences were then cast over one village only; and even there it depended on the caprices of the chief, who regulated and guarded it jealously. All other villages lived in darkness, although aware of the existence of light in that village. They made many attempts to get possession of it. Some, after a few efforts, gave up in despair. Others, not so easily discouraged, continued a longer time with the same empty result. But one village, owing to the persistent character of its chief, would never own itself defeated, and persevered in spite of past failures.

Here, in the village hall, the people gathered daily to discuss the all-important question of light, and concluded to call for volunteers to go in quest of it. To the fortunate one the following reward was held out: eternal glory and the hand of the chief's beautiful and favorite daughter. Considering the inducements, there were no lack of volunteers at first, but, as none of these returned, not even to tell the story of their failure, the list became smaller and smaller, and after a time weeks would pass without anyone offering himself. What became of these eager seekers after light was a mystery. It was generally supposed that some dropped by the wayside, and the others, on reaching the land of light and finding the task too arduous, decided to remain there always rather than go back without light.

The chief, however, was undaunted, and continued calling the meetings and for volunteers regularly. At one of these the raven was present. He listened attentively to all the speeches, and heard the chief's call for volunteers, and when a considerable time had elapsed without anyone indicating his desire to go, he rose and addressed the assembly. Sad to say, his speech has been lost in the dark ages, except the last and memorable words, "I will bring you light." This was followed by such loud peals of laughter and mocking hoots that the building almost shook. The chief, who was deep in thought during the raven's harangue, was aroused from his revery by this sudden outburst of laughter, and inquired the cause of it. With much derision the speech and boasts of the raven were repeated to him. Although he may have had as little faith in the words of the raven as the others, he was yet too wise a man to let any opportunity, no matter how slim, of obtaining light—the great object of his life—go by unembraced. Instead of joining in the laughter, he mildly reproved his followers, and then addressing himself to the raven, congratulated him on his noble resolution, encouraged him to persevere, and ended by reminding him of the prize that awaited him whose efforts should be crowned with success.

With this the meeting dissolved. The raven, satisfied with the present and rejoicing in the future, flew home to make ready for the expedition. Joyfully he related the events of the day to his grandmother, a woman. "Caw! Caw! Caw! Grandmother, tomorrow I start after the light, and on my return with it I shall marry the chief's beautiful daughter and become famous. Make all things ready, for I leave early in the morning. Caw! Caw! Caw!"

"Ai-Ai-Yah!" she exclaimed. "Better ones than you have tried and failed, and how will you, a raven, get it! Why do you want to marry? Who will marry such a one as you? You smell too strong."

This was too much for him. "You old hag!" he screamed with rage. "Who is asking your opinion or advice! How does my smell concern you? To spite you I will marry, and the chief's daughter at that. Even if I am a raven, I will do what I promise."

Early the next morning he left the village, and after several days of flight in the darkness it lightened up faintly. The farther he went, the lighter it became, and when he reached the village the light was so strong that it almost blinded him. It was a large and cheerful village. The chief's large barrabara, where the lights were kept, was in the center. Close by was a spring of water, and there the raven alighted and eyed sharply the women as they came for water. Not noticing the chief's daughter among them, he began to wish that she would appear. A moment later he saw her coming towards him, and when she had dipped out some water he murmured, "I wish she would drink some of it." The words had barely been said when she bent over to drink. Instantly he changed himself into a tiny piece of down, and, unnoticed, she gulped it down with the water.

She conceived, and in due time gave birth to a son, a raven. Being the first child of an only child, he was fondled and nursed tenderly. The chief was especially devoted to him and loved him even more than his daughter. He was indulged and humored in all his wishes. Whatever he saw he called for; whatever he called for had to be given to him; and if it was not given him immediately, he cawed, cried, pestered, clawed, and pecked until he got it. In this manner he handled everything on the premises that might possibly contain the lights except three little caskets on an out of the way shelf. These he noticed one day and asked for them. The chief was asleep, and as no one else dared touch them, the request was denied. But he would have them, and he commenced such a cawing, scratching, and hawing that the chief awoke. Not waiting to learn the cause of all this disturbance, he shouted angrily, "O, give him anything he wants, and shut him up!" And he went to sleep again.

The caskets were handed him, and he opened them one by one. In the first was night; the second contained the moon and stars, and in the third the sun was shining. He looked at them awhile, and then thrust them aside as worthless. But a few days later, when no one was about, he flew upon the shelf, grasped the two boxes containing the precious lights, and flew out with them. Some of the people outside noticed him, and raised the cry: "A raven flew out of the chief's barrabara with two boxes in his mouth!"

When the chief discovered his loss, the raven was miles away. He flew many days, and each day it grew darker and darker until he was in darkness altogether. After suffering some hardships he arrived in the village, reported himself to the chief, and requested that the people be called together. When all were assembled he addressed them, congratulated them, reminded them of the last meeting, the promises made, and concluded by saying, "I have brought you light." In the presence of all he opened one of the caskets, and instantly the moon and stars were visible in the sky. The people and chief were almost wild with joy; and the latter kept his promise, and bestowed on him his favorite daughter.

On the morrow the raven called on his father-in-law, and asked what he had to offer for a still better light than even the moon and stars. "My other daughter," replied the chief.

"Call the people, and you shall have it," said the raven.

If the villagers were wild with joy on seeing the moon and stars, imagine their emotions on beholding for the first time the sun. Since that memorable day the sun, moon, and stars have illuminated the whole world. The crow married the two daughters of the chief, with whom he is living very happily to this day.

Ojeeg, The Summer Maker

The Ojibwa have a tale describing how summer came into the world. Again, like light and fire, summer must be stolen from powerful supernatural beings. It is from this tale that Longfellow wrote these lines for Hiawatha:

> *He was telling them the story*
> *Of Ojeeg the Summer-Maker,*
> *How he made a hole in heaven,*
> *How he climbed up into heaven,*
> *And let out the summer-weather,*
> *The perpetual summer-weather,*
> *How the Otter first essayed it,*
> *How the Beaver, Lynx and Badger,*
> *Tried in turn the great achievement,*
> *From the summit of the mountain . . .*

Ojeeg was a great hunter. He lived on the southern shore of Lake Superior. Ojeeg had a wife and one son.

Now the son hunted game as the father taught him. He followed the trails over the snow. For snow lay always on the ground. It was always cold. Therefore the boy returned home crying.

One day as he went to his father's wigwam in the cold and snow he saw Red Squirrel, gnawing the end of a pine cone. Now the son of Ojeeg had shot nothing all day because his hands were so cold. When he saw Red Squirrel, he came nearer, and raised his bow.

Red Squirrel said, "My grandson, put up your arrow. Listen to me."

The boy put the arrow in his quiver.

Red Squirrel said, "You pass my wigwam very often. You cry because you cannot kill birds. Your fingers are numb with cold. Obey me. Thus it shall always be summer. Thus you can kill many birds."

Red Squirrel said again, "Obey me. When you reach your father's wigwam, throw down your bow and arrows. Begin to weep. If your mother says, 'My son, what is the matter?' do not answer her. Continue weeping. If she says, 'My son, eat this,' you must refuse the food. Continue weeping. In the evening when your father comes in he will say to your mother, 'What is the matter with my son?' She will say, 'He came in crying. He will not tell me.' Your father will say, 'My son, what is the matter? I am a spirit. Nothing is too hard for me.' Then you must answer, 'It is always cold and dreary. Snow lies always upon the ground. Melt the snow, my father, so that we may have always summer.' Then your father will say, 'It is very difficult to do what you ask. I will try.' Then you must be quiet. You must eat the food they give you."

Thus it happened.

Ojeeg then said, "I must make a feast. I must invite my friends to go on this journey with me." At once Ojeeg killed a bear. The next day he had a great feast. There were Otter, Beaver, and Lynx. Also Wolverine and Badger were at the feast.

Then they started on their journey. On the twentieth day they came to the foot of a high mountain. There was blood in the trail. Some person had killed an animal. They followed the trail of that person. They arrived at a wigwam.

Ojeeg said, "Do not laugh. Be very quiet."

A man stood in the doorway of the wigwam. He was a great manitou [spirit of nature]. He was a head only. Thus he was very strange. Then he made a feast for them. He made very curious movements, so Otter laughed. At once the manitou leaped upon him. He sprang on him, but Otter slipped out from under him and escaped.

The manitou and the animals talked all night. The manitou said to Ojeeg, the Fisher, "You will succeed. You will be the summer-maker. But you will die. Yet the summer will come."

Now when they followed the trail in the morning, they met Otter. He was very cold and hungry, therefore Fisher gave him meat.

Then they journeyed on. On the twentieth day, they came to the top of a lofty mountain. Then they smoked their pipes.

Then Ojeeg, the Fisher, and the animals prepared themselves. Ojeeg said to Otter, "We must first make a hole in the Sky-cover. You try first."

Otter made a great spring. He did not even touch the Sky-cover. He fell back, down the hill, to the bottom of the hill. Then Otter said, "I will go home." So he did.

Then Beaver tried. He fell. Also Lynx and Badger fell.

Then Wolverine tried. He made a great leap and touched the sky. Then he leaped again. He pressed against the Sky-cover. He leaped a third time. The Sky-cover broke, and Wolverine went into the Sky-land. Fisher also sprang in quickly after him.

Thus Wolverine and Fisher were in the Sky-plain, in the summer land. There were many flowers and streams of bright water. There were birds in the trees, and fish and water birds on the streams. Many lodges stood there, but they were empty. In each lodge were many *mocuks*, many bird cages, with birds in them.

At once Ojeeg began to cut the *mocuks*. The birds flew out. They flew down through the hole in the Sky-cover to the Earth-plain below. They carried warm air down with them.

Now when the people of the Sky-land saw these strangers, and their birds escaping, they ran to their wigwams. But they were too late. Spring, and summer, and autumn had slipped down the hole in the Sky-cover. Endless summer was just passing through, but they broke it in two with a blow. Therefore only a part of endless summer came down to the Earth-plain.

Now when Wolverine heard the noise of the Sky People running to their lodges, he jumped down the hole and escaped. Fisher also tried to jump, but the people had shut the cover. Therefore Fisher ran and the people pursued him. He climbed a great tree in the north, and the people began shooting at him. Now Fisher was a spirit; he could not be hurt except in the tip of his tail. At last they shot him in his tail.

Fisher called to the Sky People to stop shooting. But they did not stop until darkness came. Then they went away. Fisher climbed down. He went towards the north. He said, "I have kept my promise to my son. The seasons will now be different. There will be many moons without snow and cold."

Thus Fisher died, with the arrow sticking in his tail. It can be seen there, even to this day.

Powerful Changed

Several African American tales tell why the animals we know today are not as they were originally meant to be. It is usually their own orneryness that got them into trouble and altered what God created. In this story, the great folklorist Zora Neale Hurston recreates a tale-telling session among Southern men.

"Well, you know when de Flood was and dey had two of everything in de Ark—well, Ole Nora didn't take on no trees, so de woodpecker set 'round and set 'round for a week or so, then he felt like he just had to peck himself some wood. So he begin to peck on de Ark. Ole Nora come to him and tole him, 'Don't peck on de Ark. If you peck a hole in it, we'll all drown.'

"Woodpecker says, 'But Ah'm hungry for some wood to peck.'

"Ole Nora says, 'Ah don't keer how hongry you gits, don't you peck on dis Ark no mo. You want to drown everybody and everything?'

"So de woodpecker would sneak 'round behind Ole Nora's back and peck every chance he got. He'd hide hisself way down in de hold where he thought nobody could find him and peck and peck. So one day Ole Nora come caught him at it. He never opened his mouth to dat woodpecker. He just hauled off and give dat peckerwood a cold head-whipping wid a sledge hammer, and dat's why a peckerwood got a red head today—'cause Ole Nora bloodied it wid dat hammer. Dat's how come Ah feel like shootin' every one of 'em Ah see. Tryin' to drown *me* before Ah was born."

"A whole lot went on on dat ole Ark," Larkins White commented. "Dat's where de possum lost de hair off his tail."

"Now don't you tell me no possum ever had no hair on dat slick tail of his'n," said Black Baby, " 'cause Ah know better."

"Yes, he did have hair on his tail one time. Yes, indeed. De possum had a bushy tail wid long silk hair on it. Why, it useter be one of de prettiest sights you ever seen. De possum struttin' 'round wid his great big ole plumey tail. Dat was 'way back in de olden times before de big flood.

"But de possum was lazy—jus' like he is today. He sleep too much. You see Ole Nora had a son name Ham and he loved to be playin' music all de time. He had a banjo and a fiddle and maybe a guitar too. But de rain come up so sudden he didn't have time to put 'em on de Ark. So when rain kept comin' down he fretted a lot 'cause he didn't have nothin' to play. So he found a ole cigar box and made hisself a banjo, but he didn't have no strings for it. So he seen de possum stretched out sleeping wid his tail all spread 'round. So Ham slipped up and shaved de possum's tail and made de strings for his banjo out de hairs. When dat possum woke up from his nap, Ham was playin' his tail hairs down to de bricks and dat's why de possum ain't got no hair on his tail today. Losin' his pretty tail sorta broke de possum's spirit too. He ain't never been de same since. Dat's how come he always actin' shame-faced. He know his tail ain't whut it useter be; and de possum feel mighty bad about it."

"A lot of things ain't whut they useter be," observed Jim Presley. "Now take de 'gator for instance. He been changed 'round powerful since he been made."

"Yeah," cut in Eugene Oliver. "He useter have a nice tongue so he could talk like a nat'chal man, but Brer Dog caused de 'gator to lose his tongue, and dat's how come he hate de dog today."

"Brer 'Gator didn't fall out wid Brer Dog 'bout no tongue," retorted Presley.

"Brer Dog done de 'gator a dirty trick 'bout his mouth. You know God made de dog and de 'gator without no mouth. So they seen everybody else had a mouth so they made it up to git theirselves a mouth like de other varmints. So they agreed to cut one 'nother's mouth, and each one said dat when de other one tole 'em to stop cuttin' they would. So Brer Dog got his mouth first. Brer 'Gator took de razor and cut. Brer Dog tole him, 'Stop,' which he did. Den Brer Dog took de razor and begin to cut Brer 'Gator a mouth. When his mouth was as big as he wanted it, Brer 'Gator says, "Stop, Brer Dog. Dat'll do, I thank you, please." But Brer Dog kept right on cuttin' till he ruint Brer 'Gator's face. Brer 'Gator was a very handsome gent'man befo' Brer Dog done him that a way, and everytime he look in de lookin' glass he cry like a baby over de disfiggerment of his face. And dat's how come de 'gator hate de dog."

"My people, my people," lamented Oliver. "They just will talk whut they don't know."

"Go on, Oliver."

"De 'gator didn't fall out wid de dog 'bout no mouth cuttin' scrape. You know all de animals was havin' a ball down in de pine woods, and so they all chipped in for refreshments and then they didn't have no music for de dance. So all de animals what could 'greed to furnish music. So de dog said he'd be de trumpet in de band, and de horse and de frog and de mockin' bird and all said they'd be there an' help out all they could. But they didn't have no bass drum, till somebody said, 'Whut's de matter wid Brer 'Gator, why don't he play bass drum for us?' Dey called Brer 'Gator but he wasn't at de meetin' so de varmints deppitized Brer Dog to go call on Brer 'Gator and see if he wouldn't furnish de drum music for de dance. Which he did.

" 'Good evenin', Brer 'Gator.'

" 'My compliments, Brer Dog, how you makin' out? Ah'm always glad when folks visit me. Whut you want?'

" 'Well, Brer 'Gator, de varmints is holdin' a big convention tonight in de piney woods and we want you to furnish us a little bit of yo' drum music.'

"'It's like this, Brer Dog, tell de other animals dat Ah'm mighty proud they wants me and de compliments run all over me, but my wife is po'ly and my chillun is down sick. But Ah'll lend you my drum if you know anybody kin play it, and know how to take keer of it too!'

"'Oh, Ah'll do *dat*, Brer 'Gator. You just put in in my keer. You don't have to worry 'bout dat atall.'

"So de dog took Brer 'Gator's tongue to de ball dat night and they beat it for a drum. De varmints lakted de bass drum so well till they didn't play nothin' else hardly. So by daybreak it was wore clean out. Brer Dog didn't want to go tell Brer 'Gator they had done wore his tongue out so he hid from Brer 'Gator. Course de 'gator don't like it 'bout his tongue so he's de sworn enemy of de dog."

The Star Husband

As in the Greek myths, Native American gods and goddesses often interacted with people, and the story of a human marrying a celestial body is widespread among North American tribes. This version was told among the Blackfoot and has been adapted here by storyteller Lynn Moroney. In addition to telling the origin myth, which is its ultimate purpose, the tale includes a warning to be obedient that is similar to the warning God gave to Eve in the Garden of Eden. It is easy to see why this elegant and compelling tale survives and is often chosen by modern American storytellers.

One summer night two girls decided to sleep outside. They left the place where all the others were camped and walked until they came to a hill. They made their beds, and after they had lain down, they began to watch the stars. As the sky grew darker, the stars grew in number and brightness.

"These stars are beautiful," said one girl.

"Oh, look! One of the stars just fell," said the other.

"There in the south is a red star," said one. "And just there, there is a yellow star," said the other.

With the appearance of each new star the girls grew more delighted. They agreed that sleeping outside was a good idea, for never had they seen so beautiful a night.

In time, one of the maids noticed one special star. "Sister, see that star," she said, "that white star just over there? That is my favorite star. I wish that star could be my husband. If I married that star, I could go way into the sky and live with the stars."

The girls gazed at the stars for a while longer, but the night had worn on, and in time they fell asleep—sound asleep under a sky filled with stars.

The next day, on their way back to camp, the girls found a berry patch. They started gathering berries, and the girl who had wished for a husband wandered off. As soon as she was alone, she heard a sound. Looking up, she saw a young man standing before her. He wore a white feather in his hair, and his vest and moccasins were beaded with white and crystal beads that sparkled and glimmered like the stars.

"Do not be afraid," he said. "Last night you wished to marry the white star. I am that white star. I am White Morning Star, and I have come for you. Marry me, and we shall live in the sky world."

All fear left the girl, and she gave her hand to the young man. At once, they began their journey to the sky.

When the other girl discovered that her friend was missing, she ran back to the camp. She told the girl's mother and all the people that she had no idea what had happened to her friend. "We were gathering berries and she just disappeared," she said. Then she began to weep. The people in camp could not understand what could have happened, and for a long time afterward, they waited for the girl's return.

In the meantime, the young couple reached the sky. The girl noticed how much the sky world was like the world below. There were rivers and streams, rolling hills, trees, wildflowers, animals and birds, and all manner of good roots and berries.

The Star Husband presented his new bride to his parents. His father was the Sun, and his mother was the Moon. Moon was the first to speak, saying, "We are pleased that you have come to live with us, and to have you for our daughter." Moon liked her new daughter-in-law, and wanted her to be happy. Then Moon set about teaching the young bride many special things about the sky land.

One day Moon gave her daughter-in-law a magic digging stick. "With this stick you will be sure to find many kinds of roots. Find them and always take as many as you please, but heed this warning: there is one root that you must never dig." Then Moon took the young wife to a place where many prickly bushes and thorns grew. Right in the center there was growing one green plant. "Daughter . . . do you see that turnip plant? You must never dig for that turnip. You must never pull it from where it is growing. Do you understand?" The bride said she understood, and she and Moon went on their way.

Time passed. The Star Husband and his young wife were very happy. She learned much about the sky world. Each day she went forth to gather berries and roots, and always she was careful not to dig around the forbidden plant. More time passed, and the happy couple had a fine baby boy. The sky people brought him gifts and shared their joy.

The baby grew, and the young mother continued each day to gather food, but over time she changed. Instead of avoiding the place where the turnip grew, she passed by it each day. She began having strange thoughts: "I wonder why I cannot have that turnip. Perhaps Moon is just being selfish, and does not want me to have anything that tastes so good."

Each day it was the same. She would sometimes stare at the turnip plant for long periods of time. Soon the young mother began to brood over the plant and wondered, "What kind of turnip plant can it be? What secret does it hold?"

One day, when her baby was at the age when he could sit by himself, the maid again went to the place where the plant was growing. She sat her son down, and this time, slowly and carefully, very carefully, she began to dig around the plant with her digging stick. She poked and dug until the ground was soft. Then she reached down and pulled the turnip up and out of where it was growing. Whooosh! A rush of air came from the hole. She then looked down through the hole and, to her surprise, she could see the Earth below—tall grasses, rolling hills, many buffalo—and she could see the lodges of her people.

That night when her sky family saw the turnip, they scolded her, and Moon asked, "Did you see anything unusual when you pulled the turnip from where it grew?"

The young wife answered, "Oh, nothing unusual, just the Earth, and the lodges of my people."

The Star Husband gasped. "No! You do not know what you have done! Now that you have looked again upon the Earth, you cannot stay here in the sky. You must leave at once. You must take our son and return to your people. When you reach Earth, you must not let our son touch the Earth for fourteen days. If you do, he will turn first into a little puff ball of seeds, then he will turn into a star.

He will not move through the sky, as do other stars. He will remain always in one place."

The Sun Father called one of the sky men to help the mother and child down to the Earth. The sky man took a rope made of spider webs and, tying the mother and child to one end, he slowly let them down through the turnip hole.

Now down on Earth some boys were playing, and they saw the young woman and her child coming down from the sky. Soon she was hanging above the center of camp. One of the boys recognized her and cried out, "Look! It is the girl who disappeared while she was gathering berries." All of the people in the camp ran to her. Everyone was glad to see her, especially her mother, who quickly took her daughter and grandson to her lodgings.

The young woman told her mother all about the sky world, and for the first thirteen days, everything went well. The young mother was ever so watchful over her child, careful never to let him touch the ground.

Then on the fourteenth day, the grandmother asked her daughter to fetch some water. The girl cautioned, "Mother, while I am gone, be sure to watch my son's every moment. He must not leave his bed of blankets, for he must not so much as even touch the ground." Then the girl hurried off to gather water.

The grandmother did not understand why her grandson should not touch the Earth. She watched over the child for a while, but from time to time, she looked away. Then, while her back was turned, the baby boy crawled to the edge of the blankets. Just as the grandmother turned back around, she saw the boy place one little hand upon the ground. Quickly, she swept him up and placed him back in the center of the blanket.

But it was too late. Without a sound, the baby boy crawled inside the pile of blankets that had made his bed.

The mother returned with the water and, not seeing the boy, she was filled with fear. "Where is my son?" she whispered.

"He's down inside the blankets," said the grandmother.

The mother rushed over to the bed and began pulling the blankets away, one after another. She did not find her son. All she found was a little ball of puffy white seeds. She knew what had happened. Slowly she picked up the little puff ball and placed it close to her heart.

That evening the mother went to the top of a small hill. It was the same hill where, many moons before, she had wished for a husband. She watched as, one by one, the stars came into the sky. High in the northern sky, in the place where she had pulled up the turnip, there was a new star. The young mother knew that that little star was her son. That night and all the star-filled nights from then until the day she died, the mother of the star looked into the sky and sent her love to her son.

It was in this way that the fixed star, the star-that-does-not-move, came to be. The star is still there, for the stars go on . . . and on . . .

The Dog-Rib Legend of Ithenhiela

––•–•––

"Dog-Rib" refers to the Chipewyan tribe in northern Canada who told this story to folklorist James Mackintosh Bell in 1903. At that time, the tribe had had almost no contact with white culture. One night, Bell stood watching the northern lights with members of the tribe, and after their return to the Dog-Rib encampment, one of the elders told this fabulous tale. While following the adventures of the culture hero Ithenhiela, the story explains the formation of several important landmarks, including the Canadian Rockies. Of this tale Bell writes, "It was the most beautiful of all the Dog-Rib stories," and he adds a poignant note to the end of the story: "The influx of fur-traders into the Mackenzie River region . . . within the last two years, since my return, has, I believe, very much altered the character of the Northern Indians."

––•–•––

In the great Northwest of Canada there flows one of the mightiest rivers of the earth, known to the whites as the Mackenzie, and to the Northern Indians as the Too-Cha-Tes, or Big Water. On the very border of the Arctic Circle another great river joins the Big Water from the Southwest. This river the Dog-Ribs still know as "the river that flows from the country of the Big Man."

Naba-Cha, or the Big Man, was one of the most enormous men who ever lived. His wigwam was made of three hundred skins of the largest caribou that could be killed on the vast plains far to the northward. It had taken the bark of six huge birch-trees to make the onogan from which he daily ate his meals. And it took one whole moose, or two caribou, or fifty partridges, to feed him each day. Famous indeed was Naba-Cha throughout the whole North Country, and many were the expeditions of war he had made into distant lands to the north, east, south, and west. He had traveled northward to the mouth of the Big Water to fight the Snow-Men or Eskimo, eastward across the Great Lake of Many Slaves to the country of the Yellow Knives, where he had seen the pure copper shining in the sands of mighty rivers, southward away on to the great plains to the country of the Crees, where there were so many large animals. But westward he had never ventured far, because in that direction it was said that a bigger man than Naba-Cha dwelt. Now Naba-Cha was not only big, but he was also cruel and wicked, especially to a young Wood-Cree boy whom he had brought back from the South once when on the warpath, and who had neither father nor mother nor sister nor brother to help fight. Ithenhiela, the Caribou-Footed, as the boy was called, had, however, one great friend at the wigwam of Naba-Cha. This was Hottah, the two-year-old moose, the cleverest of all the northern animals. Truly he was clever for he had traveled all the distance from the mouth of the Too-Cha-Tes to the wigwam of Naba-Cha in three days, and this was very far indeed. Now Hottah had long thought of a plan by which he might help Ithenhiela. He knew that far to the westward, much beyond where Naba-Cha had ever gone, flowed another river almost as great as Too-Cha-Tes, and that safety for a hunted man or beast lay on its farther side, because there dwelt Nesnabi, the Good Man.

One day Hottah came to Ithenhiela and said to him, "We will go away. You get a stone, a clod of earth, a piece of moss, and a branch of a tree, and we shall escape from the cruel Naba-Cha." Ithenhiela got what he was told to get, and soon they were ready to be off. Hottah took Ithenhiela upon his back, and before long they were out on the great plains which lie many days beyond the Too-Cha-Tes. Hardly had they started when they saw coming behind them Naba-Cha on his great caribou. Then said Hottah, "Fling out behind you your clod of earth." [Ithenhiela] did so, and immediately there rose up behind them, and between them and Naba-Cha, great hills of earth so wide and so high that it was many days before Naba-Cha again came in sight. And during this time Ithenhiela ate the ripened berries, while Hottah chewed the sweet grass which grew beyond the hills.

When Naba-Cha once more appeared in sight, Ithenhiela flung out behind him the piece of moss, and a great muskeg-swamp lay behind them. And for days the great man and his caribou foundered in the thick sphagnum. Meanwhile, on and on towards the country of the Setting Sun passed Hottah and Ithenhiela. And when once more Naba-Cha appeared, Ithenhiela dropped the stone, and great indeed were the high rocky hills which intervened between them and Naba-Cha. Up to the very clouds rose the hills, white with snow, and magnificent, such as had never been seen before. Long it was before the fugitives again saw Naba-Cha and the great caribou, and far had they gone towards the West before Ithenhiela had to throw the branch of the tree from him. Then arose a great and mighty forest of which the trees were so thick that Naba-Cha could not pass between them, and had to cut his way through, while the caribou was left behind because his horns had stuck in the branches, and he could not pass on. All this delay helped Ithenhiela, and when he once more saw the cruel Naba-Cha, he and his moose-friend had already crossed the Great Western River which they had tried so hard to reach. Away into the Northwest wound Tes-Yukon, through the high rocky hills to the northward, foaming as it flowed. Soon came Naba-Cha to the other side of the Tes-Yukon, and called aloud, "Help me, Hottah, across this mighty river. Help me to reach the country that lies beyond, and I shall do no harm to Ithenhiela." Then across for him went Hottah, and as he brought him back across the great Tes-Yukon, he overturned him, and down he swept through the swirling rapids of the river and was lost. This was the last of the wicked Naba-Cha.

Then came Hottah to Ithenhiela standing upon the bank, and, turning to him, he said, "Ithenhiela, I must leave you now, and return whence I came. Go you and follow this great river, and soon you will come to a great tepee. This is the home of Nesnabi, the Good Man. Great indeed is he, and far has he traveled into our country to the eastward, among the golden rivers lost in mountains to the southward; to the great water which has no ending to the westward; and to the silent plains, all snow-covered to the northward, where live the Snow-Men. He, like Naba-Cha, is big, but he is not cruel, and he harms no one. He will aid you."

Then departed Ithenhiela, and following the bends of the great Tes-Yukon through the high spruce forest, he came to the wigwam of Nesnabi, who stood silent beside his home.

"Whence have you come, young man," said he, "and where are you going!"

At this, up spoke Ithenhiela, "Great Chief, I have come from far. I have neither father nor mother nor brother nor sister. My home was with my own people away in the South Country, and there I lived happily until the coming of Naba-Cha, who took me away with him to the cruel North Country, where the snow lasts long in winter by the sweeping waters of the Too-Cha-Tes. Hard indeed was Naba-Cha to me, and many a season passed I in misery with him, until I came away with Hottah, the two-year-old moose who brought me to your country, O Great Nesnabi, and but now has he left me."

To this answered the kind Nesnabi, "Ithenhiela, I have long known that you would come to me. Stay with me as long as you like, but if at the end of the week you wish to journey away, I will then prepare you for your journey farther into the West Country."

Thus it was that Ithenhiela stayed at the wigwam of Nesnabi. But when the week was done, he came to his protector, and said to him, "I must now leave you and travel farther. Give me that preparation for my journey that you have promised me."

Then took Nesnabi seven arrows from his wigwam, and said to him, "This is enough to help you, Ithenhiela, but should you shoot at any bird or beast in a spruce-tree and the arrow stick in the branches, take you care that you go not after it, for if you do, surely something will happen to you." Hardly had Ithenhiela left the good Nesnabi, when he saw a squirrel in the branches of a red spruce-tree, and, raising his bow he shot an arrow at it. Down fell the squirrel, but the arrow lodged in the branches. At once, Ithenhiela, forgetting what Nesnabi had told him, started to climb after the arrow. As he mounted, the arrow went up, too. Up, up, they went, until at last they came to the sky, and the arrow passed through, and he after it.

Great was Ithenhiela's surprise when he entered the Sky Country. It was so different from what he had expected. He had imagined a glorious country, where the sun always shone, and where herds of musk oxen, caribou, and moose roamed at large in plenty, with many of his own people camped in large wigwams here and there. But instead, the air was damp, dreary, and cold; no trees or flowers grew; no herds of animals ran on the silent plains; the smoke of no wigwam greeted his anxious eyes; the war-whoop or hunting-cry of no Indian of his own people was heard. Only, far in the distance against the sky shimmered a great white mass, like a pile of snow, when the sun shines upon it in the early summer. Towards this great white thing ran a winding path from the very spot where Ithenhiela stood.

"I will follow it," thought he, "and see what I come to and find out what lies in that blazing wigwam over there." As he passed along, he met an old woman who said to him, "Who are you, and where are you going?"

"I have come from far," said Ithenhiela. "I am the Caribou-Footed. Can you tell me who lives over there in that big white wigwam?"

"Ah," said Capoteka, "I know you, Ithenhiela. Long have I thought you would come here. But you have done wrong; this is no country for man. In that great wigwam over there lives Hatempka, and unhappy is he because he has lost his belt of medicine, and until he gets it again, no one will be happy in the Sky Country. The belt is at the tepee of the two blind women who live far beyond the wigwam which shines so white, and no one can get it from them. Whoever finds it, and gets it from the bad blind women, will have the daughter of Hatempka, the beautiful Etanda, for his wife." Off then started Ithenhiela, and, traveling hard, soon came he to the home of the two old blind women.

As he entered the wigwam, he saw hanging upon the side the belt of Hatempka, and many indeed were the skulls which hung about it, for many had gone to seek the belt, but none had returned. The blind women bade him welcome and said to him, "When you leave, Ithenhiela, tell us so that we may bid you good-bye."

Now Ithenhiela had noticed that each of the two old women had behind her back a knife of copper, long and sharp. "Ah," thought he. "When I leave they mean to kill me." For one sat on either side of the door in readiness. "But I shall fool them."

In one part of the wigwam lay a muskamoot, a bag of bones and feathers. To this he tied a string, which he pulled over the pole above the door. Then said he, "I am going now, blind women. Remember I am old and fat, and when I leave,

I make much noise." At this he pulled the string, and towards the door passed the bag of bones and feathers.

Immediately the two old blind women stabbed, but striking only feathers, the long knives passed through them into each other and both were killed. Then took Ithenhiela the belt of medicine, and went he unto the shining white home of Hatempka and said to him, "Great chief, be you happy now, I have brought to you your healing belt. Give me now my wife, your daughter, the beautiful Etanda, that I may leave you."

Then said Hatempka, "Oh! Much pleased am I, Ithenhiela. You have saved my people. Now shall the sun shine again. Now shall musk oxen, caribou, moose, and bear live once more in our country. Again shall we see the smoke of many wigwams. Once more shall we hear the voice of many hunters. Take you now my daughter, the fair Etanda, but leave me not. Stay with me, and be a great man after me." So Ithenhiela remained at the shining white home of Hatempka.

Hence was derived the name and country of the Big Man. Still, the Indians in that distant country, when the northern lights flit across the sky, see in them the fingers of Ithenhiela, beckoning them to the home he has found for them so far away.

Man, the Burro, and the Dog

This tale from the Hispanic Southwest of the United States is a fanciful explanation for the aging process that is a natural part of human life. Hispanic tales in North America have their roots in Mexico, and ultimately in Spain. The following tale is from a collection heard in New Mexico and southern Colorado.

When God created the universe, He also created man to rule over the earth. At the same time, He decided to give man two friends. So He first made man, and then He created the burro and the dog. Then, as the three stood before him, God spoke these words to the man:

"Your name is man, and you shall rule over everything. You will have dominion over the earth, and you will live sixty years. During this time you will see good days and bad days, but there will be more good days than bad."

The poor man thought sixty years was a very short time to live as ruler of the earth, but he agreed.

Then God turned to the burro and said:

"Your name is burro, and you will be subject to the law of man. You will live thirty years, and in that time there will be good days and bad days, but the bad days will outnumber the good days."

"Oh," said the burro, "if my life is to be so hard, I don't want that many years. Take away ten of those thirty years."

The man, who was carefully watching the proceedings, spoke up:

"Those ten years, Lord, give them to me!"

So God added those ten years to man's sixty. Then He spoke to the dog and said:

"Your name will be dog, and you will be man's best friend, and you shall live according to his law. You will live twenty years, and during your lifetime you will see good days and bad days, but there will be more bad days than good."

"Oh," the dog wailed, "if my life is to be one of torment, I don't want so many years. Please take away ten."

"Lord, give those ten years to me!" begged the man.

So God added twenty years to the man's life so that man would live to be eighty.

And that is why man lives the life of a donkey from sixty to seventy, and also why he lives the life of a lowly dog from his seventieth year on!

Possum, Turtle, and the Wolves

———————

Contemporary storyteller Doug Elliott shows us how the simple desire to explain a small feature of the natural world can lead to a ripping good story. Elliott believes that the following tale, which he adapted from a Cherokee tale heard in the late nineteenth century, has African origins. It seems only logical, since there is a clear relationship between Turtle's adventure and Brer Rabbit's famous trip to the briar patch. But there is also an element here of "The Brave Little Tailor," a widely told fairy tale from Europe.

———————

Possum is sort of a slow critter, not fast like a rabbit. He just ambles along, looking for things to eat, making a living as best he can. He can climb a tree but not quickly like a squirrel. He climbs slowly and carefully as you or I might.

Possum had a friend who was even slower than he was. His name was Turtle. Bright and early one morning Possum said, "Come on, Brother Turtle, I want to take you out to my favorite tree." So he and Turtle ambled on over to a big persimmon tree. The tree was loaded with persimmons, and they looked very ripe. They were a rich orange color, and their skins were soft and wrinkly. Possum carefully tasted one of them. They didn't have any of the mouth-drying puckery taste that unripe persimmons are famous for: They were as soft and sweet as sugar plums.

Turtle said in his slow deep voice. "Well, they look pretty good, Brother Possum, but how am I gonna get some? I can't climb a tree."

"Don't worry, Brother Turtle," Possum said as he started up that tree. "I'll climb up and throw some down to you."

He got up in the tree, climbed out on a limb, and started eating some of the persimmons and tossing others down to Turtle. He'd eat one and toss one down, then he'd eat another and toss another down to Turtle. They felt like they were having a picnic.

"Keep 'em coming, Brother Possum," Turtle shouted (as well as he could with a mouth full of persimmon). "They sure are good!" Possum continued throwing them down, and the two friends were having a wonderful time of it until all of a sudden, out of the bushes came a great big wolf. Now, Possum knew he was up in the tree, where the wolf couldn't get him. Turtle knew that he could pull into his hard shell, where the wolf couldn't get him. But that wolf still ruined the picnic by standing right over Turtle and catching and eating all the persimmons that Possum was trying to throw down to Turtle. Possum threw them all around, thinking the wolf would miss some, but that wolf jumped up and caught them all before they even hit the ground. So Possum tried throwing the persimmons down very fast, one after the other, in rapid succession, but the wolf still managed to catch every one.

Possum didn't know what to do. That wolf might never leave them alone! Then he looked up higher in the tree, and there he saw a huge persimmon that was almost as big as a grapefruit. And that gave him an idea. First he started throwing down the small persimmons as fast as he could. That greedy old wolf had his jaws open wide so he could catch every one. When Wolf's jaws were flapped open as wide as they could be, Possum heaved down the giant persimmon as hard as he could, and the wolf caught it right in the throat. That persimmon stuck there, and the wolf soon keeled over dead. As Possum climbed down the tree, Turtle remarked in his slow deep voice, "That sure was good thinking, Brother Possum. I didn't think that wolf would ever leave us alone." They stood for a moment and looked at the big dead wolf. Then Turtle said, "I didn't tell you, Brother Possum, but I'm about to go on a long journey, and the one thing I need for my traveling bag is a couple of spoons. Then if somebody offers me a meal along the way, I could use the spoons to eat with, and I could also use them for ladling water out of streams when I get thirsty."

"What has that got to do with a dead wolf?" Possum asked.

Turtle replied, "I just figured out where I'm gonna get those spoons. I'm gonna cut that wolf's ears off and make wolf-ear spoons." And that's just what Turtle did. He cut those ears off, took them over to the stream, scrubbed them out, and laid them on the rocks to dry in the morning sun.

As the sun shone down, those ears dried out, and as they dried, they curled up. It wasn't long before they looked a lot like spoons.

When the ears were all dried out, Turtle tucked them into his traveling kit and started down the trail. "See you later, Brother Possum. Thanks for that delicious 'simmon breakfast." And down the trail he went, just a-walking and a-hiking and a-walking and a-hiking. And for a turtle, he traveled quite far that morning.

As the noon hour approached, he started to get hungry, but he couldn't find anything to eat. There weren't any persimmon trees, and even if there had been, his possum buddy wasn't there to climb them for him. There were no berries or worms or snails or anything else that turtles like to eat. So he just kept on a-walking and a-hiking, getting hungrier all the time.

Soon he came to a village, and as he walked by, some people came out and said, "Hey there, Turtle! It looks like you've been traveling. Do you want something to eat?" Turtle said that, indeed, he was hungry, so the people invited him into a lodge to have a bowl of hominy.

They put the hominy in front of him and said, "Now just a minute, Turtle. We'll get you a spoon, and you can have all you want." Turtle replied, "That's all right. I've got my own spoon, thanks." And he reached into his traveling bag, pulled out one of his wolf-ear spoons, and started eating that hominy. Nobody thought anything about it at first, until someone noticed what Turtle was eating with. They started whispering among themselves, "What's that turtle eating with?"

"It looks like a wolf's ear!"

"A wolf's ear! Where would a turtle get a wolf's ear?"

"Could he have killed a wolf? I didn't think a turtle could kill a wolf."

Right then, somebody came into the lodge and heard just the last part of the whispered conversation. "Killed a wolf? Who killed a wolf! That turtle kills wolves? I'm getting out of here!" Soon the rumor was spreading through the village like wildfire. "There's a wolf-killing turtle on the loose, and he's right here in our village!" Those foolish people were thrown into a panic, and they all ran to the woods, hid in the bushes, crawled into hollow logs, or climbed up in trees.

Turtle continued eating his hominy. He didn't know why everybody had disappeared so fast. When he finished, he crawled out of the lodge and looked around. There was no one in sight, so he called out, "So long, folks. I'll be on my way now. Thanks for the meal." And down the trail he went, a-walking and a-hiking and a-walking and a-hiking.

In the meantime the people came back to the village and congratulated one another for their quick escape from the dangerous wolf-killing turtle. Everybody was talking about it. Every boy told every girl, every girl told every mama, every mama told every dad, every dad told every grandpa, told every grandma, told every dog, told every cat, told every mouse, told every rat, told every frog, told every bird, told every squirrel, told every rabbit, told every fox, told every snake, told every bug, and soon the forest was buzzing with the rumor of the wolf-killing turtle. Turtle didn't know a thing about it—he just continued slowly and steadily down the trail, just a-walking and a-hiking.

He traveled along for several more hours, and the sun was beating down. He was getting very thirsty, but he couldn't find any water to drink: not a spring or a stream or even a puddle. He came to another village, and as he approached, some people came out and said, "Hey there, Turtle, it sure is hot today. Aren't you thirsty?"

"I sure am," said Turtle.

"Well, come on over. We just made some fresh sumac lemonade. It's right here in this pot. We'll get you a ladle, and you can scoop out all you want."

"Oh, that's all right," said Turtle, "I've got my own little ladle right here." And he reached into his traveling bag, pulled out one of the wolf ears, and started slurping away. Nobody thought anything of it until they noticed what Turtle was using for a ladle.

Now, we all know that turtles travel pretty slowly. However, rumors travel a whole lot faster, and would you believe that the rumor about the wolf-killing turtle had gotten to this village long before Turtle himself had arrived? Of course, everybody figured it was just a silly rumor, and nobody believed it, because how could a little turtle kill a great big wolf anyway? It just couldn't be true.

But when they saw Turtle pull out that wolf's ear, they knew that the rumor must be true, and in an instant this village too was thrown into panic and fear. Soon everybody was running to the woods, climbing up trees, hiding in the bushes, or crawling into hollow logs.

Turtle kept on slowly slurping away at the sumac drink. When he stopped and looked around, he noticed that everyone was gone. "Now, what got into them?" he said to himself. "This bunch of humans is even stranger than the people I met in that last village." He drank his fill of the tangy juice and felt very refreshed. "Thanks for the drink, folks, wherever you are," he shouted over his shoulder as he started down the trail, a-walking and a-hiking.

Before too long the people came out of hiding and started talking excitedly among themselves, and soon the rumor of the wolf-killing turtle had spread to every corner of the forest. Turtle just kept trudging slowly along. He didn't know anything about the rumors that were being spread about him. But he did notice something peculiar as he traveled. He would hear the birds singing and the squirrels and chipmunks scurrying around ahead of him on the trail, but as he got closer to them, the woods would become absolutely quiet. All the critters were hiding because they had heard about the wolf-killing turtle, and they were afraid that he might kill them too.

It made Turtle uneasy not to hear all the other animals around him as he walked, especially as he neared a thick dark place in the woods. He just kept on slowly, a-walking and a-hiking. Suddenly, out of the bushes came a whole pack of wolves, and they surrounded him. Everywhere he looked, all he could see was growling wolves and sharp teeth. He blinked and said, "Uh oh . . ."

The leader of the pack swaggered up. "All right, Turtle," he snarled. "So you're the one who's been killing our brothers!" And he reached into Turtle's traveling bag and pulled out the wolf-ear spoons. He held the ears up to the other wolves and howled in rage. "Look. Brothers, what more proof do we need? This is the wolf-killer, all right!"

"But . . . but," Turtle protested.

"No buts about it," the wolf leader rudely interrupted. "We're gonna put a stop to this wolf-killing right here and now."

"Let's build a fire," one of the wolves suggested, "and throw him in it and burn him up. What do you think of that, Turtle?"

Turtle knew what to say. "Well, you just go ahead and throw me in that fire. I wouldn't mind at all. No sir. I'd just roll around in that fire with my hard shell and put your fire right out."

The wolves muttered among themselves. "We'd better think of something worse than that." Then one of them barked, "I know—let's get a big clay pot of water. We'll put him in it, build a big fire under it, and boil him."

Turtle said, "Go ahead and try to boil me. I wouldn't mind that at all. I'd just kick around in that old pot and hit it with my hard shell, and it would crack your pot. Then the water would come out and drown your fire—and you'd have a broken pot besides."

The wolves began talking among themselves, trying their best to think of something worse, when one of them said, "I know, let's take him to the river. We'll throw him in, and he'll drown!"

Turtle thought to himself, "I wouldn't mind that. I'm a good swimmer." But he was a smart turtle, and this is what he said: "No! Don't throw me in the river. That would be the worst thing you could do! Burn me or boil me, if you must, but please, oh please, don't throw me in the river!"

Those foolish wolves said, "If that's the worst thing we can do, let's do it." And they marched Turtle straight to a river bank high up over the water. One of those wolves grabbed his front legs, and another grabbed his back legs, and they started swinging him. One, two, three! They threw him off the river bank.

Turtle sailed through the air, end over end, down toward the river until—wham! He hit a rock and splashed into the water. When he felt the cool water all around him, he knew that all he had to do was swim across the river, and he would be home free. But as soon as he began to swim his first stroke, he felt a sharp pain. "Oh, my aching back," he moaned.

He had really hurt his back when he hit that rock. In fact, he could hardly swim at all, so he ended up having to half-swim and half-limp. Slowly, slowly he made his way across the river. When he reached the other side, he found a sloping sandbar that was overhung with wild plants and bushes. He pulled himself up on the sandbar and crawled up under the bushes to rest.

His back hurt so badly that he didn't even want to look at it. But he knew he had to, and when he finally did look, he saw that his shell was all cracked and broken. He didn't know what to do. Then he noticed some of the plants that were growing around him. They were medicinal herbs: mint and willow and comfrey and even backache root. Turtle sniffed the mint, chewed the willow bark, and rubbed the comfrey and the backache root all over his sore, broken shell.

That night he sang medicine songs and prayed to the Great Spirit, and soon he was fast asleep. The next morning when he woke, he felt much better, and when he looked back over his shell, all the pieces had come back together, and the cracks had healed. And to this day you can still see the cracks in Turtle's shell.

Getting Common Sense

Anansi, the trickster-spider who was imported in folktales from West Africa during slave times, is responsible for all manner of mischief in the world. But like the trickster of Native American tribes, Anansi is sometimes also responsible for creating things humans need to survive. In this tale the spider is up to his usual tricks. When they backfire, the world gains what Anansi loses. The nonsense line at the end of the tale is a marker of the sort used by traditional tale-tellers in many cultures to indicate the end of the story.

Once upon a time, Anansi thought to himself that if he could collect all the common sense in the world and keep it for himself, then he was bound to get plenty of money and plenty of power, for everybody would have to come to him with their worries, and he would charge them a whole lot when he advised them.

Anansi started to collect up and collect up all the common sense he could find and put it all into one huge calabash. When he searched and searched and couldn't find any more common sense, Anansi decided to hide his calabash on the top of a very tall tree so that nobody else could reach it.

So Anansi tied a rope around the neck of the calabash and tied the two ends of the rope together and hung the rope around his neck so that the calabash was on his belly. He started up the tall tree, but he couldn't climb very well or very fast because the calabash kept getting in his way. He was trying and trying so hard when all of a sudden he heard a voice burst out laughing in back of him. And when he looked he saw a little boy standing on the tree's root: "What a foolish man! If you want to climb the tree front-ways, why don't you put the calabash behind you?"

Well, Anansi was so angry to hear that big piece of common sense coming out of the mouth of such a little boy after he had thought he had collected all the common sense in the world that Anansi took off the calabash, broke it into pieces, and the common sense scattered out in the breeze all over the world. Everybody got a little bit of it but no one got it all. It was Anansi who made it happen that way.

Jack Mandora, me no choose none.

Ouiot and Frog

Of all the mysteries confronting humankind, death is the most perplexing and profound. Almost every culture has accounts of the origin of death among the tales explaining the glories of the universe and the smallest details of the insect world. The following tale explains not just how death came into the world, but also the reason some animals are used for food and the divine nature of the moon. Collected from the San Luiseno tribe in California in 1906, it may seem somewhat incomplete because the missing aspects of the story would have been understood by the hearers. Yet it is a graceful story, with its own integrity and beauty.

While they were all living at Temecula, there was a man among them, Ouiot, who was very wise and who knew more than anyone living. He taught the people and watched over them and made provision for their needs. He called them all his children.

It was a custom for all the people to take a bath every morning. Among them was a beautiful woman whom Ouiot had especially admired. She had a beautiful face and long hair that fell down to her feet, completely covering her back. She always went down to the water when no one else was there and would bathe when no one could see her. Ouiot noticed this and made it a point to watch her one day. When she jumped into the water, he saw that her back was hollow and flat like that of a frog, and his admiration turned to disgust.

The woman, Frog, observed Ouiot and read his thoughts. She was filled with anger against him. When she told her people of his feelings towards her, they conspired together saying, "We will kill him." So the four of them, Frog, Earthworm, Gopher, and Water Animal, decided to destroy him by witchcraft. As soon as they had finished their witchcraft, Ouiot fell sick. He tried in vain to ease his pain. He sent north, south, east, and west for remedies, but nothing could help him. He grew so much worse that he lay helpless, unable to rise. Frog and her helpers came and jeered at him, and because he lingered so long in his illness, they gave him the name Ouiot.

Then a man, named Rattlesnake, arose and said, "What is the matter with all you people? You call yourselves witches, yet you cannot cure our sick brother." So Rattlesnake, who knew everything, searched north, south, east, and west, trying to find some way to help Ouiot, or to learn what was the matter with him. But it was all in vain. After him another man, Horned Toad, equally great, went about searching for a remedy, trying his best, but without success. Next Roadrunner stood up. He examined Ouiot and searched about among the people to see if any of them had caused his illness. But he could discover nothing. Next came Little Bird. He did the same thing. He examined Ouiot and told the people that someone had poisoned him and that he was going to die.

Ouiot was getting worse all the time, and he called his best friend, Kingbird, a great captain and a very good man, and told him that he had been poisoned and named the four who had caused it and told him why they had done it and that he was soon to die. To Kingbird alone he revealed the truth that he would return. "Look towards the east for my coming in the early morning," he said. Thus Kingbird knew the secret. Then Ouiot summoned all the rest of the people that he might give them his final commands. When all had gathered together, some of his children raised him in their arms so that he could sit up and address them. The tears began to run down his cheeks. Coyote, Bluefly, and Buzzard crowded about him, wanting to eat his body. Coyote began licking his tears. Then Ouiot said that his death might come in the first month or in the second part of the first month. But this time passed and he was still alive. "Perhaps I shall die next month or in the second part of the next month." This also passed. So he predicted his death in each successive month, only to linger through until the last. In the last month, he died, and death came into the world. No one had died before.

There was a man, Kangaroo-Rat, who made a carrying-net in which to lift Ouiot. They sent to all four points of the compass for wood, the sycamore, black oak, white oak, tule, hemlock, and cedar, in order to build the funeral fire. They got a hollow log, and on the lower half they laid the body. Then they put the other half of the log above it for a lid. After the pile of wood was ready and the fire lighted, the men carried the body in the net, and after circling the fire three times laid it on the flames.

Coyote, who wanted to eat the body, was sent away. He ran off but looking back, he saw the smoke of the burning fire rising up to the sky. So he turned and came running back with all his might. They took sticks and tried to drive him away, and they stood in a circle close together about the fire to prevent him from approaching it. But Badger was only a little man, and Coyote ran at him and jumped over his head. He snatched the heart, the only part of the body that was not consumed by the flames, and ran off with it, devouring it.

There was a man among them named Little Squirrel, and when Ouiot was burned he stood up and addressed the people. He called the clouds from the mountains to come, and the clouds and fog from the sea to gather, and to fall in showers upon the earth to blot out all tracks that Ouiot had made when he moved upon the world. He asked that none be left. So the clouds came, and it rained heavily.

Ouiot had told them that in time to come they must have fiestas for the dead and that they must begin to kill and eat for food. Until this time they had never eaten flesh or grains, but had lived on clay. They discussed the matter, questioning who should be killed first. One man after another was chosen, but each refused in turn.

Ouiot had said that Eagle must be killed at the time of every fiesta, and Eagle did not like this. To escape, he went north, south, east, and west. But there was death for him everywhere, and he came back and gave himself up. Hummingbird said that he would like to take Eagle's place. He felt that he was a person of importance. But the people said, "No! You are a little man, not fit for that." And they would not let him.

Ouiot had also said they could eat Deer. They talked about killing Deer. "He is a nice-looking man. He would be good for meat." Lion was a strong, powerful man, and he said, "Why do you delay and discuss? This is the way it should be done." So he fell on Deer and killed him, and the others that had been selected to be animals were killed at the same time. They turned into different kinds of animals and different kinds of grain, and all the things we see now in the world.

When they killed Deer, they took the small pointed bones of the leg to use as awls for making baskets. A fine basket was made, and the bones and ashes of Ouiot were placed in it. They buried the basket in the ground. While they were burying it, they sang solemn words with groans and they danced. This was the first time there had been singing or dancing for the dead. Rabbit was the man who sang first, and Crow and Wild Goose danced first.

After the fiesta was over, they had a big meeting at Temecula, where they were still together. They had found out that death had come into the world and they didn't know what to do. They discussed the matter. All those that are now stars went up into the sky at this time, hoping to escape death in this manner. And all things that live in the ground, worms, insects, and burrowing animals, went underground to hide from death. But others decided to stay on earth. They figured that it might be possible to live for a certain number of years and then to go back and be young again. Then they all left Temecula and scattered all over, just as it is today. Now that Ouiot was gone there was no use staying in their first home. They no longer had a guide and teacher there.

No one knew that Ouiot was to come back, except Kingbird. Early in the morning he would go to the housetop and call out, "Ouiot is coming back."

"What does he say?" the people wondered. They did not understand, until Ouiot rose as the moon in the east. They saw the moon rise, and they knew it was Ouiot. It was the first time the moon had ever come, but it has risen ever since.

2

Tall Tales, Brags, and Other Lies

Americans didn't invent the tall tale, but they certainly have embraced the concept and improved on it. The ability to produce "lies" at will, to make the most outrageous story appear true, is still considered high art in North America. But what makes a tale "tall" is not just that the facts are exaggerated. The key is the teller's ability to exaggerate with a straight face. Some "liars" will pepper any conversation with one-liners beginning, "That reminds me of the time . . ." Others will begin long yarns based on one exaggeration, then add to it every other lie they can think of. Then there are those who have whoppers on the tips of their tongues all the time. I once asked my friend Don McCleod whether his new woodstove was any good at drawing air. He didn't miss a beat before he said, "It draws very well. Sucked the cat right up the chimney the first day we had it." It seemed perfectly effortless, and he never smiled.

Tall-tale telling flourished after the opening of the frontier, when early settlers sent back tales of fantastic plants, superhuman creatures, and astonishing feats of strength by ordinary men and women. Such stories entered the popular imagination, providing fertile ground for yarn-spinners and glib "liars." Most rural communities harbored a local "character" known to be "downright windy," or "a real wit," who was highly respected and popular at parties. Greenhorns heading West, or blundering into any isolated part of America, were at the mercy of the local wit, and new tall tales evolved just to describe the gullibility of outsiders.

Tall tales are widely dispersed throughout North America. They were originally passed by word of mouth along railroad lines and stagecoach trails and told as though the unbelievable had occurred at the last stop down the line. Newspapers on the American frontier entertained readers with pages of outrageous lies, which further spread the tales. As time went on tall tales became a part of the national literature, Mark Twain being only one among many writers who used them as a jumping-off point for their work. Today, many a storyteller and stand-up comedian stakes his or her fame on the audience's willingness to be roped in by a yarn.

How to Tell a Story

––•––

Not just anyone can spin a yarn, for the successful tall tale depends entirely on the teller's ability to think of something utterly outrageous and "tell it for the truth." To help make this principle clear, Mark Twain obliges us with instructions.

––•––

I do not claim that I can tell a story as it ought to be told. I only claim to know how a story ought to be told, for I have been almost daily in the company of the most expert storytellers for many years.

There are several kinds of stories, but only one difficult kind—the humorous. I will talk mainly about that one. The humorous story is American, the comic story is English, the witty story is French. The humorous story depends for its effect upon the manner of the telling; the comic story and the witty story upon the matter.

The humorous story may be spun out to great length, and may wander around as much as it pleases, and arrive nowhere in particular; but the comic and witty stories must be brief and end with a point. The humorous story bubbles gently along; the others burst.

The humorous story is strictly a work of art—high and delicate art—and only an artist can tell it, but no art is necessary in telling the comic and the witty story; anybody can do it. The art of telling a humorous story—understand, I mean by word of mouth, not print—was created in America, and has remained at home.

The humorous story is told gravely; the teller does his best to conceal the fact that he even dimly suspects that there is anything funny about it; but the teller of the comic story tells you beforehand that it is one of the funniest things he has ever heard, then tells it with eager delight, and is the first person to laugh when he gets through. And sometimes, if he has had good success, he is so glad and happy that he will repeat the "nub" of it and glance around from face to face, collecting applause, and then repeat it again. It is a pathetic thing to see.

Very often, of course, the rambling and disjointed humorous story finishes with a nub, point, snapper, or whatever you like to call it. Then the listener must be alert, for in many cases the teller will divert attention from that nub by dropping it in a carefully casual and indifferent way, with the pretence that he does not know it is a nub.

Artemus Ward used that trick a good deal; then when the belated audience presently caught the joke he would look up with innocent surprise, as if wondering what they had found to laugh at. Dan Setchell used it before him. Nye and Riley and others use it today.

But the teller of the comic story does not slur the nub; he shouts it at you—every time. And when he prints it, in England, France, Germany, and Italy, he italicizes it, puts some whooping exclamation points after it, and sometimes explains it in a parenthesis. All of which is very depressing, and makes one want to renounce joking and lead a better life.

Let me set down an instance of the comic method, using an anecdote which has been popular all over the world for twelve or fifteen hundred years. The teller tells it in this way:

The Wounded Soldier

In the course of a certain battle a soldier whose leg had been shot off appealed to another soldier who was hurrying by to carry him to the rear, informing him at the same time of the loss which he had sustained; whereupon the generous son of Mars, shouldering the unfortunate, proceeded to carry out his desire. The bullets and cannon-balls were flying in all directions, and presently one of the latter took the wounded man's head off—without, however, his deliverer being aware of it. In no long time he was hailed by an officer, who said:

"Where are you going with that carcass?"

"To the rear, sir—he's lost his leg!"

"His leg, forsooth?" responded the astonished officer; "you mean his head, you booby."

Whereupon the soldier dispossessed himself of his burden, and stood looking down upon it in great perplexity. At length he said:

"It is true, sir, just as you have said." Then after a pause he added, *"But he TOLD me IT WAS HIS LEG!!!!!"*

Here the narrator bursts into explosion after explosion of thunderous horse-laughter, repeating that nub from time to time through his gaspings and shriekings and suffocatings.

It takes only a minute and a half to tell that in its comic-story form; and it isn't worth the telling, after all. Put into the humorous-story form it takes ten minutes, and is about the funniest thing I have ever listened to—as James Whitcomb Riley tells it.

He tells it in the character of a dull-witted old farmer who has just heard it for the first time, thinks it is unspeakably funny, and is trying to repeat it to a neighbor. But he can't remember it; so he gets all mixed up and wanders helplessly round and round, putting in tedious details that don't belong in the tale and only retard it; taking them out conscientiously and putting in others that are just as useless; making minor mistakes now and then and stopping to correct them and explain how he came to make them; remembering things which he forgot to put in in their proper place and going back to put them in there; stopping his narrative a good while in order to try to recall the name of the soldier that was hurt, and finally remembering that the soldier's name was not mentioned, and remarking placidly that the name is of no real importance, anyway—better, of course, if one knew it, but not essential, after all—and so on, and so on, and so on.

The teller is innocent and happy and pleased with himself, and has to stop every little while to hold himself in and keep from laughing outright; and does hold in, but his body quakes in a jelly-like way with interior chuckles; and at the end of the ten minutes the audience have laughed until they are exhausted, and the tears are running down their faces.

The simplicity and innocence and sincerity and unconsciousness of the old farmer are perfectly simulated, and the result is a performance which is thoroughly charming and delicious. This is art—and fine and beautiful, and only a master can compass it; but a machine could tell the other story.

To string incongruities and absurdities together in a wandering and sometimes purposeless way, and seem innocently unaware that they are absurdities, is the basis of the American art, if my position is correct. Another feature is the slurring of the point. A third is the dropping of a studied remark apparently without knowing it, as if one were thinking aloud. The fourth and last is the pause.

Artemus Ward dealt in numbers three and four a good deal. He would begin to tell with great animation something which he seemed to think was wonderful; then lose confidence, and after an apparently absentminded pause add an incongruous remark in a soliloquizing way; and that was the remark intended to explode the mine—and it did.

For instance, he would say eagerly, excitedly, "I once knew a man in New Zealand who hadn't a tooth in his head"—here his animation would die out; a silent, reflective pause would follow, then he would say dreamily, and as if to himself, "and yet that man could beat a drum better than any man I ever saw."

Ab Yancey's Squirrel-Hunt

Stories of "The Marvelous Hunt" abound throughout North America. In some, the miraculous events are added to the exploits of well-known characters such as Davy Crockett. In this whopper, though, the teller wants his hearers to believe that he is the one who had the great day out.

"Wal, gentlemen, when I was a young-un powder an' ball was high an' hard t' git, so we allus had t' make ever' shot count. I recollect one time I was a-tryin' t' git two red squirrels lined up so's I could kill both of 'em with one bullet. Thar was four of 'em a-runnin' 'round in a chinkapin tree, an' I reckon I must have sot thar twenty minutes afore I got 'em set to suit me. When I pulled trigger I seen both of 'em fall, but jest then I heerd turkeys a-yoikin', an' it warn't but a lee-tle ways off I seen seven hens an' a gobbler a-settin' in a tree. Seems like that 'ar bullet done skittered over thar some way, an' split the limb they was a-settin' on, an' ketched their feet in th' crack.

"Wal, sir, I clumb up t' git them turkeys an' wring their necks afore they could bust loose on me, but just as I was a-comin' down I lost my holt an' fell slap-dab into a bresh-pile. Thar I was a-scramblin' an' a-rollin', an' afore I could git out I'd smothered a hull gang o' quails an' two big swamp-rabbits! I jest tied them eight turkeys an' them forty-one quails an' them two swamp-rabbits all t'gether with pawpaw bark, an' back I went a-packin' 'em t' whar my squirrels was at. One o' them squirrels had fell in th' creek, so I waded in atter him. Hit was deeper'n I figgered on, an' th' water was kinder riled up an' dingy like. . . . When I got out on th' bank ag'in, danged if my pockets an' boot-tops wasn't jest chuck full o' fish—mostly perch an' goggle-eye!

"Whilst I was a-stringin' them fish I retch back t' scratch a chigger bite, an' my ol' shirt was too dang-tight anyhow, so one o' th' buttons popped off'n it. I seen th' dang thing go a-whistlin' off into a bunch o' hazel bresh, an' I aimed for t'

hunt it up soon as I got my fish strung t' suit me. D'rectly I heered a turrible scufflin' round an' gaspin' an' gurglin' in them bresh, so I drapped th' fish an' snuck over whar I could peek in. Thar was a big buck a-rollin' round, an' he was a-dyin', too, but danged if I could see what kilt him. Hit kinder skeerd me. But I just cut his throat anyhow, t' let him bleed right good, an' thar was my ol' button stuck in his wind-pipe! He must of opened up his mouth for t' belch, I reckon, an' that 'ar button jest flipped in thar an' shut his wind plumb off! Hit shore was th' biggest one-bullet huntin' I ever done, seen, or hearn tell of. . . . Thar was one deer, eight turkeys, two swamp-rabbits, forty-one quails an' maybe fifty pounds o' fish, an' Pappy shore was proud when he seen me draggin' of it all home.

"Hit was a sad day at our place, though, on account of Uncle Hen. Uncle Hen was a purty good feller, but he didn't have no sense, an whut did he do but up an' call me a liar when I was a-tellin' how I got that 'ar buck. 'Liar' allus was a fightin' word in th' Yancey family, so I just naturally had t' kill him. Pap hisself said he couldn't make out t' blame me none, but it shore did gravel him t' see his own brother a-layin' thar all butchered up an' gutted that-a-way. . . . I done it with my ol' huntin'-knife, gentlemen,—same one you-uns see a-stickin' out o' my boot-top right now!"

Tall Hunting Tale

Few subjects in rural America inspire more lying than hunting does. Here is another hunting tale, told in the first person, with an outcome similar to the previous tale, but with a very different beginning.

Once upon a time I bought me a dog. I give three bushel of dried apples for him—sold the dried apples and then bought the dog. Well, the feller I bought him from said he would tree coons. So I took him a coon huntin'. He begin barkin' about ten o'clock, out on a high knob. We went up to see what the dogs was barkin' about. I looked up on a cliff about thirty feet high. The dog was lookin' up the cliff. I looked up in a tree and about ten feet above the last limb a coon was stickin', a coon on a little knot. I asked him if he couldn't climb up and catch it. And he nodded his head. So he backed off about thirty yards and clim' up on another cliff about forty feet high. I asked if he could jump from one cliff to the other, and he nodded his head. He backed off about four hundred yards. He started to jump. And he got out about halfway and saw he wa'n't aimin' to make it, so he turned around and come back.

Well, I thought it was smart of him, you see. He went ahead and I shot the coon and it rolled off the cliff. I picked it up and we took on off to the house. We got down to the creek, and my brother was with me. We started across the creek on the swingin' bridge and I dropped my flask of carbide down in the water, river about twenty feet deep. I told him I'd go down and get my carbide, if he'd wait for me, and he said, "No," said, "you've had a cold. I'll go down and get it," said, "it'd make you sick."

He dived down and was gone about thirty minutes. And I dived down to see what he was doing. He was settin' there on a log, stealin' my carbide, takin' it out of my flask, pourin' it in his'n. I asked him what he was doin', and he said, "Nothing, I just needed a little carbide and I was takin' it out of your flask—I seed you had plenty of it."

Well, my dog, see, I was gone about thirty minutes and my dog he got worried. So he come down to see what I was a-doin'. He run around to the end of this log where we was settin' and he begin barkin'. I looked in and saw an old boar hogfish and a gang of little shoats. I nodded my head and he went in after 'em. He shook his head. He couldn't make it. I kindled me up a far at the other end and I smoked them out. I smoked and smoked and smoked. About thirty minutes here they come. And the water run out of their eyes, I'd smoked 'em so much. My brother said, "How did you kindle a far?"

I said, "I jerked a few slabs off the log we was settin' on and struck me a match, and that's all there was to it."

Well, we caught the fish and come on up to the top. I had a rifle-gun, had one round of ammunition. I looked out in front of me and there laid a rattlesnake about twelve feet long. Well, I started to shoot it and about that time I heard a noise down the river. I looked and there was 5,000 wild ducks comin' up the river. Well, I didn't know which to shoot, the ducks or the rattlesnake. About the time I started to shoot the ducks I heard another noise up the river and I looked and there was 5,000 wild geese. Well, I shore didn't know what to do then. I knowed I couldn't kill the geese and the ducks, all, and the snake. So I said to myself, "I'll kill the snake and try to catch a goose as she passes." I pulled the trigger. The barrel busted. Half of it went down the river and killed 5,000 wild ducks. The other half went up the river and killed 4,999 wild geese. The gun flew all to pieces. I didn't have nothing left but the stock.

I gathered up all my ducks, killed the snake, gathered up all my geese and started across the swingin' bridge. I looked over in the corner and saw my gun locks, stickin' there on a rail, had that other goose hemmed. I walked over and picked her up and wrung her neck. Well, I had all them geese and ducks and started across that bridge, and the bridge broke with me. Down I went twenty feet deep in the water. I swimmed, I kicked, and I paddled, and when I finally got to the bank and got out I had 300 pound of fish in my hip boots. And I went on to the house and told my wife I thought I had purty good luck. And that was all of it.

The Dog Who Could Walk on Water

If hunting brings out the liar in men, competition to have the best hunting dog brings out the braggart. The following Cajun tale from Louisiana was told by Revon Reed not about himself, but about two people he claims to know. Note that the winner in this competition is the man with the wittiest remark, not the one with the miraculous dog.

You know, the typical Cajun is a terrible liar, and naturally likes to brag. And it's natural, in a way. Let's say you have a good hunting dog. Mine will always be a little better. I don't care how good your dog is. And there's a little story that I tell like that about two old guys who were always arguing about dogs and ducks. One always had a better dog than the other.

One day, one [named Olide] struck oil on his property and became a millionaire. He decided that he would travel around the world to find a dog better than Pascal's [his neighbor's] dog. And he finally found a dog which had been trained to walk on water, a retriever, but it didn't swim; it walked. It ran so fast that its feet just barely touched the water. So he bought the dog. He paid ten thousand dollars for it. Just to prove to Pascal that he had a better dog than him.

So when he came home, he said to Pascal (he told him nothing about the dog), "I found myself a dog, so," he said, "wouldn't you like to go duck hunting tomorrow!"

"Oh yeah!" he said. "You have a dog!"

"Yeah."

"He's not nearly as good as mine, eh!"

He said, "We'll see."

So they went hunting. Pascal shot first. A duck fell on the water. His dog quickly started swimming. It went to get the duck. It came back tired.

Olide said, "Look here! Watch what my dog can do!" Another duck. He shot. Fell on the water. The dog jumped out of the boat and started running on the water.

• 59 •

Pascal watched this. The other one watched, too, to see if this would impress him. So it came back, it brought the duck back. It was hardly wet.

He said, "What do you think of my dog now!"

"Well," he said, "I don't see that it's one bit better than mine." He said, "All I can say is that it can't even swim." He said, "I don't see where it's such a good dog!"

Old Gawge and the Ninety and Nine

Hunters affectionately gave names and personalities to their guns and made claims about them to rival the lies they told about their dogs. The punch line of the following whopper, told around New England, is a favorite among the nation's best liars.

Old Gawge took a heroic draft of lemonade. "Ah-h-h!"—he smacked his lips. "I ain't had a drink like that since the Spring my brother John come offa the drive an' fell over the cow-yard fence." Then he settled down to business:

"Wal, sir," he said, "they wan't nary shotgun in the back country whar I was riz. My fambly was addicted to the old Winchester 44-40, which were, an' still is, a great gun fer deer an' b'ar. But when it come to ducks, I fixed me up a scattermaran that had the old 44-40 skun forty ways fer Sunday. She was a old Revolutionary War flintlock musket with the bar'l sawed off half way betwixt the muzzle an' britch. My load was a handful or so of powder, paper waddin', an' as many rocks, dried beans, nails, and sech like as I could cram into her.

"Course, she wouldn't allus fire when you pulled the trigger, 'specially if the weather happened to be a mite damp, but when she did go off—gracious Peter! It took the rest of the forenoon fer to tote the ducks home!

"Wal, sir, this partic'lar mornin' I'm a-tellin' you about, I riz long before the sun, did the most of my chores, loaded up ol' Betsy Ann, an' traipsed down to the lake an' rowed out to a island while 'twas still dark. 'Twas early in the Fall an' they was consid'rable of a mist, which put me to some trouble fer to keep my powder dry.

"Without makin' no more noise than a weasel in a chicken coop, I pulled the boat up on shore an' crep' across that island to a leedle small cove on t'other side, whar the ducks held their lodge meetin's.

"Gosh all hemlock you should of see the sight which met my eyes! The sun was jest beginnin' fer to rise, an' that thar cove was fuller of ducks than a Grange hall on a strawberry festervule night! They was young ones, old ones, big ones, leedle ones an' meedjum-sized ones: all colors, shapes an' descriptions!

'Jeepers!' thinks I, 'I'm goin' to need help luggin' them ducks home, sure as leedle green apples'll give you the tummy-ache!'

"Cautious as a tomcat at a dog show, I creeps a leedle closter, kneels down, pours a leedle powder in the pan, an' aims right spang into the middle of them ducks. Then I braces myself, closes my eyes, and pulls the trigger.

"Nawthin happens.

"I wait a leedle while an' nawthin still happens, so I opens my eyes an' takes a peek at Betsy. The powder in the primin' pan ain't went off. I snaps the flint a couple times an' she sparks all right, but it seems like that ain't enough fer to set the powder off 'cause she's mebby a leedle mite damp.

"But this don't bother me a mite. I aims ol' Betsy again an' scratches a match an' holds it onto the pan. Z-z-z! The primin' percolates fine an' dandy this time, but it don't set off the charge. So I fills up the pan an' tries again. I kept tryin' till my primin' powder was all gone, but 'twas no use."

Here Old Gawge favored me with a meaning look: "But I didn't git on the rampage an' begin cussin' an' threatenin' like some folks I knows on. Nossir, I had too much sense fer that, even if I was leedle more than a boy. I jest riz onto my feet an' quietly went back to my boat and started to row fer home.

"Wal, sir, I hadn't got more'n a few rods offa that island when I hears a sizzlin' noise. I looks down at my feet an' thar is ol' Betsy Ann jest a-smokin' an' a-frothin' at the mouth, a-rarin' to go! The sun had riz by now an' out on the open water it had been hot enough fer to dry that powder charge out.

"Judas Priest! Now I want to tell you, mister, the way I turned that boat round and rowed fer that island again was a caution! I knew ol' Betsy was a-goin' to speak her piece right plumb sudden, an' I wanted to git her aimed at them ducks afore she started talkin'.

"I beached the boat an' run across that island to the cove so fast, the trees looked like a card of matches, an' all the time ol' Betsy Ann was a-splutterin' away like as if she couldn't hold in no longer.

"Wal, sir, to make a long story short, I jest did manage to git back to that thar cove an' draw a bead when 'Boom!' ol' Betsy Ann let a roar out of her an' a peck of rocks, dried beans, nails, and lead-foil from tea packages scattered in amongst them ducks, while I went rump-over-tea kittle in the opposite direction, on account of not havin' a chancet to git set fer ol' Betsy's kick.

"Purty soon I got myself picked up, found they was no bones busted, an' begin a-countin' of them ducks. I counted ontil my fingers was all used up an' then begun a-countin' on my toes ontil they was all used up too, when I begun all over ag'in."

Suddenly Old Gawge halted and poked a club-like finger into my chest. "I'll bet you couldn't guess how many ducks I got with that one shot if'n you was to go to Tophet fer it," he said.

"One cripple scared to death by the noise and another paralyzed just by seeing your face," I replied, just a bit sarcastically.

Old Gawge sniffed disdainfully and turned to Paxton. "S'pose yea guess," he invited.

Paxton thought a moment. He takes games very seriously, Paxton does. Once he won first prize of a fifty-cent cigar lighter in a charades contest. "Seven?" he asked hesitatingly.

Old Gawge spat disgustedly. "Nossir!" he snorted. "They was ninety an' nine ducks layin' dead in that cove when the smoke rolled away!"

Paxton and I stared open-mouthed for sixty seconds. Then I reached for and downed a liberal libation. A lemon seed choked me and it was several more seconds before I could recover my breath. "Why," I inquired of Old Gawge when I could talk again, "why didn't you call it a hundred?"

The old sinner assumed an expression of injured dignity. "I said ninety an' nine 'cause that's jest prezactly how many I counted," he said firmly. "Do you think fer one minute that I would up an' make a liar out of myself jest fer one measily duck?"

Uncle Swain

———

Swain Lupton was a classic local "character" of a type that has all but died out in North America. Admired and prized among men for his wit and strength, he was good-naturedly scorned by women who hated to see him coming, they said, because when he got around, the men quit working and sat out under the tree swapping yarns. Uncle Swain lived in the eastern-most region of North Carolina, where the barrier islands known as the Outer Banks begin. He died in 1910, so I never met him, but I spoke at length to his nephew Worth Harris, who narrated his deeds.

———

Oh, he was a character. And there was no amount to what he could eat. Had legs as big around as nail kegs.

One afternoon in particular he went to my house and my mother said to him said, "Uncle Swain, have you had any supper?"

"Ah . . . Nah . . . Ain't struck none."

Well she went to work. She'd already cooked for the rest of us. So she went to work and it was a devil lot of trouble, cause she cooked on one of them woodstoves. Went to work fixing up his supper.

The following day she went over to the neighbor's. She said, "Well I had Uncle Swain for supper last night." Neighbor said, "YOU had him for supper. Well we did, too." And one of the ladies who lived right close to the dock where the boat stopped said, "My God, did he eat to your house. He ate to my house, too."

That was three suppers he ate that one evening.

Yeah, he went to hollering, "Ah . . . Ah . . . Ain't struck none!"

My God! Tales like the day he'd be going somewhere . . . used canoes around then, dugouts. Said he tied his canoe to what he thought was a stake and turned out to be flounder's eyes. Just such tales as that. Somebody'd tell about seeing a big flounder—eighteen or so pounds—and he'd come up and tell that one. So big, he tied the skiff to his eyes. And pretty soon the flounder started to submerge and just about sunk his boat.

Another one he used to tell, said he was going deer hunting one time. And his wife's named Margaret. Says, "Marg—have I got any shot left?" "No, got no shot left, Swain." Says, "Ah . . . What am I going to do? I'll load her down with these peach pods." So he said he soaked her down with peach pods. So said he went in the woods. It wasn't long he said one of his dogs run a real big buck right by. He blazed away right into his side. He said he didn't kill him though.

Disappointed him to death. And went and told Marg, "Well I missed my first deer." Anyhow he said that the following year he went back to the same woods again and saw this peach tree in bloom. It was moving round through the bushes! "Well," he said, "I'm getting old. I'm seeing things. I gotta get out." Said when he got a little closer look—it was that deer he'd shot—that deer he'd shot with those peach kernels. He said a tree was growing out of his side that was IN BLOOM!

Said there was an uncle of his [of Swain's] shooting loons in the fall. Yeah, loons going south. They'd go on the Outer Banks and shoot loons. And Swain said there was Uncle so-and-so would always get to shoot the first one that came by. Said he and another boy went and found this uncle's gun—unbeknownst to him—poured out the shot and rammed it down with feathers. Said they went on and started waiting. Waited, and by and by he said they saw one a-coming.

Said, "Uncle so-and-so, SEE A LOON COMING BY. YOU GET READY NOW!" Old man put the gun up like this here. WHOOM! And did the whole world turn to feathers up there. Said the old man looked at the loon he thought he'd hit but was still flying and said, "Old fellow, it is a good thing you're going South. Because as many feathers I shot out of you, you'll freeze to death this winter!"

To tell you the truth, there's nobody comparable to him. Nobody even close who tells stuff like that. He went up until he died. He was on his death bed. He didn't have but one grandson. Called him—said, "Robert, come 'ere. Something I want to tell you."

Said, "Grandfather, what is it?"

Said, "I'm leaving you a fortune."

The boy, he thought he was leaving something valuable of course. He began to get excited and asked him what it was.

"Ah . . . Ah . . . I'm leaving you the whole world to make a living in."

Just such nonsense as that.

The Trained Trout

Among American tall-tale tellers, the characters who inhabit the area of Maine known as "Down East" are far and away the best known for keeping a straight face while "sawing off a whopper." This story is so movingly told, it is hard not to be roped in.

The sage of Beaver Camp sat sunning himself on the bench beside the cook camp, the bench so widely known as the scene of countless weary hours of that perpetual toiler. He seemed to be smoking an old black pipe, whereas he was only dropping matches into its empty bowl at intervals of three minutes, agreeable to the terms of his contract with the American Match trust.

As he so sat and pondered, the writer, at the time a recent arrival, approached and said: "Mr. Grant, I wish you would give me the true history of your wonderful success in taming a trout. I have heard of it in all parts of the world but I have always longed to hear the story direct from headquarters."

"Well, it really ain't so much of a story," replied the famous chronicler. "It was this way. Nine year ago the eleventh day of last June, I was fishin' out there in the pads, and right under that third yaller leaf to the right of the channel—yes, that one with the rip in it—I ketched a trout 'bout six inches long. I never see a more intelligent lookin' little feller—high forehead, smooth face, round, dimpled chin, and a most uncommon bright, sparkling, knowin' eye.

"I always allowed that with patience and cunning a real young trout (when they gets to a heft of 10 or 15 pounds there ain't no teachin' them nothin') could be tamed jest like a dog or cat.

"There was a little water in the boat and he swims around in it all right till I goes ashore and then I gets a tub we had, made of the half of a pork barrel, fills it with water and bores a little small hole through the side close down to the bottom and stops the hole with a peg.

"I sets this tub away back in a dark corner of the camp and every night after the little fellow gets asleep I slip in, in my stockin' feet, and pulls out the peg softly and lets out jest a little mite of the water. I does this night after night so mighty sly that the little chap never suspected nothin' and he was a-livin' hale and hearty for three weeks on the bottom of that tub as dry as a cook stove, and then I knowed he was fit for trainin'.

"So I took him out o' doors and let him wiggle awhile on the path and soon got to feedin' him out of my hand. Pretty soon after that when I walked somewhat slow (I'm naturally quite a slow walker some folks think) he could follow me right good all round the clearin', but sometimes his fins did get ketched up in the brush jest a mite and I had to go back and swamp out a little trail for him; bein' a trout, of course he could easy follow a spotted line.

"Well, as time went on, he got to follerin' me most everywhere and hardly ever lost sight of me, and me and him was great friends, sure enough.

"Near about sundown one evening, I went out to the spring back of the camp, same one as you cross goin' to Little Island, to get some butter out of a pail, and, of course, he comes trottin' along behind. There was no wind that night, I remember, and I could hear his poor little fins a-raspin' on the chips where we'd been gettin' out splits in the cedar swamp. Well, sir, he follered me close up and came out onto the logs across the brook and jest as I was a-stoopin' down over the pail I heard a kee-plunk! behind me and Gorry! if he hadn't slipped through a chink between them logs and was drowned before my very eyes before I could reach him, so he was." Here a tear started from the good old man's eye on a very dusty trip down his time-stained cheek.

"Of course I was terrible cut up at first—I couldn't do a stroke of work for three weeks—but I got to thinkin' that as it was comin' on cold (it was in late November then) and snow would soon be here and he, poor little cuss, wasn't rugged enough for snowshoein' and he couldn't foller me afoot all winter no how, and as he couldn't live without me, mebby it was jest as well after all he was took off that way. Do you know, Mister, some folks around here don't believe a word of this, but if you'll come down to the spring with me, right now, I'll show you the very identical chink he dropped through that night, so I will. I've never allowed anyone to move it. No, sir! nor I never will."

Here the old man dropped match number thirty-seven into his pipe and sucked at it hard in silence, while I crept softly away on tiptoes. I never could bring myself to speak of it again, after seeing him so deeply moved—I never could.

A Trip to the Moon

Tall tales make the best entertainment for children, and skillful tellers keep stories handy so that when questions come up such as, "What is the moon made of?" the answer is at the ready. The proof of the moon's famous composition is given here by Mrs. Casto (Elizabeth) Wallace of Sparta, Tennessee.

—·+·—

When I was a child I'd always heard, you know, that the moon was made of cheese; so I decided I'd see. There was a large mountain close to where we lived and I could see the moon as it would come up at night. It just come right over that mountain, and I thought I could just reach right over and touch it. And I'd heard people say that you could. So I decided that I'd go to that mountain and see.

Well, I started out walkin'; packed me a little lunch, you know, and put it on a stick across my shoulder. I walked and I walked, and oh, I got so tard. And I come to a pasture, and there was an old gray mar' grazin' thar in the field. So I had a rope in my pocket that I could tie to a tree so that when I jumped off on the moon, if I didn't land thar it would hold me, you know, and I wouldn't fall and kill myself. Well, I put that on the old gray mar' and made me a halter out of it.

I got up on her and went to ridin', and not far from the foot of this mountain, why, her back broke in two. I got off and I cut me a hickory limb and stuck it each way in her back and shoved it up her backbone and that fixed 'er up, you know. And I got back up on her and I rode to the foot of this mountain.

And I started up the mountain, and when I got almost to the top I saw a b'ar a-comin'; and Lawd, you can't imagine how fast I finished a-goin' up that mountain! But just as I got to the edge of this bluff, why, that b'ar was right thar behind me. And I grabbed hold of its tail and turned that b'ar wrong side out. And that b'ar went back down that mountain just a-laughin' itself to death, because all that fur was ticklin' it on the inside.

And about that time, why, here come the moon. And it was close enough that I tied my rope to the tree, you know, and as it came by I jumped off on it and

I got up on thar. And in a little bit, why, I thought how far that I was from it [the bluff]. And it was a little farther the next night, and the next night; so I knew that, well, maybe I couldn't never get back on that rock anymore.

And I soused [plunged] my fingers down in the moon, and found out it was really cheese. And it was just full of skippers—like cheese skippers [insects], you know, that gets in old cheese—it was so old. Well, those skippers, they were larger than any huge rats we have here. I set about skinnin' those skippers, and I skinned, and skinned, and skinned. And then I tied those skippers together until I made a rope long enough that I skinnied down it, and come back to Earth!

The Snake-Bit Hoe Handle

This time-honored tall tale has been adapted by contemporary storyteller Doc McConnell, who grew up in Tennessee "listening to stories in his family's cabin home and around the potbellied stove at John Mauk's General Store." It is one of the many fantastic stories settlers told to exaggerate the size and scope of the American land and the creatures who inhabited it.

When I was growin' up, it seemed like all I ever done was hoe corn. I'd hoe corn from mornin' to night. One day, I was out in the field a-hoein' corn and, as I was lookin' outa the corner of one eye, there in that corn patch was a great big ol' copperheaded rattlesnake. You'd never seen such a snake in your life. He rared back at me, and I rared back at him with my hoe.

I took a swing at that ol' snake, missed 'im, and hit a rock and broke the hoe outa the end of my hoe handle. That ol' rattlesnake sunk them teeth into the grain of that hoe handle and held on for dear life. Down through the cornfield we went. I would shake him awhile, and he would shake me awhile. We got clear down to the end of the corn patch before I finally shook that ol' snake offa the end of my hoe handle.

I ran to the house, throwed that ol' hoe handle down at the garden fence, and said, "Pa, you won't believe what's happened to me out there in the cornfield. I jist seen the biggest snake up there on that ridge as you've ever seen. He bit my hoe handle, and I hit a rock and broke my hoe offa the end of my hoe handle, and I ain't a-goin' back into that cornfield no more."

Pa said, "Son, I know what you're a-tryin' to do. You're jist tryin' to git outa hoein' corn. You jist go out there and git that hoe handle and bring it to me and I'll put you a new hoe on the end of that handle."

Well, I went out to the garden fence and started to pick up that hoe handle, and you ain't a-goin' to believe this. Where that snake's poison had soaked into the grain of the wood of that ol' hoe handle, it had done started swellin' up. It commenced to swellin' and swellin' and swellin' from the poison until that hoe handle was as big 'round as a baseball bat—and ten feet long. I couldn't believe it.

So, I took that ol' hoe handle to show Pa and he said, "Why, we'll jist have to make some kindlin' wood outa that hoe handle. Run out and git the axe."

By the time I got back, the hoe handle had kept a-swellin' and a-swellin' and a-swellin' so that it was as big 'round as a water bucket.

Pa said, "We'll jist have to saw that ol' hoe handle up for firewood. Git the crosscut saw."

So I went over to the woodshed to git the saw, and by the time I got back, that hoe handle was as big as a wagon wheel—and over seventy-two feet long.

"Why," Pa said, "there ain't nothin' to do now but to take that hoe handle down there to the sawmill and have it sawed up for lumber."

It was so big now that we could barely git it in our wagon. And as that ol' team of mules pulled that log to the mill, that hoe handle drug a big trench right down the middle of the road.

Well, they sawed all day Friday and 'til dinner on Saturday. And when they was done, they had sawed 746,362 board feet of lumber from that ol' hoe handle. It jist kept on a-swellin' and a-swellin', and by the time we got that lumber stacked up, we had twenty-two wagonloads of lumber. We hauled that lumber home, and Pa sat out there and looked at that pile of lumber and thought and thought.

Finally on Monday mornin', he said, "You boys git outa bed. We're a-goin' to build a chicken house."

Well, we commenced to sawin' and hammerin' them boards, and when we was done, we had one of the finest chicken houses in Tucker's Knob. It was a purty structure—twenty-two foot long, seventeen foot deep, and nine foot high in the front. We had boxes for layin', and little poles for roostin'. It was a nice-lookin' building.

And as we were standin' back admirin' our new chicken house that afternoon, Pa said, "Son, that chicken house needs one thing before we've completed our job. We need to put a good coat of paint on our new chicken house. Run and git us some paint."

So I went down to John Mauk's store and bought five gallons of the purtiest striped paint that you've ever seen. We commenced to paintin' that chicken house, and we painted way up into the evenin' 'til it was jist gittin' dusky dark. And when we finished, we stood back to admire our work, and all of a sudden, we heard this creakin' and moanin' and groanin' and that chicken house commenced to shakin' and movin' 'round.

You see, I had mixed some turpentine in that paint, and that turpentine that I'd used to thin the paint was such good medicine that it started takin' the swellin' outa that lumber. And that chicken house went to shrinkin' and shrinkin' and shrinkin'. And when it got done shrinkin', it wasn't no bigger than a shoe box. And it's a good thing we hadn't put our chickens in it, 'cause they'd ever' one been killed, I know.

Uncle Billy Hallock's Yarn

In every region of the continent people make it a point of pride to claim the largest, fiercest, most determined mosquitoes. This story was recorded at the turn of the century on Long Island. Uncle Billy Hallock would go to any lengths to prove that mosquitoes "in those days" were much bigger than "in these days."

A generation ago, when the box tree post office was in use here, travelers were wont to while away an hour between stages by listening to Uncle Billy Hallock. One of his stories ran this way:

"No, there ain't no 'skeeters here now; there used to be 'skeeters, but arter we got tu puttin' 'em on the farm for manure we used 'em all up. One summer I was kinder short of manure for turnips and I hitched up the ox cart, loaded up the old flintlock and druv down tu the beach. When I got thar I backed the cart under a beach plum bush—beach plum bushes used to grow taller than they du now—and fired the old flintlock. Talk about skeeters; I jest slaughtered 'em; the cart was full and I had tu shovel 'em away from the wheels before them blamed oxen could start the load.

"I druv hum and spread the dead 'skeeters onter the turnip patch and then I made tu more trips tu the beach and got tu more load of the 'skeeters, and put 'em on the patch. Well, I sowed the seed and yu could see them turnips grow if yu'd been thar. I use't watch 'em grow, an' I seen 'em grow an inch a minute by the watch. By the first of September they was six feet high an' still growin'.

"One dark, foggy night long toward the last of September my oxen got out of the yard an' I couldn't find 'em. I didn't think of huntin' for 'em in them turnips, but I spent a week huntin' for 'em on Quogue plains.

"I druv up tu Moriches and got Captain Smith tu lend me his deer hounds tu hunt with and blamed if them hounds didn't find them oxen in them turnips an' run 'em all day long without ever driven' the oxen out. The turnips was so high that I couldn't see the oxen and only knew they was in thar by the barkin' of the dogs.

"That night there cum on a reg'lur old-fashioned southeaster. It was one of the hardest blows I ever see—I think like a'nough yu've heard uv it—we used to call it the September gale. Well, that gale blowed every darn leaf off of them turnips and the next day I started them hounds again. Well, I could jist see the top of them darned oxens horns over the top of them turnips and made out to find 'em then.

"How big was the turnips, did you ask? Well, I couldn't measure them because they was bigger than my bushel corn basket and I had tu cut 'em up in the patch before I could handle 'em. No we don't have no 'skeeters to 'mount to nothin' nowadays."

I Wish I Could Tell a Lie

Like mosquitoes and other creatures, the weather in America has always provided a rich body of lore for use in tall tales. Seafarers, of course, had bragging rights when it came to knowing what bad weather meant, and they became famous for their ability to exaggerate "a little."

This rhyming tale was reportedly told by a sea captain in Newport, Rhode Island.

I stood one day by a breezy bay
A watchin' the ships sail by,
When a tired tar said—with a shake of his head
"I wish I could tell a lie.

I've seed some sights that would jigger your lights
And have jiggered me own—in sooth,
But I ain't worth a darn at spinnin' a yarn
That wanders away from the Truth.

We was off on the brig—the Rig—A Gig,
A mile and a half to sea,
When Captain Snook with a troubled look
He comes and he says to me—

'Hey! Bos'n Smith, make haste forthwith
An' hemstitch the for'ard sail;
Accordion pleat the dory sheet
For there's goin' to be a gale.'

I straightway did as the Captain bid
And no sooner the job was thru,
Than a North wind—Whoof! bounded over the roof,
An' sufferin' lights she blew!

She blowed the tars clean off the spars,
The spars clean off the mast,
While anchors 'n sails, 'n pails 'n nails
Went by on the wings of the blast.

And before we could look—she blowed the cook
Straight out o' the galley bin,
While pots 'n pans and kettles 'n cans
Went rattlin' after him.

She blowed the fire from the galley stove,
The coal from the galley bin,
Then she whizzed a pace past the Captain's face
An' blowed the beard off his chin.

'Now whizzle me dead,' the Captain said
An' the words blowed out of his mouth
'We're lost I fear, if the wind don't veer
An' blow a while from the South!'

An' whizzle me dead—no sooner he said
Them words that blowed from his mouth,
Then the wind veered 'round with a hurricane sound
And blowed straight in from the South.

An' we opened our eyes with wild surprise
With never a word to say,
For in changing her tack, the wind blowed back
The things that she'd blowed away.

She blowed the tars back onto the spars,
The spars back onto the mast
Back came the sails, an' the pails an' the nails
That into the ship stuck fast.

An' before we could look—she blowed the cook
Back into the galley coop;
Back came the pans an' the kettles an' cans,
Without even spillin' the soup.

She blowed the fire back into the stove
Where it burned in its proper place,
An' we all of us cheered as she blowed the beard
Back onto the Captain's face.

There's more of my tale—said the Mariner hale,
That would jigger your lights in sooth,
But I ain't worth a darn at spinnin' a yarn
That wanders away from the Truth."

Remarks Made at the Hatchet Club

"Liars' clubs" became popular during the nineteenth century, where people sat by the hour swapping tall tales, brags, and generally trying to outdo one another in exaggerating the truth. These liars' bench gatherings took tall-tale telling out of the country store and turned it into a more formal type of public entertainment.

"Talking about hard blows out west," said Mr. Lewis, of the Detroit Free Press, at a meeting of the Hatchet Club, "talking about heavy winds, why I saw a man out in Michigan sitting quietly on his doorstep eating a piece of pie. Suddenly, before he could get into the house, the wind struck him. The gale first blew the house down, and then seized the man, carried him through the air a hundred yards or so, and landed him in peach-tree. Soon afterward a friendly board from his own house came floating by. This he seized and placed over his head to protect himself from the raging blast, and—finished his pie." (Sensation.)

"That was a windy day for Michigan, I presume," said Mr. Wm. Nye, of Laramie, "but that would not compare with one of our Laramie zephyrs. Why, gentlemen, out in Laramie, during one of our ordinary gales, I've seen boulders big as pumpkins flying through the air. Once, when the wind was blowing grave-stones around, and ripping water-pipes out of the ground, an old Chinaman with spectacles on his nose was observed in the eastern part of the town seated on a knoll, calmly flying his kite—an iron shutter with a log-chain for a tail." (Hear, Hear!)

"That was quite windy," said a Boston man, who had just returned from Nevada. "We had some wind out there. One day as I was passing a hotel in Virginia City, the cap blew from one of the chimneys. It was a circular piece of sheetiron, painted black, slightly convex, and the four supports were like legs. The wind carried it down street, and it went straddling along like a living thing."

"Well, what was it?" asked a member.

"Why, it turned out to be a bed bug from the hotel, and, by George! I never saw anything like it," then he added, "outside of Boston." (Sensation.)

"You have seen some strong winds, gentlemen," observed Eli Perkins, "but I have seen some frisky zephyrs myself, and, as tonight is the 22d of February, the birthday of the patron saint of the Hatchet Club, I will tell you about them.

"Once, out in Kansas, they told me the wind blew a cook-stove eighty miles, and came back the next day and got the griddles. (Wonder and applause.)

"A reporter of the Kansas City paper was standing out in the street looking at the stove as it floated away, when the wind caught him in the mouth, and turned him completely wrong side out. (Sensation.)

"In Topeka," continued Mr. Perkins, "post holes were ripped out of the ground and carried twenty miles (hear, hear), and careless citizens who ventured out were blown right up against brick walls and flattened out as thin as wafers (Sensation, and a voice, 'that's too thin'). Yes, thousands of citizens," continued Eli, "'were thus frescoed onto the dead walls of Topeka. The next day after the wind subsided, Deacon Thompson went around with a spade and peeled off a wagon load of citizens, and—"

"What did he do with them?" gasped the members of the Club.

"Why, gentlemen, if I remember rightly, he shipped them to Texas and sold them for circus posters and liver pads."

"Arise and sing!"

Frontier Brags

———— ✦ ————

Bragging began as the spontaneous eruption of the overripe, Wild West ego in the saloons and on the streets of frontier towns. A peculiar form of American tall-tale telling, brags eventually became a form of entertainment and were "performed" at liars' clubs and other venues. In the first example below, notice the reference to "grinning the bark off a tree." It is the braggart's challenge to the famed Davy Crockett who makes political hay from the same claim in Chapter 3.

————

BILLY EARTHQUAKE

As we were passing by the court-house, a real "screamer from the Nob," about six feet four in height, commenced the following tirade: "This is me, and no mistake! Billy Earthquake, Esq., commonly called Little Billy, all the way from No'th Fork of Muddy Run! I'm a small specimen, as you see, a remote circumstance, a mere yearling; but cuss me if I ain't of the true imported breed, and I can whip any man in this section of the country. Whoop! won't nobody come out and fight me? Come out, some of you, and die decently, for I'm spileing for a fight, I hain't had one for more than a week, and if you don't come out I'm flyblowed before sundown, to a certingty. So come up to taw!

"Maybe you don't know who Little Billy is? I'll tell you. I'm a poor man, it's a fact, and smell like a wet dog; but I can't be run over. I'm the identical individual that grinned a whole menagerie out of countenance, and made the ribbed nose baboon hang down his head and blush. W-h-o-o-p! I'm the chap that towed the Broad-horn up Salt River, where the snags were so thick that the fish couldn't swim without rubbing their scales off!—fact, and if any one denies it, just let 'em make their will! Cock-a-doodle-doo!

"Maybe you never heard of the time the horse kicked me, and put both his hips out of jint—if it ain't true, cut me up for catfish bait! W-h-o-o-p! I'm the

very infant that refused its milk before its eyes were open, and called out for a bottle of old Rye! W-h-o-o-p! I'm that little Cupid!

"Talk about grinning the bark off a tree!—'tain't nothing; one squint of
mine at a bull's heel would blister it. O, I'm one of your toughest sort,—live for
ever, and then turn to a white oak post. I'm the ginewine article, a real double acting engine, and I can out-run, out-jump, out-swim, chaw more tobacco and spit
less, and drink more whiskey and keep soberer than any man in these localities. If
that don't make 'em fight . . . nothing will. I wish I may be kiln-dried and split up
into wooden shoe-pegs, if I believe there's a chap among 'em that's got courage
enough to collar a hen!"

THE PURPLE BLOSSOM OF GINGHAM MOUNTAIN

"Let all the sons of men b'ar witness!" sings this gent, as he goes skatin'
stiff-laig about in a ring like I relates, arms bent, an' back arched; "let all the sons
of men b'ar witness; an' speshully let a cowerin' varmint, named Sam Enright, size
me up an' shudder. I'm the maker of deserts an' the wall-eyed harbinger of desolation! I'm kin to rattlesnakes on my mother's side; I'm king of all the eagles an'
full brother to the b'ars! I'm the bloo-eyed lynx of Whisky Crossin', an' I weighs
four thousand pounds. I'm a he-steamboat; I've put a crimp in a cat-a-mount with
nothin' but my livin' hands! I broke a full-grown allagator across my knee, tore
him asunder an' showered his shrinkin' fragments over a full section of land! I
hugged a cinnamon b'ar to death, an' made a grizzly plead for mercy! Who'll come
gouge with me? Who'll come bite with me? Who'll come put his knuckles in my
back? I'm Weasel-eye, the dead shot; I'm the blood-drinkin', skelp-t'arin', knife-
plyin' demon of Sunflower Creek! The flash of my glance will deaden whiteoak,
an' my screech in anger will back the panther plumb oft his natif heath! I'm a slay-
er an' a slaughterer, an' I cooks an' eats my dead! I can wade the Cumberland without wettin' myse'f, an' I drinks outen the spring without touchin' the ground! I'm
a swinge-cat; but I warns you not to be misled by my looks! I'm a flyin' bison, an'

deevastation rides upon my breath! Whoop! whoop! whoopee! I'm the Purple Blossom of Gingham Mountain, an' where is that son of thunder who'll try an' nip me in the bud! Whoop! whoopee! I'm yere to fight or drink with any sport; ary one or both! Whoopee! Where is the stately stag to stamp his hoof or rap his antlers to my proclamations! Where is that boundin' buck! Whoopee! whoop! whoop!"

California

—·—·—

As statehood came to the Western Territories, so did state pride. Since inventing whoppers had already grown into a national sport, the practice lent itself perfectly to yarn-spinners who went back east and were called upon to describe the state in which they lived.

—·—

The wear and tear of this covered-wagon life on the plains discourages many, although (who can doubt it?) we are journeying to a land unexcelled in all the world—even if there isn't a single nugget of gold within its boundary lines! This is illustrated by the yarn of a man who had lived in California, until he had reached the interesting age of 250 years. In most countries a man that old would be pretty feeble and decrepit, but not in California—Oh no! In fact such were the exhilarating, life-giving, and youth-preserving qualities of that climate that our hero at 250 was in the perfect enjoyment of his health and every faculty of mind and body. But he had become tired of life. The perpetual responsibility of managing a large fortune made him long for a new state of existence, unencumbered with this world's cares, passions, and strifes. Yet, notwithstanding his desire—for which he daily and hourly prayed to his Maker—health and vigor typical of residents of California clung persistently to him. He could not shake them off. At times he contemplated suicide; but the holy padres (to whom he confessed his thoughts) admonished him that that was damnation; being a devout Christian, he would not disobey their injunction. A lay friend, however, no doubt the heir to his estate, with whom he daily consulted on this subject, at last advised him to a course which, he thought, would produce the desired result. It was to make his will and then travel into a foreign country. This suggestion was pleasing to our California patriarch in search of death, and he immediately adopted it. He visited a foreign land; and very soon, in accordance with his plan and his wishes, he fell sick and died. In his last will and testament, however, he required his heir and executor, upon pain of disinheritance, to transport his remains to his own beloved country and there entomb them. This requisition was faithfully complied with.

His body was interred with much be-candled pomp and ceremony in his own California, and prayers were duly rehearsed in all the churches for the rest of his soul. He was happy, it was supposed, in Heaven, where, for a long series of years, he had prayed to be; and his heir was happy that he was there. But who can safely mock Providence? Being brought back and interred in Californian soil, with the health-breathing, youth-preserving, Californian zephyrs rustling over his grave, the energies of life were immediately restored to his inanimate corpse! Herculean strength was imparted to his frame and, bursting the prison-walls of death, he appeared before his chapfallen heir reinvested with all the vigor and beauty of early manhood! He submitted to his fate with Christian resignation and determined bravely to live his appointed time.

3

Legendary Heroes
and Heroines

Folk heroes are made, not born. That is, the measure of a hero's fame is not necessarily what he has done, but how many stories and songs have been generated about him among the people. Take the case of such well-known heroes in North American folklore as Annie Oakley and Casey Jones. Though they possessed remarkable skill and talent in their chosen fields, they actually led rather ordinary lives—she as a performer and he as a railroad engineer. But the body of lore that surrounds their memories has made them legends. Others, such as Davy Crockett and Johnny Appleseed, certainly led extraordinary lives. But even so, their exploits might have died with them had not people kept on inventing tales and ballads about them long after they passed away.

The question of what makes a hero becomes a thorny one when we consider how many stories and songs have been created about people who would otherwise live in infamy—real criminals like Stackalee and Belle Starr who became legends thanks to the folk process. When a master tale-teller takes the core of a story about a real human being and adds to it all manner of exaggeration, then the person, who may in fact have been only remarkable, becomes a hero. So while the following tales are usually based in truth, they are heroic folktales by virtue of the fertile imagination of the North American people.

Annie Oakley Makes Her Name

———•—•———

Annie Oakley was born in 1860 in Ohio, and by the age of six she was using a rifle to hunt for food. At the age of twenty-five she joined Buffalo Bill's Wild West Show and traveled throughout the United States and Europe demonstrating her uncanny talent as a markswoman. Thrilling tales of her exploits with the rifle vary in the details, as proper folktales always do. In some stories about Annie's contest with her future husband, Frank Butler, the element of mystery about her gender is missing. This story, though, is much more entertaining than those.

———•—•———

Late in the afternoon on a day in spring of the year 1865 the manager of the Gibson House [in Cincinnati, Ohio] waited impatiently as Jesse Jago tossed the lines, sheathed his rifle and began his impressive descent from the Martin and Chenowith stage. The ritual over, he approached the driver.

"Jesse," he said, "is that A. Oakley still up in Greenville?"

"Yep," Jesse said. "Be sendin' more quail any day now, from what I hear."

"Never mind about the quail, can you get him up here?"

"What for?" Jesse asked.

In answer, the manager produced a four-sheet poster announcing in circus-style letters the appearance of, "FRANK BUTLER, WORLD'S CHAMPION RIFLE SHOT."

"Ever hear of this fellow?" the manager asked, gesturing to the poster.

"Reckon I have," Jesse said.

"You know he has a standing offer of a hundred dollars to anybody who can outshoot him?"

"Has he now?" Jesse said, stroking his chin.

"That's right. And what's more I've already bet him another hundred dollars that I know a fella who can beat him. Word's all over town. Everybody's betting on that Oakley fella. Can you get him to come up?"

"What sort of a match?"

"Rifle. Best out of a hundred."

"I'll fetch A. Oakley, providin' one thing—the match goes on regardless of Oakley's age or size or looks."

"I don't care what he looks like. He can shoot, that's all we care about."

"Oakley'll be here Saturday."

Never was there such a crowd on hand to greet the Greenville stage as there was that Saturday. Quail shot through the head had been the talk of Cincinnati for months. Word of it had passed up and down the river and now it seemed that everyone was at the Gibson House for the coming out of A. Oakley.

No one waited for Jesse Jago's ceremonious descent. Eager hands pulled open the coach door. There were two passengers, an alert, athletic-looking man and a young woman. Quickly the male passenger was hoisted to several pairs of broad shoulders. Necks were craned and excitement ran high as the crowd closed in. It was some time before the protesting stage passenger could explain that there'd been some mistake. He was Oliver Toth, correspondent for *Leslie's Weekley*, and what was going on anyhow?

The lithe, willowy girl who had also come in on the stage approached the center of excitement. A plaid skirt hung nearly to her ankles. A sunbonnet framed her finely chiseled face. There were tiny crow's feet alongside a pair of extraordinarily bright hazel eyes. The young lady addressed the man who was making the most commotion.

"I beg your pardon," she said, "I reckon I'm the one you're lookin' for. My name's Annie Oakley."

A roar of protest went up from the crowd. The quick-thinkers rushed to cover their bets, the others surged around the manager of the Gibson House demanding that the match be called off.

Jesse Jago came up then, and for once he had forgotten to sheathe his rifle. He handled it casually, almost carelessly. The hubbub died.

Jesse spoke softly, as he always did.

"One of the conditions of this match was that it goes on exactly as scheduled, no matter what A. Oakley looked like."

There was a sharp protest but it died quickly as Jesse made a particularly careless gesture with his rifle.

"Get your gun, Annie," he said.

The rest of the story is still told on winter nights when men are fondly cleaning their favorite rifles. The little girl from backwoods Ohio fired shoulder to shoulder with the world's champion rifle shot, scoring hit for hit. On the last round, the one hundredth, Frank Butler missed. Annie Oakley never missed.

Davy Crockett

―――・・―――

Having grown up with little formal education in the backwoods of Tennessee, Davy Crockett became interested in politics in the early part of the nineteenth century. He served as a state legislator, and then as a U.S. congressman before he was killed at the Alamo in 1836. His exaggerated eccentricity led to many tales being generated about him. But, in fact, Crockett was a self-made legend since he was responsible for making up most of the stories about his outlandish deeds. It has been difficult to decide whether he should be included here among our heroes and heroines, or among the rogues' gallery of liars in Chapter 2. But there can be no question of his authenticity. He is as much a hero for his ability to entertain as for his courage.

―――・―――

GRINNING THE BARK OFF A TREE

American politicians have used the fine art of braggadocio in stump speeches almost from the beginning of the nation. No one, however, has ever done it better than Davy Crockett.

That Colonel Crockett could avail himself, in electioneering, of the advantages which well applied satire ensures, the following anecdote will sufficiently prove:

In the canvass of the Congressional election of 18—, Mr. ***** was the Colonel's opponent—a gentleman of the most pleasing and conciliating manners—who seldom addressed a person or a company without wearing upon his countenance a peculiarly good humoured smile. The colonel, to counteract the influence of this winning attribute, thus alluded to it in a stump speech:

"Yes, gentlemen, he may get some votes by *grinning*, for he can *outgrin me*—and you know I ain't slow—and to prove to you that I am not, I will tell you an anecdote. . . . You all know I love hunting. Well, I discovered a long time ago that a 'coon couldn't stand my grin. I could bring one tumbling down from the highest tree. I never wasted powder and lead, when I wanted one of the creatures. Well, as I was walking out one night, a few hundred yards from my house, looking carelessly about me, I saw a 'coon planted upon one of the highest limbs of an old tree. The night was very *moony* and clear, and old Ratler was with me; but Ratler won't bark at a 'coon—he's a queer dog in that way. So, I thought I'd bring the lark down in the usual way, *by a grin*. I set myself—and, after grinning at the 'coon a reasonable time, found that he didn't come down. I wondered what was the reason—and I took another steady grin at him. Still he was *there*. It made me a little mad; so I felt round and got an old limb about five feet long, and, planting one end upon the ground, I placed my chin upon the other, and took a *rest*. I then grinned my best for about five minutes; but the cursed 'coon hung on. So, finding I could not bring him down by grinning, I determined to have him—for I thought he must be a droll chap. I went over to the house, got my axe, returned to the tree, saw the 'coon still there, and began to cut away. Down it come, and I ran forward; but d—n the 'coon was there to be seen. I found that what I had taken for one was a large knot upon the branch of the tree and, upon looking at it closely, I saw that *I had grinned all the bark off, and left the knot perfectly smooth.*

"Now, fellow-citizens," continued the Colonel, "you must be convinced that, in the *grinning line*, I myself am not slow—yet, when I look upon my opponent's countenance, I must admit that he is my superior. You must all admit it. Therefore, be wide awake—look sharp—and do not let him grin you out of your votes."

The Colonel Swallows a Thunderbolt

Davy Crockett was capable of playing the back woods rube to the hilt. The following tale, though, shows that behind the act he was a sophisticated humorist, as well.

Thar ar a grate menny kinds of larning. I found it out when I went to Kongress. That ar your mattymatticks, your jommytrees, your sighentifficks, and your axletrissity. I nose nothin about the other wons, but the axletressity is a screamer. Thar war a feller in Washington that put the thunder and litening into glass bottles, and when a feller had the roomatiz, or the Saint Vitals dance, he would put the axletressity into his corpse jist like pouring whiskey into a powder horn, and it cured him as clean as a barked tree. So I seed how 'twas done; and intarmined whenever ennything aled me to try it, only I didn't keer about the bottles, for I thort I could jist as well take the litening in the raw state as it cum from the clouds. I had been used to drink out of the Massissippy without a cup, and so I could take the litening without the bottles and whirligigs that belongs to an axletressityfying masheen. It fell out that sum two yeers arter I had ben to see this axletrissity, I got a leetle in love with a pesky smart gal in our cleering, and I knowed it war not rite, seeing I war a married man. So I combobbolated on the subject and at last I resisted that I would explunctificate my passions by axletrissity, so it must be done by bringing it rite on the hart and driving the love out of it. So I went out into the forrest one arternoon when thar war a pestiferous thunder gust, I opened my mouth, so that the axletressity might run down and hit my hart, to cure it of love. I stood so for an hour, and then I seed a thunderbolt a cummin, and I dodged my mouth rite under it, and plump it went into my throte. My eyes! It war as if seven buffaloes war kicking in my bowels. My hart spun round amongst my insides like a grindstone going by steem, but the litening went clean through me, and tore the trowsers cleen off as it cum out. I had a sore gizzard for two weeks arterward, and my inwards war so hot that I use to eat raw vittals for a month arterward, and it would be cooked before it got farely down my throte. I have never felt love since.

David Crockett Meets a Bear

Sometimes Davy Crockett told the truth, and sometimes he didn't. This story, unlike the previous tales, has the ring of authenticity about it and is one of the stories that helped make his reputation for bravery.

In the morning I left my son at the camp, and we started on towards the harricane [a stretch of timber felled by a hurricane]; and when we had went about a mile, we started a very large bear, but we got along mighty slow on account of the cracks in the earth occasioned by the earthquakes. We, however, made out to keep in hearing of the dogs for about three miles, and then we come to the harricane. Here we had to quit our horses, as old Nick himself couldn't have got through it without sneaking it along in the form that he put on to make a fool of our old grandmother Eve. By this time several of my dogs had got tired and come back; but we went ahead on foot for some little time in the harricane, when we met a bear coming straight to us, and not more than twenty or thirty yards off. I started my tired dogs after him, and McDaniel pursued them, and I went on to where my other dogs were. I had seen the track of the bear they were after, and I knowed he was a screamer. I followed on to about the middle of the harricane, but my dogs pursued him so close, that they made him climb an old stump about twenty feet high. I got in shooting distance of him and fired, but I was all over in such a flutter from fatigue and running, that I couldn't hold steady; but, however, I broke his shoulder, and he fell. I run up and loaded my gun as quick as possible, and shot him again and killed him. When I went to take out my knife to butcher him, I found I had lost it in coming through the harricane. The vines and briers was so thick that I would sometimes have to get down and crawl like a varment to get through it all; and a vine had, as I supposed, caught in the handle and pulled it out. While I was standing and studying what to do, my friend came to me. He had followed my trail through the harricane, and had found my knife, which was mighty good news to me; as a hunter hates the worst in the world to lose a good dog, or any part of his hunting tools. I now left McDaniel to butcher the bear, and I went after our horses, and brought them as near as the nature of case would allow. I then took our bags, and went back to where he was; and when we had skin'd the bear, we fleeced off the fat and carried it to our horses at several loads. We then packed it up on our horses, and had a heavy pack of it on each one. We now started and went on till about sunset, when I concluded we must be near our camp; so I hollered and my son answered me, and we moved on in the direction to the camp. We had gone but a little way when I heard my dogs make a warm start again; and I jumped down from my horse and gave him up to my friend, and told him I would follow them. He went on to the camp, and I went ahead after my dogs with all my might for a considerable distance, till at last night came on. The woods were very rough and hilly, and all covered over with cane.

I now was compel'd to move on more slowly; and was frequently falling over logs, and into the cracks made by the earthquakes, so that I was very much afraid I would break my gun. However I went on about three miles, when I came to a good big creek, which I waded. It was very cold, and the creek was about knee deep; but I felt no great inconvenience from it just then, as I was all over wet with sweat from running, and I felt hot enough. After I got over the creek and out of the cane, which was very thick on all our creeks, I listened for my dogs. I found they had either treed or brought the bear to a stop, as they continued barking in the same place. I pushed on as near in the direction to the noise as I could, till I found the hill was too steep for me to climb, and so I backed and went down the creek some distance till I came to a hollow, and then took up that, till I come to a place where I could climb up the hill. It was mighty dark, and was difficult to see my way or any thing else. When I got up the hill, I found I had passed the dogs; and so I turned and went to them. I found, when I got there, they had treed the bear in a large forked poplar, and it was setting in the fork.

I could see the lump, but not plain enough to shoot with any certainty, as there was no moonlight; and so I set in to hunting for some dry brush to make me a light; but I could find none, though I could find that the ground was torn mightily to pieces by the cracks.

At last I thought I could shoot by guess, and kill him; so I pointed as near the lump as I could, and fired away. But the bear didn't come; he only clomb up higher, and got out on a limb, which helped me to see him better. I now loaded up again and fired, but this time he didn't move at all. I commenced loading for a third fire, but the first thing I knowed the bear was down among my dogs and they were fighting all around me. I had my big butcher in my belt, and I had a pair of dressed buckskin breeches on. So I took out my knife, and stood, determined, if he should get hold of me, to defend myself in the best way I could. I stood there for some time, and could now and then see a white dog I had, but the rest of them, and the bear, which were very dark coloured, I couldn't see at all, it was so miserable dark. They still fought around me, and sometimes within three feet of me; but at last, the bear got down into one of the cracks, that the earthquake had made in the ground, about four feet deep, and I could tell the biting end of him by the hollering of my dogs. So I took my gun and pushed the muzzle of it about, till I thought I had it against the main part of his body, and fired; but it happened to be only the fleshy part of his foreleg. With this, he jumped out of the crack, and he and the dogs had another hard fight around me, as before. At last, however, they forced him back into the crack again, as he was when I had shot.

I had laid down my gun in the dark, and I now began to hunt for it; and, while hunting, I got hold of a pole, and I concluded I would punch him awhile with that. I did so, and when I would punch him, the dogs would jump in on him, when he would bite them badly, and they would jump out again. I concluded, as he would take punching so patiently, it might be that he would lie still enough for me to get down in the crack, and feel slowly along till I would find the right place to give him a dig with my butcher. So I got down, and my dogs got in before him and kept his head toward them, till I got along easily up to him; and placing my hand on his rump, felt for his shoulder, just behind which I intended to stick him. I made a lounge with my long knife, and fortunately stuck him right through the heart; at which he just sank down, and I crawled out in a hurry. In a little time my dogs all come out too, and seemed satisfied, which was the way they always had of telling me that they had finished him.

I suffered very much that night with cold, as my leather breeches, and everything else I had on, was wet and frozen. But I managed to get my bear out of this crack after several hard trials, and so I butchered him, and laid down to try to sleep. But my fire was very bad, and I couldn't find anything that would burn well to make it any better; and I concluded I should freeze, if I didn't warm myself in some way by exercise. So I got up, and hollered a while, and then I would just jump up and down with all my might, and throw myself into all sorts of motions. But all this wouldn't do; for my blood was now getting cold, and the chills coming all over me. I was so tired, too, that I could hardly walk; but I thought I would do the best I could to save my life, and then, if I died, nobody would be to blame. So I went to a tree about two feet through, and not a limb on it for thirty feet, and I would climb up it to the limbs, and then lock my arms together around it, and slide down to the bottom again. This would make the insides of my legs and arms feel mighty warm and good. I continued this till daylight in the morning, and how often I clomb up my tree and slid down I don't know, but I reckon at least a hundred times.

Mike Fink Meets David Crockett

Mike Fink gained fame as a keelboatman on the Mississippi River. He was known for his great strength and also for his outrageous behavior and speech. Whether or not there ever was such a meeting between the two legendary figures is anyone's guess.

"I expect, stranger," said Davy, "you think old Davy Crockett war never beat at the long rifle; but he war, though. I expect that there's no man so strong but what he will find some one stronger.

"If you haven't heerd tell of one Mike Fink, I'll tell you something about him, for he war a helliferocious fellow, and made an almighty fine shot. Mike was a boatman on the Mississip', but he had a little cabin on the head of the Cumberland, and a horrid handsome wife, that loved him the wickedest that ever you see.

"Mike only worked enough to find his wife in rags, and himself in powder and lead and whiskey, and the rest of the time he spent in knocking over b'ar and turkeys, and bouncing deer, and sometimes drawing a lead on an Injun. So one night I fell in with him in the woods, where him and his wife shook down a blanket for me in his wigwam.

"In the morning says Mike to me, 'I've got the handsomest wife, and the fastest horse, and the sharpest shooting iron in all Kentuck, and if any man dare doubt it, I'll be in his hair quicker than hell could scorch a feather.'

"This put my dander up, and sez I, 'I've nothing to say agin your wife, Mike, for it can't be denied she's a shocking handsome woman, and Mrs. Crockett's in Tennessee, and I've got no horses. Mike, I don't exactly like to tell you you lie about what you say about your rifle, but I'm damned if you speak the truth, and I'll prove it. Do you see that are cat sitting on the top rail of your potato patch, about a hundred fifty yards off? If she hears agin, I'll be shot if it shan't be without ears!'

"So I blazed away, and I'll bet you a horse, the ball cut off both the old tom cat's ears close to his head, and shaved the hair clean off the skull, as slick as if'd done it with a razor, and the critter never stirred, nor knew he'd lost his ears till he tried to scratch 'em.

" 'Talk about your rifle after that, Mike!' sez I.

" 'Do you see that are sow off furder than the end of the world,' set Mike, 'with a litter of pigs around her?' And he lets fly.

"The old sow gave a grunt, but never stirred in her tracks, and Mike falls to loading and firing for dear life, till he hadn't left one of them are pigs enough tail to make a toothpick on.

" 'Now' sez he, 'Colonel Crockett, I'll be pretticularly obleedged to you if you'll put them are pigs' tails on again,' set he.

" 'That's onpossible, Mike,' sez I, 'but you've left one of 'em about an inch to steer by, and if that had a-been my work, I wouldn't have done it so wasteful. I'll mend your shot.' And I lets fly, and cuts off the apology he's left the poor cretur for decency. I wish I may drink the whole Mississip', without a drop of the rale stuff in it, if you wouldn't have thort the tail had been drove in with a hammer.

"That made Mike kinder sorter wrothy, and he sends a ball after his wife as she was going to the spring after a gourd full of water, and knocked half her comb out of her head, without stirring a hair, and calls out to her to stop for me to take a blizzard at what was left on it. The angeliferous critter stood still as a scarecrow in a cornfield, for she'd got used to Mike's tricks by long practice.

" 'No, no, Mike,' sez I. 'Davy Crockett's hand would be sure to shake, if his iron war pointed within a hundred mile of a shemale, and I give up beat, Mike.' "

The Ballad of Casey Jones

An article in The Erie Railroad *magazine in 1928 describes Casey Jones as "6 feet 4 1/2 inches tall, dark-haired and gray-eyed," and it was said of him that "he always had a smile or a broad grin. The faster he could get his engine to roll, the happier he was. He would lean out of the cab window . . . and when he got her going so fast that the side rods looked solid, he would look at you and grin all over, happy as a boy with his first pair of red boots." Songs about Casey Jones have been found among railroad men all over the world, with French, German, and even South African versions. The following stanzas represent the traditional ballad that began circulating soon after Casey's death.*

Come all you rounders for I want you to hear
The story told of a brave engineer;
Casey Jones was the rounder's name
On a heavy six-eight wheeler he rode to fame.

Caller called Jones about half-past four,
Jones kissed his wife at the station door,
Climbed into the cab with the orders in his hand,
Says, "This is my trip to the promised land."

Through South Memphis yards on the fly,
He heard the fireman say, "You've got a white-eye,"
All the switchmen knew by the engine's moans,
That the man at the throttle was Casey Jones.

It had been raining for more than a week,
The railroad track was like the bed of a creek.
They rated him down to a thirty mile gait,
Threw the south-bound mail about eight hours late.

Fireman says, "Casey, you're runnin' too fast,
You run the block signal the last station you passed."
Jones says, "Yes, I think we can make it though,
For she steams much better than ever I know."

Jones says, "Fireman, don't you fret,
Keep knockin' at the firedoor, don't give up yet;
I'm goin' to run her till she leaves the rail
Or make it on time with the south-bound mail."

Around the curve and a-down the dump
Two locomotives were a-bound to bump.
Fireman hollered, "Jones, it's just ahead,
We might jump and make it but we'll all be dead."

'Twas around this curve he saw a passenger train;
Something happened in Casey's brain;
Fireman jumped off, but Casey stayed on,
He's a good engineer but he's dead and gone—

Poor Casey was always all right,
He stuck to his post both day and night;
They loved to hear the whistle of old Number Three
As he came into Memphis on the old K.C.

Headaches and heartaches and all kinds of pain
Are not apart from a railroad train;
Tales that are earnest, noble and gran'
Belong to the life of a railroad man.

Johnny Appleseed

Americans have always valued eccentricity and the freedom it brings. As a folk hero, Johnny Appleseed is as famous for being odd as for planting trees. It is rumored that Johnny graduated from Harvard and was soon after either kicked by a horse, jilted by a girl, or suffered from malaria, any or all of which events caused him to start wandering. The life of John Chapman spawned innumerable tales. Many, like the first presented here, romanticize his mission in life. Others attest to the possibility that he might have been a little bit beyond the bend.

John Chapman was born in the year 1775, at or near Springfield, Mass. In the latter years of the last century, or beginning of the present, he, with his half-brother, Nathaniel Chapman, came to Ohio, and stayed a year or two, and then returned to Springfield, and moved their father's family to Marietta, Ohio. Soon after that, Johnny located in Pennsylvania, near Pittsburgh, and began the nursery business, and continued it on westward.

He was an earnest disciple of the faith taught by Emanuel Swedenborg, and claimed that he had conversation with spirits and angels. In the bosom of his shirt he always carried a Testament and one or two old volumes of Swedenborg's works. These he read daily. He was a man rather above middle stature, wore his hair and beard long and dressed oddly. He generally wore old clothes that he had taken in exchange for the one commodity in which he dealt—apple trees. Dr. Hill says in 1801, an old uncle of ours, a pioneer in Jefferson County, Ohio, said the first time he ever saw him (Johnny) he was going down the river with two canoes lashed together and well laden with apple seeds which he obtained at the cider presses of western Pennsylvania. Sometimes he carried a bag or two of seeds on an old horse, but more frequently he bore them on his back, going from place to place on the wild frontier, clearing a little patch, surrounding it with a rude enclosure and planting seeds therein. He had little nurseries all through Ohio, Pennsylvania and Indiana. If a man wanted trees and was not able to pay for them,

Johnny took his note, and if the man ever got able and was willing to pay the debt, he took the money thankfully; but if not,
it was well.

He was such a good, kind, generous man, that he
thought it wrong to expend money on clothes to be worn just for
their fine appearance. He thought if he was comfortably clad, and in
attire that suited the weather, it was sufficient. His head covering was often a
pasteboard hat of his own making, with one broad side to it, that he wore next the
sunshine to protect his face. It was a very unsightly object to be sure, and yet never
one of us children ventured to laugh. We held Johnny in tender regard. His pan-
taloons were old and scant and short, with some sort of a substitute for "gallows"
or suspenders. He never wore a coat unless it was in the wintertime, and his feet
were knobby and horny and frequently bare. Sometimes he wore sandals
instead—rude soles with thong fastenings. The bosom of his shirt was always
pulled out loosely so as to make a kind of pocket or pouch in which he carried his
books. We have seen Johnny frequently wearing an old coffee sack for a coat, with
holes cut in it for his arms.

All the orchards in the white settlements came from the nurseries of
Johnny's planting. Even now after all these years, and though this region is densely populated, I can count from my window no less than five orchards or remains
of orchards that were once trees taken from his nurseries. Long ago if he was
going a great distance and carrying a sack of seeds on his back he had to provide
himself with a leather sack, for the dense underbush, brambles and thorny thickets would have made it unsafe for a coffee sack. I remember distinctly of falling
over one of Johnny's well filled sacks early one morning immediately after rising.
It was not light in the room, at the head of the stairs, and it was not there when
I went to bed the night before. It seems that he arrived at night, and for safe-
keeping the sack was put upstairs, while he lay beside the kitchen fire. I never saw
him sleep in a bed. He preferred to lie on the floor with his poor old horny feet
to the fire. . . .

In 1806 he planted sixteen bushels of seed on an old farm on the

Walhonding River, and he planted in Licking County, Ohio, and Richland County, and had other nurseries further west. One of his nurseries is near us, and I often go to the secluded spot on the quiet banks of the creek shut in by sycamore trees, with the sod never broken since the poor man did it. And when I look up and see the wide out-stretched branches over the place like out-spread arms in loving benediction, I say in a reverent whisper, "Oh the angels did commune with the good old man, whose loving heart prompted him to go about doing good. . . ."

On the subject of apples he was very charmingly enthusiastic. One would be astonished at his beautiful description of excellent fruit. I saw him once at the table when I was very small, telling about some apples that were new to us. His description was poetical, the language remarkably well chosen. It could have been no finer had the whole of Webster's Unabridged, with all its royal vocabulary been fresh upon his ready tongue. I stood back of mother's chair, amazed, delighted, bewildered, and vaguely realizing the wonderful powers of true oratory. I felt more than I understood.

He was scrupulously honest. I recall the last time we ever saw his sister, a very ordinary woman, the wife of an easy old gentleman and the mother of a family of handsome girls. They had started to move west in the winter season, but could move no farther after they reached our house. To help them along and to get rid of them, my father made a queer, little one-horse vehicle on runners, hitched their poor caricature of a beast to it, helped them pack and stow therein their bedding and a few movables, gave them a stock of provisions and five dollars, and sent the whole kit on their way rejoicing. And that was the last we ever saw of our poor neighbors.

The next time Johnny came to our house he very promptly laid a five dollar bill on my father's knee and shook his head very decidedly when it was handed back. Neither could he be prevailed upon to take it back again.

He was never known to hunt any animal or to give any living thing pain; not even a snake. One time when overtaken by night while traveling he crawled into a hollow log and slept till morning. In the other end of the log was a bear and her cubs. Johnny said he knew the bear would not hurt him, and that there was room enough for all.

The Indians all liked and treated him very kindly. They regarded him from his habits as a man above his fellows. He could endure pain like an Indian warrior; could thrust pins into his flesh without tremor. Indeed so insensible was he to acute pain that treatment of a wound or sore was to sear it with a hot iron and then treat it as a burn. He ascribed great medical virtues to the fennel, which he found probably in Pennsylvania. The overwhelming desire to do good and benefit and bless others induced him to gather a quantity of the seed, which he carried in his pockets, and occasionally scattered along his path in his journeys, especially at the waysides, near dwellings. Poor old man! He inflicted on the farming population a positive evil, when he sought to do good, for the rank fennel with its pretty, but pungent blossom, lines our roadsides and borders our lanes, and steals into our door-yard, and is a pest second to the daisy.

The last time we saw Johnny was one summer day when we were quilting upstairs. A door opened out upon the ground, and he stood his little bundle on the sill and lay down upon the floor, resting his head on the parcel. Then he drew out of his bosom one of his dingy books and read aloud to us.

In 1838 he resolved to go further on. Civilization was making the wilderness to blossom like the rose. Villages were springing up, stagecoaches laden with travelers were common, schools were everywhere, mail facilities were very good, frame and brick houses were taking the places of the humble cabins; and so Johnny went around among all his friends and bade them farewell. The little girls he had dandled upon his knees, and presented with beads and gay ribbons, were now mothers and the heads of families. This must have been a sad task for the old man, who was then well stricken in years, and one would have thought that he would have preferred to die among his friends. He came back two or three times to see us all in the intervening years that he lived; the last time was in the year he died, 1845. In the Spring of that year, one day after traveling twenty miles, he entered the house of an acquaintance in Allen County, Indiana, and was as usual, cordially received. He declined to eat anything except some bread and milk, which he ate, sitting on the doorstep occasionally looking out towards the setting sun.

Before bedtime he read from his little books "fresh news right from heaven," and at the usual hour for retiring he lay down upon the floor, as was his invariable custom. In the morning the beautiful sight supernal was upon his countenance, the death angel had touched him in the silence and the darkness, and though the dear old man essayed to speak, he was so near dead that his tongue refused its office. The physician came and pronounced him dying, but remarked that he never saw a man so perfectly calm and placid, and he inquired particularly concerning Johnny's religion. His bruised and bleeding feet, worn, walk the gold paved streets of the New Jerusalem, while we so brokenly and crudely narrate the sketch of his life. A life full of labor and pain and unselfishness, humble unto self-abnegation, his memory glowing in our hearts, while his deeds live anew every springtime in the fragrance of the apple-blossoms he loved so well.

A FOLKTALE OF JOHNNY APPLESEED

In Paris, France, two young men were condemned to death during the French Revolution. Disguised as laborers they escaped to London and subsequently came to America, landing at New Orleans. There they gathered together a few of their countrymen, secured a boat, and made their way up the Mississippi River to a point now known as Louisiana, Missouri. Finding the mouth of Salt River they followed the stream to where New London now stands. There one of these leaders, Dr. Antoine Saugrain, separated from his companions and, going into the Saverton Hills, built a fort, and spent the winter trapping. Afterward he joined the Lewis and Clark expedition.

The other young Frenchman, Mathuran Bouvet, and others of the company, went further up the Salt River and built a fort at what is now known as Spalding Springs. The Indians called this stream "Ohaha." The Spanish called it

"Rio de Salle," on account of the many salt springs along its course.

On a night shortly after building his fort, Bouvet was sitting in his cabin looking over some maps he had made of the country traversed, when he heard a noise at the door. When he ascertained that one man only was without he ordered the door opened. In walked a gaunt, peculiar looking character, singing:

> I sow while others reap,
> Be sure my warning keep,
> Indians will come by break of day,
> Indians hunting scalps, I say,

and he walked out. The Indians came "by break of day" and fought with burning arrows trying to fire the fort, but failed and were repulsed by the French. Bouvet then established salt works and began the manufacture of salt by boiling the water from these salt springs, and as fast as he made a load a boat took it to St. Louis. Returning from one of these trips he found the works had been destroyed by the Indians. He rebuilt them, but in a second attack by the Indians, so many of the whites were killed that those who survived abandoned the fort and made their escape to other settlements.

The man who gave this fort warning was "Johnny Appleseed," whose real name was John Chapman.

Johnny Appleseed when a young man living in Owensboro, Kentucky, was engaged to marry Sarah Crawford, a very beautiful young girl. The night before the day of their wedding she died. Johnny's grief unbalanced his mind, and in his delirium he thought he was called by the Lord as a harbinger of peace to the west and that his special mission was to plant appleseed along the way, that those who followed might reap the benefit of his sowing. So he went to the orchards where cider was being made and gathered a bag of seed and in the spring started on his mission.

Because of his mental condition and of a superstition among the Indians regarding the insane, he was allowed to go and come unmolested, even among the most savage tribes. He lived among them, learned their language, adopted their dress and habits, but never lost his loyalty to the white man and often gave them warning when the Indians were on the war path. Thus he passed through the wilderness, along the water courses and by the clearings singing, "I sow while others reap."

Johnny Appleseed married an Indian girl and lived with her in a tepee on Turkey Creek, in this (Ralls) county, Missouri. One morning he walked into his tepee, gazed longingly at his baby and walked away. He was never heard of again.

The Cherry Tree Legend

Few legends are so ingrained in the national consciousness of the United States as that of George Washington and the cherry tree he allegedly chopped down. Here is perhaps the earliest version of the story, from a book written shortly after Washington's death. (The first edition of the book appeared in 1800, but the cherry tree story wasn't added until the fifth edition, in 1806.)

Never did the wise Ulysses take more pains with his beloved Telemachus, than did Mr. Washington with George, to inspire him with an *early love of truth.* "Truth, George," said he, "is the loveliest quality of youth. I would ride fifty miles, my son, to see the little boy whose heart is so *honest,* and his lips so *pure,* that we may depend on every word he says. O how lovely does such a child appear in the eyes of everybody; his parents dote on him. His relations glory in him. They are constantly praising him to their children, whom they beg to imitate him. They are often sending for him to visit them; and receive him, when he comes, with as much joy as if her were a little angel, come to set pretty examples to their children.

"But, O! how different, George, is the case with the boy who is given to lying, that nobody can believe a word he says! He is looked at with aversion wherever he goes, and parents dread to see him come among their children. O, George! my son! rather than see you come to this pass, dear as you are to my heart, gladly would I assist to nail you up in your little coffin, and follow you to your grave. Hard, indeed, would it be to me to give up my son, whose little feet are always so ready to run about with me, and whose fondly looking eyes, and sweet prattle make so large a part of my happiness. But still I would give him up, rather than see him a common liar."

"Pa," said George very seriously, "do I ever tell lies?"

"No, George, I *thank* God you do not, my son; and I rejoice in the hope you never will. At least, you shall never, from me, have cause to be guilty of so shameful a thing. Many parents, indeed, even compel their children to this vile practice, by barbarously beating them for every little fault: hence, on the next offence, the little terrified creature slips out a *lie!* just to escape the rod. But as to yourself George, you know I have *always* told you, and now tell you again, that, whenever by accident, you do anything wrong, which must often be the case, as you are but a poor little boy yet, without *experience or knowledge*, you must never tell a falsehood to conceal it; but come *bravely* up, my son, like a *little* man, and tell me of it: and instead of beating you, George, I will but the more honor and love you for it, my dear."

This, you'll say, was sowing good seed!—Yes, it was: and the crop, thank God, was, as I believe it ever will be, where a man acts the true parent, that is, the *Guardian Angel*, by his child.

The following anecdote is a *case in point*. It is too valuable to be lost, and too true to be doubted; for it was communicated to me by an excellent lady.

"When George," said she, "was about six years old, he was made the wealthy master of a *hatchet!* of which, like most little boys, he was immoderately fond, and was constantly going about chopping every thing that came in his way. One day, in the garden, where he often amused himself hacking his mother's pea-sticks, he unluckily tried the edge of his hatchet on the body of a beautiful young English cherry-tree, which he barked so terribly, that I don't believe the tree ever got the better of it. The next morning the old gentleman, finding out what had befallen his tree, which, by the by, was a great favorite, came into the house; and with much warmth asked for the mischievous author, declaring at the same time, that he would not have taken five guineas for his tree. Nobody could tell him anything about it. Presently George and his hatchet made their appearance. 'George,' said his father, 'do you know who killed that beautiful little cherry tree yonder in the garden?' This was a *tough question*; and George staggered under it for a moment; but quickly recovered himself, and looking at his father, with the sweet face of youth brightened with the inexpressible charm of all-conquering truth, he bravely cried out, 'I can't tell a lie, Pa; you know I can't tell a lie. I did cut it with my hatchet.'

'Run to my arms, you dearest boy,' cried his father in transports. 'Run to my arms; glad am I, George, that you killed my tree; for you have paid me for it a thousand fold. Such an act of heroism in my son is worth more than a thousand trees, though blossomed with silver, and their fruits of purest gold.'"

It was in this way by interesting at once both his *heart* and *head*, that Mr. Washington conducted George with great ease and pleasure along the happy paths of virtue.

Belle Starr

———

Not all North American folk heroes are famous for their goodness or skill. Belle Starr was known as the Cleopatra of the Plains, though she was neither beautiful nor did she have access to powerful people other than outlaws. She was also known as the Bandit Queen of Dallas, which is more descriptive of her exploits. She had ties to the James brothers, and operated a safe haven for thieves on the Canadian River in Oklahoma's Indian Territory. She died a violent death in 1889, shot by an unknown bushwhacker. For all that, though, she has been lionized in books and films and remains heroic as one of the few women among the outlaws of the frontier.

———

BELLE'S ARREST

Belle was arrested twice with her husband, Sam Starr. The first time she was sentenced to one year in the Detroit penitentiary. The second time she was not sentenced, and enjoyed a week of sight-seeing in Fort Smith, Texas, while awaiting trial. The following newspaper account reveals just how seriously Belle took the charges against her.

For the past week the noted Belle Starr has been quite an attraction on the streets of this city. She came to answer two indictments in the Federal Court . . . first for being implicated in the stealing of a fine mare, the one ridden by the notorious John Middleton when he was drowned in the Poteau River, twenty-five miles above this city, in May, 1885; and second, on a charge of robbery, in which it is claimed that Belle, dressed in male attire, led a party of three men who robbed an old man named Ferrell and his three sons. . . .

Monday night Belle swung her Winchester to her saddle, buckled her revolver around her, and mounting her horses, set out for her home on the Canadian. Before leaving, she purchased a fine pair of 45-calibre revolvers . . . Belle says she anticipates no trouble in establishing her innocence in the cases against her, but thinks it terribly annoying to have to spend her time and money coming down here to court five and six times a year.

Belle attracts considerable attention wherever she goes, being a dashing horsewoman, and exceedingly graceful in the saddle. She dresses plainly, and wears a broad-brimmed white man's hat, surmounted by a wide black plush band, with feathers and ornaments, which is very becoming to her. She is of medium size, well formed, a dark brunette, with bright and intelligent black eyes. . . .

Belle is a crack shot, and handles her pistols with as much dexterity as any frontiersman. No man enters Younger's Bend without first giving a thorough account of himself before he gets out.

Belle related many incidents of her life that would be of interest, and says she has been offered big money by publishers for a complete history of it, but she does not desire to have it published yet. She has a complete manuscript record, and when she dies she will give it to the public. She spends most of her time writing when at home.

"You can just say that I am a friend to any brave and gallant outlaw, but have no use for that sneaking coward class of thieves who can be found in every locality, and who would betray a friend or comrade for the sake of their own gain. . . ."

BELLE STARR'S HORSE RACE

Stories like this one, which show Belle's trickster qualities, are popular in the Ozark region of Missouri where she was born.

———

John Hargrove, a pioneer businessman and one of the founders of this community on the Arkansas-Indian Territory border, raised the finest thorough-bred horses in the region. His black stallion had never been beaten in a race, and Hargrove's financial holdings increased greatly as his stallion outran all challengers year after year.

Belle Starr, also a lover of fine horses, acquired a spirited sorrel from a Kansas breeder. Returning with her new horse to her Youngers Bend home, she stopped in Siloam Springs and challenged Hargrove to a race. Belle and Hargrove agreed to bet $500 on the contest. Word of Belle Starr's challenging Hargrove's unbeaten stallion spread throughout the region and large crowds gathered to see the race and to wager among themselves. Belle hired a young Indian boy as a jockey, and, knowing her animal could easily beat Hargrove's stallion, she instructed her jockey to hold the sorrel back and let Hargrove's horse win by at least one length.

Belle paid Hargrove the $500 and reluctantly admitted he had the better horse. The next day she approached Hargrove again and told him she would like a rematch, but that she wanted the stakes to be raised to $5,000. Convinced his stallion had won easily over Belle's challenger, Hargrove accepted the offer wholeheartedly, and the race was scheduled for two days later. As race time approached the crowds grew even larger than before. People came from miles around to see the contest between the notorious Belle Starr and Siloam's leading citizen. This time Belle told her jockey to let the horse run with all he had. As she expected, her horse outran Hargrove's stallion by several lengths. Belle left $5,000 richer with a sorrel that was now worth a great deal as a result of its being the only horse ever to beat Hargrove's champion stallion. Hargrove was embarrassed by the trick Belle had played on him, and poorer by $4,500.

Judge Roy Bean's Necktie Justice

Judge Roy Bean lived on the Texas frontier during the latter part of the nineteenth century. He became known as the one and only representative of the "Law West of the Pecos." After living a life of questionable legality himself, Roy Bean settled in Langtry, Texas, in 1882, and was appointed Justice of the Peace. From then until 1903, he conducted court in the Jersey Lily Saloon from whence hilarious stories of his flamboyance traveled fast along the fledgling railroad lines leading back to civilization.

"Hear ye! Hear ye! This honorable court's now in session; and if any galoot wants a snort afore we start, let him step up to the bar and name his pizen. Oscar, serve the gentlemen." Thus did Judge Bean open court to try one Carlos Robles, an opening typical of his original procedure.

"Carlos Robles," he said solemnly after witnesses and hangers-on had downed their liquor, "it is the findin' of this court that you are charged with a grave offense against the peace and dignity of the law West of the Pecos and the State of Texas, to wit: cattle rustlin'. Guilty or not guilty?"

Not being able to speak or comprehend English, Robles merely grunted.

"Court accepts yore plea of guilt. The jury will now deliberate; and if it brings a verdict short of hangin' it'll be declared in contempt. Gentlemen, is yore verdict ready?"

The twelve nondescript citizens cleared their throats in unison. "It is, your honor," several spoke.

"Thank you, gentlemen. Stand up, Carlos Robles, and receive your sentence. You got anything to say why judgement shouldn't be passed on you in this court?"

Of course Carlos had not, in view of the fact that he had only the vaguest idea of what was transpiring.

"Carlos Robles," Judge Roy continued, his voice almost quaking with the solemnity of the occasion, "you been tried by twelve true and good men . . . and they've said you're guilty of rustlin' cattle.

"Time will pass and seasons will come and go; Spring with its wavin' green grass and heaps of sweet-smellin' flowers on every hill and in every dale. Then will come sultry Summer, with her shimmerin' heat-waves on the baked horizon; and Fall, with her yeller harvest-moon and the hills growin' brown and golden under a sinkin' sun; and finally Winter, with its bitin', whinin' wind, and all the land will be mantled with snow. But you won't be here to see any of 'em, Carlos Robles; not by a dam' sight, because it is the order of this court that you be took to the nearest tree and hanged by the neck till you're dead, dead, dead, you . . . son-of-a-billy goat!"

The Law West of the Pecos could be cruel in administering his brand of justice; but he was cruel only when he deemed the accused and the crime fully warranting such cruelty. He more frequently tempered justice with his own peculiar brand of mercy, especially if there was any means by which he could profit by that mercy.

One afternoon several ranchmen brought in a twenty-year-old boy accused of horse-stealing. They demanded that he be tried and dealt with according to the enormity of the crime.

Judge Bean duly opened court. He appointed six men as jurors, the actual number meaning nothing to him and depending entirely upon men available. He would not appoint just any citizens to jury duty. They must be good customers of the liquor bar at the other end of the shack during intermissions, or their services as jurors no longer were desirable or acceptable. Every transaction must be made to return the utmost in profit, and non-drinking jurors were strictly dead timber.

"Hear ye! This honorable court is again in session. Anyone wishin' a snort, have it now. This here prisoner is charged with the grave offense of stealin' a horse and Oscar, where are the witnesses?" the Law West of the Pecos opened. He appreciated his own sense of humor in varying his court openings to relieve the monotony; but he seldom varied to the extent of omitting the invitation to participate in a snort at the other bar.

"We caught him in the act of stealin' the animal," the ranchman testified. "He admitted his intentions."

"That right, young feller? You was stealin' the cayuse?"

The young prisoner dropped his head, unruly red hair tumbling down over his high forehead. "Yes, your honor," he mumbled.

"Gentlemen of the jury," His Honor instructed, "the accused pleads guilty to horse theft. You know as well as I do the penalty. I'm ready for yore verdict." And it was promptly forthcoming.

Gravely the judge passed sentence. "If there's any last word, or anything, I'll give you a few minutes," he told the pale Easterner, thus extending an infrequent favor.

"I would like to write a note—to my mother back in Pennsylvania," the doomed prisoner mumbled with obvious emotion. "Thank you."

"Oscar, fetch the prisoner a piece of wrappin' paper and a pencil. I think we got a pencil back there behind that row of bottles." Bean gently handed the convicted thief these writing facilities, got up and tendered him the beer barrel and rickety table from which sentence had just been passed. Then he took a position directly behind the boy so that he could watch over his shoulder at what he wrote.

The victim wrote at length in apology for the grief and trouble he had caused his mother and earnestly sought her forgiveness. "In small part perhaps I can repay you for the money I have cost you in keeping me out of trouble. Enclosed is $400, which I've saved. I want you— "

Judge Bean started, cleared his throat, cut in at this point. "By gobs!" he exclaimed, "gentlemen, I got a feelin' there's been a miscarriage of justice, in this case. I hereby declare it re-opened. Face the bar, young man."

The prisoner removed himself from the beer keg and stood erect in front of the judicial bench, befuddled at this sudden turn.

"After all, that wasn't much of a cayuse the lad tried to steal and he didn't actually steal him. So I rule it's a finable case. I hereby fine the accused three hundred dollars and get to hell outer this country afore I change my mind. . . . Court's adjourned and what'll it be for you down there, Slim?"

Wild Bill Hickock's Duel with Dave Tutt

What makes Wild Bill Hickock such a fascinating folk legend is the fact that, though he reportedly killed dozens of opponents in flamboyant gun battles, he is often depicted as a reluctant killer. There is a melancholy about him because it seems that trouble came to him unbidden. His appeal also lies in his unwavering self-confidence as a skilled marksman. This account, taken down by a literate man from someone who supposedly knew Wild Bill firsthand, demonstrates how oral reports were exaggerated and propelled prominent, real-life heroes into the realm of legend.

Bill was born of Northern parents in the State of Illinois. He ran away from home when a boy, and wandered out upon the plains and into the mountains. For fifteen years he lived with the trappers, hunting and fishing. When the war broke out he returned to the States and entered the Union service. No man probably was ever better fitted for scouting than he. Joined to his tremendous strength he was an unequaled horseman; he was a perfect marksman; he had a keen sight, and a constitution which had no limit of endurance. He was cool to audacity, brave to rashness, always possessed of himself under the most critical circumstances; and, above all, was such a master in the knowledge of woodcraft that it might have been termed a science with him—a knowledge which, with the soldier, is priceless beyond description.

The main features of the story of the duel was [*sic*] told me by Captain Honesty, who was unprejudiced, if it is possible to find an unbiased mind in a town of 3000 people after a fight has taken place. I will give the story in his words:

"They say Bill's wild. Now he isn't any sich thing. I've known him goin on ter ten year, and he's as civil a disposed person as you'll find he-e-arabouts. But he won't be put upon.

"I'll tell yer how it happened. But come inter the office; thar's a good many round hy'ar as sides with Tutt—the man that's shot. But I tell yer 'twas a far fight. Take some whisky? No! Well, I will, if yer'l excuse me.

"You see," continued the Captain, setting the empty glass on the table in an emphatic way, "Bill was up in his room a-playin seven-up, or four-hand, or some of them pesky games. Bill refused ter play with Tutt, who was a profession-al gambler. Yer see, Bill was a scout on our side durin the war, and Tutt was a reb scout. Bill had killed Dave Tutt's mate, and, atween one thing and another, there war an onusual hard feelin atwixt 'em.

"Ever sin Dave come back he had tried to pick a row with Bill; so Bill wouldn't play cards with him any more. But Dave stood over the man who was gambling with Bill and lent the feller money. Bill won about two hundred dollars, which made Tutt spiteful mad. Bime-by, he says to Bill:

"'Bill, you've got plenty of money—pay me that forty dollars yer owe me in that horse trade.'

"And Bill paid him. Then he said:

"'Yer owe me thirty-five dollars more; yer lost it playing with me t'other night.'

"Dave's style was right provoking; but Bill answered him perfectly gentlemanly:

"'I think yer wrong, Dave. It's only twenty-five dollars. I have a memorandum of it in my pocket down stairs. Ef it's thirty-five dollars I'll give it yer.'

"Now Bill's watch was lying on the table. Dave took up the watch, put it in his pocket, and said: 'I'll keep this yere watch till yer pay me that thirty-five dollars.'

"This made Bill shooting mad; fur, don't yer see, Colonel, it was a-doubt-ing his honor like, so he got up and looked Dave in the eyes, and said to him: 'I don't want ter make a row in this house. It's a decent house, and I don't want ter injure the keeper. You'd better put that watch back on the table.'

"But Dave grinned at Bill mighty ugly, and walked off with the watch, and kept it several days. All this time Dave's friends were spurring Bill on ter fight; there was no end ter the talk. They blackguarded him in an underhand sort of a way, and tried ter get up a scrimmage, and then they thought they could lay him out. Yer see Bill has enemies all about. He's settled the accounts of a heap of men who lived round here. This is about the only place in Missouri whar a reb can come back and live, and ter tell yer the truth, Colonel—" and the Captain, with an involuntary movement, hitched up his revolver-belt, as he said, with expressive significance, "they don't stay long round here!

"Well, as I was saying, these rebs don't like ter see a man walking round town who they knew in the reb army as one of their men, who they now know was on our side, all the time he was sending us information, sometimes from Pap Price's own head-quarters. But they couldn't provoke Bill inter a row, for he's afeard of hisself when he gits *awful* mad; and he allers left his shootin irons in his room when he went out. One day these cusses drew their pistols on him and dared him to fight, and then they told him that Tutt was a-goin ter pack that watch across the squar next day at noon.

"I heard of this, for every body was talking about it on the street, and so I went after Bill, and found him in his room, cleaning and greasing and loading his revolvers.

"'Now, Bill,' says I, 'you're goin ter git inter a fight.'

"'Don't you bother yerself, Captain,' says he. 'It's not the first time I have been in a fight; and these d—d hounds have put on me long enough. You don't want me ter give up my honor, do yer?'

"'No, Bill,' says I, 'yer must keep yer honor.'

"Next day, about noon, Bill went down to the squar. He had said that Dave Tutt shouldn't pack that watch across the squar unless dead men could walk.

"When Bill got onter the squar he found a crowd standin in the corner of the street by which he entered the squar, which is from the south, yer know. In this crowd he saw a lot of Tutt's friends; some were cousins of his'n, just back from the reb army; and they jeered him, and boasted that Dave was a-goin to pack that watch across the squar as he promised.

"Then Bill saw Tutt standin near the courthouse, which yer remember is on the west side, so that the crowd war behind Bill.

"Just then Tutt, who war alone, started from the courthouse and walked out into the squar, and Bill moved away from the crowd toward the west side of the squar. Bout fifteen paces brought them opposite to each other, and about fifty yards apart. Tutt then showed his pistol. Bill had kept a sharp eye on him, and before Tutt could pint it Bill had his'n out.

"At that moment you could have heard a pin drop in that squar. Both Tutt and Bill fired, but one discharge followed the other so quick that it's hard to say which went off first. Tutt was a famous shot, but he missed this time; the ball from his pistol went over Bill's head. The instant Bill fired, without waitin ter see ef he had hit Tutt, he wheeled on his heels and pointed his pistol at Tutt's friends, who had already drawn their weepons.

"'Aren't yer satisfied, gentlemen?' cried Bill, as cool as an alligator. 'Put up your shootin-irons, or there'll be more dead men here.' And they put 'em up, and said it war a far fight."

"What became of Tutt?" I asked of the Captain, who had stopped at this point of his story, and was very deliberately engaged in refilling his empty glass.

"Oh! Dave? He was as plucky a feller as ever drew trigger; but, Lord bless yer! it was no use. Bill never shoots twice at the same man, and his ball went through Dave's heart. He stood stock-still for a second or two, then raised his arm as if ter fire again, then he swayed a little, staggered three or four steps and then fell dead.

"Bill and his friends wanted ter have the thing done regular, so we went up ter the Justice, and Bill delivered himself up. A jury was drawn; Bill was tried and cleared the next day. It was proved that it was a case of self-defense. Don't yer see, Colonel?"

I answered that I was afraid that I did not see that point very clearly.

"Well, well!" he replied, with an air of compassion. "You haven't drunk any whisky, that's what's the matter with yer." And then, putting his hand on my shoulder with a half-mysterious, half-conscious look in his face, he muttered, in a whisper:

"The fact is, thar was an undercurrent of a woman in that fight!"

I had a curiosity, which was not an idle one, to hear what this man [Bill] had to say about his duel with Tutt, and I asked him:

"Do you not regret killing Tutt? You surely do not like to kill men?"

"As ter killing men," he replied, "I never thought much about it. The most of the men I have killed it was one or t'other of us, and at sich times you don't stop to think, and what's the use after it's all over? As for Tutt, I had rather not have killed him, for I want ter settle down quiet here now. But thar's been hard feeling between us a long while. I wanted ter keep out of that fight; but he tried to degrade me, and I couldn't stand that, you know, for I am a fighting man, you know."

A cloud passed over the speaker's face for a moment as he continued:

"And there was a cause of quarrel between us which people round here don't know about. One of us had to die; and the secret died with him."

"Why did you not wait to see if your ball had hit him? Why did you turn round so quickly?"

The scout fixed his gray eyes on mine, striking his leg with his riding-whip, as he answered.

"I *knew* he was a dead man. I never miss a shot. I turned on the crowd because I was sure they would shoot me if they saw him fall."

"The people about here tell me you are a quiet, civil man. How is it you get into these fights?"

"D—d if I can tell," he replied, with a puzzled look which at once gave place to a proud, defiant expression as he continued—"but you know a man must defend his honor."

"Yes," I admitted, with some hesitation, remembering that I was not in Boston but on the border, and that the code of honor and mode of redress differ slightly in the one place from those of the other.

Stackalee

Just as white American tradition makes heroes out of outlaws, so African American culture confers hero status on its most famous scoundrels. Stackalee—sometimes called Stagolee—reigns supreme as the most notorious bad man of all. Numerous tales have been published and countless ballads made to detail his exploits. The ballads are almost always in a rhyme scheme and rhythm that belong to the African American tradition known as the toast, a style of speech that has more recently evolved into rap.

THE LEGEND OF STACKALEE

Stackalee was a big Negro bad man born on Market Street in St. Louis in 1861. He was born double-jointed and with a full set of teeth and red eyes. "A gipsy told his mother, Told her like a friend, Your double-jointed baby, Won't come to no good end." So says one of the legends which celebrate his name.

Stackalee was named for the famous boat he worked on. He was a stoker or roustabout on the Mississippi-Ohio River packet *Stacker Lee*, which plied between Memphis, Cincinnati, St. Louis, and Vicksburg. People spell his name Stagolee sometimes, but mostly they call him Stack.

Stack was a fine musician. He could play the guitar and the piano, and he was always moaning the blues or beating out some rag. Women loved him. When he hugged the girls he squeezed the breath out of them, and they liked that.

Stack's own girl was born on Market Street in St. Louis in 1861, just like Stack himself. Her name was Stack o' Dollars. They called her that because she not only *had* a stack of dollars but always bet them all in a gambling game. She was a big fat girl with diamond teeth and *some smile*. She smoked cigars and could lick any man in town in a fist fight. Stack did like a spirited woman. She wore a Stetson hat, too—a bigger one than Stack's.

Stack always wore a Stetson hat, the five-gallon size. He dearly loved a Stetson, and had a whole row of them, all different colors, hanging on pegs in the house on Market Street. Everybody says he sold his soul to the Devil in return for a magic spell on his favorite Stetson. He could get away with anything as long as he wore that hat. And he was never caught as long as he had it.

Stackalee was a gambler, a gunman, and a killer. Nobody knows how many notches he had on his gun for the men he had killed. He feared no one. He even challenged Jesse James once, but that was a mistake. Nobody was a match for Jesse James in *any* kind of fight, and the minute Jesse let go of him Stack beat it for the mountains.

Once in the mountains he met up with two deputies who were out looking for him in order to collect the $5,000 reward on his head. So he sat down to chat with them and pass the time of day. Stack learned their names and then shot their initials in their hats before they discovered who he was. He nearly split his sides laughing to see how fast they left the neighborhood.

But every bad man gets caught up with, one way or another, it seems, and the Devil was getting tired of Stack's devilment. He was tired of waiting to snatch Stack's soul to hell, too.

Stack was in a gambling game one night in St. Louis. He was winning, seemed as if he couldn't lose, and he was so busy scraping in the money that he forgot about his hat which he had hung on the back of his chair. This was the Devil's chance. In the guise of a nice young man named Billy Lyons he took the hat and headed for a barrel house down the street, where he knew Billy Lyons to be. With a yell in his throat and a gun in each hand Stack tore after him. When he got there, there was Billy Lyons all right, smoking a cigarette, easylike, expecting nothing; but the Stetson hat was not in sight.

Stack shot him on sight and killed him dead for stealing the magic Stetson that had always saved him from the law. Onlookers said Billy had not left the barrel house all evening, but Stack did not believe that.

The police wagon came and hauled Stackalee off to jail. But the Devil got cheated out of Stack's soul, after all, for they did not hang him. The judge sentenced him to a stretch of seventy-five years in Jefferson penitentiary, and there he is. He has served thirty-four years and has forty-one still to go. So the Devil is still waiting.

THE BALLAD OF STACKALEE

———·———

It was in the year of eighteen hundred and sixty-one
In St. Louis on Market Street where Stackalee was born.
   Everybody's talkin 'bout Stackalee.

It was on one cold and frosty night
When Stackalee and Billy Lyons had one awful fight,
   All about an old Stetson hat.

Stackalee got his gun. Boy, he got it fast!
He shot poor Billy through and through; the bullet broke a lookin glass.
   Oh, oh, Lord, Lord, Lord.

Stackalee shot Billy once; his body fell to the floor.
He cried out, "Oh, please, Stack, please don't shoot me no more."

The White Elephant Barrel House was wrecked that night;
Gutters full of beer and whisky; it was an awful sight.

Jewelry and rings of the purest solid gold
Scattered over the dance and gamblin hall.

The can can dancers they rushed for the door
When Billy cried, "Oh, please, Stack, don't shoot me no more."

"Have mercy," Billy groaned. "Oh, please spare my life;
I've got two little babies and an innocent wife."

Stack says, "God bless your children, damn your wife!
You stole my magic Stetson; I'm gonna steal your life."

"But," says Billy, "I always treated you like a man.
'Tain't nothin to that old Stetson but the greasy band."

He shot poor Billy once, he shot him twice,
And the third time Billy pleaded, "Please go tell my wife."

Yes, Stackalee, the gambler, everybody knowed his name;
Made his livin hollerin high, low, jack and the game.

Meantime the sergeant strapped on his big forty-five,
Says, "Now we'll bring in this bad man, dead or alive."

And brass-buttoned policemen all dressed in blue
Came down the sidewalk marchin two by two.

Sent for the wagon and it hurried and come
Loaded with pistols and a big Gatling gun.

At midnight on that stormy night there came an awful wail—
Billy Lyons and a graveyard ghost outside the city jail.

"Jailer, jailer," says Stack, "I can't sleep.
For around my bedside poor Billy Lyons still creeps.

"He comes in shape of a lion with a blue steel in his hand,
For he knows I'll stand and fight if he comes in shape of man."

Stackalee went to sleep that night by the city clock bell,
Dreaming the devil had come all the way up from hell.

Red devil was sayin, "You better hunt your hole;
I've hurried here from hell just to get your soul."

Stackalee told him, "Yes, maybe you're right,
But I'll give even you one hell of a fight."

When they got into the scuffle, I heard the devil shout,
"Come and get this bad man before he puts my fire out."

The next time I seed the devil he was scramblin up the wall,
Yellin, "Come an get this bad man fore he mops up with us all."

Then here come Stack's woman runnin, says, "Daddy, I love you true;
See what beer, whisky, and smokin hop has brought you to.

"But before I'll let you lay in there, I'll put my life in pawn."
She hurried and got Stackalee out on a five thousand dollar bond.

Stackalee said, "Ain't but one thing that grieves my mind.
When they take me away, babe, I leave you behind."

But the woman he really loved was a voodoo queen
From Creole French market, way down in New Orleans.

He laid down at home that night, took a good night's rest,
Arrived in court at nine o'clock to hear the coroner's inquest.

Crowds jammed the sidewalk, far as you could see,
Tryin to get a good look at tough Stackalee.

Over the cold, dead body Stackalee he did bend,
Then he turned and faced those twelve jury men.

The judge says, "Stackalee, I would spare your life,
But I know you're a bad man; I can see it in your red eyes."

The jury heard the witnesses, and they didn't say no more;
They crowded into the jury room, and the messenger closed the door.

The jury came to agreement, the clerk he wrote it down,
And everybody was whisperin, "He's penitentiary bound."

When the jury walked out, Stackalee didn't budge.
They wrapped the verdict and passed it to the judge.

Judge looked over his glasses, says, "Mr. Bad Man Stackalee,
The jury finds you guilty of murder in the first degree."

Now the trial's come to an end, how the folks gave cheers;
Bad Stackalee was sent down to Jefferson pen for seventy-five years

Now late at night you can hear him in his cell,
Arguin with the devil to keep from goin to hell.

And the other convicts whisper, "Whatcha know about that?
Gonna burn in hell forever over an old Stetson hat!"
Everybody's talkin 'bout Stackalee.

4

Larger Than Life

~

Every traditional group in history has had its culture heroes—godlike people with extraordinary powers who created the physical landscape and, more importantly, symbolized the moral character of the entire group. Native Americans, for example, have a centuries-old pantheon of culture heroes, some of whose stories appear in Chapter 1. Although pioneer America had its share of flesh-and-blood heroes, by the middle of the nineteenth century the unique culture that had grown out of the frontier experience still lacked mythic heroes. And so Americans did what they always do when something is not readily available. They invented for themselves a multitude of demigods to take the place of the real heroes whose heyday was nearly over.

It stands to reason that the culture heroes of the United States would be primarily comic figures. Though their ultimate purpose was serious—to symbolize the spirit of the nation—Paul Bunyan, Pecos Bill, and all their kin were born when the tall tale was enjoying enormous popularity. The characters attracted whoppers, lies, and brags like magnets, and stories about them breathed new life into many a familiar tall tale. Not every mythical hero in American lore is meant to be funny, but the tall-tale humor in the majority of the tales reflects an important aspect of the American character of the period. What the heroes did for a living also reveals a great deal about what was happening in American society. As river workers, seamen, loggers, railroad men, plainsmen, and cowboys, they represented the national preoccupation with strength, expansion, and commerce.

Many folklorists believe that Pecos Bill, Paul Bunyan, and other American demigods began life on the printed page, the products of professional writers' imaginations. Others think it possible that the culture heroes in this chapter began as stories generated among the workers, which found their way into print only after the tales had become popular. It is, in fact, impossible to separate the stories that originated in oral tradition and those that were penned by professional writers, so the debate will probably never be resolved. One thing is certain, however: These characters are firmly entrenched in the minds of most Americans as part of our traditional lore, how ever they came into being.

The Birth of Paul Bunyan

Stories about Paul Bunyan began to circulate in the early part of the twentieth century, providing those Americans inclined to tell tall tales with a perfect vehicle for their lies. There is known to have been a Canadian logger named Paul Bunyon who, some people think, may have been a model for the stories. But the first printed mention of the hero was, of all places, in the advertising literature for a lumber company, and some suspect that the character was invented for that purpose. Of all North American folktales, those about Paul Bunyan were the quickest to be turned into literature, as frontier newspaper writers filled their pages with stories that were eventually collected in books. With so many people at work on his image, he gathered around him a bizarre array of men and beasts the like of which has seldom been surpassed in North American lore or literature.

If what they say is true, Paul Bunyan was born down in Maine. And he must have been a pretty husky baby, too, just like you'd expect him to be, from knowin' him afterwards.

When he was only three weeks old he rolled around so much in his sleep that he knocked down four square miles of standin' timber and the government got after his folks and told 'em they'd have to move him away.

So then they got some timbers together and made a floatin' cradle for Paul and anchored it off Eastport. But every time Paul rocked in his cradle, if he rocked shoreward, it made such a swell it came near drownin' out all the villages on the coast of Maine. The waves was so high Nova Scotia came pretty near becomin' an island instead of a peninsula.

That wouldn't do, of course, and the government got after 'em again and told 'em they'd have to do somethin' about it. They'd have to move him out of there and put him somewheres else, they was told. So they figured they'd better take him home again and keep him in the house for a spell.

But it happened Paul was asleep in his cradle when they went to get him. They had to send for the British Navy, and it took seven hours of bombardin' to wake him up. Then, when Paul stepped out of his cradle, it made such a swell it caused a seventy-five-foot tide in the Bay of Fundy. Several villages were swept away, and seven of the invincible English warships were sunk to the bottom of the sea.

Well, Paul got out of his cradle then, and that saved Nova Scotia from becomin' an island, but the tides in the Bay of Fundy are just as high as they ever were.

So I guess the old folks must have had their hands full with him, all right. And I ought to say, the King of England sent over and confiscated the timbers in Paul's cradle and built seven new warships to take the place of the ones he'd lost.

When Paul was only seven months old, he sawed off the legs from under his dad's bed one night. The old man noticed when he woke up in the mornin' that his bed seemed considerable lower than it used to be, so he got up and investigated. Sure enough, there were the legs all sawed off from under it and the pieces layin' out on the floor.

Then he remembered he'd felt somethin' the night before, but he'd thought he must be dreamin'—the way you dream that you're fallin' down sometimes when you first go off to sleep. He looked around to see who could have done it and there was Paul layin' there sound asleep with his dad's cross-cut saw still held tight in his fist and smilin' in his sleep as pretty as anythin'.

He called his wife, and when she came in he said to her, "Did you feel anythin' in the night?"

"No," she said. "Is anythin' wrong?"

"Well, just look here," he said. And he showed her the four-by-eights layin' there on the floor and the saw in their kid's hand.

"I didn't light the lamp when I went to get up this mornin'," she said, "and I guess I didn't notice it."

"Well, he's done it, anyway," said the old man. "I'll bet that boy of ours is goin' to be a great logger someday. If he lives to grow up, he's goin' to do some great loggin' by and by, you just see—a whole lot bigger than any of the men around here have ever done."

And they was right, all right. There ain't never been loggin' before nor since like Paul Bunyan done.

Babe the Blue Ox

It is the rare person in America who does not have the image of a big blue ox firmly lodged in his or her imagination. There are conflicting stories of how the friendship between Paul Bunyan and his faithful companion came to pass. The following tale is the most commonly accepted account.

One day when Paul was working in his father's logging camp in the Maine woods it started to snow. Day after day the soft fluffy snowflakes fell until the entire camp was covered with a blanket of snow. Log cabins disappeared from sight, and all but the tallest trees were buried under the great snowdrifts.

And the strangest thing of all was that the snow, instead of being white, was a bright sapphire blue! For miles and miles as far as one could see the forest was covered with beautiful blue snow. Loggers even today remember that year and call it the Winter of the Blue Snow.

When the snow had stopped falling, Paul put on his snowshoes and went out to find wood for his fireplace. As he was returning, he noticed two little ears sticking up through a snowdrift.

"It must be some poor animal lost and freezing to death," thought Paul. He reached down with one of his great hands and scooped the little thing out of the snow. It was a baby ox calf with thin wobbly legs. Paul put the little calf inside one of his large pockets and took him home. Soon he was curled up in front of the fireplace and as happy and warm as could be.

"Poor little baby!" said Paul as the little calf drank some warm milk and gratefully caressed Paul's hand with his tongue. Paul decided to call the little calf "Babe" and keep him for a pet.

The strangest thing about Babe was that, even after he became thawed out, his coat remained a soft glossy blue. Paul nursed his new pet back to health, but his color never changed. The Winter of the Blue Snow had colored him blue, and blue he remained forever after.

Babe followed Paul wherever he went and grew larger each day. Every time Paul looked around the little calf seemed to have grown a foot taller.

In the spring, Paul built a little barn for Babe and put the calf inside for the night. The next morning, the barn was gone and so was the little blue calf. Paul searched high and low. Finally he found Babe calmly eating grass in a neighboring valley—with the barn perched right up on his back! He had outgrown it in a single night!

Paul became very fond of Babe and took him on all his adventures in the woods. He grew by leaps and bounds and soon was almost as large as Paul himself. Woodsmen tell us that when Babe was full grown he measured forty-two axe-handles between the eyes.

His appetite was tremendous. Every evening he ate a ton and a half of hay. Even then he wouldn't be satisfied to go to bed unless he had three wagonloads of turnips for dessert.

Paul taught him to help with the logging in the woods, and would give him an eighty-pound lump of sugar if he had been a good ox during the day. Babe was always full of mischief, however. He liked to roar and stamp his feet at night so the men would run out of the bunkhouses where they slept, thinking it was an earthquake! When Paul scolded him for it, Babe only chuckled to himself and pretended he was asleep.

Once when Babe was standing beside the cookhouse he winked at Paul and put his head in the cookhouse window. Babe gave a great sneeze and blew a whole barrel of flour over Hot Biscuit Slim, the cook, and his helper, Cream Puff Fatty!

Babe was very useful in many ways. For instance, Paul had a lot of trouble with the crooked, twisting road that wound in and out through the forest. He finally tied one end of the road to a large stump and hitched Babe to the other end with a large logging chain. Babe dug his great hoofs in the ground and strained and tugged until he had pulled the entire road out straight. It was a mighty feat of strength. In doing it, he stretched the heavy iron links of the logging chain until it was a single iron bar!

During his first summer, Babe became fat and lazy and one day refused to pull the logs down the road to the river. He wanted to wait until winter when the snow was on the ground and logs would slide easier. Paul didn't say a word, but that night he had the men secretly whitewash the road. The next morning, Babe thought it was snow and pulled the logs without further trouble.

When winter finally came again and covered the Maine woods with beautiful white snow, Babe was the happiest ox in the world. He loved to roam through the woods on the new snowshoes that Paul had given him for his first birthday. The greatest trouble Paul had that winter was finding enough food for Babe, who was getting thin. One day he thought of a great idea and called Ole the big Swede. Ole was the camp blacksmith, and next to Paul, the largest man in camp.

"Ole," he said, "I want you to make the largest pair of green eyeglasses in the world." When Ole finished, Paul put the glasses on Babe, strapping them over his nose. He then turned Babe out in the snow again. To Babe, with his new green glasses, all the snow looked like nice green grass! He ate and ate and grew fat and healthy again in no time at all.

In all the woods, there was no one so kindly toward Babe as Paul Bunyan, and no ox was ever as faithful to its master as Babe, the famous Blue Ox.

Pipeline Days

It is a little known fact that, besides working as a logger, Paul Bunyan also made a name for himself drilling for oil in the American South. The following story is written as a conversation among Paul's acquaintances that evolves into a bragging contest.

. . . "Say," said Fat, "did any of you guys ever see Paul Bunyan in a poker game. The cards he used were so big that it took a man five hours to walk around one of them. Paul used to play a lot of poker that time we was digging Lake Michigan to mix concrete in when he was building the Rocky Mountains. A little while after that we dug Lake Superior for a slush pit for one of them big wells we was drilling. Any of you birds want to play some poker?"

"You know so much about Paul Bunyan," said [the Contender]. "Did you ever hear about that big steer that he had? He called her Babe and she just measured forty-two pick-handles lengths and the width of a size seven derby hat between the eyes. And strong! Why that steer could pull anything!

"I remember one time when we was drilling a well down Breckenridge way. Wasn't much of a hole, just sixteen inches. Well, we drilled and drilled and didn't ever strike nothing—except dust, and a God's plenty of that; so finally Paul he said we might as well give it up as a dry hole and let it go at that.

"But Paul was mad! He swore around for two or three days and smashed the derrick into kindling wood and was about to quit drilling when he saw a advertisement in the paper by some bird out on the plains that wanted to buy some post-holes. Ten thousand post-holes it was he wanted. Ten thousand holes three feet long.

"Well, Paul he hitched a chain around this duster [dry well] hole and hooked up Babe and pulled fifteen thousand feet of it out of the ground. He got mad again because the hole broke off and left over half of it in the ground. But directly he said that they wasn't no use of a post-hole being sixteen inches across;

so he just quartered the hole and then sawed it up into the right lengths. . . ."

"I worked for Paul on one of them deep wells once," said Fat. "It was out in Arkansas. Jimmy Blue was running the rig and we was drilling with standard tools. We got down thirty thousand feet and struck a rock formation that a bit wouldn't touch. And we was using a pretty good sized bit too, drilling a fifty-inch hole.

"Well, we worked on this formation for three weeks without doing any good and then we called up Paul. Paul he come out there and took charge of the rig himself and worked for three more weeks, day and night, without doing anything except ruin a lot of bits. And finally he got so mad that he jumped down on the derrick floor and pulled up the bit with his hands. Then he threw it down into the hole as hard as he could throw it. Well, we busted the rock that time. The bit just kept on going and when the line run out it pulled derrick, rig, and all into the hole after it.

"We got a gusher that time. But when Paul seen that the rig had pulled Jimmy into the hole with it he was just about to plug off the hole and abandon it. But in a few days we got a telegram from Jimmy in China saying that he had a 100,000 barrel gusher and was spudding in on another location."

"Did any of you guys work for Paul on that big line he laid?" asked the Contender. "Well, I worked for him on that 100-inch aluminum line that he laid from Pennsylvania to California. We laid it to pipe buttermilk out to his camp out there. Paul liked buttermilk so well himself that he had a twenty-four-inch petcock running wide open all the time to catch enough for him to drink."

"Yeh," said Fat, "I know all about that. I helped Paul drill the buttermilk well that furnished that line. We drilled down thirty-two thousand feet and then struck a formation of cornbread. We drilled for five hundred feet through the cornbread and then for twelve hundred feet through solid turnip greens—except that every few feet would be a layer of fried sow-belly. That's where the old song started: 'Cornbread, Buttermilk, and Good Old Turnip Greens.'"

. . . The Contender put in, "Did you ever hear about the cattle line that Paul Bunyan laid from his ranch to Chicago?

"Well, Paul he got tired of paying such high freight to get his stock to market; so he just laid a pipeline all the way to the stockyards in Chicago and pumped them through it. Everything went all right except that the pipe was so big that the calves and half-grown yearlin's would get lost in the threads and starve to death before they could get to the outside. And one time the line sprung a leak and Paul lost thirty-five carloads of cattle before he could get it corked [caulked]. But he sure did do a good job of corking when he did get to it."

"How the devil did he cork a hole that big?" asked Fat after a minute or two of silence.

"Why with B.S., you big windbag, same as that that you have been spouting off."

Paul's Popcorn

This favorite tale displays Paul Bunyan's ingenuity and makes clear why he became a symbol for the "can-do" spirit of America.

Having got the water meandering around to make the soil moist, Paul figured he'd test the land out with popcorn. So he picked up a good healthy looking kernel, walked out to a likely looking place that had been irrigated lately, and dug a hole about a foot deep with his middle finger. He couldn't use his forefinger or thumb, naturally, because he was holding the corn between them.

Well, Paul had no more than started back to camp to get Ole to act as a witness, than there was a sort of sputtering up of brown dirt, and a cornstalk came skyhooting through. In no time at all, the corn was up to Paul's knee. And by the time he got back with Ole, the cornstalk had grown so much that the top was buried in a cloud.

"Ole!" says Paul. "Climb up to the top of that baby and chop the top off so she won't grow any more!"

Ole started shinning up the stalk at a great rate. But the thing kept shooting up, and in a minute or so Ole, too, was out of sight in that cloud. It was a handsome cloud with cottony bumps and scallopy edges, but Ole said afterwards that being inside of it wasn't different from being inside any old cloud. "Nothing but fog inside it," he said.

"When you chop the top off, throw her down," Paul yelled.

Ole's voice came booming down. "The top's above me," he said. "I can't get *to* the thing." Ole's big voice had something like the effect of thunder, and the cloud rained away from around him. But this new moisture made the stalk grow even faster.

"This won't do!" Paul yelled. "Come down, and we'll handle her some other way!"

"Can't come down, either," Ole yelled in a minute. "Every time I go down one yard, this thing shoots up three, and I'm losing ground. I'm getting hungry, too."

Paul yelled for Babe, right then. And while he was waiting for Babe to come along, he used his shotgun to shoot up a few crullers which he hoped—for the time being, at any rate—would keep Ole from starving to death.

When Babe came along, Paul hurried with the beast over to Jim Hill's railroad, the Great Northern, which (by good luck) wasn't far away. Paul loaded Babe up with a pile of steel rails, then hurried back to the cornstalk with them.

"I'll see if I can't choke off the moisture in this cornstalk," Paul said. And with that he started tying those rails together and then knotting them around the cornstalk.

It worked, too.

Soon the ears of corn away up near the top stopped getting moisture and started to dry out. Then the hot sun hit them hard, and shortly the corn began to pop, making considerable noise, too.

After a while, this popped corn came drifting down like so many snow-balls. Babe, who'd lived through so much fierce weather, didn't do any more than shiver a little. But a big herd of cattle grazing near by decided they were in a world-beating blizzard and promptly froze to death.

Meanwhile, growing in spite of those knotted steel rails the way it had, the cornstalk had been bitten into by the things, and had cut itself off of itself. Now it started to tumble, slow but sure. Ole rode it down to the ground, just like a logger standing on a log in white water, then at the right time he jumped off lightly and headed back for Paul, following along the cornstalk.

When Ole got there, the owner of the cattle herd, who'd hurried over, was talking up right sassy to Paul. "Look what you did to my cattle, just when they were fat for market!" he yelled. "You'll have to pay for them."

"Course I will," Paul said. And he settled for the cattle, right on the spot, for Paul was always fair and square, regardless of cost.

"Hello, Ole," says Paul. "Glad to see you back. Just bought me a herd of frozen cattle."

"Goodness gracious!" Ole said. "And with our camp so far from where the cattle are, if we ship them they're likely to spoil."

"That won't do," Paul said. "We'll have to figure a way to use the critters. Teddy Roosevelt wouldn't like it if we wasted all those natural resources. Let me think."

After thinking a while, Paul snapped his fingers. "I've got it!" he said. "If the popcorn froze them, the popcorn can keep them frozen."

With that, he strolled over to the railroad and called on the head man, Jim Hill. Jim rented him a raft of box cars. Then, with the help of Babe, Paul stuffed those box cars with animals *and* popcorn. And that way, the meat kept fine until it had been delivered at Paul's camp.

So, without knowing it at the time, Paul had gone and invented refrigerator cars.

Paul Bunyan Takes Care of Mosquitoes

With mosquitoes being something of a national bird among tall-tale tellers, it is only natural that Paul Bunyan encountered some, and he knew just what to do.

Boys, did I ever tell you about the time I drove the Naubinway over to Paul Bunyan's camp on Big Mantisque Lake? Boys, I want to tell you there's some dandy mosquitoes over in that swamp even now, but the modern mosquitoes are nothing like their ancestors.

Well, just as I was pulling into Paul Bunyan's camp that day I heard some terrible droning noise like one of these modern airplanes. Even Paul, big as he was, seemed excited and yelled to me to hurry into his office. So I knew something was wrong.

Then Paul told me that some of the big mosquitoes was loose. He had trapped them several years ago, because they was bothering his cattle. Paul told me that two mosquitoes was trying to kill his prize heifer. They had the critter down and was trying to drag it off, he said, when along came a really big mosquito. The big mosquito simply killed off the other two, picked up the cow, and flew away. So Paul decided then and there to put on a campaign against them. He and his men trapped several of them in live traps, he said, and the rest got scared and flew away.

But this day, when I come to visit Paul, some of the mosquitoes had broken loose. We had barred the doors when we heard the mosquitoes droning overhead. They were landing on the roof. I shook like a leaf, but Paul wasn't scared. Overhead I heard a terrible cracking and looked to see swordlike weapons piercing the roof. Paul said they were mosquito stingers. So he grabbed his sledge and clinched those stingers like a carpenter clinches a nail. Next day he put twelve of his star lumberjacks to executing mosquitoes on that roof. He said he was through showing kindness to the mosquitoes. It didn't pay. They'd stab you in the back.

Cal Bunyan's Ireland, Jerusalem, Australia & Southern Indiana Railroad

---

Who would have thought that Paul Bunyan had a brother, and that he was a railroad man of extraordinary vision who was responsible for the longest, biggest, and fastest railroad in America?

I first heard about Cal from "Springheels" Conley, an old boomer who, in talking about some of the railroads where he had worked, mentioned the IJA&SI.

"What?" demanded Conley, when I told him I couldn't remember any railroad with those initials. "Do you mean that you've never heard of the Ireland, Jerusalem, Australia & Southern Indiana Railroad?"

I confessed that I never had, and "Springheels," after pouring himself another malted milk from the shaker the soda fountain clerk had set on the counter in front of us, told me all about Cal Bunyan and his railroad.

"You see, it was this way," said "Springheels," as he helped himself to my cigarettes. "Cal got the idea about starting the IJA&SI after Jim Hill finished building the Great Northern. I guess Cal was a little jealous of all the nice things the newspapers were saying about Hill. Anyway, Cal decided to build a road bigger than any that Jim Hill or any of those other guys could build.

"So he started laying the track of the IJA&SI. Ordinary ballast, such as cinders and gravel, wouldn't do for the tracks, so Cal used boulders which he brought from the Rocky Mountains. Each boulder weighed six tons and Cal used millions of them.

"Present-day section men think that big rails are now being used. They should have seen the kind on the IJA&SI. It took the largest steel mill in the United States, operating on a thirty-six-hour-day and nine-day-week schedule, two years to produce one rail for Cal.

"Each tie was made from an entire giant redwood tree. And the section men had to use pile-drivers to spike down the rails. One day a section foreman slipped and fell to the ground from the top of a rail. It was a 500-foot sheer drop and he was killed instantly.

"After the track was built, the next job was to get an engine and cars. They had to be made to order and it was a hard task finding machinery large enough to turn out the parts. Cal finally solved the problem by taking the two largest Ferris wheels he could find and setting them in line about a block apart to use for lathes in which to turn the axles for the new locomotive. He bought a merry-go-round and used it for a journal box boring mill. The Eiffel Tower in Paris was rigged up for a drill press.

"The rivets and staybolts used for the engine's boiler and firebox were 24 feet in diameter. A volcano was used to heat the rivets, and then the boiler-makers drove them in place by firing cannon balls at them.

"Building the coaches was some job, too. Each nail was driven by two husky carmen wielding fence post mauls. Long-stroke air hammers were used for tacking the upholstery on coach seats.

"Finally, an engine and 700 cars were ready for the first train. Before the engine was fired up, however, the 3,600 members of the road's board of directors held a banquet in the locomotive's firebox.

"There was only one tragedy to mark the day of the train's first run. When the engineer started the air pump, the first stroke sucked all of the air out of four neighboring states and hundreds of people suffocated to death.

"A roll of paper, like is used on newspaper printing presses, was used to write out orders for the engineer and conductor. The telegraphers who sent these orders were all clog dancers. They pounded out the dots and dashes by dancing jigs on the keys of their instruments.

"All of the clerks on the IJA&SI used fountain pens which, like Johnny Inkslinger's, took a barrel of ink at each filling.

"The engineer and fireman had to use a balloon to get up to the engine cab. If they had tried to climb up the gangway the 16-hour law would have caught them long before they got near the top.

"No man was strong enough to pull the throttle on this locomotive, so a stationary engine was installed on the right side to do the job.

"Mules and mine cars were used to haul coal from the tender and dump it on the deck in front of the firebox door. The fireman's scoop shovel held two tons.

"The train was so long that the conductor rode on a motorcycle to take up the tickets. He punched each ticket by shooting holes through it with a .45-caliber automatic pistol.

"On the dining car, a whole beef was used for each steak. Two cement mixers were required to stir the gravy, and potatoes were lifted out of the frying pans by steam shovels. A tank car was coupled in the front of each diner to carry the cream for the passengers' coffee.

"Just as the train started out, the engineer blew the whistle. When the steam condensed, it made a cloudburst which flooded the whole country.

"The train started to pick up speed and the engineer had to put on a pair of goggles that had lenses 18 inches thick. By and by he got going so fast that the suction from the train picked all of the leaves off the trees and pulled the farmers' corn out of the ground for eight miles each side of the right-of-way.

"No train ever went at the speed this one did. It went so fast that after it was brought to a dead stop it was still making 65 miles an hour. Two months later the schedule was speeded up so that the train arrived at its destination an hour before it left its starting point.

"At first there was a lot of trouble on the night runs—over the headlight. It was so powerful that it lighted up an area of 50,000 acres on each side of the track and kept it lighted for twelve hours after the train had passed. The farmers raised an awful rumpus about this—all of their chickens were dying from the loss of sleep. Also, the heat from the headlight was burning up wheat fields and drying up rivers. So the engineer tried to cover the headlight with a shield of six-inch armor plate, but the light shone through just the same. Finally, he took out the reflector, cut all the wires, and smashed the dynamo with a sledge hammer. This cut down the range of the light to a mile and a half, and half of the farmers stopped kicking.

"After that everything went along fine until one day when it was decided to double the speed of the train. It was no trick to do this, because at no time had the engineer ever had the throttle open more than three notches.

" 'Give her all she's got,' Cal Bunyan told the engineer when they started out on the new test run.

"The engineer opened her wide up. And did she make speed! But that was the end of the IJA&SI. The train went so fast that the friction melted all the rails and burned all the ties to ashes. And on the last half mile of the line, where the track went up a steep grade, the train was going at such a speed that when it reached the top the engine took off like an airplane and carried itself and its 700 cars so far into the stratosphere that the law of gravitation quit working. That was years ago, but the train is still rushing through space up there."

That was all of the story. "Springheels" tried to add a few more words, but his voice broke and he began sobbing. I got up quietly and slipped out a side door. The next day when I passed there, I glanced in. "Springheels" was still standing at the soda counter, crying into his malted milk over the sad fate of the IJA&SI.

The Birth of John Henry

The existence of a living railroad man named John Henry has never been proven, although many people claimed to have known him. He was embraced, especially among African Americans, as the ultimate strong man. The folklorist B. A. Botkin notes that, compared to Paul Bunyan, there has been "a surprisingly small amount of exaggeration in the stories about John Henry." In the following story, however, it is clear that the folk process has been at work.

Now John Henry was a man, but he's long dead.

The night John Henry was born the moon was copper-colored and the sky was black. The stars wouldn't shine and the rain fell hard. Forked lightning cleaved the air and the earth trembled like a leaf. The panthers squalled in the brake like a baby and the Mississippi River ran upstream a thousand miles. John Henry weighed forty-four pounds.

John Henry was born on the banks of the Black River, where all good rousterbouts come from. He came into the world with a cotton-hook for a right hand and a river song on his tongue:

> "Looked up and down de river,
>> Twice as far as I could see.
> Seed befo' I gits to be twenty-one,
>> De Anchor Line gonter b'long to me, Lawd, Lawd,
>> Anchor Line gonter b'long to me."

They didn't know what to make of John Henry when he was born. They looked at him and then went and looked at the river.

"He got a bass voice like a preacher," his mamma said.

"He got shoulders like a cotton-rollin' rousterbout," his papa said.

"He got blue gums like a conjure man," the nurse woman said.

"I might preach some," said John Henry, "but I ain't gonter be no preach-er. I might roll cotton on de boats, but I ain't gonter be no cottonrollin' rouster-bout. I might got blue gums like a conjure man, but I ain't gonter git familiar wid de sperits. 'Cause my name is John Henry, and when fo'ks call me by my name, dey'll know I'm a natchal man."

"His name is John Henry," said his mamma. "Hit's a fack."

"And when you calls him by his name," said his papa, "he's a natchal man."

So about that time John Henry raised up and stretched. "Well," he said, "ain't hit about supper-time?"

"Sho hit's about supper-time," said his mamma.

"And after," said his papa.

"And long after," said the nurse woman.

"Well," said John Henry, "did de dogs had they supper?"

"They did," said his mamma.

"All de dogs," said his papa.

"Long since," said the nurse woman.

"Well, den," said John Henry, "ain't I as good as de dogs?"

And when John Henry said that he got mad. He reared back in his bed and broke out the slats. He opened his mouth and yowled, and it put out the lamp. He cleaved his tongue and spat, and it put out the fire. "Don't make me mad!" said John Henry, and the thunder rumbled and rolled. "Don't let me git mad on de day I'm bawn, 'cause I'm skeered of my ownse'f when I gits mad."

And John Henry stood up in the middle of the floor and he told them what he wanted to eat. "Bring me four ham bones and a pot full of cabbages," he said. "Bring me a bait of turnip greens tree-top tall, and season hit down wid a side er middlin'. Bring me a pone er cold cawn bread and some hot potlicker to wash hit down. Bring me two hog jowls and a kittleful er whippowill peas. Bring me a skittletful er red-hot biscuits and a big jugful er cane molasses. 'Cause my name is John Henry, and I'll see you soon."

So John Henry walked out of the house and away from the Black River Country where all good rousterbouts are born.

The Ballad of John Henry

—·•·—

John Henry is most famous for the stance he took against the coming of the machine age, which symbolized the oppression of individual workers. Among the best known and most often sung of the American ballads, "The Ballad of John Henry" recounts the famous story of the contest between John and the steam drill, which earned him his place as hero of the workingman.

John Henry was a li'l baby, uh-huh,
Sittin' on his mama's knee, oh, yeah,
Said: "De Big Bend Tunnel on de C. & O. road
Gonna cause de death of me,
Lawd, Lawd, gonna cause de death of me."

John Henry, he had a woman,
Her name was Mary Magdalene,
She would go to de tunnel and sing for John,
Jes' to hear John Henry's hammer ring,
Lawd, Lawd, jes' to hear John Henry's hammer ring.

John Henry had a lil woman,
Her name was Lucy Ann,
John Henry took sick an' had to go to bed,
Lucy Ann drove steel like a man,
Lawd, Lawd, Lucy Ann drove steel like a man.

Cap'n says to John Henry,
"Gonna bring me a steam drill 'round,
Gonna take dat steam drill out on de job,
Gonna whop dat steel on down,
Lawd, Lawd, gonna whop dat steel on down."

John Henry tol' his cap'n,
Lightnin' was in his eye:
"Cap'n, bet yo' las' red cent on me,
Fo' I'll beat it to de bottom or I'll die,
Lawd, Lawd, I'll beat it to de bottom or I'll die."

Sun shine hot an' burnin',
Wer'n't no breeze a-tall,
Sweat ran down like water down a hill,
Dat day John Henry let his hammer fall,
Lawd, Lawd, dat day John Henry let his hammer fall.

John Henry went to de tunnel,
An' dey put him in de lead to drive;
De rock so tall an' John Henry so small,
Dat he lied down his hammer an' he cried,
Lawd, Lawd, dat he lied down his hammer an' he cried.

John Henry started on de right hand,
De steam drill started on de lef'—
"Before I'd let dis steam drill beat me down,
I'd hammer my fool self to death,
Lawd, Lawd, I'd hammer my fool self to death."

White man tol' John Henry,
"Nigger, damn yo' soul,
You might beat dis steam an' drill of mine,
When de rocks in dis mountain turn to gol',
Lawd, Lawd, when de rocks in dis mountain turn to gol'."

John Henry said to his shaker,
"Nigger, why don' you sing?
I'm throwin' twelve poun's from my hips on down,
Jes' listen to de col' steel ring,
Lawd, Lawd, jes' listen to de col' steel ring."

Oh, de captain said to John Henry,
"I b'lieve this mountain's sinkin' in."
John Henry said to his captain, oh my!
"Ain' nothin' but my hammer suckin' win',
Lawd, Lawd, ain' nothin' but my hammer suckin' win'."

John Henry tol' his shaker,
"Shaker, you better pray,
For, if I miss dis six-foot steel,
Tomorrow'll be yo' buryin' day,
Lawd, Lawd, tomorrow'll be yo' buryin' day."

John Henry tol' his captain,
"Looka yonder what I see—
Yo' drill's done broke an' yo' hole's done choke,
An' you cain' drive steel like me,
Lawd, Lawd, an' you cain' drive steel like me."

De man dat invented de steam drill,
Thought he was mighty fine.
John Henry drove his fifteen feet,
An' de steam drill only made nine,
Lawd, Lawd, an' de steam drill only made nine.

De hammer dat John Henry swung
It weighed over nine pound;
He broke a rib in his lef'-han' side,
An' his intrels fell on de groun',
Lawd, Lawd, n' his intrels fell on de groun'.

John Henry was hammerin' on de mountain,
An' his hammer was strikin' fire,
He drove so hard till he broke his pore heart,
An' he lied down his hammer an' he died,
Lawd, Lawd, he lied down his hammer an' he died.

All de womens in de Wes',
When dey heared of John Henry's death,
Stood in de rain, flagged de eas'-boun' train,
Goin' where John Henry fell dead,
Lawd, Lawd, goin' where John Henry fell dead.

John Henry's li'l mother,
She was all dressed in red,
She jumped in bed, covered up her head,
Said she didn' know her son was dead,
Lawd, Lawd, didn' know her son was dead.

John Henry had a pretty li'l woman,
An' de dress she wo' was blue,
An' de las' words she said to him:
"John Henry I've been true to you,
Lawd, Lawd, John Henry, I've been true to you."

Annie Christmas

Though some believe that the character of Annie Christmas is based on a genuine figure who lived in New Orleans, as with her male counterpart, John Henry, there has been no way to prove it. Whether she lived or not, the tales about her eventually reached legendary proportions, and they brought a feminine element to the overwhelmingly male-centered body of myth surrounding the growth of the nation. In some stories about Annie Christmas, she is depicted as a white woman; in others she is black, and there continues to be disagreement among folklorists and storytellers about which was the original character.

Once upon a time in New Orleans there lived a woman who could only be described as extraordinary. For starters, she was strong, stronger than any man; stronger, some said, than any horse or ox that worked the river hauling wagon loads of cotton and goods to and from the riverboats that brought the world to New Orleans and took New Orleans to the world. Though she's been dead a long time, if you hang around New Orleans to this day, you will hear somebody say of a man, "Why, he's as strong as Annie Christmas."

And then Annie Christmas was tall. Some said she stood seven foot; some said eight. Some said anywhere in between. She wore the clothes of a riverman and worked her own keelboat. She worked faster and longer than any man alive. "Said little and done much," that's what they said, for she did not speak except to call out a warning or make it known what she thought of any man who mocked her.

Oh, she'd been known to fight, and any man who fought her once knew better than to fight her again. Once a newcomer to New Orleans named Mike Fink was hanging around the dock with all the other rivermen waiting for an empty flatbed to arrive to take a load of cotton up to Natchez. He commented that her ladyship ought to be home darning cotton socks and not out making a fool of herself hauling cotton bales. He said this to her back while she was hunched over a half-ton bale getting ready to hook it with a grapple. Without a word, Annie laid down the grapple, picked up the cotton, and stood up . . . and up . . . and up. At her full height, and with a half-ton bale of cotton stretched up over her head, she looked like Atlas holding up the world. And though some say Mike Fink was tall of stature, and some say he was short, on that day it probably didn't matter if he was tall or short in comparison to ordinary people.

Fink's eyes, that had been narrowed in sarcasm a minute before, were round, now, and popping. It was the only time anyone ever noticed him lose his wisecracking voice. For he sputtered and stuttered and put his stubby little arms out as if he was going to catch that bundle on the way down.

Annie spoke then. Her voice was soft as cotton fresh from the gin. "It seems clear to me, suh, that you have a somewhat narrow viewpoint on the subject of who should be where, when." That was all she said. And then she threw that bale with all her might, but not at Fink. She threw it down, straight down into the water off the dock by his feet. The tidal wave that swept Fink away was small, but powerful, and it carried him, still standing, to Natchez with his mouth open but no sound coming out, all the way. And that's why Mike Fink was never seen in New Orleans again.

"Not much of a fight," was all the rivermen could think of to say about the incident.

When she felt like it Annie would dress up. She would dress up *fine!* She had her dresses made by Miz Lacy Lusterfellow, who knew just where to tuck and sew to show off a figure like Annie Christmas. To make the midnight blue gown Annie wore when she wanted to look particularly pretty, Miz Lacy used an entire bolt of the finest China silk, which Annie had taken in pay for a week's work in August the year before. The dress had more gathers than the opera house curtains, and more bows about the bodice than the Christmas tree at the governor's mansion. And when Annie walked down the street she'd nod her feather-crowned hat to her friends, who would marvel aloud how a woman so big and so strong could look so ladylike, so *royal*, in a dress.

The only thing that could take Annie Christmas out was love. Strong as she was, she was powerless when that old bug bit her, and she was tireless in pursuit of a way to scratch that itch. Once she fell for a man, he'd just as well come along, 'cause she'd dog his tracks, rest her oars in the wake of his keelboat, or gamble the night away on his boat, as in the case of her last love, the gamesman in a riverboat gambling hall. Annie had twelve sons, and they were all as tall and black as she was. And when they all dressed up to go have themselves a time on the river, they were a sight to behold. Six sons escorted her on the right, and six sons escorted her on the left. She aimed to have more sons, so they said, but her last chance came and went on the night Annie Christmas died.

On this particular night, Annie and her sons rowed out on a flat boat to the *Lacey Mae*, a riverboat with a sweet name and a reputation for the fiercest gambling on the Mississippi. Annie fell in love that night for the last time, with a man named Easter, Jimmy Easter. She stood behind him while he played blackjack, and he had more luck than a copper penny. He knew she was there, but he ignored her something awful. He didn't know— how could he have known?—that she was his lucky charm. When he turned to collect his winnings, Annie put her hand on his shoulder and smiled. He smiled back and said, "Howdy, ma'am."

Jimmy Easter was nigh as tall as Annie and equally handsome. He winked at her, but didn't tarry, brushed by her shoulder and walked off to the roulette wheel to try his new found fortune there. Annie's girlfriend, Sis McQueen, saw what was coming and told Annie the truth, that Jimmy Easter was a married man and she'd better watch out. But Annie was smitten, and she strolled over to the roulette wheel and just *leaned* on Jimmy's arm. The closer she got, the more he won. It was a match made in gambler's heaven, and Jimmy seemed to be about to realize that when the door to the casino opened and in walked his wife, Charlene. It only took her a second to assess the situation, and she being the jealous type, she wasted not a word or a minute, pulled a gun, and shot Annie Christmas once through the heart.

What the rivermen said was, "River couldn't kill her; birthing twelve big strapping boys couldn't kill her; Mike Fink couldn't kill her; but love, careless love, that's what killed her."

Annie's sons knew what to do after that. Seemed they'd known this day would come. They dressed her in her midnight blue dress, and had a coffin made to fit her. They carried the coffin through the streets of New Orleans so her admirers could pay their last respects. They walked her to the river, and at the dark of the moon, put her on a keelboat. Then they stood, each taking a turn with the pole, and pressed themselves out of sight down the river, into the mist, singing a slow sad song, never to be seen again.

The Saga of Pecos Bill

As the popularity of America's new mythological heroes grew, writers invented new ones who were quickly embraced by the public. In 1923, Edward O'Reilly wrote "The Saga of Pecos Bill" using the formula that had proved so successful with Paul Bunyan and other demigods. That is, he strung together many of the tall tales that were circulating about cowboys in the early part of the century, creating one long story of the most remarkable cowboy who ever lived.

According to the most veracious historians, Bill was born about the time Sam Houston discovered Texas. His mother was a sturdy pioneer woman who once killed forty-five Indians with a broom-handle, and weaned him on moonshine liquor when he was three days old. He cut his teeth on a bowie-knife, and his earliest playfellows were the bears and catamounts of east Texas.

When Bill was about a year old, another family moved into the country, and located about fifty miles down the river. His father decided the place was gettin' too crowded, and packed his family in a wagon and headed west.

One day after they crossed the Pecos River, Bill fell out of the wagon. As there were sixteen or seventeen other children in the family, his parents didn't miss him for four or five weeks, and then it was too late to try to find him.

That's how Bill came to grow up with the coyotes along the Pecos. He soon learned the coyote language, and used to hunt with them and sit on the hills and howl at night. Being so young when he got lost, he always thought he was a coyote. That's where he learned to kill deer by runnin' them to death.

One day when he was about ten years old a cow-boy came along just when Bill had matched a fight with two grizzly bears. Bill hugged the bears to death, tore off a hind leg, and was just settin' down to breakfast when this cow-boy loped up and asked him what he meant by runnin' around naked that way among the varmints.

"Why, because I am a varmint," Bill told him. "I'm a coyote."

The cow-boy argued with him that he was a human, but Bill wouldn't believe him.

"Ain't I got fleas!" he insisted. "And don't I howl around all night, like a respectable coyote should do?"

"That don't prove nothin'," the cow-boy answered. "All Texans have fleas, and most of them howl. Did you ever see a coyote that didn't have a tail? Well, you ain't got no tail; so that proves you ain't a varmint."

Bill looked, and, sure enough, he didn't have a tail.

"You sure got me out on a limb," says Bill. "I never noticed that before. It shows what higher education will do for a man. I believe you're right. Lead me to them humans, and I'll throw in with them."

Bill went to town with this cow-hand, and in due time he got to enjoyin' all the pleasant vices of mankind, and decided that he certainly was a human. He got to runnin' with the wild bunch, and sunk lower and lower, until finally he became a cow-boy.

It wasn't long until he was famous as a bad man. He invented the six-shooter and train-robbin' and most of the crimes popular in the old days of the West. He didn't invent cowstealin'. That was discovered by King David in the Bible, but Bill improved on it.

There is no way of tellin' just how many men Bill did kill. Deep down he had a tender heart, however, and never killed women or children, or tourists out of season. He never scalped his victims; he was too civilized for that. He used to skin them gently and tan their hides.

It wasn't long before Bill had killed all the bad men in west Texas, massacred all the Indians, and eaten all the buffalo. So he decided to migrate to a new country where hard men still thrived and a man could pass the time away.

He saddled up his horse and hit for the West. One day he met an old trapper and told him what he was lookin' for.

"I want the hardest cow outfit in the world," he says. "Not one of these ordinary cow-stealin', Mexican-shootin'

bunches of amateurs, but a real hard herd of hand-picked hellions that make murder a fine art and take some proper pride in their slaughter."

"Stranger, you're headed in the right direction," answers the trapper.
"Keep right on down this draw for a couple of hundred miles, and you'll find that
very outfit. They're so hard they can kick fire out of a flint rock with their bare
toes."

Bill single-footed down that draw for about a hundred miles that afternoon; then he met with an accident. His horse stubbed his toe on a mountain and
broke his leg, leavin' Bill afoot.

He slung his saddle over his shoulder and set off hikin' down that draw,
cussin' and a-swearin'. Profanity was a gift with Bill.

All at once a big ten-foot rattlesnake quiled up in his path, set his tail to
singin', and allowed he'd like to match a fight. Bill laid down his saddle, and just
to be fair about it, he gave the snake the first three bites. Then he waded into that
reptile and everlastingly frailed the pizen out of him.

By and by that old rattler yelled for mercy, and admitted that when it
came to fightin', Bill started where he left off. So Bill picked up his saddle and
started on, carryin' the snake in his hand and spinnin' it in short loops at the Gila
monsters.

About fifty miles further on, a big old mountain-lion jumped off a cliff
and lit all spraddled out on Bill's neck. This was no ordinary lion. It weighed more
than three steers and a yearlin', and was the very same lion the State of Nuevo
León was named after down in old Mexico.

Kind of chucklin' to himself, Bill laid down his saddle and his snake and
went into action. In a minute the fur was flyin' down the cañon until it darkened
the sun. The way Bill knocked the animosity out of that lion was a shame. In
about three minutes that lion hollered:

"I'll give up, Bill. Can't you take a joke?"

Bill let him up, and then he cinched the saddle on him and went down
that cañon whoopin' and yellin', ridin' that lion a hundred feet at a jump, and
quirtin' him down the flank with the rattlesnake.

It wasn't long before he saw a chuck-wagon, with a bunch of cow-boys squattin' around it. He rode up to that wagon, splittin' the air with his war-whoops, with that old lion a screechin', and that snake singin' his rattles.

When he came to the fire he grabbed the old cougar by the ear, jerked him back on his haunches, stepped off him, hung his snake around his neck, and looked the outfit over. Them cow-boys sat there sayin' less than nothin'.

Bill was hungry, and seein' a boilerful of beans cookin' on the fire, he scooped up a few handfuls and swallowed them, washin' them down with a few gallons of boilin' coffee out of the pot. Wipin' his mouth on a handful of prickly-pear cactus, Bill turned to the cow-boys and asked:

"Who the hell is boss around here?"

A big fellow about eight feet tall, with seven pistols and nine bowie-knives in his belt, rose up and, takin' off his hat, said:

"Stranger, I was; but you be."

Bill had many adventures with this outfit. It was about this time he staked out New Mexico, and used Arizona for a calf-pasture. It was here that he found his noted horse Widow-Maker. He raised him from a colt on nitroglycerin and dynamite, and Bill was the only man that could throw a leg over him.

There wasn't anythin' that Bill couldn't ride, although I have heard of one occasion when he was thrown. He made a bet that he could ride an Oklahoma cyclone slick-heeled, without a saddle.

He met the cyclone, the worst that was ever known, up on the Kansas line. Bill eared that tornado down and climbed on its back. That cyclone did some pitchin' that is unbelievable, if it were not vouched for by many reliable witnesses.

Down across Texas it went sunfishin', back-flippin', side-windin', knockin' down mountains, blowin' the holes out of the ground, and tyin' rivers into knots. The Staked Plains used to be heavily timbered until that big wind swiped the trees off and left it a bare prairie.

Bill just sat up there, thumbin' that cyclone in the withers, floppin' it across the ears with his hat, and rollin' a cigarette with one hand. He rode it through three States, but over in Arizona it got him.

When it saw it couldn't throw him, it rained out from under him. This is proved by the fact that it washed out the Grand Cañon. Bill came down over in California. The spot where he lit is now known as Death Valley, a hole in the ground more than one hundred feet below sea-level, and the print of his hip-pockets can still be seen in the granite.

I have heard this story disputed in some of its details. Some historians claim that Bill wasn't thrown; that he slid down on a streak of lightnin' without knockin' the ashes off his cigarette. It is also claimed that the Grand Cañon was dug by Bill one week when he went prospectin'; but the best authorities insist on the first version. They argue that that streak of lightnin' story comes from the habit he always had of usin' one to light his cigarette.

Bill was a great roper. In fact, he invented ropin'. Old-timers who admit they knew him say that his rope was as long as the equator, although the more conservative say that it was at least two feet shorter on one end. He used to rope a herd of cattle at one throw.

This skill once saved the life of a friend. The friend had tried to ride Widow-Maker one day, and was thrown so high he came down on top of Pike's Peak. He was in the middle of a bad fix, because he couldn't get down, and seemed doomed to a lingerin' death on high.

Bill came to the rescue, and usin' only a short calf-loop, he roped his friend around the neck and jerked him down to safety in the valley, twenty thousand feet below. This man was always grateful, and became Bill's horse-wrangler at the time he staked out New Mexico.

In his idle moments in New Mexico Bill amused himself puttin' thorns on the trees and hems on the toads. It was on this ranch he dug the Rio Grande and invented the centipede and the tarantula as a joke on his friends.

When the cow business was dull, Pecos Bill occasionally embarked on other ventures; for instance, at one time he took a contract to supply the S.P. Railroad with wood. He hired a few hundred Mexicans to chop and haul the wood to the railroad line. As pay for the job, Bill gave each Mexican one fourth of the wood he hauled.

On another occasion Bill took the job of buildin' the line fence that forms the boundary from El Paso across to the Pacific. He rounded up a herd of prairie-dogs and set them to dig holes, which by nature a prairie-dog likes to do.

Whenever one of them finished a nice hole and settled down to live in it, Bill evicted him and stuck a fence-post in the hole. Everybody admired his foresight except the prairie-dogs, and who cares what a prairie-dog thinks?

He threw in with a bunch of Kiowa Indians one time on a little huntin'-trip. It was about the time the buffalo were getting scarce, and Bill was huntin' with his famous squatter-hound named Norther.

Norther would run down a buffalo and hold him by the ear until Bill came up and skinned him alive. Then he would turn it loose to grow a new hide. The scheme worked all right in the summer, but in the winter most of them caught colds and died.

The stories of Bill's love-affairs are especially numerous. One of them may be told. It is the sad tale of the fate of his bride, a winsome little maiden called Slue-Foot Sue. She was a famous rider herself, and Bill lost his heart when he saw her riding a catfish down the Rio Grande with only a surcingle. You must remember that the catfish in the Rio Grande are bigger than whales and twice as active.

Sue made a sad mistake, however, when she insisted on ridin' Widow-Maker on her weddin'-day. The old horse threw her so high she had to duck her head to let the moon go by. Unfortunately, she was wearin' her weddin'-gown, and in those days the women wore those big steel-spring bustles.

Well, when Sue lit, she naturally bounced, and every time she came down she bounced again. It was an awful' sad sight to see Bill implorin' her to quit her bouncin' and not be so nervous; but Sue kept right on, up and down, weepin', and throwin' kisses to her distracted lover, and carryin' on as a bride naturally would do under those circumstances.

She bounced for three days and four nights, and Bill finally had to shoot her to keep her from starvin' to death. It was mighty tragic. Bill never got over it. Of course he married lots of women after that. In fact, it was one of his weaknesses; but none of them filled the place in his heart once held by Slue-Foot Sue, his bouncin' bride.

There is a great difference of opinion as to the manner of Bill's demise. Many claim that it was his drinkin' habits that killed him. You see, Bill got so that liquor didn't have any kick for him, and he fell into the habit of drinkin' strychnine and other forms of wolf pizen.

Even the wolf bait lost its effect, and he got to puttin' fishhooks and barbed wire in his toddy. It was the barbed wire that finally killed him. It rusted his interior and gave him indigestion. He wasted away to a mere skeleton, weighin' not more than two tons; then up and died, and went to his infernal reward.

Many of the border bards who knew Pecos Bill at his best have a different account of his death.

They say that he met a man from Boston one day, wearing a mail-order cow-boy outfit, and askin' fool questions about the West; and poor old Bill laid down and laughed himself to death.

5

Life Lessons

~

Tale-telling offers a way of passing the time and entertaining one another, but some stories have a more serious purpose. They convey meaning and instruction that are important to the community that has generated the stories. Cautionary tales—or moralizing tales, as they are sometimes called—reinforce social values, sometimes with humor and sometimes with tales meant to frighten children and adults away from behavior that will harm them or disrupt community life.

Many stories that are not overtly moralizing have strong lessons embedded in them. Such stories have the power to persuade because they entertain as they teach, and their lessons are remembered long after a simple warning or admonition is forgotten. As a nation of immigrants, North Americans have taken their cautionary tales from many lands, and the values they support represent many cultures. Yet every such story, no matter what its source, has a life lesson to teach all of us, since the most important values—generosity, honesty, common sense—cut across time and cultural boundaries.

Looking for Trouble

———•+•———

This tale, which encourages common sense, is a traditional cautionary tale from the Sea Islands off the coast of Georgia and South Carolina, where Gullah is spoken. Because of their isolation, the people of the Sea Islands retained a rich body of lore until well into the twentieth century.

———•+•———

One day long ago, Alligator was floating in his home creek thinking how satisfy life is.

In those days, he's dress-up in a white suit good enough for Sunday all the time. He lives in the water with all the fish he can eat so he never has to work for a living. And he never, never meets up with trouble.

Well, Alligator is lazy in the sun-hot when here comes Bo Rabbit projecting along the creek shore.

"G'morning, Alligator. How're you today?" asks Bo Rabbit, stopping to pass the time of day and other sociabilities.

"Doing just fine, thank you kindly. How's everyone to your house?"

"Oh, we making out. But so much trouble, Alligator. So much trouble."

"Trouble! What's that, Rabbit? I ain't never seen trouble."

"You ain't never seen trouble! Great Peace! I can show you trouble, Alligator."

"I'd like that, Bo Rabbit. I'd surely like to see how trouble stands."

"All right," Bo Rabbit makes response. "Meet me in the broomsage field tomorrow morning time the sun dries the dew off the grass good and I'll show you trouble."

Next morning time the sun gets high, Alligator takes his hat and starts to leave the house. Miz Alligator asks him where he's going.

"I'm going to meet Bo Rabbit so he can show me how trouble stands."

"Well, if you're going to see trouble, I'm going, too."

"Hush up, you ain't going nowhere," says Alligator, high and mighty. "You best let me go see how trouble stands first. Then I can show you."

This makes Miz Alligator so mad she starts to arguefy.

They quarrel so loud till all the little alligators hear them and come sliding into the room, *hirr, hirr, hirr, hirr, hirr, hirr.*

All the little alligators holler, "If you're going to see trouble, we're going, too. If you're going, we're going, too."

They make such a racket that to save his ears, Alligator roars, "Quiet! All right, all right. You *all* can come."

They cross the marsh and time they get in the broomsage field there's Bo Rabbit sitting on top a stump waiting for them.

"G'morning, Bo Rabbit," they say. And all the little alligators make their curtseys, *sazip, sazip, sazip, sazip, sazip, sazip.*

Bo Rabbit tells them "G'morning" back. "You all come to see trouble this morning, isn't it so!"

"It's so," says Alligator.

"It's so," say all the little alligators.

"All right. Stand out in the middle of the field and wait. I'll go get trouble and bring it."

Alligator, Miz Alligator and all the little alligators slither into the field, KAPUK, *Kapuk, kapuk, kapuk, kapuk, kapuk, kapuk, kapuk.*

Bo Rabbit runs to the far edge and cuts him a hand of broomsage. Then he puts fire to it and runs it round and round the field till the fire runs round and round the field.

Miz Alligator sees the fire jumping up red and the smoke rising. "What's that yonder, Alligator?" She lives in the river and the wet marsh and never sees fire.

Alligator runs his eye around and shakes his head in puzzlement.

"I think that's the trouble Rabbit is bringing to show us," says Miz Alligator.

All the little alligators jump up and down and holler, "Ain't trouble pretty, Ma? Ain't trouble pretty!"

Soon the fire hot gets close and the smoke gets bad and all the alligators take out for one side of the field. They meet the fire.

They turn around to the other side. They meet the fire.

The fire gets so close it feels like it's going to burn them.

They all shut their eye and throw their head close to the ground and bust through the fire and never stop till, SPASHOW, Alligator jumps in the creek.

Right behind him, *Spashow*, Miz Alligator jumps in the creek.

Then all the little alligators come, *shu, shu, shu, shu, shu, shu,* in the creek.

As they scramble out, Bo Rabbit yells across the stream, "You've seen trouble now, Alligator. You like to see it again? I can show you."

"No, suh, Bo Rabbit. No, suh," says Alligator.

He looks at his suit. His white suit good enough for Sunday is gone.

He is blackish-green and rough and bumpy just the way he stands till yet.

"It's all Bo Rabbit's fault. Him and his Judas ways," says Alligator.

But even as the words come out his mouth, Alligator knows in his spirit that's not rightly so. He's the one asked to see trouble.

"I've learned one lesson for all my life," says Alligator. "Don't go looking for trouble, else you might find it."

The Bird That Was Ashamed of Its Feet

Children of all ages spend a lot of time scrutinizing themselves and agonizing over any-thing that doesn't seem normal. How do we, by the time we are adults, learn to appre-ciate what makes us unique? This Cherokee tale, adapted by storyteller Gayle Ross, offers all of us a new way to look at ourselves.

This is what the old people told me when I was a child, about the days when the world was new and all creatures still spoke the same language. Now, in those days, there was a bird called Meadowlark, whose feet grew so big that he was ashamed of them. While the other birds flew through the air and sang in the treetops, Meadowlark hid himself in the tall grass where no one could see him. He spent all his time staring down at his big feet and worrying about them.

"Provider must have made a terrible mistake," thought Meadowlark, turn-ing his feet this way and that. No matter how he looked at them, all Meadowlark could see was how big his feet were. "Perhaps Creator thought this would be a funny joke to play," said Meadowlark. "I'm sure anyone who saw my big feet would laugh at them, but I do not think this is funny at all." And so Meadowlark con-tinued to hide himself away in the tall grass.

One day Grasshopper was going about his business, making his way through the tall grass, when he bumped smack into Meadowlark, sitting on the ground and staring sadly at his feet.

"What are you doing here?" asked Grasshopper. "You are not one of those birds who live on the ground! You should be in the treetops with the other birds. Why do you not fly and sing as they do?"

"I am ashamed," answered Meadowlark. "These feet that Provider gave me are so big and ugly that I am afraid that everyone will laugh at me!"

Grasshopper looked down at Meadowlark's feet, and his eyes grew big with amazement. It was true; Meadowlark's feet were huge! Grasshopper did his best not to smile; he did not want to hurt Meadowlark's feelings.

Finally he said, "Well, it is true that your feet are perhaps a bit larger than those of other birds your size. But Creator does not make mistakes. If your feet are big, you may be sure that they will be useful to you someday. Big feet will not keep you from flying. Big feet will not stop you from singing. You are a bird and you should act like one!" And Grasshopper went on about his business.

After Grasshopper had gone on his way, Meadowlark sat and thought about his words. "Perhaps he is right," said Meadowlark. "The size of my feet cannot change the sound of my voice or the power of my wings. I should use the gifts Creator gave me." And so Meadowlark took Grasshopper's advice and flew out to sing. He landed in the top of a tree, threw back his head, and let his song pour from his throat. Meadowlark could really sing! Piercingly sweet and beautiful, the liquid notes of Meadowlark's song spread through the forest.

One by one, the animal people stopped what they were doing and gathered to listen to Meadowlark's voice. Raccoon, Possum, and Skunk; Deer, Bear, and Wolf; even Rabbit paused in his scurrying about to listen in wonder to this marvelous singer. The other birds flocked around Meadowlark, listening. Even Mockingbird fell silent, entranced by the melody that Meadowlark sang.

When Meadowlark began to sing, he forgot everything else, even his big feet. He closed his eyes and lost himself in the joyful song Creator had given him. When at last he finished his song and looked around, there were all the other birds and animals, staring at him. With a rush of shame, Meadowlark remembered his feet. Thinking that the others were staring at him because he was so ugly, Meadowlark flew back down to the tall grass and hid. And this time he would not come out.

Not very far from the tall grass where Meadowlark hid, there was a wheat field planted by the Human Beings. Now there was a Quail who had made her nest and laid her eggs in the middle of this wheat field. Every day she sat on her nest and waited for her eggs to hatch. As the wheat grew ripe and her eggs had still not hatched, Quail began to worry. Sure enough, one afternoon she heard the people talking about how they were going to come out and cut the wheat the very next day. Quail knew that her nest would be trampled and her eggs crushed, and she began to cry.

Now Grasshopper heard Quail crying, and he came to see what was wrong. "The men are coming to cut the wheat," Quail cried, "and my family will die!"

Suddenly Grasshopper had an idea. "Wait here," he told Quail. "I think I know someone who can help."

Grasshopper hurried to find Meadowlark. "Quail needs help to move her family," said Grasshopper, "and I think your big feet are the answer."

When Meadowlark heard of Quail's trouble, he agreed at once to try to help. He flew to Quail's nest. There he found that his big feet were just the right size to pick up Quail's eggs. Very carefully, Meadowlark lifted Quail's eggs and flew with them to the safety of the tall grass. There Quail built a new nest, and it was not long before the eggs hatched. As Meadowlark watched Quail tending her beautiful babies, he thought to himself, "My feet may be big and ugly, but they did a good thing. I should not be ashamed of them!"

And so Meadowlark flew out of the tall grass, back to the treetops where he began to sing. He is singing to this day, and his song is still so beautiful that everyone stops to listen.

A Boy and His Donkey

Every book of etiquette makes it clear that one fundamental rule of good manners is to take the smaller portion and leave the larger for others. We can tell our children this, but it is much more likely that they will remember it after reading this tale from the Hispanic Southwest.

Once there lived a very poor woman who lived alone with her only child.

One day the son, who was only ten, decided to seek work. "Mother," he said, "let me go out and look for work."

His mother would not permit him to go because he was too young. But the boy insisted that he should go out and look for work to help support her. He bothered her so much that one day she finally relented. She prepared a packsack with provisions for her brave young son, gave him her blessing, and sent him on his way. The lad then loaded the provisions on his donkey and set out to look for work. He didn't know which direction to take, so he wandered until he was far from home.

But the Virgin Mary, who was the boy's patron saint, and the prayers of his mother guided him. On the road he traveled he met a woman dressed in a blue robe.

"Where are you going, my son!" asked the woman, who was in truth the Blessed Virgin.

"I am looking for work to support my mother."

"You are a good son, but you must be very careful because there are many evil men on this road who may harm you," she warned him.

"They can't harm me," the boy answered, "because I have nothing they can steal."

The Virgin smiled. "Since you are determined to continue your journey, here, take these three apples. Whenever you meet someone who wants to travel with you, cut an apple in half, but always cut one half smaller than the other. Offer both halves to the person; and if he takes the bigger half then do not count that person as your friend. He is a bad person, and may harm you. But the person who takes the smaller half will be a good friend whom you can trust."

The boy tucked the three apples in his coat pocket and continued on his way. That evening he met a man who asked him if they could travel together as companions and the boy agreed. When they stopped to rest that evening the boy cut one of the apples in half, remembering to leave one half smaller than the other. He offered them to the man. The man reached for the bigger half.

This is not a good companion, the boy thought. And he was right because it was the intention of the man to steal the donkey once the boy was asleep.

That night, although he was very tired, the boy didn't sleep. When he was sure the man was asleep he got up very quietly, gathered his provisions and hurried to his donkey. He loaded his burro and fled.

When the thief got up to steal the burro he found both the boy and the donkey gone. The thief cursed his luck and wondered how the boy had known his intentions.

Later on his journey, the boy met another man. The man suggested to the boy that they could travel together since they were going in the same direction. The boy agreed. That evening he cut the second apple in half, again cutting one half smaller than the other. He offered them to the stranger and the man immediately took the bigger half. So the boy knew this was another sly man to beware of.

That night as soon as the man had fallen asleep the boy got up very quietly and carried his pack to where his burro was hobbled. He packed his provisions and was far away by the time the thief awakened to find himself alone with his evil intentions.

The very next day the boy met up with an old man.

"Where are you going, my son?" the old man asked.

"I am going to the city to look for work," the boy replied.

"There are many thieves on this road. They might harm you."

"They can't harm me," the boy answered, "because the prayers of my mother and the Blessed Virgin Mary protect me."

"Very good, my son," the old man nodded. "I am going in the same direction. Why don't we travel together?"

The boy agreed and they continued together. That evening when they had arrived at a campsite, the boy cut his last apple in half, again leaving one half smaller than the other. He offered them to the old man, and the old man took the smaller piece.

And so the boy knew that he had met a good companion with whom he could travel. That night he slept soundly, confident that he had met a good friend. When he awoke the sun was already high in the sky. He rubbed his eyes and looked around, but the old man was gone.

The boy leaped out of his bedroll and ran in search of his burro. But when he went down to the pasture he found them both. The old man had simply moved the burro to where there was better pasture. From that day on they traveled together and became good friends, and eventually the boy found work, and sent money to his mother.

Brer Possum's Dilemma

Storyteller Jackie Torrence was told this tale by her grandmother after she was bitterly disappointed by the betrayal of a friend. She says that, though it was a bitter lesson to learn that some people are ungrateful by nature, stories like this one comforted her.

Back in the days when the animals could talk, there lived ol' Brer Possum. He was a fine feller. Why, he never liked to see no critters in trouble. He was always helpin' out, a-doin' somethin' for others.

Ever' night, ol' Brer Possum climbed into a persimmon tree, hung by his tail, and slept all night long. And each mornin', he climbed outa the tree and walked down the road to sun 'imself.

One mornin' as he walked, he come to a big hole in the middle of the road. Now, ol' Brer Possum was kind and gentle, but he was also nosey, so he went over to the hole and looked in. All at once, he stepped back, 'cause layin' in the bottom of that hole was ol' Brer Snake with a brick on his back.

Brer Possum said to 'imself, "I best git on outa here, 'cause ol' Brer Snake is mean and evil and low-down, and if I git to stayin' around 'im, he jist might git to bitin' me."

So Brer Possum went on down the road.

But Brer Snake had seen Brer Possum, and he commenced to callin' for 'im.

"Help me, Brer Possum."

Brer Possum stopped and turned around. He said to 'imself, "That's ol' Brer Snake a-callin' me. What do you reckon he wants?"

Well, ol' Brer Possum was kindhearted, so he went back down the road to the hole, stood at the edge, and looked down at Brer Snake.

"Was that you a-callin' me? What do you want?"

Brer Snake looked up and said, "I've been down here in this hole for a mighty long time with this brick on my back. Won't you help git it offa me?"

Brer Possum thought.

"Now listen here, Brer Snake. I knows you. You's mean and evil and low-down, and if'n I was to git down in that hole and git to liftin' that brick offa your back, you wouldn't do nothin' but bite me."

Ol' Brer Snake just hissed.

"Maybe not. Maybe not. Maaaaaaaybe not."

Brer Possum said, "I ain't sure 'bout you at all. I jist don't know. You're a-goin' to have to let me think about it."

So ol' Brer Possum thought—he thought high, and he thought low—and jist as he was thinkin', he looked up into a tree and saw a dead limb a-hangin' down. He climbed into the tree, broke off the limb, and with that ol' stick, pushed that brick offa Brer Snake's back. Then he took off down the road.

Brer Possum thought he was away from ol' Brer Snake when all at once he heard somethin'.

"Help me, Brer Possum."

Brer Possum said, "Oh, no, that's him agin."

But bein' so kindhearted, Brer Possum turned around, went back to the hole, and stood at the edge.

"Brer Snake, was that you a-callin' me? What do you want now?"

Ol' Brer Snake looked up outa the hole and hissed.

"I've been down here for a mighty long time, and I've gotten a little weak, and the sides of this ol' hole are too slick for me to climb. Do you think you can lift me outa here?"

Brer Possum thought.

"Now, you jist wait a minute. If'n I was to git down into that hole and lift you outa there, you wouldn't do nothin' but bite me."

Brer Snake hissed.

"Maybe not. Maybe not. Maaaaaaaybe not."

Brer Possum said, "I jist don't know. You're a-goin' to have to give me time to think about this."

So ol' Brer Possum thought.

And as he thought, he jist happened to look down there in that hole and see that ol' dead limb. So he pushed the limb underneath ol' Brer Snake and he lifted 'im outa the hole, way up into the air, and throwed 'im into the high grass.

Brer Possum took off a-runnin' down the road.

Well, he thought he was away from ol' Brer Snake when all at once he heard somethin'.

"Help me, Brer Possum."

Brer Possum thought, "That's him agin."

But bein' so kindhearted, he turned around, went back to the hole, and stood there a-lookin' for Brer Snake. Brer Snake crawled outa the high grass just as slow as he could, stretched 'imself out across the road, rared up, and looked at ol' Brer Possum.

Then he hissed. "I've been down there in that ol' hole for a mighty long time, and I've gotten a little cold 'cause the sun didn't shine. Do you think you could put me in your pocket and git me warm?"

Brer Possum said, "Now you listen here, Brer Snake. I knows you. You's mean and evil and low-down, and if'n I put you in my pocket you wouldn't do nothin' but bite me."

Brer Snake hissed.

"Maybe not. Maybe not. Maaaaaaaybe not."

"No, sireee, Brer Snake. I knows you. I jist ain't a-goin' to do it."

But jist as Brer Possum was talkin' to Brer Snake, he happened to git a real good look at 'im. He was a-layin' there lookin' so pitiful, and Brer Possum's great big heart began to feel sorry for ol' Brer Snake.

"All right," said Brer Possum. "You must be cold. So jist this once I'm a-goin' to put you in my pocket."

So ol' Brer Snake coiled up jist as little as he could, and Brer Possum picked 'im up and put 'im in his pocket.

Brer Snake laid quiet and still—so quiet and still that Brer Possum even forgot that he was a-carryin' 'im around. But all of a sudden, Brer Snake commenced to crawlin' out, and he turned and faced Brer Possum and hissed.

"I'm a-goin' to bite you."

But Brer Possum said, "Now wait a minute. Why are you a-goin' to bite me? I done took that brick offa your back, I got you outa that hole, and I put you in my pocket to git you warm. Why are you a-goin' to bite me?"

Brer Snake hissed.

"You knowed I was a snake before you put me in your pocket."

And when you're mindin' your own business and you spot trouble, don't never trouble trouble 'til trouble troubles you.

The Red Rag Under the Churn

The Devil figures mightily in the cautionary tales of North America where many folktales teach the values of religious faith. Avoidance of the Devil is the obvious message in the following tale from Kentucky, but a more subtle message is implied: "Be suspicious when you are offered something for nothing."

One day a man went over to his neighbor's to see him about trading hogs. When he got there the old woman come to the door an' told him her man's off somewheres in the field, but would he come in an' wait a spell till he'd git back. He done so, and when he got hisse'f set down he took notice that she's doin' her churnin'. Hit come to him how quick she's gittin' her butter, too, a heap faster'n his old woman ever got hern. He asked her could he have a drink, an' quick 's she got out the door after him one he lifted up the churn and looked under it, and thar were a little bitty red rag, like off'n a flannel petticoat. He got out his knife and cut him off a piece, and put the rag back under the churn, against she got back with his drink. Then he told her he 'lowed he'd not wait longer, but go out an' see if he could find her man in the field.

But he never went ary a step after that man. He went home to his wife fast's he could ever git there. He says to her, "Sary, git up what cream you have, an' do some churnin' fer me."

She looked at him wonderin'-like, an' says, "What fer ye wantin' me to churn? I ain't got but a dab o' cream, an' they's heaps o' butter, down to the spring-house."

He just says to her, "Sary, you git out what cream they is, an' do a churnin' fer me right off!"

Well, when a man spoke to his old woman thataway, she done what he said. Leastways, in them days she did. She brought out her churn, an' her dab o' cream, an' was just fixin' to begin her churnin' when he says, "Here, Sary, let me hitch up your churn an' put this here little bitty red rag under it."

• 182 •

She looked at him funny-like, but she never said nothing. So he put his rag under the churn an' she begun. Well, will ye believe what I'm tellin' ye? They wasn't scarcely enough cream in that churn to make a splash, but right off she could tell hit was gittin' fuller'n fuller. Hit wasn't no time till the butter was comin' so fast hit scared her. She jumped up and grab up her churn an' started out the door, sayin' she didn't aim to git mixed up in no bewitchment. Her old man picked up the red rag and stuffed it in his pocket.

That evenin', when he'd done finished up his chores, he was just startin' from his milkin'-shed back to the house when all to onct they was a huge-big figger standin' square in front of him. The sun-ball was settin', and this figger looked plumb queer, with the red glare from the sun-ball lightin' up all the sky behind him.

Hit come up, a-bowin' and smilin', and helt out his hand with a little book in it to the man. He says to the man, "Sign your name right here, if you please."

The man was feelin' mighty queer by this time, but he pulled hisse'f up the best he could an' says, "If you're aimin' fer me to sign your book, bring it over here to me your se'f!"

The feller looked at him surprised an' says, "Why, I can't come over to you."

Then he saw as how they was a circle plumb round him, an' hit come up clost to where the figger was standin', but not quite. So he reached over and took the book and opened it. They was writin' at the top of the page an' hit said, "WE, AND ALL THAT WE POSSESS, BELONG TO THE DEVIL." Below hit was the names of all his neighbors, an' the name of the woman what had the red rag under the churn headed the list!

Well, he looked acrost at the figger, an' hits eyes were glarin' at him like coals of fire, but he says, "I ain't goin' to sign nothing like that! I don't belong to the devil!"

The figger glared at him worse'n ever, an' says, "Hit's strange if ye don't belong to the devil. Ye have took part in witchcraft! What about that there red rag under your churn?"

Right then the man he felt somethin' movin' in his pocket, an' fore he could bat his eyes twict, out come the purtiest little bitty red bird, an' hopped up on his wrist. Hit cocked one eye up at him an' then flew acrost an' lit plumb on the shoulder of that awful-lookin' figger. An' all the time hit were lettin' out the horridest loud chuckles, like a demon laughin' at him.

The man he turned to the book real quick an' writ somethin' down on the other side of the page, an' signed his name. He writ, "WE AND ALL THAT WE POSSESS BELONGS TO THE LORD." Then he reached the book back to the figger. He give just one look at it, an' then he—he—, well, I 'low he jist went up in smoke! Leastways they was a flash, like a fire, an' a smell of brimstone, an' the man fell to the ground in a sort o' fit.

Soon's he come to hisse'f he got up an' run in to his wife. He told her what had happened to him, an' said they was aimin' to pack up an' leave thar the very next mornin'. He wasn't aimin' to stay where all his neighbors belonged to the Devil!

I reckon they moved right off. Leastways they hain't no one lived there up on the side of the hill since I can recollec'. An' will ye believe what I'm tellin' ye? Right thar where the figger stood, they hain't nothin but sage-grass growed from that day to this. I reckon that's the reason they've allers named that thar patch of sage-grass THE DEVIL'S GARDEN.

The Two Wagoners

In the largely Catholic Hispanic culture, stories whose characters include God and the saints are frequent. Although capable of miracles, they are presented in folktales as quite human; sometimes they are even roguish. But generally the tales they inhabit are meant to instruct people in the right relationship with the deity.

One hot summer day two men with wagons were delivering firewood to the villagers of the Villa Real de Santa Fe. When they came to the steep and narrow path which climbed La Bajada hill, the carts got stuck. Try as they might, the two pairs of oxen couldn't pull the heavily loaded carts up the steep hill.

One of the wagoners worked diligently with his oxen, cracking his whip over their backs and cussing and coaxing them to pull harder.

His *compadre* in the second cart didn't seem too concerned about the predicament. He calmly lay down in the shade to take a nap.

God will help me out of this dilemma, he thought to himself. I'll just say a few prayers before I take my nap!

Now it so happened that the Lord and St. Peter were on their way to Santa Fe that same day. They often traveled the old Camino Real to watch over their flock and perform good deeds for worthy people. When they came upon the two wagoners the Lord said, "Come now, St. Peter, let's help this honest man push his wagon up the hill."

So they put their strong shoulders to the wagon of the man who was working so diligently and they soon had it up the steep grade and on its way to Santa Fe.

The Lord and St. Peter then continued on their way. St. Peter, who had been reflecting on the ways of the Lord, finally stopped and said, "Lord, I am perplexed. Why did we help the man who was cursing in his work, but didn't help the man who remembered you in his prayers!"

"Well, St. Peter, I can see you have some things to learn about human nature and the way of the Lord. The man we helped did not curse from his heart. His language was that of affection for his oxen. He is a good man who works hard and is concerned with the well-being of his family. But the second man is a lazy one who thinks that I will solve all his problems if he only mumbles a few prayers before he sleeps. He is a hypocrite who remembers me only when he is in trouble. He can stay where he is!"

Annancy and the Yam Hills

This African American story was recorded in the 1890s and recounts the prodigious greed of the famous African trickster-spider, Annancy. Annancy is still a major charac-ter in tales told in North America. In some areas the name has been changed to Nancy, and the character takes on female traits. Like tricksters in other cultures, Annancy roams the world doing pretty much what he pleases. Sometimes he gets away with his decep-tions, and sometimes, as here, he doesn't.

A long time before time dere was a Queen, who was bery wicked; an' she was a witch, an her name was Five; but she didn't like dat name, so she say, who eber say Five, mus' fall down dead!

An' one time, it was bery hungry times, an' all the rivers were from bank to bank—an' nobody could get across to go to market side. An' Annancy get to be bery hungry, so he was cunning an' go an' build five piles of yams by de riber side. An' he build a nice little house dere, too.

An' when de rainy season over, de people day come fetch water at de rib-ber. An' by dis time Annancy was getting more an' more hungry. So when any-body come along him would say:

"I beg you, come tell me how many yam hills I have here; I can't count bery well."

So den de friendly ones would come to where de yam hills was an' count dem.

"One, two, three, four, five"—an' when dey say "five" dey fall down dead, and den Annancy eat dem!

So time go on an' on; an' Annancy lib bery well, an' in plenty, till one time Guinea Fowl come along, on her way to de grand market; an' Annancy say:—

"Oh, Missus Guinea Fowl! I beg you come count my yam hills for me. I make some, an' I don't know how many. Do come tell me!"

So Guinea Fowl come to where de yam hills dem was. An' den she go an' sit upon one of dem an' say:

"I see, one, two, three, four an' de one I sittin' on!"

"Cho!" say Annancy; "you don' count right at all!"

An' Guinea Fowl say again, "One, two, three, four, an' de one I sittin' on!"

An' Annancy say again, "Cho! you don' count right, at all!"

So den Guinea Fowl say, "How you count it, den?"

An' Annancy say: "One, two, three, four, f-i-v-e!—five!"

An' him fall down dead, an' Guinea Fowl eat him up.

Dis story show dat "Bein' greedy choke de puppy!"

Words of Wisdom

An almost identical version of this Hispanic story has been recorded in Kentucky from Italian immigrants, and yet another version comes from Ireland. What seems nonsensical at first makes more sense after you have a bit of experience.

Once there were three poor men. Two of them had large families, but the third had only his wife and one son who was studying for the priesthood. One day they discussed the poverty of their small village and the job of feeding their families, and the three decided that it was best to leave their depleted farms and look for work in the city. So they prepared provisions and set out to look for work.

After they had traveled some distance they met an old man who asked them where they were going. They explained their situation and told him they were looking for work.

"Well," the old man said, "suppose I make you an offer. Which would you prefer to take: a bagful of money, or three wise pieces of advice that would serve you in life!"

"We'll take the money, of course!" two of the men said without any hesitation.

The man with the one son thought awhile and finally said, "I believe I will take the words of wisdom."

The old man gave the full sacks of money to the first two men, then he turned to the third and said:

"Don't leave the well-traveled road for the path. Don't ask about what does not concern you. And, don't jump to conclusions about what you hear and act too hastily."

Then he said goodbye to the three men and disappeared. Immediately the two who had chosen the money turned to the third man and exclaimed, "Oh, what a foolish thing you've done! What good is that advice going to do you?"

The man smiled. He knew the advice of the old ones was not to be taken lightly. "It may be that the three rules will serve me better than the gold will serve you. And I will gladly part with my wealth, so I am going to give you free the first piece of advice: As you return home, *don't leave the well-traveled road for the path.*"

"Bah! What do you know!" they answered and went off laughing. And to get home sooner they decided to take a path through the forest instead of the road. On the trail they were assaulted by thieves who killed them and took their gold.

The man who had been given the advice continued his journey until he came upon a very large ranch house where he asked for lodging for the night. The gentleman of the house invited him in and gave him supper. After supper, the master of the house took the man to meet his wife. She was very frail and thin, a mere skeleton. The man felt like asking why she was so thin, but at the same time he remembered the second proverb for guiding his life, so he remained quiet. The man then asked for work and was given a job.

Now it so happened that his host was a rich man who owned much land and had many servants, and in all his years he had never met a man who minded his own business. When anyone saw his wife they invariably asked why she was so thin and then he would become angry and run them off. If his rage was aroused enough he would have them killed. He had purposefully instructed his servants to feed her only leftover food, bones and pieces of dry tortillas, and that is why his poor wife was so thin. He had made a solemn vow not to better her condition until he met a person who would not ask why he kept his wife in such a state. On the other hand, if he met such a person, that person would acquire all of his wealth.

Now, the master thought, this last man I hired has not stuck his nose in my business; I will ask him why.

"Señor," he said to the worker, "why haven't you asked me why I keep my wife as I do?"

"Sir," the man replied, "a husband and a wife's business is their own, and I do not ask about what does not concern me."

"Well spoken," the master answered. "At last I have found a man who doesn't meddle in the lives of others. From this day forward you shall be the owner of everything I have, and I will ask my wife's forgiveness and treat her well."

The rich man gave the worker everything he had and then he and his wife left for another city. The man, now that he was the new owner of a vast ranch, decided to go fetch his family. He made preparations, packed his pistol and hurried home.

Now, he had been gone a long time, so when he arrived he decided to surprise his wife. He went to the window and peeked in and what he saw made his blood boil! A young priest had just embraced his wife! He immediately thought of killing his wife and reached for his pistol, but then he remembered the third piece of advice and calmed himself. He listened closely and heard his wife speak to the young priest, and then he recognized this man as his son.

The third maxim had served him well. He entered the house and greeted his family and they cried with joy. And the fortune which the rich man had left them was more than enough for the husband and wife to live well the rest of their lives.

So now you've heard my story
Of do's and of don'ts
And men who mistreat wives.
If you don't like my cuento
Tell your own to make us wise!

The Golden Rain

Kindness and generosity almost always pay off in folktales. Likewise, characters who are mean and selfish always receive their just deserts. Aunt Lizbeth Fields of Kentucky transforms this timeless fairy tale into a story for the children of her community to take warning by. Much of Aunt Lizbeth's archaic language reflects the Old World origins of the tale as well as of her ancestors.

In all the years I was a granny midwife I never tended but one woman that birthed twin babies, and them as like as two peas. It was different with the twins in an olden tale I aim to tell you while I wait for Dicie to get her business tended to.

The twin girls in the olden tale weren't no ways like each other. One of them was ugly as homemade sin and lazy and idlesome. T'other was pretty as a picture and helpsome and work brittle. Their mammy favored the ugly, idlesome girl and made a pet of her. The pretty, helpsome girl they made do all the work around the place. She had to spin and weave and pack water from the spring. They never let her rest or have a minute's peace.

One day they got so mad at her that they drove her off out of the house and made her sit by the spring and spin yarn. Maybe she liked better to be out away from the house where she couldn't hear them quarrel at her. She spun so fast she stuck her finger with the spindle and made the blood come. She stooped down to wash off the blood with spring water, and she fell into the spring.

She fell down and down through the water and on down past the water. When she came to herself and looked about, she was in a fine meadow, all over green and pretty with flower blooms and with birds a-singing. Falling straight down for such a far piece had made her feel scatter-wit. She sat there till she gathered up her wits, and then she got up and set out walking across the meadow.

First she came to a little house with some bread baking in the oven. The bread said to her, "Please take me out of this here hot oven or I'll burn up. Hurry, for I'm already a-scorching." She took the bread out of the hot oven and set it to cool. The bread said to her, "Thank you, mam, and put a piece of good fresh bread in your pocket to eat on while you are a-traveling."

Next she came to some walnut trees, all bending down clear to the ground with a heavy load of nuts. The walnut trees said to her, "Please to shake our limbs and make some of the nuts fall off so we won't break down with such a heavy load." She shook off nuts till the walnut trees' limbs raised up some. The walnut trees said, "Thank you, mam, and take some nuts for your journey."

Last she came to a little house where a little old woman was a-working. "Please," the old woman said, "come in the house and cook me some supper; I'm all tired and wore out and I can't cook me a bite to eat."

She fixed the old woman and herself a good supper. She washed up the dishes and cook pots and shook up the old woman's feather bed so she would rest easy. Weeks and months passed by and she went on living at the old woman's house, doing all the house work and spinning, and weaving goods to make the old woman some new wearing clothes. She hoed out the garden and tater patch and sang song ballads while she was a-working.

After a time she got homesick and wanted to go back for a visit. Seems like she was lonesome for her kin, no matter how bad they had treated her. The old woman asked her how much wages were owing, and the girl said, "You don't owe me nary penny."

To show her thanks the old woman made a shower of gold around the girl. The golden rain fell on her till she was all over covered with gold. She went back home like that, and they mirated over how she was all over covered with gold. She let them pick off her gold and hide it away to spend for things, and she told them where she had been and what took place.

The ugly, idlesome girl wanted to have a shower of gold fall on her. So she set a spinning wheel by the spring and stayed there a while. She never got no blood on her finger, for she never spun no yarn. She just stood up (after a time) and jumped into the spring.

It happened the same way with her, only she wouldn't help the things that begged her to. She walked right on and let the bread burn black as a cinder, and she let the walnut trees break down with such a heavy load of nuts. At the old woman's house she said she wouldn't do a lick of work lessen she got high wages. The old woman agreed to that. The girl turned out lazy and hateful and just sat around and collected her wages. After she stayed long as she figured she had to for the gold to rain down on her, she left the old woman's house to go back home. No shower of gold for her, though. It rained down sticky, black tar all over her, and she never could wash it off. Though she scrubbed and scoured till she wore the skin off of herself, she never could clean herself up; and she had to live that way, all black and sticky, to the end of her days.

Why Men Have to Work

This African American story offers modern Americans a cautionary tale about selfishness toward the environment. Though it is an ancient tale with mythological elements, it is freshly relevant given modern attitudes toward nature.

The sky used to be very close to the ground. In fact, it wasn't any higher than a man's arm when he raised it above his head. Whenever anybody got hungry, all he had to do was to reach up and break off a piece of the sky and eat it. That way, no one ever had to work.

Well, it was a fine arrangement for a while, but sometimes people would break off more than they could eat, and what they couldn't eat they just threw on the ground. After all, the sky was so big there would always be enough for everybody to eat. What did it matter if they broke off more than they actually wanted?

Maybe it didn't matter to them, but it mattered to the sky. In fact, it made the sky angry to see itself lying on the ground, half-eaten, like garbage. So one day the sky spoke out and said, "Now look-a-here! Can't have this! Uh-uh. Can't have you people just breaking off a piece of me every time your stomach growls and then taking a little bite and throwing the rest away. Now if y'all don't cut it out, I'm going to move so far away no one will ever touch me again. You understand?"

Well, people got the message. In fact, they were pretty scared, and for a while they made sure that no one ever broke off more of the sky than he could eat. But slowly they began to forget. One day, a man came by and broke off a chunk big enough to feed forty people for a month. He took a few little bites, licked around the edges, threw the rest over his shoulder, and walked on down the road just as happy and dumb as anything you've ever seen. Well, the sky didn't say a word, but with a great roar, the sky lifted itself up as high as it could, and that was pretty high.

When the people realized what was happening, they began crying and pleading with the sky to come back. They promised that they would never do it again, but the sky acted like it didn't hear a word.

The next day, the people didn't have a thing to eat, and they had to go to work to feed themselves, and that's why man is working to this very day.

A Bundle of Troubles

One of my favorite African American tales, "A Bundle of Troubles," reminds us not to think too much about that grass on the other side of the fence.

One night Mose went to bed 'bout bowed down with his troubles.

Seem like all of 'em was a-hoppin' on him at oncet. He turned and twisted, but by 'n by he went to sleep and then he had the dream.

Seem like, in the dream, ever'body had all a-sudden started miratin' and fussin' 'bout their troubles. Seem like they couldn't talk 'bout nothin' else. Fin'ly, the debbil, he got tard of all this loose talk 'bout troubles, caze most of 'em was blamed on him. Then one Sadday, 'thouht nobody 'spectin' him, he 'peared uptown, jes as the streets was most crowded, and he rung a bell to call all they 'tensions to him.

When ever'body gathered 'round, he say like this:

"I bin hearin' a powerful lot 'bout all you folkses' troubles. Yo'all thinks you is got more troubles as anybody. And I's a-gittin' mighty tard a-hearin' 'bout nothin' else. Yo'all nussin' your troubles so hard you ain't got no time for no real sinnin'.

"I tell you what I's a-gonna do. I's a-gonna take up all of you troubles. Ever'body what has got troubles, jes wrop 'em up in a bun'le and bring 'em down to the depot check-room right away and I'll take 'em up and rid each and ever'body of you troubles. Now go home and wrop them troubles up and hurry down to the depot with 'em."

Well, it didn't take Mose more'n a minit to git home. He say he warn't runnin' 'zactly, but he was a-passin' a lot of folks what was.

He got the biggest thing he could find to hold all of his troubles, which was a big paper box with "Saunders Tripe" printed on the outside. Mose didn't think it would begin to hold all his troubles, but he started in a-packin' anyway.

First went in his old rhumatiz, and then his cawns.

"Yo'all bin hurtin' me for many the year," he say, "and I's sho glad to part company with you."

Then went in the lan'lord, and the sto'keeper what Mose owe for his fertilize. Then there was his back church dues what he hadn't paid, and that yeller gal over at Marse John Simmons' place. I don't know why he put her in, but he did. Then he throwed in his sore tooth, and his boy what got drunk all the time, and the old plow what never would foller a straight furrow. Then went in his old black skin, all his gray hair, and his wife's naggin', and the hatchet what would fly offen the handle. He throwed in his old mule, Bess, what kicked the daylights outen him ever time she got a chancet, and that sportin' nigger what was a-slippin' 'round his youngest gal.

He throwed in a heap more tribalashuns, and it seem like the box jes' wouldn't hold all of 'em, but there was allus a lil room at the top.

By'n by he had 'em all in, and then he took a big breaf and a piece of old plow line and tie them troubles up hard and fast in the box. He made a nice bun'le and throwed it on his wheelbar' and started for the depot.

It took him a long time to git there, caze the streets was packed with folks all loaded down with bun'les. There was old Sis Thompkins what didn't anybody know ever had a trouble in her life, and what was allus a-laffin', and a-jokin', and a-goin' on. She was loaded down with such a big bun'le that she had three of her lil gran'chillun a-helpin' her tote it. There was the preacher with a good-size load. There was even white folks, and Mose was surprise at that, but they seem to have the biggest bun'les of all. There was old Cunnel LeRoy, the biggest man in the town; even he had a bun'le. It warn't a very big bun'le, 'bout the size of a dozen eggs wropped up, but it was a bun'le just the same.

When Mose got to the depot, the check-room was piled up to the ceilin' with bun'les, and the debbil had three-four of his imps a-helping him with the checkin'. Mose put down his bun'le, and a perlite lil imp put a check on it and handed Mose a stub.

"What fo' you gimme this check?" say Mose. "I don't want the bun'le back—no time atall."

"'Tain't you check," say the perlite lil imp. "It's somebody else's check. You see it's like this: Next Chusday all yo'all what's checked a bun'le of troubles comes back here with these checks and you gets somebody else's bun'le of troubles. Ever'one of you has been a-sayin that you troubles was worser yit, so the Old Man he gonna let each'n of you trade and git somebody else's troubles."

"Well," say Mose. "I sho won't mind that. Maybe I git some nice easy troubles like dander, or a good-lookin' wife, or too much money." And then he put out for home.

Long 'bout cain't-see time, when Mose was a-settin' on his porch, he got to thinkin' 'bout the propersition, and the more he think 'bout it the lessen he likes it. He 'members somethin' 'bout ole Cunnel LeRoy, and some of the other folks, too. Seem like it jes warn't workin' out like he had thunk. By'n by he got down his hat and his walkin' stick and he went down to the depot to see how things was a-comin'. When he got there, first thing he heerd was somebody laffin', and he looked 'round the corner of the pile of bun'les and there was the debbil and the imps a-laffin' fit to kill. Seem like they had jes heered the bestest joke anybody ever told.

"Now look here," say Mose to hisself, "When the debbil gits to laffin' somebody bound to git the worst of it. I ain't never heerd of the Old Boy a-doin' anybody a favor yit lessen he gits the best of the deal."

So he went up to the debbil, perlite-like, and he say, "Mister Debbil, mebbe I make a mistook today. I left a big bunch of troubles with you, but I ain't so sure now that I wants to part with 'em. They bin with me so long I thinks that I's growed kinda fond of 'em. Wonder could I get 'em back 'thouht nobody axin' me no questions?"

The debbil he open his mouf wide and laff. And when he laff it was worser as when he frowns. His eyes didn't have no whites in 'em and was all shiny like they bin polished. His funny skin was a-twitchin and his tail was a-lashin' back'rds and for'rds.

"Br'r Mose," he say, 'tween laffs, "I's powerful sorry to tell you, but the check for you bun'le is in somebody else's hands now, and I don't see how you can git it back."

"Well, then," say Mose, "I won'er iffen you can show me what kinda lookin' bun'le this here check of mine calls for?"

"To be sho," say the Old Boy, and he looked at the check, and went 'round comparin' it with the checks on the bun'les.

"Here it is," he fin'ly say, and he holds up the lil bun'le of troubles of Cunnel LeRoy. "Looks like a mighty nice lil bun'le of troubles you gonna git Chusday, Br'r Mose. I congratulates you. Jes a lil bun'le of white folks troubles. That ought'n worry a old darky like you."

When Mose see that bun'le he scairt most to death.

"Please, suh, Mister Debbil," he say, "please, suh, gimme my old bun'le of troubles back. That's it right over there by that lil green imp, in the box marked with the tripe. I bin a-thinkin' it over and my troubles ain't so bad. I kinda miss the ole cawns and the rhumatiz, and the game tooth. By rights I owes the lan'lord, and the sto'keeper, and it wouldn't be right not to pay 'em. That yeller gal ain't gonna bother me no more, caze she's gittin' crazy 'bout somebody else. I kin take a firmer hand with the chillun, and I don't mind being mule-kicked, or throwed by the plow, and I kinda misses the old woman's naggin already. To tell the truf, I don't believe they was troubles after all—jes lil worries, and I misses 'em tubble. Won't you please to give 'em back, suh?"

The debbil he laff agin, and he laff and laff. And Mose begin to back off a lil way. Then the debbil look mad, and he say: "Take you bun'le of troubles, Br'r Mose," he say, "but don't you ever let me hear you fussin' 'bout 'em agin, or I'll give you some sho-nuff troubles."

Mose grab up his troubles and toss 'em up on his shoulder like they was no more'n a box of feathers. It didn't take no wheelbar' to git 'em away from that depot.

Why didn't Mose take old Cunnel LeRoy's troubles when he had a chancet? I axes him that.

Mose say he see a coffin in that bun'le, and he 'members jes in time that the Cunnel's trouble was a lil old cancer of the stummick.

The Robe

———•◦•———

La Llorona is a ghost who haunts many areas of the North American Southwest region as well as regions of Central and South America. Legend has it that La Llorona lived in Aztec times, though many tales place her much more recently. The story goes that her children were drowned; in some accounts she drowned them because she didn't want them; in some her husband forced her to drown them; and in others the drowning was an accident. Whatever the cause of her sorrow, La Llorona, "the weeping woman," roams the countryside crying for her children and warning others against wrongdoing. This story is not a traditional tale, but it is likely to provide a cautionary story in this young man's family for generations.

———•◦•———

As a young boy growing up in the Belen area in the early 1950s, there were many times when I used to hear the story of *La Llorona*. There were several versions, but the one I used to hear the most often from my grandmother was that *La Llorona* had lost her two children and desperately needed to find them, and that she might see a child who looked like one of hers, and she would start screaming in agony. The reason she was always near the river was because that's where she had lost them, supposedly by drowning. My grandma also used to say that *La Llorona* had the ability to judge others because she lived in another world where the past, present, and future were one.

My understanding of *La Llorona* came into play during the summer of 1956, when Billy Segura moved into the neighborhood. Billy and I were both 12 years old and we hit it off right away. I liked Billy because he was afraid of absolutely nothing. He brazenly smoked Pall Malls, cussed up a storm, and dismissed as "stupid" all of the things that I had been taught to value from birth. Not only that, he talked about getting himself tattooed when he was 16 and joining the Navy. Billy was from Los Angeles and knew everything—a real sophisticated kind of a guy, I thought. My parents differed on this appraisal and forbade me to associate with him in any way whatsoever.

I was an obedient, well-behaved kid and I tried to oblige my parents but it was pretty useless in the face of Billy's constant insistence that we break the rules whenever possible. He also berated me for being "chicken" and for allowing my parents and grandmother to "push me around." This was around the time of the Korean conflict and there was a lot of publicity in the papers about American soldiers being brainwashed by the Koreans. Billy warned me about losing my ability to even reason in the face of their manipulation. I was putty in his hands.

I began climbing out of my bedroom window some nights to meet Billy and his wayward friends down by the river, or at the dump, or wherever they decided to congregate. Most of his friends were older kids—some of them even had their own cars and they carried chains or tire irons around the way some women carry purses. They had nicknames like "Killer" or "Loco" or; "Hitter," and I found out that one of the major reasons they all met so late at night was for the purpose of acquiring parts to their automobiles at minimal, if any, cost.

I began to wise up at some point and realized I was in over my head. I knew it was a matter of time before I would be placed on assignment as a "runner" or something illegal. I was also growing tired of this deception and I was still young and impressionable enough to fear my grandmother, fear *La Llorona*, fear my parents, and fear punishment. One hot night in August, I snuck home with a new resolve—I would not see Billy Segura or his weird friends anymore. I carefully removed the screen, climbed into my bedroom in the usual way, replaced the screen, and got into bed.

As I lay back against the cool pillow, relieved that I had finally made this decision to straighten out my twisted and corrupt life, I happened to look down toward the end of my bed, and there she was, the light of the half moon showcasing her like a Renaissance painting in a museum—*La Llorona*, seated in my rocking chair, as motionless as a statue. As I lay there in a state of complete terror, my eyes riveted to her darkened but distinctive form, a cloud moved across the moon and plunged us both into near total darkness. As the minutes—and then hours—ticked by on my trusty lit-tle alarm clock, *La Llorona* continued her vigil, staring at me in final judgment of my deeds. I knew, then, that it was probably too late to do anything—it was your classic example of the sinner repenting, only to find out that Judgment Day had already arrived, that the Grim Reaper—or, in this case, *La Llorona*—was already at the door.

I could see that she looked almost exactly as I had always pictured her, with the exception of a long braid that fell over her left shoulder. And, despite the heat of that endless summer night, she wore her dark cloak securely wrapped around her with a hood that almost completely covered her pale, twisted, and ancient face. Her mouth lay slackly open as if prepared to emit a silent scream, and I could see tiny little fangs glistening in the dim moonlight. As I lay there waiting for death or whatever fate *La Llorona* had chosen for me, I thought of my loving family, of this wonderful house we lived in, of the beans and chile and tor-tillas that I would never taste again in the awful netherworld that I would call home for all eternity. And I wondered why *La Llorona* was not sitting in Billy Segura's bedroom instead of mine. What had I ever done to deserve this?

And so, I have come to the end of my story. As you can see, I am still here. Of course, it was not *La Llorona* sitting in my rocking chair that August night. It was my bathrobe, a dark brown corduroy thing thrown carelessly over the back of the chair, a robe that my mother had made on her Singer sewing machine. It was an unusual bathrobe because it had a gold braid that served as a tie around the waist, which used to be a pull for some old draperies we had in the basement. And it had a hood that I could wear over my head on those cold nights when it was necessary to make a trip to the outhouse.

To this day, I regard the dawn as the most exciting, revealing part of the day, when a person is most susceptible to learning the truth about life.

What happened to Billy Segura? I have no idea. His family moved back to Los Angeles a few months later. I am glad I knew him for that brief period, though—the best lessons are always learned early in life.

6

Tricks and Tricksters

The trickster is one of the most enduring characters in the oral traditions of North America. Tales chronicling the exploits of Rabbit and Coyote originated around ancient Native American campfires, and the characters still influence Native American culture. In a less serious vein, but testifying to the lasting quality of the trickster, people enjoy seeing similar characters pulling similar tricks on the Saturday morning cartoons. In many of the best-known tales, the hero-trickster is a small, weak creature who gets the better of his stronger antagonist through wit and deception. We love the trickster because he (rarely she) flouts the laws of polite society, challenges the high and the mighty, and wins! He does what we would all like to do if we only dared.

European immigrants brought to North America tales in which a human *trickster outwits other people, and such stories have never waned in popularity. Elements from trickster stories turn up in the Jack Tales (a fine example of which appears in this chapter), in tales about outsmarting the Devil, and in tales in which one member of a culture group consistently gets the better of everybody else, as in the stories of the Yankee Peddler. In some stories, such as those about Big John the Conqueror, the ability to pull the wool over the*

eyes of the unsuspecting has elevated characters in North American lore to leg-
endary status. Though the tales below are from oral tradition and generally out
of the past, the contemporary trickster is everywhere. Look for him at the
movies!

Brother Rabbit Breaks Up a Party

When they were brought to America, African slaves lost almost everything but their folklore. It is significant that the central figure in the tales they preserved is Brer Rabbit, who is small and weak and in constant danger, but who manages to stay alive by using his wits. When Joel Chandler Harris published the Uncle Remus stories in 1880, he helped to fuel an interest in understanding and preserving African American traditions. Since then, the stories of the fruitless efforts of Brer Fox to outwit Brer Rabbit have been retold, updated, and republished in countless forms.

"One time," said Uncle Remus, "Brer Fox, he took and asked some of the other creatures to his house. He asked Brer Bear, and Brer Wolf, and Brer 'Coon, but he didn't ask Brer Rabbit. All the same, Brer Rabbit got wind of it, and he allowed that if he didn't get to go, he expected he'd have as much fun as the next man.

"The creatures that did get the invite, they took and assembled at Brer Fox's house, and Brer Fox, he asked them in and got them some chairs, and they sat there and laughed and talked, until by and by, Brer Fox, he fetched out a bottle of rum and lay her out on the side board. And then he sorter stepped back and said, says he:

"'Just do step up gentlemens, and help yourselves.' And you better believe they helped theirselves.

"Well, while they was drinkin' and drammin' and drammin' and goin' on, what do you expect Brer Rabbit was up to? You can just as well make up your mind that Brer Rabbit was monstrous busy, 'cause he was sailin' around fixin' up his tricks. Now, a long time before that, Brer Rabbit had been at a barbecue where there was a fit of playing the pipes and drums. And all the while all the folks was down at the spring eatin' dinner, Brer Rabbit, he crept up and ran off with one of the drums. There was a big drum and a little drum, and Brer Rabbit he snatched up the littlest one and ran home with it.

"Now, then, when he heard about the other creatures going to Brer Fox's house, what did Brer Rabbit do but get out this rattlin' drum and make his way down the road towards where they were. He took that drum, and he went down the road towards Brer Fox's house, and he made it talk like thunder mixed up with hail. It talked like this:

"'*Diddybum, diddybum, diddybum-bum-bum—diddybum!*'

"The creatures, they was a drinkin' and a drammin' and a goin' on at a terrible rate, and they didn't hear the racket, but all the same, here comes Brer Rabbit:

"'*Diddybum, diddybum, diddybum-bum-bum—diddybum!*'

"By and by Brer 'Coon, who always has got one ear hung out for the news, he up and asked Brer Fox what was that, and by that time all the creatures had stopped to listen. But all the same, here came Brer Rabbit:

"'*Diddybum, diddybum, diddybum-bum-bum—diddybum!*'

"The creatures, they kept on listenin,' and Brer Rabbit kept on gettin' nearer, 'til by and by Brer 'Coon reached casual-like under the chair for his hat and says, says he:

"'Well, gents, I expect I better be going. I told my old woman that I wouldn't be gone a minute, and here it is a long way in the day.'

"With that, Brer 'Coon, he skipped out, but he hadn't got much further than the back gate, for here came all the other creatures like they was running a foot-race. And old Brer Fox was working in the lead—he was that scared.

"Yessir! there they all were, and there they all went. They took short cuts, and they scrambled over one another, and they didn't rest 'til they got in the bushes.

"And meanwhile, old Brer Rabbit, he kept comin' on down the road:

"'*Diddybum, diddybum, diddybum-bum-bum—diddybum!*'

"And bless gracious! When he got to Brer Fox's house, there wasn't nobody there! Brer Rabbit is that audacious that he hunted all around 'til he found the air hole of the drum, and he put his mouth to that hole and sang out, says he:

"'Is there anybody home?' And then he answered himself, says he:

"'Law, no, honey. Folks all gone.'

"With that, old Brer Rabbit broke loose and laughed. He did! Fit to kill himself. And then he slammed Brer Fox's front gate wide open and marched up to the house. When he got there, he kicked the door open and hailed Brer Fox, but nobody was there. And Brer Rabbit, he walked in and took a chair, and made himself at home with puttin' his feet on the sofa and spittin' on the floor.

"Brer Rabbit didn't sit there long, though, before he caught a whiff of that rum. And then he *saw* it on the side-board, and, of course he stepped right up and dropped about a tumbler full somewhere down in the neighborhood of his goozle. Now, Brer Rabbit is mighty like some other folks I know. He took one tumbler full, and it wasn't long before he took another one, and as you know when a man does this a-way, he proceeds to get rummy.

"Now, all this time the other creatures was down in the bushes listenin' for that diddybum, and makin' ready for to light out from there at the drop of a hat. But they hadn't heard no more fuss for a while. And by and by Brer Fox, he says he's going back and look after his plunder. And the other creatures say they believe they'll go along with him. They started out, they did, and they crept towards Brer Fox's house. But they crept mighty careful, and I'm bound if somebody didn't shake a bush and make a racket, and all stopped stock still and listened. Yet they still didn't hear no fuss, and so they kept on creepin' 'til they got in the house.

"Well! When they got in there, the first sight they saw was old Brer Rabbit standin' up by the rum bottle, mixin' up a toddy, and he wasn't so stiff-kneed, neither. He sort of swang from side to side, and he looked like he was mighty limber, which goodness knows a man gets to be limber when he drinks the kind of liquor that Brer Fox provided for them creatures.

"When Brer Fox saw Brer Rabbit makin' free with his doins that way, what do you expect he did? What he didn't do, he didn't cuss; he didn't holler; and he didn't chase Brer Rabbit away like you'd think he would.

"In fact, to be sure, he was glad, because he saw right away that he had a good chance to catch Brother Rabbit once and for all.

"So he stood there, Brer Fox did, and he watched Brer Rabbit's motions. By and by he hollered out, says he:

"'Ah yi! Brer Rabbit!' says he. 'Many a time you've done made your escape, but now I got you!' And with that, Brer Fox and the other creatures closed in on old Brer Rabbit.

"Seems like I told you that Brer Rabbit had gone and taken more rum than what was good for his wholesomeness. Yet his head wasn't swimming so bad that he didn't know what he was doin'.' And 'bout the time he laid eyes on Brer Fox, he knew he had done got himself in close quarters. As soon as he saw this, Brer Rabbit made like he was down in the cup even deeper than he was. And he took and staggered around like a town gal standin' in a canoe. It seemed like he was just as limber as a wet rag.

"So he staggered up to Brer Fox, he did, just as sassy and audacious as you please. And he rolled his eyeballs around, and slapped Brer Fox on his back and asked how he be. Then when he saw the other creatures, he hollered out, he did:

"'Put up your dukes, gentlemens! Put up your dukes! If you'll just gimme hand-room and come one at a time, the tussle'll last longer. Now you all come on,' says he.

"Ole Brer Rabbit talked so crazy that the other creatures had more fun than you can shake a stick at. But by and by Brer Fox said they better get down to business. So then they all closed in on Brer Rabbit, and there he was.

"Now, in them days, ole man Bear was a judge amongst the creatures, and they all asked him what they was goin' to do with old Brer Rabbit. And Judge Bear, he put on his specs and cleared up his throat and said that the best way to do with a man that kicked up such a racket and run the neighbors out of their own house and went in there and leveled the pantry was to take him out and drown him. And old Brer Fox, which was sittin' on the jury, he up and smacked his hands together and cried and said, says he, that after this he was going to believe that Judge Bear had got ahold of some lawyer-books, because that was exactly what they say when a man levels his neighbor's pantry.

"Then Brer Rabbit, he made out like he was scared, and he hollered and cried, and he begged 'em, in the name of goodness, 'Don't fling me in the spring branch. Oh! don't fling me in the spring branch! 'Cause y'all know I don't know how to swim!' But then he hung down his head like he was meeting his fate and said sadly, but if y'all are just dying for to pitch me in, then for mercy's sake, give me a walkin' cane, so I can have somethin' to hold onto while I'm a'drownin'.

"Ole Brer Bear scratched his head and said, says he, that as far as his remembrance goes back, he ain't come across nothin' in the lawyer-book to the contrary of that, and then they all agreed that Brer Rabbit could have his walkin'-cane.

"With that and a cheer, they caught up Brer Rabbit and put him in a wheelbarrow and carried him down to the branch, and flung him in.

"They flung him in, all right," continued Uncle Remus. "And Brer Rabbit lit on his feet, same as a tomcat, and picked his way out with the help of the walkin'-cane. The water was that shallow that it didn't more'n come over Brer Rabbit's slippers. And when he got out on the other side, he hollered back, says he:

" 'So long, Brer Fox!' "

Tío Conejo and the Hurricane

It is almost impossible to trace the path of folktales as they travel from culture to culture, and this tale demonstrates why. It is a Latino story, but its roots are in the original Brer Rabbit stories. (In Spanish, Tío Conejo means "Uncle Rabbit.") Mary Ann Brewer, who tells this tale, says that it is popular in many places where hurricanes are frequent: in Mexico, Texas, North Carolina, and in the Caribbean. Wherever he lives, whether he is Uncle Rabbit, or Brer Rabbit, or simply Rabbit, the animal who is the smallest and weakest in the forest is the classic trickster who does more than just protect himself. When he has a chance to make a clean escape, Tío Conejo remains to bedevil his nemesis for the sheer joy of it.

A long time ago, all the animals in the jungle got along with each other, except for one, Tiger, better known as Señor Tigre. Señor Tigre vowed to eat all the small animals he could get his claws on, and he loved to chase after Rabbit, better known as Tío Conejo.

But Tío Conejo was quick and smart, and he loved to play tricks on slow, gullible Señor Tigre. Like the time when Tío Conejo was cleaning out some vines and making a rope out of them. It was hot, and the sun was blazing down. Tío Conejo wasn't paying any attention, when who should come sneaking up behind him? Why, his favorite enemy, *el gato malo y tonto*, that mean dumb cat, Señor Tigre.

"OK, Tío Conejo, I've caught you now. You are one dead rabbit!"

Señor Tigre was too close. Tío Conejo knew he didn't have time to get away. He had to think fast. "OK, Señor Tigre. Just eat me up right now. I don't want to be around when—it happens!" Tío Conejo gave a little shiver of fear and rolled his eyes dramatically.

"What's going to happen, Tío Conejo?"

"Oh, Señor Tigre, haven't you heard? A terrible hurricane's coming. It'll be here any minute. This sudden heat is a sure sign."

"*¿El huracán? ¡A mi no me gustan los huracanes!*" Señor Tigre replied with a shaky voice.

"I know you don't like hurricanes. I don't like them either. That's why I'm making this rope. I'm going to tie myself down to something so I don't blow away." Tío Conejo held up his rope for Señor Tigre's inspection.

"That's a good idea, Tío Conejo. But you just wait a minute! I want you to tie *me* down. I don't want to blow away either."

"Oh, Señor Tigre, I like the way your mind works. Let's see what we can find to tie you down to." Tío Conejo's eyes danced as he grabbed Señor Tigre by the paw and led him through the jungle. Suddenly, Tío Conejo stopped short. "Oh, Señor Tigre, look at this big tamarind tree. I bet it has stood right here through lots of hurricanes. Let's tie you to this!"

"OK, *pero, bien fuerte.*"

"Oh yeah . . . good and tight, I'll tie you good and tight!" Tío Conejo couldn't help but smile.

So Tío Conejo tied Señor Tigre to that tamarind tree with his long rope of vines, wrapping it around and around Señor Tigre's chest. "*¿Bien fuerte, Señor Tigre?* Tight enough?"

But Señor Tigre was still uncertain. "*Un poquito mas.* Just a little tighter, Tío Conejo."

So Tío Conejo grabbed the rope with both paws and pulled with all his might. "*¿Bien fuerte ya?* Tight enough now?"

Señor Tigre's eyes nearly bulged out of his head. He managed to gasp out, "*¡Bien fuerte!*" But when he looked at the other end of the rope, Tío Conejo was nowhere to be found. *¡Tío Conejo se fué como una chispa!* Tío Conejo was outta there!

Now it should come as no surprise that Señor Tigre was not the most popular guy in the jungle. It took him well into the next day just to find someone who was willing to untie him. He finally talked a couple of monkeys into letting him loose. Just as they untied him, he grabbed one of the monkeys and started to pop it into his mouth. At that moment he heard a voice up on the tree.

"Uh-uh-uh! That's no way to eat a monkey, Señor Tigre. Don't you know how to eat a monkey?"

"Well, I *thought* I knew how to eat a monkey."

"No, Señor Tigre. You've got to throw that monkey up into the air, close your eyes, open your mouth, and let the monkey fall in. That's how you eat a monkey!"

Señor Tigre shrugged his shoulders. "OK," he said. He scratched his head and closed his eyes. Repeating the instructions to himself, *"Cierra los ojos, abre la boca, tira el chango,"* he threw the monkey up in the air. But the monkey caught a branch of the tree, and he was gone.

Tío Conejo was waiting in that tree. He had a big tamarind seedpod, and as soon as he got a good aim, he threw that big old seed right down Señor Tigre's throat. Oh, Señor Tigre was in terrible shape. He was coughing and sputtering, trying to get his breath. Finally, he blew that tamarind seed through the air. Then he ran back into the jungle, yelling for Tío Conejo.

Now, some people say that he's still out there—that somewhere in the thick, green, Latin American jungle lurks a slow, dull-witted, big cat with a bad temper. They say you can hear him as he runs through the jungle, yelling for Tío Conejo. "Tío Conejo, someday I'm going to catch you! You are one dead rabbit! *¡Tu eres un conejo muerto!"*

But you'll never hear Tío Conejo answer back. He's nowhere to be found. *¡Tío Conejo se fué como una chispa!* Tío Conejo is outta there!

Coyote Tricks the White Man

———·•·———

Folktales almost always have a function beyond their entertainment value. Stories about Brer Rabbit in the African American slave culture, for example, offered encouragement to people to find subtle ways to rebel. Some Native American tales took on the same function as white settlers became more and more a threat. In this example, where the white man is the butt of the joke, the point is unmistakable.

———·———

Coyote was walking down a road when he saw somebody riding toward him on horseback. When the rider came up Coyote saw that it was a white man. Coyote kept looking at him, already thinking up some way to cheat him.

The man pointed toward Coyote and said, "I'm looking for the cleverest coyote. Are you the one that tricks all the people; are you that clever one?"

Coyote said, "No, I am not that one."

But the white man insisted, "You are the man that cheats the people." Coyote kept denying that he was the clever one. "Hurry up," said the white man, "cheat me, perform some trick on me."

Coyote said, "Oh, I'm not that kind of man. They just call me that."

The white man said, "I know about you; let's have a match."

Finally Coyote said, "It's true, I'm that one, but my medicine for cheating people is at home. I left it way back west and it would take me a long time to go get it."

The white man said, "Well, you go get it."

Coyote answered, "I'm pretty tired. I've traveled a long ways. If you want to have a match, you lend me your horse and I'll go get my medicine."

The man got off his horse and said, "All right, you go get your medicine."

Coyote picked up a little stick and went to the opposite side from the white man in order to get on the horse. Coyote then jabbed the horse as he pretended to try to get on him. The horse gave a snort and jumped away from him. "Your horse is afraid of me because I have no hat," Coyote said.

"All right, I'll give you my hat," the man said.

Coyote pretended to get on the horse, jabbing him again. "Your horse is afraid of me because I have no coat," Coyote explained. The white man gave Coyote his coat.

Coyote again caused the horse to snort and jump. "Your horse is afraid of me because I have no boots." The man gave Coyote his boots.

Again Coyote tried to get on the horse, but as usual the horse appeared to be afraid. "Your horse is scared of me because I have no pants." The man took off his pants and gave them to Coyote.

Coyote did the same thing to the horse and said, "I haven't any gun." The man strapped his gun on Coyote. This kept up until the white man did not have a stitch of clothes.

When Coyote got all the white man had, he got on the horse and rode away, leaving the man with nothing on. After riding a short distance he turned and said, "Say, white man, you know it now. I am a clever Coyote; this is how I cheat people." The white man called him to come back, but Coyote did not listen and rode off and left him there. He took everything the man had.

Big John the Conqueror

Big John the Conqueror represented a human version of Brer Rabbit, having all the survival skills of that famous trickster, and then some! Although there is no firm evidence that he ever lived, stories about Big John were widespread among slaves, and they demonstrate how the slaves used the character as an escape valve in the face of oppression.

Every night Big John used to go up to the Big House and stand in the chimney corner and listen to what Old Massa talked about. That way he learned a lot about what was goin' to happen. If he heard Old Massa say he was gonna kill hogs the next day, Big John would slip back to the quarters and tell the other niggers, "Tomorrow we kills hogs."

"How you know that?" they asked him.

"I can tell fortunes, that's how," said Big John. "Ain't noth'n' hid from me."

And the next mornin' when Old Massa come out and told all the niggers to get ready for a big hog killin', they decided Big John was a fortune teller for true. From then on they believed anything he told them.

One day when Big John was hangin' around the back door of the Big House, he seen his Mistress throw the water out of her wash basin, and in it he saw her diamond ring. But before he could pick it up, a turkey gobbler gobbled it down.

Soon the whole house was raisin' a ruckus lookin' for the lost ring, so Big John went to Old Massa and told him he knew where it was. Old Massa promised him if he could find the ring he would make him a present of a fine fat shoat. So Big John told him to kill the gobbler and he would find the ring.

At first Old Massa didn't want to kill his prize gobbler, and he told Big John that if he was foolin' him he would kill him sure. But when he killed the gobbler, there was the ring. From then on Old Massa thought Big John was a fortune teller too.

One day Old Massa was braggin' to some white folks that he had a nigger who could tell fortunes. One man disputed his word, so Old Massa said, "I'll bet you forty acres of good bottomland my nigger can tell fortunes!"

" 'f you so sure, what you spuddin' for?" asked the man. "Why don't you make a real bet? I'll bet you my whole plantation."

"Since you really wants to make a bettin' thing outa my statement," said Old Massa, "let's make it worth my time. We'll bet our whole plantations and every horse and mule and hog and nigger on the place."

So they agreed on it, and decided to prove the thing out a week from that day. Old Massa took Big John aside and told him about the bet, and said, "I bet everything I got in this world on you, and if you make me lose I'll kill you!"

The provin' day came and Old Massa was up bright and early. He was up so early he had to saddle his own horse and then go wake up Big John. Big John climbed on a mule, and off they rode to the provin' ground. When they got there it looked like everybody and their brother was on hand to see the sight. The other bettin' man had the privilege of fixin' the proof, so Big John was led away a little piece. Then they brought him back and showed him a great big old black iron washpot turned upside down, and they asked him what was under it.

Everybody knew but Big John. Old Massa told him he better think good if he wanted to live. Everybody kept quiet waitin' to hear what Big John would say. He looked hard at the pot and walked around it three or four times, but he didn't have the least idea what was under it. He began to sweat and scratch his head and Old Massa looked at him and began to sweat too. At last Big John decided he might just as well give up and get the killin' over with.

"You got the old coon," he said.

When he said that Old Massa threw his hat up in the air and let out a whoop, and everybody else was yellin' with surprise, cause that's what was under the pot,—a big old coon. So Old Massa went off to Philadelphia to celebrate, but before he left he give Big John his freedom and a hundred dollars and left him in charge of the plantation.

Old Massa and Old Miss had no sooner got on the train than Big John sent word to the niggers on all the plantations, "Massa is gone to Philamayork and won't be back for three weeks. He done left me in charge of everything. Come on over to the Big House for a big time." While the invite was bein' carried round, he told some of the hands to go into Massa's lot and kill hogs till you could walk on 'em.

That night Big John really spread a scrumptious table. Everybody that could get hold of white folks' clothes had 'em on. Big John, he opened up the whole house and took Old Massa's big rockin' chair and put it on top of Massa's bed. Then he climbed up and sat down in it to call the figures for the dance. He was sittin' in his high seat with a box of Massa's cigars under his arm and two in his mouth when he seen a couple of poor-lookin' white folks come in.

"Take them poor folks out of here and carry them back to the kitchen where they belongs," Big John said. "Don't allow 'em back up front again.

"Nothin' but quality up here."

He didn't know that they was Old Massa and Miss, who had slipped back to see how he would behave while they was gone. They washed the dirt off their faces and came back up front where Big John was still sittin'.

"John," said Old Massa, "after I trusted you with my place you done smoked up my fine cigars and killed all my hogs and let all these niggers in my house to act like they was crazy. Now I'm goin' take you out to the persimmon tree and hang you. You is entitled to a good hangin', and that's what you gon' get."

While Old Massa was gone to fetch a rope, Big John called his friend Ike to one side and said, "Ike, Old Massa is gonna take me out and hang me to the persimmon tree. Now I want you to hurry out to that tree and climb up in it. Take a box of matches with you, and every time you hear me ask God for a sign, you strike a match."

After a while here come Old Massa with a rope, and he led Big John out to the tree. He tied a noose in the rope and put it around Big John's neck and then threw the other end of the rope over a limb.

"I got just one favor to ask of you, Old Massa," said Big John. "Let me pray before I die."

"All right," said Old Massa, "but hurry up and get it over with, cause I never been so anxious to hang a nigger in my life."

So Big John kneeled down under the tree and prayed, "O Lord, if you mean for Massa not to hang me, give me a sign."

When he said that, Ike struck a match and Old Massa seen it and began to shake. Big John kept on prayin', "O Lord, if you mean to strike Massa dead if he hangs me, give me a sign." Ike struck another match and Old Massa said, "Never mind, John, you done prayed enough—the hangin' 's off!" But Big John prayed right on, "O Lord, if you means to put Old Massa and all his family to death unless he turns us niggers loose, give me a sign." This time Ike struck a whole handful of matches, and Old Massa lit out from there as fast as he could run.

And that's how the slaves was freed.

Jack and the Giants' New Ground

———— ·•·•· ————

The Jack Tales are sometimes called American fairy tales because, though they are set in the ordinary coves and hollows of the backwoods, they are nonetheless peopled with the kings, queens, and fantastical beings common in European lore. Though Jack (or sometimes John) is known in folktales throughout the world, the tales most identified with North America are those told in the Appalachian region of the eastern United States. Popular culture was slow to come to the mountains, and modern tellers remember hearing the Jack Tales from their parents and grandparents who told them while the entire family worked at tedious tasks such as carding wool and weaving cloth. Skilled storytellers took an hour or more to finish a long rambling tale. Here, Mrs. Maud Long, of Hot Springs, North Carolina, evokes that earlier time when there was no need to hurry through a story.

———— ·•·•· ————

A long time ago Jack and his folks lived way back in the mountains and they were just as poor as people could be. Will and Tom, the two older brothers, were just fine workers—they helped in everything. But Jack was just so lazy—half the time they couldn't get a lick of work out of him. Now, of course, this made for a lot of quarreling and fussing with the two older brothers and his father and mother.

So one day Jack said, "You know what I'm going to do? I'm going to clear out of this place. I'm going out into the world and see if I can't find me a fortune. I'm tired of this little old rocky farm."

So his mother fixed him up a poke of vittles and he threw 'em over his back and away he went. He walked and he walked, and the sun just a-beating down on him so hard. He got hungry and ate up his poke of vittles, and went a-walking on, and the sun getting hotter and hotter every step he took. And yet it wasn't twelve o'clock. And he thought, "I wonder where I'm gonna get a bite of dinner . . . for I sure am getting hungry."

Just then he noticed a nice-looking road that turned off from the main highway and he thinks to himself, "I'll just follow this a little way and see where it leads to." And pretty soon he came to a great big rock wall with a gate of pure gold. "Hm-m-m," said Jack to himself, "they's well-doing folks a-living here. I just wonder if they'd give me a bit of dinner. I believe I'll holler and find out."

"Hello-o-oo!"

Pretty soon a man came out on the porch and said, "Hello, stranger. What are you doing, what are you looking for?"

"Well, I'm a-lookin' for a job of work," says Jack.

"Well, I don't know as I'm hiring anybody right now, but come on in anyway, stranger, and sit a while."

Jack pushed that gate open and walked right in. And the man reached around and brought out two chairs, and says, "Come on, sit down, I reckon you can rest a little while, can't you? You're not in much of a hurry."

"No," Jack says, "I guess I can rest a little while anyway." So he took out his old corncob pipe and leaned back and went to smoking. Looked around after a while and he says, "And what did you say your name was, Mister?"

"Why, I'm the King. What's your name?"

"Jack's my name. Now, Mister King, I'm just mighty glad to know you. I'm mighty glad. And I know with all of this land that you have around here, you've got a sight of work. Don't you want to hire somebody?"

"Well," the old King says, "now Jack, I'd like to know, are you a good worker?"

"Oh, yes sir," Jack says, "I'm the finest worker there is back home."

"Well, can you plow?"

"Sure I can."

"Well, can you clear a new ground?"

"Why, you know, King, that's just all I do back home, I just clear new ground."

"Well, can you kill a giant?"

"Huh?" says Jack. Dropped his old pipe and he reached down and picked it up. Said, "Well, I ain't never killed one yet, but I guess I could try."

"Well, now," the King says, "if you can clear a new ground and if you're a giant killer, you're just the man I've been looking for. But I tell you, Jack, I have a new ground at the top of that mountain yonder that I've been trying to get cleared for a year. I've sent more than a dozen men up there, and they've every one been killed by that giant. Because you see, down in that other holler, there lives a family of giants that claim that new ground is theirs and they won't let anybody clear it. Well, if you can go up there and kill them, and then clear that new ground, Jack, I tell you, you're the man I'm looking for. Besides paying you good wages for clearing that new ground, I'll pay you a thousand dollars for every giant head you bring here to the house. And I'll give you ten cents an hour for every bit of work you do besides. And that's a good price."

"Yes, sir," Jack says, "that's a good price and that just suits me fine. I'll be ready to go up there and see what I can do."

"Yes," the King says, "after you eat a bite of dinner. Now come on in, I think the old woman has us some dinner ready. And let's see if we can't eat a little, and then you can go up there and see what you can do."

Jack went in to the table and, my!—it was just loaded with good things to eat. Chicken and ham and pie and cake, and biscuit and butter and honey. Oh, Jack just ate such a dinner!

But he looked across and the old King was still eating, and the Queen just piled his plate up full of food again and, lord, Jack didn't want those folks to think that he couldn't eat as much as the King.

So he reached down under the table and drew up that old leather apron that he always wore, fastened it good in his pants-belt, and drew his belt right good and tight to hold it down good and strong, and he begun eating all over again. He'd take a bite and then he'd slip a whole lot down into that leather apron. Poured four or five glasses of milk down in there, bread and chicken and cake— just everything.

After a while, the King pushed back his chair and said he was through.

And Jack pushed back his chair, went out on the porch and he said, "Now I guess, bedads, I'd better be about that giant killing."

"Yes," the King said, "go on down yonder to the woodpile and you'll see there some axes. Pick you up the sharpest-edged looking one you can find, and go on. Up on the top of the mountain there, you'll find the tree with a chip or two taken out of it, where the other fellows have tried to begin chipping. But just about the time you begin a-whacking, Jack, right then the giants will be a-coming."

Well, Jack went on down to the woodpile, looked back and waved to him and said, "I'll be back in time for supper."

Picked him up a little old bit of a tommy-hatchet there, and the King said, "Jack, Jack! you'll need one of them big axes! Don't take that little old thing."

"No," Jack says, "bedads, this axe is just what I want." Stuck it in his belt and went a-climbing on to the top of the mountain.

Now when Jack got up there, he was sure worried. He didn't know what he was going to do. Gracious sakes, he didn't want to begin a-hacking on that tree, for those giants'ud come a-running up on him. And he knew that if he didn't hack some, the King would know that he hadn't been doing any kind of work and he wouldn't give him any supper. Well, he thought and he thought. What could he do? He just didn't know.

He looked around and he saw a tall slim poplar tree, the highest thing on the mountain. Climbed into the very tip top of that, took off that little old tommy-hatchet from out of his belt and begun hacking at the little bitty limbs. Ka-whack! Ka-whack!

He hadn't made more than six whacks till he heard something coming through the underbrush, and he looked down there and, gracious sakes alive, there was that two-headed giant that the King had told him about! (Yes sir, this one just had two heads, but the twins had three heads apiece, the old mother had three heads, and the old daddy had four.)

"Oh, boy," Jack says, "there comes $2000, but do you reckon I'll ever get 'em?"

He just kept right on a-whackin', though, just like he didn't know a thing was down underneath.

The old giant came right up to the very tree where he was a-whackin' and looked up at him, and he says, "Howdy, stranger, what in the world are you doin' up there?"

"Ah," Jack says, "bedads I'm clearing the new ground."

"Clearing the new ground!"

"Yes, I'm clearing the new ground for the King."

The giant said, "Now lookee here, stranger, what's your name?"

"Jack's my name, bedads."

"Well, Jack, you must be plumb crazy. Clearin' a new ground and a-beginnin' at the top of the tree. I never heard tell of no such."

"Why," Jack says, "that's the way we clear the new grounds back home all the time."

"Well," the giant says, "listen, Jack, we're not havin' that new ground cleared. No siree, we're not! This new ground belongs to us, and the King or nobody else is goin' to clear it. Now you just come down on out of that tree and go on home with me for supper."

Well, the old giant thought Jack wouldn't understand what he meant. But Jack did. But he came sliding down the tree, but he stayed well up in the limbs above that old giant's reach. He looked down at him and he said, "I tell you, I've always heard that giants is powerful strong. How 'bout it, sir?"

"Well," the old giant said, "some of us is and some of us ain't. Now as for me, I can kill any thousand Englishmen that ever dare face me, just barehanded."

"Well," Jack says, "I tell you what, I bet you I can do something that you can't do."

"Huh," the old giant says, "what is that?"

"Why," says Jack, "I can squeeze milk out of a flint rock."

"Now you can't do it, and I know it!"

"Well," Jack says, "just a-hunt me up a flint rock down there and chunk it up here, and I'll show you."

So while the old giant was hunting around to find an old flint rock, Jack took a little old knife—the sharp point of it—and jabbed a little old hole in that little leather apron. The giant threw him up the flint rock and Jack caught it in his hand, squeezed it right up tight next to that little old hole in that leather apron, and drip, drip, drip went the milk right down at that old giant's feet.

"Well," he says, "lands sakes, Jack, do that again."

So Jack pushed it up good and tight against the little old apron and squi-i-i-r-rt the milk came out just like you was a-milking a cow.

"Well," that giant says, "throw that rock down here to me. If you can do that, I can do it."

Jack threw the rock down to the giant, and he squeezed down on it and he didn't get a drop of milk. And he squeezed again, and there didn't any milk come. And the old giant got so mad, he just squeezed down with all his might and just ground that flint rock into powder in his hands.

"Well," Jack says, "I can do something else you can't do, too, giant."

"Now," the giant says, "what can you do this time?"

"Why, laws a-massy, I can just take my knife and rip my stomach right open, sew it up again, and I'm just as good as new."

"Hah, now," the old giant says, "now I know you're lying, Jack."

"All right," Jack says, "bedads, just watch me."

Took his knife and he ripped open that little old leather apron and out came pouring milk and chicken and everything. And Jack just took him a little old rawhide string that he had, and punched him some holes, and sewed that old leather apron right back up again.

The old giant says, "Jack, for lands sakes, throw me down that knife. I know if you can do that, I can do it."

Jack threw him down the knife and the old giant picked it up and r-rripped open his stomach, and blood and everything come flying out—and first thing you know the old giant just reeled around there and keeled over dead.

Jack slid down that tree, took his little old tommy-hatchet, hacked off those two heads, and went a-dragging them down to the King's house.

Well, when the King saw him coming he says, "Land a-sakes, Jack, if you're not the finest killer I ever saw! You're sure the man I've been a-lookin' for.

And here's your $2000 for those two heads. Now come on in, Jack, and eat you some supper and rest up a bit."

Well, Jack went in and he had him a good supper. And he had a good bed to sleep in and, oh!, he had $2000. "Ho," Jack thinks to himself, "boys, as soon's I can get away from here, I'm a-lightin' back out home."

After breakfast he said to the King, "Now I tell you, I'd better be going home. The folk's are missing me powerful back there, and I betcha my pappy's a-wanting me to help him set out tobacco. I'd better just be goin' on back."

"Oh, no," the King says, "Jack, you can't go back now. Why, gracious sakes, you're the finest giant-killer that there is. No sir, you go back up in that new ground and kill me some more of those giants. That's what you do. Why, I believe you can destroy the whole bunch of them."

"Well," Jack says, "bedads, I guess I can go back and try."

So he started back up the mountain.

Oh, my, how he wished he could get out of there without passing back by the King's house. He didn't want to mix up with those giants any more.

But he didn't have much time to think, because just about the time he reached there, a-coming up the holler he heard tramp! break! scrape! down through the thicket there. He looked and there came the twins with the three heads, just a-stepping over those big old rocks and thickets, coming just a-brushing up that mountain.

"Law," Jack thought, "what will I do? what will I do?" He was just shaking all over.

He saw a great old big hollow log over there, and ran into that just as hard as he could go, scooping his shirt-tail up full of rocks as he went in. Got in there and laid down. It was so big, why, he could stand right up in it. He just crawled down among some of the big old leaves and things that had blown in there, and lay as still as a mouse.

When those two giants came up and saw their brother lying there with his heads cut off, oh, my land, such taking on you've never heard! They screamed and they cried, and they said, "Oh, what will Pappy and Mammy say when they know about this! And don't we wish we knew who did it! Look, the ground's not tore up a bit. It don't look like there's been a sign of a fight, and yet his head's whacked clear off and gone. Oh, if we could just find the feller that did that, wouldn't we go for him! You know, he could have killed a thousand Englishmen if every one of them had come at him at one time. Now who do you reckon could have done that? Well," they said, "we'd better pick him up and take him on down home."

And one of them said, "You know what, Mammy sent us up here for some firewood. We'd better not go back without it either. But let's just pick the handiest thing there is. Let's just take this hollow log over there. That'll be just fine."

All right, one of the twins got at one end of it and the other at the other.

Of course Jack got jostled around a good bit laying in there, but finally they kind of got it up on their shoulders and settled down a little bit.

The giant in front had it just laying right up on his shoulders, just right with his head showing right square to Jack.

Jack waited until they got down the hill a little ways.

He picked him out one of those pretty good sized rocks and with all his strength—kavim!—he took the old giant right in the back of the head.

The old giant stumbled a little and he said, "Looky here, don't you be a-rocking me! Goodness knows we've got enough carrying this old log with brother laying on top of it. Don't go a-rocking me now, sir!"

"Oh," the other giant said, "why I didn't touch you with no rock. What's the matter with you? I've not got a rock anyway." He said, "Go on down that mountain."

Well, they started on down the mountain a little.

Traveled a little bit further, and Jack picked him out a little bit bigger rock. And ka-whack! he took him right in the back of the head. Oh, boy, that hurt, I know!

The old giant stumbled around and he said, "Now listen here, that's the second time you've done it. You hit me with another rock, and if you don't take a lickin' it will be because I can't give it to you. Now you mind what you're doing."

His brother said, "Well, what in the world are you a-talkin' about? I've not hit you with no rock."

Well, they just fussed and quarreled and gave each other the lie and everything you could think about. They finally started on down the hill, though, carrying the big old log with the brother laying on top.

Well, Jack reached around in among his rocks and got a real sharp-edged one, the biggest one of the whole bunch. And just let go with it—ka-wham!—right in the same spot. And just cut that old giant's head till the blood begun to ooze down there. Oh, it just almost knocked him down!

And he threw down that log and he took back at that other giant, and he said, "I tell you, I told you I'd whip you if it was in me if you hit me with another rock—and you've cut the blood out of my head!"

And such a fight you've never seen.

Why, they clawed and kicked and bit and pulled hair, and finally they just got clinched so tight, they rolled over and over on the ground. They kicked up great trees and rocks, and they just fought until they were so weak they couldn't even let go of each other.

When Jack saw them in that kind of a fix, he just crawled out of the end of that old log and—ka-whack, ka-whack, ka-whack, ka-whack, ka-whack, ka-whack!—the six heads of those giants were off.

Jack took the six heads and he went a-walking back down to the King's house.

Well, there was $6000 more. Oh, boy, Jack was feeling good.

The King says, "Now, Jack, you've killed all the young ones. There's just the old man and the old woman, and I know good and well you can go back up there and get them."

"Well," Jack says, "I tell you, this is enough. I guess I'd better be going for home, sure. I know my folks is worried about me by now. They're expecting me back to the house. I'd better go on."

"Not now, Jack," the King says, "go on back up there and kill the rest of those giants. And then the only thing in the world you'll have to do will be to clear that new ground."

"Well," Jack says, "bedads, I'll go on back up there and try."

So back up the mountain he started. And this time he didn't climb no trees. He wasn't a-shaking, he wasn't scared. He just took his little old tommy-hatchet and he begun a-hacking on that tree—ka-whack, ka-whack! And my land, it sounded like thunder coming up that mountain—this old big giant with four heads, just right charging on him. And he saw his boys lying there dead, their heads cut off.

He said, "Huh, stranger, howdy. What's your name?"

Says, "Mister Jack is my name, sir."

"Well," he says, "Mister Jack, do you know anything about who's killed my boys here?"

"Yes, sir," Jack says, "you're looking right at the man now. I killed 'em. Come up here sassin' and a-cussin' me around. I'm not takin' that off of anybody. And you want to be mighty careful, sir, what you say to me or I'll fix you the same way."

"Oh, yes," the old giant pappy says, "come on, Mister Jack, and come on down to the house with me and meet the old lady. Why no, I'm not going to sass you nor say nothing bad at all. I'm going to be powerful careful of what I say."

"Well," Jack says, "bedads, I don't care if I do, then. Let's go." And down the mountain they started to the old giant's house.

The old giant said when he got pretty close, he said, "Now, Jack, you'd better wait out here and let me go in, for when I tell the old woman about these boys being killed and your being out here, she's a-going to take on powerful. Law, they's no telling what she might do. So, Jack, you just stay out here and wait on me a little while, and I'll go in. And then if it's all right, why, we'll be glad to have you come in for some supper."

"Well," Jack says, "bedads, I'll just wait out here on you."

He just waited until the old giant got in the house and

he went a-slipping up to the door as fast as he could and put his ear right to the keyhole, and he heard the old man say, "Old woman, they's a little old man out there named Mister Jack. Jack's killed all three of our boys. He's cut their heads off. You've never seen such a fight in your life as they fit up on that mountain . . . it's just cleared up pretty near!" And he said, "This Mister Jack says he done it. Now I don't know whether he did or not. He don't look powerful strong to me, but out there's the boys. I brought 'em down. They're laying out there in the yard."

Well the old woman *did* throw a fit. She screamed and she cried and she raved, and then she said she'd kill Mister Jack. . . .

"Now, now, now," the old man said, "don't you go out there. He's killed those three boys. Now don't you dare go. Old woman, you're a-kind of weak and feeble compared to them. Don't you go out that way. You just wait. I'll test out Jack's strength, I'll see if he's as strong as he says he is."

So the old woman calmed down a little.

And the old giant said, "I'm going out and find out about him, and you just kind of straighten up the house in here—and get the oven good and hot! I think maybe we might have him for a little supper."

So Jack went a-pounding back out into the yard and was a-standing out at the edge, just like he was a-walking up to where the old giant and the house was.

The old giant came out and he reached down in the yard and he picked up four great big old buckets. You've never seen such things! Slung 'em on his arm and said, "Come on, Jack, let's go down here to the creek and bring the old woman up a little bit of water so she can get her some supper."

So they went down to the creek and the old giant reached in with one hand and he dipped up one big piggin full, and he reached in the other hand and he dipped up the other. And he said, "Now, Jack, over there's your two buckets."

Jack didn't pay him a bit of attention. He just rolled up his britches-legs and rolled up his shirt-sleeves way up to his elbows, and he went a-wading right out into the middle of that creek, feeling around in under a big old rock that was out there.

And the old giant says, "Jack, what in the world are you doing out there?"

"Why," he says, "bedads, just as soon as I can find a place to take hold of, I'm going to tote this creek up there to the old woman so we won't have to be a-toting loads of water up there. She can just come out there and get it when she wants it."

"Oh, law, no," the old giant says, "don't be getting this creek up there, Jack. No, no, don't do that." Says, "Land sakes, don't you know it would ruin my cornfield. And besides, the old woman's getting kind of old and tottery. She might fall in and get drowned. Come on, come on back to the house."

"Well," Jack says, "bedads, if I can't take the creek up there, I'm not taking no little old piggin of water."

"Well," the old giant says, "just leave the creek alone, Jack, and you don't need to mind about the little old buckets of water. Come on. These two's enough for her anyway." And on back up to the house they went.

The old man went in the house again, and he said, "Land sakes, old woman, I had the hardest time in the world getting Jack not to bring that creek up here. Lord, he's the mightiest man I ever did see or hear tell of. I just had to beg him to leave it down there." Said, "Now listen, you see if you can't do something with him. I'll get him to come on in the house here, and you see if you can't get him in that oven over there. I'll go out, and I'll be out here somewhere. Well, wait," the old man said, "wait a minute. Let me . . . let me try him first with throwing that crowbar. Just wait a minute, I'll see what he can do with that."

So he comes on back out. And Jack had heard every word that he said, but he was standing way off down in the yard just like he hadn't heard a thing.

The old man says, "Come on, Jack, this is what me and the boys used to do while the old woman was a-getting supper. We'd pick up this crowbar here and see who could throw it the furthest. Now come on, I'll give it a send way out yonder in the field, and you go out there and get it and bring it on back over here. Throw it on back over here to me."

So the old man picked up this great old big crowbar—why, it must have weighed a half a ton!—and give it a sling through the air. Went about a hundred and fifty feet out there.

Well, Jack went a-running on out to where the old crowbar lit up in the ground. Just standing there. He didn't even pay a bit of attention to the old giant. He cupped his hands up to his mouth and shouted: "UN-N-CLE! UN-N-CLE!"

"Ah!" the old giant says, "what'd you call me 'Uncle' for?"

"Oh," he says, "I'm not a-talking to you, I'm not a-talking to you at all . . . UN-N-CLE! . . . I'm a-hollerin' to my uncle way over yonder in Ohio. Why I've got a uncle over there that's a blacksmith, and he needs this here crowbar about making some horseshoes. The very thing. I'm just getting ready to throw it over to him, and I want him to be ready to catch it. UN-N-CLE!"

"Listen, Jack, Jack, don't throw that crowbar away! Why, that's all the one I've got. Don't do that. Now take your hand off of that crowbar and come on back here. Come on to the house and let's go on in. I think the old woman's got some supper ready. If she hain't, she pretty soon will have."

So the old giant took Jack into the house and said, "Now, old woman, here's Mister Jack, and he's going to come and have a little supper with us. I'll go out and split you up a little bit of wood while you go on finish the supper."

Well, the old woman she made like she was real glad to see Jack, and she picked up a comb and a washrag and said, "Come on here now, Jackie, let me comb your hair and wash your face and get you nice and cleaned up, ready for supper."

"Oh, no, bedads," Jack says, "I can wash my own face, and I can comb my own hair, too."

"Oh, no, no, now," the old woman says, "come on and just let me do it. This is the way I always fixed up my own boys. Now come on and let me do it, Jackie. Just get right up there on that shelf, and I can just reach right over and get you without having to stoop over a bit."

And Jack looked—and he saw that that shelf was right where it could be tipped right off into the old oven.

Well, Jack he acted like he'd like to get up on the shelf and he couldn't.

And he'd wiggle off and he'd get always off on the wrong side.

And the old woman said, "Well, Jack, didn't you ever sit on a shelf before in your life?"

"No, sir," Jack says, "bedads, I never did. I don't know a bit more know how to sit on this shelf than anything. You get up here and show me."

"Well," the old woman says, "I'm kind of heavy to get up on that little shelf. But you just put your shoulder right under the edge of it there and hold it up so it won't break, and I'll get up there and show you how to sit on a shelf."

So the old woman, the old giant, got up on that shelf, and Jack just gave his shoulder a little hunch and a good push and right into that old oven he threw the old giant mother. And he worked around there with a great old big iron hook and he finally pulled the lid on it. Went over and hid in behind the door.

After a while the old man pushed open the door, come walking in, and says, "Old woman, old woman! Jack's a-burning, I smell him, I smell him!"

Jack didn't say a thing.

The old man run over and pulled the top off of that big old furnace there . . . "Law have mercy," he says, "that's not Jack. That's my old woman, and she's burned to a coal! There's your three heads, there's your three heads! That's her!"

"Yes," and Jack stepped from behind the door. And he said, "Mind what you say to me, I'll just sure put you in there, too."

"Oh, yes, Jack, I'm a-minding what I say to you. I'm not going to say a thing in this world out of the way. No, sir, Jack, I'm not!" But he says, "Listen, Jack. Help me get out of this country some way." He said, "Here you've killed the boys and now you've killed the old woman . . . just help me get out of the country."

"Well," Jack says, "I'd be glad to, sir, but, you know, I'm afraid it's a little too late."

"Too late? What do you mean?"

"Why," Jack says, "the King's a-sending a thousand soldiers down here right now, maybe two or three thousand of them. And they're going to kill you just as soon as they get down here."

"Oh, Jack, Jack! Can't you hide me somewhere? Can't you do something for me, Jack?"

"Yeah," Jack says, "get into that old big chest over there and I'll see what I can do."

So he got the old giant down in the chest, and Jack ran out on the back side of the house. And he took up big sticks of wood, and he thumped and he beat on the old house, and he hollered and he whooped. And you'd have thought there was two or three thousand men out there, the noise Jack was a-making.

And he was a-fussing with them: "Now go on back, go on back. I tell you I've done away with all of them. You go on home and tell the King he didn't need to send you over here. Go on back, every one of you!"

But he acted just like they'd pushed right on into the house. And Jack came on in the house, throwing over the chairs, and breaking up the tables, and ker-whacking and ker-banging. And finally Jack acted like he was just driving them every one back out, and he took up a big stick and he said, "Now, if you don't get out of here, I'm going to do you just like I did the giants. Get out, I tell you! I've already killed the old giants."

Finally it went like they'd all went off and the noise kind of died down. And Jack went over to the chest and raised up the lid a little bit, and said, "Now crawl out there," he said, "the last one of 'em's gone. You get out of there easy like, and get away from here."

The old giant came out. He was just a-trembling and a-shaking. "Oh, Jack," he said, "what'll I do for you, what'll I do? Here you've saved my life from all them three thousand Englishmen." Said, "I know they'd a-killed me, they'd a-tore me limb from limb. Now, Jack, now, Jack, what do you want me to do?"

Jack says, "Mister, just star t right over that mountain and don't let me see you stop anywhere. Just keep a-walkin' and that'll be all I ever ask of you. Just don't you ever come back here!"

The old giant said, "Jack, I'll be so glad to get away from here I'll never want to come back." And great steps he went taking right over that mountain.

And the last Jack saw of him, he just tipped the ridge and went right down on the other side.

Well, Jack looked around. There was the three old heads of the old woman giant. He could take them in . . . but, boys, what was he going to do about the old man? He'd sent him away.

Took those three heads back down to the King, and the King says, "Now, Jack, I just owe you $3000 more, but I sure can't pay you a thing for them giant's heads that went walking off over the mountain. You just lost $4000 right that-away."

"Well," Jack says, "bedads, this is plenty to do me and my folks the rest of our lives anyway." And he says, "Now listen, King, I'm kinda tired and wore out fightin'. I'm goin' on back home, and tomorrow I'll send Will and Tom to clear that new ground for you."

The Boy That Was Foolish-Wise

The following story was told in the 1920s by Uncle Tom Dixon of Kentucky. Collector Marie Campbell writes of Uncle Tom's beautiful speaking voice and his love of "lingering" over a tale. This story is clearly related to the Jack Tales, but notice that there are no Old World elements included here.

What I'm starting to tell now ain't much of a tale. Mostly it's just a pack of foolishness about a boy that hired out to a farmer and acted foolish-wise and outsmarted the farmer. The boy's two brothers had been hired out to the farmer for a year and a day, and they came back home all wore out and sick from slaving in the garden and corn patches—and no wages in their pockets. The farmer cheated them out of the last penny.

The boy that had stayed at home and worked around the place got mad. "I'll show that farmer," he said. "I'll collect your wages for you, and I'll outsmart him so he can't cheat me out of what will be owing."

He went and hired himself to the farmer, and he laid down a hard bargain. He said, "You'll have to pay me twenty [dollars] for a year's working, and some more things I want to set straight; it's a bargain that every time I won't do what I can do I lose a month's wages, and every time I'm stopped from doing what I was told to do you pay me an extra month's wages."

The farmer agreed, thinking all the time that he'd figure some way to get out of living up to what he promised.

The first day the boy worked, he never got much to eat. He stole a half a goose and made out to keep from starving.

The next day he had a scant bite for breakfast, so he called for his dinner and ate it right after his breakfast. He asked for his supper and ate that too, along with breakfast and dinner. Then he went out and asked the farmer, "What do you tell your work hands to do after supper?"

The farmer said, "I tell my work hands to go to bed after they eat their supper."

The boy went to bed and lay there all day, resting up from slaving the day before. The farmer found out he weren't working, and hunted and found him in the bed.

He made the boy get up out of the bed, and the boy collected an extra month's wages according to their bargain, for the farmer had told him to go to bed and then made him get up.

The day after that, the farmer told the boy to keep the old brindle cow out of the corn patches. There he sat all the morning minding Old Brindle, and keeping her out of the corn patches while the other cows and the sheep and hogs were tromping down the young corn.

The farmer saw how things were, and he hollered at the boy, "Leave Old Brindle be and chase them other critters out of the corn patches!"

The boy let Old Brindle alone for a while and chased the other critters out of the corn patches. He collected another extra month's wages for being stopped from doing what he had been told to do.

Another day the farmer told the boy to make a path across a swampy place. The boy said, "What made the path over the mountain?"

The farmer said, "Sheep's feet made the path over the mountain."

The boy sharpened his pocket knife and started to cut off the sheep's feet, saying, "I reckon sheep's feet made a path over the mountain, they can make a path across a swampy place. Reckon I'll just have to cut off all the sheep's feet and strow them along in the miry places, like filling up mudholes with rocks." The farmer made him stop, and that was another extra month's wages.

Things went on like that for some time, with the boy collecting an extra month's wages every day of his life. The farmer couldn't stand it no longer, and he told the boy he was fired. The boy said he wouldn't quit, but the farmer begged him to. After some time, the boy agreed to go home if the farmer would pay him the wages owing to his brothers. The farmer paid the brothers' wages, and then he said, "Now you are fired. You got to quit working for me and go home."

"There goes another extra month's wages," the boy said. "You hired me to work for you, and now you're making me stop what you hired me to do."

And the farmer was bound to pay.

The Arkansas Traveler

Pity the poor traveler on the back roads of America! Stories of the taciturn farmer who simply will not give a straight answer have made their way into jokes and popular songs. In some regions of the country, especially where there are a lot of tourists, the local people revel in such tales as "The Arkansas Traveler," letting the trickster do what they are, in fact, too polite to do.

A tall, well-dressed stranger made his way through the backwoods of Arkansas, a place where the roads weren't but dirt paths and the cabins scarce as hens' teeth. Suddenly he came to a small clearing, in the middle of which sat an old cabin. It had sagging walls and a mighty poor roof, and out on the porch, sitting on a whiskey barrel playing the fiddle, was an old, bearded man. The stranger, who has come to be known as the Arkansas Traveler, heard the old fellow playing the same notes over and over again as if he couldn't bear to part with them. The Traveler rode up, and all during their conversation the old man continued right on playing those same notes.

Arkansas Traveler: Hello, stranger.

Fiddler: Hello, yourself.

T: Sir, can you tell me where this road goes to?

F: It ain't never been any whar since I've lived here. Least it's always thar when I git up in the mornin'.

T: Well, I'm supposed to take it to where it forks. How far is it to there?

F: It don't fork at all, but it shore splits up like the devil.

T: Have you any spirits here?

F: Lots of 'em. Sal saw one last night by that ol' holler gum tree, and it nearly skeered her out of her skin.

T: You don't understand what I mean, sir. Have you any liquor?

F: Had some yesterday, I did, but ol' Blue he got in and lapped it right up out of the pot.

T: No, I don't meant pot liquor. I mean whiskey. I'm wet and cold and would like some whiskey. Have you got any?

F: Oh, sure I do. Certain. Why, I drank the last this very day.

T (growing more annoyed): Well, I'm as hungry as I am thirsty. I haven't eaten since this morning. Might you have something to eat?

F: Stranger, thar ain't a damned thing in the house and that's a fact. Not a mouthful of meat, not even the dust of a meal round here.

T: Can you give my horse something?

F: Got nothin' to feed him on.

T: Sir, I'm not likely to get to another house tonight and I would be very grateful if you would let me sleep in yours. I'll tie my horse to that tree and will just have to do without anything to eat or drink.

F: Cain't. See, my house leaks. Thar's only one dry spot in it and me and Sal sleeps on that'n. As for your horse, that thar tree is the ol' lady's persimmon tree. You cain't tie to it, 'cause she don't want it shuk off. She aims to make beer off it.

T (staring hard at the fiddler): Why don't you repair your roof and stop the leaks?

F: It's been rainin' all day long.

T: Why don't you do it when the weather is dry?

F: It don't leak then.

T: How far is it to the next house?

F: Stranger, I don't know. I ain't never been thar.

T: Well, do you know who lives here?

F: I do.

T (waiting to hear): Who, then?

F: I do.

T: If I may be so bold, what might be your name?

F: It might be Tom and it might be Dick, but it lacks a damned sight of it.

T: This place of yours is pretty quiet. Seems the only thing alive is you. How do you do for a living here?

F: Perty well, thank you. How do you do yourself?

T: I mean what do you do for a living, sir?

F: Keep a tavern and sell whiskey.

T (exasperated): I told you that was what I wanted!

F: Stranger, hear tell of this. I bought a bar'l more'n a week ago. Me and Sal we went shares. But after we got the bar'l here, we found we only had one bit 'tweenst us, and Sal she didn't want to use her'n first, nor me mine. I had me a spiggin' in one end and she had her a spiggin' in t'other. So, you see, Sal takes a drink out of my end and pays me the bit fer it. Then I'd take one out'n her'n and give her the bit back. My, we was getting along fust rate, 'til Tom, damned skunk that he be, bored a hole on the bottom to suck at and the next time I went to buy myself a drink from Sal, they weren't none thar.

T (giving up): Well, sir, I'm sorry your whiskey's all gone.

The Arkansas Traveler had finally gotten the message and turned his weary horse away from the porch determined to follow the road until he found a place more hospitable. He heard those crazy fiddle notes going over and over, and couldn't resist a parting shot at the old man on the porch.

T: My friend, why in the hell don't you play the balance to that tune?

F: It's got no balance to it.

T: I mean that you aren't playing the whole tune, just part of it.

F: Stranger, kin you play the fiddle?

T: Yes, a little, sometimes.

F: Well, you don't look like a fiddler to me, but if you think you got a tune in you or if you think you kin pull any more out'n the tune I been playing, you kin just git down and try.

The Traveler climbed off his horse and stepped up onto the man's porch. He took up the fiddle and played those same notes, only he added a whole music book more. He played the whole tune, and then some.

F: Stranger, take a half a dozen chairs and set down here. Sal, stir yourself round like a six-horse team in a mud hole. Go round in the holler whar I killed that buck this mornin', cut off some of the best pieces, and bring 'em up for me and this gentleman directly. Raise up the board under the head of the bed and git that old black jug I hid from Tom (the skunk ain't so smart as he'd have me think), and give us some whiskey. Thar's plenty in that. Mose, drive ol' Blue out of the bread tray, then climb up in the loft and git that rag that's got the sugar tied in it. Dick, carry the gentleman's hoss 'round the back and under the shed and give him some fodder and corn, as much as he can eat.

Mose: Daddy, thar ain't enough knives for to set the table.

F: Whar's big butch, little butch, ol' case, cob-handle, granny's knife, and the one I handled yesterday? That's enough to set any gentleman's table with. Damn me, stranger, if you cain't stay as long as you please, and I'll see to it that you git all the plenty you need to eat and drink. Will you have coffee for supper?

T: Yes, sir.

F: Play away, stranger. You kin sleep on the dry spot tonight.

T (after playing steadily for two hours): Friend, can you tell me about the road I'm to travel tomorrow?

F: Tomorrow! Stranger, you won't git out'n these diggings fer six weeks and a day. But when it gits so you can start, you see that big sloo over thar? Well, you have to git cross that, then you take the road up the bank, and in about a mile you come to a two-acre-and-a-half corn patch; the corn is mightily in the weeds, but you needn't mind that one bit, just ride on. About a mile and a half, maybe two miles from that, you'll come to the damnedest swamp you ever struck in all your travels; it's boggy enough to mire a saddle blanket. Thar's a fust-rate road near about six feet under thar.

T: How am I to get at it?

F: You can't git at it nary time till the weather stiffens down some. Well, about a mile beyon', you come to a place whar thar's two roads. You can take the right-hand road if'n you want to, and you'll follow that a mile or so 'til you find it runs out. So then you got to come back and try the left hand road. When you git about two miles down that-a-one, you'll know fer certain you're on the wrong path, for thar ain't any road thar. You'll then figure you're mighty lucky if'n you can find your way back to my house, whar you can come and play that tune fer as long as it suits you.

The Yankee Peddler

One of the masters of deception in American folklore is the Yankee Peddler. Tales of his shrewd business deals were published in newspapers all over the country during the nineteenth century and thus went from oral tradition to the printed word. Then they were read and retold in backwater towns as if the events had happened locally. Like many tricksters, the Yankee Peddler is regarded with a mixture of scorn and admiration.

THE YANKEE FINISHES HIS MEAL

There was once this stagecoach route in Texas that ran through a little town called Camden, where a notorious tavern was situated. A stage full of folks was nearing Camden one evening when one man aboard remarked to another, "We aren't but five miles from town."

"Pesky glad to hear it," said a Yankee-lookin' feller. "I'm as hungry as a hound."

"Sorry for you, then," answered the other man. "I'm as hungry as you, but we won't get three mouthfuls down before the stage is ready to leave. It's an old trick at the tavern."

"Trick or no trick," said the Yankee, "I'll have a hearty dinner."

"You might at that," said the man, "but you'll lose your seat on the stage for sure."

The Yankee smiled and looked at everyone. "I'll bet you supper for this whole group that I get my dinner and I don't lose my seat."

"I hate to steal your money, but I'll take that bet, because I know this tavern too well. You can throw cigars and wine into the deal too, for we'll be in Columbus later on this evening in time for a real supper."

Sure enough, when the stage got to Camden,

the dinner that was supposed to be for the passengers wasn't ready yet. When it was, a man stood at the door and taxed folks four bits apiece as they went in to eat. But before the passengers could get four bits' apiece worth of food down their throats, the tavern-keeper came in shouting that the stage was ready, mail was behind time, and the driver wouldn't wait a minute not even for his own grand-mother. The travelers raced outside as fast as they could, no one wanting to miss his seat on the stage and get stuck in Camden, except for the Yankee, who stayed where he was and continued to eat. Plate after plate, he made those vittles walk down his throat most amazingly fast.

"You'll lose your seat, friend," said the tavern-keeper.

"Don't care much. I want the dinner I paid for, and then some," replied the Yankee, eating his way through a turkey that no one else had had time to touch. "And to finish up," he said to the tavern-keeper, "I guess I'll take a bowl of bread and milk."

The keeper went out of the room and presently came back and put the bowl down before his customer.

"Thank you kindly," the Yankee said. "I reckon I'll need a spoon, though, to eat this stuff with; cain't be eatin' bread and milk with my fingers."

"Spoon, sir!" said the keeper, his eyes popping out of his head. "There were a dozen spoons on the table just a while ago, and they were real silver spoons at that!"

"Well, there may have been," said the Yankee, "but you cain't blame them folks on that stage, now, can you? They weren't goin' to pay four bits an' come away with nothin' to show for it."

"Thunder and lightning!" roared the keeper. "If I don't bring the whole lot of those thieves to justice, then there's not a snake to be found in Virginny!" and he rushed to his horse out back.

About a half an hour later, after the Yankee had finished every scrap of food on the table, the same stage returned rattling and clattering. The Yankee got up, went outside, and climbed aboard the stage among the passengers.

"Hold on! Hold on, stranger!" yelled the keeper, who had brought the stage back with the sheriff. Quite a crowd had gathered. "I want you to point out the robbers that took those spoons. Now I got the law and some friends and they'll help me straighten these thieves out for good."

"Well, mister," drawled the Yankee, "I guess if you look in your coffeepot, I calc'late you'll find them spoons. Seems I made a mistake. Goodbye, and thanks for the best meal I ever got for four bits. And don't be tellin' this to the next stage, neither."

Away went the stage, the driver cussin' because his stage was late, the passengers roarin' with laughter, and behind them a tavern-keeper who was madder than a blind hornet.

RAZOR-STROP TRADE

"I reckon I couldn't drive a trade with you to-day, Square," said a "ginooine" specimen of a Yankee peddler, as he stood at the door of a merchant in St. Louis.

"I reckon you calculate about right, for you *can't*," was the sneering reply.

"Well, I guess you needn't git huffy 'beout it. Now here's a dozen ginooine razor-strops—worth $2.50; you may have 'em for $2.00."

"I tell you I don't want any of your traps [tricks]—so you may as well be going along."

"Wal, now look here, Square, I'll bet you five dollars, that if you make me an offer for them 'ere strops, we'll have a trade yet."

"Done!" replied the merchant, placing the money in the hands of a bystander. The Yankee deposited a like sum.

"Now," said the merchant, "I'll give you a picayune [sixpence] for the strops."

"They're your'n!" said the Yankee as he quietly pocketed the stakes.

"But," said he, after a little reflection, and with great apparent honesty, "I calculate a joke's a joke; and if you don't *want* them strops, I'll trade back."

The merchant's countenance brightened.

"You are not so bad a chap, after all," said he; "here are your strops, give me the money."

"There it is," said the Yankee, as he received the strops and passed over the sixpence. "A trade is a trade; and, now you are wide awake, the next time you trade with that 'ere sixpence, you'll do a little better than to buy razor strops."

And away walked the peddler with his strops and his wager, amidst the shouts of the laughing crowd.

How Pedro Urdemalas Got Into
and Out of Heaven

In the Hispanic Southwest, a cycle of tales grew up around one Pedro Urdemalas, who exhibits all the lawless traits of Coyote. Since the trickster finds his greatest delight in flouting the power of authority, it follows that in a largely Catholic society, Pedro would match his wits with the highest authority of all. In the following hilarious example, the original collector of the tale, Frank Goodwyn, includes the dramatization offered by the tale-teller.

It seems that Pedro Urdemalas, swindling his bosses out of fabulous sums, had lived a long life on earth. When it was over, he climbed the clouds to heaven and knocked on the golden gate.

"Who is it?" asked Saint Peter, who was Pedro's *tocayo*. That is, they had the same name.

"This is your *tocayo*, Pedro Urdemalas. Let me in."

"Where is your passport? Where were you born?" To Nicolas [who told the story], Saint Peter was a customs officer, the golden stairs were the bridge across the Rio Grande, and Pedro was himself trying to get home again.

"I was born in a valley between two hills." Imitating Pedro, Nicolas made his voice thin and plaintive as the baa of the freshly branded calves that had not yet found their mothers.

"What was the name of the valley?" Imitating Saint Peter, Nicolas made his voice heavy and demanding as the bawl of bulls plaguing the worried mothers of the calves.

"Oh, it has many names, *tocayo*." Nicolas squinched his shoulders and stuck out his upward-turned palms in imitation of

Pedro. "Different people gave it different names. I think it ran east and west. All kinds of good things were there. Watermelons, beans, grass for the cows, corn for the hogs, oats for the horses. And a river ran through it, with water which went all the way from its head in the hills to its mouth in the sea. When there was rain, everything grew green, but when it was dry, the grass died and the cows and hogs and horses became thin."

Nicolas shook his fist and told me that Saint Peter's angry yelling shook the stars. "Stop wasting my time! What do I care for watermelons, beans, grass for the cows, corn for the hogs, and oats for the horses? Am I a cow or a hog or a horse? No! I am a saint! A spirit! And spirits do not eat, for there is no body to need eating. Only spirit, thin as the air. Nor do I care for your rivers or hills, nor for your green grass of rainy weather or your dead grass of dry times. I am here by command of Dios, to see that no man passes in without permission from the bosses. If you do not know the day and place of your being born, you cannot get a passport, and without a passport you cannot pass this gate. It is the law."

"But I was born a long time ago, *tocayo*. I cannot remember."

"That is your bad luck. Not mine."

"But please, *tocayo*. Have pity on a poor *pelado* who wants only to get a glimpse of your beautiful place, so that he may tell the others of his land what it is like. Nobody from Texas has ever seen inside heaven. Just one little peep is all I ask, *tocayo*."

Now Saint Peter, being a man of mercy, opened the gate just a little. Instead of looking, Pedro stuck his finger in. Quickly, Saint Peter tried to shut the gate, but Pedro cried, "Ouch! *Tocayo*! My finger got caught in the gate! Please do not cut it off! Open the gate a little more, so I can get it out."

Saint Peter, who could not bear to see a man suffer, opened the gate a little more. Instead of taking his finger out, Pedro stuck his whole hand in.

"Ouch! *Tocayo*! You will cut off my hand! Open the gate just enough for me to get it out."

This was not going as Saint Peter had intended, but his kindness of heart would not let him do otherwise than open the gate a bit more for Pedro to get his hand out. This time Pedro stuck his whole arm in.

"Ouch! *Tocayo*! Now you have caught my arm! You should not be so careless with your gate!"

Saint Peter, who would not think of cutting off a man's arm, opened the gate a little more. Instead of taking his arm out, Pedro took off his big straw hat and threw it into heaven. It went bouncing and rolling over the clouds behind Saint Peter.

"Oh, what a shame, *tocayo*!" Pedro lamented. "It seems that I can never have anything but bad luck. The wind has blown off my hat! It is the only one I have, and hell is such a hot place, I am told. Almost as hot as Texas when the Texans are branding calves. You cannot send me away without a hat. Please let me come in and find it."

Now as all the world knows, Saint Peter has no hair himself. He could not bear to think of a man going bareheaded in hell, to say nothing of Texas. So he let Pedro in to find his hat. Pedro, very happy, went running over the clouds behind his hat. Saint Peter looked at the sun, which was his clock. Thirty minutes passed, then thirty hours, then thirty days, but still there was no sign of Pedro.

One day an angel came and knelt before the throne of Dios, our Señor, saying, "Sir, I lost a feather from one of my wings. Do you think there could be a thief around here?"

"Hush!" whispered Dios. "You must not mention thieves in this holy place! You will ruin my good reputation! Go back and play on your harp, and maybe you will find your feather. Here is a fresh cloud that I have just made. You may use it for a pillow." He tossed the new cloud to the angel, who took it and flew away pacified if not happy.

Next day a second angel came. "Our Sir, I lost a ring from my finger. Are you sure that no—"

"Hush! Do not say that word. Go back and play on your harp and maybe you will find your ring. Here is a fresh cloud, one of the softest I have ever made. You may cushion your knees on it when you kneel before the cross." For even angels must kneel before the cross of Christ.

Next day a third angel came. "Our Sir! I lost—"

"Hush!" said Dios. "I know what you are going to say. We will go and talk to Saint Peter. We must find out what kind of persons he has been letting in lately."

So they went to see Saint Peter, but he only shook his head. Then he thought a moment and said, "Now that I remember, a man from Texas named Pedro Urdemalas came in after his hat some time ago. He has not yet gone back out. I suppose he has not found it."

"Pedro Urdemalas!" gasped Dios, turning pale, for Pedro Urdemalas was known everywhere to be terrible for his deviltry.

"Pedro Urdemalas!" echoed the angels, also turning pale.

"Find him," commanded Dios, "and throw him out."

They hunted and they hunted but they never found Pedro. One by one the angels came back dragging their tired wings, bringing the bad news of failure.

Saint Peter scratched his bald head and tried to be helpful. "He may have slipped out through the cellar."

"My cellar!" screamed Dios, shaking his long beard with such thundering terror that the foundations of the sky almost came loose. "And I've got fifty gallons of good mescal down there! Go get him, you deadbeats! Hurry! Don't stand there like idiots! Get him out of here!"

The angels scattered like a flock of frightened turkeys, rushing in every direction at once, lifting up big clouds and little clouds to look under them, sometimes stopping and panting a moment behind a half-formed star, temporarily hidden from the wrath of Dios. After a long time they came back with sweat dripping from their wings. They had found nothing.

At last Dios, who knows all things, thought of a plan. He sent an angel to the earth after a Texan. Soon the angel returned, carrying a Texan by the collar.

"Bring him a chair," said Dios.

They brought the Texan a chair and he sat down beside the golden gate.

Dios asked, "Do you know a song called 'La Cucaracha'?"

"Oh, sure," said the Texan. "Everybody in Texas knows that song." He crossed his legs and used his hat to brush the stardust off his boots.

"Sing it," said Dios.

The Texan put his hat on one side of his head, tuned his guitar—for, as you know, all good Texans have guitars—and began to sing: "The *cucaracha*, the *cucaracha*, he will pace along no more. . . ."

The angels had never heard such a song before. They were very quiet.

"Again!" commanded Dios.

The Texan sang again. Nothing happened.

But the third time he sang, a straw hat went spinning into the sky beyond the faraway clouds. Dust began to rise in that direction, and the angels heard somebody yell, "Long live Mexico!"

Dios pointed his long, bony finger. "Yonder he is. I knew that he would not be able to stay quiet when he heard that song." Then Dios reached over the clouds, lifted Pedro out by the back of his neck as a mother cat lifts kittens, held him out over the edges of heaven, and dropped him back down to the earth, where he still works cattle in the Texas sun.

Bobtail and the Devil

———•—•———

The notion of outsmarting the Devil is very popular in the folklore of North America. In many tales, especially in the southeastern United States and in African American lore, the Devil is presented as just another scurrilous character who wants to cheat the hero, and the hero must use his wits to win. In the following tale, the Devil is just plain dumb and lazy.

———•—•———

Well, oncet upon a time there was two people lived in the world. Of these two people it was always questioned by other people which one was the smartest, Bobtail or the Devil. Now Bobtail he was just a Bobtail, just a-running around, and the old Devil he had other things. So one day Bobtail said, "Well, Devil," says, "we can't decide which one is the greatest. So I tell you what le's do. Le's raise a big patch of potatoes." The Devil agreed to do it.

Well, they planted 'em a big patch of potatoes. Bobtail planted him a big patch in his lot and the Devil planted him a big patch in his lot. Now Bobtail, he took and put manure on his potatoes. But the Devil he was lazy and sorry—he just run around, getting anything for nothing—and he didn't put anything on his.

Well, when digging time come Bobtail went and dug his potatoes. He had old big potatoes. The old Devil he had just little old small ones. He didn't like that much. So he—as the Devil is—he thought he had been cheated. He said, "Well, Bobtail," said, "you had your choice. Now I don't think it was fair. Le's raise some hogs."

Well, Bobtail said, "O.K., we will."

So Bobtail and the Devil got their hogs and they begin to raise hogs. They put 'em all in a lot together. Well, they fed their hogs, fed 'em corn, just anything they could feed 'em. When killing time come—when the hogs got up big enough—the question come up how they was going to divide 'em. Well, Bobtail says to the Devil, says, "Devil, I'll give you the first choice," says, "you take out you a hog and then I'll take out mine and we'll divide 'em."

So the Devil he went in and he looked over the hogs. As the Devil is, he wanted to cheat him, you know. So he retch down and picked up the biggest one he could find, an old big fat one. It went, "Weeeeeeennh!" and he picked it up and threwed it over the fence. Bobtail went down and he picked up his'n. It squealed right big and he threwed it over his fence into his lot. The Devil looked around and he picked the next biggest one he could find and he threwed it over the fence. Bobtail picked up another and put it over his fence into his lot. Well, there was just one more hog left, and the Devil said to himself, "Now I've got it on Bobtail, I've got it on him—that's sure!" So he picked up this small hog and threwed it over in his lot. The Devil was pleased. Bobtail he kindly scratched his head, you know, and he said to himself, "I've been cheated!"

But he got to looking around directly, and the Devil he was looking around. And then the Devil hollered at Bobtail, said, "Bobtail!"

Bobtail said, "Yes, Devil, what do you want?"

"Looks like your hogs are in your lot, but I haven't got any hogs."

Bobtail said, "Why?"

Said, "I've fooled around and my fence has got holes in it and my hogs have got over in with your hogs."

Bobtail said, "Ah, that's all right. You see, when I picked up my hogs," said, "I twisted their tails," said, "I know mine."

As far as I know the Devil is still looking yet, trying to find them straight hog tails.

7

The Fool

~

In the lore of all lands there are famous characters who are fools, and North America has its fair share. Two kinds of fool dominate this group of tales. There is the simpleton who is invariably foolish—a noodle, a silly, who can always be counted upon to do the wrong thing. Then there is the wise fool, the one presumed to be too stupid to take seriously, but who, in the end, surprises everyone by coming up with the clever idea that wins the day. Both types of tales have high entertainment value in oral traditions.

Some of these tales will be familiar as jokes, for there is a close relationship between jokes that have been popular in North America and traditional tales about fools. In a less politically correct era than this one, characteristics of the fool were given to members of ethnic groups partly to emphasize the stereotypes of an outsider culture. Telling such tales in order to appear superior to another group seems part of human nature. When I was young my friends and I, being North Carolinians, told our noodlehead tales about, who else, South Carolinians. Later, I met South Carolinians who told identical tales with numbskulls from, you guessed it, North Carolina. No one likes to be the butt of noodlehead stories, but it seems that plenty of people like to tell them.

The Three Sillies

This classic noodle story, known throughout the world, is well told in a Southern version by Lee Drake. Other versions give different reasons for the daughter's distress: An ax is stuck in the ceiling and might fall on her someday; she can't decide what to name her firstborn child; or she can't figure out who the father of her children will be. This tale attaches another well-known story, usually told separately, about the foolish wife who is saving money for hard times and loses it all when she meets a man on the road who says his name is Mr. Hard Times. There are many variants of this tale because it is so easy to incorporate new jokes about fools.

This boy was goin' to see his girl, and he had promised to marry this girl. So he 'cided he would have dinner with the girl before he married her. That's back a long time ago. Instead of goin' to town and buyin' syrup [molasses] like they do these days, they made it, and they kept it in barrels. And when they wanted syrup on the table, they'd take a container out and turn the keg up over it and let the syrup come out; and it would come out slowly, y'know, until it filled the container up, and then they'd take it back to the kitchen.

So they had dinner fixed—mother, father, and everybody—for this guest. And this boy, they called him in and they got to the table and the mother says, "Oh, Sister, we forgot something. We don't have any syrup on the table." Says, "Sister, will you go draw some syrup?"

Sister say, "Yes, Mother, I'll go draw some syrup." So she went out there to draw the syrup, and she turned the keg up over the container and let the syrup start runnin' in. And she put her hand to her jaw, and she was thinkin'. She says, "Lawd, I'm tryin' to think what Brother's oldest son is named." And she set there and thought.

And so she stayed so long, her mother say, "Lemme go see what's wrong with Daughter." Say, "She's stayin' too long." So she goes out. She say, "Daughter, what are you doin'?"

Daughter say, "Mother, I'm just tryin' to think what Brother's oldest son is named." So Mother, she started helpin' think, too! She stays a long time.

So Father, he say, "Let me go see what's wrong with Mother and Daughter." So he goes out. "What are you all doin'?" he says.

"We . . . Sister's jus' tryin' to think what Brother's oldest son is named, and I was jus' here tryin' to help her think."

So this boy he still sit there, he sit there. He 'cided he would go out and see what all of 'em was doin'. So he went out there and looked. Syrup done run all out on the groun'! And he says, "Hey, what are you all doin'?"

Mother say, "Daughter was jus' tryin' to think what Brother's oldest son is named, and I started tryin' to helpin' her think."

And Father say, "Well, I tried to help them think what Brother's oldest son is named."

The fellow that was goin' to marry the daughter say, "Damn!" Says, "I'm goin'. I don't want no dinner." He say, "Now, if I find three more fools like y'all, I'll marry your daughter. Unless that, I won't." And he left.

So he went on down the road. He got down the road, he saw a lady goin' 'round and 'round the house with an empty wheelbarrow, 'round and 'round the house. So he stood and watched the lady. He say, "Lady, what you doin'?"

She says, "I jus' washed off my back porch, son, and," says, "it ain't no sunshine around there," says, "I'm tryin' to roll some of this sunshine around there to dry the back porch."

He say, "I'll be damned!"

He went on up the road a little further and a man had a pretty, nice brick house, pretty lawn with fine grass on it. And the man had a rope th'owed across the housetop and he was jus' swingin' down on that rope for all he's worth. Jus' sweatin' up everything. Boy asked him, "Hey, mister," say, "what are you doin'?"

He say, "Son, I'm goin' tell you somethin'." Say, "I got some old oxen 'round behind the house there." And say, "They so poor, I'm tryin' to pull 'em over on the grass."

He say, "Mister, take the rope off and drive the oxes around." And say, "They'll come on around."

He told him, "I hadn't thought of that." He took the rope and drove 'em on around, and they went to eatin'.

He say, "Damn, look like I'm goin' to have to marry that gal anyway." He say, "I'm goin' to leave the road; I'm goin' down through these woods."

So he went down through the woods, turn off the road so he wouldn't meet nary another fool. He got thirsty and wanted some water. He say, "Well, there's an old spring down here; I'm goin' to stop at this spring and get me some water." Got to the spring. Happened to look up: man had a hog by its back legs jus' pushin' him, y'know. Juggin' him like he's tryin' to push a wheelbarrow or somethin'. Says, "Hey, mister, what are you doin'?"

He say, "I got a hog here and he's so poor, he won't even root." He says, "I'm tryin' to make him root."

He say, "Mister," say, "put him down; he'll go out there and go to rootin'." So he put the hog down and he went on out there and jus' started to rootin' and eatin' up everything, sticks and all.

He says, "I'll be damn. I guess I'll go back and marry her." He turned around and went on back. And he married the girl.

So he told her, "Honey," says, "here's ten dollars," and say, "I want you to keep this for Mister Hard Times, hear?"

She say, "Okay, Honey."

And he says, "I got a big old ham of meat in there." Says, "That's to go on these cabbage greens during the summer." He says, "Okay?" That means the cabbage greens they was goin' to raise, y'know.

So they went on, made it up 'til the summer, y'know. They had nice greens and everything, plenty to eat. Then things got kind of hard, and he wanted some of that ham meat that he had told her to go in the greens. So he asked her, says, "Honey," say, "you say you don't have anything to eat." Say, "How 'bout some of that ham meat I told you we goin' to put in them greens this summer?"

She say, "Honey," says, "when those cabbage first come up," says, "I cut it [the ham] up in little thin slices and put a thin slice on every head."

So that made him mad. He says, "I shouldn't a married this fool at the start with." He say, "Where my ten dollars?"

She say, "Next day after we got married," say, "Mister Hard Times come by here and I give it to him."

So he quit her, and that's the end of that story.

Two Tales of Foolish John

One of the most famous and long-lived fools in North American folklore is found among the French-speaking people in the American South. In the Creole and Cajun cultures of Louisiana and Missouri he is often known as John Sot, or Jean Sotte. He is probably related to our old friend Jack, often journeying far and entering into contests that he, unlike Jack, loses more often than not. For he is usually presented as an utter fool with no redeeming intelligence. In the following two tales, Foolish John shows his colors as an authentic noodlehead, keeping company with the three sillies in the previous story.

THE DOLLARS AND THE FROGS

Foolish John's mother and father were very poor people. Foolish John, who was the eldest, was their sorrow instead of their solace. The more they tried to correct him, the more he showed himself to be stupid and no account. What I am going to relate will give you a good idea of what his parents had to tolerate and forgive in him. My goodness, what they went through!

One day Foolish John's mother sent him to his uncle's to borrow ten dollars. She warned him to take good care of the money, because there would be ten one-dollar bills, not to lose a single one. Foolish John assured his mother that he understood the errand very well, leaving on the run.

While returning from his uncle's house, Foolish John passed near a pond, where the frogs, springfrogs and bullfrogs, were carrying on a racket, like nobody's business. Foolish John stopped to listen. He heard the tiny voices of the small springfrogs, saying: "You have eight! You have eight! You have eight!" [*"Tu as huit!"*] The silly lad believed the creatures were making fun of him, meaning that he didn't know how to count the money he had in his pocket. He became furious and replied: "You lie! Mama says I have ten, do you hear!" The springfrogs continued more loudly: "You have eight! You have eight! You have eight!" Beside himself, Foolish John cried out to them: "If you know so much about it, here, look!" and he threw the bills out upon the water to the frogs. "Count them for yourselves, if you wish," continued he. "There you are—one, two, three, four, five, six, seven, *eight*, nine and ten! Well now, is that not right? You see that you were wrong. Now return them all to me. I must be off. Mama is waiting for me."

Naturally the springfrogs paid no attention at all to him, and the pretty dollar bills went floating off upon the water like so many leaves in the breeze. Foolish John, poor thing, did not know what to do. He stepped into the water of the pond, while saying: "I'll get them in a little while. Mama needs that money more than those springfrogs and bullfrogs." But just then a huge bullfrog, seated by a cypress tree, began to go: "No bottom! No bottom!" [*"Pas de fond!"*] Foolish John, who did not know how to swim and was afraid to get drowned in a deep pond, was frozen with fear. He stopped instantly and began to back up toward the bank of the pond. As soon as he felt the good, firm ground under his feet, he hastened homeward to relate his adventure to his mother. The poor woman! One can imagine what her sorrow was on learning what had happened to her money—borrowed money at that, which had to be returned without having spent it!

Now don't tell me, my little children, that in such a fool there was not something to make an angel lose patience.

FOOLISH JOHN AND THE RAIN

Foolish John had just put on a nice, clean suit of clothes and was ready to go somewhere for his mother.

"Foolish John," warned his mother, "be careful not to get caught in the rain with your nice, clean clothes. It looks like bad weather. Don't forget to duck out of the rain if it begins to fall."

"All right, Mother," answered Foolish John as he set out on his way. However, he had hardly reached the bayou bridge when a great peal of thunder brought down a shower of rain. Foolish John realized he was in the rain and wanted to get out of it, remembering what his mother had told him. He saw no shelter nearby as he stood on the bayou bridge. So he thought and thought. Finally he jumped from the bridge into the bayou, in order to get out of the shower. As he stood in the muddy bayou water, his hat remained over the water on his head that stuck out of the bayou. He took off his hat and held it under the water.

When Foolish John reached home, his mother saw him all wet and covered with mud from head to feet.

"Foolish John!" she exclaimed. "Didn't I warn you to keep out of the rain? You are not only wet but all covered with mud."

"Well, Mother," explained Foolish John, "you told me to duck out of the rain if it came. When it did, I ducked into the bayou. I even held my hat under the bayou out of the rain."

Fido est mort (Fido Is Dead)

―――・―――

It is easy to see how Jean Sot got to be the principal character of this delightful joke-tale,
versions of which are told elsewhere in the world, including France, England, and other
regions of the United States. This version was told to Barry Jean Ancelet by Revon Reed
in Louisiana.

―――・―――

And then, the tale which makes me feel like laughing—He [Jean] had gone to work for a man who had a big plantation, a big planter, a rancher. He left to go on vacation. He put Jean Sot in charge of the farm, with the servants, the blacks, and the others, and his wife and his wife's mother, his mother-in-law in other words, and he went on a vacation.

And after a week, he decided to call Jean Sot on the telephone. He called him. He said, "Uh, Jean Sot, how is everything over there?"

"Oh, sir! Everything is going very well, sir," he said. "All is well."

"Are you sure that everything is okay?"

"Well, there's just Fido," he said, "Fido is dead. The little dog."

He said, "Fido is dead?! How did he die!"

"Well, sir," he said, "he died while eating some burnt, uh, mule meat."

"Oh, no!" he said. "What happened, Jean Sot! How did this happen?"

"Well, sir," he said, "your barn caught fire. The mules couldn't get out of their stalls. They burned." He said, "Then, the little dog went and ate some of that burnt mule meat. It gave him a stomach ache, and he died."

Then, the other fellow grabbed his head on the other end of the telephone. He said, "How did the barn catch fire, imbecile? Tell me quickly!"

"Well," he said, "the barn caught fire because of the house that had caught fire before."

He said, "How did this happen, Jean Sot?"

"Well," he said, "you see, sir, your mother-in-law had a heart attack and she died suddenly and she was enshrouded with candles all around and," he said, "one of the candles ignited the curtains and, before we knew it, the house was on fire and the barn caught fire and the mule burned and Fido ate some of the burnt meat and he died. Otherwise, everything's fine."

"And what killed the poor old woman!"

He said, "Well, it's her daughter, your wife." He said, "When she found out that she had secretly run off with one of the workers on your plantation, that she had eloped with one of the servants, it killed the poor mother."

And with this, the other fellow fell into a fit. He did not know what was going on anymore. It all started with Fido who had eaten some burnt meat, but Jean Sot did not want to say too much all at once.

The Devil and the Lord Dividing Souls

Fear of the local graveyard has made a fool of many a person. This is an African American version of a tale that is widely told throughout North America.

Here's a story about two slaves. Long years ago, they worked for the old master, and the old master never would give 'em enough to eat. And so, why, so they didn't git enough to eat, they would steal stuff and take home, and they would cook it at night after they git home. They would do all their stealing at night after they done gone home.

And so one day they had a lot of potatoes, and they knowed people didn't fool around the graveyards at night. And so they took these potatoes and carried 'em in the graveyard. Both of 'em had a sack apiece, and had two great big uns they laid down at the gate 'cause they was so tired when they got there with those big bags of potatoes apiece. And they went on inside. They was goin' to divide the potatoes up. Neither one of them could count, and the way they had to do to divide anything they had, they always say, "You take this one and I'll take that one."

So here come up another slave; he stayed at this other master's house. He'd go off at night, but he'd come back and spend the night 'cause he had to tote the old [crippled] master everywhere he went. He came by this graveyard that night and he heard this, "You take this one and I'll take that one. You take this one and I'll take that one." He stopped; thought that might have been a ghost or somethin'. And he stopped still and listened, see was it his heart beatin'. He felt his heart right tight, see was it his heart beatin'; and it wasn't his heart beatin'. Still he heard this sound: "You take this one and I'll take that one. You take this one and I'll take that one." So old John 'cided he'd run on up to the house and tell Boss about this God down there dividin' up souls!

So he went on up to the house. "Hey, Boss! Hey, Bossman!"

"Yes, John; what is it, John, what is it?"

He said, "God and the Devil down here dividin' up souls at the grave-yard!"

He said, "Aw no, John, ain't no such thing!"

"Yes it is, yes it is. You don't tell me, 'cause I heard 'em!"

He says, "Okay, take me down there and let's see God and the Devil dividin' 'em up. I want to hear it, too."

So John picks him up and take him on down there. Sit him down 'side the gate. And so, sho' nuff, he heard this noise. "You take this one and I take that one. You take this one and I'll take that one." Sound went on for a long time.

Old Boss reach over and touch John: "You, you was right, John. You was right! You was right!"

Later on they got through dividin' up what they had in there. They had two real large potatoes they left at the gate; they was so tired, they just dropped them at the gate. One say, "Oh, you forgot somepin'."

He says, "What is it?"

"You know. You remember dem two we drop at the gate, don't ya?"

So John cut out! See, he didn't take time to pick up Old Master that time. So when John got to the house, Old Master was already in there, done slammed the door in his face!

Pat and the Devil

Pat and Mike are two Irishmen whose antics are famous in folktales among Irish immigrants to North America. In Ontario, where Pat is a well-known fool, he becomes the main character in a variant of the previous graveyard story. The following tale from Ontario was told by Mr. G. N. Waugh and published in The Journal of American Folklore *in 1918.*

There was once a country parson badly crippled with rheumatism, who had an Irishman employed to carry him about on his back.

Quite late one evening the parson was being brought home, when he discovered that he had forgotten his sermon at the church. Shortly before this, so it happened, a wealthy parishioner had died, and willed that all his money was to be buried with him. A couple of rascally fellows were about to dig up the body and steal the money, being totally unaware that the dead man's relatives had already removed the coin. When they dug the body up, the thieves found nothing but hickorynuts, which had been substituted by the relatives. Not so easily disappointed, one of them said, "Remain here while I steal a sheep from the farm over there." Pat and the parson were then returning for the sermon. The thief in the churchyard, thinking it was his companion returning with the sheep, cried out, "Is he fat or lean?" Pat dropped the parson at once, saying, "Fat or lean, be jabers! you can have him," and he quickly ran for home. Getting up, the parson also ran, never again to be bothered by rheumatism.

Pat, ever after, thought it was the Devil he had seen in the churchyard, cracking nuts on a tombstone.

The Riddle Test

In "The Riddle Test" from Nova Scotia, Pat, from the previous story, suddenly crosses the line between the fool and the wise man. Usually depicted as an unmitigated fool, here he turns tables and makes a fool of the boss.

There was an Irishman out looking for a government job. So he went up to one fellow, an' he said, "Look a here, I've been voting for you all me life. I ought to get a job of you." So the man said, "I guess we've got something for you to do, but before I give you the job you have to answer three questions. Now you go home and consider the questions, then come back tomorrow with the answers. And if you answer them correctly you get the job." Pat said, "Go on with your questions." The man said, "The first is, the weight of the moon. The second is, how many stars are in the sky. And the last is, what I'll be thinking on when you come." So the next morning the Irishman come back. He found the old fellow in. He said, "Well, Pat, I guess you thought of what I told you. Now let's hear your answers. The first question was, 'How much does the moon weigh?' Well, how much?" The Irishman said, "One hundred weight." . . . "One hundred weight! Why how do you make that out?" Pat said, "Well, the moon has four quarters, and four quarters make a hundred, don't they?" The man said, "I guess you're right. Well, now, answer the second question. How many stars are in the sky?" The Irishman said, "Seven billion, eight thousand million, four hundred and fifty-two thousand." The man said, "How now, how do you make that?" "Well," said the Irishman, "if you don't believe me, you can go count them yourself." "That's right, that's right," said the old fellow. "We'll let that pass. But how about the last question. What am I thinking?" . . . "Well, you think that I'm Pat, but I'm his brother Mike!" . . . It wasn't Pat. He had sent his brother Mike to answer the questions.

Jean Sotte and the Riddle

———•·•———

Riddles are often used in tales as tests that separate the wise from the foolish. One of the oldest recorded riddles to come down through oral tradition was posed to Oedipus by the Sphinx, "What goes on four legs in the morning, two legs at noon, and three legs at night?" That question crops up in this next story of Jean Sotte. Here, however, as in the previous tale, the fool manages to blur the distinction between the wise and the foolish, surprising everyone and winning the day. The following story, though clearly of European origin, was collected among former slaves and told in the Creole dialect. The folklorist Alcée Fortier then translated the tale.

———•·•———

There was once a fellow who was so foolish that everybody called him Jean Sotte. He was so simple that everyone made fun of him. He would light the lamp in daytime, and put it out at night; he would take an umbrella with him only when it was very dark. In summer he would put on a great coat, and in winter he would go nearly naked. In short, he did everything contrary to common sense. King Bangon, who loved to play tricks, heard of the sayings and deeds of Jean Sotte, and sent for him to amuse his friends. When Jean came to the king all began to laugh, as he looked so awkward. The king asked him if he knew how to count. Jean replied that he knew how to count eggs; that yesterday he had found four and two. "How much does that make?" said the king. Jean went to count the eggs, and on returning said there were four and two.

"Exactly," said the king, "but tell me, Jean Sotte, they say that Compair Lapin is your father. "

"Yes, he is."

"No, no," said some one else; "I think it is Compair Bouki."

"Yes, yes," said Jean Sotte, "it is he also."

"No, no," said an old woman who was passing; "it is Renard who is your father."

"Yes," said Jean Sotte, "all of them; they are all my fathers. Every time one of them passes by me he says, 'Good-morning, my child.' I must believe, then, that they are all my fathers."

Everybody laughed at Jean Sotte; then the king said: "Jean Sotte, I want you to bring me to-morrow morning a bottle of bull's milk. It is to make a drug for my daughter, who is sick, and has a sideache in her back."

"All right," said Jean Sotte, "to-morrow morning early I shall bring it."

King Bangon then said:—

"On the first of April, in one month, you will come. I want you to guess something. If you guess, I will give you my daughter in marriage, but if you try three times, and do not succeed, my executioner will have to cut your neck."

"All right," said Jean Sotte, "I will try." And then he went away, pretending to go and get the bull's milk.

When he reached home, he related to his mother all that had happened, and the old woman began to cry, and could not be consoled, because, however foolish her boy was, she loved him, as he was her only child. She forbade him to go to the king, and threatened to tie him in her cabin, or to have the sheriff throw him in prison. Jean Sotte paid no attention to his mother, and started before day-break, with his axe on his shoulder. He soon arrived at the house of the king, and he climbed into a big oak tree which was before the door. He began, *caou, caou, caou*, to cut down the branches with his axe, and he woke up everybody in the house. One of the servants of the king came out to see what was the matter; and when he saw Jean Sotte on the top of the tree, he said: "But what is your business there? Fool that you are, you are disturbing everybody."

"It is not your business,—do you hear!" said Jean Sotte. "Are you the watch-dog to be barking thus in the yard? When your master, King Bangon, comes, I will tell him what I am doing here."

The king came out, and asked Jean Sotte what he was doing there. He replied that he was cutting the bark to make some tea for his father, who had been delivered the day before of two twins.

"What!" said the king, "for whom do you take me, Jean Sotte. Where did you ever hear of a man in childbirth? I think you mean to make fun of me."

"How is it that yesterday you asked a bottle of bull's milk? If you were right, I am also."

The king replied: "I believe that you are not so foolish as you want to make people believe. Go to the kitchen, and they will give you your breakfast. Don't forget to come on the first of April, that we may see which of us will be the April fool."

On the first of April Jean Sotte mounted his horse and went out without his mother seeing him. Compair Bouki, who is deceitful and evil-minded, said: "I shall prevent Jean Sotte from going because I know he is so foolish that they will cut his neck and keep his horse. It is better that I should profit by it, and take his horse. Don't you say anything; you will see what I shall do."

He took a large basket full of poisoned cakes, and put it on a bridge where Jean Sotte was to pass. "If he eats those cakes, he will die, and I shall take the horse."

Bouki knew that Jean Sotte was greedy and that he would surely eat the cakes. Compair Lapin liked Jean Sotte, because one day, when he was caught in a snare, Jean Sotte had freed him. He did not forget that, and said: "I want to protect the poor fellow," and before daybreak he waited on the road for Jean Sotte. When he saw him, he said: "Jean Sotte, I am coming to render you a service, listen to me: don't eat or drink anything on your way, even if you are dying of hunger and of thirst; and when the king will ask you to guess, you will reply what I am going to tell you. Come near; I don't want anybody to hear."

Compair Lapin then told him what to say. "Yes, yes, I understand," said Jean Sotte, and he began to laugh.

"Now," said Compair Lapin, "don't forget me when you marry the king's daughter; we can have good business together."

"Yes," said Jean Sotte, "I shall not forget you."

"Well, good luck, pay attention to all you see, look on all sides, and listen well."

Then Jean Sotte started, and a little while afterwards he arrived at a bridge on the river. The first thing he saw was the basket full of cakes which Compair Bouki had placed there. They smelled good and they were very tempting. Jean Sotte touched them and felt like biting one, but he remembered what

Compair Lapin had told him. He stopped a moment and said: "Let me see if they will do harm to my horse." He took half a dozen cakes and gave them to his horse. The poor beast died almost immediately and fell on the bridge. "See, if I had not been prudent, it is I who would be dead instead of my horse. Ah! Compair Lapin was right; a little more and I should have been lost. Now I shall have to go on foot."

Before he started he threw his horse into the river; and as the poor beast was being carried away by the current, three buzzards alighted on the horse and began to eat him. Jean Sotte looked at him a long time, until he disappeared behind the point in the river. "Compair Lapin told me: 'listen, look, and don't say anything'; all right, I shall have something to ask the king to guess."

When Jean Sotte came to the king nobody was trying to guess, for all those who had tried three times had been put to death by the king's executioner. Fifty men already had been killed, and everyone said, on seeing Jean Sotte: "There is Jean Sotte who is going to try, they will surely cut off his head, for he is so foolish. But so much the worse for him if he is such a fool."

When he saw Jean Sotte the king began to laugh and told him to come nearer. "What is it," said he, "that early in the morning walks on four legs, at noon on two, and in the evening on three legs?"

"If I guess, you will give me your daughter?"

"Yes," said the king.

"Oh! that is nothing to guess."

"Well, hurrah! hurry on if you don't want me to cut your neck."

Jean Sotte told him, it was a child who walked on four legs; when he grew up he walked on two, and when he grew old he had to take a stick, and that made three legs.

All remained with their mouths wide open, they were so astonished.

"You have guessed right; my daughter is for you. Now, let anybody ask me something, as I know everything in the world; if I do not guess right I will give him my kingdom and my fortune."

Jean Sotte said to the king: "I saw a dead being that was carrying three living beings and was nourishing them. The dead did not touch the land and was not in the sky; tell me what it is, or I shall take your kingdom and your fortune."

King Bangon tried to guess; he said this and that and a thousand things, but he had to give it up. Jean Sotte said then: "My horse died on a bridge, I threw him into the river, and three buzzards alighted on him and were eating him up in the river. They did not touch the land and they were not in the sky."

Everybody saw that Jean Sotte was smarter than all of them together. He married the king's daughter, took his place, and governed the kingdom. He took Compair Lapin as his first overseer, and hanged Compair Bouki for his rascality. After that they changed Jean Sotte's name and called him Jean l'Esprit.

Jean Sot and Bull's Milk

Different storytellers choose to emphasize different details in the stories they tell. In this fine example of a Cajun folktale, the teller expands on one brief episode from the previous Creole tale, creating a different story altogether.

Down around Mamou, there was once a boy who was so foolish that everybody called him Jean Sot, Foolish John. He and his *maman* were dirt poor, and he was less than no help at all. It seemed like Jean Sot just couldn't do anything right. Everything he touched ended in ruin, and he believed any silly story he was told. His *maman* would shake her head and sigh, "Oh, that boy must have moss between his ears!"

The people in his village loved to tease and play jokes on him. They'd say, "Jean Sot, the sky is fallin'!" The poor thing would run and hide, sure the world was ending for true. But their best joke was to ask, "Hey, boy, whatcha gonna be when you all grown up?"

Jean Sot loved that question. He would grin from ear to ear and say, "Me, I'm gonna marry the prettiest girl and be the richest man in all the parish." How the people laughed and laughed!

In time, the foolish boy became a foolish young man. One day as he was walking down the road, he passed by a big, fancy house. A beautiful girl was sitting up on the *galerie*, combing out her golden hair. She had the face of an angel but the brains of a duck. She was every inch as foolish as Jean Sot! Wouldn't you know, those two took one look at each other and fell right in love.

Jean Sot begged her to marry him. The girl says, "Oh, yes, *cher, mais oui!* But you must ask Papa for my hand!" The foolish boy ran to the girl's daddy, little knowing that this was the richest man in the parish, and asked to marry his daughter. But the rich man knew all too well about Jean Sot, and he had not the least intention of seeing his only child marry a fool, much less a poor one. Still, he thought it might be a good joke to play along and see just how foolish Jean Sot could be.

"Hmm," says the rich man, pretending to think it over, "I don't know if you are good enough for my daughter. Maybe you can prove yourself to me?"

"Oh, *oui*, Papa, anything you say!"

"Well, then, take this silver flask and fill it up for me."

"What do you want?" asks Jean Sot. "Wine, whiskey?"

"*Non*," says the rich man, keeping a straight face. "Take this flask and fill it up with . . . bull's milk. That's right! If you can fill this flask with the milk of a bull, then you can marry my daughter, and all my wealth will be yours someday."

So Jean Sot eagerly took the flask, and away he went down the road to find a bull to milk. He ran until he came to the countryside. There in a pasture, sure enough, was a big ol' mean-lookin' bull.

He walked right up to that bull and looked him over, trying to figure where to get started. But ol' bull was getting madder and madder, pawing the ground, shaking his horns. The next thing you know, he was charging and Jean

Sot was running for his life. He just barely escaped!

That evening Jean Sot thought harder than he'd ever thought in his life. Suddenly, it came to him. The girl's father had tricked him! Now, after a lifetime of being the target of everyone's practical jokes, even Jean Sot had learned a little something, you see. He thinks, "The time has come to show them all." Soon he had made a plan.

Late that night, with a little hatchet in hand, he went back to the rich man's house and shimmied up a slippery willow tree growing beside the man's bedroom window. He perched on a limb and took to chopping on that tree, chip-chop, chip-chop, chip-chop. All the while he's moanin' and groanin', "Oh, *mon pauvre papa!* Oh, my poor *papa!*"

Before long, the whole neighborhood comes running to see what all the commotion's about.

The shutters of the rich man's window fly open and he hollers out, "Jean Sot, is that you? What the devil are you doin', choppin' on my tree and moanin' to raise the dead in the middle of the night? I know you're foolish, but I didn't know you was crazy too!"

"Oh, my poor *papa*, he's havin' such a hard time of it," says Jean Sot. "This bark'll make a good tea, don't ya know, and help 'im get stronger."

"What's the matter with your *papa*, boy?" asks the rich man, taken aback. "Is he sick-sick? Has he got the fever?"

"Oh no, it's much worse than that!" says Jean Sot. "Never has a poor man had it so rough. You see, tonight my papa gave birth—to twins!"

"*Mon Dieu!*" the rich man exclaims. "Did he have boys, or girls, or one of each?"

With that, Jean Sot started in to laughin' so hard he nearly fell out of the tree. The neighbors were slappin' each other on the back and sputterin'. Well, the rich man realized he'd been had, and he starts to cussin'.

"Of all the . . . Jean Sot, you better get outta that tree and quit tellin' lies 'fore I get my shotgun after you!"

"I don't think I'd be talkin' 'bout lyin' if I was you," says Jean. "I don't want to call you a liar, but if you say a bull can give milk, then my *papa* can give birth to twins, for true!"

The rich man was ashamed. His neighbors had witnessed the whole thing, and so he was forced to hold up his end of the bargain or be ridiculed as a greater fool than Jean Sot.

And so, just as he had predicted, Jean married the prettiest girl and became the richest man in the whole parish. The people started thinking that he must really be smart-smart after all. They even made him captain of the Mardi Gras riders. It just goes to show that even the greatest of fools can sometimes become a leader.

The Mule Egg

---·---

Contemporary storyteller Doc McConnell carries on an age-old tradition when he takes a traditional tale and plugs in characters from his own experience. In this case it is his brother, Steamer, who becomes the main character in the tale of a gullible child.

---·---

I'd like to tell you a story about my brother Steamer. Now, ol' Steamer liked a lot of different things. Vienna sausage. Frog legs. Girls. Goin' to town. But best of all, he liked mules. He said that a mule was all a mountain boy should ever need.

He said, "Why, a mule'll plow all day long. He won't talk back. You can't push 'im off a bluff. He don't eat much, and he don't cost much to keep. Any man needs 'im a good mule."

Steamer would take any kind of mule.

He said, "If I could jist git me a little baby mule, I'd even take the runt of the litter. Jist a little ol' mule about twelve inches long with nice floppy ears, soft, fluffy fur, big, strong hind legs. Why, if I had me a little baby mule, I'd feed it and take care of it. And when it'd git up about waist high, I'd put my little harness on it, hook it up to my toy plow, and I'd plow ever' corn patch in Tucker's Knob."

That's all Steamer would ever talk about. He even begged Mama and Daddy to put 'im a baby mule in his sock at Christmastime.

Well, one day Steamer went down to John Mauk's General Store and begun to look around. John asked 'im, "Steamer, did ya ever find yourself a little baby mule?"

Steamer said, "No, I didn't. You don't know anybody that's got any little baby mules, do ya?"

John said, 'No, I don't know nobody that's got a baby mule, but . . ."

And about that time, Steamer looked over on the shelf and saw John's shipment of big, ol', brown, round, hairy coconuts, a whole basketful of 'em. Steamer looked at them things and said, "John, what in the world are those big, ol', brown, round, hairy things over there!"

He said, "Why, Steamer, them things is mule eggs. Ain't you never seen a mule egg before?"

Steamer said, "A mule egg?"

John said, "Yeah, you know how an ol' hen sits on a hen egg and hatches out little baby chickens? Well, these old mare mules sit on them big nests full of mule eggs, and that's where you git little baby mules."

And ol' Steamer says, "Where in the world did you ever find that many?"

John said, "Well, there was an old mare mule that had a nest down there in the brier patch, and we gathered 'em up this mornin'. Folks is always askin' for a good mule egg. *You* need one of them mule eggs, Steamer."

"You mean I could hatch it out myself?"

John said, "Why, Lordy, yes, son. You could hatch it yourself. Jist fix yourself a little nest, and sit on that ol' mule egg for 'bout two weeks, jist like an ol' hen. But don't ever let the egg git cold. You have to keep it warm all the time, or it won't hatch, Just sit on that egg for two weeks, don't ever git offa it, and when two weeks is up, that mule egg will pop open and there'll be a little ol', hairy, long-eared baby mule jist like you've always wanted."

Well, ol' Steamer was excited. "What will you take for one of them mule eggs!"

John said, "I'd have to have thirty-five cents for one, I guess."

So ol' Steamer picked up some pop bottles and pumped a little gas for ol' John and he gave 'im one of them mule eggs. Steamer carefully carried it home and showed it to Mama.

Well, Mama went along with Steamer—helpin' 'im git an ol' tobacco basket and some straw, settin' up Steamer's nest in our woodshed behind the house.

Ol' Steamer laid that mule egg right on top of that pile of straw, climbed on top, and sat down. And Mama brought Steamer an ol' quilt because she jist knew he was a-goin' to git chilly sittin' out there in the shed for two weeks.

Well, ol' Steamer started sittin' on that ol' coconut, thinkin' it was a mule egg, and he started countin' the days. One, two, three . . . And when Steamer would git hungry, Mama would bring his meals out to 'im. Four, five, six, seven, and finally, eight days had passed. Ol' Steamer was gittin' excited 'cause it wasn't goin' to be long 'til that mule was a-goin' to hatch out and he was a-goin' to have 'im a nice, fluffy, long-eared, baby mule.

Steamer counted the days. Nine, ten, eleven, twelve, thirteen, fourteen, fifteen, and finally, eighteen days come and went. Two weeks had already passed and no baby mule. He couldn't figure out why that baby mule hadn't kicked open that shell, so he held it up to his ear to see if he could hear 'im kickin' inside. He didn't hear a sound.

Well, Steamer got mad, and out there behind that woodshed he threw that ol' mule egg as hard as he could down into the brier patch—hopin' it would bust open and, if there was a baby mule inside, it would git out.

Well, sittin' out there in that brier patch was a floppy-eared jackrabbit. And that ol' mule egg hit that jackrabbit on the side of the head, addled 'im, and that rabbit jumped from the brier patch and commenced to runnin' 'round in circles and, finally, run off across the cabbage field.

When Steamer saw that ol' floppy-eared jackrabbit, he thought it was his baby mule and commenced to chasin' it, hollerin', "Come back! Come back! I'm your mammy! And your pappy, too!"

Steamer chased that ol' jackrabbit 'til he was jist give out, and he watched 'im run over the hill and out of sight.

"Oh, go on then," yelled Steamer. "I don't want ya. I can't plow that fast nohow."

The $50,000 Racehorse

Carrying on her family's storytelling tradition, Hannah McConnell Gillenwater tells this tale that she heard from her uncle "Steamer" McConnell, who was the subject of the previous story.

When I was a girl, I was my dad's shadow. Everywhere he went, I tagged right along. One of my favorite places to go was John Mauk's country store in Stony Point, Tennessee.

I remember that store's screen door and how the hinges would squeak. John kept those old wood floors oiled, and I can still recall the smell. That was *the* store in Stony Point, complete with a pot-bellied stove. All the gentlemen would sit around that stove, and it'd be red-hot at the bottom. They'd sit there, chewin' and spittin'. I'd sit there too and listen to the stories they had to tell.

Now, John Mauk was quite a character. Long before I was even a gleam in my daddy's eye, they say that John was probably the meanest man in Hawkins County. He never would go to Sunday school, church, or revival meetings—in fact, he'd cheat you blind. He'd charge you a little more than he should and keep his finger on the scales when he weighed out fruit or vegetables. He was a pretty ornery fellow.

Well, John was getting up in years, and the people in the community were starting to worry about his soul and what would happen to him in the hereafter. There happened to be a traveling Baptist revival coming through Hawkins County, and some of the little old ladies down at the Baptist church commenced to praying for old John. They started tellin' him, "John, you need to come to this revival." Well, they hounded him, and the men of the church hounded him too, until finally he said, "All right, I'll come."

It was on the last night of the revival that John Mauk came, and he got religion. He said, "I've turned over a new leaf. From here on out, I'm going to be living at the foot of the cross." He got such a good case of religion that afterward, every time he went to ring up a sale in his store, he'd quote a verse of Scripture.

Well, this particular day in October—the sun was shinin' down, but there was a definite nip in the air—we were all sittin' around the stove in John's store, and I was listening to stories and wantin' a chew of tobacco, but they wouldn't let me have one. And in the door came this little girl.

John said, "Well, howdy, honey. What can I do for you today?" She said, "I want some candy." So John handed the big old glass candy jar down to her, and she filled her pockets full, gave him her money, and left. She must have gotten 15 cents' worth of candy for a nickel. We couldn't believe that he'd been so kind to that kid. Old John never had liked young 'uns much.

He went around to the cash register and looked up into the heavens. Then he rang up the sale, and he said, "Suffer the little children to come unto me."

About 10 minutes later Cougar Myers's mama came in there, hunting a birthday present for her daddy. John let her come around behind the counter, and he showed her the bandana handkerchiefs and the pocket combs and the sock supporters and the Barlow knives and Aqua Velva and stuff. She picked her out a nice present for old man Myers, and John gift-wrapped it for her for free with some old Christmas paper he had left over.

She paid him and went out the door, and as he went to the register to ring up the sale, he looked heavenward again and said, "Honor thy father and thy mother."

Boy, by then, we were impressed with all that Scripture. It wasn't long afterward that we heard a big commotion outside the store. We looked out, and a brand-new bright blue pickup truck with a matching horse trailer had pulled up in front of the store. It had out-of-the-county license tags. Nobody knew that old feller.

Sure enough, he got out of the truck and came into the store. He had on a sheepskin coat, a big old 10-gallon hat, and pointy cowboy boots. He came a-struttin' in, walked up to the counter, and growled, "I want to buy me a horse blanket."

John said, "I'll see what I got." So he went to the back room, and he had three horse blankets there. They were all the very same kind, but each one was a different color. Naturally, John got the top one off the shelf and brought it out and laid it on the counter. The man said, "All right, how much is that?" John said, "Sir, that'll be $9.95."

That man yelled, "Nine ninety-five? Nine ninety-five? Buddy, I've got a $50,000 racehorse in that trailer out there, and I'm not about to put a cheap blanket like that on my horse! You can just forget it if you haven't got anything better." Old John said, "You want a better blanket." The man said, "Yeah, I want a better blanket."

John went to the back room again and took the next one down the line—same thing, just a different color—and brought it out and put it down on the counter. The man said, "All right, how much is that one?" John said, "Sir, that'll be $19.95."

The man said, "Buddy, I thought I told you I had a $50,000 racehorse out there, and no cheap stuff like that is going on the back of my horse!"

John said, "Sir, I aim to please. I think I got another one. I know what you want now."

So John took back that horse blanket and brought out the last one, carrying it as if it were some royal gem, and he laid it down real gentle in front of that man. Old John turned back one corner of the blanket, rubbing his hand over it, and he said, "Now, how is this?" The man said, "How much is that one?"

John said, "Sir, that's the best blanket in the house. That'll be $99.95."

The man said, "I'll take it." He whipped out the fattest wallet I've ever seen. Now, it might have been filled mostly with ones—I don't know. But he thumbed through there and pulled out a crisp $100 bill and laid it on the counter. He stuck that blanket under his arm and said, "Keep the change." Then he went out that squeaky screen door, jumped into his pickup truck, and took off.

There was dead silence. We couldn't believe what had just transpired. John stood behind the counter, holding that hundred-dollar bill in his hands. He looked over at us, and we looked at him. He waited. We reckoned he was waiting for some divine inspiration.

Finally he went over to the cash register. He looked toward heaven, rang that sale up, and said, "He was a stranger, and I took him in."

Jim Baker's Bluejay Yarn

Animal tales have always been a feature of North American folklore. Storytellers have given animals every human trait, including foolishness. Mark Twain, who was known as one who didn't suffer fools lightly, told this tale when he went on his lecture tours in the nineteenth century.

Animals talk to each other, of course. There can be no question about that; but I suppose there are very few people who can understand them. I never knew but one man who could. I knew he could, however, because he told me so himself. He was a middle-aged, simple-hearted miner who had lived in a lonely corner of California, among the woods and mountains, a good many years, and had studied the ways of his only neighbors, the beasts and the birds, until he believed he could accurately translate any remark which they made. This was Jim Baker. According to Jim Baker, some animals have only a limited education, and use only very simple words, and scarcely ever a comparison or a flowery figure; whereas, certain other animals have a large vocabulary, a fine command of language and a ready and fluent delivery; consequently these latter talk a great deal; they like it; they are conscious of their talent, and they enjoy "showing off." Baker said, that after long and careful observation, he had come to the conclusion that the bluejays were the best talkers he had found among birds and beasts. Said he:

"There's more *to* a bluejay than any other creature. He has got more moods, and more different kinds of feelings than other creatures; and, mind you, whatever a bluejay feels, he can put into language. And no mere commonplace language, either, but rattling, out-and-out book-talk—and bristling with metaphor, too—just bristling! And as for command of language—why *you* never see a bluejay get stuck for a word. No man ever did. They just boil out of him! And another thing: I've noticed a good deal, and there's no bird, or cow, or anything that uses as good grammar as a bluejay. You may say a cat uses good grammar. Well, a cat does—but you let a cat get excited once; you let a cat get to pulling fur with another cat on a shed, nights, and you'll hear grammar that will give you the lockjaw. Ignorant people think it's the *noise* which fighting cats make that is so aggravating, but it ain't so; it's the sickening grammar they use. Now I've never heard a jay use bad grammar but very seldom; and when they do, they are as ashamed as a human; they shut right down and leave.

"You may call a jay a bird. Well, so he is, in a measure—because he's got feathers on him, and don't belong to no church, perhaps; but otherwise he is just as much a human as you be. And I'll tell you for why. A jay's gifts, and instincts, and feelings, and interests, cover the whole ground. A jay hasn't got any more principle than a Congressman. A jay will lie, a jay will steal, a jay will deceive, a jay will betray; and four times out of five, a jay will go back on his solemnest promise. The sacredness of an obligation is a thing which you can't cram into no bluejay's head. Now, on top of all this, there's another thing; a jay can outswear any gentleman in the mines. You think a cat can swear. Well, a cat can; but you give a bluejay a subject that calls for his reserve-powers, and where is your cat? Don't talk to *me*—I know too much about this thing. And there's yet another thing; in the one little particular of scolding—just good, clean, out-and-out scolding—a blue-jay can lay over anything, human or divine. Yes, sir, a jay is everything that a man is. A jay can cry, a jay can laugh, a jay can feel shame, a jay can reason and plan and discuss, a jay likes gossip and scandal, a jay has got a sense of humor, a jay knows when he is an ass just as well as you do—maybe better. If a jay ain't human, he better take in his sign, that's all. Now I'm going to tell you a perfectly true fact about some bluejays.

"When I first begun to understand jay language correctly, there was a little incident happened here. Seven years ago, the last man in this region but me moved away. There stands his house,—been empty ever since; a log house, with a plank roof—just one big room, and no more; no ceiling—nothing between the rafters and the floor. Well, one Sunday morning I was sitting out here in front of my cabin, with my cat, taking the sun, and looking at the blue hills, and listening to the leaves rustling so lonely in the trees, and thinking of the home away yonder in the states, that I hadn't heard from in thirteen years, when a bluejay lit on that house, with an acorn in his mouth, and says, 'Hello, I reckon I've struck something.' When he spoke, the acorn dropped out of his mouth and rolled down the roof, of course, but he didn't care; his mind was all on the thing he had struck. It was a knot-hole in the roof. He cocked his head to one side, shut one eye and put the other one to the hole, like a 'possum looking down a jug; then he glanced up with his bright eyes, gave a wink or two with his wings—which signifies gratification, you understand—says, 'It looks like a hole, it's located like a hole,— blamed if I don't believe it *is* a hole!"

"Then he cocked his head down and took another look; he glances up perfectly joyful, this time; winks his wings and his tail both, and says, 'Oh, no, this ain't no fat thing, I reckon! If I ain't in luck!—why it's a perfectly elegant hole!' So he flew down and got that acorn, and fetched it up and dropped it in, and was just tilting his head back, with the heavenliest smile on his face, when all of a sudden he was paralyzed into a listening attitude and that smile faded gradually out of his countenance like breath off'n a razor, and the queerest look of surprise took its place. Then he says, 'Why, I didn't hear it fall!' He cocked his eye at the hole again, and took a long look; raised up and shook his head; stepped around to the other side of the hole and took another look from that side; shook his head again. He studied a while, then he just went into the *de*tails—walked round and round the hole and spied into it from every point of the compass. No use. Now he took a thinking attitude on the comb of the roof and scratched the back of his head with his right foot a minute, and finally says, 'Well, it's too many for *me*, that's certain; must be a mighty long hole; however, I ain't got no time to fool around here, I got to 'tend to business; I reckon it's all right—chance it, anyway.'

"So he flew off and fetched another acorn and dropped it in, and tried to flirt his eye to the hole quick enough to see what become of it, but he was too late. He held his eye there as much as a minute; then he raised up and sighed, and says, 'Confound it, I don't seem to understand this thing, no way; however, I'll tackle her again.' He fetched another acorn, and done his best to see what become of it, but he couldn't. He says, 'Well, *I* never struck no such a hole as this before; I'm of the opinion it's a totally new kind of a hole.' Then he begun to get mad. He held in for a spell, walking up and down the comb of the roof and shaking his head and muttering to himself; but his feelings got the upper hand of him, presently, and he broke loose and cussed himself black in the face. I never see a bird take on so about a little thing. When he got through he walks to the hole and looks in again for half a minute; then he says, 'Well, you're a long hole, and a deep hole, and a mighty singular hole altogether—but I've started in to fill you, and I'm d—d if I *don't* fill you, if it takes a hundred years!'

"And with that, away he went. You never see a bird work so since you was born. He laid into his work . . . and the way he hove acorns into that hole for about two hours and a half was one of the most exciting and astonishing spectacles I ever struck. He never stopped to take a look any more—he just hove 'em in and went for more. Well, at last he could hardly flop his wings, he was so tuckered out. He comes a-drooping down, once more, sweating like an ice-pitcher, drops his acorn in and says, '*Now* I guess I've got the bulge on you by this time!' So he bent down for a look. If you'll believe me, when his head come up again he was just pale with rage. He says, 'I've shoveled acorns enough in there to keep the family thirty years, and if I can see a sign of one of 'em I wish I may land in a museum with a belly full of sawdust in two minutes!'

"He just had strength enough to crawl up on to the comb and lean his back agin the chimbly, and then he collected his impressions and begun to free his mind. I see in a second that what I had mistook for profanity in the mines was only just the rudiments, as you may say.

"Another jay was going by, and heard him doing his devotions, and stops to inquire what was up. The sufferer told him the whole circumstance, and says, 'Now yonder's the hole, and if you don't believe me, go and look for yourself.' So this fellow went and looked, and comes back and says, 'How many did you say you put in there?' 'Not any less than two tons,' says the sufferer. The other jay went and looked again. He couldn't seem to make it out, so he raised a yell, and three more jays come. They all examined the hole, they all made the sufferer tell it over again, then they all discussed it, and got off as many leather-headed opinions about it as an average crowd of humans could have done.

"They called in more jays; then more and more till pretty soon this whole region 'peared to have a blue flush about it. There must have been five thousand of them; and such another jawing and disputing and ripping and cussing, you never heard. Every jay in the whole lot put his eye to the hole and delivered a more chuckle-headed opinion about the mystery than the jay that went there before him. They examined the house all over, too. The door was standing half open, and at last one old jay happened to go and light on it and look in. Of course, that knocked the mystery galley-west in a second. There lay the acorns, scattered all over the floor. He flopped his wings and raised a whoop. 'Come here!' he says. 'Come here, everybody; hang'd if this fool hasn't been trying to fill up a house with acorns!' They all came a-swooping down like a blue cloud, and as each fellow lit on the door and took a glance, the whole absurdity of the contract that that first jay had tackled hit him home and he fell over backwards suffocating with laughter, and the next jay took his place and done the same.

"Well, sir, they roosted around here on the housetop and the trees for an hour, and guffawed over that thing like human beings. It ain't any use to tell me a bluejay hasn't got a sense of humor, because I know better. And memory, too. They brought jays here from all over the United States to look down that hole, every summer for three years. Other birds, too. And they could all see the point, except an owl that come from Nova-Scotia to visit the Yo Semite, and he took this thing in on his way back. He said he couldn't see anything funny in it. But then he was a good deal disappointed about Yo Semite, too."

The Killer Mosquitoes

Mosquitoes turn up all the time in North American folklore presumably because they are a common pestilence in almost every region of the country. They most often appear in the tall tales, but this story from Louisiana, with versions all over the South, is told to poke fun at foreigners who are not familiar with our critters.

There were once three Irishmen called O'Leary, O'Bleary, and O'Neary who decided to leave the old country and come to Louisiana. They'd heard about the rich, black, delta dirt and the great plantations. They figured they'd find some work, save their money, and start farming. They'd grow sugar cane and cotton, beans and rice, everything but potatoes—they were just sick and tired of eating potatoes. O'Leary, O'Bleary, and O'Neary took passage on a ship bound for New Orleans. After weeks at sea, the Irishmen arrived in Louisiana at last. They got off the boat and started walking around to see what they could find for themselves.

They kept to the river, looking for a plantation where they could find work. Before long they were lost in the middle of the river bottom. Everywhere there were only swamp woods as far as they could see. The *mousse* hung down from the trees like an old man's beard, and *boscoyo* [cypress] rose up from the water like knobby knees. Alligators snapped at them and cottonmouth snakes hissed. But they weren't afraid, for they'd heard about the strange creatures that lived in La Louisianne: fish with cat whiskers and big as a man; giant snapping turtles; *pichou*, the bobcat that screamed like a woman. They fancied they knew all they needed to know to get by, so on they tramped, deeper and deeper into the swamp.

The sun began to sink low, so they decided they better make camp for the night. They found a little sheltered piece of dry ground and settled down there. The sun set and darkness fell. The three Irishmen were so tired, they were soon fast asleep. They'd slept only a few winks when suddenly they woke up howling and slapping at their faces and arms. A high, whining sound whirred in their ears.

They were being attacked by some kind of tiny beasts with a bite like the stick of a needle!

"What is it?" hollers O'Leary.

"I dunno, but it bites like the devil!" O'Bleary yells.

"I can't see it," says O'Neary, "but I can hear it whinin' for our blood!"

All night long the Irishmen slapped and cursed at the little monsters. When morning came they were red-eyed and covered with itchy red bumps. At last they got a look at the beasts that had nearly eaten them alive. They didn't know what to make of the little bloodthirsty creatures. They had never heard of mosquitoes!

"We better get out of here before they come back with their mates and kill us for good," says O'Leary. O'Bleary and O'Neary agreed, and they hurried away as quickly as they could through the swamp.

Well, the three men didn't have a notion of where they were going, and they wound up on the river right back where they started. They'd been walking in a circle. They turned in the opposite direction and walked until the sun was low in the sky. A little deserted cabin lay before them, perched on the river bank. They thought it looked like a good place to spend the night.

The three Irishmen barred the door and pulled the shutters. "We'll be safe here from those creatures. They'll not bite us tonight," they said. They settled in, with stomachs growling and the three of them just itchin' all over. They were dog-tired, and pretty soon they fell fast asleep. O'Neary's snoring woke up O'Leary, and when he sat up he saw blinking lights buzzing about the room.

"Wake up, mates!" he shouts. "Those blood-suckin' devils are back!" The others woke up trembling. "They mean to kill us for sure!" hollers O'Neary. "Faith and begorra!" shouts O'Bleary. "Look! They brought lanterns so they could see us and suck us dry. Run for it, boys! Aaiieegghh!"

The three Irishmen were running so wildly to get out of that cabin that they broke the door down. They didn't know that the blinking, buzzing lights in the cabin were only harmless *mouches à feu*, fireflies.

O'Leary, O'Bleary, and O'Neary didn't stop running until they got back to New Orleans, where they took the first ship they could find back to Ireland. After that they never minded eating potatoes at every blessed meal. For at least at home they were safe from those whining, needle-nosed, lantern-carrying, blood-sucking, killer mosquitoes!

The Yankee Peddler and the Innkeeper

────◆◆◆────

Two famous American characters are brought together in this tale of deception and fool-
ishness. The Yankee Peddler makes a frequent appearance in stories from the
Northeastern United States, not as a fool but as a clever bargainer who does his best to
make fools of his customers. He finds an easy mark in the Dutchman, who, in nine-
teenth-century Pennsylvania Dutch culture, was the object of many jokes the people told
on themselves.

────◆────

A Yankee peddler westbound with his team of horses and load of notions was held up at a Dutchman's Inn for almost a week because of a very severe storm. Rains had made the roads impassable and the streams were in a flooding state.

Finally after days of eating and sleeping and drinking at the Inn, and after demanding considerable service from the Dutch innkeeper, he asked that his horses be hitched and be made ready to depart.

Finally he asked the innkeeper, "How much is my fare?" and the Dutchman thinking a dollar a day enough, but seeing the man wasn't a regular customer, said, "$10.00."

The Yankee said, "Maybe it would be better if I paid you on the way back, then I could give you $20.00 for my stay and it would allow me time to make more sales and have more ready cash after I sell my supplies." But to this the Dutchman was suspicious and insisted on being paid cash THEN.

The Yankee paid him the $10.00 and the Dutchman, feeling that he had made a good profit, seeing that he charged him almost half again as much as he usually did to other people, said, "It's a custom for the innkeeper to offer a trav-eller a drink for the road," to which the Yankee said, "Fine." (This was a time hon-ored custom, to be expected by the Yankees.)

The innkeeper handed the Yankee a mug of cider and the Yankee said, "This certainly would make fine wine if you put it through that new secret wine-making process." And the Dutchman thought, "If I could convert cider into good wine, I'd be rich and have hundreds more visitors, etc."

The Dutchman said, "Tell me how to make it." And the Yankee said, "It is new and valuable and I'll charge you $10.00 now and when I return, if the cider is wine, you will have to agree now to pay me an additional $50.00."

After the agreement was made, the Dutchman and Yankee went into the cellar, and the Yankee asked for a half-inch auger, bored a hole into one end of the barrel of cider and asked the Dutchman to place his thumb to this, and stretch his arm so he could cover the other hole also.

"Hold this position while I go up and get the spigots from my wagon."

With this he left the Dutchman, arms spread out holding the barrel with holes in it, and jumped in his wagon and left.

8

Love Stories

~

Woven into the fabric of many homespun North American folktales are recognizable elements from European fairy tales. More than any other type of tale, love stories inherit their themes from these ancient sources. Regional North American tellers have for centuries taken half-remembered stories, placed them in settings close to home, and rendered them in dialects from all over the continent. As the tellers adapt the stories to reflect their own surroundings, they change characters' names, add some details and omit others, and, in some cases, combine several stories into one. "Cinderella" is frequently used as the basis for a love story, and it is closely followed in popularity by "East of the Sun and West of the Moon" and "Beauty and the Beast."

In addition to Old World tales that have been altered to fit North American storytelling styles, several purebred American love stories are represented here. Just as with every other aspect of life, North Americans have developed their own peculiar way of courting each other and of talking about it later. Some of these stories are legendary. That is, they are probably based on real events that are either very funny or are significant to the culture group that keeps them alive. Other tales are pure romantic fiction.

The Girl That Married a Flop-Eared Hound-Dog

This remarkable American version of one of the world's most frequently repeated fairy tales was told to Marie Campbell by Uncle Tom Dixon of Kentucky in the 1930s. Readers will recognize in this tale elements of "East of the Sun and West of the Moon."

That old flop-eared hound-dog laying there on the hearth with his head to the fire 'minds me of a tale my foreparents used to tell of evenings gathered about the hearth. While we wait for Suzanne to call supper, I aim to tell you the old time tale called "The Girl That Married a Flop-Eared Hound-Dog." Musta looked pine-blank like that old hound-dog laying right there by the fire.

They was a man—a king maybe—that had a fine castle and lands that stretched from here to yonder. His wife died and left him all lonesome. One day when he was out in the woods, not hunting but just walking around nearly about to lonesome to death, a fine hound-dog with long flop-ears come up to him wagging its tail and acting friendly. The king thought maybe it had got lost from some folks hunting in his woods. So he sat down on a log and called the dog up to him and said to it, "What you doing here, flop-eared hound-dog? How come you got lost from hunting? What you want me to do for you?"

He never thought a breath about no answer. He was just making friends with a good hunting dog. But the flop-eared hound-dog set itself down in front of him and said, "I want to marry one of your girls; that's what I want, and I can take good care of her and keep her happy if she's a-mind to have me."

Well, the king was so addled in his mind with hearing a hound-dog speak out that way that he said, "Come along home with me, and I'll let you ask one of my girls will she marry you, and I'm willing if she is."

The flop-eared hound-dog asked the oldest girl first would she marry him. She flew mad and screeched and screamed, "No I won't marry no flop-eared hound-dog! I won't marry nothing but a natural man! Who ever heard tell of such an idea!"

Then the flop-eared hound-dog asked the middle girl would she marry him. And she had a bigger fit than the oldest girl done had. And she wouldn't marry him neither.

When he asked the youngest girl would she marry him, she said she would if she could come back home now and again to see her folks. She never 'peared to feel no shame about who she was marrying but asked a big passel of folks to the wedding just like she was going to marry a natural man. And she fixed a heap of fine wedding clothes.

Then the very minute of the wedding ceremony when the sisters had their eyes covered up with their hands, for they couldn't bear to see a flop-eared hound-dog stand up and marry their sister in front of a whole crowd of folks that never had no hint that she weren't marrying a natural man—well, that very minute the groom came in, and it weren't no flop-eared hound-dog no more but a good-looking young man dressed up in his Sunday clothes. A mean old witch had put him under a spell till some nice girl was willing to marry him of her own free will. He was so good-looking and rich that the oldest girl and the middle girl turned mighty jealous. And folks said it was the best wedding they been to that season.

After the wedding frolic was over, the bride and groom went to their fine home in some place a far piece off. I don't know where it was nor no more about it. It was just a fine big house and they lived happy together.

Then in a year and a day the girl hankered to go see her folks, and she wanted to stay there till she birthed her baby. Her man was willing for her to go on a visit to her folks, but he cautioned her not to tell his name to nobody even if they begged mighty hard. If she told that his name was Sunshine on the Dew, she wouldn't never see him no more.

Well, she had the baby at her old home place, and it was a mighty pretty boy baby. When it was two days old, in the night folks heard fairy music; and in the morning the baby was gone. Whoever had stole the baby left sweet cakes and wine at the head of the bed. But no trace of the baby.

The sisters blamed the baby's daddy and they tried to find out what his name was—but the youngest girl shut her mouth up tight and wouldn't tell. Her man came in a month's time and took her home with him.

Another year and a day passed by and the youngest girl hankered to visit her folks again and stay till she birthed her [next] baby. Her man cautioned her again not to tell his name to nobody or she wouldn't see him no more. When the second baby—a girl this time—was two days old, they was fairy music in the night. And the baby gone—nobody could guess where. Whoever had stole this baby had put sweet cakes and wine at the head of the bed like the time before.

The sisters blamed the baby's daddy again and tried to find out his name. But the youngest girl shut up her mouth tight and wouldn't tell. In a month's time her man come and took her back home with him.

Three times the youngest girl went home to visit her folks and stayed till she had birthed her baby—the last one another boy. Three times her man cautioned her not to tell his name or she wouldn't see him no more. But the sisters threatened her with her life if she wouldn't tell. So she said in a low whisper that his name was Sunshine on the Dew.

When the last baby was two days old the fairy music in the night came again. And the next morning—no baby—no sweet cakes nor wine at the head of the bed neither. And no man come to take her home with him no matter how long she waited.

After she waited some months for her man to come and he never showed up, she set out on foot to go to her married home. Nobody home when she got there. No sign of nobody. So she set out to travel till she found her man. She traveled all day till she had holes in her shoes. At nighttime she saw a little house in the woods. The door stood open and a fire was blazing in the fireplace. An old woman in a rocking chair by the hearth made her welcome. She said her man with three babies different sizes had been there three nights before. The old woman gave her a good supper and warm water to wash herself and a soft bed to her sides. In the morning she gave the girl some scissors that she said would cut by themselves whatever the girl wanted her cloth to be.

The second night at the same kind of little house an old woman made her welcome and said her man with three babies different sizes had been there two nights before. This old woman gave her a good supper and warm water to wash herself and a soft bed to her sides. In the morning she gave the girl a thimble that would sew by itself.

The last night another old woman in a little house made the girl welcome and told her her man with three babies different sizes had been there just the night before. The girl wouldn't stay for no supper nor no warm water to wash herself nor no soft bed to her sides. She wanted to hurry on and try to catch up with her man. The old woman tied up a snack to eat in a budget (small sack) and gave it to the girl along with a needle that would sew fine things by itself.

The girl went on till she came to a fine big house with a crowd of folks gathered about. It was her man fixing to marry again. But the girl swapped her magic sewing tools that could cut and sew fine things without no help from any person. She swapped them things to the other girl to give back her man to her. I don't call to mind the details and particulars of how it come about—but when the man that had been a flop-eared hound-dog saw his first woman, it all come over him again how he loved her with all his heart; and he gave the fine new house to the woman he wasn't going to marry, and took his babies three different sizes and the girl that had birthed him the babies and they went back to their own home place to live out all the days of their life.

The Algonquin Cinderella

The basic story of Cinderella is told in almost every culture on Earth, and some experts think that it is thousands of years old. Whether the Native American Algonquin tribes heard it from European settlers and altered it or generated their own version, we will never know. But this beautiful tale stands as one of the best renditions I have ever heard.

There was once a large village of the MicMac Indians of the Eastern Algonquins, built beside a lake. At the far end of the settlement stood a lodge, and in it lived a being who was always invisible. He had a sister who looked after him, and everyone knew that any girl who could see him might marry him. For that reason there were very few girls who did not try, but it was very long before anyone succeeded.

This is the way in which the test of sight was carried out: at evening-time, when the Invisible One was due to be returning home, his sister would walk with any girl who might come down to the lakeshore. She, of course, could see her brother, since he was always visible to her. As soon as she saw him, she would say to the girls:

"Do you see my brother?"

"Yes," they would generally reply—though some of them did say "No."

To those who said that they could indeed see him, the sister would say:

"Of what is his shoulder strap made?" Some people say that she would enquire:

"What is his moose-runner's haul?" or "With what does he draw his sled?"

And they would answer:

"A strip of rawhide" or "a green flexible branch," or something of that kind.

Then she, knowing that they had not told the truth, would say:

"Very well, let us return to the wigwam!"

When they had gone in, she would tell them not to sit in a certain place, because it belonged to the Invisible One. Then, after they had helped to cook the supper, they would wait with great curiosity, to see him eat. They could be sure that he was a real person, for when he took off his moccasins they became visible, and his sister hung them up. But beyond this they saw nothing of him, not even when they stayed in the place all the night, as many of them did.

Now there lived in the village an old man who was a widower, and his three daughters. The youngest girl was very small, weak and often ill, and yet her sisters, especially the elder, treated her cruelly. The second daughter was kinder, and sometimes took her side, but the wicked sister would burn her hands and feet with hot cinders, and she was covered with scars from this treatment. She was so marked that people called her *Oochigeaskw*, the Rough-FacedGirl.

When her father came home and asked why she had such burns, the bad sister would at once say that it was her own fault, for she had disobeyed orders and gone near the fire and fallen into it.

These two elder sisters decided one day to try their luck at seeing the Invisible One. So they dressed themselves in their finest clothes, and tried to look their prettiest. They found the Invisible One's sister and took the usual walk by the water.

When he came, and when they were asked if they could see him, they answered: "Of course." And when asked about the shoulder strap or sled cord, they answered: "A piece of rawhide."

But of course they were lying like the others, and they got nothing for their pains.

The next afternoon, when the father returned home, he brought with him many of the pretty little shells from which wampum was made, and they set to work to string them.

That day, poor little Oochigeaskw, who had always gone barefoot, got a pair of her father's moccasins, old ones, and put them into water to soften them so that she could wear them. Then she begged her sisters for a few wampum shells. The elder called her a "little pest," but the younger one gave her some. Now, with no other clothes than her usual rags, the poor little thing went into the woods and got herself some sheets of birch bark, from which she made a dress, and put marks on it for decoration, in the style of long ago. She made a petticoat and a loose gown, a cap, leggings and a handkerchief. She put on her father's large old moccasins, which were far too big for her, and went forth to try her luck. She would try, she thought, to discover whether she could see the Invisible One.

She did not begin very well. As she set off, her sisters shouted and hooted, hissed and yelled, and tried to make her stay. And the loafers around the village, seeing the strange little creature, called out "Shame!"

The poor little girl in her strange clothes, with her face all scarred, was an awful sight, but she was kindly received by the sister of the Invisible One. And this was, of course, because this noble lady understood far more about things than simply the mere outside which all the rest of the world knows. As the brown of the evening sky turned to black, the lady took her down to the lake.

"Do you see him?" the Invisible One's sister asked.

"I do, indeed—and he is wonderful!" said Oochigeaskw.

The sister asked:

"And what is his sled-string?"

The little girl said:

"It is the Rainbow."

"And, my sister, what is his bow-string?"

"It is The Spirit's Road—the Milky Way."

"So you *have* seen him," said his sister. She took the girl home with her and bathed her. As she did so, all the scars disappeared from her body. Her hair grew again, as it was combed, long, like a blackbird's wing. Her eyes were now like stars. In all the world there was no other such beauty. Then, from her treasures, the lady gave her a wedding garment, and adorned her.

Then she told Oochigeaskw to take the wife's seat in the wigwam: the one next to where the Invisible One sat, beside the entrance. And when he came in, terrible and beautiful, he smiled and said:

"So we are found out!"

"Yes," said his sister. And so Oochigeaskw became his wife.

La Cenicienta Huasteca

It is possible that the story of Cinderella was brought to southwestern North America from Spain, where it has always been popular. This Mexican version characteristically changes the main setting for the story from a fancy ball to the church. "La Cenicienta" is Spanish for Cinderella; "Huasteca" is probably derived from Aztec.

Maria la Cenicienta was a girl who worked for a woman who had a daughter. She had to do all the housework and besides was compelled to labor at night carding wool. However, there was a little lamb that helped her. And this story tells us that the woman learned about this and ordered the lamb killed. Also, she called this girl, La Cenicienta, and told her to take the stomach of the lamb to the river and wash it and prepare it for *menudo*. While she was at the river preparing the meat for *menudo* some fish came and carried the little stomach away. La Cenicienta began to cry.

Then a fairy woman appeared and told her to weep no more. She said that near by La Cenicienta would find a small house and in the house was a baby crying and some large *tinajas* (large earthen jars) turned upside down.

"Sing to the baby and put it to sleep," she said; "then turn the *tinajas* upright."

La Cenicienta did as that fairy woman ordered. She found the small house and the baby crying. She sang and the little one went to sleep. Then she turned a *tinaja* upright, and immediately a golden star fixed itself upon her forehead and she was dressed in fine clothes. She turned another *tinaja* and there found the *menudo* meat prepared for cooking.

When she returned home the woman and the girl wanted to know how she got the fine clothes and the star. La Cenicienta told them what had happened at the river.

Envy entered the hearts of the woman and the girl, and they took the clothes from La Cenicienta. Then the woman had another lamb killed and sent her daughter to the river with the stomach of the animal.

"Do as La Cenicienta did," she said. "You will get more beautiful things."

The daughter took the meat to the river and while she was washing it, some fish came and carried the little stomach away. Then the girl pretended to weep. A fairy woman came to her and said:

"Weep no more. Go to the little house near here. You will find a baby crying. Sing it to sleep. Then the *tinajas* you see in the house are to be turned upright."

That girl went to the small house, and she whipped the baby hard. She turned a *tinaja*, and the *moco* of a *guajolote* (a turkey-cock's comb) attached itself to her forehead. She went home and wrapped a cloth about her head to hide the *moco*.

Later, the woman and her daughter went to mass. La Cenicienta was in the kitchen weeping and working when a fairy woman came to her and asked why she was sad.

"I wanted to go to mass," said La Cenicienta, "but they wouldn't let me." And then the fairy woman gave her a wand of *virtud*. "When you wish with your heart for something that is good, touch the star on your forehead with this wand and your wish will come true," she said.

Immediately La Cenicienta wished for elegant clothes and golden shoes and a carriage *mejor que ninguno* with a span of fine horses.

She went to mass. Everyone was amazed, and a prince fell in love with her.

When later the woman and her daughter came home, they found La Cenicienta in her ashy clothes working in the kitchen as usual. They told La Cenicienta of the miracle that they had seen at mass.

"The miracle was I," said La Cenicienta.

They laughed and mocked and said the star on La Cenicienta's forehead was taking the salt from her brain.

The following Sunday the woman and daughter went to mass, and as before left La Cenicienta home. However, this time La Cenicienta did not weep. She used her wand of *virtud* as she had done before, and behold she was at mass as beautiful as the most beautiful fairy.

When La Cenicienta left the church she lost one of her golden shoes near the door. The prince found it and went to the home where the woman lived with her daughter. He said he intended to marry the girl whose foot would fit that shoe. The woman's daughter crammed her big foot into the shoe. The prince put her in the carriage and was on his way to his palace when a little dog began barking and saying, "*Moco de guajolote va en coche y estrella de oro está en casa* (the turkey-cock's comb goes in the carriage, and the star of gold is in the house)." The prince was puzzled and went back to the house where the woman lived. He found the beautiful servant La Cenicienta. The golden shoe fitted her foot. They were married, *y fueron muy felices.*

Fabiano and Reyes

This dramatic tale, which is told in the Hispanic Southwest in North America, clearly has roots in the romantic fairy tales of Europe's Middle Ages. As the European ancestors of modern Hispanics crossed paths with the Indian populations of the American Southwest, tales such as "Fabiano and Reyes" were given more homely settings, though the notion of royalty was retained. This blending of the Old and the New Worlds produces a story of extraordinary love, and serves as a caution, as well.

Once there lived two kings and their wives who were very good friends. When one of the queens gave birth to her first child, the neighboring king and queen were asked to be godparents, and they named the baby boy Fabiano. Two years later the other queen gave birth to a baby girl, and she and the king, in turn, invited their friends to be godparents, and they named the girl Reyes.

Fabiano and Reyes grew up like brother and sister, and they loved each other very much. When they were growing up they would visit each other, spending one week in one palace and the next in the other. And later when they went to study at school Fabiano always took care of Reyes, because he cared for her as if she were his sister.

Fabiano grew to be a very handsome young man, one without equal in the region. When he was only fifteen he began writing love notes to his many girlfriends, and he shared all his secrets with Reyes because she was his confidante. When he showed her a letter from a girl whose heart he had broken he would say, "My dear Reyes, I only want a beautiful girl. If I had to marry an ugly girl I'd rather be blind."

And Reyes, who didn't consider herself a beautiful girl, would bow her head in shame and answer, "Fabiano, you deserve the most virtuous woman on this earth, one who is as beautiful as you."

Time passed and Fabiano continued his flirtations, and he always told Reyes everything, including his dislike for ugly girls. When school was over they returned home, and they still visited each other as before—one week in one palace and the next in the other.

In those days the kings often entertained people by holding big fiestas at their palaces. There were dances, bullfights and many other diversions. And as usual, Fabiano and Reyes were always together. Fabiano always found the most beautiful girls to dance with, and when he introduced them to Reyes he would always whisper, "I'll never marry an ugly girl, better to be blind than that!"

One summer, after the dances had come to an end in the palace of Fabiano's family, the entertainment was moved to the palace of Reyes' father. Her father had vowed to outdo his compadre—he was going to bring singers and bullfighters from across the sea!

And so it was at a dance at Reyes' home that Fabiano found a pretty American girl. When he introduced her to Reyes he said, "Look, I have finally found my sweetheart. This is the kind of girl for me, is she not a beauty?"

"I agree," Reyes answered courteously. "Also, the woman who marries you should be the most virtuous woman in the world."

The following night Fabiano saw that Reyes was not dressed in her silk dress and jewelry; instead she had made a very simple linen dress for herself.

"Reyes!" Fabiano exclaimed, "Why aren't you dressed in your silk dress! That simple linen dress doesn't become a rich princess who has all the virtues of the world."

"Fabiano," she answered, "a woman as ugly as myself doesn't deserve to wear silk and fine apparel. I should wear only the most simple dress."

"I will be ashamed," he said, "for you to be seen with my American sweetheart; she will be dressed in her best silks and you in simple linen."

"Oh, she deserves the best," Reyes answered. "She is a lovely woman. But I don't deserve silk as I am ugly. So I will dress in a simple manner."

The following night, which was the last night of entertainment at the palace of Reyes' father, the singers who had been invited failed to arrive. Fabiano, who was eager to show off his new sweetheart, waited for them all afternoon, but there was no sign of the singers. Finally a servant arrived with the message that there had been a shipwreck and the singers had drowned.

Reyes grew very worried. "I don't want my father to be ashamed in front of his guests because he has no entertainment," she said. "Perhaps I can take their place."

"Oh, no!" Fabiano objected. "It would be a disgrace to have you, a princess, sing in public!"

Nevertheless Reyes decided to sing for the sake of her father. Even as Reyes began to sing Fabiano continued to insist that she should not. It wouldn't look right, he said, for such a handsome man as he to be seen with a plain and common singer.

But Reyes sang and when Fabiano heard her he was astonished. Never had he heard such a beautiful voice. He then became so enamored of Reyes that he didn't know what to do. When Reyes finished singing Fabiano was immediately at her side telling her how beautifully she had sung, but Reyes reminded him that she was an ugly woman and unworthy of his attention.

That evening when the festivities were concluded, Fabiano could hardly bear to leave. He had fallen completely in love with Reyes. The next day he told his parents that they should go and arrange for him to have Reyes' hand in marriage. The king and queen were overjoyed to hear of this plan.

But Reyes refused the offer by sending back a pumpkin, which according to the custom of that time meant a refusal. She also sent a letter in which she told Fabiano that she didn't deserve a man like him. She reminded him he had often derided ugly women, and since she was not beautiful and didn't wish him to be blind he should marry someone else. Fabiano waited a month but then became impatient and sent a friend to again ask Reyes to marry him. The friend went to Reyes but she explained that a marriage with Fabiano was impossible because of his conceit. It was true, she loved Fabiano, but as things were, the situation was impossible.

When Fabiano heard Reyes' answer he was brokenhearted. To try to forget his love he left his parents and moved to a foreign country. But he couldn't forget Reyes and every week he wrote her of his love.

Now it so happened that one afternoon Fabiano went hunting. He fired at a rabbit and the gun exploded. The gunpowder burned his eyes and blinded him. To make matters worse, while Fabiano was recovering from the accident his parents died, and shortly afterwards he heard that Reyes' parents had died also.

Later, when Fabiano returned home, he found himself alone. He had kept all of the letters he had written to Reyes but had never sent in a small box, but since he was now blind he was unable to read them as he used to. Now his only companion was a friend who came to visit him. His friend saw that Fabiano was very sad because he was alone and blind. One afternoon when he was visiting Fabiano, the friend inquired about Reyes.

"Has Reyes come to see you?" he asked.

"No," Fabiano answered, "she doesn't come to see me because of the way I treated her, but I know that without her I will die. She doesn't know that I truly love her and that she is my only consolation in life."

Then the friend went to see Reyes, and she asked about Fabiano.

"As you know, he is home, and he is blind, but you are such a hard woman it seems you have forgotten you grew up together."

"You are wrong, sir," Reyes answered. "The love I have for Fabiano cannot be destroyed by death itself."

"He doesn't know that," the friend said. "He thinks you don't love him. His life is very difficult. Because he is blind, his servants take advantage of him and feed him only when they want to. The food is poorly prepared and he is neglected. He needs someone to care for him. Would you be willing to be his nurse?"

"I will be Fabiano's nurse on one condition," Reyes answered, "and that is if you swear not to tell him it is I. I still believe he fell in love with me only because he heard me sing. Perhaps this way I will discover if he truly loves me."

"You have my word that I won't tell him anything," the friend said, "and you can see for yourself if his love is real."

The friend went back to Fabiano and asked him if he could bring a nurse to care for him. "Yes," Fabiano agreed, "but bring me a nurse who can read, one who will care kindly for me and see that I am fed."

So the friend brought Reyes to Fabiano's palace, and she was so overjoyed to see him again that she turned away and wept secretly. Then with great care she prepared his bath, and after he had bathed she helped him dress in the clothes of a prince. She fed him well and took good care of him because she loved him very much.

One day after she had been there a month Fabiano asked her for a favor. "Nurse," he asked, "can you keep a secret?"

"I believe I can," Reyes answered.

"Then go to the storage room near my bedroom. There you will find a small box. Bring it to me. But remember, this is a secret only you and I will share."

Reyes brought the box and when Fabiano opened it she saw it was full of his old love letters to her. He asked her to read the letters and when she read them Fabiano grew very sad and his eyes grew wet with tears. Reyes, too, wept silently, but because Fabiano was blind he could not see the tears which rolled down her cheeks.

The next day Fabiano's friend came to visit and he found Reyes in the kitchen, her eyes red from crying. He asked Reyes what was the matter.

"Yesterday I discovered that Fabiano's love for me is real," she said, "and I cried all night after reading the letters he wrote to me."

"What do you plan to do?" the friend asked.

"I must put aside the mistakes of the past and marry Fabiano," she answered. "I have always loved him, and I love him even more now and want to care for him."

The friend was overjoyed. He immediately went to Fabiano and said, "My friend, I believe you should be married. You have many good years of life left; perhaps you should consider marrying this good woman who is your nurse."

Fabiano sighed. "Who would love a blind man?" he said. "And although the nurse is a good woman, the only love in my heart is for Reyes."

"Then I shall go and ask her for you," the friend said.

Fabiano shook his head. "She refused me when I was young and hand-some. Why should she accept me now that I am blind?"

"I will ask her anyway, and we shall see if she loves you or not!" the friend insisted.

For a moment hope stirred in Fabiano's heart. "Oh, if Reyes would marry me I would give you half of all I own, my friend!"

So the wedding was arranged, and the next day the friend and his wife, who were to be the witnesses, brought Reyes to Fabiano.

As they left for the church, Fabiano, who still didn't know that it was Reyes who had been his nurse, called for the nurse and told her to prepare a banquet table for the wedding feast.

Then the wedding party went to the chapel and Fabiano and Reyes were married. When they returned everyone was happy and excited. Fabiano called his nurse to come and serve them. Only then did his friend turn to him and tell him that the nurse who had served him so loyally all that time was Reyes herself: "Don't call for your nurse, for she is in truth Reyes. She is the bride at your side!"

Fabiano then took Reyes in his arms and understood at last that the real beauty of a woman lies in her soul.

A Bunch of Laurel Blooms for a Present

The theme from "Beauty and the Beast" begins this Kentucky story, and "The Frog Prince" ends it. But in "The Frog Prince," the princess is usually angry at the frog and throws him against the wall, which brings about a magic transformation. Here, we are given a stronger, braver heroine who takes the decisive step to release her lover from the spell.

Brought you some laurel buds to make a flowerpot to pretty up your house. Mary always loved laurel blooms the best when they were still little, knobby, pink buds, kinda square-shaped. Giving you a bunch of laurel blooms puts me in mind of an olden tale about a girl that wanted laurel blooms for a present.

It starts with a man going off from home a far piece to tend to some business, and he asked his three girls what they wanted him to bring them back for presents. The oldest girl said she wanted him to bring her back a green silk dress. The middle girl said she wanted him to bring her a pair of gold beads. The youngest girl wanted him to bring her a bunch of laurel blooms for a present. Maybe they had moved down to the level country from the mountains, and she was used to seeing laurel blooms back where they used to live. I don't know. The tale don't say.

The man bought the green silk dress and the pair of gold beads as soon as he got to the far-off place. But he waited about the laurel blooms till he was ready to start back home, so they wouldn't get all wilted. Then he couldn't find any laurel blooms. He looked and he looked. After a time he saw some laurel blooms on the edge of a woods. Seemed like they didn't belong to nobody, so he picked some to give his youngest girl for a present.

After he picked the laurel blooms, an old witch came out of the laurel bushes and said they belonged to her, and she didn't aim to let nobody pick them. She said he had already picked some, and he would have to die. He told her the flower blooms were for a present to his youngest girl. Then the old witch said he could live if he would give his youngest girl to her.

He would rather die than do that. He begged the old witch to let him go home and give the presents to his girls. She said he could do that. He gave the green silk dress to the oldest girl and the pair of gold beads to the middle girl. They put on their finery and primped in front of the looking glass. He gave the laurel blooms to the youngest girl, and she hugged his neck and kissed him. Then she put her present of flower blooms in a flowerpot of water to keep them fresh. Her sisters made fun of her for asking for nothing but flower blooms when she coulda had fine things to wear.

The man told his girls he had to go to the witch, and the youngest girl ran off in the night and went in his place to save him from the old witch. The old witch put her to live in a nice little house with an upstairs. A good supper was fixed and on the table waiting. The youngest girl saw two places at the table. Then in came the biggest toad-frog she ever did see.

It sat down in one chair, and she sat down in the other chair, and they ate supper together. The toad-frog washed up the dishes and told her to rest from the long journey. She went upstairs and found a room with a nice bed and lay down to sleep. In the night she could see by the candle the big toad-frog climbing into her bed. She went back to sleep, and in the morning when she woke up, he was gone. He had breakfast ready when she went downstairs, and all the time he cooked and kept house. He treated her kind and good, but she couldn't like his warty old skin and his toad-frog eyes. Living with a man-size toad-frog would give a girl the creeps, it seems like to me. But she learned to love his kind and helpsome ways, though not his looks.

He picked laurel blooms every day and brought them to her for a present. She felt like she could live out her days with him, if only he looked like a natural human. One night she woke up thinking about it. In the moonlight she could see a handsome young man laying in the bed beside her and the warty old frog skin hanging on a bed post.

She eased out of bed, got the warty

old frog skin in her hands, and tipped downstairs. She flung the warty old frog skin into the fireplace and watched it crackle and burn. Then she went back to bed and slept sound till morning.

It was a handsome young man woke her up next morning. He told her he could stay a man now. Burning up the warty old frog skin had lifted the witch's spell on him. They lived there amongst the laurel blooms together in the nice little house with an upstairs.

Her sisters were jealous all their lives for her having such a handsome man that would cook the breakfast, and give her a house with an upstairs. Maybe they learned their lesson about being greedy and wanting costly presents and ending up with not as much as the youngest sister that asked for nothing more than a bunch of laurel blooms.

The Toadfrog

Herewith an inevitable, all-American takeoff on the fairy tales that play so big a part in North American love stories. It comes from the Ozark Mountains and, like the previous story, has elements of both "The Frog Prince" and "Beauty and the Beast."

One time there was a pretty girl walking down the street, and she heard somebody say, "Hi, Toots!" But when she looked around there was nobody in sight, just a little old toadfrog setting on the sidewalk.

So then the pretty girl started to walk on down the street, and she heard somebody say, "Hello, Beautiful!" But when she looked around there was nobody in sight, just this little old toadfrog.

So then the pretty girl started to walk on down the street, and she heard somebody say, "You got anything on tonight, Baby?" But when she looked around there was nobody in sight, just this little old toadfrog setting on the sidewalk.

The pretty girl looked down at the little old toadfrog. "I know it ain't you a-talking," she says.

"It's me, all right," says the toadfrog. "I'm a handsome young man, by rights. But I'm turned into a toadfrog now, because an old witch put a spell on me."

The pretty girl studied awhile, and then she says, "Ain't there anything you can do to break the spell?"

The toadfrog says there is only one way, and that is for a pretty girl to let him sleep on her pillow all night. The pretty girl thought it was the least she could do, to help this poor fellow out. So she took the little old toadfrog home and put him on her pillow when she went to bed.

Next morning the pretty girl's father come to wake her up, and he seen a handsome young man in the bed with her. She told her father about the little old toadfrog, and the witch that put a spell on him, and how it all happened. But the old man didn't believe the story, any more than you do!

Old Black-Oak Knows Best

Sometimes it takes a "supernatural" effort to win the girl. The teller of this tale, Mr. Frank Payne, of Missouri, claimed he heard it first in 1904. Other versions have the boy hiding in church and waiting for his girl to come and pray for a husband.

One time there was a pretty girl named Josie, and her folks was well fixed but they had trouble with the law, so the town boys didn't come around much. There was a young farmer name of Pete wanted to go with her, but Josie wouldn't do it because she figured them high-collar town boys was better. She give old Gram French two dollars for a charm, but it didn't do no good. Finally Gram told her to hang the charm on the old black-oak at midnight, and then say a little rhyme.

When Josie come to the old black-oak she done just like Gram told her, and then set down to see what happened. Pretty soon she heard a voice away up in the air a-mumbling. Josie was kind of scared, but she stood still a minute and listened. There was some more mumbling, and then the voice says, "You got to marry Pete." Josie run for home when she heard that and never told the folks nothing.

The next night she went back to the old black-oak and done just like Gram told her, and then set down to see what happened. Pretty soon she hears some more mumbling up in the air, and then the voice says, "You got to marry Pete." Josie went home and thought about it a long time.

The third night she went back to the old black-oak and done just like Gram told her, and then set down to see what happened. Pretty soon she heard something a-mumbling up in the air, and then the voice says, "You got to marry Pete." Josie went home just like she done before, and never slept a wink all night.

Next day she went and told Gram French what happened. "If you heerd the same thing three nights a-runnin', you better go ahead an' marry Pete," says Gram. "What's the use to marry a fellow like that?" says Josie. "Why, he ain't got a pot to cook in, or a window to throw it out!" Gram just set and looked at her awhile. "Old black-oak knows best," she says. "It takes more'n pots an' windows to make a good husband." Gram didn't say no more, and Josie didn't return no answer.

Josie told the folks she knowed all the time it was Pete a-talking out of the old black-oak, and she says Gram French must have put him up to it. But Pete just grinned, and he never did admit nothing. Him and her got hitched in the dark of the moon, all right. But the neighbors say they done about as good as any other married folks.

Hard of Hearing

Persuading the girl to look twice at him is sometimes the easy part of a young man's courtship. Dealing with her father might prove the greatest challenge of all. "Jonathan" in the following story is an old slang term referring to a man from the New England states.

A young Jonathan once courted the daughter of an old man that lived "down east," who professed to be deficient in hearing, but, forsooth, was more captious than limited in hearing, as the sequel will show.

It was a stormy night in the ides of March, if I mistake not, when lightning and loud peals of thunder answered thunder, that Jonathan sat by the old man's fireside, discussing with the old lady (his intended mother-in-law) on the expediency of asking the old man's permission to marry "Sal." Jonathan resolved to "pop it" to the old man the next day. Night passed, and by the dawn of another day, the old man was found in his barn-lot, feeding his pigs. Jonathan rose from his bed early in the morning, spied the old man feeding his pigs, and resolved to ask him for Sal.

Scarce had a minute elapsed, after Jonathan made his resolution, ere he bid the old man "good morning." Now Jonathan's heart beat; now he scratched his head, and ever and anon gave birth to a pensive yawn. Jonathan declared that he'd as lief take thirty-nine "stripes" as to ask the old man; "but," said he aloud to himself, "however, here's go it, a faint heart never won a fair girl," and addressed the old man thus:—

"I say, old man, I want to marry your daughter."

Old Man—"You want to borrow my halter. I would loan it to you, Jonathan, but my son has taken it and gone off to the mill."

Jonathan—putting his mouth close to the old man's ear, and speaking in a deafening tone—"I've got five hundred pounds of money!"

Old Man—Stepping back as if greatly alarmed, and exclaiming in a voice of surprise— "You have got five hundred pounds of honey, Jonathan? Why, it is more than all the neighborhood has use for."

Jonathan—(Not yet the victim of despair, and putting his mouth to the old man's ear, bawled out)—"I've got gold."

Old Man—"So have I, Jonathan, and it's the worst cold I ever had in my life." So saying, he sneezed a "wash up."

By this time the old lady came up, and having observed Jonathan's unfortunate luck, she put her mouth to the old man's ear, and screamed like a wounded Yahoo:

"Daddy, I say Daddy—you don't understand; he wants to marry our daughter."

Old Man—"I told him our calf halter was gone."

Old Lady—"Why, daddy, you don't understand—he's got gold!—he's rich!"

Old Man—"He's got a cold and the itch, eh! What's he doing here with the itch, eh!" So saying the old man aimed a blow at Jonathan's head with his walking cane—but happily for Jonathan, he dodged it. Nor did the rage of the old man stop at this, but with angry countenance, he made after Jonathan, who took to his heels; nor did Jonathan's luck stop here, he had not got out of the barn yard, nor far from the old man, who run him a close race, ere Jonathan stumped his toe, and fell to the ground, and before the old man could "take up," he stumbled over Jonathan and fell sprawling in a mud hole. Jonathan sprung to his heels, and with the speed of a John Gilpin, cleared himself. And poor Sal! she died a *nun. Never had no husband.*

Farmer Smith and Ma'am Jones

Courtship among the conservative and reserved residents of New England had a style all its own. It is entirely possible that this story is based on a real incident, the retelling of which became a popular way to describe the unique character of New England dwellers.

Widower Smith's wagon stopped one morning before widow Jones' door and gave the usual country signal, that he wanted to see somebody in the house, by dropping the reins, and sitting double, with his elbows on his knees. Out tripped the widow, lively as a cricket, with a tremendous black ribbon on her snow white cap. Good morning was said on both sides, and the widow waited for what was further to be said.

"Well ma'am Jones, perhaps you don't want to sell one of your cows, no how, for nothing, any way, do you?"

"Well there, Mr. Smith, you couldn't have spoke my mind better. A poor, lone woman like me, doesn't know what to do with so many creatures, and I should be glad to trade if we can fix it."

So they adjourned to the meadow. Farmer Smith looked at Roan—then at the widow—at Brindle—then at the widow—at the Downing cow—then at the widow again—and through the whole forty. The same call was made every day for a week, but Farmer Smith could not decide which cow he wanted. At length, on Saturday when widow Jones was in a hurry to get through with her baking for Sunday—and "ever so much" to do in the house, as all farmers' wives and widows have on Saturday, she was a little impatient—Farmer Smith was as irresolute as ever.

"That 'ere Downing cow is a pretty fair creature"—but he stopped to glance at the widow's face and then walked round her—not the widow, but the cow.

"That 'ere short horn Durham is not a bad looking beast, but I don't know"— another look at the widow.

"The Downing cow I knew before the late Mr. Jones bought her." Here he sighed at the allusion to the late Mr. Jones, she sighed, and both looked at each other. It was a highly interesting moment.

"Old Roan is an old milch, and so is Brindle—but I have known better." A long stare followed this speech—the pause was getting awkward, and at last Mrs. Jones broke out—"Lord Mr. Smith, if I'm the one you want, do say so!"

The intentions of widower and the widow Jones were duly published the next day as is the law and custom in Massachusetts; and as soon as they were "out published," they were married.

Strawberries

Storyteller Gayle Ross draws upon her native Cherokee myths and legends for many of her performances. This magnificent ancient love story is also an origin myth about the reason for the creation of "love berries."

Long ago, in the very first days of the world, there lived the first man and the first woman. They lived together as husband and wife, and they loved one another dearly.

But one day, they quarreled. Although neither later could remember what the quarrel was about, the pain grew stronger with every word that was spoken, until finally, in anger and in grief, the woman left their home and began walking away—to the east, toward the rising sun.

The man sat alone in his house. But as time went by, he grew lonelier and lonelier. The anger left him and all that remained was a terrible grief and despair, and he began to cry.

A spirit heard the man crying and took pity on him. The spirit said, "Man, why do you cry?"

The man said, "My wife has left me."

The spirit said, "Why did your woman leave?"

The man just hung his head and said nothing.

The spirit asked, "You quarreled with her?"

And the man nodded.

"Would you quarrel with her again?" asked the spirit.

The man said, "No." He wanted only to live with his wife as they had lived before—in peace, in happiness, and in love.

"I have seen your woman," the spirit said. "She is walking to the east toward the rising sun."

The man followed his wife, but he could not overtake her. Everyone knows an angry woman walks fast.

Finally, the spirit said, "I'll go ahead and see if I can make her slow her steps." So the spirit found the woman walking, her footsteps fast and angry and her gaze fixed straight ahead. There was pain in her heart.

The spirit saw some huckleberry bushes growing along the trail, so with a wave of his hand, he made the bushes burst into bloom and ripen into fruit. But the woman's gaze remained fixed. She looked neither to the right nor the left, and she didn't see the berries. Her footsteps didn't slow.

Again, the spirit waved his hand, and one by one, all of the berries growing along the trail burst into bloom and ripened into fruit. But still, the woman's gaze remained fixed. She saw nothing but her anger and pain, and her footsteps didn't slow.

And again, the spirit waved his hand, and, one by one, the trees of the forest—the peach, the pear, the apple, the wild cherry—burst into bloom and ripened into fruit. But still, the woman's eyes remained fixed, and even still, she saw nothing but her anger and pain. And her footsteps didn't slow.

Then finally, the spirit thought, "I will create an entirely new fruit—one that grows very, very close to the ground so the woman must forget her anger and bend her head for a moment." So the spirit waved his hand, and a thick green carpet began to grow along the trail. Then the carpet become starred with tiny white flowers, and each flower gradually ripened into a berry that was the color and shape of the human heart.

As the woman walked, she crushed the tiny berries, and the delicious aroma came up through her nose. She stopped and looked down, and she saw the berries. She picked one and ate it, and she discovered its taste was as sweet as love itself. So she began walking slowly, picking berries as she went, and as she leaned down to pick a berry, she saw her husband coming behind her.

The anger had gone from her heart, and all that remained was the love she had always known. So she stopped for him, and together, they picked and ate the berries. Finally, they returned to their home where they lived out their days in peace, happiness, and love.

And that's how the world's very first strawberries brought peace between men and women in the world, and why to this day they are called the berries of love.

Lovers' Retreat

Among the romantic tales of love in North American folklore there are many stories of star-crossed lovers who, for reasons of birth or parental condemnation, have had to take risks in order to be together. "Lovers' Retreat" is one of many legends that give names to places in North America.

Many years ago, in the northern part of Texas, lived a small band of Indians among whom were a young brave and a young maiden lost in love. For the sake of convenience, we shall call the young brave Running Elk and the maiden Laughing Water. She was the daughter of old Chief White Eagle, but in the veins of the warrior lover there was no royal blood, and the father refused to allow the marriage that both of the lovers so greatly desired.

The refusal was not, however, based primarily on the difference in rank. Running Elk was an ideal young brave. He was the best hunter in the band; no other could run so swiftly, ride so skillfully, or shoot an arrow so truly as he. His bravery had been tried more than one time. In a battle he had once, single handed, fought and killed six of the enemy. Many a chieftain would have been proud to claim such a warrior for son-in-law. Indeed, Chief White Eagle was pleased with the suitor, but his tribe was a weak tribe and he wanted his daughter to marry into a strong tribe. Such an alliance he regarded as necessary against powerful enemies.

After many pleadings with the old chief and as many refusals, the lovers saw that there were but two courses left to them. They could give up all hope of marriage and let the negotiations that were already under way for the marriage of Laughing Water into a powerful tribe proceed; or they could run away and seek united refuge in a strange tribe. They chose the latter course.

It was dark midnight when Laughing Water met Running Elk at the outskirts of the Indian village. He had two ponies ready, and the lovers were on their way immediately. They rode during the remainder of the night and almost all the following day. Late in the afternoon they saw a cloud of moving dust rising perhaps an hour's ride behind them. The pursuers were gaining ground rapidly.

The runaways were now at the edge of a strange, mountainous country. Their horses were tired and further journey on them meant capture, then torture. Running Elk called a halt, and when the girl had dismounted, he tied a thorny stick to the tail of each horse, gave the horses a slash with the thong of buffalo hide that he used for a bridle, and saw them disappear down a draw. Then he and the maiden set out on foot, selecting rocks and hard gravel for a path. Their tribesmen would be baffled by the trail for a little time at least.

After the couple had traveled in this way for what seemed to them a long while, they reached the top of a mountain covered with cedar, walnut, and scrub oak. All at once they came upon a wide crevice. They turned their direction and were as suddenly confronted by another crevice, narrow and forty or fifty feet deep. This they descended, taking care not to loosen rocks or earth.

The two Indians were surprised to find that this break led to a network of such passages, the widths of which varied from a foot to twenty or thirty feet. The walls were of solid rock and rose to a height of from forty to sixty feet. On the tops of these rocks had formed a soil that sustained a variety of vegetation. A greenish moss covered the sides of the rocks and against them clung straggling vines; from the tops and from niches along the sides, prickly pears hung; here and there a tree grew up out of the bottom of the fissures and swept its branches over the tops of the cliffs. A cold spring trickled from the bottom of one of the rock walls.

The lovers knew that there must be a cave somewhere amid such surroundings. They began to search for it, and had searched only a little while when they came to a small mountain lake. It was at a kind of gateway between mountain and plateau, and on the mountain side was the cave. It opened into the lake, its floor well above the level of the water, and extended back into the enormous boulder.

Running Elk swam to the mouth of the cave and climbed in, and with his senses as alert as those of the panther explored the darkness. He found that the recess ran back some twenty feet and that it was clear of harm. He swam back to the shore, got his beloved, and returned to the cave. The two had not been hidden ten minutes when they heard their tribesmen making camp by the water.

Presently a few of the young bucks went into the lake for a swim. One of them discovered the mouth of the cave and called to his companions. They all came to him and began to talk of exploring the place.

Huddled close to each other in the remotest part of the cave, the lovers waited. Though they were themselves in pitchy darkness, they could see the world outside; however, dusk was approaching. Then they saw one of the bucks raise his body into the edge of the cave. He paused, fixed himself, and reached down to give a hand to a companion. Just then the lovers heard a wild shouting. They recognized the voice of their Medicine Man. He was screaming to the braves to come away from the cave, and telling them that all caves with their openings in or just above water were inhabited by evil spirits. The braves left the cave with frenzied strokes and soon the silence told that all the Indians had deserted the region of the lake. Again the lovers breathed freely.

But they would not leave their refuge until they were sure of safety. All that night, all the next day, and all the next night, they remained in hiding. Then they left in search of a friendly tribe to take up with, and the story generally goes that they found hospitality and security.

The white man has changed the looks about the picturesque region where the couple wandered and hid; but the cave and lake where they evaded their pursuers bears in memory of them the name of Lovers' Retreat.

Poke-o'-Moonshine

Another legend that lends its name to a landmark, "Poke-o'-Moonshine," with its tragic ending, is more typical of the tales of lovers who are denied the right to be together.

———

One of our few satisfying mountain names is Poke-o'-Moonshine, or Peekamoonshine, in the Adirondacks. In this lonely height is a cave with a crack in the roof through which, in certain phases of the moon, a ray of light will enter; and this peek or peep or poke of moonshine has given a name to the mountain itself. In 1757 a young Huguenot noble, François du Bois, came to America to join his regiment in Canada. He came the more willingly because he knew that his sweetheart, Clemence La Moille, would presently follow him, for her father had incurred the dislike of certain political enemies and had been virtually banished from the kingdom. And, true enough, it was not long ere Emil La Moille and his daughter left their home, forever. From New Rochelle, where they lived for a little time, they went northward with an Indian guide and eventually settled in a lovely valley, east of Lake Champlain, on the bank of that river now called La Moille. Clemence found a way to let her lover know their whereabouts. He ascended the lake at that time with Montcalm's force, which some days later attacked the English near Lake George, and no doubt he cast a longing eye at the peaceful hills that walled Champlain on its eastern side, for somewhere among them his lady awaited him.

Possibly he did not then imagine that in a few days he should be seeking her, a disgraced and heart-sick soldier, but so it fell out. Truth is, he had little stomach for his business. He was less in love with war than with Clemence; being Protestant, he could not sympathize heartily with the scheme of a Catholic government against a Protestant people; and especially he loathed the brutalities that the Indians committed under permission of his fellow officers. The horrible massacre that followed the French victory on Lake George ended his endurance. He stole away from camp at night, found a canoe, and in a few days he had reached the La Moille cabin, weak, discouraged, but with no jot of his love abated. He did not dare to meet the father. Exile though he was, the old man still revered his France and loved his old profession of arms. When he learned that this proposed son-in-law was a deserter he would spurn him indignantly from his presence.

But with the girl it was otherwise. Du Bois gained audience with her, and with pity for his mental and bodily suffering mingled with her love she sheltered him. The French army would soon be returning toward the St. Lawrence, and he might be seen, chased, captured, and imprisoned, if not shot. Clemence lived almost as free a life as an Indian, and she was a willful girl withal. It was an easy matter to absent herself for a day or two from home. In a night journey across the lake the young couple reached a trail leading into the fastness of the Adirondacks, and there Clemence left François, after directing him how he should reach Poke-o'-Moonshine, and promising to join him so soon as she could replenish their ammunition and recover some of her belongings.

A few days later she kissed her father and said she was going upon the lake. She never returned. Her dog reached home that evening with a letter in his collar, but rain or dew had made it illegible. Years afterward old La Moille, while hunting in the mountains, took shelter from a storm in the grotto of Poke-o'-Moonshine. The tempest lasted so long that he gave up the thought of leaving it that night, so he made himself comfortable and went to sleep. In the small hours he awoke to see a slender ray of moonlight falling through a chink in the rock. It rested on a scrap of gold lace from a military coat, and on a necklace—his daughter's. Was he dreaming? He reached out and took the pearls into his hand. They were real. Had the cave become the tomb of the young pair? Had they fallen victim to bears or panthers? It will never be known. But the cross that stood at the cave door for years after has banned all shadows, and the figures that glide over Lake Onewaskra by moonlight are said to be François and Clemence.

A Tale of Love

Perhaps the most endearing of all North American traditional tales, this one is not about human love at all. Yet this story, which is perennially popular in Mexico, evokes all the themes so popular in folk legend.

It was that time when the swallows return. They leave on the feast day of San José and come back on the feast day of San Juan. They say that many cross the ocean but few return, because they are eaten by the Moors.

They waste no time, once on land, but begin immediately to gather mud and build their nests. Most of them choose the eaves of houses and barns, but one young and especially pretty swallow chose the belfry of a little church.

In the churchyard there was a large mesquite tree where a pitacochi came and sang every day. One morning, when the swallow stuck her neck out to hear better, he noticed her and began to sing as he had never sung before. It was truly love at first sight.

From then on the two birds spent every moment together. In the mornings, they would circle low around the village and then fly away into the countryside. And in the evenings, they would rest on the branches of the mesquite and he would serenade her. Indeed, the little swallow made a wonderful summer for the pitacochi.

Time flew by and the green leaves turned to gold. One day, as they sat on a branch of the mesquite, the pitacochi noticed how sad the swallow's eyes were and how she bent her head.

"What's the matter?" the pitacochi asked. "Why are you so sad?"

The little swallow was silent for a moment, then looked up at him. "The time for us to leave is almost here and I wish I didn't have to go. It will hurt me to leave you," she said, bending her head down again.

"That's right," said the pitacochi. "I'm so in love that I had forgotten you have to leave." The pitacochi tried to comfort her. "You can stay here with me. I'll take care of you."

The swallow looked up at him again. "We must all go away together," she told him. "If I stay here, I will surely die."

"Then I'll go with you," said the pitacochi.

Though his decision made the little swallow happy, she still tried to change his mind. "You'll never make it," she said. "We have to fly clear across the ocean and you're too heavy." But despite all her pleading, the pitacochi was determined to go with her.

Swallows always carry two small twigs in their beaks, when they fly over the sea, so they can rest on the waves when they become tired. And so, when the feast day of San José arrived, the swallow had two little twigs ready for the pitacochi. When they reached the edge of the sea, they stopped on a cliff top to rest, and once more the swallow tried to persuade the pitacochi to change his mind.

"It's best for you to remain here," she said. "If you should have to turn back, I'll never stop worrying about you."

In the distance the flock made crooked little lines against the blue horizon.

"You wait here," said the swallow, "and if God grants, I'll return and we'll be together again."

The pitacochi looked out at the mighty sea. "We'd better catch up with the rest," he said.

The land kept sinking deeper each time the swallow turned around, "Drop your twigs in the water," she would tell the pitacochi when she noticed him getting tired. They would stop to rest for a while and then start up again. But after many tries, the pitacochi lost all hope.

"You're right," he cried. "I cannot make it. I'm not good for anything. I wish I were dead." He tried to make the swallow catch up with the flock.

"We're not too far out yet," he said. "You must go on."

"No," said the swallow. "If I let you go back alone, I will surely die of grief."

The two birds slowly made their way back to shore. When they were on the cliff top once again, they began to weep.

"Wait for me," the swallow told the pitacochi, "and pray to God that I can return."

They embraced each other for the last time and the little swallow spread her wings and took off. "Adiós," she called as she swooped out toward the sea.

The pitacochi stood on the cliff watching, with tears rolling from his eyes, until he could no longer see the fading form of his love.

Summer came once more and it was time again for the swallows to return. When they arrived, they began as usual to build their nests in the eaves of houses and barns. The pitacochi waited and waited for the little swallow to return. But he was still sitting alone in the mesquite tree when the stars came out that evening.

And so it was every summer until one day, he waited no more.

9

Of Ghosts, Witches, and the Devil

North America was and is fertile ground for the growth of spine-tingling tales. From the earliest times the spirit world has infused every aspect of life for Native Americans, giving rise to an elegant supernatural tradition. Early European settlers, whose belief in the existence of witches and devils was highly developed, confronted a continent where unimaginable stretches of wilderness provided the perfect atmosphere for supernatural lore. Later, African slaves brought tribal traditions that blended with Christianity to form voodoo and other forms of "black magic."

Although the twentieth century has been hard on people's belief in the supernatural, tales about witches and demons are popular to this day. Ghost stories are different in that they are most often legendary in nature. That is, they are the result of people really seeing a ghost, or at least thinking they did. There are thousands of such tales in North America. They are usually regional, involve an identifiable landmark, and sometimes recount the lives and deaths of real people. For example, I can find published accounts of the Hessian soldier who haunts the basement of my own Revolutionary War–era house. I have not yet made his acquaintance, but I know several previous residents who say they've felt his benign presence on dark and stormy nights.

Choosing from among the tales in this most popular folktale genre, I have tried to represent several regions and culture groups in North America. This chapter, then, offers a variety of supernatural encounters—some legendary, some cautionary, and some that have been handed down just to give you the creeps.

The Haunted House

This is the essential ghost story, containing everything a tale needs to spook the innocent listener. It also provides the satisfaction of knowing that justice is done in the end. "The Haunted House" was recorded in Wise County, Virginia.

One time a preacher went to see if he could put a haunt to rest at a house in his settlement. The house had been haunted for about ten years. Several people had tried to stay there all night, but they always would get scared out by the haunt.

So this preacher took his Bible and went to the house—went on in, built himself a good fire, and lit a lamp. Sat there reading the Bible. Then just before midnight he heard something start up in the cellar—walking back and forth, back and forth. Then it sounded like somebody was trying to scream and got choked off. Then there was a lot of thrashing around and struggling, and finally everything got quiet.

The old preacher took up his Bible again, but before he could start reading, he heard footsteps coming up the cellar stairs. He sat watching the door to the cellar, and the footsteps kept coming closer and closer. He saw the doorknob turn, and when the door began to open, he jumped up and hollered, "What do you want?"

The door shut back easy-like, and there wasn't a sound. The preacher was trembling a little, but he finally opened the Bible and read awhile. Then he got up and laid the book on the chair and went to mending the fire.

Then the haunt started walking again and—step!—step!—step!—up the cellar stairs. The old preacher sat watching the door, saw the doorknob turn and the door open. It looked like a young woman. He backed up and said, "Who are you? What do you want?"

The haunt sort of swayed like she didn't know what to do—then she just faded out. The old preacher waited, waited, and when he didn't hear any more noises, he went over and shut the door. He was sweating and trembling all over, but he was a brave man and he thought he'd be able to see it through. So he turned his chair to where he could watch, and he sat down and waited.

It wasn't long before he heard the haunt start up again, slowly—step!—step!—step!—step!—closer, and closer—step!—step!—and it was right at the door.

The preacher stood up and held his Bible out before him. Then the knob slowly turned, and the door opened wide. This time the preacher spoke quiet-like. He said, "In the name of the Father, the Son, and the Holy Ghost—who are you and what do you want?"

The haunt came right across the room, straight to him, and took hold of his coat. It was a young woman about twenty years old. Her hair was torn and tangled, and the flesh was dropping off her face so he could see the bones and part of her teeth. She had no eyeballs, but there was a sort of blue light way back in her eye sockets. And she had no nose to her face.

Then she started talking. It sounded like her voice was coming and going with the wind blowing it. She told how her lover had killed her for her money and buried her in the cellar. She said if the preacher would dig up her bones and bury her properly, she could rest.

Then she told him to take the end joint of the little finger from her left hand, and to lay it in the collection plate at the next church meeting—and he'd find out who had murdered her. And she said, "If you come back here once more after that—you'll hear my voice at midnight, and I'll tell you where my money is hid, and you can give it to the church."

The haunt sobbed like she was tired, and she sunk down toward the floor and was gone. The preacher found her bones and buried them in the graveyard.

The next Sunday the preacher put the finger bone in the collection plate, and when a certain man happened to touch it, it stuck to his hand. The man jumped up and rubbed and scraped and tore at that bone, trying to get it off. Then he went to screaming, like he was going crazy. Well, he confessed to the murder, and they took him on to jail.

After the man was hung, the preacher went back to that house one midnight, and the haunt's voice told him to dig under the hearthrock. He did, and he found a big sack of money. And where that haunt had held on to his coat, the print of those bony fingers was burned right into the cloth. It never did come out.

Marie Jolie

When she was a child in Louisiana, J. J. Reneaux heard this Cajun story from her grandmother, and now she incorporates it into her storytelling performances. An encounter with the Devil is the subject of hundreds of North American folktales, and elements of this tale are common in many of them.

Down in the bayou country there was once a beautiful girl named Marie. She was so pretty, so *jolie*, that all the people called her Marie Jolie. She was as sweet as sugar cane, but if you did her wrong, look out, for that girl could show a temper as hot as cayenne pepper.

Now, Marie Jolie grew to be of a marrying age, but to her maman's disappointment, she wasn't yet of a mind to be married. First she wanted to have adventures and see the big world. So she found something wrong with every young man who came to court her. This one was too short; that one was too tall; the next one had the ears of an *éléphant*.

After a while her maman got impatient with Marie, for she worried that her daughter would wind up an old maid—a terrible fate in those days. So Maman said, "Marie Jolie, it is time for you to take a husband. You can't pick one to suit you, so me, I'm gonna do it for you. We gonna have us a contest. You see this pumpkin? I'm gonna get M'su Carencro, the buzzard, to put it on the highest, skinniest branch of that big cypress tree out there in the swamp. *Chère*, the man who can fetch that pumpkin down without fallin' in the water is gonna be your husband!"

"Well, Maman," said Marie, "if it's got to be, I s'pose that's as good a way as any of choosin' a man."

The contest was held the following week. Men came from parishes far and near, each one more eager than the last to win the hand of Marie Jolie. But one, a tall, dark, handsome man, stood out from the crowd. "Ooh, Maman," said Marie, "I hope he gets the pumpkin! He's a good lookin' devil for true."

One after the other, the men tried to climb the great cypress, but they all ended up spitting swamp water. At last the good lookin' stranger's turn came. Quick as lightnin' he scaled that tree like a cat, snatched the pumpkin, and landed with his boots on dry land. Before she knew it, Marie Jolie was a married woman.

She climbed proud as could be into her husband's wagon, and they started driving down the road. It wasn't long, however, before she noticed that things were getting strange. The path was growing darker and darker, and her new husband uglier and uglier.

Suddenly a fearsome man appeared beside the path. "Gimme my tie and collar that I lent ya!" he called out. Marie's husband took off the tie and collar. "Here then," he said, "take back your ol' tie and collar!"

A little further down the road, they met another man. He said, "Gimme back my coat that I lent ya!" "Take your ol' coat," said her husband. Yet a third man appeared and demanded his trousers; a fourth demanded his hat. Her husband stopped the wagon, disappeared briefly into the swamp woods, and returned just as well dressed as before.

Finally, a fifth man, fiercer than all the others together, his face hidden in the shadow of his tall hat, appeared before them and pointed a long, bony finger. "Give me the horses that I lent ya!" he roared. "Go to the devil, then," said her husband with a wicked laugh, "and take your ol' horse with ya!"

He watched as the man led the animals away, and then he turned to his wife and hissed, "Girl, get down and hitch y'self to the wagon, and pull us home!" Marie Jolie could feel her temper rising. She was gonna tell him a thing or two! But a terrible change had come over her husband. His icy glare and ugly scowl frightened her. She thought she had better do as he said—at least for a little while.

She climbed down, hitched herself to the wagon, and began to pull with all her strength.

At last they arrived at her husband's *cabane*. It was a gloomy lookin' place, set way back in the swamp woods. "Marie Jolie," said her husband, "I must leave. While I am gone, you will stay here, and my maman will take good care of you." And he disappeared in a burst of flames and smoke.

Marie was scared for true. She begged her new mama-in-law, "Please, Belle-mère, tell me why my husband is so strange!"

Belle-mère, who was a kind woman at heart and felt worse than anybody about how her son had turned out, sadly shook her head. "Oh, *chère fille*!" she said. "You've made a terrible match. You have gone and married M'su Diable, the devil himself!"

Marie couldn't believe her ears. "Old woman, you are only jealous. You just want to break up my marriage!"

"You do not believe me, *'tite fille*? Come with me," the old woman whispered. She led Marie Jolie inside the house to a secret door. She unlocked it with a big brass key, and the heavy door creaked open. There inside that dim room Marie saw the devil's other wives—each one hanging from a hook.

Now Marie Jolie knew the truth. "Oh, please. Belle-mère," she cried. "You gotta tell me how I can escape! How can I get out of here?"

"Girl, do you not see what became of the others who tried to escape? Stay with me, little one. I will keep you comp'ny and ease your suffering," Belle-mère pleaded. "Do not bring down the terrible wrath of my son, the devil!"

But Marie Jolie was growing angry, and in her anger she grew bold. "No," she insisted, "I will not be the devil's wife! If you won't help me escape, I'll find a way on my own!"

Belle-mère sighed. "The devil knows many tricks. He can change into fire and smoke and ride the wind. You cannot outrun him, but maybe—if you are brave enough—you can outsmart him. Even the devil cannot defeat a strong heart. But if your courage fails, he will destroy you!"

Marie was determined. "My heart is strong, and my mind is made up," she said. "M'su Diable will not destroy me!"

"All right then," said Belle-mère, "here is what you must do. M'su Diable will return in the deepest night, at three o'clock, the soul's hour. He hates dawn and the rising sun. In its light he cannot hide his true self, so he sleeps. His spy, L'Gaim, the rooster, keeps watch. If he catches you tryin' to escape, he will crow. Tonight you must feed L'Gaim three bags of corn instead of one so that he will oversleep. At sunrise go and gather six dirty eggs. They will protect you. Do not take the clean eggs, for they are bad luck. Then, *chère*, run as quick-quick as you can away from this place!"

Marie did as she was told. Rooster overslept, and she got the six dirty eggs. She tiptoed out, soft-soft, but the gate hinge squeaked. and L'Gaim woke up crowin' full-throat. "M'su Diable, M'su Diable, Wake up! *Vite-vite!* Your wife is gettin' away!"

Marie ran for her life as M'su Diable came screaming after her. She had not gone far when she turned and saw a cloud of smoke and fire approaching. She took one dirty egg and threw it over her shoulder. BOOM! It exploded right in the devil's path, and a fence of wood as high and wide as the eye could see sprang up. M'su Diable snorted and stomped in fury and flew back to his *cabane*. When he returned he had his magic golden ax. The ax chopped through the fence at once, and the devil was again hot on the trial of his runaway wife.

Marie grabbed a second dirty egg and heaved it straight at the devil. CRACK! It flashed like a bolt of lightning, and a fence of brick sprang up as high and wide as the eye could see. The devil cursed and spat, but his magic ax smashed the brick to bits.

Marie took aim and flung the third dirty egg. It shattered like thunder, and a fence of stone sprang up as high and wide as the eye could see. The devil shrieked and set his ax to ripping through the wall, and soon the cloud of fire and smoke again threatened to destroy her.

Marie took the fourth egg and hurled it through the air. The earth shook with its force, and a fence of iron sprang up as high and wide as the eye could see. But it too was little trouble for M'su Diable's fearsome magic.

Marie ran as fast as she could, but M'su Diable was almost upon her. She grabbed the fifth egg and pitched it straight into the fireball behind her. A wall of flames roared to the sky, and a deep bayou appeared before the devil. The water stopped him cold. But suddenly a great gust of wind blew the evil cloud of smoke and fire over the bayou, and the waters began to boil.

Marie's blood ran cold as ice when she looked back this time. For M'su Diable had dropped his disguise, and now she saw the ol' devil himself as he truly is. His forked tail whipped wildly about, his cloven hooves raised clouds of dust, and his goat beard flapped wickedly in the wind. The bright sun glinted off his sharp, curved horns, and his beady eyes burned like hot coals. Crusty red scales covered his body. For true, M'su Diable looked a whole lot like a boiled crawfish!

Only one dirty egg remained, and Marie threw it with her last ounce of strength. But her hand trembled, so that she completely missed her mark. The egg fell at her own two feet and exploded. The earth rumbled and cracked. A mighty river came rolling by. It was the Mississippi. Marie was trapped. How could she ever swim such a wide, dangerous river?

But wait—wasn't that old Grandmaman Cocodrie [the alligator] sunning herself over there in the shallows? Marie cried out to the gator. "*Te prie, Grandmaman, traversez moi! Grandmaman, te prie sauvez ma vie! Aidez moi, Cocodrie!* Grandmother, I pray you, carry me across. Grandmother, I pray you, save my life! Help me, Old Cocodrie!"

Grandmaman Cocodrie, always on the lookout for an easy meal, swam up to Marie without a moment's hesitation. "Maybe I will carry you across," she growled. "But tell me, what makes you think I won't eat you up?"

"Grandmaman," said Marie, "I'd rather be your supper than be the devil's wife!"

"Climb on my back, *'tite fille*, I like your courage!" said the old alligator, and she carried Marie quickly and safely to the other side.

Just then, M'su Diable came runnin' up to the bank. In his most charming voice he called out, "*Traversez moi, Grandmaman, traversez moi! Belle, belle Cocodrie!* Carry me across, old Grandmother, carry me across! Beautiful, beautiful Cocodrie!"

"Climb on my back, M'su. I'll give you a ride for sure!" said the ol' gator with a snap of her jaws. M'su Diable stepped onto her scaly back, holding his forked tail out of the muddy water, and Grandmaman Cocodrie swam out into the deep river.

Things were looking awfully bad for Marie, with M'su Diable closing in on her. But if there was anything that Grandmaman Cocodrie hated, it was a mean ol' devil on her back, and suddenly, way out where the water was swiftest and darkest, she dived. M'su Diable didn't have a snowball's chance in August. M'su Diable, of course, can't swim a lick—not much water down where he comes from. The Ol' Muddy took that devil kickin' and sputterin' all the way downstream to New Orleans. Some say he washed up in the French Quarter, right smack dab in the middle of Bourbon Street—but then, that's another story altogether.

As for Marie Jolie, she lived to be *une très vieille femme*, a very old woman. She had many adventures before her black hair turned snow white. People began to call her Marie Esprit, the spirited one. When they asked why she never married again, she'd just smile and say, "You know, *chère*, once you been married to one devil, there's no need to go out and look for another one!"

Sammy and His Fiddle

The following legend surrounds a man who lived in the Pine Barrens region of New Jersey during the first half of the nineteenth century. Though near the densely populated, supersophisticated Northeast region of the United States, the Pine Barrens have a history of deep-woods isolation, and the lore of the place is steeped in mystery.

Folk writers have long been fascinated with the ancient legend in which an old man bargains with the devil—his soul for a return to youth. It has appeared in many forms, in many lands, including two operatic versions.

The Southern Jersey Pinelands story tellers have their own version of this tale. It concerns the Giberson family, who were pioneers in the Ocean County and Little Egg Harbor regions of the Pines. Many of the Gibersons still reside in the area.

Samuel Gordon Giberson, one of the well-known clan who lived deep in the woodlands of Ocean County during the middle 1800s, was known throughout the area as "Fiddler Sammy Buck." Every door was open to him and his fiddle. Sammy had two joys in life: to play for the social gatherings of his Pines neighbors and to enjoy a nip or two, preferably two, in the taverns of the area.

One night at a small backwoods inn near New Gretna, Sammy and another character by the name of Bill Denn began swapping tales over a few bolts of Jersey Lightnin' (Pineland applejack) and doing a bit of bragging. Eventually a dispute arose as to who was the better fiddler and dancer.

They decided on a contest. Sammy played for Denn while the latter displayed his dancing skill, and Denn played fiddle for Sammy. As the night progressed, so did the drinking and dancing until finally Sammy boasted, "I can beat you or any man I ever seed dancin' and fiddlin'. Could even beat the devil in a showdown."

The contest ended inconclusively, with both participants exhausted. Sammy weaved out of the tavern and along the road to his shack. As he approached a bridge he stopped for a nip from his flask, as a precaution against the morning damps. A dark figure blocked his way.

"Sammy Giberson?" asked the stranger.

"Yeh," replied the tired and slightly tipsy Sammy.

"I hear you think you can beat me dancing and fiddling!" said the figure on the bridge.

Considering this a challenge, Sammy replied, "I can beat anybody. Who are you?"

"The devil. Start playing!"

According to the tale repeated many times in the woodlands, Sammy took out his fiddle and started a tune. The devil began dancing. The more he danced the wilder became the music and the steps. Then it was Sammy's turn. The contest continued to dawn.

Apparently an understanding was reached in which the devil promised Sammy to teach him tunes that no one else knew or could play, including an "air tune," and Sammy would become the greatest fiddler the Pines had ever known, or would ever know.

Giberson continued to delight the Pinelands with new and fancy fiddling, including tricks of playing he had never attempted before. He'd fiddle with the instrument above his head, behind his back, even on the ground. One of his favorite tricks to astonish listeners was to remove violin strings one by one until only a single one remained. Sammy could play as expertly and as beautifully upon the single string as upon the normal four. He was always well supplied with refreshment during these performances, the termination of which varied according to Sammy's mood of the moment.

Following Sammy's encounter on the bridge that one early morning, listeners detected something different about their favorite musician. He was not only playing strange tunes but given to telling tales of a close association with a creature he called the devil. According to the Pines people, Sammy would disappear on moonlight nights and from the deep woods would come the sounds of not one, but two fiddles! These became known as the devil duets.

Sammy Giberson soon began to feel his oats and play games on his duet partner, every so often slipping in a well-known hymn tune while they were playing. At this, the devil was forced to stop fiddling and vanish.

No one knows for sure the final outcome of this strange relationship. Sammy continued playing for the Pinelanders, especially the much requested "air tune," which Giberson would inform one and all he "just picked outta the air." This he would not perform unless well fortified with his special brew and then, according to stories told by listeners, he would rise to the heights of a Paganini. Although many tried to copy the "air tune," none could master it. Sammy would ignore requests for this melody until a late hour. As soon as he played it, he would end his performance, pack his fiddle, and disappear into the woodlands.

Eventually Sammy died. According to some reports he is buried in a Little Egg Harbor Township woods cemetery. To those with livelier imaginations, Sammy still roams the Pines. Recalling the legend that the devil never gave anything without demanding something in return, many believe that Satan finally collected Sammy as payment for his fiddle lessons.

The fiddle itself was locked in its black box and put upon an attic shelf. From time to time, some say, it would break into melody of its own accord, an added embellishment to the folklore that has sprung up around Sammy. Whether that is true or not, we do know that the fiddle eventually vanished.

However, those who frequent Pineland trails during brisk autumn evenings when the leaves begin to turn swear they still hear the sounds of Sammy and his fiddle playing the "air tune."

Or is it just the night winds among the trees?

Tom Dunn's Dance on Rag Rock

———•—•———

The following tale resembles "Sammy and His Fiddle," except that it is a much older story with a Puritan flavor. There are dozens of folktales in North America that follow the theme set down in literary form as the stories of Doctor Faustus, or "The Devil and Daniel Webster." Some tales, like Sammy's, give no real moral lesson, and other's, like Tom Dunn's, offer an unforgettable lesson about resisting temptation.

———•———

Rag Rock, in which Wabanowi had his long sleep, was a home of sprites and demons down to the nineteenth century. Thomas Dunn knew this, and on ordinary nights he would have taken all manner of long cuts around it, for he had no fondness for things not of this world, whether they were ghosts or gospels. But on the night of his dance, having been to a husking-bee where he had "kept his spirits up by pouring spirits down," and having found so many red ears that he was in a state of high self-satisfaction, for he had kissed his pretty partner twenty times, he spunked up and chanced it straight across the hill. As he approached he saw a glow among the trees and heard a fiddle going—going like mad. He buffeted his way through the thicket to see who of his towns-people were holding a picnic in the moonshine and dancing to such sacrilegious music; for there was dancing; he could hear the shuffle of feet. In a minute he had reached the edge of a grade lighted by torches and found there a richly dressed and merry company tripping it with such spirit as he had never seen before. He dearly liked to shake a leg in a jig or reel, and a chance like this was not to be withstood. He entered the ring, bowing and all a-grin, and was welcomed with a shout. On a hummock of moss sat a maid without a partner, a maid whose black eyes snapped with mischief, whose cheeks and lips were rosy, and whose skirt, raised a trifle higher than common, showed a pair of marvelous neat ankles. The invitation in her smile and sidelong glance were not to be resisted. Tom caught her by the waist, dragged her to her feet, and whirled off with her into the gayest, wildest dance he had ever led. He seemed to soar above the earth. After time he found that the others had seated themselves and were watching him. This put him on his mettle, and the violin put lightning into his heels. He feated it superbly and won round on round of applause. He and the girl had separated for a matter of six feet and had set to dance each other down. As he leaped and whirled and cracked his heels in the air in an ecstasy of motion and existence Tom noticed with pain that the freshness was leaving his partner's face, that it was becoming longer, the eyes deeper and harder. This pain deepened into dismay when he saw that the eyes had turned green and evil, the teeth had projected, sharp and yellow, below the lip, the form had grown lank and withered. He realized at last that it was the demon crew of the hill with which he was in company, and his heart grew so heavy that he could barely leap with it inside of him, yet leap he must, for he was lost unless he could keep up the dance till sunrise or unless a clergyman should order him to stop— which was not a likely thing to happen. So he flung off his coat, hat, vest, and tie and settled into a business jog. The moon was setting. In two hours he would be free, and then—a cramp caught him in the calf, and with a roar of "God save me!" he tumbled on his back.

The cry did save him, for a witch cannot endure to hear the name of God. He saw a brief vision of scurrying forms, heard growling, hissing, and cursing in strange phrases, realized for a second that a hideous shape hung threatening over him, was blinded by a flame that stank of sulphur, then he saw and heard no more till daylight. If he was drunk, and imagined all this, how can one explain the two portraits of the witch he danced with? They were etched in fire on the handle of his jack-knife, one as she appeared when he met her, the other as she looked when his eyes were closing. A fever followed this adventure. After he had regained his health Tom took to himself a wife, joined the church, forsook all entertainments, drank tea, and became a steady workman. He recovered his peace of mind, died a deacon, and was rewarded by having a cherub with a toothache sculptured on his gravestone.

Whickety-Whack, Into My Sack

Like Maud Long, who told "Jack and the Giants' New Ground" in Chapter 6, Ray Hicks grew up in the southern Appalachian Mountains, where the Jack Tales were a main feature of his childhood. He is among the handful of people in the second half of the twentieth century who can tell the Jack Tales from memory. "Whickety-Whack" is a favorite, and one that he particularly enjoys telling.

Well, Jack went into the army and stayed thirty years. And at that time, all you got when they discharged you was two loaves of bread. And when they discharged Jack, they give 'im two loaves of bread, and he headed off into the woods, tryin' to git home.

When he got into a little old town, he met a beggar who was a-beggin' fer somethin' to eat. So Jack—he was what they called good-hearted—give 'im one of them loaves of bread.

Jack went on and hadn't went but jist a little ways 'til he met another beggar, and he was a-beggin' for somethin' to eat. So Jack took out the second loaf, cut it in half, and give it to the second beggar.

Well, Jack went on down the road a little ways and got to studyin' that he'd cheated that last beggar. He'd give the first beggar a whole loaf. So Jack run back and overtook 'im and says, "I cheated you. I met a beggar before you and I had two loaves, and I give 'im a whole loaf. Here's the other half of yours."

So the beggar took it and thanked 'im. "Being you're so honest," the beggar says, "I'm a-goin' to give you somethin'." And he pulled out a sack. "Take this sack with you. If anything gits to botherin' you or you need anything, just say, 'Whickety-whack, into my sack.'"

And then he says, "Here's a drinkin' glass. Take it along. If anybody is sick, git the glass a third or half full of water. If the blubbers goes to the bottom, that person's a-goin' to die. If they come to the top, he's a-goin' to live."

Jack thanked 'im and went on his way. But he hadn't walked too fer outa town 'til he come to some woods, and he seed twelve wild turkeys a-sittin' up in a tree.

"Bedad," he says, "right here is a good time to try this sack out."

So Jack eased as close as he could—them turkeys were awful wild—and he got the sack between his legs, a-holdin' it, and he looked up at those turkeys and said, "Whickety-whack, into my sack."

And he said it was a sight to watch them twelve turkeys crowd down into that sack. Twelve big ones. And he shet it up, slung it across his back, and went on down the road 'til he came to another little old town. It was a-gittin' late up into the night, he was hungry and tired, and he seed he had to stay over.

So Jack went into a hotel and showed them folks the turkeys, and he made a deal with 'em. They kept 'im all night for them turkeys, and Jack got fifteen cents to boot.

Well, the next mornin', he started out and purty soon made it home. He went to a-workin' on his cabin, repairin' his old home place, to live in it 'til he got to where he could do better.

In a few days, he heerd that there was a man in that settlement who had a big farm, and it was hainted. Ghosts were 'bout to run 'im off his place. So the farmer put the word out that if there was any man in that country that could whip them ghosts, he'd deed' 'im the house and land, give 'im a clear title to it.

So Jack went out the next day, inquirin' and findin' out about it, and finally he found the man. Jack took 'im up on it, and the man gave Jack a fryin' pan and some vittles. Jack got settled in at the house, and when it got dark, he fixed 'im some supper and eat and laid down aside the fireplace to take 'im a nap.

He hadn't laid there but jist a few minutes 'til he heerd somethin' a-comin' down the stairs. He shook his head and said, "What do you reckon that is?" And directly, they come down and it was six little black devils and each had a sword apiece, a bag of money apiece, and a deck of playin' cards apiece. They rousted Jack up and begin to beggin' 'im to play cards.

Well, they got to playin', and finally at three games, Jack had lost all but a nickel of the fifteen cents he got in his boot fer them twelve wild turkeys on his way home from the army. But Jack watched careful and purty soon got one pot, and he began to gain, and directly, Jack broke them six little black devils. He had all of their money in his pocket.

So them little devils said, "We'll jist kill you and take it back." So, they got to makin' at Jack with their swords, and Jack was dodgin' 'em. And they thought they had 'im, but Jack happened to think of his sack. So when them little devils got to puffin' for wind and begin to give down a little, Jack grabbed his sack, jerked it open—it had a drawstring on it—and said, "Whickety-whack, into my sack."

Jack said it was somethin' to see them six little devils stuff themselves down in that sack. He jist shet it up, throwed it over in the comer, and laid down to finish his nap.

The next mornin', the farmer come up, jist a-knowin' certain that Jack was gone. He'd done buried fifty men who'd tried. "You're a-livin' and they ain't a scratch on ya," the man said. "What happened here last night?"

Jack says, "It's a-layin' over there in that sack. It's six little black devils shet up in there."

The man says, "As much trouble as them devils have been to me, I won't be satisfied until I see 'em beat up on a blacksmith's anvil. There's a fellow down yonder in the holler who runs a blacksmith shop. Will you go with me?"

Jack says, "Yes, I'll go."

So him and Jack went down there and got the man that run the blacksmith shop to hammer them devils up on the anvil. And when he begin to hammer, so many sparks flew outa them little devils that it set the blacksmith shop on fire and burnt it down.

Well, anyhow, Jack got the deed to the land and begin to stay there and work on the place.

But then, the king's daughter got sick and death was on 'er. And he'd had all of the doctors beheaded 'cause they couldn't cure his daughter. So the king put out an advertisement that if any man, just any community country man, could cure 'er, the money, the gold and silver, wouldn't be a-lackin'.

So Jack took that drinkin' glass and his sack and begin to hunt up the old king to see 'im and see if he could do 'er some good. So he went to the king's house and hollered 'im out.

And the king says, "What're ya here for!"

Jack says, "I hear that you had out word that if any man could cure your daughter the money wasn't a-lackin', and if he couldn't cure 'er, you'd behead 'im."

And so the king says, "Yeah, but you don't look like you could do a job like that."

"Well, bedad," Jack says, "I might look like that, but you said *anybody*."

So the king says, "That's right. I'll have to give ya a try."

Well, they took Jack into the room where the king's daughter lay sick, and Jack sent the king to git his special glass a third or half filled with water. And the king brought it to 'im, and Jack looked, and, sure enough, the blubbers went to the bottom. Death was on 'er.

So Jack got his sack down beside 'er bed and said, "Whickety-whack, come into my sack." And Death went down in that sack, and Jack shet it up. And the girl, the king's daughter, went to jumpin' over the floor, a-praisin'.

The king offered to pay Jack, but he wouldn't take nothin'. He said, "I didn't come for wealth. I come to save your daughter."

Jack went on back home and got some boys to climb a tree, a big poplar in the yard, and take that sack with Death in it and tie it way up on a big limb.

Well, years passed and one day, Jack decided he'd take a little walk down the road. And he hadn't went but a little ways 'til he heerd somethin' a-comin' 'round the turn. Rickety-rack. Bumpety-bump. Rickety-rack. Bumpety-bump. And he looked beyond the curve, and he saw it was an old woman who'd jist went to bones and hide. Her bones was a-creakin' as she walked, and her nose was a-bumpin' her knees.

Jack says, "Howdy do, ma'am."

"Howdy do," she says. "Law me, I can't git around no more. I'm so poor. I've jist went to bones and hide. It seems like I've been a-livin' a million years. And I can't die. I've heerd that some rascal has Death tied up in a sack, and we can't die."

Well, that made Jack think. And after a while, he went back home and tried to climb that poplar tree to git the sack. But he had gotten so poor 'imself that he had to git a younger boy to go up that poplar. So that boy got that sack and brought it down to Jack, and they said when Jack opened it, he was the first one that fell dead.

And that was the end of Jack in that tale.

The Grouse Girl

This haunting tale of the creature who sheds her skin to become human was recorded on Kodiak Island in Alaska. It has many versions around the world, the best known being the tale of the Silkie, a seal who frequents the islands near Ireland, Scotland, and Canada, and who, if caught, becomes the prisoner of whoever holds the skin.

Two men, the older lame and unattractive, the younger sound and handsome, lived by themselves in a barrabara far from other human beings. When they arose in the morning, they drank some oil—to keep hunger away the rest of the day—and then went out hunting; one to the hills, and the other to the beach. In the evening one returned with seal meat, while his partner brought bear meat. Many years they lived in this manner without seeing or even knowing that other people existed.

After the usual breakfast one morning, the older man went to the beach to hunt, and the younger man to the hills, and in the evening both returned loaded with seal and bear meat respectively. By rubbing together two sticks of wood, they soon had a fire over which they cooked some meat, and, after eating, put on their parkas and sat outside on the barrabara, with their faces toward the sea. While sitting there, a grouse appeared and lit on the barrabara, near the younger man, and commenced pecking. "Why does the grouse come here?" the man asked, and pushed her away. She flew up, but returned a moment later to the place occupied before. Seeing her there again, the handsome fellow said to the other one: "What is the matter with the bird? Her home is on the hills, and yet she is bothering here." He drove her off, but she, not discouraged, came back to him. "What does she want?" he exclaimed impatiently, and forced her away rather roughly. When she descended the fourth time, it was by the side of the lame man who took her in his hand, began stroking her, and finally decided to keep her as his pet. Before retiring, the lame man made a nest for the bird near him, and then all turned in for the night.

The next morning the men went hunting as usual. As they approached the barrabara in the evening, they were greatly surprised to see smoke coming out of it, and on entering to find it clean, a warm supper waiting for them, and a pair of new leather suspenders hanging over the lame man's bed. "Somebody has been here to-day," said the younger man; and although they looked outside and inside, they found no one. The grouse was on her nest, her head hidden under her drooping wings, and looked altogether tired. Perceiving her condition, the lame man remarked: "The bird has had nothing to eat or drink the whole day; she must be both hungry and thirsty."

This little excitement did not prevent them from enjoying their supper, nor did it disturb their sound sleep during the night; and the next morning they proceeded with their daily occupation. As the evening before, they found their home in order, the meat cooked, and a pair of new *torbarsars* (shoes made of seal-skin) hanging where the garters had hung the day previous. The grouse was on her nest, her head under the drooping wings, but no one else was to be found, although they searched a long time. After eating their supper, the older man fed and played with the grouse, and then they all went to sleep.

On account of the stormy weather, the several days following the men remained at home. During that time the bird tried once more to gain the good grace of the handsome man, but he treated her roughly, and would not let her come near him, and she avoided him after this. The first favorable day the two men went in different directions to hunt. As soon as the younger man was out of sight, the lame man squatted down, saying: "I will watch to-day and see who cleans and cooks for us, and makes torbarsars for me." Slowly and cautiously he crawled back quite close to the barrabara and waited. The morning passed without giving him a clue, but towards evening he saw smoke coming out of the smoke hole. He crept still closer, and heard footsteps within. While he lay there, guessing who it might be, a young and beautiful girl stepped out. Her face was white, hair and eyebrows black, the parka was of white grouse feathers, and the leggings of the fur seal torbarsars were white with various trimmings. He gazed at her, and when she went in, he followed her, watched her a moment at her work, and then seized her.

"Ai-Ai-Y-a-h!" she exclaimed. "You scared me. Let me go." Instead he drew her fondly to him, and when he did so, her face reddened with blushes.

"I will not let you go," he said; but when he noticed a grouse skin on the nest, he freed her, and although she begged to have the skin back, he took it outside, and hid it.

The handsome man was both scared and amazed, but he asked no questions. Since it was customary for a newly married man to stay at home with his wife for a certain time, it was a long time before the old man went out hunting again. When he did so, he always returned before his partner, and generally found a pair of torbarsars or some other present waiting for him; but the younger man found nothing.

Though the younger man asked no questions, and knew not who the girl was and where she came from, he did a great deal of thinking. It puzzled him to know why the girl preferred a lame, old man to him a young, handsome man. She did not like him, he knew, for she never made anything for him, while the lame man had presents forced on him. He finally decided to take matters in his own hands, and make the girl his wife. One night, when the married couple were asleep, he arose and killed the lame man. Going back to his bed, he called to the girl to leave her dead husband and be his wife. This she refused to do. "You cannot go away from here," he said; "you will have to be my wife."

"I will never be your wife," she answered; and getting up, she searched for the grouse skin among her husband's things and found it in his tool bag. This she hid under her parka. When he called her again, saying, "Come, you are my wife," she replied: "I came here to be your wife, but you did not take me. Three times I came to you, and three times you chased me away. The last time you hurt me. I will not be your wife now." While speaking, she pulled out the grouse skin, shook it three times, and, when she had finished, pulled it on herself and flew out through the smoke hole, leaving a young, sound, and handsome man wifeless and partnerless.

Aunt Tucky

This is one of the creepiest tales I have ever heard. Witches have long been known to shed their skins when they go out haunting at night, and tradition has it that the way to catch them is to make it impossible for them to get back in. Storyteller Harriet Lewis heard this African American tale as a child from a woman in her community who claimed to know it for the truth.

Back when I was a girl, there was a woman lived way back on the Cypress Bayou, away from everybody else. She had a shabby little cabin. To the front, she had two plank boards for steps and a rough board door. Across the back, there was a porch built out over the edge of the bayou. She was a couple of miles above us on the right fork of Linton Road and about a quarter-mile down the first dirt trail to the right. She was a witch-woman; everybody said so.

She had a bunch of children out at the little place—which was passing strange since she wasn't married. We thought maybe she stole them. Anyhow, she would never let them around other people, church, school, or nothing. She just kept them out there working them, and teaching them witch-woman ways.

We all knew that if a man had a fight with someone, all he had to do was walk down that dirt path to Aunt Tucky's place—that's her name, Aunt Tucky. He could walk up those two wooden steps, rap on the board door and call out, "Aunt Tucky, Aunt Tucky!" The door would crack open. The old woman would peer out and snap, "What you want?"

That man could tell her how he was mad at whoever. He could say, "I want you to give him a whammy. Put a bad spell on him!"

And from behind the door, Aunt Tucky would say, "Cross my palm with money." One bony hand would stretch out, palm up, fingers waiting. (It did not take much. Two bits would do.)

When that quarter was placed in Tucky's hand, she pulled it in. Still behind the door, she'd say, "Name the man." After the name was named, business was done. That man on the doorstep could go on home.

Within five days, guaranteed, something would happen to the one named. It could be that the man would be cutting firewood to sell for Christmas money. He could be cutting with a brand new axe or a trusty old one. Didn't matter. His axe was going to break! Old or new, it would break. And he'd have to spend all his money on a new one! Bad luck! Or, that man's best, favorite coon-hunting dog—perfectly strong and healthy—would be turning around to take a nap. That dog would fall over, *blap!* Dead on the ground! A friend gone and lots less meat on the table 'til he's replaced. Bad luck from Aunt Tucky! Or one of the feller's children—run those fields, climb those trees, swim that bayou—one of them would fall off his own back porch. The child would break all four legs! Yes! Four legs. I said that to show you *double* bad luck! That man would have to take off work, take the child to the doctor. See, he lost money from his work, and lost money on the doctor. Double bad luck from Aunt Tucky the witch-woman.

We all knew about hexes and spells, but some people claimed there was more. Some heard that at the moment the sun set and the night breeze began, Aunt Tucky could shed her skin. She could slip out of her skin and become like a spirit or a ghost or a haunt. The children whispered that Tucky could catch the night wind and ride it across the bayou waters, sifting herself through the moss and stirring the foggy, black water. Going who-knows-where and doin' who-knows-what! All night, until the dawn. Then she'd ride the wind across her back porch and call, "Skin, my skin. Let me in." Tucky would slide back into her skin. She'd walk back into the house just as if she'd been on God's green earth all along. That is what she'd do back in those woods, and nobody around to see!

One summer evening, Tucky called her children together and told them she was going away. "You big ones take care of the little ones," she said. "Sit by the fireplace, keep the front door locked. If anybody comes knocking on the door and calling 'Aunt Tucky,' don't open the door. Just answer them and say, 'Ain't no Aunt Tucky here!' They will think they got the wrong place and go away. Stay here, sit still. Watch for me and wait. I'll be back."

Then she called one of the big children to come to the back porch with her. Aunt Tucky told the child to pick up the skin when Tucky shed it. Most important, the child had to hang the skin on the nail on the wall next to the porch. That was so Aunt Tucky could get back in it easy.

Tucky began to moan, "Skin, my skin. Let it begin." She simmered; she glowed. Her old brown skin slid down to the porch floor. Aunt Tucky was like a spirit or a haunt! Floating up and out, lighter than a spider's silk thread, she hitched to the night wind and rode away across the dark bayou waters.

The poor child did what she was told. So Aunt Tucky's skin, all wrinkled up, was hung on the nail on the back porch wall: and the children sat inside by the fireplace waiting. But Aunt Tucky did not come back the next morning. They all got hungry; the little ones cried. Still the big ones made them stay put because Tucky had told them to stay. They's scared of her. So, they waited through another day and night. The big ones were so hungry they wanted to cry, too.

When the sun rose proud-high, on the third day, the big ones took the little ones by the hand saying, "Come on! We're going somewhere where people take care of their children—where people care about being with their families." They walked out that wooden front door, down those two plank steps, to the road, and to the first neighbor's house they could find. Before those children could finish telling her about being hungry and Aunt Tucky being gone, that good neighbor-woman was already cooking. She filled those empty stomachs with biscuits and white gravy 'til they were full satisfied. Then she told them to go back to their cabin place. Aunt Tucky would be looking for them if she had come back, you see. "But I'll come check on you before the day is over," she promised. So they went back to sit still, and watch and wait.

The neighbor lady took some of her egg money,

caught a ride to town and bought a ham and a big bag of salt. How she got all that out to Aunt Tucky's before dark, I don't know. But she did. Late in the day, the neighbor-lady came down the path. She called to the children—not knocking—so they let her in. Seeing that Tucky hadn't come back, she fried them some ham. They ate, then sat by the fireplace again, watching the neighbor-lady in Aunt Tucky's house. She told the big ones that she wanted to show them how to use the salt to cure ham. That could wait 'til tomorrow though. She needed to start home before dark.

"But," she said, "we've got to do something about this salt before I go. It would be rock hard if that damp air off the bayou gets to it over night!"

She began looking for a bucket with a lid, a jar or canister with a top. But she couldn't find anything. She went to the back porch. She looked up the porch—nothing. She looked down the porch—nothing. Bare, clean, empty, nothing! When she turned to go back into the house, the woman spotted something hanging on the wall by the door. The children heard her say, "Here! This old hide-y-side-y thing will do!" And she lifted Aunt Tucky's skin from the nail on the wall.

The little children were scared. What should they do? What should they say? The big ones decided they should do exactly what Aunt Tucky told them. They did not say one word. They just sat still and watched and waited. They kept quiet and watched out the back door as the neighbor lady shook out the skin. She opened it wide at the top and began to scoop salt into it. They watched the lady fill the brown hidey-skin bag with the white salt, then take off a shoelace to tie tight 'round the neck of it. They kept quiet as she leaned the salt-filled skin against the back porch wall, brushed off her hands, and came back inside. She told them the sun was going down and she had to go. She'd be back tomorrow, and she told them to lock the doors after she left.

Doors locked, the children waited quietly. It was that night that Aunt Tucky returned from wandering the bayou. Her voice moved across the porch, calling, "Skin, my skin. Let me in."

But something was wrong! The salt! The salt poured into Aunt Tucky's skin had dried and shrunk the skin! The hide was shriveled so that Aunt Tucky could not fit. Also, the knot of shoelace at the throat top was pulled tight. Being a spirit-thing, Tucky couldn't force the knot undone! Aunt Tucky forced the breeze across the porch again; her voice was anxious.

"Skin, skin, always lucky. Welcome home your Aunt Tucky."

Nothing happened.

Again and again they heard her beg, "Skin, my skin. Let me in."

But she could not get in.

Tucky whipped up a fury wind and began to howl and moan. She rode the wind full force, battered the front door—*blam! blam! blam!*—calling, "It's Aunt Tucky-y-y, it's Aunt Tucky!" But the children had been told what to do when someone knocked against the door. They huddled close, and shouted, "Ain't no Aunt Tucky! No Tucky here. No Tucky here. Go away!"

Tucky went some kind of mad! She started trying to tear down the house. She'd make those children help her get back her skin. She whipped the wind 'round the house, rattled the cracked windows, shook walls. She pulled shingles from the roof. Those poor children sat waiting and watching. Tucky and the wind seemed to be shaking the house apart.

Through the night Aunt Tucky's voice called, "Skin, my skin. Let me in-n-n. It's-s-s Aunt Tucky . . . y!" Through the same night, the big ones and the little ones held each other close waiting and waiting and hoping.

Their hope came through the east window. They saw the sky lighten to gray, then the earth edged with pink. Tucky's voice seemed to fade; the wind slowly went away. A beautiful golden ray of sunlight reached up from the east and glorified the cloudless morning! The night wind began to weaken. The night air had to go back to the foggy bayou and its shadow places. And Aunt Tucky had to ride away with it.

Soon as there was light enough, the big ones took the little ones by the hand and explained, "Aunt Tucky ain't never coming back. We're going to find a place where people care about their children, where people come home to their families. And we'll stay there." So they went out and down the Linton Road where they found good people. Several families took those children in and cared for them. Raised them.

Even today, people can go up Linton Road and out on that dirt path to the little cabin. It's still there and in fair shape. Nobody lives there though. I hear that if a person can walk out on the porch just at sunset, the evening breeze will begin to stir from across the bayou as dark comes. I've heard some say that on that porch just at dark . . . if they are very still, and will watch and wait, they'll see the moss move. They can feel the night wind, and they can still hear a thin old voice saying, "Skin, my skin. Let me in." That witch-woman can't come back and she can't leave here, either. To this day, it's still Aunt Tucky.

The Yellow Ribbon

This story, with its can't-miss shock value, is a classic among schoolchildren all over North America. Folklorist Maria Leach reports that the tale is quite old and is told in many parts of Europe, as well as in North America.

John loved Jane. They lived next door to each other, and they went to first grade together, and John loved Jane very much. Jane wore a yellow ribbon around her neck every day.

One day John said, "Why do you wear the yellow ribbon?"

"I can't tell," said Jane. But John kept asking, and finally Jane said maybe she'd tell him later.

The next year they were in the second grade. One day John asked again, "Why do you wear the yellow ribbon around your neck?" And Jane said maybe she'd tell him later.

Time went by, and every once in a while John asked Jane why she wore the yellow ribbon, but Jane never told. So time went by.

John and Jane went through high school together. They loved each other very much. On graduation day John asked Jane please to tell him why she always wore the yellow ribbon around her neck. But Jane said there was no point in telling on graduation day, so she didn't tell.

Time went by, and John and Jane became engaged, and finally Jane said maybe she would tell him on their wedding day.

The wedding day came, and John forgot to ask. But the next day John asked Jane why she wore the yellow ribbon. Jane said, "Well, we are happily married, and we love each other, so what difference does it make?" So John let that pass, but he still did want to know.

Time went by, and finally on their golden anniversary John asked again. And Jane said, "Since you have waited this long, you can wait a little longer."

Finally Jane was taken very ill, and when she was dying John asked again, between sobs, "*Please* tell me why you wear the yellow ribbon around your neck."

"All right," said Jane, "you can untie it."

So John untied the yellow ribbon, and Jane's head fell off.

The Ghost of Jean Lafitte

Every region of North America has its legends of famous ghosts. In Louisiana, the pirate Jean Lafitte haunts the bayou where it is believed he buried his treasure before he died.

A young, war-weary Confederate soldier was making his long way back home, following the snaking path of a bayou, when a terrible storm fell upon him. The wind wailed as thunder boomed and rain fell like needles. The soldier saw that he had better find shelter, so he left the bayou and began to wander through a thicket. He soon became lost in the blinding rain.

The soldier came to an abandoned house in the middle of nowhere. The door stood open. He called out but nobody answered, and since it was nearly dark he went inside to escape the howling wind. He struck a match and found dry firewood left behind by some other lost soul. The young man quickly made a fire and settled down for the night. He was dead tired from his journey, and he soon fell into a heavy sleep.

Sometime in the deep of the night he waked with the strange feeling that he was not alone in the house. And there by the light of the dying fire, he saw the ghostly figure of a man standing in tall, muddy boots. His arms were folded across his chest and a pirate's cutlass hung at his side.

The man pointed at him and says, "Come with me."

"Who—who are you?" whispers the soldier.

"I am Jean Lafitte," he wails. "*Viens avec moi!* Come with me, save my soul, help me!"

The man disappeared into thin air without another word. The soldier's heart was pounding hard, but he told himself it was only a dream. He stoked the fire and lay back down. The apparition had unsettled him, and now he jumped at every creak and groan of the old house, until at last his tired body gave in to sleep.

The fire had died down when the soldier again waked with a start. A strange, icy draft of wind whistled through the room and the ghostly pirate appeared once more before him.

"Help me, free my soul," the pirate's spirit pleads.

The young man could barely speak for fear. "Wh—what do you wa—want from m—me?" he asks.

"I am condemned," wails the ghost, "a slave to my treasure—bought with human tears and broken hearts. Now I must pay the price of my fortune. My soul is bound to my blood money. Take my treasure and set me freeeee!"

The young man could feel himself being lifted against his will and forced to follow the ghost of Jean Lafitte. The spirit brought him to a secret room. There, with a wave of the pirate's hand, the boards in the floor disappeared to reveal a huge chest, spilling over with treasure. The room was lit up by the shining glow of silver, jewels, and golden coins.

Jean Lafitte stretches out his hands, crying, "Take it! Take my treasure. Help me save my soul!"

The spirit's hands were gory, and bloody tears dripped from his burning eyes. He reached out, closer, closer, until the young man felt the bloodstained fingers grasp his arm like an icy claw—it was the touch of death itself. The soldier's terror rose beyond the power of the spirit's spell and he broke away, running like a madman into the stormy night. The wind tore at him and booming thunder shook the ground. He crashed through the thorny thicket in the blinding rain. Behind him he could hear the ghost crying in the wind, "Take my treasure. Ohhhhh, help meee!"

The young man lived to tell the story, and he warned all who would seek the treasure to beware. The pirate's bloody curse, he would say, follows whoever takes the treasure. To this day, when a storm booms down the bayou, many believe that the wailing wind carries the pitiful cries of the ghost of Jean Lafitte. For his spirit is condemned to wander forever through the dark night, begging, pleading for somebody to take his cursed treasure and free his tortured soul at last.

The Weeping Woman

In the Southwestern United States, and in Mexico, the reigning queen of ghosts is La Llorona, the weeping woman. So many tales exist about the origin of her presence that looking at a few of them provides a fascinating look at the folk-process at work.

I.

A long time ago, an Indian couple was to be married, another ordinary marriage as it may appear. But as time went on, the economic status of the family went from fair to very poor. When the couple had its first baby, a boy, the father knew he couldn't feed him, so after thinking about what was best for the child, he went to the river, and after asking God for forgiveness, he dropped the child in the river. The husband believed he was doing the right thing and repeated his feat as each child was born. Each time the town's people heard the wife screaming, "Ay, my hijo" [Oh, my son] in an eerie tone.

When her last son was born [all previous ones were boys], she was determined to have him live. She went down to the river, and after her husband dropped the boy, she went after him. Since she wasn't skilled in the art of swimming, she drowned along with her son.

Nobody thought much of it after the death, but one foggy night, one of the farm workers saw the ghostly figure of a woman and child in the river. The woman screamed in her high pitched voice, "Oh, my son." After that night, the ghost appeared on the water and the nearby land. The husband couldn't sleep because he heard these eerie sounds. Finally the husband, knife in hand, jumped into the river and tried to kill the woman. After his unsuccessful try, his body was never found.

After the story was spread around, people reported seeing her in different places. But the local people said that she appeared only on rainy, foggy nights.

II.

La Llorona hated men, especially men who have two or more women. She appears to them dressed in a white robe and makes a pass and when they follow her they are always found drowned, sometimes in the canal, but sometimes they will be in the street. They always die with their eyes open like they were looking up at something and couldn't stop.

III.

There was a woman who had gone out into the fields one day to help her husband with the crop. She left her children unattended. When she came home that evening, she found all of her children dead. Somehow they had poisoned themselves. When she saw this, she went out of her mind and killed herself. Since a suicide cannot be admitted to heaven, the Llorona was condemned to wander the earth.

IV.

When she was born, she was a twin. She and her sister were so identical, that when they were baptized, the other one was baptized twice. La Llorona was never baptized. She married when she was nineteen and had a son and a daughter. But she did not love them, so she drowned them in a ditch. When she died and went before God, He punished her by having her cry and search throughout the world for her children until the day the world ends. Then she will be pardoned. They say that she appears where there are lakes and ditches, and her weeping and wailing can be heard.

V.

Well, my friends told me there once lived this lady who had a bunch of kids. Well, you see, she couldn't feed these kids. So she decided to kill them. She took them to the river and told them they were going to go swimming. They believed her. She drowned them. And God punished her for this. So He said, "You will always cry when a person puts a broom in the corner and it's raining." She regretted what she had done. But every time someone puts a broom in the corner when it rains at night, she has to go out and kill someone.

La Llorona Teaches a Hippie a Lesson

In most stories about sightings of La Llorona there is one common feature: She usually appears to people who are in danger of straying from the straight moral path. First-person accounts are often given by people who had been drinking, had been contemplating stealing, hadn't been to church in a while, or were guilty of some other misdemeanor, until the sight of La Llorona convinced them to leave their evil ways behind.

There are many stories here in Chimayo about La Llorona. This is one of my favorites.

Back about 1970, the first hippies moved here. Some of them were okay, but some of them were very disrespectful. This story concerns one of the disrespectful ones, who was also a thief.

This hippie was named after some animal or bird—the hippies used names like that. He was named "Bear," or "Crow." I can't remember. Maybe it was "Mole." No, now that I think of it, "Mole" was someone else's name—a friend of his, I think. I'll call him "Bear" for the purposes of this story. He had a wife who also had a strange name like "Sunshine" or "Ocean" or something like that, and a couple of little children who ran around with runny noses and no pants or shoes. They bought a little piece of land that no one else would want and built a house that was all underground, with boards over the top for a roof. It was a terrible place to live. At least, my husband and I thought so. But who am I to judge? *"Cada chango a su columpio"*—each monkey to his own swing.

Now, this "Bear" was from California and had a very rich family, so he never had to work and he didn't have any respect for people who worked hard.

The first trouble we had with "Bear" was when he would go riding horses across our pasture and leave the gates open so the cows would get out and my poor husband would spend days chasing them back into the pasture. This caused a lot of trouble for us, believe me. A couple of people even shot in his direction, but he didn't pay any attention. He thought the land belonged to everyone and there shouldn't be any fences, but my husband says, "Good fences make good neighbors."

The other thing we all thought was strange was that this hippie had some idea he was an Indian. We would see him riding his horse along the arroyo and all he wore was this little leather thing like Tarzan, with beads and feathers around his neck and moccasins.

People tried to ignore this "Bear," but soon they started to notice signs that something had been in their gardens. At first it was like the skunks do when they get at the corn, with all the ears broken off. Then, other vegetables started to disappear and some fruit, too. We soon realized it wasn't a skunk—not the four-legged kind, anyway.

Nobody had caught "Bear" stealing, but people knew it was him anyway. As we say up here in the north, *"Cuando el sartén chilla, algo hay en la villa"*— "When the frying pan sizzles, something's up in the village."

So, this stealing went on through the summer and then, that fall—in October, I think—it all stopped. We had a long summer that year with no frost in September, so there was still food in many gardens. One of the best gardens belonged to Mrs. Martinez and she told me this story.

Late one night in this particular October, when the moon was almost full and the leaves were dry and rustling on the trees, Mrs. Martinez could not sleep. She has sciatica, *pobrecita*, so she was up at her table late, drinking *atole* and look-ing out the window. Hearing a noise, she looked closer and saw this "Bear" in her garden with a sack and all of a sudden she realized that he was taking her carrots! He was wearing his Tarzan costume and had smeared himself with something dark like mud, probably so he couldn't be seen.

The wind was blowing that night, so there were noises from the loose tin on Mrs. Martinez' roof and the tree branches. Now, you should know that Mrs. Martinez' garden is right below the Martinez *acequia*, which is the big one that runs through the plaza, and it is well known that La Llorona likes the ditches.

So, as Mrs. Martinez was watching this "Bear" through her window, she heard the wind really start to howl louder and louder. Then she realized that it was not just the wind—it was the cry of La Llorona! She saw this "Bear" straighten up all of a sudden after bending over the carrot patch, and even through the mud on his face, she could see his eyes get big. Across the ditch came floating La Llorona, tall like she is, and all dressed in black, increasing her howling by the minute. The "Bear" dropped poor Mrs. Martinez' carrots and began to run. He was so scared he ran right into the fence and fell down. He tried to get up, but his body failed him and so he scrambled along on all fours.

All along the road, as "Bear" ran, the howling continued and all the porch lights came on and the dogs began to bark. Everyone saw "Bear," running as fast as he could, his Indian braids standing out straight behind him as he ran for his life.

After that night, this "Bear" took his family to live somewhere else. He is probably still stealing because, as we all know, "*La zorra mudara los dientes pero no las mientes*"—"The fox may lose its teeth but not its ways."

But, thanks to La Llorona, this doesn't happen in our village anymore.

A Pretty Girl in the Road

Readers will instantly recognize the story of "the vanishing hitchhiker." This tale is ever-popular, usually features a car and two boys, and often includes the detail of the girl's borrowing a sweater that is later found draped over her gravestone. This simple rural version is from Missouri.

One time there was a fellow a-riding along and it was getting dark and coming on to rain besides. He seen a girl a-standing beside the road, where a old house had burnt down but the chimney was still there. She was a tall slim girl with a poke bonnet on, but he seen her face plain. He stopped and says if you are going somewheres I will give you a ride, because my horse carries double. She says her name is Stapleton, and her folks live down the road a piece. So then she jumped up behind him light as a feather. Pretty soon he spurred the horse a little, so she had to put her arms round his waist.

They rode on about a mile and he found out her first name was Lucy, and she wasn't married neither. He could feel her breath on his neck while they was a-talking, and he liked it fine. He got to thinking this was the kind of a girl he'd li' to marry up with, because he liked her better than any girl he ever seen befor'

So they rode another mile and it was pretty dark by this time, and come to a graveyard. And there was a big house with lights in the window little way off. She says that's where my folks live, but I'd better get down figured she was going to take a short cut home, so her paw wouldn't kno' been riding with a stranger. Folks was awful particular about what the' done in them days. The girl jumped off and walked over to the gate. be seein' you pretty soon," but Lucy just waved him goodbye and graveyard.

The fellow waited awhile so she would have time to g' he rode up in front of the big house. Soon as the dogs begun com come out, and he says, "My name is Stapleton." He says the have supper with them and stay all night, as they have got plenty of room. And then he hollered a boy out of the barn to take care of the traveler's horse.

They had a mighty good supper, but there wasn't nobody at the table, only Judge Stapleton and his wife. The fellow kept looking for Lucy to show up any minute, but she never come. So after while he went to bed in the spare room. It was a fine shuck mattress too, but he didn't sleep very good.

Next morning after breakfast they got to talking, and the Judge says him and his wife just moved here a year ago. "We used to live two miles down the road," he says, "but our house was lightnin'-struck and burnt plumb down. There ain't nothing left now but the old chimney." The fellow says yes, he seen that chimney when he rode by there last night. "I didn't mind losing the house," says the Judge, "only our daughter was sick in bed. We carried her out to the gate, but the shock was too much for her, and she died that same night."

The fellow just set there, and the Judge went on a-talkin' about what a fine girl his daughter was, and how him and the old woman was pretty lonesome nowadays. "We buried her in that little graveyard," says the Judge. "You can see stone from the front gallery. There ain't a day goes by, rain or shine, that my don't walk over there an' set by the grave awhile."

Everything was mighty still for a minute, and then the traveler says, as your daughter's name?" It sounded kind of funny, the way he said it, obliged to know.

name was Lucy," says the Judge.

The Spectre Bride

———·•·———

The major supernatural element of "The Spectre Bride," a tale told among Osage tribes in the early part of this century, is remarkably similar to that of numerous versions of "the vanishing hitchhiker."

———

Fighting Buffalo, a young hunter of the Osages, left camp on the Nickanansa to sell his furs in St. Louis and to buy there some ornaments worthy to be worn by Prairie Flower, the girl who had promised to marry him, on his return. This journey, eighty or ninety years ago, was a matter of toil and difficulty, so that he was absent for about three weeks, during which time he had no news of affairs at home. When he regained the Nickanansa and had neared the site of his village he quickened his pace, for there were no lodge peaks above the earth waves of the prairie, no wisps of smoke to promise the comfort of supper. Not greatly wondering at this, as he knew and shared the migratory habits of his people, he looked about to find some picture-writing that should guide him to the new village of the tribe, and was pleasantly surprised on seeing at a distance the figure of a young woman, seated among the ashes and refuse of the vanished camp, and bent, as if weeping. The pleasure of this discovery was in the recognition of the girl. It was Prairie Flower. He ran forward eagerly, and would have embraced her, but she turned her head sadly, and would not look at him.

"I have jewels and ribbons for you, my bride," he said, tossing off his pack. She gave a little sob.

"Where are our people?" he asked.

"Gone. Gone to the Wagrushka."

"But you are here, alone."

"I was waiting for you."

"Then we will go to our people at once, and to-morrow we shall be married; and you will be the most beautiful of all the girls; yes, in all the flat country."

She still averted her face. "I will carry your pack," she said. Among

Indians the burdens that are not borne by horses are usually carried by women, so that this was quite the thing to do. Fighting Buffalo laughed a little as his sweetheart picked up the bundle, for it was filled with gifts that would make her happy. But why did she hide her face? and now that they had started on the march for the Wagrushka, why did she gather her cloak about her in that fashion, and cover her head, like the head of a corpse that is ready for burial? "There's no accounting for women's tempers," thought the hunter. "She will be more kind tomorrow." Plodding on through the tall grass, she following silently in his footsteps, seldom speaking, and then but quietly, they came at sunset to the new camp of the Osages and saw the blue smoke curling pleasantly above the tepees. The girl stopped. "It is better that we should not enter the camp together. You know that is the custom only with married people. I will wait for a time beneath this tree."

Fighting Buffalo ran on ahead, aroused the village with a joyful shout, and called greetings to his relatives, while yet a quarter of a mile away. To-morrow Prairie Flower would be his wife, and he was happy. As he went nearer he was chilled by a boding. The people were sad and silent. Even the children desisted from their play. "What ails you all?" he asked. "Has any one died since I left you?"

There was no answer. Then he addressed his sister: "Feather Cloud, go back and tell Prairie Flower to come to us."

His sister recoiled. "Do not speak like that," she murmured, with a side-long glance toward her parents, as if she feared they might have heard her brother's words.

"Tell me, what has come over every one? Why have you moved? Why will you not bring my bride to me?"

"Prairie Flower is dead, and is buried beneath that tree."

"This is poor fun, if you intend to joke. She came with me from the Nickanansa, and brought my pack as far as that tree. Faugh! I will go after her myself."

He walked hastily back in the twilight, his people following at a distance. His pack lay at the tree-foot, on a new grave. With a choking cry he pressed his hands upon his heart and fell on the mound, dead.

Acknowledgments

CHAPTER 1

"The Boy of the Red Sky" adapted from "The Boy of the Red Twilight Sky" by Cyrus Macmillan from *Canadian Fairy Tales*, The Bodley Head.

"What Makes Brer Wasp Have a Short Patience" from *Afro-American Folktales* edited by Roger D. Abrahams. Copyright © 1985 by Roger D. Abrahams. Reprinted by permission of Pantheon Books, a division of Random House, Inc.

"Oppossum Steals Fire" from *The Mythology of Mexico and Central America* by John Bierhorst. Copyright © 1990 by John Bierhorst. Reprinted by permission of Morrow Junior Books, a division of William Morrow & Company, Inc.

"Light" from "Tales from Kodiak Island" collected by F. A. Golder in *The Journal of American Folklore*, Volume 16: April–June 1903.

"Ojeeg, The Summer Maker" from *Myths and Legends of the Mississippi Valley and the Great Lakes* edited by Katherine B. Judson. Copyright 1914 by A. C. McClurg & Company, Chicago.

"Powerful Changed" from *Mules and Men* by Zora Neale Hurston. Copyright 1935 by Zora Neale Hurston. Renewed 1963 by John C. Hurston and Joel Hurston. Reprinted by permission of HarperCollins Publishers, Inc.

"The Star Husband" by Lynn Moroney from *Best Stories from the Texas Storytelling Festival* published by August House Publishers, Inc. Copyright © 1995 by Lynn Moroney. Reprinted by permission of Lynn Moroney, Oklahoma City, OK.

"The Dog-Rib Legend of Ithenhiela" from *The Journal of American Folklore*, Volume 16, 1903.

"Man, the Burro, and the Dog" from *Cuentos: Tales from the Hispanic Southwest* selected and adapted by Jose Griego y Maestas, retold by Rudolfo A. Anaya. Copyright © 1980 by the Museum of New Mexico Press. Reprinted by permission of The Museum of New Mexico Press.

"Possum, Turtle, and the Wolves" by Doug Elliott. Reprinted by permission of Doug Elliott, 3831 Painter Gap Road, Union Mills, NC 28167. Doug Elliott is a naturalist, an herbalist, and a storyteller. He has written several books and produced a number of award-winning recordings, including one of "Possum, Turtle, and the Wolves."

"Getting Common Sense" from *Anansi and Miss Lou* by Louise Bennet, Sangster's Book Stores, Ltd., Kingston, Jamaica.

"Ouiot and Frog" from *The Journal of American Folklore*, Volume 19, 1906.

CHAPTER 2

"How to Tell a Story" from *How to Tell a Story and Other Essays* by Mark Twain. Copyright 1897, 1898, 1899 by Harper & Bros., New York.

"Ab Yancey's Squirrel Hunt" from *Ozark Mountain Folks* by Vance Randolph. Copyright 1932 by Vanguard Press, Inc.

"Tall Hunting Tale" from *South from Hell-fer-Sartin: Kentucky Mountain Folk Tales* by Leonard W. Roberts. Copyright © 1964 by the University Press of Kentucky. Reprinted by permission of Edith R. Roberts, Stanville, KY.

"The Dog Who Could Walk on Water" from *Cajun and Creole Folk Tales: The French Oral Tradition of South Louisiana* collected and annotated by Barry Jean Ancelet. Copyright © 1994 by Barry Jean Ancelet. Reprinted by permission of Barry Jean Ancelet and Garland Publishing Inc.

"Old Gawge and the Ninety and Nine" by Walter H. Martin in *Sun Up*, September 1932.

"Uncle Swain" adapted from "Local Character Anecdotes Down East" by Catherine Peck in

The North Carolina Folklore Journal, Volume 39, No. 2 (Spring 1993). Used by permission of Catherine Peck.

"The Trained Trout" from *The Tame Trout and Other Fairy Tales* narrated by Ed Grant of Beaver Pond, Maine, chronicled by Francis I. Mauls. Published in 1904 by Maine Woods and Woodsman Printing.

"A Trip to the Moon" from *Storytellers: Folktales and Legends from the South* edited by John A. Burrison. Copyright © 1989 by the University of Georgia Press. Reprinted by permission of the University of Georgia Press.

"The Snake-Bit Hoe Handle" by Doc McConnell as it appeared within *Homespun: Tales from America's Favorite Storytellers* edited by Jimmy Neil Smith. Copyright © 1988 by Doc McConnell. Reprinted by permission of Doc McConnell, Rogersville, TN.

"Uncle Billy Hallock's Yarn" from the *New York Folklore Quarterly*, Volume 9, No. 1 (Spring 1953). Reprinted by permission of the New York Folklore Society, P. O. Box 130, Newfield, NY, 14867.

"I Wish I Could Tell a Lie" from *The American Imagination at Work: Tall Tales and Folk Tales* edited by Ben C. Clough. Copyright 1947 by Alfred A. Knopf, Inc. and renewed 1975 by Ben C. Clough. Reprinted by permission of Alfred A. Knopf, Inc.

"Remarks Made at the Hatchet Club" from *Library of Wit and Humor by Mark Twain and Others, with the Philosophy of Wit and Humor* edited by Melville D. Landon. Published in 1898 by Star Publishing Company, Chicago.

"Billy Earthquake" as it appeared within *An American Glossary, Being an Attempt to Illustrate Certain Americanisms upon Historical Principles* by Richard H. Thornton, Vol. II. Published in 1912 by J. B. Lippincott Company, Philadelphia. This story was originally published in a Florida newspaper, circa 1840.

"The Purple Blossom of Gingham Mountain" from "Old Man Enright's Love" in *Wolfville Days* by Alfred Henry Lewis. Published in 1902 by Frederick A. Stokes, Company, New York.

"California" from *Forty-Niners* by Archer Hulbert. Copyright 1931 by Archer Butler Hulbert, by permission of Little, Brown & Company.

CHAPTER 3

"Annie Oakley Makes Her Name" from *The Female Hero in Folklore and Legend* by Tristram Potter Coffin. Copyright © 1975 by Tristram Potter Coffin. The Seabury Press, Inc.

"Grinning the Bark off a Tree" published in *Sketches and Eccentricities of Colonel David Crockett of West Tennessee* in 1833 by J. & J. Harper, New York.

"The Colonel Swallows a Thunderbolt" as it appeared in *Davy Crockett, American Comic Legend* selected by Richard M. Dorson. Published in 1939 by Rockland Editions, New York. This story was originally published in the 1854 *Crockett Almanac* by Cozans, New York.

"David Crockett Meets a Bear" from *The American Imagination at Work: Tall Tales and Folk Tales* by Ben C. Clough. Copyright 1947 by Alfred A. Knopf, Inc. and renewed 1975 by Ben C. Clough. Reprinted by permission of the publisher.

"Mike Fink Meets David Crockett" from *The American Imagination at Work: Tall Tales and Folk Tales* edited by Ben C. Clough. Copyright 1947 by Alfred A. Knopf, Inc. Renewed 1975 by Ben C. Clough. Reprinted by permission of Alfred A. Knopf, Inc.

"The Ballad of Casey Jones" as it appeared in *Erie Railroad Magazine*, Volume 28 (April 1932), No. 2, p. 12.

"Johnny Appleseed" from *Rosella Rice's Recollections*, reprinted for the Ohio Valley Folk Research Project of the Ross County Historical Society, Chillicothe, Ohio, by Dave Webb from *History of the Ashland County Pioneer Historical Society*, Ashland, OH.

"A Folktale of Johnny Appleseed" from "Frontier Preacher and Planter" by Iantha Castillo in *The Missouri Historical Review*, Vol. XIX, No. 4, July 1925.

"The Cherry Tree Legend" from *The Life of George Washington* by Mason Locke Weems, 1806. Weems was an itinerant preacher and book peddler who published *The Life and Memorable Actions of George Washington* in 1800.

"Belle Starr's Horse Race" from *Ozark Tales and Superstitions* by Philip W. Steele. Copyright © 1983 by Pelican Publishing Company, Inc. Reprinted by permission of the publisher.

"Belle's Arrest" from the *Dallas News*, June 7, 1886, as published in *Legendary Ladies of Texas*. Francis Edward Abernathy, ed. Dallas: E-Heart Press, 1981.

"Judge Roy Bean's Necktie Justice" from *Vinegarron: The Saga of Judge Roy Bean* by Ruel McDaniel. Copyright 1936 by Ruel McDaniel. Southern Publishers, Kingsport, TN.

"Wild Bill Hickock's Duel with Dave Tutt" from "Wild Bill" by Ward Nichols in *Harper's New Monthly Magazine*, Vol. XXXIV (February 1867), No. CCI.

"Stackalee" from *The Rainbow Book of Folktales and Legends* by Maria Leach. Copyright © 1958 by Maria Leach. Reprinted by permission of HarperCollins Publishers, Inc.

"The Ballad of Stackalee." Onah L. Spencer. From *Direction*, Vol. IV (Summer, 1941), No. 5, pp. 14–17. Copyright 1941, by Direction, Inc.

CHAPTER 4

"The Birth of Paul Bunyan" from *Paul Bunyan* by Esther Shepherd. Copyright 1924, renewed 1952 by Esther Shepherd. Reprinted by permission of Harcourt Brace & Company.

"Babe the Blue Ox" from *Paul Bunyan Swings His Axe* by Dell J. McCormick. Copyright 1936 by Caxton Printers, Ltd. Reprinted by permission of the publisher.

"Pipeline Days" abridged from *Foller de Drinkin' Gou'd*, Publications of the Texas Folklore Society, 1928. Reprinted by permission of the Texas Folklore Society.

"Paul's Popcorn" from *Tall Tale America: A Legendary History of Our Humorous Heroes* by Walter Blair. Copyright 1944, renewed 1972 by Walter Blair. Reprinted by permission of Coward, McCann & Geoghegan, a division of The Putnam & Grosset Group.

"Paul Bunyan Takes Care of Mosquitoes" from *Paul Bunyan: Last of the Frontier Demigods* by Daniel Hoffman. Copyright 1952, renewed 1980 by Daniel Hoffman. Published by Temple University Publications and reprinted by permission of Daniel Hoffman.

"Cal Bunyan's Ireland, Jerusalem, Australia & Southern Indiana Railroad" from *The Signalman's Journal*. Reprinted by permission of the Brotherhood of Railroad Signalmen, Mount Prospect, IL.

"The Birth of John Henry" from *John Henry* by Roark Bradford. Copyright 1931 by Roark Bradford. Published by Harper & Bros., New York.

"The Ballad of John Henry" collected, adapted, and arranged by John A. Lomax and Alan Lomax. Copyright 1934, renewed Ludlow Music, Inc., New York. Used by permission of The Richmond Organization, New York.

"Annie Christmas" by Catherine Peck. Used by permission of Catherine Peck.

"The Saga of Pecos Bill" as it appeared in *A Parade of Heroes* by Tristram Potter Coffin. Copyright © 1978 by Tristram Potter Coffin. Published by Bantam Doubleday Dell.

CHAPTER 5

"Looking For Trouble" from *Bo Rabbit Smart for True* by Priscilla Jaquith. Text copyright © 1981 by Priscilla Jaquith. Reprinted by permission of Philomel Books.

"The Bird That Was Ashamed of Its Feet" by Gayle Ross as it appeared in *Best Stories from the Texas Storytelling Festival* published by August House Publishers, Inc. Copyright © 1995 by Gayle Ross. Reprinted by permission of Gayle Ross, Fredericksburg, TX.

"A Boy and His Donkey" from *Cuentos: Tales from the Hispanic Southwest* selected and adapted by Jose Griego y Maestas and Rudolfo A. Anaya. Copyright © 1980 by Museum of New Mexico Press. Reprinted by permission of the publisher.

• Acknowledgments •

"Brer Possum's Dilemma" by Jackie Torrence from *Jackie's Tales*, by Jackie Torrence, 1998 (New York: Avon Books).

"The Red Rag Under the Churn" by Alice Childs from *American Speech*, Vol. V, December 1929, No. 2.

"The Two Wagoners" from *Cuentos: Tales from the Hispanic Southwest* selected and adapted by Jose Griego y Maestas and Rudolfo A. Anaya. Copyright © 1980 by Museum of New Mexico Press. Reprinted by permission of the publisher.

"Annancy and the Yam Hills" adapted from *Annancy Stories* by Pamela Colman Smith. Published in 1899 by R. H. Russell, New York.

"Words of Wisdom" from *Cuentos: Tales from the Hispanic Southwest* selected and adapted by Jose Griego y Maestas and Rudolfo A. Anaya. Copyright © 1980 by Museum of New Mexico Press. Reprinted by permission of the publisher.

"The Golden Rain" from *Tales from the Cloud Walking Country* by Marie Campbell. Copyright © 1958 by Indiana University Press. Reprinted by permission of the publisher.

"Why Men Have to Work" from *Black Folktales* by Julius Lester. Copyright © 1969 by Julius Lester. Reprinted by permission of Grove/Atlantic.

"A Bundle of Troubles" collected by W. E. Hennessee of the Writer's Program of the Works Progress Administration in the State of North Carolina, in *Bundle of Troubles and Other Tarheel Tales* edited by W. C. Hendricks. Copyright 1943 by Duke University Press. Reprinted by permission of Duke University Press.

"The Robe" from *The Weeping Woman: Encounters with La Llorona* edited by Edward Garcia Kraul and Judith Beatty. Copyright © 1988 by Edward Garcia Kraul and Judith S. Beatty. Reprinted by permission of Judith Beatty, Santa Fe, NM.

CHAPTER 6
"Brother Rabbit Breaks Up a Party." Adapted from *Nights With Uncle Remus* by Joel Chandler Harris.

"Tío Conejo and the Hurricane" by Mary Ann Brewer, adapted from *Best Stories from the Texas Storytelling Festival* published by August House Publishers, Inc. Copyright © 1995 by Mary Ann Brewer. Reprinted by permission of Mary Ann Brewer, Richardson, TX.

"Coyote Tricks the White Man" from *Kiowa Apache Tales* edited by J. Gilbert McAllister. Publications of the Texas Folklore Society, 22, 1949. Reprinted by permission of the Texas Folklore Society.

"Big John the Conqueror" from *Stetson Kennedy: Palmetto Country*. Copyright 1942 by Stetson Kennedy. Published by Duell, Sloan & Pearce.

"Jack and the Giants' New Ground" as it appeared in *Folklore on the American Land* by Duncan Emrich, Little, Brown & Company, 1972.

"The Boy That Was Foolish-Wise" from *Tales From the Cloud Walking Country* by Marie Campbell. Copyright © 1958 by Indiana University Press. Reprinted by permission of Indiana University Press.

"The Arkansas Traveler" as it appeared in *Great American Folklore* compiled by Kemp Battle. Compilation copyright © 1986 by Kemp Battle. Published by Doubleday & Company, Inc.

"The Yankee Finishes His Meal" as it appeared in *Great American Folklore* compiled by Kemp Battle. Compilation copyright © 1986 by Kemp Battle. Published by Doubleday & Company, Inc.

"Razor-Strop Trade" originally published by *Cyclopaedia of Commercial and Business Anecdotes* by Frazar Kirkland, Vol. II, p. 555. D. Appleton and Company, 1864.

"How Pedro Urdemalas Got Into and Out of Heaven" from *Life on the King Ranch* by Frank Goodwyn. Copyright 1951 by Frank Goodwyn. Published by A & M University Press, 1983. Reprinted by permission of Frank Goodwyn, Silver Spring, MD.

"Bobtail and the Devil" from *South from Hell-fer-Sartin: Kentucky Mountain Folk Tales* by Leonard W. Roberts. Copyright © 1964 by the University Press of Kentucky. Reprinted by permission of Edith R. Roberts, Stanville, KY.

• ACKNOWLEDGMENTS •

CHAPTER 7

"The Three Sillies" originally titled "The Foolish Bride" from *Storytellers: Folktales and Legends from the South* edited by John A. Burrison. Copyright © 1989 by the University of Georgia Press. Reprinted by permission of the publisher.

"Two Tales of Foolish John" from "The Legend of Foolish John" by Marie Theriot and Marie Lehaye in *Southern Folklore Quarterly*, Vol. BII, September 1943, No. 3. Copyright 1943 by the University Press of Kentucky. Reprinted by permission of the publisher.

"Fido est Mort (Fido Is Dead)" from *Cajun and Creole Folktales: The French Oral Tradition of South Louisiana* by Barry Jean Ancelet. Copyright © 1994 by Barry Jean Ancelet. Reprinted by permission of Garland Publishing, Inc.

"The Devil and the Lord Dividing Souls" from *Storytellers: Folktales and Legends from the South* edited by John A. Burrison. Copyright © 1989 by the University of Georgia Press. Reprinted by permission of the publisher.

"Pat and the Devil" from *The Journal of American Folklore*, Volume 31, January–March 1918.

"The Riddle Test" from *Folklore from Nova Scotia* collected by Arthur Huff Fauset. Reprinted by permission of the American Folklore Society from *The Journal of American Folklore*, 38:148, 1925.

"Jean Sotte and the Riddle" from *Louisiana Folktales* collected and edited by Alcée Fortier. Published in 1895 by Houghton Mifflin Company.

"Jean Sot and Bull's Milk" from *Cajun Folktales* by J. J. Reneaux. Copyright © 1992 by J. J. Reneaux. Reprinted by permission of August House Publishers, Inc.

"The Mule Egg" by Doc McConnell as it appeared in *Homespun: Tales from America's Favorite Storytellers* edited by Jimmy Neil Smith. Copyright © 1988 by Doc McConnell. Reprinted by permission of Doc McConnell, Rogersville, TN.

"The $50,000 Racehorse" by Hannah McConnell Gillenwater from *More Best-Loved Stories Told at the National Storytelling Festival*, 1992, selected by the National Association for the Preservation and Perpetuation of Storytelling. Copyright © 1992 by Harriet McConnell Gillenwater. Reprinted by permission of Harriet McConnell Gillenwater, Rogersville, TN.

"Jim Baker's Bluejay Yarn" from *A Tramp Abroad* by Mark Twain. Published in 1907 by Harper & Bros., New York.

"The Killer Mosquitoes" from *Cajun Folktales* by J. J. Reneaux. Copyright © 1992 by J. J. Reneaux. Reprinted by permission of August House Publishers, Inc.

"The Yankee Peddler and the Innkeeper" from *Pennsylvanian Republican*, York, PA, March 23, 1942.

CHAPTER 8

"The Girl That Married a Flop-Eared Hound Dog" from *Tales from the Cloud Walking Country* by Marie Campbell. Copyright © 1958 by Indiana University Press. Reprinted by permission of Indiana University Press.

"The Algonquin Cinderella" from *World Tales: The Extraordinary Coincidence of Stories Told in All Times in All Places* by Idries Shah. Copyright © 1979 by Technographia, S. A. and Harcourt Brace & Company. Reprinted by permission of Harcourt Brace & Company.

"La Cenicienta Huasteca" from the Publications of the Texas Folklore Society. Used by permission of the Texas Folklore Society.

"Fabiano and Reyes" from *Cuentos: Tales from the Hispanic Southwest* by Jose Griego y Maestas and Rudolfo A. Anaya. Copyright © 1980 by Museum of New Mexico Press. Used by permission of the publisher.

"A Bunch of Laurel Blooms for a Present" from *Tales from the Cloud Walking Country* by Marie Campbell. Copyright © 1958 by Indiana University Press. Reprinted by permission of Indiana University Press.

"The Toadfrog" and "Old Black-Oak Knows Best" from *The Devil's Pretty Daughter and Other Ozark Folk*

• ACKNOWLEDGMENTS •

Tales by Vance Randolph. Copyright © 1955 by Columbia University Press. Reprinted by permission of Columbia University Press.

"Hard of Hearing" from *The Yankee Blade*, March 1, 1851 (Vol. X).

"Farmer Smith and Ma'am Jones" by H. Hastings Weld from *Burlington Daily Free Press*, May 19, 1948.

"Strawberries" by Gayle Ross from *Homespun: Tales from America's Favorite Storytellers* edited by Jimmy Neil Smith. Copyright © 1988 by Gayle Ross. Reprinted by permission of Gayle Ross, Fredericksburg, TX.

"Lovers' Retreat" from the Publications of the Texas Folklore Society, Number III, 1924. Reprinted by permission of the Texas Folklore Society.

"Poke-o'-Moonshine" from *American Myths and Legends* by Charles M. Skinner. Published in 1903 by J. B. Lippincott, Philadelphia.

"A Tale of Love" from *Mexican Folk Tales* translated and edited by Anthony John Campos. Copyright © 1977 by the Arizona Board of Regents. Reprinted by permission of the University of Arizona Press.

CHAPTER 9

"The Haunted House" from *American Folktales and Songs* by Richard Chase. Copyright © 1956 by Richard Chase. Reprinted by permission of Dover Publications, Inc.

"Marie Jolie" from *Cajun Folktales* by J. J. Reneaux. Copyright © 1992 by J. J. Reneaux. Reprinted by permission of August House Publishers, Inc.

"Sammy and His Fiddle" from *Pine Barrens Legends, Lore and Lies* by William McMahon. Copyright © 1980 by William McMahon. Reprinted by permission of Middle Atlantic Press.

"Tom Dunn's Dance on Rag Rock" from *American Myths and Legends* by Charles M. Skinner. Published in 1903 by J. B. Lippincott Company, Philadelphia.

"Whickety–Whack, Into My Sack" by Ray Hicks from *Voice of Appalachia* by Ray Hicks, 1998 (Winston Salem, NC: John F. Blair). By permission of Lynn S. Salsi, Box 3404 Greensboro, NC 27410. Lynn Salsi is Ray Hicks' biographer.

"The Grouse Girl" from *The Journal of American Folklore* collected by E. A. Golder. Published in 1903 by Houghton Mifflin Company.

"Aunt Tucky" by Harriet Culbertson Lewis from *Best Stories from the Texas Storytelling Festival* published by August House Publishers, Inc. Copyright © 1995 by Harriet Culbertson Lewis. Reprinted by permission of Harriet Culbertson Lewis, Benton, LA.

"The Yellow Ribbon" from *The Rainbow Book of American Folk Tales and Legends* by Maria Leach. Copyright © 1958 by Maria Leach. Reprinted by permission of HarperCollins Publishers, Inc.

"The Ghost of Jean Lafitte" from *Cajun Folktales* by J. J. Reneaux. Copyright © 1992 by J. J. Reneaux. Reprinted by permission of August House Publishers, Inc.

"The Weeping Woman" from *Legendary Ladies of Texas* edited by Francis Edward Abernathy. Copyright © 1981 by the Texas Folklore Society. Reprinted by permission of the Texas Folklore Society.

"La Llorona Teaches a Hippie a Lesson" from *The Weeping Woman: Encounters with La Llorona* compiled and edited by Edward Garcia Kraul and Judith Beatty. Copyright © 1988 by Edward Garcia Kraul and Judith S. Beatty. Reprinted by permission of Judith Beatty, Santa Fe, NM.

"A Pretty Girl in the Road" from *The Devil's Pretty Daughter and Other Ozark Folktales* by Vance Randolph. Copyright © 1955 by Columbia University Press. Reprinted by permission of the publisher.

"The Spectre Bride" from *American Myths and Legends* by Charles M. Skinner. Published in 1903 by J. B. Lippincott Company, Philadelphia.